LORDS & LADIES
COLLECTION

*Two Glittering Regency
Love Affairs*

A Matter of Honour
by Anne Herries

&

The Chivalrous Rake
by Elizabeth Rolls

The Regency

LORDS & LADIES
COLLECTION

The Regency

Lords & Ladies
COLLECTION

Anne Herries &
Elizabeth Rolls

*M&B™ and M&B™ with the Rose Device
are trademarks of the publisher.
Harlequin Mills & Boon Limited, Eton House,
18-24 Paradise Road, Richmond, Surrey TW9 1SR*

First published in Great Britain in 2000 and 2003

THE REGENCY LORDS & LADIES COLLECTION
© Harlequin Books S.A. 2008

The publisher acknowledges the copyright holders of the individual works as follows:

A Matter of Honour © Anne Herries 2000
The Chivalrous Rake © Elizabeth Rolls 2003

ISBN: 978 0 263 86649 0

052-0208

*Printed and bound in Spain
by Litografía Rosés S.A., Barcelona*

A Matter of Honour
by
Anne Herries

Anne Herries, winner of the Romantic Novelists' Association's Romance Prize 2004, lives in Cambridgeshire. After many happy years with a holiday home in Spain, she and her husband now have their second home in Norfolk. They are only just across the road from the sea, and have a view of it from their windows. At home and at the sea they enjoy watching the wildlife and have many visitors to their gardens, particularly squirrels. Anne loves watching their antics and spoils both them and her birds shamelessly. She also loves to see the flocks of geese and other birds flying in over the sea during the autumn, to winter in the milder climes of this country. Anne loves to write about the beauty of nature and sometimes puts a little into her books, though they are mostly about love and romance. She writes for her own enjoyment and to give pleasure to her readers.

Chapter One

'Marry the Thornton gel!' The Dowager Lady Longbourne almost sat up, and she would have, had it not been
positively too warm for any such exertion. She lay amongst
silken cushions on her elegant daybed and waved a languid
hand at her visitors. 'Carlton, you really shouldn't make
such tasteless jokes. I confess I am surprised at you.'

'It was not meant as a jest, Mama.' Lord Vincent Carlton's lazy smile flickered over his mouth. He was exceptionally good looking and far too wealthy for his own good;
though generous to anyone he cared for, he was considered
by some others to be stand-offish and rather too high in the
instep. 'That is why I have come to see you this afternoon.
If you will be so kind, I want you to invite Cassandra to
stay here so that we can get to know one another properly
before I propose.'

'Ask the Thornton chit to stay *here*?' Lady Longbourne's
limpid blue eyes took on an expression of dismay. 'You
surely cannot mean that, Carlton? You are not seriously
considering a mésalliance?'

'He has to,' the second of her visitors said. 'It is a matter
of honour, Mama. Vinnie has to marry her.'

One satin-shod foot touched the ground, followed closely

by the second. Lady Longbourne sat up! An expression of shock mixed liberally with disbelief on a face that still retained some measure of the outstanding beauty which had been hers in youth. She stared at Sir Harry Longbourne, her younger son and her favourite, being the precious fruit of her second marriage, which had been happier than the first.

'What are you talking about, Harry? Why should Carlton be obliged to marry this gel?' she demanded. Her cheeks turned pale as she looked at her eldest son incredulously. 'Carlton! Surely, you…haven't dishonoured the girl, have you?'

The smile left Vincent's eyes. He was deeply offended by the suggestion that he would stoop so low as to dishonour any woman—especially a lady of quality! However, he was too fond of his mother (despite knowing only too well that she had always favoured his brother) and too much a gentleman to let his anger show.

'Of course he hasn't!' Harry jumped in before he could think of a suitable reply. 'What a hummer! You ought to know Vinnie better than that, Mama. It was a promise we all made to Jack Thornton just before he was killed at Waterloo.'

'Promise? What promise?' his mama asked, irritated at having her peace disturbed on such a warm day. 'What has a promise to Cassandra's brother have to do with Carlton offering for her?'

'Jack had just heard the news of his father's death,' Harry went on patiently, while Carlton rose to his feet and wandered over to the windows of the small back parlour Lady Longbourne favoured at Carlton House. He stood gazing out at the neatly manicured lawns and rosebeds as Harry elaborated for their mother's benefit. Behind him, an enamelled French clock ticked relentlessly on the rather fine mantelpiece designed by Mr Adam. 'Naturally, he was shocked—'

'As anyone would be,' interjected Lady Longbourne. 'To throw most of one's fortune away at the gambling tables while one's son and heir is fighting for King and country. And then to…' She gave a shudder of distaste. 'It must have been terrible for Cassandra to find her father dead by his own hand…'

'Exactly, Mama.' Carlton turned to take up the story, his expression carefully controlled and giving no sign of the horror any decent person must feel. 'Jack was distraught. Out of his mind with grief and shock. He implored us to take care of his sister, begging all of us to promise that one of us would marry her if he died…'

'But why must it be you?' inquired his mama. 'You could make a much more prestigious match, Carlton.'

'You mean I should marry an heiress—or the daughter of a duke, perhaps? To restore the family fortunes…'

He was a tall man, lean, but wiry and with the bearing of a soldier. His dark hair was cut short in one of the new styles that were just now fashionable amongst the *ton*, and his clothes bore all the hallmarks of the very best tailors; his boots were a work of art. He looked what he was, a gentleman in possession of a large fortune with the liberty (since his return from France after Napoleon's defeat) to do exactly as he pleased.

'Well…' She saw the mocking look in his eyes and pulled a face at him. 'No, I do not, Vincent! I know well enough that you have taken good care of the estate since you came into it—and that we have all benefited from your good sense. But the daughter of a mere baronet…you should think of your own consequence and the family pride.'

The dark eyebrows rose, a challenge in Vincent's quizzing gaze which brought a flush to her cheeks. Because, of course, little as she liked to be reminded of it, his late father had also been a reckless gambler and, had he not died suddenly, might have brought them all to ruin.

'Yes, I know it was only an accident that saved us from your father suffering a similar fate to Sir Edward Thornton—but that isn't the point.'

'The point is, Mama,' Lord Carlton reminded her gently, 'that you have been saying for an age that you wished I would marry to provide an heir for the Carlton family and—'

'Well, how could I not?' she spoke indignantly. 'With your uncle Septimus forever telling me it is time you did your duty—and as for that odious wife of his, preening over her abominable brat as if she could already see him in your place. I vow I hardly knew how to hold my tongue the last time they stayed here. She was examining the curtains as if she saw herself moving in at any moment. You may be past the first flush of youth, Carlton, but you ain't about to drop down dead! And since you returned safely from the war, I have every hope of your living for some years yet.'

'Thank you for your confidence, Mama. I am heartily relieved to hear it.'

'Oh, you!' She gave him a fulminating stare. 'You will always have your joke—not that I find them at all funny. You have a very odd notion of humour, Vincent!'

'Forgive me, Mama.' There was a gleam in Lord Carlton's grey eyes. 'I am very sorry you do not appreciate my jokes.'

'What I do not appreciate is this absurd idea that you must marry the Thornton gel,' Lady Longbourne said on a sigh. 'If Jack Thornton asked all of you to look out for his sister, which was not so unreasonable after all, in the circumstances of our having been neighbours while my dear Bertie was alive…' she dabbed at the corner of her eyes with a wisp of filmy lace kerchief '…and still would be, I dare say, if you had not been generous enough to allow me to return here to Carlton, which I much prefer to Longbourne, being much less draughty in the winters—why must you be the one to marry her?'

Having had years of practice of unravelling his mama's often tangled speeches, Lord Carlton understood immediately what was on her mind.

'It was less generous than you imagine,' he replied, smiling at her reassuringly. 'I do not care for this house. I prefer my own house in London—and do not forget I have Grandfather Hamilton's estate in Surrey, which would make a very pleasant country home if I had it refurbished in a more modern style.'

'Well, with your wealth I suppose you may do as you please,' Lady Longbourne said, sinking back against her piles of silken cushions with relief. 'I dare say you could afford to buy a dozen houses. I always thought it was a little unjust of my father to leave the lion's share of his fortune to you.'

'No, no, Mama,' Harry rushed in as always, a flush in his cheeks. He had often benefited from his half-brother's generosity after a night's ill luck at the gaming tables, and was embarrassed at the suggestion that he should have been left part of the Hamilton estate. 'I have Papa's estate, which, though not as large as Vinnie's, was flourishing when it was passed down to me. Vinnie had hard work of it to bring the Carlton estate about after he inherited the title, you know.'

'Yes, well, I suppose that is true enough,' Lady Longbourne admitted. 'I know Papa thought Vincent had an excellent head on him and said as much to me just before he passed away…' Again she sighed and dabbed at the corners of her eyes. 'And we've all felt Carlton's generosity…but what I still don't understand is why he has to marry the gel.'

'Jack's body was never brought in,' Vincent said, a haunted look in his eyes. 'He was my friend, Mama. His body lies in an unmarked grave somewhere in France. I owe him this at the very least.'

Lady Longbourne was temporarily silenced. Her son's passionate words and the pain in his eyes had surprised her. It was unlike Carlton to show his feelings so plainly.

'There were five of us,' Harry said before his brother could stop him. 'We drew straws for it and—'

'I won,' Vincent said, glaring at Harry. 'I remember Cassandra as being a little thin and plain, but she was only twelve or so at the time so I imagine she must have changed somewhat by now. Besides, a promise given on the field of battle to a comrade is a matter of honour, Mama—and I intend to keep it.'

'Supposing she won't take you?' Harry asked, wrinkling his smooth brow. He was four and twenty, fair of skin and hair, blue-eyed and possessed of a sunny nature which won him friends easily. He was seven years younger than the brother he admired more than he would ever dare show— because if there was one thing Vinnie couldn't stand, it was people fawning over him! 'What shall we do then?'

'I won the first shot at courting her,' Vincent said. 'If she turns me down, it will be up to the rest of you.'

'Turn you down?' Lady Longbourne's eyebrows rose incredulously. 'Whatever else Cassandra Thornton may be, I do not think her a fool. She will snatch at such an offer, Carlton. In her circumstances, you must appear to be a gift from the gods…and she may have changed, but plain is plain and there's no way she could ever be a beauty.'

'I do not expect her to be a beauty, nor do I particularly wish for beauty in the woman I marry,' replied a man who was famed for the remarkable looks of the various mistresses he had kept since reaching his majority. 'I find the young ladies described in London's drawing rooms as

''Fair Beauty'' and ''Goddess'' rarely have natures to match their faces; they are usually spoilt and often vain. No, no, Mama, I am not to be put off by your cavilling.' He smiled at her to ease the sting of his words. 'Now, my very dear Mama—will you oblige me by inviting Cassandra to stay here as your guest?'

'Of course. You had no need to ask, Carlton. You are my son, and the only desire left to me in life is to serve my dearest ones. Much as I fear for your happiness married to such a girl—as plain a gel as could be, she was!—I shall naturally do all in my power to promote the match, if you wish it. If you will be guided by me, you will give up the notion at once…but invite her here by all means. I am completely at your command.'

Which meant, of course, that she considered the visit an inconvenience, but felt obliged to do as he asked because of past favours.

Lord Carlton sighed inwardly. Lady Longbourne had for some time considered herself to be delicate and spent many hours lying indoors when she might have been employed in some more rewarding activity. Her indolence had been brought about through a genuine illness following the un-happy demise of her beloved husband (a chill had turned to a malevolent fever and carried Harry's father off in a matter of days) and it saddened Vincent to see his mother this way. He remembered her as the glowing bride of Sir Bertram Longbourne, and wished he could see her as happy again.

He acknowledged privately that there was justice in her words. Cassandra Thornton had indeed been a plain, often quiet, child, but she had also had a bright smile and plenty of spirit when it was aroused. It was Vincent's hope that, in taking temporary charge of a girl who had been left with no relatives to care for her, his mother might recover her own spirits.

'You are very good, Mama,' he said and bent to kiss her cheek. 'Will you write to Cassandra this afternoon?'

'Before dinner,' she said, half smothering a sigh. 'You must know that I would do anything to oblige you, Carlton…' She reached up and patted his cheek. 'I do love you, you know.'

'I know that,' he replied, smiling at her. 'I have never doubted it.'

'You are a comfort to me in my autumn years,' Lady Longbourne said, then looked at Harry mistily. 'I am very fortunate to have two such devoted sons. Some sons hardly ever visit their mother—they prefer to racket about London, enjoying the pleasures of town without a thought for those unable to do so…'

'Mama…' Harry looked uncomfortable, as though he wished to escape. 'If you will excuse me…I think I shall go for a walk before dinner.'

'We are both devoted to you,' Vincent said as his brother made a hasty exit. 'But I think I should warn you, Mama—Harry is unlikely to stay here long, unless you can persuade him. He has lost his heart to a lady…but pray do not look so alarmed. I do not imagine my revered brother has marriage in mind. *She* is at least ten years his senior and of dubious reputation. Harry is not so lost to reason that he cannot see the drawbacks of such a connection; he will no doubt make her his mistress for as long as it suits him—but I thought it best to tell you something you might otherwise have heard from a less well-informed source. I have been instructed to tell you that Uncle Septimus intends to visit you very soon.'

'Oh, no!' cried Lady Longbourne, sensibly dismayed more by the impending visit than her son's intention of taking a mistress. 'Pray do not say so. I hope he means to come alone, for if he brings Felicity and Archie with him I shall be pressed beyond bearing.'

'Since he does not come for another few weeks, you may have Cassandra with you. I am persuaded that, together, she and I may protect you from submitting to too many of my uncle's lectures.'

'I hope you do not mean to desert me until after your uncle has gone?'

'I shall stay until Cassandra has either accepted or refused me. After that, we shall have to see…'

Vincent was thoughtful as he strolled around his estate later that evening, noting various details which must be brought to the attention of his bailiff. It *was* time he married and provided the family with an heir. Since he had never yet encountered a woman he felt in the least inclined to make his wife, the obvious answer was to make a marriage of convenience to a woman who would not demand too much of him.

When Jack had first suggested he marry Cassandra, Vincent had been reluctant. Had he given his word that first time, that nonsense with the straws would never have been necessary. After Jack's death, he had known it was his duty to marry Cassandra. He was honour-bound to it!

Why, then, had he delayed all this time? It was almost eleven months since Napoleon had been defeated and banished to the island of St. Helena, and nine since Vincent had come home. His own wounds had long healed, but still he had done nothing about redeeming his promise to Jack Thornton, though of course he had written to Cassandra from France.

He had his reasons for not going to see her. Against all hope, he *had* hoped—but that was nonsense. The fact that all his efforts to trace Jack's body had been futile did not mean that he was still alive. He had seen his friend fall, knew that the shot must have been fatal. Many soldiers had been buried where they lay, some too badly mutilated by the French cannon to be recognised even by their friends.

'God damn it, Jack!' Vincent cursed aloud as he stood alone, watching the sun go down. 'I never wanted you to die. Why won't you let me be at peace?'

But he would never be at peace, unless he atoned in some way for letting Jack down. And the only thing Jack had ever asked of him was to take care of his sister.

'She ain't pretty,' Jack had said to him once as they sat talking over a dying fire. 'But she will make someone a damned good wife. She needs a decent man, Vinnie. I can't stand to think of anyone hurting her. I've always thought you and Cassie might suit.'

Vincent had denied him then, but days later, after the news of Sir Edward's terrible suicide, he had given his word with the others.

'All right, Jack,' he said now, glaring up at the night sky. 'You win, damn you! I'll marry her—if she'll have me.'

It was two days later and Miss Cassandra Thornton was in the bedchamber of her home, staring at the array of gowns spread over her bed. They gave her some considerable pleasure. She had never owned so many new clothes before in her life, and though she knew they would not carry her through the London season that she had been planning since the news of her rather startling inheritance had arrived, she could not help but feel some satisfaction.

'They are lovely,' her companion said, stroking a particularly pretty green cloth walking gown. 'You are so lucky, Cassie. I've never seen anything so fine.'

'Do you like that one?' Cassie asked, picking up the gown and holding it against the younger girl. 'Yes, the colour is just right for you. It brings out the gold lights in your hair, and the green of your eyes. You must have it, Sarah.'

'Oh, I couldn't possibly,' cried Miss Sarah Walker. The fifth daughter of a country parson, she had been unable to repress a little stab of envy on seeing the clothes, since her parents, though kind and generous within their means, would never be able to afford a season for her. 'You haven't even worn it yet. I was only admiring it. I did not expect you to give it to me.'

'I know that, silly!' Cassie laughed, her brown eyes as warm as melted chocolate as she pushed the dress into her friend's hands. 'I shall still have as many gowns as I need until I go up to London.'

'When do you leave?' Sarah asked, looking at the gown with undisguised longing, yet still hesitating. 'Are you sure you don't want this, Cassie?'

'Quite sure. It will suit you far better than it would me. I was misguided in my choice of style in that gown. I shall do better in future. In fact, I believe the brown velvet and the blue muslin would look well on you. I think you should have them all.'

'Cassie! You are too generous. You cannot possibly afford to give me all these clothes.'

'Yes, I can,' Cassie said, snatching up a paisley shawl and two rather fetching bonnets, and adding them to the growing pile. 'Aunt Gwendoline was so very, very rich, Sarah. I am sure I nearly died when that lawyer came all the way up from Cornwall to tell me she had left me everything. She was Mama's elder sister, of course, and I vaguely remember seeing her once when Mama took me to stay…it was a few months before she died.'

Tears hovered on her thick, dark lashes but she blinked them away.

'Dearest Cassie,' her friend said. 'You still miss her, don't you?'

'I know it was a long time ago. I was only fourteen when she fell ill, but I loved her very much,' Cassie said. 'Yet I had Father and Jack. To lose them both so suddenly…' She smothered a sob. 'But losing Jack was the worst of all. We were always such good friends. I miss him so much, Sarah.'

'I know…' The two girls embraced affectionately. 'And it was awful when the lawyers told you you had only months to find somewhere else to live. I think it is so unfair when an estate is entailed to some distant cousin or other.'

'There wasn't much left after the debts were paid. Just the house and a few bits and pieces—but it was still up-setting to be told I must go. Particularly when Father's cousin Kendal is so odious,' Cassie said. 'I could not wait to leave…and yet I had nowhere to go.'

'You could have come to us,' Sarah reminded her. 'I should have been glad to have you. Papa told you you could share my room, and stay with us for as long as you wished.'

'Your father is so kind,' Cassie said, 'but I did not want to be a burden to him. No, I had almost made up my mind to hire myself out as a governess or a companion…and then poor Aunt Gwendoline left me her fortune. I wish I had written to her more often now—but she did not encourage it.'

'Was she not almost a recluse in her last years?'

'So I have been told. She did not particularly welcome us when Mama took me to visit—but she *has* left me her whole fortune.'

'And now you are off to London to find yourself a hand-some beau!'

'Oh, at least a dozen of them,' Cassie said, her dark eyes alive with mischief. 'I mean to be the toast of Lon-don…despite not being a beauty. Money, you know, makes up for many faults in a lady's appearance.'

'You are not plain,' said Sarah loyally. 'Papa says you are a handsome woman—and, you must know, that's a compliment from him.'

'Yes, indeed!' Cassie laughed deep inside her. She was

not what most people would describe as beautiful; she did not have the fair, delicate looks she knew to be all the rage—but neither was she plain. Or not so plain that it would discourage gentlemen from offering for her once they discovered she possessed a considerable fortune. 'I know it to be so. And I am gratified.'

'So when do you leave?'

'When Mrs Simmons sees fit to answer my letter. She was recommended to me by Lady Fitzpatrick as a chaperon—and, as you know, I cannot go to London without a respected chaperon to lend me consequence or I shall never do more than flutter at the edges of society.'

'She will surely write soon,' Sarah said, slightly wistful. 'I shall miss you, Cassie.'

'Well, you need not,' Cassie said, making up her mind to something that had just occurred to her. 'Why do you not come with me? It would not be fitting for us to visit alone, because you are only nineteen—and though I am one and twenty, it would not be considered proper for us to go unchaperoned. But I should be much happier if you accompanied Mrs Simmons and me…'

Sarah stared at her, in disbelief. 'You cannot mean it? No, no, Papa could never afford to let me go.'

'You will not need to trouble your father for money,' Cassie said. 'The clothes I've already given you will do for a while, and when we go to London I shall buy more for us both. It will be my present to you for all the kindness you and your family showed me after my father…died.'

Cassie's eyes reflected the grief and hurt she had felt at the shocking circumstance of her father's suicide. Although the elderly Lady Fitzpatrick had continued to welcome her to her house at the other side of the little Hampshire village, many of the neighbours who had been to dine with her father had shunned her. Had it not been for the Reverend

Walker and his family, Cassie might have given way to the despair that had been so very overwhelming.

She had, in fact, struggled bravely against a series of misfortunes—the worst by far her discovery of her father's lifeless body in his library. His death had not caused her as much grief as her beloved brother's, but it had given her a horror of guns and led to nightmares. For some weeks she had been unable to sleep without waking with tears on her cheeks, and though the bad dreams had finally ceased, the memory still lingered at the back of her mind.

Only a girl of strong resolution could have put such a terrible time behind her, retaining both her sanity and her determination not to be crushed. There *had* been moments when Cassie had felt there was no reason for her to go on living, but some months had passed since her world fell apart. She had slowly come to terms with her loss, making up her mind to rebuild her life, and the news of her inheritance had aroused her fighting spirit once more.

Until the double tragedy that had almost destroyed her, Cassie had always been able to live well within herself. Her parents had always treated her fairly, but they had both idolised Jack. He was the son and heir both had wanted: a laughing, confident young man who must make any parent proud. As a young child, Cassie had not blamed her parents for putting Jack first. She had adored him herself, and he had always been her champion.

From the very beginning, they had been close. Cassie still ached for the loss of him. She was sure she would never be as close to anyone again. Perhaps because of that, she had made up her mind not to look for love in her choice of a husband. Love was too painful: she had no wish to be hurt again. She had money; what she needed now was a man of some consequence. Someone who could give her a place in society.

Cassie had spent long enough being looked down at by

her neighbours. She wanted neither pity nor condescension, but a respect that was hers by right. As the daughter of a gambler who had taken his own life, she could only achieve her heart's desire by marrying a man of good family—a leader of the *ton*!

'Oh, do not look like that, dearest,' Sarah begged, recalling her thoughts to the present with a touch of her hand. 'I cannot bear to see you so unhappy.'

Cassie shook her head. 'I am not precisely unhappy, Sarah. I was thinking of Jack. I shall always miss him, but it is getting better. I am determined to put it all behind me. And you can help me by agreeing to come to London with me.' The sparkle of mischief was back in her eyes. 'In fact, I shall not go without you. I shall persuade your father to agree.'

'I am sure he will if *you* ask him,' Sarah said, excitement dawning in her eyes. 'But only if we are properly chaperoned, of course.'

'Lady Fitzpatrick promised…' Cassie began, pausing as there was a knock at the door. Then a maid entered. 'Yes, Ellie, what is it? Do you have something for me?'

'You asked me to bring any letters to you, miss.'

'Has it come at last?' Cassie eagerly took the letters she was offered, breaking the seal of one which had come from London. 'This is from Mrs Simmons…' She scanned the first few lines. 'She will join me as a companion…oh!' Her disappointment was sharp. 'But not until the end of next month.'

'Next month?' Sarah looked at her. 'That is not so bad, is it?'

'It will be August by the time we are in London,' Cassie replied. 'The season will be as good as over. Perhaps we should go to Brighton instead?'

'Brighton is fashionable in the summer…'

'But it is not London,' Cassie said, frowning. 'Oh, well,

I suppose it will have to do…' She was opening the second letter and, as she began to read it, gasped in surprise. 'Good gracious!'

'Is something the matter?'

'No…' Cassie gave her an odd look. 'It is from Lady Longbourne. Do you remember Sir Bertram? When he died, his widow moved to Lord Carlton's house. The Longbournes' house, which belongs to Sir Bertram's heir, of course, has been let to tenants for some years.'

'I do just remember the family,' Sarah said. 'I never knew them well, but Papa visited after Sir Bertram died— it must have been eight years ago. I went with him, but I stayed in the garden with Sir Bertram's son…I think his name was Harry.'

'That's right. Lady Longbourne has two sons, Harry and his half-brother Vincent.' Cassie blushed. 'I mean Lord Carlton, of course.'

'Did you know them well?'

'Quite well. My mother often had tea with Lady Longbourne. I remember once…' She hesitated, then shook her head. 'It doesn't matter. I was only a child.'

'Oh, do tell,' Sarah pleaded. 'It must have been something particular or it would not have stayed in your mind.'

Cassie laughed, her cheeks still a little pink. 'I had been given a kitten as a present from Jack. It was for my birthday. I was twelve.'

'What happened?'

'My kitten climbed a tall tree. I called and called, but she would not come to me. She was mewing so pitifully and I couldn't bear to hear her. Jack was out riding with Father—so I climbed up the tree to rescue her and got hopelessly stuck.'

'Cassie!' Sarah stared at her, halfway between amusement and dismay. 'Whatever did you do?'

'I sat on a branch and waited for Jack to come home—

but Vincent Carlton came first. He had called to see Jack, of course: they were such good friends.' A strange, reminiscent expression had crept into Cassie's eyes. 'I shouted to him and he climbed the tree after me. I made him take Kitty first and then come back for me. He was wearing a pair of pale cream riding breeches—and he tore them in a very revealing place.' She laughed, looking a little embarrassed. 'They were new, too, as he informed me in no uncertain manner.'

'Was he angry?'

'No—just embarrassed, I think. He went off at once without stopping to see Jack. I never saw him to speak to again. He went away to London, and a year or so after that Sir Bertram died. I haven't heard from Lady Longbourne in years, though Lord Carlton wrote to me from France and begged me to send to his own lawyers in London if I was in any sort of difficulty. It was a very kind letter…'

'He must have forgiven you, after all.'

'Or he felt it his duty. His friendship with Jack had continued out there. My brother often mentioned him when he wrote…'

Again, Cassie's eyes clouded with sadness. However, she was not a girl to feel sorry for herself, and she had made up her mind that the time for grief had passed. Jack would not have wanted her to go on breaking her heart for him. He had thought too much of her for that!

'Do you care to go riding?' she asked Sarah. 'You can have my mare and I'll ride Jack's bay. We used to ride him together sometimes. So he will allow me to exercise him, though he can be restive and difficult to manage.'

'What will you do with the horses when you leave here?'

'I shall take them both with me. I told Kendal Saracen was my brother's personal property, his to do with as he pleased—and Jack's own will left his possessions to me. I've had everything else of Jack's packed into large trunks and sent them to Nanny Robinson's cottage. I refuse to let Kendal get his hands on anything that belonged to my brother!'

'Is he so very awful, Cassie?'

'Detestable!' Cassie replied and shuddered. 'He visited me not three weeks after Jack was killed and used his title! Then he dared to—to offer me the chance of becoming his wife. It was so very obvious that he could not wait to get his hands on what little was left of Papa's estate—or Jack's as it was by then. And that he imagined he was doing me a very great favour by offering for me!'

'That was most insensitive of him. How fortunate that you refused him. Now that you have so much money of your own, you may choose where you will.'

'No doubt he would have tried to get his hands on that had he known.' Cassie's eyes sparked. 'He implied that he had a right to guardianship over me, because he is Father's cousin—though the relationship between him and my father was never friendly. To be plain, they hated each other. After meeting Kendal once, I can understand why he was never invited to stay here.'

'What did you say to him?'

'I told him I was old enough to do without his help—and that I had a lawyer to look after my affairs. He was not best pleased with me, and went off in a huff.'

'Do you suppose he could have known of your aunt's intention to leave you her money?'

'How could he? There had never been the slightest hint of it. I'm sure he could not have known about her fortune.'

'No, I suppose not,' Sarah said, still frowning. 'Perhaps he was only doing what he felt to be his duty?'

'I dare say we shall never know. For he was in such a way when he left—and it was after that I was given notice to quit.' Cassie shook her head. 'I am sure I've seen the last of Kendal, for he is not likely to repeat his offer again.'

Privately, Sarah thought it was extremely likely that the odious Sir Kendal Thornton would make his presence felt once he had heard of Cassie's inheritance. She was thankful that her friend had at least one influential acquaintance.

'And what did Lady Longbourne's letter say?' she prompted after a short silence. 'You did not tell me.'

'Did I not?' Cassie laughed. 'We were diverted by other topics.'

'Lord Carlton's unmentionables!'

Cassie nodded, her eyes carrying secret thoughts that seemed to please her. 'She was so kind as to ask me to go and stay at once.'

'Oh, that is nice of her.'

'Yes, so I thought.'

'And shall you?'

'Only if you will come with me. You have been my constant companion these past months, Sarah. I do not know how I should have managed alone. I cannot bear to part from you now. I shall write and tell Lady Longbourne to expect us next week. I am sure she will be happy to have us both, since she says she is in need of companionship.'

'If only Papa will permit it!'

'He can surely have no objection. He must remember Lady Longbourne.' Cassie smiled at her, sensing her dawning excitement. 'We shall walk down to the vicarage and beg his indulgence,' she said. 'I shall take Janet, of course. She has guarded me well since Father…and she will be glad to look after us both.'

Janet had been Lady Thornton's personal maid from the moment she was a bride and, though she was now nearing sixty, a thin, no-nonsense lady who never hesitated to correct her young mistress's behaviour if she thought it necessary, she was devoted to Cassie.

'Papa thinks well of your Janet.' Sarah's eyes glowed. 'Let us go and speak to him at once!'

* * *

It was not until much, much later that evening, when Cassie was alone, preparing for bed, that she had a chance to reflect on the day's events.

The Reverend Mr Walker had agreed to the visit after only a moment or two of reflection, professing himself pleased with the idea of his daughter accompanying her, both to Lady Longbourne's, and to Brighton. The younger son of an impoverished baronet, who had had no choice but to take up the church for his living, he was still worldly enough to know that a better chance for his daughter to mix in good society was never likely to present itself, and while he would not have dreamed of saying it, he had every hope that his charming and pretty daughter might find herself a husband whilst staying with her friend.

Cassie had been sure Sarah's dear papa would see the advantage of a visit to Lord Carlton's estate, as she did herself. Nothing could be more fortunate. Indeed, it would be much better if she could have made her come out in London under Lady Longbourne's patronage, but she did not expect that: yet it would do her no harm if it were generally known that she had visited with the family, and no doubt she could trust Mrs Simmons to publish the fact once they were settled in Brighton later that summer.

Now, Cassie sat brushing her long, rich brown hair, staring vaguely at her reflection in the dressing mirror without truly seeing herself. A little smile played about her full, generous mouth as she let herself remember that long-ago incident in the garden of her home.

'Come down, Cassandra,' Vincent had commanded with all the force of his superior years. 'I'll get the kitten later.'

'You must take her first,' she had insisted, defying his efforts to rescue her. 'She's more frightened than I am and, if you try to take us both, she may struggle and fall.'

Her eyes danced with laughter as she recalled the very improper expressions he had uttered when, on the return journey, he had snagged his breeches on a branch, revealing the fact that he was wearing nothing underneath the tight-fitting garment.

She had laughed then, too, and he had looked furious, but apart from that first startled oath, had said nothing out of place. She recalled that he had always had perfect manners—and a truly amazing smile.

The young Cassie had dreamt about her rescuer for some nights afterwards, but the memory had faded after he went away and she had eventually forgotten her knight—until his kind letter from France, which had brought her to tears.

There had been other letters from Jack's friends, but only Lord Carlton's had made any real impression on her. It had seemed he really cared how Cassie felt, while the rest merely conveyed sympathy in a conventional way.

It would be pleasant to meet Lord Carlton again, if only to thank him for the consideration he had shown her. She wondered if the invitation from Lady Longbourne had been at his instigation, and the thought made her oddly restless.

She rose from her dressing table and went to gaze out of her bedroom window. There was a pale round moon in the sky, throwing its silver light over the garden and arousing a wistful longing in her—a longing for what?

She did not know what she wanted, or at least, she did know—but to hope for something that could never be was futile.

'Oh, Jack my dearest,' she sighed. 'If only you were here to share Aunt Gwendoline's legacy—what fun we could have had spending it together.'

For one moment Cassie's skin tingled as she caught sight of something moving amongst the shrubbery. Was there someone down there? She put up the sash window and leaned out, straining to see, but a cloud had passed across the moon and she could not be sure that anything had been there in the first place.

Of course there was no one there! Cassie closed her window and turned away. She was imagining things…but just for a moment she had thought there was a man out there watching the house.

Chapter Two

The next few days were extremely busy for Cassie as she, Sarah and Janet packed their trunks and sorted through their closets for forgotten scarves, shawls and bonnets. With a little industry, the scarves could be freshened, the bonnets refurbished with ribbons and made to look almost new.

Cassie was pleased that she had given Sarah some new gowns, because at least they could both arrive looking presentable. She wished she had had time to order more for them both, but there was not a moment to be lost, for she wanted to make the most of the summer season.

'We might just persuade Lady Longbourne to take us to London for a few days,' she confided to Sarah, as they were packing trifles they could not possibly manage to live without into one of the large trunks. 'I do not count upon it, for it is kind enough of her to ask us to stay—but it would be nice to have our clothes ready for when we go to Brighton later. Even if she does not wish to trouble herself, she may know a reliable seamstress who could be trusted to work from our measurements.'

'I am sure I never expected to own anything so fine as this,' Sarah replied, stroking the material of the green walking dress Cassie had given her. 'I shall wear it to travel in, for the journey is no more than three or four hours, so Papa says, and it will not be creased.'

'It does look well on you,' replied Cassie. 'With your honey-blonde hair and green eyes…' She glanced at her own dark hair, which was thick and glossy enough, but unremarkable beside her friend's. 'You are so pretty, Sarah. I do not doubt that you will have all the dashing young men running after you when we get to Brighton.'

'Only if they are not in need of a fortune,' Sarah said, laughing at her enthusiasm. She was a practical girl and knew that it would probably take more than a pretty face to secure the kind of marriage Cassie was hoping for. 'Poor Papa cannot give me more than a hundred pounds when I marry and an allowance of fifty pounds a year, just as he does now.'

Cassie said nothing, but made up her mind to write to the lawyers in London and see if it would be possible to settle a small sum of money on her friend. She did not yet quite understand the terms of her aunt's will, but she knew she had a great deal of money in her possession, though there were some restrictions on the disposal of capital—at least until she married.

She said nothing to her friend, who she knew would protest, nor would she until it was all settled but, being a generous girl, she tucked the idea away in her mind for future reference.

At last it was time for the girls to set out on their travels. As the Reverend Mr Walker had said, it was a journey that should take them no more than four hours at most.

The carriage was brought round at ten that morning, and after some discussion as to whether all their boxes had been safely stowed on the baggage coach, the carriage went off at a good pace.

Cassie turned round to look back at her home for one

last time. The remainder of her personal things were to be sent to Nanny Robinson for safekeeping, and a groom was to walk her precious horses over to Lady Fitzgerald's stables that very morning. She might, had she wished, have lingered at the house for another month but, although torn by memories, both happy and sad, she was relieved to be leaving early.

She had always loved the old house where she had been born, but she would not want to live there without her family. No, it was for the best, she thought, relaxing back against the cushions of the very comfortable carriage Lady Longbourne had sent over the previous night to fetch her.

Cassie could afford to set up her own carriage now if she wished, and she would probably do so when she had her own establishment—but although she was a reasonable judge of horses, she could not buy them for herself. She needed a male representative, someone who could be trusted not to saddle her with bone setters or old nags: she wanted a bang-up pair, and fashionable equipage to show them off.

It was all so very exciting, so much to look forward to that she found no trouble in keeping up a flow of chatter with her friend, and it was not until they had been travelling for nearly two hours that she heard a shout from the coachman, and glanced out of the window. The horses were slowing to walking pace, and when Cassie saw what was going on just ahead of them, she pulled the cord to let her driver know that she wished to stop.

'What is it?' Sarah asked. 'Why are we stopping?'

'Someone is ill,' Cassie replied. 'She has fallen on the ground. I think…yes, I am sure she is in some trouble.'

Sarah looked out of the window and gasped. Although a kindly girl, she was the product of a strict upbringing and what she saw shocked her. 'But—but she is—'

'Yes, exactly,' Cassie said, and, as the carriage stopped,

jumped out without waiting for assistance. 'You stay there, Sarah…I shall see what needs to be done.'

Janet had been snoozing quietly in her corner, oblivious to what was happening. She woke up and looked about her in a daze.

'Are we there?'

'No…' Sarah nodded unhappily towards the open door. 'It's Cassie…she insisted on stopping.'

Janet glanced out of the window, snorting in disgust over the impetuous behaviour of her mistress. She got out of the carriage with the assistance of the groom, who had jumped down from the box and was watching his mistress warily. Having assessed the situation, she then went to where Cassie had knelt on the grass verge. She was bending over a woman who was clearly in pain—a rather dirty-looking creature wearing what Janet would most certainly describe as rags.

'Now, what are you at, miss?' she asked in a voice heavy with resignation.

Years of coping with stray animals, wounded birds and ragamuffins brought home by Miss Cassandra to be fed in the kitchen had prepared Janet for the inevitable. And she was not in the least surprised when her young mistress suggested that they must take the vagabond into the carriage with them.

'Now that would not be wise,' she began, but a flash from Cassie's eyes silenced her. 'Might I suggest that the proper place for her is in the baggage—'

'No, you may not,' Cassie said firmly. 'If you and Sarah are not prepared to ride with this poor woman, you may both ride in the coach.'

'Now, there's no need to take on,' Janet said, accepting her fate. 'Give the poor lass to me. She shall sit next to me and I'll attend her if…well, let's hope it does not come to that!'

'I knew you would see it my way,' Cassie said, smiling in a way that would have charmed the sourest temper. 'I want to be with her, Janet. Just to make sure that she does not suffer…'

'Aye,' the long-suffering Janet replied with a wry grimace, 'of course you would.'

Lord Carlton was in the salon with his mama at Carlton House, awaiting the arrival of Miss Cassandra Thornton and her friend Miss Sarah Walker. It was well past three in the afternoon and they had begun to wonder where their guests could have got to, as they had been expecting them any time this past hour or more.

Lady Longbourne was looking exceptionally fine that day in her simple but elegant pale grey gown with a Norwich silk shawl draped negligently over her shoulders and her hair dressed with a lace cap of such fetching ingenuity that her son was moved to remark on it.

'That cap becomes you very well, Mama. I like it exceedingly.'

'Well, I am glad that you do, for you paid for it together with several more and various other items you insisted I should order for my birthday, besides giving me those sapphires, which were far too extravagant for a woman of my age.'

'But became you very well…'

'You had no business to be wasting your money on a woman of my wretched health,' his mama replied, suffering an irritation of the nerves. Really, it was so inconsiderate of Carlton to expect her to entertain two young and probably very silly gels! The afternoon was warm and it was well past the time for her nap. 'I dare say I shall never have the occasion to wear them.'

'I see no reason why you should not,' her unfeeling son replied. 'We must give some dinners for our guests,

Mama—and perhaps a little dance if Cassandra agrees to be my wife.'

'You surely do not expect—' Whatever Lady Long-bourne had been about to say was lost as the butler opened the door and announced, in hushed and important tones, the arrival of their guests.

'Miss Cassandra Thornton and Miss Sarah Walker.'

Lady Longbourne raised her quizzing glass as two young ladies walked in. They were both wearing dresses of good quality material, but made in a way which her ladyship's experienced eye knew at once for the work of a provincial seamstress: the latest fashions had been faithfully copied, but would not do for the lady who was to become Carlton's wife. She must obviously take Cassandra's wardrobe in hand!

But which of them was Miss Thornton? She could not remember the girl, who had usually preferred to play in the garden rather than venture into the salon, when she and Lady Thornton had been taking tea.

'Cassandra, my dear!' she said and stared directly at Sarah, who looked younger and slightly less modish than her companion. 'And Miss Walker…'

'Forgive me, Mama,' Vincent said, 'I believe this young lady is Cassandra.' His grey eyes held a hint of amusement as he walked towards them and held out his hand to her. 'It is some years since we met, but the circumstances were such as to have somehow imprinted your features into my mind. Am I right, are you indeed Miss Thornton?'

'Yes, I'm afraid I am, sir.' Cassie laughed as she gave him her hand, her cheeks a little pink, yet managing to meet his teasing gaze. 'Though I would as lief not be reminded of that incident. I fear you must have been quite cross with me that day, though you did not allow it to show.'

Vincent raised her hand to his lips, placing a chaste sa-lute on the back. 'I felt a little foolish, I admit—but hope

I should never be churlish enough to subject you to bad temper.' Then, turning from her to Sarah, he kissed her hand in the same manner and welcomed her to Carlton House. 'For any friend of Miss Thornton's must always be welcome here—must she not, Mama?'

Vincent was pleasantly surprised by Cassandra's looks. He, too, recognized that style was sadly lacking in her dress, but she had an attractive, open, healthy look about her, as if she spent her days outside as often as possible, and he liked the laughter in her eyes. He had feared her troubles might have changed her, but now he could see that her spirit had not been crushed.

Lady Longbourne had come forward and was smiling. 'You are both very welcome, my dears,' she said and kissed each of them in turn on the cheek. 'You have no idea how dull it can be for a widow alone in the country, especially when one's health does not favour one—it is a pleasure for me to have such delightful company.'

As she spoke, she realized that it might after all be quite a refreshing change to have two young ladies staying with her—and the matter of Cassandra's wardrobe was something she intended to oversee personally. It struck her then that she would have to accompany the gel to London, and she was horrified at the thought—and yet her duty was to see Carlton's fiancée safely established in society. Naturally, she would do whatever was necessary, even though it would be very troublesome and might put her own health at risk.

Cassandra had seen at once the rather languid manner of her hostess, noticing the droop of her mouth and a certain pallor, which she thought might have been caused by lack of exercise and fresh air.

'I am truly sorry to hear you have been unwell, ma'am,' she said. 'It was kind of you to invite us, and I hope we shall not be too much trouble for you.'

'No, no, I am sure you could not be the slightest trouble to me. I have often wished for a daughter—and now for a time I may pretend that I have not one but two.'

'Prettily said, Mama,' Vincent said, a wry smile in his eyes. 'Let me assure you, Miss Thornton, we have been eagerly awaiting you...'

'You must forgive us if we are late,' Cassie said. 'We were delayed for an hour or more—were we not, Sarah?'

'It was so awful,' Sarah said, shedding her reserve as the thoughts uppermost in her mind burst forth. 'We came upon a band of travelling folk on the road, and one of the women was near fainting. Cassie insisted on stopping the carriage and we took her up with us—'

'You took a gypsy woman up with you?' Lady Longbourne stared at Cassandra in horror. 'But she could have had fleas or an infectious disease...or anything!'

'Pray do not disturb yourself, ma'am,' Cassie replied. 'She was big with child and clearly near her time. She was trying to reach a camp where the wise women of the band could care for her and...'

Lady Longbourne gasped. Had it not been so clearly her duty to instruct this ridiculous child her son was determined to marry, she would have fainted and retired to her bed at once.

'Cassandra,' she said in hushed tones that conveyed her very real sense of horror, 'you must not...you *really* must not speak of such things so openly. Especially when gentlemen are present. You will be thought of as fast...or worse.'

'Oh, dear, shall I?' Cassie smiled inwardly. 'I am so sorry if I have upset you, ma'am. Please do sit down. You look quite faint. You must forgive me for my execrable manners. I fear am not used to the rules of society. My only thought was that I could not leave the poor woman to...lie there on the ground and...' She subsided with a blush as she noticed that Lord Carlton was, far from being shocked, hard put to contain his laughter. 'But it was very wrong of me. I promise you she was not infectious—and I do not think we have taken harm from the encounter. But I just could not abandon her.'

'No, that would indeed have been very unkind in you,' Vincent said, managing to look grave notwithstanding his desire to laugh. 'You could not leave a fellow creature in such extremity. Despite the discomfort it must have incurred for you—to say nothing of your travelling companions!—I am persuaded you were refreshed by the satisfaction of having done a good deed.'

'Vincent!' Lady Longbourne gave her son a quelling look. 'I beg your pardon, Miss Thornton. I dare say you might not realize it, having not come across my son's very odd notion of humour before which is hardly surprising, for I'm sure no one else could possibly imagine such remarks to be funny—but I can assure you in all good faith that he *was* teasing you.'

Cassie's startled eyes flew to Carlton's face. She had never doubted that he was making fun of her and, as she saw the expression of indulgence on his face as he looked at his mother, she was hard pressed not to laugh out loud. What a wicked sense of humour he had, very much like that she and Jack had shared!

'I am indebted to you for telling me,' she replied in a deceivingly flat tone. 'But Lord Carlton is very good to remind me that I have inconvenienced poor Sarah, and I dare say she is itching to tidy herself—just in case the poor woman did have fleas.'

At this, Vincent was betrayed into a laugh—a laugh so deep and husky that Cassandra found it difficult not to join in. However, Lady Longbourne was clearly affronted by her son's amusement. She turned her back on him and smiled on Sarah, reassuring her she would find clean water waiting in her room.

'I shall ring for Mrs Midge to take you up at once,' she said. 'For I should not like to be subjected to such an encounter myself, and understand perfectly how you feel. If I were you, I should let one of the maids take your gown and give it a good shake, my dear, and then you may feel better. You may both come down as soon as you feel ready, and we shall have tea—for you must both be starving, having missed your lunch.'

'Oh, we were well prepared,' Cassie said blithely. 'Janet never travels without a basket of food, since, as she says, one never knows what one may encounter on the road.'

'I dare say she has travelled with you before, Miss Thornton?'

Lord Carlton's quip was neither helpful nor deserving of a reply, so Cassie wisely ignored it.

She went on unheedingly, 'And despite giving most of Janet's food to the companions of the poor woman we helped, we ate a piece of pie and a biscuit each, did we not, Sarah?'

'Yes…but I confess I am still a little hungry, Cassie.'

The housekeeper had arrived by this time and, having been asked by Lady Longbourne to show the young ladies to their rooms, obliged immediately. Sarah was only too anxious to go, and Cassie followed, pausing briefly at the door to glance back. Her eyes encountered Lord Carlton's and, meeting his thoughtful gaze, she felt an odd flutter of her heart.

How very handsome he was! Far more so than she had remembered. She thought perhaps this visit might be even more useful than she had first thought. It was a happy chance that he was staying with his mother, when he might so easily have been in town with his friends. And a gentleman of Lord Carlton's standing would naturally have a great many friends. If he were to show his approval of her publicly, Cassie would be invited everywhere. If only she could somehow get to London before the season was over.

Vincent toyed with his wineglass as the butler was serving the second course at dinner that evening. It was a very decent dinner by country standards, consisting of pigeons in red wine, a roasted cockerel and a leg of pork removed with a dish of creamed sweetbreads, some green peas, a dish of buttered asparagus and tiny sautéed potatoes, together with a curd junket and some crab tartlets. Not quite up to the standards of the French chef he employed in London perhaps, but not so badly presented as to give offence. Yet Vincent had discovered he had no appetite.

He noticed that Cassandra ate a little of the cockerel and the side dishes, but touched neither the pork nor the pigeons. However, when the sweet course was served, she did justice to the various jellies and trifles. She was clearly a healthy girl, with a lively, intelligent manner. Very suitable for the mother of the children he must provide in order for the family line to remain unbroken.

He had wondered if he would be able to go through with his promise to Jack, but, observing her now from beneath his long, dark lashes, he thought perhaps the task need not be so very burdensome after all. She was not pretty—his mother had been right about that—but not so very plain as to be without charm.

He knew that it was fashionable amongst the married men of his acquaintance to take mistresses, and perhaps Cassie would be content with that, since she had made it clear she did not want a love match. Yet Vincent knew that it was not what he really wanted.

What then? A wry smile touched his mouth. Was he truly such a fool as to believe in the perfect love? If only one were fortunate enough to find it...

* * *

Cassie was acutely aware of Lord Carlton watching her during dinner. He seemed not to be interested in his meal, and she had seen a brooding expression in his eyes that was so at odds with his usual manner that it intrigued her. However, when he joined the ladies in the drawing room after dinner, he was his normal charming self.

'Would you care to see over the house, Miss Thornton?' he asked. 'It is not of any great age, and therefore I can promise you no ghosts or fascinating antiquities. But we do have an extensive library, which has a rather splendid ceiling.'

'Cassandra will not want to see that,' said his mama. 'You should show her the orangery, that is far more suitable.'

'I should very much like to see the house, sir,' Cassie said.

'And you, Miss Walker?' Vincent looked smilingly towards Sarah, who begged to be excused on the grounds that Lady Longbourne had just asked her to play the pianoforte for her.

Cassie stood up, then accompanied her host out into the hall and through a large open parlour, which had several rather hard, uncomfortable-looking sofas ranged against the walls but no other furniture.

'This is where we have sometimes held little dances,' Vincent informed her. 'Not grand enough for an important ball, of course. I have thought about building an extension, but my grandfather's house in Surrey is much larger. I believe, when I settle to country life, it is there I shall make my home.'

'I dare say you have not wished particularly to hold many balls before this,' Cassie said politely. 'And I am sure you could set up at least twenty couples here if you wished.'

'Yes, perhaps.' Vincent's mouth curved in a lazy smile.

'As you say, I have not felt the need to hold a ball—but I may well do so in future.'

'When you marry, your wife may wish to entertain frequently,' Cassie said wisely. 'Some ladies are more fond of company than others. I suppose your mama does not entertain as often as your wife might wish?'

'Exactly so. When I marry, things will undoubtedly change.'

'I should imagine they must.' Cassie's eyes met his candidly. 'I suppose you have been much accustomed to coming and going as you please, without a word to anyone. I have often thought gentlemen fortunate to have so much freedom. But I suppose there are compensations to being a lady.'

She sounded so doubtful that Vincent's attention was caught.

'I suppose there must be.' His eyes danced with a wicked amusement. 'What can they be? Do tell me, Miss Thornton, for I am not certain that I know. And I would venture to suggest that you have given some thought to the subject.'

'One of them is to take refuge in dignity and refuse to answer when one knows a certain gentleman is being excessively provoking.' Cassie gave him a sparkling look. 'I am eager to see the ceiling in your library, sir—if I may?'

'Just through here,' Vincent invited. 'It was designed and executed by an obscure but talented Italian artist my father brought here at some expense. I do hope you approve.'

Cassie followed him into what was obviously a magnificent apartment. The walls were lined with tasteful, restrained bookcases of rich dark mahogany with a fine stringing of a lighter wood. Two large tables dominated the central run of the room, and three leather-covered matching sofas, which looked enticingly comfortable, were set to catch the light from the long windows.

However, it was undoubtedly the magnificent ceiling

which drew the immediate attention of anyone entering the room. At either end there were large semi-circles which had been painted with a delicate duck-egg-blue background. Against this was drawn a scene of half-naked nymphs partly covered by flimsy drapes, and what appeared to be a satyr. The remainder of the ceiling was garlanded with swags of grapes, vine leaves and cherubs.

'Oh,' Cassie said, a little surprised by the lascivious expression in the satyr's eyes. 'It is very unusual. Beautiful, of course, but not quite what one might expect.'

'It is exactly what one might have expected of my father,' Vincent said, a chuckle escaping him as he realized she had taken it completely in her stride. 'Mama detests it, of course. She would have me paint it over—but whatever one's personal feelings, it is a work of art. Would you not say so?'

'Oh, yes,' Cassie agreed without hesitation. 'I do not believe you should cover it over, sir. After all, one is not forced to look unless one wishes.'

'No,' Vincent replied, giving her an appreciative look. 'One does not have to look.'

Cassie was exploring the room a little further, picking up pieces of sculpture and discovering that the theme of the ceiling had been repeated in the marbles and porcelain. Noticing a door at the far end, she moved towards it. 'And what is through here, sir? Is one permitted to see?'

'The billiard room. Not of interest to a lady, I dare say?'

Cassie turned her dark, melting gaze on him, her brows arched. 'This particular lady would like to see it,' she said. 'May I?'

'Be my guest,' Vincent invited, that lazy smile she had remarked earlier playing about his mouth.

He followed Cassie in, watching from beneath thick black lashes as she stroked her hand reverently over the velvet-smooth surface of the huge table that dominated the room. She hesitated, then with seeming care selected a cue from the racks, chalked the tip and eyed the balls which had been left carelessly on the table.

'May I?' she asked.

He nodded, his gaze narrowing keenly as she lined up the balls and proceeded to pot three of them one after the other with pleasing precision. He applauded, which brought a flush to her cheeks. She replaced her cue, looking conscious as he continued to stare at her.

'So you play,' he said. 'I suppose Jack taught you?'

'We spent hours practising trick shots,' Cassie said, a little shy now. 'I suppose it is an unusual pastime for a lady—but I always preferred to be with Jack if he would have me. Mama scolded me, of course, but I fear I am sometimes inclined to be wilful and I did not always heed her as much as I ought.'

'Yes, I see.' Vincent's eyes quizzed her. 'It *is* a fault, Miss Thornton. Undoubtedly, you would raise eyebrows in some houses if you admitted to such a terrible vice—but I promise not to hold it against you.'

'Oh, I should not dream of admitting it in mixed company,' Cassie said, an answering gleam in her eyes. 'But somehow I do not think you would betray a lady's confidence.'

Vincent made her a little bow. 'Now I am on my mettle, am I not? You make it a matter of honour that not one word of this conversation shall ever pass my lips.'

Cassie laughed, a deep husky sound from a well inside her—a sound that was wholly enchanting to the man who listened. 'I believe that must be one of those compensations we spoke of earlier, sir—do you not think so?'

It was a hit. Vincent acknowledged it with a smile, but made no comment.

'I believe we should return to the others now, Miss

Thornton. I have enjoyed our little tête-à-tête. It has been most enlightening.'

Cassie blushed at the look in his eyes. Had she said too much? His teasing humour had led her into thinking she might be open with him, but now she wondered if he might think her fast.

She hoped not. It mattered what Lord Carlton thought of her, because he and his mama could open the doors of London society for her.

Alone in her bedchamber an hour or so later, Cassie brushed her long hair as she sat before the dressing mirror. In the candleglow it was a rich chestnut, the red highlights picked up by the play of the flickering flame. She had sent Janet to bed after she had unhooked her gown, because she was not yet ready to retire herself.

It had been an interesting evening. Lady Longbourne was a thoughtful hostess, but more than that, she had a charm about her that was impossible to resist. She might have little airs about her, imagining herself an invalid when she was perhaps in much better health than she allowed, but she could be lively when she chose, and Cassie had not enjoyed herself as much in an age.

Lord Carlton was much more difficult to gauge. She liked what she knew of him, but felt he kept his own feelings carefully hidden behind a mask of affability. Could he really be as pleasant as he appeared?

Blowing out her candle, Cassie went to the windows and drew back the curtains. It was dark outside, the moon obscured by clouds, and she could see nothing. She sighed, feeling unaccountably restless, and wishing that she had thought to beg a book from Lord Carlton's library before she came up.

A little smile touched her lips as she recalled his air of expectation when she first saw the ceiling. Had he thought she would blush and turn away in embarrassment? He had looked at her with approval after that, and she had the feeling she had passed some sort of test.

And yet why Lord Carlton should be pleased that she was not a missish creature, she could not imagine.

Cassie laughed at herself. Perhaps she was letting her thoughts run away with her, as she had been accused of in the past.

'You're always arranging things the way you want them in your head,' Jack had told her once. 'Life isn't like that, Cassie. If you're not careful, little sister, you're going to be hurt one day. And I shouldn't like that. I shouldn't like that at all.'

Cassie smiled to herself at the memory. She had known what it was to be truly loved, if only as a sister. Only a fool would expect to find such real devotion a second time.

Alone in the garden, Vincent stared at Cassie's window. Her room was in darkness and he supposed she was sleeping. A smile touched his mouth as he thought of her, of the way she had countered his mockery earlier that evening. His memories of Jack's sister had not played him false. She was an exceptional woman, just as Jack had always insisted.

Vincent's thoughts returned to the last time he had seen Jack alive and the pain twisted inside him. God damn it! Would he never be free of this torture?

'I did what I thought was right,' he muttered. 'I did not mean you to die, Jack. Forgive me…I did not mean you to die…'

It had become clear to him how much Cassie had cared for her brother, and that made his situation even more difficult…made his guilt even heavier to bear.

Would he ever be able to tell her the truth…and if he did, would she forgive him?

Chapter Three

'And where,' said La Valentina, addressing Sir Harry Longbourne with a glint of temper in her magnificent eyes, 'is Carlton? I have not seen him this past week.'

La Valentina was an opera singer, admired as much for her dark, exotic beauty as her wonderful voice. Her company was avidly sought by a bevy of eager gentlemen, but only the wealthiest amongst them could have afforded her extravagant tastes. It was said that her greed for the good things of life matched her temper—which was formidable—but that she could also be generous when she chose.

She had been Lord Carlton's mistress for six months, or so it was rumoured, and some disappointed gentlemen were beginning to hint that wedding bells were in the air. No one actually believed such nonsense, of course—Carlton marry an opera singer? Never! He was far too conscious of his duty to his family, and his pride would in any case forbid it. All the same, it was deliciously amusing to speculate on such a scandalous outcome and the busy tongues could not resist such a juicy morsel.

'Well?' La Valentina threw the shakes into Harry with a flash of her eyes. 'Have you an answer for me, sir—or have your wits gone begging?'

'The thing is…' began Harry and then hesitated. He was not one of the lady's many admirers, and having heard the malicious gossip circulating the gentlemen's clubs decided to nip it in the bud. 'The thing is, madam, Vinnie has gone down to the country. His intended bride is coming to stay with Mama and…' He quailed as those Valkyric eyes darted flaming arrows at him.

'Am I to understand that Carlton is to be married?' The shock and anger in La Valentina's face revealed that she might have allowed herself to hope that there was some truth behind the rumours of an impending proposal. Uneasy, but determined to stand his ground, Harry bore up bravely.

'Oh, lord, yes,' he replied carelessly, lying through his teeth. 'It has been understood since Cassandra was in leading strings. Not publicly known, of course, but the families were all aware of it.'

'Indeed!' La Valentina seemed at a loss for words. She nodded to Harry and sailed away, the picture of outraged dignity as she disappeared into the crowded reception room of Rochester House, mingling with duchesses, dukes, earls, and making straight for the regent, who had just arrived and was one of her greatest admirers.

Harry felt a flicker of apprehension as he wondered what his half-brother would say if news of this got out, as it was bound to do, of course. Vinnie would give him a facer if nothing more. And since Vinnie, when he was first on the town, was one of the Corinthians who had been privileged to go a few rounds with Gentleman Jackson—acquitting himself so well that he was allowed to pop one in on the champion—it was useless for Harry to imagine that he could defend himself. Vinnie would give him a bloody nose—and he deserved it. He could not imagine what had driven him to lie so wildly!

As the evening wore on, however, and the calming effect

of Lord Rochester's excellent champagne began to work in him, he saw that it was all for the best and worth being milled down by his brother. It was far better for everyone to think the match had been arranged years ago, than for the truth to be generally known—and so he would tell Vinnie after he had taken his punishment, which he would, of course. He began to think it had been very clever of him to have come up with such a tale, and when friends came to congratulate him and sent their felicitations to his brother, he was able to respond with a smile and a nod.

Vinnie would probably thank him for it—after he'd knocked him down, naturally. Besides, by the time Vinnie came back to town, it would all have been settled. Cassandra would gratefully accept Carlton's offer, and once the engagement had been announced the gossips would have nothing to say.

Harry left his club feeling a little woozy and rather pleased with himself as he sauntered home. What a very clever fellow he was to be sure!

Happily unaware of his half-brother's meddling in his private affairs, Vincent was the next morning engaged in providing his guests with suitable mounts.

'I know you are a great horsewoman,' he told Cassandra. 'Jack often talked with admiration of your style over the fences.' He had spoken naturally of his friend but, as he saw the flicker of shadows in her eyes, cursed himself for a fool. 'Forgive me. I did not mean to upset you.'

'No, no, you did not,' Cassie replied, banishing the shadows. 'For a long time I could hardly bear to think of Jack, the sense of loss was too overwhelming, but...' She hesitated, unable to explain her feelings. 'I do not know why it should have happened, but just recently Jack has come back to me. He had gone—but now I feel him near me somehow.' She blushed as Vincent looked at her oddly. 'You will say my grief has turned my mind?'

'I shall say no such thing. You were very close, as close as two people can be. At first your grief was too great to be borne, but now you are beginning to remember the happy times.'

Cassie nodded but did not reply. He was right, of course, but it was more than that. To voice her thoughts too plainly might drive Jack away from her. She knew any sensible person must doubt it, but she had the strangest notion that her brother was trying to communicate with her by the power of thought. Impossible, of course! Yet so often as a child she had known when Jack wanted something of her without his saying it out loud…but he had been alive then!

Finding her unwilling to converse further on the subject, Vincent turned to Sarah, who was walking quietly at his other hand. 'And you, Miss Walker, do you ride as well as Miss Thornton?'

'Oh, no!' Sarah disclaimed. 'Cassie has a way with horses. I am a mere novice compared with her. I do not often have the chance to ride, unless Cassie lends me her mare.'

'Then I shall find a gentle mount for you,' Vincent said, smiling at her. 'I bought such a mare for Mama's use, but she will not be bothered to ride these days.'

'That is a shame,' Cassie said, joining the conversation. 'Will her health not permit her to exercise more?'

Vincent hesitated, brows wrinkling in thought. 'There is no real reason why Mama should be an invalid, but she seems to lack the desire to venture out into the fresh air. She was very ill after Sir Bertram died, but now…'

'She has gone into a decline,' Sarah said. 'I had an aunt who was much the same.'

'Might it not be boredom?' Cassie wondered aloud. 'If

she has been often alone…with both you and Sir Harry away?'

Vincent frowned and for a moment she felt she had offended him, but then he gave what she took to be a nod of agreement. 'I have often felt Mama might find happiness again, if she could be persuaded to mix more in society, as she once did—instead of confining herself to receiving the vicar and a few old friends.'

'Is that why you persuaded Lady Longbourne to invite me here?'

Cassie's clear gaze made Vincent vaguely uneasy. She was an intelligent woman, spirited and more independent than he had expected. When he, Harry, Richard Cross, Freddie Bracknell and Major Saunders had drawn straws to determine who should honour the promise they had all made, with varying degrees of enthusiasm, Vincent had made certain he drew the short straw. Jack's fate had lain heavy on his mind, and he had felt very keenly that it was his duty to take care of Cassandra. And although he had had doubts afterwards, which caused him to delay making his proposal, he still felt he was honour-bound to at least ask her to be his wife.

'Partly,' he said. 'I knew you to be in awkward circumstances, and I hoped to be of service to you. You had my letter?' She nodded. 'But you have never taken advantage of my lawyers.'

'No,' Cassie said, and hesitated. She was not sure why, but she was disinclined to tell him that she was a considerable heiress. 'I was in difficulty for a while, but I am not now. My mother's sister left me some money—'

'I was not aware you had any relatives—apart from a cousin of Sir Edward's?' Vincent's brows arched. 'And I understood that he was rather an unpleasant fellow? Jack did not care for him, at all events.' He had begged Vincent to save her from falling into Kendal's hands!

'He is quite odious!' Cassie cried. 'I dislike him very much. He had the effrontery to offer me marriage out of a mistaken sense of duty! As if I should marry for such a cause. I may not be beautiful, but I believe I am not hopeless.'

'No, not hopeless at all!' His eyes appreciated her, a smile quivering at the edges of his sensuous mouth.

'It is my intention to visit London if I can—or Brighton,' Cassie went on, blithely unaware that she had given him a facer. 'Mrs Simmons has promised to chaperon me at the end of next month. With some stylish clothes and a few introductions to the right people, I do not think it impossible I shall find someone, a *gentleman*, of course, with whom I might be comfortable—do you?'

'Is comfort your main requirement in a husband?' Vincent studied her profile with interest. He was fascinated by this show of confidence. Did she disregard him totally as a suitor—or was this a ploy to arouse his hunting instincts? No, no, he did not think her so calculating. She must consider him too old, as perhaps he was, being almost eleven years her senior.

'I believe comfort—the ability to be easy with one's chosen partner—to be of the first importance.' She turned her innocent but beguiling gaze on him. 'Do you not think so, sir?'

Vincent was much amused at her idea of marriage, but held his smile inside. Her frank way of speaking was revealing a young lady of character and he was enjoying himself immensely.

He supposed he ought to have known, for Jack had often told amusing stories of his sister's escapades, but Vincent had seen them as childish pranks—like the incident of the kitten in the tree—never suspecting there was so much depth to a girl he had met only a few times.

It had been his intention to wait a few days and then

make his offer, leaving her in his mother's care, while he went off to town until the wedding—but now he thought there might be far more to gain by delaying for a while.

'Oh, paramount,' he agreed in answer to her question. 'To be forever at odds with one's partner, not to be thought of. But what a charming notion, Miss Thornton! A novel way of describing marriage. A partnership. Indeed, yes. I like that idea.'

'Do you not think marriage should be for the mutual benefit of both husband and wife?'

'Oh, yes, indubitably!'

Vincent mentally reviewed the marital arrangements of his friends and acquaintances. Most had been entered into as a contract, for the protection of land and fortunes. A few *were* love matches, but even in these he had found the distribution of power lay with one or the other: whichever was the less besotted of the two usually held the bridle, however gently.

'Do you suppose the ideal is obtainable?' he asked.

'If you mean, do I expect perfect happiness—then my answer must of course be no,' Cassie replied seriously. 'Yet I believe it must be possible to live in harmony if one is prepared to give and take.'

'Ah, I see.' His mouth quivered but he controlled his desire to laugh. 'And have you considered love, Miss Thornton?'

'Love?' Cassie hesitated, then shook her head. 'I do not think being in love would be at all comfortable. I shall not allow such a consideration to cloud my judgement.'

'Will you not?' Vincent said softly. 'What a truly sensible young lady you are.' He directed a very odd look at her as they reached the stables. 'I see my groom has our horses ready. I believe we must continue our conversation another day…'

* * *

'Augusta Simmons!' Lady Longbourne's face assumed an expression of loathing. 'No, Carlton, I cannot allow it. Why, the woman is both a fool and—and a toad eater. She is not the proper person to present your future bride to the *ton*. No, indeed! I have never liked her: she is too puffed up in her own conceit. I wonder you could think of it!'

'Forgive me, Mama,' Vincent corrected calmly. 'It was not my notion, but Miss Thorton's own. It seems she has had some money bequeathed to her, and means to spend it on a season if she can but contrive to get herself presented.'

'That is my task,' his mother replied, getting to her feet in some agitation. 'I had already decided on it. I shall suggest to Cassandra that we all go up to town next week. We shall give a dinner the following week, after we have had time to refurbish our wardrobes and send out invitations.'

'Are you sure it will not be too much for you, dear Mama?'

'I am not quite in my dotage yet,' snapped Lady Longbourne. 'I have been feeling a little better these past two days. Besides, nothing, no considerations of self, shall stand between me and duty in this matter. Your wife must have every attention due her position in society,' she said. 'My health is nothing to the point. You know I have always put the best interests of my sons first, Carlton.'

'Then, if you are sure it will not be too much for you, I should think it best to put the idea to Miss Thornton, so that she can write to Mrs Simmons. And, Mama…thank you for your kindness, but please remember Cassandra has not yet consented to become my wife.'

'Do you intend to propose before we go up to town, or later?'

'I think we must give her time to get to know us, don't you?'

'Just as you wish.' Her ladyship frowned. 'You know I did not wish for this alliance, Vincent, but having Cassandra here with us has made me think again. She has a tendency to speak more frankly than she ought, but apart from that she has pretty manners—and breeding. From her mother, I make sure! All in all, I think her a nice gel. Not a beauty, of course, but presentable—and thoughtful. I believe she will do very well for you, Carlton. Indeed, I am persuaded you could not do better.'

'Are you indeed, Mama?' Vincent smiled inwardly. 'For myself, I do not dislike her open way of speaking, I think it engaging—but whether or not we shall suit is something we shall decide in good time.'

'I thought it was a matter of honour with you?'

'Yes, so did I,' Vincent replied, smiled oddly at his mother and kissed her hand. 'But I find that is not after all the case.'

'What do you mean?' Lady Longbourne glared at him. 'Do you intend to make the girl an offer or not?'

He smiled mysteriously, leaving her standing as he went out of the French windows and into the garden.

'Well!' she exclaimed. 'Of all the tiresome creatures…'

It was really most provoking of him. Only duty would have persuaded her to give up her peaceful seclusion in the country and now… For a moment she gave in to righteous indignation, but gradually the realisation dawned on her that she did not wish to give up her plans for Cassandra. She had indeed felt much more lively since the arrival of the two young ladies, and she was looking forward to taking them both in hand.

Even though Sarah had no expectations, she did not despair of contriving a suitable match for her. And as for Cassandra, well, if Vincent did not make up his mind, there would surely be others who would. Especially if she had a little money.

She would make a push to discover the gel's fortune. It could not be much, of course, but even a thousand or two would help Cassie to find a husband. Yet it would be rather pleasant to have the gel as her own daughter-in-law.

'Take us both to London next week?' A look of delight dawned in Cassie's eyes. 'Oh, dearest Lady Longbourne! How good you are to me. But are you sure it will not be too tiring for you?'

She looked at her hostess anxiously. The inquiry must be made but, oh, she did hope nothing would happen to prevent them going to London!

Lady Longbourne gazed up at her with an expression nicely balanced between self-sacrifice and affection.

'It will be no trouble at all, my dear child. Your mother was my closest friend. Had it not been for my precarious health I must have taken you under my wing long ago, but I am feeling much recovered of late—and I am determined not to think of myself. Whatever happens, I shall not permit that odious Augusta Simmons to present you; that shall be my pleasure.'

'I do not know how to thank you,' Cassie said, truly grateful. She was well aware that to appear in London with a paid companion could not give her a quarter of the credit that a visit with a lady of her hostess's consequence would naturally bestow on her.

'Come, sit with me for a few minutes,' Lady Longbourne said, patting the sofa seat beside her and smiling fondly. 'I think we must discuss the very urgent matter of your clothes, for what you are wearing now is very pretty, but it will not do for town, my love.'

'Oh, I know. I must buy lots of new clothes.'

'You will need a considerable wardrobe.'

'And so will Sarah,' Cassie said. 'I have promised her some new clothes as a present for all her family's kindness. And I know her papa is hoping she may find herself a husband.'

'Is he of good family?'

'Oh, yes—but there is no money, of course.'

'Well, she is very pretty so there is no telling what may happen. Are you sure you can afford to provide sufficient clothes for both of you? Because, if not, I should enjoy helping you, Cassie.'

'You are very kind, ma'am, but I believe my funds will be sufficient.'

Lady Longbourne nodded, her curiosity aroused. 'Who was your aunt, my dear?'

'Mama's eldest sister. Aunt Gwendoline. She married a gentleman from Truro, and we visited her only once that I recall.'

'Indeed?' Lady Longbourne's eyes widened. 'Who was her husband?'

'A Mr Belham,' Cassie replied. 'I never met him—and they had no children.'

'That was a source of sadness to them, I dare say?'

'I suppose it must have been,' Cassie said. 'I hardly knew her.'

'Well, well, it does not matter.' Lady Longbourne patted her hand. 'At least she thought of you, my dear. A little money is always useful.'

'Yes…' Cassie felt guilty at concealing the truth from her generous hostess. 'It is quite a lot of money. I do not precisely know the amount, but I think it could make the matter of my marriage easier to accomplish.'

'Yes…' Lady Longbourne nodded thoughtfully. 'I imagine it would…even a few thousand is a great persuader.'

'Yes.' Cassie flushed and dropped her gaze. 'I think, rather…I have been told…I can expect to be quite an heiress.'

'An heiress?' Her hostess looked startled. 'What good fortune you came to me, Cassie! Had you fallen into the clutches of that odious creature Augusta Simmons, you might have been prey for fortune-hunters and ruthless gamblers.'

Cassie smiled at her, relieved the truth was out. 'I did not like to say before, but I am persuaded that you have my best interests at heart, ma'am.'

'Oh, yes, indeed,' her ladyship said, smiling to herself. 'This alters the case, Cassie dear. I had hoped for a modest success—but now I am determined that you shall be the toast of the season. Oh, yes, this changes everything...'

Cassie and Sarah were walking in the formal gardens, having left Lady Longbourne lying comfortably on her daybed in the small front parlour, a book lying unread beside her and a glass of cordial on the table near to hand.

'This is such a beautiful house,' Sarah said as they came upon a little Greek temple. 'We are so lucky to have been invited here. And now we are to go to London next week. Could anything have been so fortunate? I wonder why Lady Longbourne has agreed to take us?'

'Yes, so do I,' mused Cassie, looking thoughtful. 'It is exceedingly kind of her, but I had thought her health too fragile to allow it.'

'Perhaps she felt it her duty to help you?' Sarah suggested. 'Since she and your mama were such friends.'

'Yes, perhaps she did,' Cassie agreed. 'But I suspect the suggestion came from Lord Carlton—though I cannot think why he was kind enough to persuade his mama for our sakes. Unless he has fallen in love with you, Sarah? You are so pretty that it is possible he might.'

Sarah blushed and shook her head at her. She knew that Lord Carlton was only being a good host when he smiled and inquired after her well-being, but she had her own ideas as to his reasons for making sure they had a season in London.

'I think perhaps—' she began, then stopped as she saw Lord Carlton coming towards them. 'Oh, here he is…'

'Ladies…' Vincent tipped his hat to them. 'I was persuaded I should find you here. It is a very pleasant afternoon, is it not?'

'Very pleasant,' Cassie said. 'Lady Longbourne felt it too warm for walking, and we left her resting. But perhaps we should return now. I should not like her to feel that we have neglected her.'

'Mama is perfectly happy,' he assured them. 'When I left her a moment ago she was wishing to have a little sleep. I came after you, because I thought it a perfect afternoon to take a rowing boat on the lake—if that would please you?'

'Oh, yes,' Sarah responded at once. 'I should like that of all things—if you would, Cassie?'

'It would be nice and cool on the lake,' Cassie said, shading her eyes as she looked towards the expanse of glistening water. 'You were very thoughtful to come after us, sir.'

'Mama told me I am to remind you that we have company for dinner this evening, but if you think it would not be too tiring to be rowed out to the island…?'

Both ladies agreed that they would find it relaxing and so the party walked down a sloping, grassy bank to the jetty where a rowing boat had been tied ready for their jaunt. Vincent handed Sarah in first, then Cassie, taking up the oars himself.

Cassie put down her sunshade, but Sarah kept hers up to protect her fair skin from the sun.

'You are not afraid of freckles, Miss Thornton?' Vincent asked.

'My skin does not freckle,' Cassie said. 'It just gets a little darker. You may have remarked that I do not have Sarah's delicate complexion?'

'No, you do not,' he said. 'I believe the sun likes you more than it does Miss Walker.'

'Oh, I never burn,' Cassie said carelessly. 'Jack and I were forever in and out of boats on the river. And sometimes we lay on the banks in the sun—as children, you know. I loved to make daisy chains…'

She blushed as she saw his gaze narrow, turning her head aside to look at the beauty of her surroundings. The banks of the lake were deeply wooded, and in the middle there was a tiny island with a summerhouse and wrought iron seats.

'This looks a pretty place for a picnic,' she remarked.

'Yes. I should have thought to bring one,' Vincent said, and his smile had disappeared. 'But perhaps another time…'

Cassie glanced at him, but his expression made her heart catch. Just what was he thinking? Had she said something to make him angry?

In fact, Vincent had been remembering another visit to the island, when he, Jack and other friends had taken a picnic there. It was just after they had all decided to join the army, and Jack had been telling them a story about his sister.

It had been the first of many, for Jack was an excellent teller of stories, and, according to her brother, Cassie had spent the best part of her life in some scrape or other.

Once again, Vincent felt the pain twist inside him as he watched her laughing in the sunshine. He wished with all his heart that Jack could have been here with them…that he was not lying in an unmarked grave somewhere in France.

There were six persons besides themselves who sat down to dinner that evening. Cassie had been introduced to the Reverend Mr Simpson, his sister, who kept house for him, a gentleman of advancing years who was placed next to her, and seemed a little deaf, and three elderly ladies who lived together.

It was not particularly scintillating company, and Cassie was amused as she saw that Lord Carlton was struggling to hide his yawns. He would have been distressed to let his guests see his boredom, of course, for he had excellent manners, but it was obvious to her that he was finding the evening exceedingly tiresome.

He very soon followed the ladies into the drawing room, having summarily dispensed with the custom of the port, and came to sit by Cassie's side on a sofa near the window.

'Forgive us for such a tedious evening,' he said, 'but these ladies are Mama's nearest neighbours and it would have been unforgivable had they not been invited to meet you. However, I do assure you that tomorrow the company will be more lively. I have invited some of my own acquaintances, and there will be cards and music.'

'You are very kind,' Cassie said, 'but *I* am not bored. Your mama's friends may be old, sir, but I find them interesting enough. They have many stories to tell if one is prepared to listen.'

'Yes, but *I* have heard them so many times before,' Vincent murmured with a wicked look that almost overset her. 'This is your first time, Miss Thornton—so you are unkind to judge me so harshly. I dare say you may find them a little less entertaining after you have heard them fifty times.'

'Indeed, you may be right, sir,' Cassie replied demurely. 'But ladies, you know, are more accustomed to listening— even if they are not always interested.'

'Not one of the privileges?'

Cassie smiled but would not answer, and after a moment Vincent left her to go and talk to the Vicar's sister.

Cassie noticed that he was perfectly attentive. Indeed,

she could not fault his manners. Yet she was not in the least surprised when he excused himself after the tea tray had been brought in, suspecting that, if she had been another man, he might have invited her to join him in his billiard room.

However, it would have been quite shocking had she followed him there, and so she was obliged to remain and listen to more of the stories she had not quite truthfully assured Lord Carlton she found so very interesting.

Being a caring girl, she did not let her mind stray more than once or twice to what his lordship might be doing, and she certainly did not allow a sigh to escape her even when her companion began to tell her the same story she had heard not twenty minutes earlier.

'I dare say you'll be glad to be off for some gallivanting in town,' Miss Simpson said to her. 'Well, you will be in good hands, Miss Thornton. Lady Longbourne knows what she's about—and as for that son of hers, handsome fellow, ain't he? And quite charming…'

'Oh, yes,' Cassie said. 'A perfect gentleman.'

'Well, as to that, there's more to young Vincent than meets the eye,' the wise old spinster said. 'But he has a good heart…yes, you can rely on that. He always had a good heart, no matter what larks he got up to.'

Now this was more like it! Cassie turned her opportunity to good advantage, listening with genuine interest to stories of her host when he was a lad.

'Of course, my brother wouldn't have it that Vincent was the one who put a pair of ladies' corsets on the spire, but I saw the look in those wicked eyes of his, and I knew. His stepfather would have had to thrash him had he known, so of course I never said a word to anyone.'

Cassie met her eyes and smiled. 'How very, very interesting,' she said. 'Thank you so much for telling me.'

'I thought you'd want to know,' the elderly lady said and

gave a cackle of delight. 'Never know when you might want to take him down a point or two!'

'No,' Cassie said, much amused. 'No, one never knows…'

Chapter Four

Cassie had been walking within the grounds of Carlton Park for almost an hour when she first heard the whimpering sound. It was another very warm day, and Sarah had declined to accompany her, protesting that she would prefer to stay in the cool of the house with a book. Feeling a little restless, Cassie had decided to go alone, her walk leading her through shaded, tree-lined avenues, by a charming stream, which rushed and bubbled over large boulders and into this wood.

Despite having just recently wondered once or twice if there was someone behind her, she had dismissed it as sheer imagination and was neither fatigued nor oppressed by the heat. Her frown of concentration was for her thoughts, which were a little disordered and concerned Lord Carlton. She could not quite place its origin, but she knew there had been a subtle change in his manner towards her of late…not exactly a withdrawal, but a distance which troubled her.

Could she have done something to offend him? She had not thought so, but found it worrying just the same.

However, the whimpering noise broke through her thoughts and she was instantly alert. What could it be? Someone or some animal was in pain. She stopped walking, listening intently to the pitiful cry. It was a child! She was sure it was a child.

Forgetting any idea she might have had of being followed, Cassie was immediately alert to another's plight. Turning to her right, she followed the sounds of distress along a twisting path, then stood still as she suddenly saw the huddled creature lying on the ground. A child…a small girl of perhaps ten years was curled up into a ball, arms hugging her knees and making the kind of sounds one might expect from an injured cat.

'Oh, you poor child,' Cassie murmured and went over to her. 'What is wrong? Have you hurt yourself?'

The girl lifted her head as Cassie approached, alarm in her rather dirty, thin face. She attempted to rise, the instinct to flee showing in her pale blue eyes, but her efforts to stand were hopeless and she fell back to the ground with a cry of despair as her ankle gave way.

'Please, do not be frightened,' Cassie said. 'I do not mean you harm. I should like to help you, if I may?'

Now that she was closer, Cassie could see that the girl was older than she had first guessed, but pale and undernourished. She knelt down on the dry grass and looked at the ankle which was obviously causing the child pain.

'Have you hurt yourself? Your ankle looks swollen. Did you fall and twist it?' The girl nodded, her eyes still wary, frightened. 'May I look? Just to be sure you have not broken any bones.'

'It ain't broke,' the girl said, catching back a sob. She wiped her nose on her sleeve, which was already less than clean. 'I was running and my foot caught in some tree roots what had lifted out of the ground. It was the wrench what hurt.'

Cassie moved her fingers carefully over the injured ankle. The girl flinched once or twice but made no sound.

'It seems not to be broken,' she agreed, feeling thankful

that the injury was no worse. 'But a nasty sprain can be very painful. I am not surprised you were crying.'

'I weren't crying for this,' the girl said, encouraged by Cassie's tone. 'It were 'cos he'll come after me and take me back. Then he'll beat me and set me to work again.'

'Oh, you poor thing,' Cassie said. 'He sounds a cruel master.'

'Ain't me master,' the girl replied, smothering a sob of fear. 'Leastways, he don't pay me nuffing. He was me muvver's fancy man. When she up and snuffed it, he made me work for me keep—runs an inn in the village, he does, makes me scrub and clean, and serve in the taproom. But I don't mind that so much, nor that he's a mean ole skinflint. It were the other thing…'

'The other thing?' Cassie was puzzled until she saw the girl flush and look ashamed. A shudder of disgust went through her. 'You don't mean that he…but you're only a child!'

'I'm nearly thirteen,' the girl said. 'He says it's time I started me proper work. He says me ma were a whore and I ought to fetch a few guineas being as it's me first…but I don't want to lie with that rotten Morgan, so I ran away.'

'Is Morgan the name of your—your employer?' Cassie supplied for want of a better word. Having been sheltered and protected for most of her life, she was shocked and horrified that a young girl should be subjected to such wickedness!

'No, Morgan's the one old Carter wants to sell me to. But I ain't gonna let him. I was gonna walk to London to make me fortune, but now I've hurt meself and he'll find me and take me back.'

'Well, he shan't do that,' Cassie said. 'For you shall come back with me and—' She remembered all at once that she was not in her own home, but a guest in the house of Lady Longbourne. 'I shall help you. I shall bind your

A Matter of Honour

ankle, then give you money for your coach fare to London.'
She finished on a flash of inspiration. 'In London you may
find work for a good master, who *will* pay you, will not
beat you—and certainly will not expect you to—to do *that*.'

'Why should you help the likes of me?' The girl looked
at her suspiciously. 'You're a lady, and it's true what old
Carter says, me ma wasn't no better than she ought ter be.'

'Because I want to help,' Cassie replied. 'I am Cassandra, but my friends call me Cassie. You need not be afraid
of me. I am your friend, and always shall be. Do you believe me?' The girl gazed up at her, then nodded. 'Will you
tell me your name now?'

'Tara,' she said, looking at Cassie with a touch of awe.
'Will you really pay me fare, miss?'

'Yes, certainly,' Cassie answered with a smile. 'But first
I must get you to the house so that I can look after you. If
I help you to stand, do you think you can hold on to me
and hop? Otherwise I must leave you here and go for help.'

'Don't go!' Tara looked fearfully behind her. 'Old Carter
will fetch me back if he finds me 'ere.'

'I doubt he will come here in search of you,' said Cassie,
a half-smile on her lips. 'This is Lord Carlton's land and
he would be trespassing—he could be arrested for that.'

This did not seem to reassure Tara. She looked nervously
at Cassie. 'Will I be sent to prison, miss? I didn't know
this wood was private property. And I know some of old
Carter's friends come 'ere poaching game; they bring pigeons and suchlike to the inn sometimes.'

'Indeed? I think Lord Carlton would be interested to
know that.'

'Shall you tell him, miss? Will he be cross with me for
being 'ere?'

'Lord Carlton is my friend,' Cassie said. 'He is a very
kind man and would not dream of harming you, but I dare
say he would deal very differently with your master—es-

pecially if we tell him what he has done to you.' She smiled at the girl. 'And now, if I help you, I think you should try to walk.'

It took some minutes of trial and error before Tara was able to get the right balance, but with Cassie's arm supporting her, and her hand on Cassie's shoulder, she managed to hop a few steps before having to rest. Their progress would obviously be slow, and it was almost time for tea. Lady Longbourne would worry if Cassie was late, but there was no help for it. She could not and would not abandon a girl who was little more than a child to a fate that was, in her opinion, worse than death. So they would just have to do their best and hope that one of Lord Carlton's servants chanced to see them and came to aid them.

Help arrived at last in the person of Lord Carlton himself some three-quarters of an hour later, when they were within sight of the formal gardens. Vincent had in fact been sent by an anxious Lady Longbourne in search of their errant guest.

'For you never know if some unscrupulous adventurer may have tried to snatch her from our care,' she told her son. 'An heiress with no family to protect her! She is vulnerable, Carlton. It is our duty to guard her vigilantly.'

'I doubt if anyone knows of her inheritance as yet,' he replied, hiding his smile at the idea of some fortune-hunter venturing to kidnap his guest in the grounds of his own estate. 'Miss Thornton was reluctant to tell even us, it seems. Why should that be, do you think, Mama?' He raised his mobile eyebrows.

'Because she is a properly brought up young gel and does not boast of her good fortune,' said his mama promptly. 'Do not waste time in asking foolish questions, Carlton. You are sometimes so unperceptive, I despair of you. Go and find her!'

'You are certain she is not in the house?'

'Quite certain.'

Vincent set off obediently, more to placate his anxious parent than for any fear of harm having come to Cassie, but as soon as he saw her he hurried to offer his assistance.

'We were worried about you,' he said. 'What has happened here?'

'Tara fell and hurt her ankle,' Cassie replied, pausing to catch her breath. The girl was by no means heavy, but it had been a long, exhausting walk. 'I could not leave her, so…'

'No, of course not. Please allow me, Miss Thornton. And, Tara, I must carry you. Do not fear, I shall not hurt you.'

'You're *him*, ain't you?' Tara said, looking at him in awe. 'His lordship what owns the land. Miss Cassie said you're kind. She says you'll likely throw old Carter in the clink or give him a bloody nose.'

Vincent's eyes betrayed him, though he controlled his very great desire to laugh. 'Did she, indeed? I think I am indebted to her, though I am not sure. May I know who old Carter is?'

Carried safely in his lordship's arms, Tara repeated her story, adding details she had not disclosed to Cassie. As Vincent heard of beatings and threats to make her submit to her master's vile plans for her, his mouth hardened and the smile faded, his eyes becoming the colour of wet slate.

'You ain't angry, are you?' Tara asked, sensing the suppressed fury in him. 'It were Miss Cassie's idea to bring me here.'

'And a very good one!' He glanced down at her. 'I *am* very angry, but not with you or Miss Cassie. In fact, I am indebted to you for telling me, Tara. Mr Carter is my tenant. I own the Hare and Hounds and, I can assure you, you will not be returning there. Indeed, Mr Carter will not be there much longer himself.'

They had reached the front of the house. Cassie hesitated as she looked at him. 'I was wondering…where to take Tara?'

Vincent smiled as he read her thoughts. 'Not to Mama's parlour, certainly. I believe you should present yourself at once to calm her fears. She was worried in case you might have been carried off by some scoundrel or other. As for Tara, you may safely leave her to my care. If she is agreeable?'

'Best take me to the kitchens,' Tara said, looking hopeful. 'Mebbe they'll give me something to eat.'

'Janet will treat her ankle and find her something clean to wear,' Cassie said. 'She always did when…' She faltered under his quizzing gaze. 'At home, you know.'

'Ah, yes, the redoubtable Janet.' He could not prevent a chuckle escaping. 'I shall take Tara to the kitchens and send for Janet at once!'

Cassie smiled, acknowledging a hit, but did not answer as she went into the house. She paused before one of the tall pier mirrors in the hall to tidy herself before entering the parlour. Her hair was a little windblown and the hem of her dress was dirty where she had knelt on the ground. She brushed away the debris before making her way to the parlour.

Between them, Tara and Lord Carlton had solved her immediate dilemma, for she did not care to imagine her hostess's shock and dismay had she presented her with the runaway. Which, of course, she must have done for politeness' sake had Lord Carlton not arrived at the eleventh hour! Thinking about it, Cassie decided it might be for the best if she did not mention the incident at all.

'Ah, there you are!' Lady Longbourne exclaimed, jumping up as she saw Cassie and coming to greet her as she entered the parlour. 'It is nearly time for you to change for dinner. You have missed tea—though I will send for a tray should you wish it?' Cassie declined with a shake of her head. 'Wherever have you been, my love? I have been imagining you lost this past hour.'

'I fear it was my own fault,' Cassie apologised. 'Please forgive me, dearest Lady Longbourne. I did not realise it would take so long to…walk home.'

'Since you are safe, there is nothing to forgive.' She gave a little sigh. 'My only worry now is that you have tired yourself. You have not forgotten that we leave for town tomorrow? Travelling is so excessively tedious, is it not?'

'I never seem to find it so,' Cassie confessed. 'There is so much to see—and all the excitement of what lies at the journey's end. I am so looking forward to this visit, ma'am. And so is Sarah! We are so fortunate to have you as our hostess. You have such style, such lovely clothes. I cannot wait to be guided by you in the matter of our wardrobes. If only it will not make too much trouble for you?'

Well pleased with Cassie's genuine concern and pretty manners, her ladyship assured her that she could never be a trouble to her.

'When Carlton first suggested your visit to me, I was doubtful that my health would stand it—but to be quite truthful, my love, you have done me good. It is so pleasant to hear young voices in the house again. I am looking forward to introducing you into society—and I do not mean the old tabbies and bores you have met here, who are all kindly folk and mean well, but not lively enough for a young gel. You will much prefer the company we shall entertain in town, Cassie.'

At this Cassie kissed her cheek, told her that she had enjoyed her stay at her home excessively, then begged pardon because if she did not hurry away she would be late for dinner. However, Lady Longbourne kept her talking a while longer, and it was almost twenty minutes later when she reached her own room.

Janet was waiting for her, her frown one of exasperation mixed with affectionate understanding.

'Oh, do not scold me,' Cassie cried, knowing that particular look of old. 'I know it was wrong of me to burden Lord Carlton and Lady Longbourne as I did—well, not Lady Longbourne precisely, because she does not know of Tara's predicament, and I dare say his lordship will think it best not tell her—but she was in such distress, poor child. I could not leave her there to be captured by her cruel master, could I?'

'No, Miss Cassandra, *you* could not. But it is as well his lordship is so understanding. It is not exactly the proper behaviour expected of a guest, to be bringing dubious kitchen girls into your hostess's home. You have only Tara's word that she wasn't running from the law. She might be a thief—or worse.'

Cassie considered, wrinkling her brow. 'Oh, no, I do not think that likely, Janet. Poor Tara is only a child.'

'So was that dirty little vagabond you found crying outside the gate and brought in to be washed and fed only last Easter. He stole a pie and one of the butler's best bottles of brandy before he absconded in the middle of the night.'

'Well, that was very bad of him,' Cassie agreed, 'but he could have stolen something far more valuable if he had tried, so I do not think him so very bad after all.'

Janet made a clucking sound in her throat, giving her mistress a dark look and shaking her head. 'One of these days you'll come unstuck, my girl. And I don't mind telling you!'

'I am sure you *will* tell me, Janet dear,' Cassie said with a wicked smile. 'Please, will you fasten this hook at my neck? I must not keep everyone waiting for dinner—that would be very bad of me.'

Janet continued to scold as she fastened the back of Cassie's very pretty, yellow silk gown, but knowing it meant nothing, Cassie let her mind wander. Lord Carlton had indeed stepped into the breach with admirable aplomb, taking the care and disposal of Tara out of her hands. She could not but be grateful for his understanding, because Janet was right and the situation might have been difficult.

She had never forgotten the incident with her kitten, but Lord Carlton had been younger then, not quite as self-possessed as he now was, and she had not known what to expect from him as a man of maturity. Over the past few days, she had discovered that he was both kind and generous—with a sense of humour that matched her own. He was, she thought, the kind of gentleman she had hoped to meet. No one could help being comfortable with someone of his temperament, which seemed almost perfect to her. Unfortunately, he did not show any signs of feeling anything more than friendship towards her.

Dismissing the very pleasant idea which had just occurred to her, she turned her thoughts to the coming trip to town. In London she was sure to find other gentlemen who would find her—or her fortune—attractive.

When Lady Longbourne set out on journey she did not do things by halves. Besides her own, very comfortable carriage, there was a smaller one in which travelled her personal maid, Margaret, her dresser Anne, Janet and, as yet unbeknown to her, Tara: behind them came the baggage coach, filled to the point of collapse with her ladyship's indispensable possessions crammed into so many trunks and band-boxes that some of the young ladies' boxes had had to be strapped on to the second carriage.

Lord Carlton shook his head over the sight, but allowed no hint of his amusement to show. He kept clothes at all his homes, preferring to travel light. Refusing Sarah's offer to sit beside her in the carriage, he smiled and assured her that he intended to ride on ahead of them, but would always be within call if it should be necessary.

'Not that I anticipate any trouble,' he assured his mama as she shot him an anxious look. 'There have been no reports of highwaymen for months on this road, but I shall be near—so you need not look so worried, dearest one. I promise you are all quite safe.'

'And so I should hope,' Lady Longbourne said. 'For we may perfectly well take another groom or two with us if need be, Carlton.'

As each coach had beside the driver a groom to assist him, and another riding behind—just in case of accidents—Vincent did not think it necessary to make any last-minute adjustments to his arrangements. He merely smiled at his mother, tipped his hat to the young ladies, and prepared to mount his horse. It was a particularly fine-looking black stallion, which was already restive from the delay and pulled at the bit as soon as it felt its master on its back.

'Steady, Hermes. I know you are ready to speed like the wind, good fellow, but we must think of others today. No, no, do not show off. Remember your manners, sir!'

Calmed by the soft voice, which hid the strength beneath, like iron covered by a velvet sheath, the thoroughbred ceased to fret, controlling the wild, fierce urge to take off on one of the mad gallops he often enjoyed with his master.

And so the cavalcade set off at last, proceeding down the long drive and out on to the country road which would lead in time to the high road. Because of the recent dry weather, there were not so many ruts as there might have been and the carriage swayed gently behind the team of four, perfectly matched greys, personally chosen for his mother by Lord Carlton.

'And so now we may be comfortable,' Lady Longbourne said. 'Dear me! Have I forgotten my vinaigrette?' She began to look about her for her reticule, but Cassie felt beneath her skirt on the seat and found it for her. 'Oh, thank you, my love. I should not have liked to ask coachman to stop so soon.'

'No, indeed, ma'am,' Cassie said, smiling at her. 'Nor indeed Lord Carlton. Gentleman do not seem to understand that one must have certain things with one, do they?'

'You are very right,' her hostess replied approvingly. 'Not that Vincent ever shows he is impatient. His father was very difficult. He often refused to travel with me…' A sigh escaped her. 'My dear Bertie was so very different. Nothing was ever too much trouble for him. I do not think I could ever find his like again.'

'Is that why you have not thought of remarrying?' Cassie asked, then blushed as Lady Longbourne stared at her. 'Forgive me, that was impertinent—but surely you are still young enough to enjoy the companionship of a gentleman?'

'Yes, I suppose I am,' Lady Longbourne said, looking thoughtful. 'Carlton is one and thirty—but I was a mere child when I married his father, not more than seventeen. I am not yet…well, not old enough to think myself a greybones just yet.'

'Indeed you are not!' Sarah and Cassie exclaimed in unison.

'It was my health, you see,' explained Lady Longbourne. 'After Bertie died, I…did not wish to live. We were so in love.' She blushed like a young girl. 'Of course, it was not fashionable to care so much for one's husband. As a gel, I was always told that love did not matter, that one man was very much as another—but I must tell you, my dear, that is simply not so! If you have a choice, choose a man who can make your life happy. Considerations of fortune and consequence are nothing beside it.' She laughed. 'There! I have been indiscreet. You will not hear such advice from others, believe me. Yet I would not see either of you made miserable by an unwise marriage.'

Cassie leaned towards her, kissing her cheek. 'How lucky we are to have found you, ma'am,' she said. 'I do not know how it is, but I have come to be so very fond of you in such a short time.'

Sarah agreed to it, and they began to converse very comfortably about all the delights that awaited them in town. Fields and trees gave way to villages, and towns, then countryside once more. They passed the time by little games of guessing, telling stories and making up new and very silly words, much as country folk often did when they had nothing else to amuse them.

'''So,'' Squire Come'ereanddoasyou'retold said to his wife, Lady Ishan'tunlessIwant, ''you are nothing but a ditheryfeatheryhalfwit.'' And said she, ''You are a numbskulldiggerynincompoop!''' Cassie finished on a whoop of triumph. 'Twenty-five! I think that is one more letter than yours, Sarah. I win.'

'Indeed, you are both quite mad,' cried Lady Longbourne, laughing until the tears ran down her cheeks. 'No, no, do not expect me to top that, Cassie. You are much cleverer than me at this game. I can do no better than hithercomescatterbrain.'

'I think I have one,' Sarah said and was just about to pronounce her almost unpronounceable word when all three ladies were startled by the sound of a pistol shot, closely followed by two more.

'Mercy me!' Lady Longbourne cried, her hand going to her heart. 'What on earth was that?'

The carriage had come to an abrupt halt. Cassie pulled the sash and put her head out of the window, to see Lord Carlton riding up to them at some speed. He reined in tightly as he came near, and, catching a glimpse of his face, she saw he was frowning.

'What happened, sir? We thought we heard shots?'

'There is nothing to worry about,' Vincent said roughly. 'I have scared the rogue off. He thought to take me by surprise, but I had been aware of him skulking in the bushes for some time.' He dismounted and opened the carriage door, looking anxiously at Lady Longbourne, who was fanning herself and looking as if she might faint. 'Forgive me, Mama. I would not have frightened you for the world, but I thought it best to scare the rogue off by firing at him before he attempted anything untoward.'

'My…my vinaigrette,' Lady Longbourne said faintly. She moaned a little as Sarah waved the little silver box under her nose, but the restorative effects of the vinegar soon brought her round. 'I thought you assured me there were no highwaymen on this road, Carlton?' Her tone was accusing, as if she held her son personally responsible for the outrage.

'Forgive me, Mama, I was not aware of any attacks. Nor am I sure the rogue meant us any harm—but when I knew we were being followed, I thought it best to put a fright into him.'

'You have made me feel quite odd,' his mama said with a frown, but as she was sitting up by this time and had recovered her colour, he was not too anxious. 'But there, it is all the same. Your father never thought of my feelings either.'

Cassie saw the slight shadow of pain in Vincent's eyes and was a little cross with Lady Longbourne for having put it there. He had acted swiftly and with no thought for his own safety, for had the rogue been intent on harm he might well have fired back. She was not sure why the thought of Lord Carlton lying wounded—or dead!—in the road was so very distressing to her, but could not prevent a gasp of dismay. She flushed as his eyes were instantly directed at her.

'How very careless I have been,' he apologized at once. 'I was too impulsive and fear I have upset you, Miss Thornton—and Miss Walker, too.'

'No, not at all,' Cassie said, rallying immediately. 'I was a little startled, that's all—but I am sure you acted with the best intentions, sir. It would indeed have been very shocking if the wretched creature had shot you in the back and then attacked our carriage—especially as the other coaches are still some distance behind us. We might have been quite at his mercy…whoever he was. I think we must thank you for your prompt action.'

'As to that…' Vincent frowned. 'I am not so sure he did mean harm, for he was trying to conceal himself and rode off at some speed the moment I fired.'

'Indeed, yes, quite shocking,' agreed Lady Longbourne, recovering her composure. 'Well, well, I forgive you, Carlton, for I dare say you did not mean to give me palpitations.'

'I am truly sorry,' Lord Carlton replied with a look of affection for her. 'I think you may be easy, ladies, for I do not imagine the rogue will trouble us again.'

A groom had come down from the driving box and closed the door of the carriage as his lordship indicated that they should set out once more.

'We shall stop for some refreshment at an inn a few miles further down this road,' Vincent said, tipping his hat to them. 'Once again, my apologies for any disturbance I have caused you, ladies.'

Cassie leaned out of the window to watch as he rode off once more. What a fine figure of a man he was! She thought that he had behaved with great restraint, and wondered if he had ever lost his temper with anyone. Perhaps he was not a man who felt things deeply? And yet at times she had seen something in his eyes that told a very different story.

Had Cassie been privileged to see Mr Carter being sum-

marily thrown out of the Hare and Hounds by his enraged
landlord the previous evening, she would have been very
surprised to discover that he was a man of violent passions
and some considerable skill in the art of the pugilist. However, since Lord Carlton was a gentleman of the first water,
who still held to his somewhat old-fashioned notions that
ladies were to be protected and never subjected to the least
unpleasantness if it could be avoided, she was not likely to
learn that the brute who had so mistreated Tara had been
well punished for his sins.

It was to Vincent's credit, however, that he always behaved well in the face of his mama's undoubted provoca-
tion, and, with a little flutter of her heart, Cassie had suddenly discovered that she had begun to like his lordship
very much indeed.

It would be interesting to get to know him a little better.

'I do hope you have recovered from your fright, Miss
Thornton?' asked Lord Carlton as they walked towards the
inn. Lady Longbourne was just ahead of them, leaning on
Sarah's arm and seeming none the worse for their adventure. He looked at her anxiously, having remembered the
unfortunate circumstance of her father's suicide. 'It was
most unfortunate that I should be forced to shoot my pistols.'

'I do have a dislike of guns,' Cassie admitted, and for
one brief moment her face reflected a deep sadness as she
recalled a certain afternoon she had tried very hard to forget. 'But I was only startled for a second. Once I looked
out and saw you, I knew there was no reason to be afraid.'

Vincent was gratified by the compliment she had made
him, for it was said so openly and unthinkingly, that he
knew her to be speaking from the heart.

'Believe me, I would never let harm come to you if it
were in my power to prevent it.'

'I know that, sir, and I am sure Lady Longbourne must also. She was just so—so shocked that she spoke thoughtlessly.'

Vincent's smile almost took away Cassie's power to breathe. For some unaccountable reason her heart suddenly raced violently, and she wondered what could be wrong with her.

'You need not be upset for my sake, Miss Thornton,' he said gently. 'Mama has been used to blaming me when she is suffering from a fit of the blues, or feeling out of curl. I do not defend myself, because I know myself to be in part responsible for her unhappiness.'

'Why, whatever can you mean?'

Cassie's eyes widened as she stared at him.

'Sir Bertram was fishing with me the day he caught the chill that led to his developing a virulent fever,' Vincent explained. 'We had gone out early, thinking it would be a dry day. Unfortunately, there was a sudden storm. We were both soaked to the skin. I took no harm, but he…became ill and died soon after.'

'But that was not your fault!'

'No,' he acknowledged. 'But it was my suggestion that we spend a day fishing. I teased him into the trip, believing he spent too much time indoors. Mama warned me he was not robust, but I did not believe her. I thought the fresh air would do him good. Alas, I was quite wrong. I have regretted what followed a thousand times or more.'

'But your intention was good,' Cassie said. 'I cannot find that you are to blame, sir. Had he been a child in your care…but even then such things are often beyond our control.'

'You would absolve me of all sin, Miss Thornton.' Vincent's eyes reflected the warm, deep laughter he felt, but his expression did not falter. 'I am indebted to you.'

'A fig for that!' cried Cassie. His teasing made her heart

do curious things. 'You cannot flimflam me, sir. I am awake on all counts.'

'Yes, I rather thought you were.'

Cassie laughed. 'Why have you brought Tara with us? I gave her money for her fare on the Mail Coach, and something to see her by until she found work. I cannot think that Lady Longbourne would be pleased to have the girl included in her household.'

'No, nor I,' Vincent said, his mouth quivering. 'Indeed, Tara told me about the money, and offered to return it.' The laughter left his eyes as he became serious. 'But I cannot believe that having rescued her from one evil master, you would want her to fall into the clutches of another?' He smiled as she shook her head. 'No, I did not think so. She was determined to go to London, so I suggested she should try working in my kitchens there. Apparently, she likes to cook given the chance, and I thought of making her Monsieur Marcel's assistant.'

'Is he your cook?' Cassie asked innocently.

For a moment Vincent relished the thought of Monsieur Marcel's reaction to being called a cook, but dismissed the tantalising vision with a suppressed laugh.

'I myself would not dare to call him that,' Vincent murmured, his eyes dancing with mischief. 'He is French, you know, and a little temperamental. He is more used to being called an artist, or a miracle of culinary genius.'

'Ah, yes, I recall Jack telling me once that you were fortunate in having an excellent chef.'

'Fortunate? Perhaps. Though I sometimes wonder if life might not be easier—more peaceful—if I were to employ a cook.'

'You cannot have tasted Mrs Horton's milk puddings,' Cassie said, her eyes brimming with wickedness. 'Or what she mistakenly calls porridge. It would serve any master builder well as plaster, I promise you!'

'Indeed, I have been fortunate to escape that fate. I collect Mrs Horton is your own cook?'

'She was, but I have bequeathed her to Kendal with my very best wishes.'

Vincent nodded. 'That will just serve him right, will it not? For being so presumptuous as to imagine you were an object of pity.'

Cassie blushed. 'Perhaps I was too forceful when we spoke of this matter before, Lord Carlton. I dare say Kendal may have meant well, but it was the way he proposed to me…so full of his own importance. So sure that I had no choice in the matter.' Her eyes flashed. 'And Jack was hardly cold in his grave.'

'That was both tactless and unfortunate,' Vincent said, and for a moment his eyes held a very peculiar expression that puzzled her. What could he be thinking?

'It was painful,' Cassie replied. She blinked hard as the tears stung behind her eyes, then looked up at him, determined to change the subject. 'Tell me, sir, do you think Monsieur Marcel will be pleased with Tara as his assistant?'

'I have every hope of it,' Vincent lied. 'One must assume he has a heart—and of course she will be only one of many under his command.'

Cassie suspected him of ulterior motives. Perhaps he wished to prick Monsieur Marcel's pretensions a little, but it was undoubtedly kind of him to take Tara into his own household. She was not sure it was quite wise to foist the girl on his chef, but if it suited his humour, it was not for her to question his decision.

'Then perhaps if there are so many he will not notice,' she suggested.

Vincent hoped she was right, but thought it a vain hope. Little did she know that he was running the risk of losing the services of one of the most sought-after chefs in London, and would find it difficult to replace him. However, he thought it worth the gamble and kept his own counsel. 'No, perhaps not.'

'Well, you can always find her something else to do,' Cassie replied blithely. 'She might become a parlour maid or some such thing, you know—or a lady's dresser.'

Carlton faced this thought without blanching. 'Yes, indeed she might. I wonder why I had not thought of it?'

Lady Longbourne turned to look back at them. 'Carlton! Why do you linger? Sarah and I are ready for our dinner.'

'I think we must join the others,' he said to Cassie. 'I shall of course let you know how Tara goes on, Miss Thornton.'

'I shall be very pleased to hear well of her.' She gazed up at him a little uncertainly. 'Do you not think that…when we are private together…do you not think you might call me Cassie?'

'Oh, I think I might,' he murmured. 'If you will return the compliment. My closest friends call me Vinnie.'

'Yes, I know. Jack always did in his letters to me. He was very proud of his friendship with you.' She took a deep breath. 'I have not thanked you for your letter to me. It—it was a comfort to me. To know that Jack and you were together just before he died…'

'You are kind to say so.'

Was that pain or guilt in his eyes? Cassie could not be sure. She did know that he had been deeply affected by her words, but there was no time to discuss the matter further even had she wished. They had caught up with Lady Longbourne, and his attention was claimed by others.

Cassie was thoughtful as she followed behind, glancing about her with interest. It was a good clean hostelry, the yard swept and tidy, and inside it smelt sweet. The landlord, who had obviously been expecting them, ushered the party reverently into a private parlour, which was well furnished in polished oak. His manner was respectful, a little anxious as he assured Lord Carlton that everything was in readiness.

It was clear to Cassie that Lord Carlton had thought of everything for their comfort. Lady Longbourne still found cause for complaint, but that was her way and her son seemed not to notice. He was unfailingly polite and considerate to all of them. And yet, beneath the surface, Cassie was becoming increasingly aware of a private grief.

Just now and then, when he thought himself unobserved, she caught a strange look in his eyes: a look she thought could best have been described as haunted, and somehow that touched her deeply. She longed in those moments to reach out to him, to comfort him, understanding what it was to feel so alone—to carry a grief that no one else could share.

Cassie suspected another very different man behind the careless, polite, laughing face Carlton showed to the world.

And it made her wonder what was the secret sorrow he held in his heart.

It also made her remember the young man who had rescued her kitten, and the memories made her wistful. She had been a young girl then, untouched by grief…and not afraid to love.

Sometimes she thought that her feelings for Lord Carlton might be more than friendship, but when that happened she fought them, not wanting to admit that she was beginning to like him too much.

His lordship had been very kind to her, but she could not convince herself that he cared for her more than any other pretty young girl his mother might invite to stay with them. It was possible that when this visit was over she would not see him again for a long time.

If Cassie allowed herself to become too fond of Lord Carlton, it could cause her pain. She had lost too many people she loved, and she did not want to be hurt again.

Chapter Five

Lord Carlton's London residence was a very large spacious house in a pleasant garden square. As she was ushered in, to be waited on by the housekeeper, Mrs Dorkins, Cassie saw at once that everything was of the first elegance. The furnishings were in what she imagined to be the latest vogue, and with a French influence: chairs and cabinets of gilt and ebony in the Empire style were just some of the items that caught her eye as she was conducted to her own apartment.

'I hope you will be comfortable here, miss,' the housekeeper said. 'His lordship had it specially refurbished on his return from France.'

'Oh…' Cassie was surprised by the look in the woman's eyes. Almost as if there was some special meaning for her in what she had just said. 'It is very elegant. Rose and cream…quite charming. And I particularly like the embroidery round the curtains—it is a pattern of daisies, I believe.'

'Yes, miss. His lordship's apartments were done over at the same time, in crimson and gold.'

'Really? How suitable.'

'I thought you would like to know…'

'Thank you. I'm sure I shall be happy here, Mrs Dorkins.'

After the housekeeper had left, Cassie explored a little further. Besides the pretty bedroom, there was a sitting room in shades of green and yellow. One door, which she thought might have led to a dressing room, was securely locked. She tried the handle, then turned away, walking over to the window to look down at the small but colourful garden. Then, hearing a knock followed by a clicking sound behind her, she looked round with a little start to see Lord Carlton enter through the door which had previously been locked. The surprise showed in her face, making her frown.

'Forgive me if I startled you,' he said. 'I discovered the key to the dressing room had been mistakenly left my side. These rooms were of course meant to connect, but in the circumstances it is more fitting that the key remains this side. I must apologize for disturbing you. You need have no fear that I shall enter your room that way again; I did so only to give you this.'

He seemed oddly ill at ease as he laid the key on a chest of drawers and turned to leave.

'Am I to understand that these rooms would normally be occupied by Lady Carlton?'

'Were I married, yes. Forgive me, Miss Thornton. My orders were misunderstood. I asked for the best guest rooms to be prepared and...' He shrugged, clearly embarrassed. 'As you see, Mrs Dorkin's assumed I meant these rooms. If it makes you uncomfortable to be so near...'

'Not at all,' Cassie replied, her cheeks warm. 'You have given me the key. Besides, I know you to be a gentleman, sir.'

'I could have another room prepared at once.'

'I see no reason for it. These are lovely rooms and I feel privileged to use them.'

'Then I shall leave you to make yourself comfortable.

Please, lock the door after me and place the key somewhere for safe keeping.'

He still seemed slightly awkward over the mistake and withdrew at once. Cassie locked the door and placed the key on the dressing chest, which was a very handsome piece of marquetry furniture.

At that moment a maid knocked, and, having been invited to enter, asked if she might unpack Miss Thornton's things. Cassie naturally gave permission, taking time to change her gown for a fresh one before going downstairs for tea. By which time any awkwardness she might have felt over being given the wrong rooms had been forgotten.

It was odd that the housekeeper should have made such a mistake, since most young, unmarried females would naturally be placed in rooms away from the gentlemen's, yet there was no real harm in it. Lord Carlton had acted exactly as one would expect on discovering the key his side of the door, and the door remained locked. As it would from now on, of course.

Over the next few days, Cassie had no occasion to regret her decision to remain in her pleasant room. She heard nothing of her host, nor did he attempt to enter her room. Indeed, she would have been surprised and not a little shocked if he had.

Now that they had returned to town, Lord Carlton was not often at home. He dined with them twice during the first week, but left afterwards to visit one of his clubs. And though he always made a point of speaking to Cassie at least once a day, asking her if she was comfortable and had all she needed, his manner unfailingly polite, she thought him more distant than ever. She was a little sad that this should be the case, for on the journey to town, they had seemed to be becoming friends.

Surely he could not still be feeling awkward because of

a mistake over the rooms? Cassie had accepted the situation without a second thought. She could have insisted on being moved, but it would have occasioned gossip amongst the servants, and she saw no need for it. Indeed, she thought it would have been an insult to her host. She was in no moral or physical danger. Lord Carlton was hardly likely to creep into her room at the dead of night and seduce her!

Lady Longbourne was in any case occupying the rooms which had been intended for Cassie, and would not have liked to be moved. And if any of the servants sought to read anything improper in the rather unusual arrangements, they would soon be put to rights by Mrs Dorkins, who had seen the key amongst Cassie's things and apologized abjectly for her blunder.

'I am sure I do not know how I misunderstood his lordship, miss.'

'It is of no importance,' Cassie assured her. 'And as these are the very finest rooms in the house, there is nothing to apologize for, Mrs Dorkins.'

Slightly worried by Lord Carlton's withdrawal, Cassie found herself thinking about him more and more. It could not possibly be the rooms that made him look at her so particularly from time to time? No, no, surely there must be more behind Lord Carlton's very odd manner? Perhaps some personal problem of his own?

Had Cassie been a fly on the wall at a very heated exchange between Lord Carlton and Sir Harry—which had not ended with Vincent giving his half-brother a facer, but a truly awesome set down!—she would have understood immediately. However, she was to remain in blissful ignorance of the situation for a while longer.

'Damn you for a gabblemongering fool!' Vincent had said, encountering his half-brother at White's after having been congratulated for the fifth time on his forthcoming nuptials. 'What on earth did you imagine you were about?'

All Harry's champagne-induced notions of a smiling, grateful Vinnie vanished like a summer mist. He stood silent and ashamed, wishing his half-brother would knock him down rather than look at him so accusingly.

'I spoke without thinking. I am most awfully sorry. But surely, it won't matter what people say or think once your engagement is announced?'

'And what makes you so sure it will be? Cassandra may not wish to marry me—or you. Or any of Jack's friends. She is an heiress and has come to town to look for a suitable match. This Banbury tale has scotched her chances before she has begun. Everyone believes she is about to become engaged to me. If she rejects me now they will call her a jilt—and what do you suppose they will call me if I do not ask her to marry me? *And* if I do, come to that! I shall be branded either as a rogue or a fortune-hunter.'

Harry wished fervently the ground would open and let him through, but, as usual in these situations, nothing of the kind happened and he was left to face his half-brother's anger.

'Were you foxed?' Vincent demanded furiously.

'No, not at the time.' Harry cringed beneath Vincent's contemptuous look. He had never seen his half-brother in such a temper. 'It was La Valentina. She asked where you were…and people were gossiping, laying bets about the possibility of your marrying her. As if you would! I decided to end the rumour—'

'And started another!' Vincent frowned as his anger began to cool, and he saw that in other circumstances it might have been amusing. 'You are an idiot, Harry. You've put me in an impossible situation.'

Far worse than Harry could ever have imagined. He was not privy to his half-brother's thoughts, but would not have learned much if he had been able to read them at this precise moment. Vincent's mind was in some considerable turmoil, torn as he was between making a clean breast of the whole thing to Cassie, and risking a scandal—or far worse, some hurt to her!—if the truth came out.

Quite unaware of the storm brewing, Cassie was enjoying all the visits to the dressmakers, milliners, glovemakers, and other shops where she purchased the various bits and pieces that were essential for a successful come out.

Several days passed before she had had time to catch her breath, and it was not until the day of her very first evening party that something happened which was to turn her world upside down.

'I have never had so much fun in my life,' Cassie said, twirling before the mirror in her room wearing one of the many new gowns which had been delivered that very afternoon. 'This is such a lovely evening dress, ma'am. It makes me look elegant. Not pretty, of course, but passable, I think.'

'You are more than that,' said Lady Longbourne, looking at her thoughtfully. Over the past few days, her feelings for the girl had grown ever more fond. It was true that Cassie was not pretty. She would never be that, but there was something rather special about her—an inner loveliness that might not be appreciated by all, but was plain to those who really looked. 'You are a handsome gel, Cassie. Any gentleman of sense will see that. I do not fear that you will be a wallflower this evening, my dear.'

'I hope not!' Cassie laughed and pulled a face at her in the mirror. 'I mean to be a success, ma'am.'

'And so you deserve,' replied her hostess with a smile.

It was to be Cassie's first venture into the critical world of London society, which was very different from dining with friends in the country. She had, of course, already met some old friends of Lady Longbourne's, who had been delighted to discover she was in town and called to present their cards, take tea or issue invitations. Most of the ladies had brought their daughters to meet Cassie; they had all been amazingly kind and friendly, though as yet none of them had been accompanied by the gentlemen of their family. Which was, when one thought about it, a little strange, Cassie thought. But perhaps the news of her fortune had not yet gone round. She was a little disappointed, for it would have been pleasant to get to know a few gentlemen before she attended her first dance, but at least she was on nodding acquaintance with some rather important ladies.

'As I was saying—' Lady Longbourne was interrupted by a knock at the door of Cassie's sitting room. 'Come in!'

The housekeeper entered. 'Lord Carlton asks if Miss Thornton will do him the honour of speaking to him in his study, ma'am.'

'I shall come down directly,' Cassie said at once and thanked her.

'I wonder what Carlton can want?' Lady Longbourne said, frowning as Mrs Dorkins departed. 'You had best go down as you are, Cassie. I dare say he will not keep you more than a few moments. It is most inconvenient. We had not yet decided on your gown for this evening.'

'I believe I have decided,' Cassie replied, 'but if Lord Carlton wishes to see me, I must not keep him waiting.'

She ran from the room with a smile on her lips. Having seen very little of her host for the past several days, she had discovered that she missed him. It was the most ridiculous thing, but the very mention of his wanting to see her had set her foolish heart racing.

She paused outside the door of his study, momentarily disconcerted. Why had he sent for her? She could surely not have done anything to displease him? Unless Tara was in trouble?

Knocking once, Cassie heard his voice requesting her to enter and did so, peeping uncertainly round the door.

'You wished to see me, sir?'

'Yes, Cassie. Please come in.' He smiled at her as she did so. 'Thank you for coming so promptly.'

She was surprised at his use of her name, because although she had given him permission to address her as Cassie, he had not—until now. His own reserve had made her too shy to use his name, in case he thought her presumptuous.

She advanced slowly into the room, which was panelled in light oak and had many pictures of horses and dogs on the walls. There was a very large desk, its leather top spread with papers and various trinkets, two matching bookcases and several sofas and chairs. Obviously a gentleman's room, it yet had a light, airy atmosphere that Cassie immediately liked.

'Is something wrong, sir?'

'You promised you would return the compliment,' he reminded her gently. 'My name is Vincent—or Vinnie, if you prefer.'

A pale rose colour crept into her cheeks. 'Yes, of course I did—but I thought you might have changed your mind.'

'Because I have been distant these past few days?'

His directness startled her. 'Well…yes. I did wonder if I had offended you in some way.'

'You? How could you?'

Vincent was standing by the fire grate, which was laid with logs but not lit because of the warm weather. Now he moved towards her, and the expression in his eyes made Cassie's heart jerk. Why did he look so serious? Her heart raced and she felt oddly breathless. What was it about him that could make her feel so very peculiar sometimes?

'I must tell you that I have been wrestling with my conscience,' he declared with the air of a man who had come to a decision. 'It has been in my mind to ask you to do me the honour of becoming my wife, Cassie.' He heard her gasp of surprise, but ploughed on bravely. 'I have been distant these past days, because I felt it would be unfair to speak before you had had a chance to have your season. However, I find I cannot wait any longer…I must speak out now or forever be damned.'

There was no doubt in Cassie's mind that he was labouring under a heavy burden of emotion—and passion! Usually so calm, there was evidence of real torment in his eyes. His voice held a tremor and he could hardly bear to look at her.

Was he so much in love with her that he could not countenance the risk of losing her to another if he did not speak now? Cassie was shaken to the core by this revelation of a man she had only suspected might exist beneath the surface. To be regarded with such passion was more than she had ever dared contemplate—and it overwhelmed her.

Her voice was steadier than her heart as she said, 'Am I to understand you are making me an offer of marriage?'

'Yes, of course. Did I not make myself clear? How foolish of me.' He smiled oddly, then took her hand in his before going down on one knee before her. 'I have the highest regard for you, Cassie, and if you would consent to be my wife, I should count myself the most fortunate of men.'

'Yes. Yes, I will marry you.' The words flew out of Cassie's mouth before she'd had time to consider them. 'I had not expected to find great passion. I am not a beauty, sir. No, no, do not deny it. If indeed you have formed a *tendre* for me, my lord, it is not for my face. However, I do not question your regard, for I too have come to—to like you very well. And I think I could be comfortable as your wife.'

Vincent kissed her hand and stood up. 'I think we shall suit,' he said, a faint smile in his eyes. 'I am indebted to you for looking kindly on me, Cassie—and I hope you will always be pleased with your choice.' He took a ring from his waistcoat pocket. It was shaped like a daisy and set with beautiful diamonds. 'This is merely to seal our bargain. I shall send at once for the Carlton jewels, and you will no doubt find something you like amongst them.'

'I am quite content with this,' Cassie said. The ring fitted her hand perfectly and had a sweet simplicity about it that pleased her. 'This could almost have been made for me.'

It had indeed been made for her for several months, but Vincent did not mention this fact. One day he hoped to tell his wife the whole truth, but to do so now would only raise doubts in her mind, and that was something he wished to avoid. He kissed her gently on the cheek and smiled.

'You look very well in that gown,' he said. 'That particular shade of yellow becomes you, Cassie. Were you trying it on for this evening?'

'Yes.' She laughed up at him, perfectly at ease. His proposal had surprised her, but she was beginning to feel extremely pleased at the idea of becoming his wife. She did not know why, but it seemed right, as if everything had somehow fallen into its proper place. 'I'm glad you approve, sir...I mean Vincent.'

'I approve of everything you do,' he assured her. His eyes suddenly leapt with mischief. 'Ah, yes, now I think of it—I have been meaning to tell you about Tara...'

'Oh, dear,' Cassie said, pulling a face. 'Was Monsieur Marcel terribly displeased?'

'Only when she allowed some tartlets to spoil in the oven,' Vincent replied. 'He was, in fact, very appreciative of the trust I had placed in him. At least, I am reliably informed that he said that he would move heaven and earth to please me and that it would not be his fault if she went straight to—' He stopped short, recollecting that he was talking to a lady, though funnily enough it did not seem wrong to tell Cassie things he would never have repeated to his mother. 'Well, it was somewhere rather warm, but we need not go into that, I think.'

Cassie's laughter rang out. Vincent was struck by her looks at that moment, realising that there was a new sparkle about her. His surprise turned swiftly to admiration. Her beauty was not conventional, but it *was* there, inside her. At times she could, and did, appear almost plain. Yet now she was so vibrant that desire surged within him and he knew an urgent longing to sweep her up in his arms and make love to her.

'When shall we be married?' he asked, his voice husky with suppressed passion. 'It is very bad of me, Cassie, but I find myself impatient to have you to myself.'

Cassie blushed and looked down, her heart beating so fast she could scarcely breathe. 'We could announce our engagement this evening—and marry as soon as you could arrange it.'

'Thank you.' He bent to kiss her cheek once more. 'I shall tell Mama at once—and we shall have champagne. Yes, this must be a celebration. I will let you go and change your gown, Cassie, or it will be too crushed for you to wear this evening.'

She smiled and left him. Walking upstairs, she felt slightly dazed. It had all happened so quickly. Just over two weeks ago, Lord Carlton had been only a hazy memory. Now they were to marry, and Cassie could feel the beginnings of a very real, sharp joy spreading through her.

Vincent's proposal had left her in no doubt that his feelings for her ran deep. He had been very moved when he confessed his need to propose to her at once, that could not be doubted—even though it was hard for her to believe he could love her so much. He could have found a much prettier woman! And he had no need of her fortune.

For her part, Cassie had liked him at their first meeting, no, the second! At the first she had thought him a hero!

For a few days she had in fact believed she was madly in love with him, but that was a girl's foolishness, of course.

Her feelings for Carlton now were very confused. She was aware of her own inexperience where gentlemen were concerned, and did not know what to make out of what was happening to her. Cassie had never had a love affair, nor yet a mild flirtation. As a young girl she had adored her brother and, apart from the incident when Carlton had rescued her kitten, had never met anyone who came close to touching that private inner core of her.

But now her sleeping heart had begun to respond to a man's teasing smile, to a wicked sense of humour and kindness. She had not looked to find real love in her marriage, yet now she could see how very pleasant a loving relationship might be. She remembered the look in Carlton's eyes when he had asked her how soon they could be married and was shocked at the immodesty of her own thoughts. Properly brought up young ladies were not supposed to think about things of that nature—at least until they were married. But she could not help imagining what it would be like to be kissed on the lips by her fiancé and...other things that made her blush and tingle all over.

Was it possible that she was falling in love with him? Cassie considered the idea. It was true that she always felt happier when Carlton was with her, that his kiss had aroused new sensations of excitement in her—but love?

She had not planned to love her husband, had convinced herself that she did not want to love anyone again—that it would be too painful—but now she was not sure. Perhaps this rather odd breathlessness she had begun to experience at the thought of Carlton kissing her was love. And she rather liked it.

If she was loved in return, might not that be the greatest happiness any woman could ever know?

And surely Vincent did love her? He had certainly

seemed to be powerfully affected by his feelings for her. She felt a sudden glow of happiness as she hurried upstairs to impart the news to Sarah. How surprised she would be!

Sarah embraced Cassie, assuring her that she thought it all quite wonderful, but adding that she was not in the least surprised.

'I was sure Lord Carlton would make you an offer,' she told Cassie a moment or so after they had hugged. 'I could see it in his eyes when he looked at you. You are very lucky, Cassie. I like Lord Carlton, and I am certain you will be happy as his wife. Any woman must be content with such a man. He is so kind and has such pleasant manners.'

'Yes…' Cassie was thoughtful. All that her friend had said was true, but there was far more to Carlton than he let show. The secret nature he concealed from the world intrigued her, making her want to learn more of the man she had promised to wed—the real man. 'Yes, I suppose so. He does seem to be everything he ought…though can any man really be as perfect as he appears?'

'What an odd thing to say.' Sarah looked at her in surprise. 'You do wish to marry him, do you not? You do not sound very certain.'

'Yes. Oh, yes,' Cassie replied. 'I am quite sure of that. I was merely thinking aloud.' She was just not sure of her feelings! A marriage of convenience was one thing, a passionate love match quite another, and her thoughts were too confused, too private to share with anyone. She smiled at her friend, hiding her doubts. 'Now I am settled, we must concentrate on finding you a husband.'

'Oh…' Sarah sighed. 'I am afraid that will not be so easily achieved.'

'You are so very pretty,' Cassie said, sliding an arm

about her waist. 'I am sure someone will fall in love with you instantly.'

'Perhaps.' Sarah blushed, avoiding her gaze. 'You will not go down to Brighton now, I suppose?'

'We shall remain in London for a few weeks, I expect. I am not sure where the wedding will be…but you will stay with me for that, Sarah. Please, say yes! I want you to be my chief bridesmaid. And I am certain we can find you someone you like before that.'

Sarah smiled but said nothing. She knew that her own case was very different from her friend's. She had overheard something Mrs Dorkins was saying to the butler—something she had thought a little strange. However, she was a sensible girl, and she genuinely liked Lord Carlton. Besides, servants' gossip was often misinformed, and to mention a few odd remarks when there was no way of knowing the truth could cause terrible harm. She had no wish to put doubts in Cassie's mind that were not already there, for she was extremely fond of her. No doubt Sarah was mistaken. Mrs Dorkins could not possibly have said that she had given Cassie the rooms adjoining his lordship's, because she knew they had been secretly engaged for years!

Cassie had no notion of her friend's anxieties on her behalf. Life had suddenly become much more exciting. Lady Longbourne had seized on the news of the engagement with delight.

'Oh, I knew how it would be when I first saw you,' she exclaimed. 'Your clothes were wrong, but I could see you had something about you, my dear. You were exactly what Carlton needed in a wife, not a cold, spoiled beauty, but a lady who will grace his household with charm and dignity. Septimus will not be able to scold me in future—nor will his odious brat step into Carlton's shoes. Felicity will be wild with disappointment, of course, but I am so happy! I shall enjoy having you as a daughter, my love.'

Having lived with Lady Longbourne for just over two weeks now, Cassie was well aware of her ladyship's dislike of her brother-in-law and his family. Although she had not yet met the infamous Septimus and his *odious* son, she had heard sufficient to be able to sympathise.

Lady Longbourne presented her with a pair of diamond-and-pearl bracelets as she was dressing for the evening.

'You should have the Carlton diamonds, of course, but no doubt Vincent will give them to you when you marry.'

In fact, Vincent sent her a gift a few minutes later. It was a choker of large creamy pearls with a small diamond pendant in the shape of a daisy. Very suitable for a young lady, but also stylish and obviously of the best quality.

Opening the box to exclaim in pleasure over the gift, Cassie wondered how Vincent had managed to match the ring so perfectly in such a short time. And how had he known about her love of daisies? As a small girl, she had spent hours making daisy chains. She had often crowned both herself and Jack with them.

'One day I'll buy you a real diamond necklace shaped like a daisy,' her brother had told her once. 'When I inherit the estate, you shall have everything you want, Cassie.'

'You will grow up and get married,' Cassie had teased. 'Then you'll forget me.'

'I might marry. I dare say I shall one day,' Jack had said, grinning at her. 'But you're my little sister, Cassie. I shall never neglect you. I shall always be there to take care of you—and when you marry, I shall make sure your husband treats you as he ought.'

'What will you do if he beats me?'

'I shall kill him!'

They had been children then, playing King and Castle in the sunshine, but Cassie had never forgotten her brother's words—or the chill that had run down her spine as he'd said them. She recalled them now in the midst of all the excitement.

Jack was so close to her, in her thoughts, as if she could almost reach out and touch him. She was drawn to her window, looking out into gardens shaded as the sun began to dip lower in the sky. What a glorious summer evening. Just as many evenings had been when she and Jack played together.

'How I wish you were here to give me away,' she whispered as she took a last glance at herself in her dressing mirror. 'But I know you would be pleased for me, Jack. Vincent was your best friend. You would approve of my marrying him. I know you would. You wrote to me about him so often.'

Jack's letters had glowed with praise for his friend. Everyone in the regiment looked up to him, he was always there for them, supporting them, pushing them to do better. Remembering the last letter her brother had sent her from France, just a few days before the war started, Cassie took it from her dressing case and read it through again. Jack had written:

Sometimes I am afraid for my life. More than that, Cassie, I am afraid I shall not acquit myself with honour. I could tell only you this, my dearest one, for I know you will understand. I do not want to die. I want to come home to you and all I hold dear—but if I deserted my friends now (or worse still, under fire) I should never forgive myself. If it were not for Vinnie, I do not think I could bear this waiting—it is the dread of what may happen rather than the fighting itself. God knows, I do not think myself a coward, Cassie—but there is so much good in life. Yet, if Vinnie is by my side, I believe I can face even death. With his help, I shall hope to do my duty and maintain the family honour.

Her poor, darling Jack! Cassie's heart ached for him, knowing how much he must have suffered before writing her such a letter. He was not a coward, could never have been a coward, but the thought of a violent death and the blood shed by his comrades had filled him with horror— as it must any man of sensitivity.

She blinked away her tears, replacing the letter in the secret drawer of her dressing case. She had shown it to no one and never would. Jack had died two days after it was sent. His grave was somewhere in France. She had never known exactly where. One day she would ask Carlton to tell her. Perhaps he would take her there.

Determinedly, Cassie locked her grief away. This was meant to be a happy night. She was about to make her début in society—and she was already engaged to a man who had been hunted by matchmaking mamas since he was first on the town! She was already a success. No one could possibly look down their noses at her now.

Besides, she would be with Lord Carlton, and they would probably dance together. Cassie's heart raced as she thought of being in his arms.

Was she foolish to let herself think of love?

She put away her doubts and fears. This was to be an exciting night—and she meant to enjoy herself!

It would have been impossible for a girl of Cassie's nature not to have enjoyed herself that evening. People were so amazingly kind to her. She had wondered if she would find herself short of partners, for she was already engaged and not on the marriage market. However, after she had danced first with Carlton and then with his brother Harry—

who was just as charming and handsome as she had re-membered—she found herself besieged with eager partners.

Many of the gentlemen were friends of her fiancé. Some had known Jack and spoke of him as a fine soldier. All were charming, attentive and willing to make her feel wel-come in society. She was several times offered felicitations on her engagement, and everyone seemed aware that she was going to marry Lord Carlton.

'He and Jack were such good friends,' said a certain Freddie Bracknell. 'We might have known Vinnie would snatch the prize from under our noses. He always was a lucky devil!'

Cassie laughed, not quite sure of his meaning, but taking it as a compliment. 'We have known each other for years,' she said. 'Carlton was a good friend to me as a child.' She did not mention the incident of the kitten, but the reminis-cent look in her eyes and the soft smile on her lips con-vinced her partner that this story of a long-standing en-gagement—which he had had good cause to doubt—must after all be true.

Strange, though, that Jack had made all five of them promise that one of them would marry her if he was killed. Freddie Bracknell thought wistfully of the long straw he had drawn. Had he had the presence of mind to have snapped it short, he might have been standing in Carlton's shoes. It was a damned shame! He could have done with the fortune Miss Thornton had inherited from some obscure aunt. Certainly he had had no suspicion of such an aunt, nor had the others…though Carlton was a damned knowing one. And, being Jack's closest confidant, he might have known in advance.

The idea rankled. The more he thought about it, the more convinced he became that he had somehow been cheated. After his dance ended, he went off to share a drink with

Harry and commiserate with him over the prize they had both lost.

'What was all that nonsense with the straws?' he muttered, feeling considerably put out. 'If Vinnie knew he was going to marry her all the time?'

'It—it was understood but not spoken of,' Harry replied uneasily. 'I dare say either of them might have changed their minds—indeed, Vinnie was uncertain what to do right up to this afternoon.'

'You mean he hadn't asked her?' Freddie Bracknell frowned. It was months since Jack had been killed. Why had Carlton delayed all this time? 'I should have thought he would have done it an age ago. Damned smoky, ain't it?'

'No, of course it isn't,' Harry replied, uncomfortably aware that once again he had put his foot in it. 'He just wanted to be sure they would suit, that's all.'

'Might have given the rest of us a chance,' Bracknell muttered. 'If it ain't just like Vinnie to draw the short straw, then find out the girl's an heiress. Luck of the devil, that's all it is!'

Harry pokered up. 'If you're going to insinuate there's something havey cavey about it...'

Seeing the glint in his eye, Bracknell backed down hastily. Harry might not have as much skill in the art of boxing as his half-brother—who did!—but he was a damned fine shot.

'No, no, it was just a thought,' he muttered. 'Miss Thornton has obviously been expecting the proposal for years anyway. I gather they were great friends when she was still in the schoolroom.'

If they were, Harry knew none of it but he nodded slightly, allowing his companion to believe what he liked. Since Vincent had obviously decided to let the rumour stand, Harry wasn't going to risk another set down like the last one!

Such is the stuff of rumour and innuendo! Freddie Bracknell's conclusions were much as most other interested bystanders' that evening. And, as always, rumour builds upon rumour.

'I hear it was a love match when they were in leading strings,' one dowager repeated to another as they sat watching the young ones dancing. 'They were far too young to think of marriage, of course, and then circumstances parted them. Now Carlton has honoured his childhood promise to wed her.'

'I heard it was a match made by their parents when she was in her cradle,' replied her friend. 'I think that is more likely. Carlton has spread himself on the town for years, now he has done the decent thing and kept the promise made in his name. It is a matter of honour, Rosalind. Nothing more or less. You can't say she's a beauty.'

'No, she ain't a beauty—but there's something about her.'

'Her fortune? They say she has ten thousand a year!'

'As much as that? I heard it was less. No wonder Carlton made up his mind to have her in a hurry!'

Blissfully ignorant of all the gossip and speculation, Cassie danced on, round and round, enchanted by the music and the glittering jewels reflected in the light of many candles. It was a magic night, a night when sadness was far away and everything seemed dreamlike and wonderful. She wished it might go on and on forever.

Sarah was dancing every dance as well. For the third time that evening with Harry Longbourne! Which was a little unwise, perhaps. Cassie noticed and wondered at it, then forgot as Carlton came to claim her for the dance before supper.

His eyes were soft with amusement as he looked down at her glowing face. 'Are you enjoying yourself, Cassie?'

'Oh, very much,' she sparkled up at him. 'I wish I might go on dancing for ever.'

'You would tire of it eventually, I dare say.'

'Perhaps. But not tonight.' She gave a little gurgle of sheer pleasure. 'I have danced with so many of your friends.' She mentioned a few names, then paused as she saw something flicker in his eyes. 'Is anything wrong?'

'No, nothing at all. Shall we go down to supper now?'

Cassie laid her hand on his arm. She thought he was looking very splendid that evening in a coat of blue super-fine that fitted him perfectly, accentuating the wiry strength of his body; his cravat was tied in a magnificent style that she knew was called *à la Fortuna*, and favoured by the more sophisticated dandies: there was some amusing story behind the style, but it was shared only by the gentlemen and no lady had yet been able to discover it!

Cassie was aware of a subtle change in his manner when she had mentioned Freddie Bracknell, or Captain Bracknell to give him his correct title. She knew they must have been in France together, in the same regiment as Jack—so what had caused that wary look in Vincent's eyes? Was there something she ought to know?

'Do you dislike Captain Bracknell?' she asked as he was silent.

'Lord, no,' Vincent said, glancing at her uncomfortably. She seemed to read him too well! 'Freddie is decent enough. He was one of us out there—but not a special friend to me.'

'Not like you and Jack?'

'No, not like that.'

For the briefest time Vincent's eyes took on the bleak, distant expression she had noticed before. She wondered what it meant, but this was neither the time nor the place to ask. One day soon, she would. After they were married, when they had the leisure to really talk of things that mattered.

Cassie became aware that someone was staring at them. A rather tall, statuesque lady, very beautiful in a dark, exotic way. She had the most compelling, magnificent eyes!

'Who is that?' Cassie asked, pressing on Vincent's arm. 'That very striking, slightly plump lady. She is staring at us rather peculiarly. Do you know her?'

La Valentina would not have been best pleased to hear herself described as plump, and only the foolish or the brave would do so in her hearing. Statuesque was the word usually applied to a figure such as hers.

Vincent hesitated momentarily, then inclined his head towards the beauty. 'Everyone knows La Valentina. She is an opera singer. Her voice is beyond anything you have ever heard.'

'Oh…' Cassie had the oddest feeling he was trying to hide something from her. She waited for him to introduce her, but he merely nodded again to La Valentina in passing and drew Cassie on into the crowded supper room. 'I should have liked to meet her.'

'Another time. She is to sing after supper, and when she gives a performance she likes to save her voice.'

'Yes, I suppose so,' Cassie agreed, but felt that he had deliberately avoided the meeting. 'She must take care of her voice.'

'Forget her,' Vincent commanded, his harsh tone startling Cassie. 'Some things are best left alone. She is not important.'

Cassie was silent. Although largely innocent of the ways of the world, she was not stupid. She knew very well that men sometimes had mistresses, especially when they were unmarried. It was inconceivable that a man of Vincent's age and experience would have lived like a monk. She sensed there had been an intimate relationship between La Valentina and her fiancé quite recently, and she told herself it did not matter. It was over, of course. It must be, mustn't it? Yes, she was certain it was—and yet she could not help feeling hurt. Which was very foolish of her!

It would not do to let Vincent or anyone else see she had been upset by the chance meeting. She lifted her chin, looking about her and waving at Sarah, who was taking supper with Harry and Lady Longbourne.

'Shall we join your mother and Sarah?' she asked, her smile bright, fixed.

'Yes, of course. If you wish it.'

Vincent was frowning. Cassie was a very perceptive young woman. She had picked up the vibes coming from La Valentina at once, and he had spoken more harshly than he had intended in an effort to stop any doubts entering her mind. He had sensed her withdrawal, and knew she had been hurt, as much by his tone as the realisation of what was behind it. He was sorry she had been distressed by the meeting, but it was brief and could not have been avoided for ever. She must have learned of it one day: the gossips would see to that sooner or later. There was no help for it. His main worry was that she would hear something she might find even more disturbing. Cassie had intelligence and a sharp mind. She must know that his relationship with La Valentina had been merely a diversion, and had ended before he had proposed marriage to her.

Vincent had caught snatches of the gossip circulating that evening. People whispered that his marriage was a matter of honour—a promise redeemed at last after years of delay. That was Harry's doing, of course. The damned idiot! Yet had the truth got out…that might have hurt her even more. She had, even before her inheritance made her independent, been angered by her father's cousin's clumsy assumption that she would be glad to marry him. He could not imagine what she might think if she learned that her brother had extracted a promise from his friends that one of them would marry her—and that they had all solemnly drawn straws to see who went first!

She would be both hurt and angry. He had realised that almost at once after meeting her, and it was this that had made him withdraw. He had decided to let things drift, watch over her through her season, and then talk to her if she did not find someone she liked well enough to marry. Harry's blunder had forced him into proposing that afternoon. It was the only way he could think of to protect Cassie from the far more dangerous gossip that would have been occasioned had she not made her début as his fiancée.

He would not harm her for the world! Vincent smiled as he watched her talking and laughing with her friend and his family. Her hurt was easing now. She was coming to terms with the idea that he had had mistresses, as he had known she would. She looked directly at him, shy and yet wanting to believe in him, to believe that he cared for her, would not shame or distress her deliberately.

He felt an odd pain in his heart. What had begun as a duty, as a way of absolving his conscience—of banishing the dreams that sometimes haunted his sleep—had become very much more.

Cassie was so much finer than he had ever imagined. She had been his best friend's sister—a spirited girl he had once rescued from a tree. But now…now she was a woman he had begun to admire very much, and he was afraid he might actually be falling rather desperately in love with her. He was struggling to keep afloat against a flood tide, but thought he might be about to go under.

He believed she liked him very well. She trusted him, looked up to him as a gentleman and a friend of Jack's. The open, warm, sharing glances she sent him sometimes were enough to make him realise that he had never expe-

rienced anything like this in his life: it showed him a new
world, a new, exciting way to live and he was anxious to
explore all that that might mean.

But what if she ever learned the truth? Not just the foolish ceremony of drawing straws to see who honoured the
promise to Jack—but the terrible, shameful truth that had
overshadowed his life for a long time now, keeping him
from seeking her out. The damning, terrifying reality that
haunted his dreams and made him wonder if he would ever
be free of this crushing guilt!

He had lived with guilt eating at him for months. Sometimes he woke from a nightmare, sweating, calling a name.
And there was never a waking moment when he did not
wish that he could turn back the clock...change what had
happened. Especially now that Cassie had come to mean
so much to him.

How would the woman he had learned to respect and
care for feel if she ever discovered that he was responsible
for the death of her beloved brother? That if it had not been
for him, Jack might well still be alive? She would not smile
at him so trustingly then. She would turn from him in disgust and horror—and how could he bear that?

Chapter Six

The past ten days had passed in a whirl of pleasure. Mornings were usually spent either driving or walking in the park, visiting the lending library, or shopping; afternoons, either visiting or outings to places of interest. Any of these innocent pastimes was liable to lead to a meeting with some of the new friends Cassie was making, and were all equally enjoyable to both her and Sarah.

Quite often Vincent escorted her and Sarah in the afternoons, and sometimes he took her driving alone in his carriage. She had mentioned her wish for a smart turnout, something that she might learn to drive herself in the country, and he had promised to look into it. Once again, they seemed to be becoming friends and Cassie was well pleased with her situation.

The memory of that look in La Valentina's eyes—which had spoken volumes, letting Cassie know exactly what the opera singer thought of the plain dab of a girl Carlton had chosen to marry!—had lingered like a nasty odour. Despite all her efforts to dismiss it as unimportant, Cassie had not quite been able to put her thoughts aside; they rankled and pricked at her like a stone in her shoe. Because, of course, La Valentina was so beautiful. And Cassie could not understand why any man should prefer her to such a woman. Had Lord Carlton been in an awkward financial position, she would have understood perfectly, and, had he been honest with her, she believed she would still have accepted him—but he was one of the wealthiest men in London. So why did he wish to marry her? She was not exceptional in any way.

The thing Cassie hated above all else was falseness. She had always been a very honest girl herself, and hated lies and deliberate deception.

However, her fiancé had made it plain by his manner that evening that the beautiful opera singer meant nothing to him, and she had tried very hard not to be jealous of his affair with her.

'You must not expect too much,' she told herself seriously when she was alone in her bedroom, gazing into a mirror which refused to lie. 'Why should he have fallen desperately in love with you, Cassie Thornton? You read too much into that look. It is enough that he likes you! He does not have to love you.'

It was and must be enough. Cassie knew there was no turning back, nor did she wish for there to be. Whether Vincent loved her or not, she was sure that they could at least be friends. Besides, everyone took it for granted that she would marry Carlton. Indeed, of late, she had begun to realise that many people seemed to believe that theirs was a long-standing affair. She wondered how the rumour had sprung up. Because of the friendship between Jack and Vincent, she supposed, and the fact that they had been close neighbours for some years.

'It is so amusing,' she told Sarah that morning as they were strolling together in the park. 'People must always gossip and make up stories!'

Sarah was silent for a moment, then, 'It does not bother you that they should say such things?'

'Good gracious, no!' Cassie laughed out loud, causing one or two heads to turn. People smiled to see the two young girls walking together in the park, a maid following just behind should she be needed, as was proper. 'Why on earth should it? I know the truth. We hardly met in those days—except for the time Carlton rescued my kitten. And then we exchanged only a few words before he hurried away to change his breeches.'

'You are wise to ignore the gossips,' Sarah said. 'It is obvious that Lord Carlton cares for you. He would not otherwise have proposed so soon.'

'Yes. I think—' Cassie stopped speaking, gasped and caught her friend's arm as she recognised the man coming towards them. 'Oh, no! What can I do to avoid him? He is coming this way and he has seen us. What a nuisance...'

'Who?' Sarah looked about her, startled by the urgency in Cassie's tone. 'Do you mean that man in the ill-fitting brown coat and grey breeches?'

'Who else would walk in a London park dressed like that?' Cassie groaned. 'It is Kendal Thornton—Father's cousin.'

She looked so dismayed, poised, as if on the verge of flight, that Sarah laughed and shook her honey-gold curls at her. 'You cannot run away from him, even though he *is* sadly lacking in town bronze. He is your only relative, after all. You must at least say good morning to him, dearest.'

'It is not only a sense of style he lacks,' Cassie hissed agitatedly. She would have said much more, but was obliged to desist as Sir Kendal approached, planting himself firmly in her path and clearly determined to address her.

'Good morning, Miss Thornton.' His thick eyebrows knitted in a frown, and Cassie thought he resembled nothing so much as a bad-tempered bulldog. 'Can it really be you? I must confess I am surprised to see you here.'

His eyes went over her, noting her stylish gown and all the accompanying trifles that proclaimed her a lady of fashion.

'Indeed?' Cassie bristled. 'I cannot imagine why anything I choose to do should surprise, or even interest, you. I believed when we last parted we had nothing more to say to one another.'

'Now, now, Cassandra,' he said, giving her his irritating, pompous smile. 'No need to fire up like that. I have realised it was foolish of me to have spoken so soon. I was concerned to set your mind at rest as to your future standing, but did not reckon with your natural grief. You were upset and that was my fault. I shall not hold your rash words against you. In fact, I am perfectly willing to make you another offer here and now, if you wish?'

'You would be foolish to do so, sir,' Cassie replied, eyes flashing. 'I meant what I said the first time. Forgive me if I am rude, but I must make it plain to you that I have no wish to marry you—nor to meet you again. Or at least, only as a distant relative, with whom I am on nodding terms.'

'You are a very stubborn girl, Cassandra. I have no idea where you found the money to come to town, but…'

'That is none of your affair,' Cassie said, very angry now. 'I have touched nothing that was by law yours. As it happens, I am the guest of Mama's closest friend. Lady Longbourne wrote to me, inviting me to stay with her and—'

He glowered at her, clearly put out by the news. 'That is as may be, but you cannot put a mere acquaintance before kinship. You ought properly to have sought my permission for the visit. You deny it, Cassandra, but as your only living relative, I do have some say in how you conduct yourself.'

'No, you do not!' Cassie said, holding her temper by a whisper. 'My father never liked you, sir. He would never have left me to your care. And if you have anything further to say on this matter, please address it to my fiancé—Lord Vincent Carlton. If you care to trouble yourself, you will soon discover that our engagement is of a long-standing nature, arranged by my father years ago. I am sure Lord Carlton will be happy to put your mind at rest on this matter if you have any doubts about my future.'

Sir Kendal's mouth fell open. Cassie saw her thrust had gone home, leaving him temporarily at a stand, and, taking Sarah's arm, she walked on. He stood, staring after her for several minutes, but made no attempt to follow.

It was a moment or two before she was calm enough to speak, and when she did so, it was of a balloon ascension they were to attend on Hampstead Heath later that day.

'Carlton says it will be an awe-inspiring sight,' she said conversationally. 'I am rather looking forward to it, you know. I imagine it must be very exciting to ride in the basket, don't you?'

'Oh, no,' Sarah said faintly, but with a look of admiration in her eyes. 'I should be terrified.'

'That awful man!' Cassie burst out, unable to hold back a second longer. 'I could not speak of him for a moment, for fear of offending your ears with words unbecoming to a lady. Words Jack sometimes used, you know.' She coloured slightly. 'I should not, of course. But it makes one feel so—so cross. How dare he? Oh, I wish I were a man. I would make him sorry he had ever been so presumptuous as to force his attentions on me when I have already made it plain they are unwelcome.'

'But, dearest,' Sarah pointed out reasonably, 'were you a man, he could not have done so.'

Cassie stared at her for a moment, then began to gurgle with laughter, her anger melting. 'Oh, how foolish of me! Of course he couldn't. I should have inherited the title and estate, shouldn't I?' She sighed. 'Why does he wish to marry me? Do you suppose he knows of my inheritance but is pretending not to? I cannot see why he should persist otherwise, can you? If only Jack had not been killed. I do miss him! He should have been here, sharing this with us, Sarah. He would have loved it so!'

'Yes, dearest. I wish he was, too, for your sake.'

Cassie smiled and hugged her arm. It was very odd, but she had a very strong feeling of Jack being close to her at that moment. She almost expected him to come riding up on his horse, jump down and swing her up in his arms as he was used to when they were together, and the tingling in the nape of her neck was so fierce that she glanced around as if to see him.

She could, of course, see no one resembling her brother. There were several gentlemen walking or riding along the bridle paths, sometimes in small groups, with ladies or alone, but no one who looked in the least like Jack. She caught a glimpse of a beggar hobbling towards her, a crutch under one arm, but just as she was thinking of looking for a shilling to give him, she heard a shout and turned to see Lord Carlton striding towards her. She waved and called his name, and when she looked again, the beggar was shuffling away in the opposite direction.

'Cassie!' Vincent cried as he came hurriedly to join them. 'Mama told me she thought I might find you here. I hoped I should, because the time of the balloon ascension has been brought forward an hour. If you do not wish to miss it, you must come home and change at once.'

'We were just about to do so,' Cassie said as Vincent companionably offered an arm to both of them. 'We would not miss such a sight for the world!'

'No, indeed, we would not,' agreed Sarah. 'We were only just talking of it, were we not, Cassie?'

'Then there is not a moment to be lost,' said Vincent, smiling at them.

The occasion was one of huge excitement that afternoon. A great many fashionable ladies and gentlemen had turned out in their carriages to watch the exciting event. Many had brought hampers with them, intending to picnic on the Heath afterwards. Some intended to follow the balloon's flight for as far as they could in the carriages or on horseback.

'Is this not thrilling?' Cassie asked as she, Sarah, Vincent and Harry sat together on a grassy bank, watching all the preparations. Several men were at that moment engaged on spreading the balloon on the ground. 'How will they ever get such a large contraption to fly? It does not look possible.'

'What are they doing now?' Sarah asked. 'Pray tell me, what is that pump thing for?'

Lord Carlton explained the principles of heating a gas that was lighter than air, which made the balloon float. 'The first balloons were invented by the Montgolfier brothers and flew in 1782 at Annonay near Lyons. They were filled with heated air, but soon after hydrogen was tried successfully. Once the balloon is filled with the gas, they have to tie it down to stop it breaking away. That is what those ropes are for. They have to be very careful or it would float off without them—indeed, that has been known to happen to some amateurs. However, I think our balloonist today is an expert.'

Cassie nodded, watching in fascination as the huge, colourful bag began to inflate. Just as Vincent had said, several men were hanging on to the ropes, pegging them down and shouting to one another as it heaved and tugged this way and that.

'I understand how they get up—but what happens when they want to come down?' Sarah was asking.

Leaving Vincent to satisfy Sarah's curiosity, Cassie moved a little nearer the balloon. It was very noisy and confusing, and she hovered at the edge of a group of excited children, knowing she must not get any closer for fear of getting caught by a stray rope should one break free.

'Cassie…' The sibilant whisper sent a little shock through her. 'Cassie, I need you…I need your help.'

'Jack!' She whirled round, looking for her brother amongst the crowd. That was his voice! She was certain of it. But where was he? She looked and could not see him. People were milling all around her, pressing forward to secure a better view as the balloonist announced he was almost ready to take flight. 'Jack—where are you?'

Suddenly, a rope snapped and the huge balloon lurched drunkenly on one side, scattering those who had ventured too close. Several ladies screamed and a man rushed past Cassie, nearly knocking her flying; the next moment Cassie's arm was caught and she was firmly guided away from the crowd.

'You must not stand so near,' Vincent said, looking at her in concern. 'It is not just the balloon itself which might be dangerous, Cassie. When people panic, others can sometimes suffer. I would not have you crushed.'

'No. It was foolish of me.'

Cassie's voice was breathless, her face very pale. She had scarcely noticed the panic over the wayward rope, which had now been secured while the balloon was righted once more. Surely she had heard Jack's voice close behind her? She could not have been mistaken! That voice had been—was still!—so dear to her. Jack had been there with her. She felt it in her heart. And yet that was impossible. Jack was dead.

'You are distressed,' Vincent said. 'Would you like to go home? Are you feeling unwell?'

Cassie shook her head, forcing a smile. 'No, no, I am perfectly well, thank you. It was just the shock…just the shock.'

The shock of hearing Jack's voice from beyond the grave. She had felt him close to her for some weeks now, but this was the first time he had tried to speak to her. Why here? Why now? Why not when she was lying alone in bed and could listen to him?

'Thank goodness I was close at hand,' Vincent said, bringing her back to the present. 'Are you faint?'

What a missish creature he must think her to make so much fuss over a silly fright! Cassie tugged her composure back into place. She could not tell her fiancé the true reason for her distress, because he would think her mind was wandering—as indeed it must be!—but she did not like him to think her such a sad case.

'Not at all,' she cried, rallying. 'It is all very exciting. Oh, Vinnie, do look! I believe it is going to fly.'

She hugged his arm, looking up at him in such a way that he was moved to kiss her, very gently on the lips. Cassie blushed and smiled at him.

'I could not resist,' he excused himself. 'You looked so much like an excited child.'

Cassie was not certain she cared for such a description, but made no reply. Then her attention was diverted as a heartfelt sighing issued from the onlookers. She looked skyward as the magnificent balloon rose majestically into the air, carrying its wicker basket and two passengers beneath it.

Cassie shaded her eyes to watch as it rose steadily, then

began to move with the currents of air, gradually drifting further and further away across the Heath.

'Oh, it has almost gone…' she said regretfully.

'Do you want to follow?'

'No—not unless Sarah or Harry does.'

'Shall we ask them?'

Sarah having declared herself satisfied with what they had already seen, Vincent popped the bottle of champagne his butler had packed for the occasion and they drank toasts to each other and ate some of the delicious trifles Monsieur Marcel had conjured up for them.

The afternoon passed away in pleasant idleness until at something past the hour of three, it suddenly became much darker overhead.

'We ought to be getting back,' Vincent said as he heard a rumble of distant thunder.

Harry and Sarah had been strolling together a little way from the carriage but, realising there was a threat of rain, came rushing back. Then, all at once, it began, tumbling down in a torrent of huge drops that hit the ground and bounced up again. The sudden downpour made everyone else hurry to pack up picnics and take shelter. Those fortunate enough to have closed carriages gave the order to move off, though the general rush made the narrow roads congested.

It was as they were passing a stand of thick trees that Cassie happened to notice the figure taking shelter there. He was huddling into a shabby greatcoat. An old soldier by the look of him, long, straggling grey hair sticking out beneath the shapeless hat jammed down tight over his forehead. Cassie was not certain why she turned her head to get a closer look as they passed. She had an odd feeling that she might have seen the man before…quite recently.

The beggar in the park that morning? No, she did not think so. Both were obviously vagrants, but this man did not have a crutch. He was just standing there, looking dejected and getting very wet. She could not know him. It was all in her imagination. Just like hearing Jack call her name!

Cassie sat back with a sigh. Of course she hadn't heard Jack call her. How could she? In her heart, she did not really believe it was possible for someone to return from the grave—though it was possible to feel them near you in spirit: that she knew for certain.

'Is something troubling you?' Vincent asked softly in her ear. 'You have not seemed yourself this afternoon.'

'Nothing is troubling me,' Cassie replied, not quite meeting his eyes. When he looked at her that way it made her heart do strange things. And she was not sure she ought to let herself care too much: gentlemen did not always appreciate clinging vines. 'Thank you for taking us to the balloon ascension. It was exciting.'

'You know I would always please you if I could, Cassie.'

'Yes, of course. You are so thoughtful. Please do not worry about me, I am perfectly happy and well.'

Vincent nodded, but his eyes were watchful. Something had seriously disturbed her that afternoon, but she had made up her mind not to tell him what it was that had caused her to come close to fainting. He regretted the fact that she was not inclined to confide in him, but he could only hope that she would learn to do so in the future. Perhaps when they were married, she would feel able to trust him…and then perhaps he could find a way to explain to her what was in his heart.

The pleasures of London continued apace: escorted rides in Rotten Row, visits to Almack's, that hallowed place of patronesses and privilege, the gardens at Vauxhall where the fireworks were only one of the delights on offer, and a succession of private lunches, dinners, musical evenings and dances. Cassie gave herself up to the excitement, forgetting everything else as the day of her wedding came nearer.

Jack seemed to have gone away from her again, and she knew it was time she let go of her grief. She had a new life ahead of her, and she was looking forward to it more and more as the days passed.

Because surely Vincent must care for her? She must forget that look in La Valentina's eyes, the look that had told her she was a mere nothing. Vincent had asked Cassie to marry him—why would he do that if he did not feel some strong emotion towards her?

She must forget she had ever seen his mistress!

And yet he had called her a child the day they had watched the balloon ascension. She wanted him to think of her as a woman he could share his life with, not someone he must always flatter and indulge as he did his mama.

They were to be married from Sir Harry Longbourne's house. A town affair had been discussed and dismissed. It was fitting that Cassie should be married at the village church in which she had always worshipped. After the ceremony, Lord and Lady Carlton would spend a few days alone at his Hampshire estate, then leave on an extended tour of France, and perhaps Italy if they cared for it. When they returned from their trip, their house in Surrey would be prepared to receive its new mistress. Lady Longbourne would have returned to Carlton House, and they would divide their time between the two estates and the house in London.

'It will be very suitable,' Lady Longbourne declared herself satisfied with the arrangements. 'Carlton can take himself off to Surrey for a few days after he has seen us safely to Longbourne, and come back a day or so before the wedding. I am sure he can find somewhere to put up for a night or two. We shall be at Longbourne. It will be almost as if you were being married from your own home, my love.'

'Yes, but much better,' said Cassie. 'For I should not want to be living there now that Sir Kendal has taken it over.'

Cassie had not chanced to meet her father's cousin again since that morning in the park, and was truly grateful for it. She hoped she would not have to see him again, and was at first adamant that he was not to be invited to the wedding.

'But surely you must,' Lady Longbourne said, slightly shocked by this obstinacy in a girl who was usually so amenable. 'I know you do not care for him, and I understand that you would not precisely wish to have such a man present at your wedding feast, but not to invite him—it cannot be done. I heartily dislike Septimus and his family, but I shall invite them. I could not do otherwise for politeness' sake.'

Cassie held out for as long as she could, but was forced to give in when Vincent told her very firmly that in this case his mother was right.

'It would be unforgivable,' he said. 'You must send him an invitation, Cassie.'

'Oh, very well,' she said, realising that her husband-to-be was not quite as easygoing as she had imagined. There was a very firm hand beneath the velvet glove he used to stroke his mama with, and even Lady Longbourne knew that there was a point beyond which she might not go. 'If it is your wish.'

'Sir Kendal is your only family,' Vincent said, giving her an odd look which she was not able to interpret, not having been present at a certain interview with her distant cousin. 'If he upsets you, you may safely leave him to me, Cassie. I will engage to put him in his place for you.'

Cassie said nothing, merely looking at him from beneath

her thick, dark lashes. It struck her then that she really knew
very little about the man she was so soon to marry. She
had seen only his public manners, which were very pretty,
but perhaps not a true representation of the real man.

Something in his eyes at that moment disturbed her,
making her heart jerk, and she turned from him to Sarah,
beginning to talk to her about the ball they were to attend
the following evening. It was given by the Duke of De-
vonshire and his duchess and was one of the grandest affairs of the season.

'Shall we go and try on our new gowns?' she said, then
looked at Lady Longbourne. 'Will you come with us,
ma'am? To advise whether or not we need any last-minute
adjustments?'

Lady Longbourne agreed at once and the three of them
went off together. Excluded from their plans, Vincent sat
frowning over his own thoughts. Cassie was keeping something from him, he was sure of it. Something that had disturbed her at the balloon ascent. And since that afternoon,
he had felt a slight withdrawal in her. He was sure there
was something on her mind—yet what could it be?

She appeared to be perfectly happy with the arrangements for the wedding; however, he had caught an odd
thoughtful expression in her eyes at times when she thought
herself unobserved. What was worrying her? He would
have liked to ask, but found it difficult. She was entitled to
her private thoughts, as he was to his—but he could not
help wondering whether perhaps he had been unfair to her
in proposing to her so swiftly.

Might she have found someone she preferred if she had
been free? The question played on his mind, especially
when he saw her looking at him as if she did not quite
understand why she had promised to wed him. Or was that
his imagination? Was there something else upsetting her?

If she would only confide in him. Yet he could not blame

her when he carried a far more terrible secret in his own breast—a secret he was not sure he would ever be able to confide in her.

The ballroom was a sad crush and therefore the evening a huge success, just as it had always been meant to be. Cassie was wearing a very elegant gown of saffron yellow with a scooped neckline, a white ruched sash, and little puffed sleeves. A band of white daisies had been embroidered on the hem of her gown, and round the edge of the sleeves. Her dark hair had been swept back into a smooth chignon at the nape of her neck, one shining ringlet allowed to fall on her shoulder. In her ears she wore a pair of magnificent diamond earrings, shaped like daises, and the pendant Vincent had given her on the occasion of their engagement was around her throat.

'You look charming, Cassie,' Vincent told her just as they entered the crowded room. He touched her hand, setting her pulses racing like the wind. 'I am very proud of my fiancée. Please save the supper dance and at least one other for me?'

'Of course.' She smiled up at him, her heart catching as she caught a look in his eyes. 'You may have the first waltz, sir.'

He preferred it when she called him by his name, but she did so only on rare occasions. Usually when she was excited—as she had been at the balloon ascension.

'Enjoy yourself, Cassie,' he murmured as he saw a group of her friends beckoning. 'We have only another few days before we leave for the country, and this is the last ball we shall attend before then.'

'Yes. I have not forgotten.'

'I shall leave you now,' Vincent said. 'But I shall return to claim my dances.'

Cassie nodded as he raised her hand to his lips briefly,

then wandered off to speak to various acquaintances. She knew that, like many other gentlemen present, he would probably play a hand or two of cards during the evening. She did not think him reckless at the tables, but amongst his friends gambling was very much favoured, and he would have been thought very odd had he stayed by his fiancée's side all evening.

Nor did she expect it of him, of course, though sometimes she thought privately that it might be pleasant to spend some time alone with him, to really talk to one another. That was not possible, however; they were both engaged with friends every day, and the evenings were often so filled with entertainments of every kind that they were forced to go from one house to another. This evening was one of the big events of the season, and would be spent entirely at the Devonshires' magnificent house.

Cassie was now very much at home amongst these people, having made a large acquaintance and several friends whose company she really enjoyed. So when she was introduced to a gentleman called Major George Saunders, who immediately asked her to dance, she merely handed him her card and forgot him until he came to claim his dance.

'I have only just come to London,' he told her with a frank, open look that was immediately appealing. 'I have long wanted to communicate with you, Miss Thornton, but rather than write I felt it would be better if we could meet in person. Had I not been detained on family matters, I should have called on you in Hampshire months before this. I wanted to tell you that I had the highest regard for your brother. Jack served under my command, and I believe he trusted me. We were certainly friends.'

'Yes, sir. I believe he did mention your name in his letters once or twice,' Cassie said. She liked him immediately. 'It is a pleasure to meet you, Major Saunders.'

'The pleasure is all mine. Jack spoke of you so often, Miss Thornton. He made many a lonely evening by the camp-fire seem brighter by telling us stories about his sister. There were usually five or six of us, including Jack himself, and I must tell you that you won all our hearts. I particularly recall a story about an irate man and a donkey...'

'Oh, no!' Cassie gazed up at him, a wicked sparkle in her eyes. The laughter bubbled up inside her. This man was reminding her of the happy times, and it was good to talk so easily of her brother with him. 'Did Jack truly tell you about that? It is too bad of him! My father was furious with me. I suppose I must have been about thirteen at the time.'

'Did you really steal the donkey from the tinker and smuggle it up to the nursery while your parents were out dining with friends?'

'Yes.' Cassie's laughter rang out. 'But she made such a terrible noise when I left her alone. The servants came running to see what was going on, so I was discovered. And the next morning the tinker came up to the house to claim his donkey; he threatened terrible things but Jack had a fight with him, and then Father had to pay him ten guineas to compensate him for the loss of his donkey. And it cannot have been worth a fraction of the price, for it was half-starved and its hooves needed attention from the farrier.'

Major Saunders was obviously hard put not to laugh as he asked, 'But you kept the creature?'

'Oh, yes! I could not have let the poor thing go back to be beaten and starved again. Especially after my father had made such an investment in its well-being.'

This time Major Saunders let out a bellow of laughter, that caused heads to turn and stare at them. 'What a remarkable young lady you are!'

'My father scolded me for days afterwards, but Jack bought me a fine leather harness and we used to take Miss Carrot Stubbornhooves for walks.' Cassie dimpled naugh-

tily as his eyebrows rose. 'We called her that because sometimes she simply stood her ground and would not move—
unless we gave her a carrot.'

'Stubborn creatures, donkeys. I often think some ladies
are much the same—at least my dear mama and sisters have
very similar characteristics.'

This time it was Cassie's turn to laugh. She was caught
by a fit of the giggles and for a moment they were forced
to stop dancing until she recovered enough to continue. She
gave him a look of warm approval as he stood patiently
for her to recover. He was such an amusing, understanding
companion. Not a particularly handsome man, of course,
rather too large and bluff to be thought fashionable, but
comforting to have around one. The kind of man who
would always be there in a crisis, she thought.

She was still smiling as they parted. When she returned
to Lady Longbourne, she found Vincent waiting for her.
He was frowning and she sensed that he was displeased
about something.

'Is it our waltz now?' she asked. 'Did you see me dancing with Major Saunders a moment ago? He said that Jack
often told stories about me by the camp-fire. We were
laughing about a donkey I once stole from a tinker—' She
caught her breath at the look in Vincent's eyes. 'Is something wrong? Are you angry with me?'

'How could I be angry with you?' he asked. 'Forgive me
if I seemed distant. I was thinking of something…'

Jack had told the story of the donkey the night before he
made the five of them promise that one of them would
marry his sister. George Saunders had agreed instantly. Indeed, he had seemed disappointed not to draw the short
straw later. Vincent had noticed the inquiring look sent his
way. Had he guessed then that all the straws were the same
length, and that Vincent had snapped his own in half, mak-

ing certain that he would be the one to ask Cassie first? If so, he had made no comment.

As he took her hand to lead her out on to the dance floor, Vincent decided he must have a word with George later that evening. Saunders was a decent fellow, but apt to say whatever was in his mind. Vincent did not want his fiancée to hear the story of the straws from anyone else but him.

Cassie could not read Vincent's thoughts as they danced. He held her carefully so as not to crush her gown, one hand placed lightly at her waist, his manner slightly distant. When she spoke to him, he looked down and smiled, but answered as if his mind was far away.

Was he angry with her? Cassie wondered. She could not see that she had done anything to upset him. Yet she felt that he was holding back from her. Or was his reserved manner simply indifference? Was this how it would always be between them? He would be polite, charming, but not really interested in her.

The thought hurt more than she had imagined it could. His proposal had been made with such passion! She had been misled into thinking he really wanted her for his wife, but now she had begun to doubt. But, oh, she must not doubt him now!

Why else would he have asked her to marry him? She simply did not understand his reasoning. If he did not feel any more than liking...why ask her in such a rush? Surely he had not spoken merely out of pity? Had he thought her too plain to ever find a husband unless he offered for her? If so, he was mistaken. No one had spoken to her openly, of course, but had he waited, it might have been different. She knew well enough that one or two gentlemen had shown a decided preference towards her—or her fortune.

'That was very pleasant, thank you, Cassie,' Vincent said

as the strains of the music died. 'Please do not forget the supper dance is also mine.'

He escorted her to Lady Longbourne, kissed her hand and walked away. Watching him go, she felt a sense of loss inside her, a terrible aching that threatened to destroy her composure.

To her horror, Cassie discovered that she was feeling weepy. She excused herself to Lady Longbourne, saying that she wished to tidy her gown, but instead of going upstairs to the bedchamber provided for the ladies' comfort, she slipped through a small anteroom into the garden.

It was a moonlit night, the grass, trees and bushes bathed in silver. A night for lovers and romance.

Why had everything suddenly changed? She had gone along blithely in a daze of excitement and pleasure, but now she was feeling oddly empty and a little nervous of the future—but that was so foolish of her! Nothing had really changed. She was letting her imagination run away with her. There was no reason to feel like this, no reason at all.

Just because Carlton had had a mistress, who was all the things Cassie was not and never could be! It was so foolish of her to mind—but she did. Oh, she did! And she had no right, absolutely none.

Cassie searched for her kerchief and dabbed fiercely at her eyes. She was not going to cry! She refused to be so foolish. What a very missish creature she was to be moping over something that could not be helped. She had always known it was unlikely she would ever find true love. Indeed, she had not wanted to love, had been afraid of the pain it might bring; she had expected to settle for a comfortable life—but now she had suddenly realised that it was not enough for her.

She wanted to be loved. Truly, deeply, whole-heartedly loved! She wanted her husband to give up all other women, to forgo his mistress for her sake. But how could she expect that when La Valentina was so very beautiful?

She gave a little sigh, blinking back her tears as she caught the unmistakable scent of cigar smoke.

'Are you unwell, Miss Thornton? May I be of some assistance?'

Cassie swung round, startled as she peered into the gloom of the garden, then she smiled as the rather large shape of Major Saunders loomed closer.

'Thank you, but I am better now,' she replied. 'I…I had a little headache and came out for some air.'

'These large affairs can be overpowering,' George Saunders agreed. 'I much prefer more intimate gatherings—but one cannot be in town and miss the Devonshires' ball.'

'No, of course not,' Cassie agreed. 'I am being very foolish. I shall go back inside now and apologise to the gentleman who was to have been my partner for the dance I have just missed.'

'Are you sure there is nothing I can do for you?' He moved towards her as she would have gone inside, his expression one of grave concern. His hand reached out to touch her, then dropped to his side as she stepped back. 'I would serve you in any way I could, Miss Thornton. If you are unhappy…or in distress?'

Cassie was surprised at the sincerity in his voice. 'No, no,' she said, blushing at this evidence of his concern. 'You are very kind, but I am not at all unhappy. I assure you it was merely a headache, and now it has gone.'

'Then forgive me for having spoken too plainly.'

'No…no such thing,' she said, blushing. 'Of course you have not. You are very kind…'

The look in his eyes at that moment shocked her. They had only just met, but he quite clearly felt attracted to her and she was uncertain what to do, embarrassed.

'Please excuse me, sir. I must go in or I shall be missed.'

George Saunders stood on in the semi-darkness of the garden after she had disappeared inside, still smoking his cigar. He was quite unaware that someone else was there, watching from behind a large bush of rosemary. When he disposed of his cigar and went into the house, the silent observer stayed on.

Vincent had come in search of the major, but having found him indulging in what was clearly a tête-à-tête with Cassie, had waited in the shadows to watch.

It was obvious that both had been affected by whatever had been said between them. Cassie was upset, embarrassed—distressed. And Major Saunders looked thunderstruck, like a man who knew the woman he most desired in the world was lost to him, as of course Cassie was, being engaged and on the verge of marrying another man.

He was reading too much into what might be a chance encounter. Saunders had come out to smoke a cigar, and perhaps Cassie had felt the need of some air. It did not have to be an assignation. Yet if that were so, why had she seemed so distressed?

He knew she had been enjoying herself in London. She had shown every sign of being content with her lot—though she had never indicated by a word or a look that she was in love with him. She had talked of liking, but nothing more. Was it possible that she had suddenly realised how much more there could be in a marriage between two people who loved one another?

It was possible for two people to meet and fall instantly in love, Vincent knew that only too well. What he could not know was whether that was the case here. If it was, then he had ruined the life of the woman he had hoped to make happy.

Chapter Seven

Cassie was feeling very tired when she parted company with her hostess in the early hours of the next morning. Vincent had escorted them home, but, after bidding them a brusque goodnight in the entrance hall, remained downstairs in his study, not having spoken a single word in the carriage.

'I vow I do not know what is the matter with Carlton,' his mama said, vainly trying to smother her yawns as she paused on the landing with Cassie and Sarah. 'I have seldom seen him so out of temper. Why, he almost snapped poor Harry's head off after supper.'

'He has seemed quiet all evening,' Cassie agreed. 'Do you suppose he is worried about something?'

'I am sure I do not care at this moment,' Lady Longbourne declared. 'His father was sometimes very disagreeable, but Vincent has always been even-tempered. This cold reserve is most unlike him.'

'Perhaps he had lost at cards?' Sarah suggested. 'That always makes Papa out of reason cross, though he never plays for anything but pennies. I think perhaps gentlemen do not like to lose at anything.'

'Carlton is not a heavy gambler,' his mother said, frowning. She stretched and yawned behind her hand. 'Well, I am for my bed. I think I shall sleep until past noon.'

Cassie kissed her, then Sarah, and they all went to their various rooms. She was yawning as she entered her bedroom, where Janet was waiting to undress her. Instantly, she was full of concern for her elderly maid.

'You shouldn't have sat up all night, Janet dear. One of the other maids could have helped me.'

'A nice thing it would be if I left you to strangers,' Janet grumbled to hide her emotions. 'Besides, I wanted you to hear about this nonsense from me. At least then you will have the truth and not some garbled version of it.'

The tone of Janet's voice alerted Cassie. She wrinkled her brow as she looked at her. 'Is something wrong? What has happened to upset you?'

'It's all a storm in a teacup, if you ask me.' Janet gave a sniff of disapproval as she began to unfasten Cassie's gown. 'If you ask me, it's the fault of that Monsieur Marcel with his airs and graces! Who does he think he is?'

'What has Tara done?' asked Cassie, feeling a sinking sensation in her stomach. 'Tell me at once, Janet, for I can tell by your face it is serious.'

'She put some salt in a special stock he was making. Apparently it has a very delicate flavour and was ruined, according to his highness! He threw it away, shouted at her for several minutes and raised a right old rumpus in the kitchen. He was heard to declare that he was not appreciated in this house and would return to France.'

'Oh, dear.' Cassie sighed. She had been expecting something of the sort since Tara was introduced into the great man's kitchen. 'That was indeed very bad of her, but did Monsieur Marcel need to make quite so much fuss?'

'One would not think so,' muttered Janet darkly. 'But it seems it was hours of work wasted and he was furious. He said that he would not tolerate her in his kitchen another moment—and the upshot of it is that she has run away.'

'Run away? Oh, no!' Cassie was dismayed. 'Where can she have gone? She knows no one in London. Are you sure she isn't hiding somewhere in the house?'

'We've looked everywhere,' said Janet pulling an odd face, as if she were battling her tears. 'Dorkins had a soft spot for her and he has fallen out with Monsieur Marcel over it. And Mrs Dorkins says she won't stay in a house that's ruled by a mad Frenchie, and now all the servants have taken sides for and against and we've had Bedlam.' Janet shook her head. 'To tell you the truth, Miss Cassie, I think they've all gone mad. All this fuss over a pinch of salt! In my opinion, the stock tasted all the better for it.'

'But it is not up to us to have an opinion, is it?' Cassie reminded her. 'Monsieur Marcel is in sole charge of the kitchen, and Tara was at fault. What she did was as bad as my going to church without a hat or gloves. She broke the rules, Janet. And I do not think Lord Carlton would be pleased to lose his chef, do you?'

'Well, if you put it that way, I suppose she *was* wrong.' Janet frowned. 'But I've grown quite fond of the little lass. I don't like the idea of her being out on the streets, at the mercy of all the nasty folk waiting to pounce on girls like her.'

'Nor do I,' agreed Cassie, vainly trying to smother a yawn. It had been such an exhausting evening! 'I hope she will be found, or that she will think it over and decide to come back to us. It really is very distressing. Especially as we leave for the country next week. We must make an effort to find her tomorrow. No, it's tomorrow now, isn't it?'

'You're exhausted and need your bed.' Janet saw the signs of strain in her face. 'And here's me chattering on about a naughty girl who didn't know when she was well off. Get to bed, lass, and don't worry about Tara. I dare say she'll come back when she's ready.'

'I do hope so.' Cassie kissed her cheek. 'Goodnight, dearest. Thank you for telling me yourself.'

Cassie carried her candlestick to the bed as Janet closed the door behind her. She set it down on the bedside chest before pulling back the covers and climbing into bed, then blew out the flame. She was so tired, but her mind was going round and round in confusion.

There was the problem of Tara's disappearance, and the domestic upset she had caused—then there were the more worrying problems of Cassie's own making. What a very foolish person she was! She had been so happy, swept along by all the excitement of the wedding preparations, her new clothes and the gifts which had been showered on her—but all at once she had begun to really think about what was happening.

Did she truly want to marry Lord Carlton? The answer was yes, but only if he cared for her.

Cassie knew she could be very happy as Vincent's wife, but not if he were marrying her simply to provide an heir for his title and estates. She had thought and thought, and the only explanation she had been able to come up with was his need to satisfy his family's expectations. She was a very suitable candidate for such a position: a plain, complaisant wife who would be content to stay at home in the country and not cause any scandals!

The thought was so painful it made her almost cry out, but she controlled the urge to give way to her disappointment. She had been foolish to allow herself to expect more. It was exactly the kind of marriage she had told Lord Carlton she was looking for, so she could not blame him for offering it. She knew in her heart it was a very sensible arrangement, but she wanted more.

Cassie tossed restlessly in her bed, sighing as she tried

to come to terms with her own feelings and could not. Her meeting with Major Saunders had unsettled her, bringing back vivid memories and making her aware that there had been other alternatives. Had she not been engaged to Vincent, she felt something might have developed between her and the major— Oh, but she could not know that! Besides, she did like Vincent so very well.

Liking? Was that truly what she felt for him? Or was it something more? Was that the reason for her restlessness now?

She shifted position and sighed again, then stiffened as she heard the whimpering sound. It had come from somewhere close by. And she knew exactly what it was!

Sitting up, Cassie lit her candle. She got out of bed, looking about her. Where was the foolish child hiding?

'Come out, Tara,' she said. 'I know you are here, so there's no point in hiding from me. I am not angry with you, so you do not need to fear that I shall punish you.'

For a moment nothing happened, then the frilled covers at the bottom of the bed moved and Tara crawled out from beneath it. She stood up, standing with her head bent, hands clasped in front of her, then raised a tear-streaked face to look at Cassie.

'I never meant to upset him,' she sniffed, wiping the back of her hand across her face and smearing it with fluff from beneath the bed. 'I was interested in what he was doing, and I tasted the stock when he wasn't looking. I thought he had forgotten the salt so I put it in for him. I was only tryin' to help. Honestly, Miss Cassie. I didn't mean to make him cross. I like him. I think he's clever and I like his funny ways.'

'You like Monsieur Marcel?' Cassie was surprised. Everyone else seemed either to fear the Frenchman or think him too full of his own importance. 'You have enjoyed working for him?'

'Oh, yes, miss!' Tara's face lit up. 'I've never bin so happy in me life. He gives me bits of his special stuff to try and talks to me about soul and fings. Only now he hates me and won't 'ave me in his kitchen no more.'

'Would you behave in future?' Cassie asked, looking at her thoughtfully. She had put on a little weight and looked much healthier, her eyes bright and her hair clean. There was, in fact, a vast improvement in her. 'If I could manage to persuade him to give you another chance—would you promise faithfully to do exactly as he says?'

'Cross me heart and hope to die,' Tara said suiting her action to the words. 'Honestly, miss.' Tears welled up and she sniffed miserably. 'Only he won't, because I ruined hours and hours of work, and he's so clever and I'm stupid.'

'Well, as long as you remember that in future.' Cassie smiled inwardly. Was the talented Frenchman aware of the devotion he had inspired in this child? 'I shall speak to Monsieur Marcel in the morning and see what can be done—but what shall I do with you in the meantime? I cannot send you back to the servants' quarters until this is settled. So I suppose you must stay here with me.'

'I'll curl up on the floor, miss, and I won't disturb you no more.'

'You did not wake me,' Cassie said truthfully. 'I was… thinking of something.' She smiled at Tara. 'You cannot lie on the floor all night. I should be awake all night worrying. Get into bed with me, you foolish child! And don't you dare kick or snore, or I shall very soon push you out again.'

Tara laughed, knowing her mistress was only teasing her. She was a right good 'un! Almost as nice, in Tara's opinion, as his lordship himself!

Alone in his study, his lordship sat with a glass of brandy in his hand and stared into space. The truth was hard but he must face it. He had made a mess of this whole affair from start to finish, and there was no point in blaming Harry. Had he gone straight to Cassie on his return from France and made her an offer of marriage as he ought, none of this need have happened.

She would have refused him, of course. But they might have become friends… Vincent allowed himself to dwell on various possibilities, some of them so impossible that only a moonstruck fool would have dreamed them up, which just showed what kind of a state he was in! A rueful smile twisted his mouth, as he saw the amusing side of his situation. He had set out with the wrong attitude, and now he was well and truly caught in a trap of his own making.

What to do about it?

He could of course tell Cassie the whole story now. He could give her the chance to cry off before it was too late. He would have to shoulder the blame, naturally. Far better that he should be branded a jilt than that she should be made unhappy.

He could go abroad, take a grand tour. Perhaps in a few years he might return. The scandal would have died down, though some would always hold it against him. Or he might decide to settle abroad somewhere…Italy, perhaps.

'Damned fool!'

Vincent got up and began to pace about the room. Live his life alone and in exile? Or as a disgraced scoundrel on the fringes of society! He wanted to do none of these things. His heart and mind were firmly rooted in England— and with Cassie. Yet he could not forget that scene in the garden of the Devonshires' home earlier that evening.

Cassie was attracted to Major Saunders. He had seen them laughing together as they danced. He could not convince himself that she had ever been quite as carefree in his company, or only once or twice. Why should she have gone to meet George Saunders secretly in the gardens? And why had Cassie been so upset?

Was it possible that there was more to this than he guessed? Had they known each other before this evening? Could they have been lovers previously?

For the first time in his life, Vincent was the victim of the green-eyed god of jealousy. He had watched Cassie with George Saunders and for a moment he had wanted to strike out at them both. His anger had been such that he had not spoken a word on the way home lest his temper betrayed him.

It was a new experience for Vincent. He had always managed to see the amusing side of his mother's little ways, indulging her and giving her whatever she wanted—but he had never felt this torment inside before, tearing him apart.

Damn it! He did not want to give Cassie up! Why should he? He wanted to make her keep her promise to wed him—but what if she regretted it afterwards? What if she had fallen in love with George Saunders? If she were to have an affair with him at some time in the future…

No! He would never allow that, never! Vincent's temper, though slow to rise, could be fearful. He did not trust himself in such an event. Much better to let her go now if she wished it.

Leaving his study, Vincent climbed the stairs to his own apartments. His limbs felt heavy and all his nerve ends were screaming, but he forced himself to hold line. If this was to be done, it must be done properly, in a civilised manner befitting a gentleman.

Once inside his room, he took the spare key to the dressing room from a drawer in the military chest which had served him well during his time as a soldier. Cassie might be sleeping, but it was best to get this over and finished before he had time to change his mind.

Opening the door very softly, he went in to Cassie's

room, then stopped, frozen to the spot as the glow from his candle fell across the bed. His expression softened, his mouth curving as he saw the protective way Cassie's arms held the sleeping child beside her.

She was so beautiful! They had all dismissed her looks as not being pretty, but now he saw her as she truly was, relaxed and flushed in sleep, and he knew that for him she was the most beautiful woman in the world. For a moment he could not tear his eyes away and he felt an ache somewhere inside him, a longing that he had never known was there deep within his soul.

He had been informed by Dorkins earlier of Tara's disappearance, but of course no one had thought to look for her here. Yet where else would she come but to the woman who had found her in the first place? The one person she had been sure would protect her—and Cassie had not failed her.

He could not disturb them. Returning as silently as he had come, Vincent re-locked the dressing room door and returned the key to its resting place. He knew he would not speak to Cassie now. God forgive him, he could not! He did not have the will. Unless she came to him, asked him for her freedom, the wedding would go ahead as planned.

Monsieur Marcel was making pancakes. Tiny, wafer thin little morsels of deliciousness, which would be flambéed later with brandy and dressed with plump raspberries and orange juice. It was one of his favourite dishes and he was making it because his conscience would give him no rest. Well aware that everyone was avoiding him that morning, he concentrated on his work and did not look up until he noticed that all the others were standing almost to attention, staring at the doorway. Turning to look, Monsieur Marcel saw that his employer's fiancée had entered the kitchen and was looking in his direction.

Such a thing was unheard of in the grand houses of London society! Ladies gave instructions to their housekeepers, who were summoned to the parlour to wait on the mistress. Never, never, did a great lady descend to the bowels of the house herself!

Cassie met his startled gaze and smiled. Monsieur Marcel dropped his spoon on the floor. One of his minions moved to retrieve it, but was stopped by a flick of the artist's hand. He moved out from behind the table and made a surprisingly elegant bow for one of his rather generous stature, and as Cassie came towards him, took the hand she offered and raised it briefly to his lips.

'*Mademoiselle,*' he said, 'I am by your visit, honoured. This ees *magnifique.*'

'So this is where you create all those wonderful dishes I have so much enjoyed,' Cassie said, glancing round in fascination. 'I have often wondered. Tell me, *monsieur*, have you everything you need? Is there anything that can be changed to make your work easier?'

'I have all I require, *mademoiselle*.' He was visibly glowing. 'Yet perhaps the oven ees a little…'ow shall we say… *ancien*? There ees marvels of modern invention to be found now, I believe. I 'ave thought perhaps…?'

'Of course. I shall speak to Dorkins later. He will arrange for you to have whatever you feel necessary.' She gave him a smile that would have devastated lesser men. 'Now, *monsieur*, I have come personally to apologise on behalf of a very silly girl, and to beg you to forgive her.'

'You have spoken to Tara?' Monsieur Marcel's ears went quite red. 'She ees not dead or lying broken and bleeding in the gutters?'

'No, indeed not. The foolish child had crawled under my bed and spent the night with me. She is inconsolable because she knows she has betrayed your trust. And she admires you so much, *monsieur*. Of course she never could, but she would like to follow in your footsteps to be a great culinary artist one day. Alas, I suppose she has lost all chance of studying under your guidance? Or is it just possible that, from the generosity of your heart, you might forgive her? Just this once…'

'She admires me?' Monsieur Marcel blinked his sparse lashes. He knew these cold English did not understand him or his dedication to perfection. To them, food was merely food; they could not see that cooking was a precise art known only to a few. How could they? They had no soul! But he had taken to the young waif Lord Carlton had introduced into his kitchen and was sorry that he had frightened her. Besides, who could resist the charm of this lady: a very great lady as he would forever after tell anyone who would listen! 'She ees a foolish child, no? But I shall do my best with her. She must learn not to take my rages so seriously—and to respect the food.'

'I have already scolded her,' Cassie murmured, not quite truthfully. 'I am sure she will do better in future.'

'Then she may return.' Monsieur Marcel's graciousness hid the emotion he was feeling. He could not shed tears before these English; they would laugh at him behind his back and they could never understand the passion that was so necessary to an artist of his calibre. Yet perhaps the future Lady Carlton had soul. Yes, perhaps she might just begin to appreciate him for his true worth. 'Tell Tara I am not now angry with her, *mademoiselle*. All ees forgiven in my heart.'

'Thank you. You are very kind, *monsieur*. But I always knew it must be so. No one who could serve such delicious food could possibly be unfeeling towards a child who needs his compassion.'

She did understand him! Emotion welled up inside him, and his eyes blinked rapidly. He abandoned all idea of returning to his native France. He must stay forever here to

serve the mistress who had shown such sensitivity: it was
his mission in life, his reason for being. He would create a
dinner for her this evening such as never before!

As she turned to leave, he was all activity. A clean spoon
was fetched, his underlings sent flying about their business,
and once more the delicate task of producing mouth-
melting crêpes fit for a goddess was continued.

A little later in the small parlour, Dorkins and Mrs Dorkins responded to Cassie's stroking in much the same manner. Dorkins confessed himself to have been a bit hasty,
and his wife promised to keep an eye on Tara while Miss
Thornton was away.

'Dorkins and me…all of his lordship's people, really.
We were wishful to say how pleased we are, Miss Thornton, that you are marrying Lord Carlton. It has been a pleasure to serve you, and we shall be happy to see you back
when you next come to town.'

Cassie thanked them for their kindness, said she had been
well looked after and went upstairs to Lady Longbourne's
rooms. She had risen earlier than usual to sort out the troubles with Tara, and Lady Longbourne was still in bed, a
tray set with a dainty porcelain pot of hot chocolate and a
dish of soft rolls balanced across her lap.

'Cassie, my love,' she said, smiling up at her as she
spread the warm roll with thick honey. 'You are up already.
I made sure you would sleep all morning. You were so
tired last evening.'

'Yes, I was a little tired,' Cassie replied. 'But I feel perfectly refreshed now. I have just this moment spoken to
Sarah, and she is getting ready to go out. We have remembered two books which must be returned to the lending
library before we leave town, and we thought a little walk
would do us good.'

'Thank you for coming to tell me,' said Lady Longbourne, sighing as she snuggled back against her pillows. 'I think I shall stay here and rest for most of the day. We have a long journey before us tomorrow, and then all the preparations for the wedding.'

Cassie felt a prickle of alarm. Her hostess did look a little fragile this morning. 'Has all this junketing about been too much for you, ma'am? You are not feeling unwell, I hope?'

'No, not at all,' her ladyship replied. 'To be honest, my dear, I have not enjoyed myself so much for ages. It was wonderful to meet so many of my old friends again. I shall be sorry to leave—except that we have your wedding to look forward to, of course.'

'Yes. You will have the pleasure of entertaining your friends at Longbourne.'

She was a little hesitant, which made her hostess frown and look at her. 'Is something wrong, Cassie? You do not seem quite yourself this morning.'

'I am perhaps a tiny bit tired after all,' Cassie admitted, knowing that she could not speak of what was truly in her mind to anyone, least of all her kind friend, who had been so generous and taken so much trouble on her behalf. 'But a walk will do me the world of good. Fresh air always blows the cobwebs away, do you not think so?'

'I must admit I have not always thought so,' said Lady Longbourne, bravely repressing a shudder. 'But if you say it does you good, Cassie, I shall believe you. As long as you do not expect me to walk out at this hour. The streets are hardly aired, my dear!'

'No, no, I do not expect it of you, dear Lady Longbourne. I should not dream of asking you to come with us. Sarah and I will be perfectly safe on our own, you know. We mean to go straight to the library and come back immediately. We shall not even trouble to take a maid with us. I cannot think it necessary, can you? Besides, they are all so busy packing and preparing for the journey tomorrow.'

'There is not the least need for you to be accompanied,' Lady Longbourne said, relaxing against her pillows with a sigh of content. 'Go along then, my love. I shall see you later.'

'It has been such an enjoyable time,' Sarah said as they were returning from the library an hour or so later, having lingered a while for a last look in the shops. 'I've had such a lovely time, Cassie—and it is all thanks to you. When I am back at home, I shall often think of this visit. I know I may never come to London again, but I shall never forget how wonderful it was. Thank you so much for all you have given me.'

Cassie looked at her thoughtfully, detecting a slight wobble in her voice. 'I am glad you have enjoyed it, Sarah. We have been so busy going here, there and everywhere that we have not had time to have a really good chat, but I was sure you were having a good time.'

'Oh, yes, wonderful!'

She looked so downcast that Cassie squeezed her arm.

'You do not know for sure that you will not come again,' Cassie said. 'You may well do so.'

'I do not expect it,' Sarah replied, avoiding her eyes. 'Papa could not afford it—besides, I've had my turn. My sisters would give anything for a chance like this. No, I shall have to be satisfied to be at home and help Mama. It is truly my duty to do so, Cassie. I have been much indulged of late.'

'As to that, I dare say your papa will let you come and stay with us sometimes. I shall certainly invite you.' Cassie hesitated, then, 'Did you meet no one you particularly liked? Was there not one gentleman who showed an interest in you?'

Sarah's cheeks were very pink. 'One gentleman—do you recall Mr John Barker? No, perhaps not. I do not believe you ever danced with him. He did show an interest in me for a while, but I did not encourage him.'

'Why?' Cassie stared at her curiously. 'Did you not like him?'

'He—he was quite pleasant, but…'. Sarah faltered, not wholly able to prevent a little sigh escaping her. 'I suppose I ought to have encouraged him. It would have pleased Papa if I had found a husband, but…' She stopped, quite unable to continue. She fiddled with her reticule, twisting it round and round her fingers. 'Oh, I am so very foolish!'

'Was there someone else?' Cassie sensed some deep emotion in her. 'I thought you might rather like Sir Harry…oh, Sarah, of course you do! How foolish of me not to have realised it before. Has he not spoken or shown any partiality?'

Sarah bit her lip, tears hovering on her dusky gold lashes. She was such a pretty girl! It would be a terrible waste if she were to live her life out as a spinster.

'He…he has been amazingly kind to me, Cassie. I dare say you may not have noticed, but we have danced often. And he has fetched me drinks and little trifles at supper. Oh, you know! But of course he was only being himself. He is so very charming, and pleasant to everyone. However, I believe there is someone else. A lady he is in love with but cannot marry. He did hint at something once, but I was not properly sure what he meant.' Sarah's cheeks went bright red. 'I think she might be his mistress, though of course he did not say that to me.'

'Oh, I see.' Cassie nodded. 'He would not marry her, I suppose?'

'His mama would not approve. Harry would never marry to disoblige her. So of course he would never ask me to be his wife, even if he was not in love with someone else.'

'Why ever not? Lady Longbourne likes you, Sarah. You know she does. It is always you she asks to run little errands for her.'

'But I am not an heiress.'

'Must marriage always be about property and money, then?'

'Not always, but it often is. You must know that, Cassie.' Sarah sighed deeply, her face wistful. 'You are so fortunate in marrying Lord Carlton. He likes you very well, and you like him. I shall probably have to marry Papa's curate, who I do not like much at all—or stay at home with my mother.'

Sarah's words struck home. It was very likely that she would have to be satisfied with a marriage of convenience or remain unwed. Even if Cassie settled some money on her, which she intended to do once her capital was her own, there would be few chances for Sarah to meet someone suitable in the quiet village where she normally lived. Had Cassie's circumstances not taken a turn for the better, she might well have been in a similar position.

'Yes, I am lucky,' she replied. 'Lord Carlton is a real gentleman and very kind. I think I shall be comfortable with him.'

'But surely…' Sarah gave her a puzzled look. 'I thought you… I mean, your case is different.'

'Why?' Cassie asked. 'Why do you say that?'

She had stopped walking, and was looking at Sarah so intently that she did not notice the shabby figure lurking to one side of her. Suddenly, he lunged at her, snatching the beaded purse she was carelessly holding by its strings. For a moment Cassie held on, then released it, letting him take it and turning her head to watch as he ran off down the street.

Sarah gasped with shock, her face going as white as a sheet. Cassie was also pale, but more stunned than frightened.

'Cassie…' Sarah caught at her arm, her chest heaving as she fought for breath. 'He—he stole your purse. That terrible old man, he stole your purse.' Her voice sounded faint and Cassie looked at her in concern. 'Are you all right?'

'Are you?' Cassie inquired, a little worried by her friend's odd colour. Sarah really was shaken by the incident. 'Do you want to sit down? You look quite ill.'

'It was the shock.' Sarah was beginning to recover, her colour coming back. 'You were wise not to struggle, Cassie. Far better to let the purse go than be hurt. Was there much in it?'

'A few guineas,' Cassie said. 'I thought I might purchase a small gift for Lady Longbourne, but we have another two days before we leave. Besides, I dare say I can find something to give her as a thank-you present. I have not worn half of the pretty scarves and shawls I've bought since we came to town.'

'Several guineas!' Sarah frowned. 'It was a considerable loss, then.'

'It doesn't matter,' Cassie said, dismissing it as of no importance. The colour was returning to her cheeks, and though her heart was still beating rather fast, she had recovered her composure. 'I should not precisely want to lose the money, but you know, dearest, I think he must have been an old soldier—and desperate!—to rob me here in broad daylight. We should be grateful to men who have served us so well in the fight against Napoleon. And I can spare the money. Especially to a man who needs it so badly.'

There was an odd, faraway look in her eyes, and Sarah realised Cassie was thinking about her brother. 'Yes, now you put it that way, I can see what you mean, Cassie. He must have needed the money desperately—but it was still a terrible shock.'

'He did not harm me,' Cassie said, still thoughtful. 'But I am sorry you were upset, Sarah.'

'I am better now,' Sarah replied, tucking her arm through Cassie's. 'I dare say it was our own fault for coming out without some kind of escort. If only Lord Carlton—or even one of the maids!—had been with us. He would not have dared to approach you like that for fear of being pursued and caught.'

The truth of this struck Cassie very forcibly. This *was* the first time she had been out without an escort of some kind. There was usually a maid or a footman to carry parcels if they went shopping, and in the afternoons and evenings both Lady Longbourne and Lord Carlton went everywhere with them.

'No,' she said, an odd, speculative expression in her eyes. 'You are very right, Sarah. This *was* his chance to approach me...he could not do so before. Even if he had wanted to...'

'What do you mean?' Sarah stared at her in bewilderment. 'Have you seen that particular man before? Where? Has he been following you?''

'I believe I may have seen him—once or twice.'

'Oh, Cassie!' Sarah cried, looking over her shoulder in sudden alarm. 'We should have called the watch or something. Supposing he is a—a wicked murderer? Or a kidnapper!'

'If he had meant me harm, he had his opportunity,' Cassie said. 'No, Sarah, I dare say I am mistaken. One old soldier is much like another, I expect—and now the war is over, London has its share of them amongst those forced to beg for their bread on the streets.' She caught her friend's arm. 'You will not say anything of this—to anyone? Not Lady Longbourne, or Lord Carlton—or even Harry. Please? I do not want to make a fuss about this.'

'But surely...'

'Please, Sarah. I should be grateful if you would keep this incident to yourself. I have lost only a few guineas. There is no need for anyone else to know what happened.'

'If that is what you want.' Sarah clearly did not understand but she agreed as she saw the appeal in Cassie's eyes. 'But I do not see why.'

'Let us forget it,' Cassie pleaded, smiling at her. 'Now, tell me about Sir Harry—are you very fond of him? Would you like to marry him if he asked you?'

Chapter Eight

Cassie did not exactly put the odd incident of her purse from her mind, but that evening something happened which pushed it to one side. She had known they were to attend a musical party, and that the opera singer La Valentina was to perform, but had made up her mind not to let it upset her. She would have Vincent at her side, and she did not imagine the singer would attempt to speak to her.

However, at the last moment, Vincent apologised and said that he was forced to cry off. 'I have an appointment at my club I must keep,' he told them. 'Forgive me, but it is a matter of business and I cannot accompany you this evening. I am sure Harry will be pleased to escort you in my stead.'

'That is not the point,' his mama said, frowning her displeasure. 'Cassie will be disappointed not to have you there.'

'I am sure she will excuse me this once.' He smiled at her, asking for her indulgence.

Cassie could do nothing but smile and say she perfectly understood. If it was in her mind that he had deliberately avoided another meeting with La Valentina in her presence, she did not allow her doubts to show either by a word or a look.

'Yes, of course,' she replied and smiled at him. 'You must do just as you think best, sir.'

'Such an understanding wife you will make,' Vincent said, an odd quizzing expression in his eyes that made her heart race wildly. 'I wonder if you will always be so willing to please me, Cassie?'

Since she did not know how to answer, she remained silent. In her turn, she wondered what he might have said if she had expressed her true feelings and complained of his neglect as Lady Longbourne had, as she might well have done.

'Vincent has never been overfond of musical evenings,' his mother confided as they were driven to their host's house. 'I dare say he is going to a boxing match or some equally barbaric sporting occasion. It is all of a piece, and his father was just the same.'

Cassie nodded, but said nothing. She was not exactly dreading the evening, but she did not particularly wish to meet the beautiful woman who had been Vincent's mistress for several months. She had been prey to a few unkind whispers over the past weeks, and certain spiteful ladies had not hesitated to let her know that the opera singer had lasted longer in her position than any other light o' love of Carlton's before her—which surely meant that Vincent must have cared for her.

The evening was begun with a quartet of men singing in harmony; they were followed by a tenor, and finally La Valentina took the centre stage. Her singing was so beautiful that even Cassie was moved to the verge of tears. She could not deny that the woman was both beautiful and talented.

After her performance, there was a general movement towards the supper room. Following behind Lady Long-

bourne and Sarah—Harry having long ago disappeared to
the card room—Cassie felt a firm touch on her arm and
turned to find herself being detained by none other than La
Valentina.

She had hoped to avoid such a confrontation, and her
heart sank as she saw the purpose in the other woman's
eyes.

'You wanted to speak to me, ma'am?'

'I know you are to marry soon,' La Valentina said, a
flash of fire in those magnificent eyes. She touched a necklace of sapphires at her neck, as if wanting to draw Cassie's
attention. 'This was *his* gift to me. Now I shall give you a
gift, Miss Thornton. For the moment he is yours alone.
Carlton is too much a gentleman to keep a mistress while
he courts his wife. You may have him for as long as it
takes you to produce the heir he needs, but he is mine.
When you are with child, he will come back to me.'

Cassie's throat was too tight to speak. Besides, what
could she say? If she denied La Valentina's words, she
would be treated to one of those condescending smiles. And
if she did what she really wanted and slapped her, it would
cause a scandal, which was very probably what the singer
had hoped to provoke.

She nodded her head, then moved off, her back straight.
She was the very picture of dignity. It was the best she
could do. As long as no one knew how much she was
hurting inside, it could not matter.

She had almost reached the supper room when Harry
came up to her. He looked at her white face and swore.

'What did that witch say to you, Cassie? Whatever it
was, ignore it. She was hoping Vinnie would marry her,
which he never would, of course—and she was trying to
hurt you.'

'She did not tell me anything I did not know,' Cassie
said, forcing a smile. 'Forget it, Harry. I intend to—and I

would be obliged if you would not tell Carlton that you
saw her speak to me.'

He looked at her for a moment, then nodded. 'Just as
you like, but had Vinnie been here she would not have
dared to speak to you like that. He finished it, you know—
before he even asked you to marry him. If she is hoping
he will go back to her, she will be disappointed. Stands to
reason. No man would be fool enough to leave your bed
for hers—' His ears went bright red with embarrassment.
'Forgive me. I ought not to have said that...'

Cassie laughed and tucked her arm through his, smiling
up at him. 'Oh, yes, you did, Harry. You have made me
feel very much better, I assure you.'

'Vinnie is no fool,' he said. 'Shall we go into supper
now, Cassie?'

'Yes,' she replied. 'I think we ought...'

Alone in her bed that evening, Cassie allowed herself a
few tears. She was so foolish to have let the little incident
hurt her. No doubt Harry was right. Vincent had done the
honourable thing and finished his affair. La Valentina had
merely been trying to get her own back. She must be sensible and ignore her spite.

Her mind turned to the moment when her purse was
snatched. She thought about it for a while, trying to decide
whether or not she had seen something in the man's eyes
that had reminded her so much of her brother she had let
go of her purse. Or was that just her imagination?

Oh, of course it was! She dismissed it as nonsense,
thought again about La Valentina's spite, then turned over
and closed her eyes.

It was their very last day before leaving for the country.
Cassie, Lady Longbourne and Sarah had spent a very enjoyable morning doing their last-minute shopping, and Cas-

sie had managed to buy a little silver-beaded evening purse as a gift for her hostess while her back was turned. She was feeling very pleased with herself for managing to keep her gift a secret, when she heard herself addressed from behind and jumped.

'Miss Thornton?' a gentleman's deep voice said. 'How pleasant to meet you. I understood you had left town.'

'Oh, no, not until tomorrow,' Cassie said, her cheeks pink as she saw who had spoken to her. 'I hope you received your invitation to the wedding, Major Saunders?'

'Yes, I did, and have written to accept,' he said. 'I wondered…have you thought about who is to give you away, Miss Thornton? If you have by some chance not decided, I hope it would not be too forward of me to offer my services—as Jack's friend?'

Cassie felt herself blushing. She supposed she ought to have asked Kendal, but it had not actually occurred to her until that moment.

'It is not forward at all,' she said. 'Indeed, I should be grateful, for there is no one else I would rather have, sir.'

'Then I shall come down a day or so earlier,' said Major Saunders. 'I have friends near by where I may stay. And I shall take the liberty of calling on you to discuss the arrangements. It will give me great pleasure to be of service to you, Miss Thornton.'

'You will be most welcome.'

Cassie gave him her hand, blushing as he raised it to his lips. She could not mistake the very real warmth in his eyes as he looked at her. It was quite clear that he liked her very well.

'Who was that gentleman, my love?' asked Lady Longbourne a moment or so later. 'I was not quite sure.'

'Major Saunders,' Cassie replied, avoiding her curious gaze. 'He was Jack's friend and has offered to give me away. Do you not think that was kind of him? He says he will call on us a day or so before the wedding to make certain of the arrangements.'

'Yes, very kind,' said her ladyship, frowning. 'Although, had you thought, you might have asked Harry.'

'But will he not stand up with Vincent as his best man?'

'Carlton could very well have found someone else,' said Lady Longbourne. 'But since it is arranged, I dare say no harm will come of it.' She glanced at the gold watch pinned to her gown. 'And now I think we really must go home...'

Some twenty minutes later, Cassie took off her bonnet and handed it with her gloves to Mrs Dorkins, who was attending her in the hall of Lord Carlton's house.

'His lordship was asking for you, Miss Thornton,' the housekeeper said. 'He asked most particularly that you would oblige him by going to the study as soon as you returned home.'

'Thank you,' Cassie replied. 'I shall go to him now.'

She left Sarah talking to Mrs Dorkins and went through the house to the study, which was at the back and looked out at the gardens. Her knock was answered by an invitation to enter and she did so, pausing just inside the door. Vincent had been staring out of the window and she was at leisure to observe that he was dressed for riding before he turned and smiled at her.

For a moment her heart stopped, then raced on wildly.

'Ah, Cassie, you have returned. I trust you enjoyed your shopping? The air is very fresh this morning, is it not?'

'It was pleasant,' she replied. 'One cannot but enjoy shopping, sir.'

'One of the privileges, I presume?'

Cassie laughed at the long-standing joke between them. 'Oh, most definitely, sir! Though I must admit it can be wearing if one has to visit too many shops to find what one particularly wants.'

His eyes were bright with amusement. 'Yet you seem to enjoy walking for its own sake?'

'I believe I prefer to walk in the country, especially when the dew is still upon the hedges, but the town has many pleasures to offer, does it not? For gentlemen as well as ladies.'

'I have always thought it enjoyable to be able to divide one's time between the two,' Vincent said. 'I dare say we shall visit London often when we are married—if you would like that?'

His eyes seemed to watch her intently. Cassie flushed and dropped her gaze. Why did she feel that there was so much more behind the simple question?

'Yes, of course,' she murmured. 'I am sure we shall find an agreeable routine that suits us both if we try.'

'Monsieur Marcel has told me you paid him a visit the other morning.' Cassie's eyes flew to his as she heard the new note in his voice. 'He came to the study, to discuss the week's menus with me as has been our custom, you know. He told me he was honoured to be consulted by my future wife as to his welfare. I believe you promised a new oven or some such thing?'

'Oh, yes. I hope you do not mind?' Cassie was slightly awkward beneath his probing gaze. Was he annoyed with her for interfering? 'I dare say it will be expensive, but one must always strive to keep one's people happy—don't you think?'

'Undoubtedly.' Vincent's eyes danced with suppressed mirth. 'I am only too glad to be relieved of all domestic responsibility and shall in future be glad if Monsieur Marcel receives his instructions from you. Particularly as you seem to have him eating out of your hand, Cassie. Yes, you may deal with him in future if you please. I confess I found the man's tantrums a little wearing.'

'Oh, no, did you?' Cassie smiled, relieved as she saw he

was teasing her as usual. His odd mood of the other evening seemed to have left him. 'I think he is feeling rather lonely here and misses his own people. But I shall be happy to take over the task. I know you have much to concern you. Besides, gentlemen do not care for such things—settling domestic disputes is what you would expect from your wife, is it not, sir?'

'Must you call me sir?' Vincent asked, a hint of irritation in his voice—or was it agitation? 'I think I would prefer Carlton, as Mama says—or Vincent, as you once promised.'

Cassie was surprised at his tone. 'Forgive me,' she said. 'I shall do better when we are married, I promise.'

'Shall you?' The expression in his eyes was unreadable. 'When we are married…'

'Do you not find our present situation a little strange?' she asked, meeting his frowning gaze with her own, which was clear and candid, putting him to shame. 'We have known each other for several weeks, and yet we are no closer to truly knowing one another than we were at the beginning. I think…I believe that must change when we are husband and wife.' She paused, giving him a shy look. 'Do you not think the same, Carlton?'

'Yes, Cassie.' Vincent smiled, making her heart race. He came towards her as a breeze lifted the curtain at the open window, standing so close that her heart fluttered like the rippling silk of the drapes. She felt suddenly breathless yet expectant. 'I believe many things will change then—and I am looking forward to having you as my wife.'

Cassie trembled as she heard the husky, intimate note in his voice. He was going to kiss her! She sensed it, welcomed it, standing very still as he reached out to draw her a little nearer. Then she was in his arms; he was holding her pressed close against his body, his eyes compelling her to look at him. A tiny shiver of anticipation ran through her as he lowered his head and touched his lips to hers.

At first it was a gentle kiss, but then his arms tightened about her and his mouth became demanding, wrenching a response from her. A response that shocked and disturbed her by its very force. Oh, she was going to swoon! It was so very, very exciting and—and terrifying to be kissed in this manner. Very different from the chaste kisses he had given her before. It aroused all kinds of new sensations in her: feelings and longings she had never dreamed of experiencing.

When at last Vincent let her go, Cassie was so confused she could hardly bear to look at him. He had aroused such longing in her, such need!

'So,' he said. 'We *shall* be married, Cassie.'

'Yes, of course. In ten days from now.'

She was puzzled. He had spoken as though it had been in doubt but was no longer.

'In ten days.' He nodded, as if he had something on his mind. 'I am sorry to have to tell you that I shall not be able to escort you to Longbourne, Cassie. I must leave almost immediately for Surrey. Some estate business needs my attention. I have asked Harry to accompany you and Mama. He has promised to do so, and you may rely on him to see you safely there.'

'You must attend to your business, s…Carlton.' Cassie hid her disappointment that he would not be with them behind a smile. 'I am glad your brother is to come with us. It will ease the leavetaking for Sarah. She likes Sir Harry, I believe.'

Vincent nodded. 'I have noticed the attraction. Well, why not, if it suits them both?'

'Would Lady Longbourne agree—if a proposal was made? And I must make it clear that none has as yet. I have been told of Sarah's preference in confidence—but I know nothing of how Sir Harry may feel about the situation.'

'It would not surprise me if his feelings were much the same as Miss Walker's. I believe he would hesitate to ask a girl of no fortune, for fear of distressing Mama. She might not be pleased at first—but I believe she might be brought to see the advantages,' Vincent said, a little smile playing about his mouth. 'Sarah is a country girl at heart and I do not think Mama will return to London for a while. I had hoped she might find someone to share her exile—but I have seen no sign of it.'

'No, nor I,' Cassie admitted with a little frown. 'But she will have us now. We shall visit her and she may like to come to us sometimes. Indeed, I am sure she will.'

'Well, we shall see what transpires.' Vincent took out his gold pocket watch and checked the hour. 'I must ask you to excuse me, my love. I shall see you again two days before our wedding.'

'Yes, of course.' Her cheeks flushed as she remembered that kiss and the response it had evoked in her. 'I shall be waiting for you.'

Cassie remained in Carlton's study after he had left. She sat down at his desk, glancing idly at the menus Monsieur Marcel had brought him, picking up various objects and turning them over in her hand. The blade of a silver paper knife had an inscription. She read it without thinking and her heart caught as she saw it had been a long ago birthday gift to Vincent from *'Your friend Jack'*.

'Jack…' The word stuck in her throat. 'Jack…'

Cassie's eyes clouded with tears. She blinked them away. It was so very odd. She could not explain the feeling that had come over her that morning when her purse was stolen. She had been determined not to let go, then, for one brief moment, she had looked into the eyes of that old soldier and her heart had almost failed her. She had thought for one brief second that it was Jack.

It could not be. Of course it could not be! The man was years older than her brother. He had a scar on his cheek and his hair was long and grey. But his eyes… Oh, his eyes were so like Jack's. Surely she could not be mistaken? She knew those eyes as well as she knew her own.

She had since that morning told herself she was wrong again and again, but gradually the feeling had taken root that she had not been mistaken. The old soldier's eyes were Jack's eyes.

Yet how could that be? How could she have seen her brother, when she knew very well that he was dead?

But if by some chance, some wonderful miracle, Jack had not died on the field of battle, why had he not come home to her? Why had he not claimed his inheritance?

Oh, this was madness. To let herself hope, knowing that hope must founder on the rock of disappointment!

She knew it could not possibly have been her brother who had snatched her purse. And yet the same man *had* been following her in London, waiting for his chance to approach her. She was almost sure of it—sure she had seen him at the balloon ascension. The afternoon when she had thought she heard Jack's voice call to her.

'Cassie, I need you…I need your help.'

Had her brother been there in that crowd of onlookers? Had he tried to reach her?

She remembered hearing the voice, then the rope snapped, panic followed and Vincent took her arm, leading her back to Sarah and his brother.

The old soldier had been there, too, that afternoon. She remembered seeing him sheltering from the rain, the shabby coat pulled up around his ears. Surely it was the same man? She was almost certain of it.

Could he possibly be her brother?

His eyes had been so like Jack's. The scar could have been gained in battle—but the hair and the way he had aged?

Actors on the stage were sometimes aged by the paint they put on their faces—and a grey wig would make anyone look older.

It could be done, she realised. If Jack wanted to disguise himself, to hide his identity, he could change his appearance—but not his eyes!

'Why, Jack?' she whispered to herself as she sat on in Vincent's chair, playing with the paper knife he had given to a friend. 'Why snatch my purse? I would have given it willingly. I would share all I have with you. You must know that? You must!'

Cassie would like nothing more than to have her beloved brother home again, to share her fortune with him. Jack must know that, so why not come to her openly?

If it was Jack—and of course she was most probably catching at straws!—but if it was, why was he in some sort of disguise? What could keep him from revealing himself to his sister and friends?

The only answer she could think of was that he was in some kind of trouble...

That evening seemed to Cassie the dullest they had spent for an age. It was just the four of them to dinner, and Sir Harry left immediately afterwards for reasons he did not disclose.

'How delightful to spend an evening quietly at home,' declared Lady Longbourne, sighing with content as she lounged negligently on the sofa. 'Would you play for us, Sarah? You have such a sure touch. Something restful if you please, my dear.'

Sarah obliged with a sad, melancholy piece that reflected her mood. Cassie saw the tears she could not hide and, feeling restless herself, got up and went over to the window. To make matters worse, it had begun to rain. She blinked hard, telling herself sternly not to be so foolish. All she had wanted was a comfortable marriage, much like her own parents' had had, but now she longed for something vastly different.

Carlton's kiss that morning had awoken a fierce hunger in her. She felt as if she had been sleeping all her life, waiting for this moment in time. And now Carlton had gone away, leaving her to a burning frustration that could not be satisfied until she was in his arms again.

Oh, how tiresome it was of him to choose this moment to abandon her! What business could possibly be as important as furthering their relationship?

If he had gone on business, of course.

The unworthy thought wormed its way into her mind. Gentlemen did not always tell the exact truth to their wives and sweethearts. Carlton's business could easily be a race meeting at Newmarket, a bare-knuckle fight at some secret location—or an assignation with a lover.

No, no, she would not believe that last of him! Jealousy tore at her heart, wounding her so deeply that she could not prevent a gasp of pain escaping her.

'Is something the matter, my love?'

Cassie avoided the searching gaze turned on her by Lady Longbourne. 'No, nothing is wrong, ma'am,' she lied. 'I am a little tired, I suppose.'

'As well you might be,' her hostess replied. 'You do not rest as you should, Cassie. We have all been racketing around with no thought of our health.' She yawned behind her hand. 'It is past nine, my dears. Why do we not dispense with the tea tray this evening and go to bed?'

All three ladies agreed on an early night, though, knowing she would not sleep, Cassie had the forethought to fetch a book from Carlton's study. She spent a few minutes looking at the variety ranged in the bookcases, then settled on a small, leather-bound volume of Shakespeare's sonnets lying on the desk. It seemed to have been well used, and when she opened it, she discovered that Carlton had marked his place with a piece of straw.

How very odd! She smiled, imagining him using it for want of something better. He must have carried it with him while campaigning in France, and just holding it seemed to bring him back to her. She clasped the book to her breast, feeling once again the strange but very exciting sensations his lips had created in her earlier that day.

'Oh, bother,' she said and, sighing, went to bed.

The return journey—first to Carlton House, where they rested for a night, and then to Longbourne—was uneventful. There were no highwaymen to frighten them, or gypsy women lying at the point of giving birth by the side of the road to be rescued.

For some obscure reason, Cassie was almost inclined to agree with Lady Longbourne when she complained that travelling was tedious.

Sir Harry was just as attentive and considerate as his brother, but somehow nothing was quite the same. Even his mama told him that Carlton had procured better rooms for them at the inn where they stayed one night, and that the supper was barely tolerable after the culinary delights Monsieur Marcel had prepared for them.

However, once they arrived at the Hall, things took a turn for the better. Sir Harry had decided not to relet after his previous tenants had taken themselves off to an archaeological expedition to Greece. He had, without telling anyone, given instructions that the whole house be modernised and refurbished.

'Oh, Harry!' his delighted mother exclaimed. 'You have

made it comfortable at last. I believe it compares favourably with Carlton's house now.'

Harry looked pleased with himself. 'I am glad you like it, Mama. I—I shall quite possibly spend more time in the country in the future, and naturally I hope you will visit me from time to time.'

'Oh, I shall, my dearest,' said Lady Longbourne. 'What a good son you are to go to so much trouble on my behalf!'

Harry's ears went red and he looked oddly guilty, but did not deny that his efforts had been meant solely to gratify his mother.

Cassie wondered. However fond a son he might be, she thought it unlikely that he would have gone to so much effort unless he had another, more personal reason. Was it possible that Sir Harry was considering marriage—and if so, to whom?

Sarah did not look like a young woman nursing a happy secret. Indeed, she seemed in danger of falling into a sad decline.

Cassie was not surprised when on the morning following their arrival, she said that she felt it her duty to return home to the vicarage.

'Oh, but I thought you would stay with me until after the wedding,' Cassie cried. 'Please, do not leave me just yet, Sarah. We both need another fitting for our gowns, just in case they need a slight adjustment. Besides, I need you to keep me company. And there is the dance two nights before the wedding. You will have to come and stay for that!'

Sarah was persuaded, but insisted she must visit her parents that morning. Cassie agreed and, since it was a lovely day, decided to walk to the vicarage with her friend.

'It will do us good to have a really long walk,' Cassie said. 'I shall come in to greet your parents, of course, Sarah, then go on to visit Nanny Robinson at her cottage. We can walk home together later.'

Mrs Walker greeted her daughter with a loving embrace and a suspicion of tears in her eyes. She would not hear of Cassie leaving without a glass of her own raspberry wine and a slice of seed cake. So it was at least half an hour before she set out for Nanny's cottage.

Her old nurse greeted her with smiles, accepting the basket of small gifts she had brought and plying her with questions about her forthcoming marriage.

'I remember his lordship well,' she said, a gleam in her eyes. 'He and Master Jack were always up to some lark or other.'

'Yes, they were good friends, Nanny.'

'And now you are to wed Lord Carlton.' Nanny Robinson nodded her satisfaction.

Cassie was silent for a moment, then, 'You still have Jack's things? In the trunks I sent?'

'I stored them in my barn,' Nanny replied. 'I have not looked recently, but I am sure they are still there.'

'I shall send for them as soon as we go to Carlton House.'

'Just as you wish, Cassandra.' Nanny shook her head. 'Though no good will come of clinging to the past, my dear.'

'I couldn't let anyone else have them.'

'No, of course you couldn't.'

The subject was dropped. Cassie spent another half an hour chatting to her old nurse, of whom she had always been fond, then set out to return to the vicarage. Her walk led her through secluded country lanes and past the drive of Thornton House. She glanced towards the house, which was just visible through the trees, but had no thought of visiting. However, just as she was about to pass by, she heard her name called, and, turning, saw Sir Kendal hurrying towards her.

Dressed for riding, he looked more at home in the country than he had in town. Cassie would have avoided him if she could, but in her heart she knew that would be impossibly rude of her.

'I was just coming to visit you,' he said as he came up to her, slightly out of breath. 'I am sorry, but I must report something unpleasant to you, Cassandra. Something I imagine must cost you some pain.'

She stared at him in dismay. 'Whatever can you mean, sir?'

'When I came into your late father's estate, it was my intention to be a good custodian. And though you chose to think ill of me, I asked you to be my wife because I thought it wrong that you should be driven from your home.'

Cassie blushed for shame. She realised that, despite his irritating manners, and thoughtlessness in making her an offer so soon after her brother's death, he had meant well. She had never really given him a chance to explain himself.

'I have misjudged you,' she admitted. 'Please forgive me if I have been impolite.'

'Well, we need not say more of this,' Sir Kendal said. 'His lordship assured me that I need have no fear for your future, so all that remains is for me to wish you well…as I do.'

'Thank you, sir. You are most kind.'

Oh, how very lowering! She still could not like him, but she knew Vincent had been right to insist on an invitation being sent.

'I shall naturally attend your wedding,' Sir Kendal went on. 'But first I must acquaint you with the shocking news…' He paused to give importance to his next words. 'There has been a burglary at Thornton House.'

'A burglary?' Cassie was startled. 'Oh, how very shocking! Was anyone hurt?'

'Fortunately, no one was injured. I myself disturbed the rogue, having risen to investigate a noise I heard. I sleep very lightly, Cassandra. Had I not gone to see what was wrong, I fear the damage might have been worse. As it was, only a pair of your father's pistols and a silver tankard were taken.'

'A pair of pistols?' Cassie stared at him. 'Oh, yes, I remember them. Father never used them because he said they were not reliable. I should think your thief would be very disappointed to get so little.'

'Then they were not of sentimental value to you?' Sir Kendal looked relieved. 'I am glad of that. I was afraid you would blame me for not taking care of your father's estate. Since it is unlikely that I shall marry, it is probable that Thornton House will one day return to your son, Cassandra, and I should not want you to blame me for any neglect.'

Cassie discovered she was touched by his concern. Seemingly, he was not so very odious after all.

'No, no,' she said. 'You must do just as you wish with the estate, Kendal. I shall not blame you for anything. Indeed, I think you very brave to investigate strange noises at night. Had it happened when I was there alone, I should have put my head under the covers and ignored it.'

She would not have, of course, but wished to make up for her former curtness to him.

'Well, as to that, I had a blunderbuss with me. And I fired it out of the window after the rogue.'

'Did you actually see him?'

'Not his face—just a glimpse as he ran away. He was wearing a shabby greatcoat and I took him for an old soldier, for there was a military look about his clothes.'

Cassie's heart jerked. Her mouth went dry, and for a

moment she could not speak. 'Did—did you hit him with your shot?'

'I doubt it,' Kendal said regretfully. 'He was too swift for me. The scoundrel! Fellows like that deserve to be hung.'

'He was probably desperate,' Cassie said, not daring to say what was truly in her mind. 'Indeed, he must have been to break into the house.'

'Well, he will not try it again in a hurry,' Sir Kendal said, a gleam of satisfaction in his eyes. 'He knows I shall not hesitate to shoot if he does.'

Cassie murmured something complimentary, though she hardly knew what she said as she parted company with him. Her thoughts were tumbling over themselves in confusion.

The old soldier who had taken her purse and the intruder who had broken into Thornton House—were they the same man? It was such an odd coincidence!

Yet not so strange if that man were Sir John Thornton. Her brother Jack!

Cassie could not help the well of hope that all at once sprang up in her. Jack was alive! She was suddenly so sure of it that she felt like screaming aloud for sheer joy.

Jack had not been killed in France. He was here in England, perhaps near by. She glanced over her shoulder as if expecting to see him following her, but he was not here at this moment: she could not feel him. Somehow she knew that he had been here in order to break into the house—presumably because he was in need of money.

Cassie thought about the times when she had sensed Jack trying to contact her. Once she had thought there was someone following her in Carlton's woods—but then she had found Tara crying. Then she had heard Jack's voice at the balloon ascension, but Vincent had come to drag her away. And the incident of the purse…when her brother had been so desperate he had been driven to steal from his own sister.

'Why, Jack?' she whispered to herself. 'Why not come to me? Why steal Papa's pistols when they belong to you?'

Cassie was now quite certain in her own mind that her brother was alive but in trouble. He must be afraid to reveal his identity to her—or to any of his friends. It was the only possible reason for his behaviour.

'Jack,' she said, urgently willing him to hear her, drawing him to her by the power of her thoughts. 'Come to me, dearest. Come to me. I shall help you. Come to me and I will help you—whatever you've done.'

In that moment, Cassie longed for her fiancé. If only he were there, so that she could confide her thoughts to him! Even though her feelings were in such a turmoil over her coming marriage, she knew that Vincent would have understood her fears and shared her excitement.

No one would be more pleased if Jack really had come back to them, and she knew that he would help her find her brother. He was the one person she could truly trust…

Chapter Nine

Cassie had collected her composure by the time she reached the vicarage. Sarah was waiting for her, and had clearly recovered her spirits. The visit with her mother had done her good, and she chattered happily enough about the wedding as she and Cassie walked back to Longbourne Hall, besides telling her lots of news about her own family.

As they drew close to the house, they stared in surprise at the rather antiquated coach which had just drawn up outside the front door. A portly gentleman was getting out. He was followed by a small dog which jumped down and proceeded to yap excitedly at the footman who was attempting to help a tall, thin lady and a spotty-faced boy of perhaps nine years from the coach.

'Whoever can that be?' Cassie said, then, turning to Sarah as they both laughed, their eyes met in shared mischief. 'Do you think it is the dreaded Septimus?'

'And the odious Archie!' cried Sarah, clapping her hands. 'Oh, dear, we must hurry to poor Lady Longbourne's aid. She was hoping they would not arrive for at least another two days.'

Entering the house a few moments later, the two girls looked at the piles of luggage littering the spacious hall.

Judging from the amount Sir Septimus and his family had brought with them, they were intending to visit for far longer than the week leading up to the wedding.

'It looks as if they mean to stay a month at least,' Cassie whispered, forcing poor Sarah into a fit of the giggles, which she did her best to hide behind her kerchief. 'Poor Lady Longbourne! She will be driven to despair.'

Sir Septimus was loudly directing the disposal of the baggage when Cassie and Sarah encountered him. All hope of escape vanished as he turned and saw them.

'One of you will be Miss Thornton, no doubt?' He eyed them both with barely hidden disapproval.

'I am Cassandra Thornton, sir.' Cassie lifted her head proudly and went forward to offer her hand. His reputation had gone before him, but she was not a coward and would not let him browbeat her as he did Lady Longbourne. 'And I believe you must be Carlton's uncle Septimus? I, too, have heard much of you, sir.'

'Humph!' His narrow-set eyes fixed on her intently. 'I had heard you were a plain, sensible, no-nonsense sort of girl. I dare say you will do. It is high time Carlton did his duty by the family. I was afraid he might marry one of these sylphlike, fair girls. No good for breeding. You look to me as if you might be capable of producing an heir. And high time, too.'

Cassie blinked. Was she meant to take that as a compliment? He was surely the bluntest man she had ever met!

'I hope I shall do all that my husband expects of me,' she said, and turned as his wife and son came up to them.

'Lady Felicity and the sprig,' Sir Septimus said, looking sourly at his wife. 'I'll leave you to get to know each other. Where is that damned butler of Longbourne's? Is nothing ever ready in Emmeline's house?'

He was, of course, referring to his former sister-in-law. Cassie knew at once why Lady Longbourne lived in fear of his visits. His loud voice was almost guaranteed to bring on one of her headaches.

'I believe you were not expected until tomorrow at the earliest,' Cassie said. 'However, I am sure I speak for Lady Longbourne when I say you are most welcome whenever you choose to visit. If you would all care to go into the green salon, I shall arrange for refreshments to be brought to you immediately.'

'And what about all this?' Sir Septimus waved his hand at the piles of luggage.

'I am sure the servants will manage better alone, sir. I know you would naturally wish to help, but I am sure Lady Felicity is exhausted and would be glad to rest.'

'Yes, I would.' The lady in question glared at her husband and pushed her son in front of her. 'Archie, say how do you do to Miss Thornton, if you please.'

Archie extended a hand that looked suspiciously sticky. Cassie smiled and bent to kiss his cheek, which was marginally more presentable. She also kissed Lady Felicity, then firmly directed her towards the front parlour. By this time Sir Harry's butler had arrived and was directing several strong, young footmen to carry up the luggage. Sir Septimus, suddenly discovering himself superfluous to requirements, followed behind his son and heir.

Cassie set herself to making their visitors comfortable, and a tray of sherry wine, biscuits and comfits was brought in. So, when Lady Longbourne arrived looking flustered some minutes later, she found there was nothing for her to do but kiss her relatives and sit down with a restorative glass of wine.

'Forgive me for not being down to receive you myself,' she murmured faintly. 'But there has been so much to do and—and I was resting.'

'You do not take enough exercise, in my opinion,' commented Sir Septimus with a frown. 'Do you good to ride out with the hunt as Felicity does.' He glanced at his wife, who Cassie could not help thinking looked much like a horse herself with her long nose and prominent teeth. 'Shake yourself up, Emmeline.'

'Poor Lady Longbourne has had an exhausting few weeks.' Cassie jumped in to save her. 'We have been simply everywhere. And the Devonshires' ball—such a sad crush. I am sure it is no wonder we all needed some time to recover from it.'

Sir Septimus turned his piercing gaze on her. His nostrils quivered and his ears pricked as if sensing a more worthy adversary.

'Humph! I do not approve of too much racketing about town. No time for it, nor has Felicity. Too expensive—but I dare say you won't care for that. An heiress, aren't you?' He tossed that one into the conversation with the air of a gladiator entering the arena.

'I believe I am,' Cassie said, a faint curve about her mouth as she prepared to give battle. 'And, no, I do not mind what I spend. Money is so boring, do you not think so? One either has none, in which case it is a worry, or so much that there is not the least point in thinking about it.'

Lady Longbourne gasped in admiration. Cassie was so brave! She herself had never dared to use Septimus's own weapons against him, and it afforded her not a little satisfaction to see him—however temporarily—at a loss for words.

He made a recovery, scowled and said, 'A fool and his money are soon parted.'

'Yes, indeed,' Cassie agreed, giving him one of her devastating smiles. 'You are so right, sir. I could not agree more with that sentiment—but there is a difference between spending money for the good of oneself and one's friends, and throwing it away. I do not care to see money wasted, naturally. But to hoard it as a miser! Can anything be so ridiculous? I am persuaded that no person of sense could wish to waste life's opportunities in such a sad way.'

Unknowingly, Cassie had hit upon Septimus's besetting sin. Although not as rich as Carlton, he had inherited an estate that provided him and his family with a satisfactory living. But he lived in fear of exceeding that income and would never spend a penny more than necessary.

'A penny saved is a penny gained.' He glared at her as if daring her to deny him, but a warning look from Lady Longbourne to Cassie saved the day.

'Oh, I am sure you are right there, sir,' Cassie said, 'and now I really think Lady Felicity's rooms will be ready for her.'

'Oh, yes, I am sure they are,' said Lady Longbourne, rising hurriedly to her feet. She had sensed a storm brewing and felt much too fragile. 'Do please come up, Felicity, for I am perfectly sure you need to rest after such a tiring journey.'

Cassie excused herself as they went out, leaving Sir Septimus to turn his attention to his son, who had been steadily eating his way through the almond comfits and now looked slightly green.

'If you are going to be sick, Archie, you may go outside,' his father said. 'Indeed, you should go out anyway, for I am fed up with the sight of you. And take that miserable dog with you! Why your mother should want to own such a puling creature I do not know. I have put up with it all the way here and cannot do so any longer!'

Cassie fled up the stairs before either Septimus or his son could come out and delay her. They really were too awful for words. Beside them, Kendal was a perfectly pleasant man!

Thinking about what Kendal had told her earlier, Cassie frowned to herself. Was she jumping to conclusions? Letting herself believe there was a chance of Jack coming back to her, when there was really no hope? It would be so foolish to build her expectations if it was all in her head!

If only there was someone she could talk to about all this!

Cassie realised with a little shock that the one person she could possibly unburden herself to was Vincent. Insensibly, she had come to rely on him to share her thoughts. She saw now that she ought to have mentioned her suspicions to him. She should have told him about what had happened the day her purse was snatched, but she had been foolishly determined to keep the peculiar incident to herself.

And the next time they had really talked, he had kissed her and everything else had been driven from her mind by her longing to have him hold her in his arms again.

'Oh, why are you not here when I need you?' she muttered to herself as she hurriedly changed into a fresh gown for luncheon. 'I miss you, you wretched man. I do wish you would come home!'

Vincent closed the estate books with a sigh. He had been in his library at Hamilton Manor, poring over them for hours and he was not sure why. His manager was always so efficient that he had no real need to go through them, except that it had become a habit from the days when he had needed to watch the pennies in order to bring himself and his family back from the edge of ruin.

The agents and managers sent in after his father's death to look after the Carlton estate, until he reached his majority and could take over, had near bankrupted him, and it had taken a lot of effort and some skill to put the estate in good heart. Indeed, had he not been left the Hamilton estate by his maternal grandfather in its entirety, he doubted it could have been done. But over the years he had acquired more and more land, building up his wealth by careful husbandry and some inspired investments, and now he knew he could afford to sit back and enjoy his life.

One thing he was sure of, his son would not find himself close to ruin when the time came for him to inherit.

His son. A smile curved Vincent's lips as he remembered the moment he had walked into Cassie's bedroom and discovered her with her arms about that wretched child Tara. It had made him realise he wanted to see his children—his son—in her arms.

'Sentimental fool,' he spoke aloud as he got up and walked over to the sideboard to pour himself a glass of brandy. It was a warm night and he had left the long windows to the garden open to get what breeze there was. 'She doesn't love you, why should she? She merely wants a comfortable marriage.'

Behind him a rustling sound at the windows alerted Vincent. He froze as a prickling at the nape of his neck alerted his sixth sense and warned him he was not alone.

'Stay where you are,' the voice commanded. 'I've a pair of pistols pointed at you and, by God, I'll use them if I have to!'

The chills ran down Vincent's spine. He was going mad! He had to be. That voice…it could not be. Jack was dead. He had killed him. As sure as if he had held the gun to his head and fired himself. He knew he had to be dead, there was no way he could have survived such an injury.

'Jack…' Vincent turned slowly, the colour leaving his face as he saw the man standing just inside the open windows. He was holding a pair of old-fashioned duelling pistols and they were both levelled at Vincent's heart, cocked and ready. 'Good God, man! It can't be you. You were dead. I saw the blood gushing from the wound to your head. The shot was fatal. I was sure you were dead.'

'Damned nearly.' Jack's eyes glinted with anger. 'For all the help you gave me, Vinnie, I might as well have been.

You left me for dead. You led me into that blasted ambush, and then left me there to die.'

'No! It wasn't like that,' Vincent cried hoarsely. The guilt, grief and regret he had been nursing for months flared up in him. 'You know it wasn't, Jack. You were in a blue funk, on the verge of running when I found you. I couldn't let you do that. I couldn't let you desert the field of battle. I had to make you go back and face the enemy again. You would never have forgiven me if I hadn't—or yourself.'

'You threatened to shoot me yourself if I didn't go with you,' Jack said, still angry. 'You took me into that ambush, and then you abandoned me to my fate.'

'I thought you were dead,' Vincent said. 'I was on a mission for Wellington. He told me to pick my own man to back me up—and you were about to run. It was my duty to ride on once you had fallen. Had I stopped to make sure you were really dead, I should have been killed and the documents I carried would have been captured by the enemy.' He turned away as the emotion surged in him. 'Good grief! Do you think I haven't been to hell and back since then? Blamed myself a thousand times for forcing you to go with me! I returned later, when the fighting was over, to search for you. I searched for days, everywhere. I went to all the field hospitals, convents, churches, wherever they told me the wounded had been taken. I scanned every list of the injured and dead. There was not a trace of you anywhere.'

'No, there wouldn't be,' Jack said, some of the tension draining out of him as he read the truth in Vincent's eyes. 'Louise found me. Apparently a finger twitched when they were going to put me on the dead cart, and she believed I was still alive. She had me carried to her home. I was more dead than alive, I promise you—and when I finally came to myself some weeks later, I did not know who I was. My memory had completely gone. I could neither walk nor speak, though I was not paralysed. I had to be taught to use every bodily function all over again, as if I were a child. If it had not been for that angel…'

'Louise? A Frenchwoman?' Vincent's eyebrows rose. 'She took you in and nursed you back to health? From what I heard, you were more likely to get a ball through the heart to finish you off.'

'Louise is not like that, she helped all those she could. She fed me, bathed me, taught me how to walk again. She is an angel, Vinnie.' Jack stepped further into the room and took off his hat. His hair was very short, as if it had been shaved close to his head and there was a deep scar and indentation near his temple where the bullet had lodged in his skull, saved from entering his brain by bone. He smiled as he saw the stunned expression in Vincent's eyes. 'They tell me my hair will grow again eventually, but it has gone grey from the shock of my illness. When you get that close to dying, it does strange things to you. I think I was near mad for a time.'

At first glance he looked an old man but, as Vincent looked into his eyes, he realised that the friend he had cared for so deeply was still there inside.

'You look awful,' he said gruffly, to hide his emotion. 'And your clothes—have you been living rough?'

'Sleeping under the stars, near starving at times. I came back six weeks or so ago,' Jack said. 'Louise gave me what she could, but she has nothing, poor darling. I intended to see Cassie as soon as I got home. In fact, I went to the house one night, and she leaned out of her window. I think she sensed someone was there, but when she looked out I lost my nerve.'

'Why? You must have known she would be glad to see you. She grieved for months over your loss. Indeed, she has hardly got over it now, though she is trying to rebuild her life.'

'I was afraid to just walk in on her looking like this,' Jack said. 'I mean, she would probably have screamed blue murder and sworn I was an impostor.'

'You know Cassie better than that,' Vincent said. 'So what was your true reason?'

'Why did you try to shoot me about a month ago?' Jack answered his question with another. 'After I couldn't bring myself to face Cassie, I came to Carlton House. She was walking alone in your woods. I followed for a while. I had almost made up my mind to speak to her then, but backed off when she found that child crying. So I decided to follow you to London…'

'That was you?' Vincent stared at him in stunned disbelief. 'Why the hell did you skulk in the trees like that? I thought you were a damned highwayman!'

'I was very nearly reduced to it.' Jack pulled a wry face, lowered his pistols and tossed them on to the desk. 'They aren't loaded. Father always said they were lethal. I wouldn't have taken them if that idiot Kendal hadn't come blundering in the way he did—I was looking for something decent to wear, but Cassie must have thrown all my clothes out.'

'I believe she sent them to Nanny Robinson for safekeeping,' Vincent said apologetically. 'She wasn't going to let Kendal get his hands on anything of yours, apparently.'

'If that isn't just like her!' Jack chuckled, obviously relieved that his sister hadn't decided to sweep his possessions out the door. 'I was pretty cut up when I thought she couldn't wait to get shot of my things. I mean, it seemed as if she had forgotten me.'

'Oh, no,' Vincent said. 'She hasn't done that. She told me you had come back to her a few weeks ago— Good grief! She was right, wasn't she? Is that when your memory returned, just a few weeks ago?'

'Yes.' Jack was smiling now, at ease. 'It came in bits

and pieces, then it was suddenly all there and I thought of Cassie, willing her to think about me. Until then, I hadn't really thought much about her. Once I remembered, Louise told me I had to come back. I was reluctant, but she insisted. She said I must at least let Cassie know I was alive.'

'Surely you will reclaim your inheritance?' Vincent looked at him hard.

Jack shrugged. 'There isn't very much, you know. I suppose I could sell the house, but my life is in France with Louise now.' His mouth softened into a smile of tenderness. 'She lives in a dreadful old château with her grandmother Madame Moreau. The roof has holes in it, and when the rains come we have to put out buckets to catch the drips. They have lost most of their land over the years, but there is a decent little farm and a vineyard. I worked with the grapes when I was recovering my strength but still did not know who I was. It was good, satisfying work, Vinnie. I think I could be happy there. Besides, Louise would never leave everything to come to England—and I love her.'

'But what if you change your mind in a few years?' Vincent said with a frown. 'Besides, there's your family to consider. Cassie…'

'She will be fine,' Jack said. 'She was always able to cope with anything life threw at her. I came back to make certain. But when I realised she was engaged to you, I knew everything was all right. So I thought I would tell you the whole story and go back to France. You can tell her when you're ready. You can bring her out to see us when you've prepared her for the shock.'

'You're going without seeing her?' Vincent was suddenly angry. 'No, damn you! You shan't do that. I shall not permit you to hurt her like that, Jack. I cannot believe you would even consider such a course of action.'

'I have seen her,' Jack said, looking awkward. 'I've been

close to her a couple of times, but she…well, you couldn't expect her to see me as her brother, could you?'

'But does she know you're alive?'

'Well, as to that, I'm not sure. I think she might have started to suspect. When I stole her purse a few days ago she looked at me a bit suspiciously—'

'When you stole her purse?' Vincent was thunderstruck. 'Where did this happen? I've heard nothing of it.'

'She didn't tell you? I thought she would be sure to.' Jack frowned. 'Why *did* you ask her to marry you, Vinnie? Was it just because of that stupid promise I forced you and the others to make?'

'That's none of your damned business!'

'Forgive me.' Jack stared him out. 'But I think it is my business. Because so much time had passed, I imagined you had become friends, got to like one another—but if she didn't tell you about losing her purse she doesn't trust you much. If this isn't a love match, I want to know. I want to be sure Cassie is happy with the arrangement.'

Vincent controlled his very great desire to give him a bloody nose. 'Then you will just have to stay around for a while, won't you? Claim your rightful place in the world and stop running around stealing other people's property.'

'Come off it, Vinnie! Cassie wouldn't grudge me a few guineas. Besides, I was desperate. I had no money. I was hungry—and I'd caught a chill at that damned balloon ascension.'

'You were there!'

'I almost spoke to Cassie then, but you took her away. I can tell you, Vinnie, you've been a thorn in my side these past weeks.'

'What I cannot understand,' Vincent said, 'is why you did not come to me? If you were afraid your appearance would upset Cassie—why not come to me and let me break the news to her?'

Jack's gaze fell away. 'You must know why I hesitated, Vinnie.'

'I'm damned if I do!'

'You knew I was a coward. You knew I had run from enemy fire. I thought you had abandoned me to my fate. I thought you must hate and despise me.' He looked up suddenly, a glint of anger in his eyes. 'Damn it, Vinnie! You had tried to shoot me once. I thought you might make a thorough job of it if I came to you, that's why I brought Father's pistols with me this evening. After all, I couldn't blame you if you did decide to shoot me. I am a disgrace to my name and family.'

'What you are is a numskull,' said Vincent, a flicker of amusement in his eyes. 'Do you think I could turn against you because of a moment's panic? You're no more a coward than any of us, Jack. We were all scared out there, believe me.'

'Not you,' Jack said, frowning. 'Nothing ever frightens you.'

'You would be surprised,' replied Vincent, a wry smile on his lips. 'Quite a few things terrify me—but I shan't tell you what they are.'

'So you don't despise me? You haven't told anyone I ran under fire?'

'Do you take me for a gabblemonger? I blamed myself for forcing you to return with me. I was your murderer, Jack—and I have had your death on my conscience these many months. I thank God that you are alive, and I am very glad to see you again.'

Jack stared at him. 'Then I can come back? I can give Kendal notice to quit and claim what is left of the estate?'

'I believe you will find Mr Thornton pleased to be relieved of the burden,' Vincent said. 'But whatever you decide, you must speak to Cassie first. And before you do that, we must make you look presentable. We are much the same size. I can find you something decent to wear. If I were you, my friend, I should take a long soak in the hot tub and then we'll have supper and talk about the future.'

Cassie paused on the stairs as she heard the voices coming from the rear of the entrance hall at Longbourne. Surely that was Vincent? She had not expected him for another two days at least and her heart took a flying leap. She ran down the last few steps and saw him removing his capped greatcoat.

'Cassie,' he said, coming towards her with his hands outstretched. 'How are you, my love?'

'Very well,' she replied, blushing at the warmth in his eyes. 'I am very happy to see you returned sooner than you thought.'

She offered her cheek and he kissed it. 'My business took less time than I had imagined,' he said. 'Besides, I wanted to see you. We must talk—'

'Ah, there you are!' Sir Septimus boomed, coming into the hall from the parlour. 'Couldn't stay away from her, eh? Well, I cannot say that I blame you. You've got yourself a spirited filly there, Carlton. More spunk in her little finger than your mother ever had.'

Vincent frowned. He did not mind his uncle's blunt manner towards himself, but was not about to countenance an insult to his mother, even if it was meant to be a compliment to Cassie.

'Lady Longbourne's health has never been as good as it might be,' he said stiffly.

'You mean she uses it as an excuse to twist you round her little finger,' Septimus crowed, looking for all the world like a Bantam cock shaping up to a full-sized cockerel. 'You won't get that from your wife. I'll wager a hundred guineas on it!'

Vincent's mouth went hard, but Cassie jumped in before he could answer.

'You should not gamble so wildly, sir,' Cassie quipped, a sparkle in her eyes as she saw Vincent's hands clench at his sides. 'You told me yourself last night that I am a wicked jade, and there's no saying what I might do to get my own way.'

'Damned if you ain't right again!' Septimus looked startled. 'Don't know what's come over me of late. You'll have me tipping my blunt like a regular gamester if I don't watch it!' He laughed as if hugely amused at the idea, nodded to Vincent and walked into the parlour, where he could be heard telling his son to take himself off to the garden and keep out of his way.

'What was all that about?' Vincent asked Cassie, looking bewildered. 'Was that really my uncle—or have I walked into the wrong house? I have never heard him talk that way to anyone. He was almost good humoured.'

'Yes, it *was* Septimus,' said Lady Longbourne, coming down the stairs to greet her son. She smiled at Cassie as Vincent kissed her cheek. 'This fiancée of yours has bewitched him. I vow I have been near hysterics at the battles between them these past two days—but it seems your uncle enjoys having her stand up to him. I have never seen him so mellow.'

'He seems just as rude as ever,' Vincent remarked drily.

'Oh, but that is just his way,' said Lady Longbourne. 'However, he has not been half as horrid to me as usual. In fact, he called me his dear Emmeline yesterday—*and* he squeezed my hand.' The look in her eyes spoke volumes to Cassie.

'Oh dear, did he?' She gave Lady Longbourne a sympathetic look. 'How very uncomfortable for you, dearest Mama.'

'Well, it was,' replied Lady Longbourne. 'For I have not

been used to it and it gave me quite a turn. But I am better now and I shall not feel so—so odd next time.'

'You cannot expect it to happen again? This is merely the shine of the new,' Cassie murmured wickedly. 'I dare say he will be himself again before you are aware of it.'

'Do you think so?' Lady Longbourne laughed. 'Well, I suppose I had better go and find Felicity. She was talking of going through the linen cupboards to make sure there were enough clean sheets to make up all the guest rooms. I am persuaded Harry's housekeeper has already seen to it so I must try to divert Felicity if I can.'

'Mama seems to have more energy than usual,' Vincent said with a lift of his eyebrows as she went off.

'There is so much to do,' Cassie said. 'I was about to walk down to the church to make sure there are enough vases—for the flowers, you know. Mrs Walker says they have plenty, but I think we might borrow some from Sir Harry's storeroom to be safe.'

'You are *very* busy,' Vincent said, feeling a little disoriented by what was happening around him. 'I do have something important to say to you, Cassie. If I shall not be in your way—perhaps I could walk down to the church with you?'

'Yes, of course.' She smiled at him. 'If you would not find it too boring. I should like to have your company. I too have something I have been wanting to discuss with you.'

'Have you, Cassie?' His eyes met hers searchingly but learned nothing. She was adept at hiding her thoughts.

They left the house together, walking through the formal gardens at the front of the house and entering the wood beyond. Neither of them spoke for several minutes, then both began at once.

'It is about Jack—' said Cassie.

'Cassie, prepare yourself for a shock. I do not know how much you have guessed but—'

They both stopped speaking and stared at one another. Cassie gazed up at him, her eyes wide and dark with emotion. 'Jack is alive, isn't he? Have you seen him, too?'

'Yes, I have seen him. You knew, didn't you? Somehow, you sensed him near by. And then you recognised him when he snatched your purse.' Vincent looked at her steadily—how frightened she looked. He wanted to comfort her but knew what he had to say would hurt and upset her. 'He thought you might have done.'

Cassie nodded, looking thoughtful. 'I had been aware of him for some time. He had gone, you know—out of my head. We had always been so close in thought, but then I thought he must be dead because he was no longer with me.'

'He nearly did die,' Vincent said gently. 'He was very ill. For a long time he could not remember anything. He had to learn to walk again.'

A sob rose to her lips. 'Oh, my poor Jack! No wonder he is so changed.' She gasped. 'Is that why he did not come to me? Was he afraid I should reject him?'

'Something like that,' Vincent agreed. He could not, would never tell her the true reason for Jack's hesitation. 'I believe he needed time to come to terms with what had happened to him. However, I shall let him tell you his own story himself. I have arranged for him to come to the house this evening, and will engage to make sure that no one disturbs you. You can meet after everyone else has gone to bed. It will be easier for him that way. And for you, I think.'

'Oh, how thoughtful of you!' Cassie frowned. 'Is he much changed—other than his looks?'

'I think him quieter, not so ready to laugh,' Vincent said

and frowned. 'He is not as he was, Cassie. You could not expect it.'

'No,' she said, looking sad. 'No, it is not to be expected.'

'I assured him you would be happy to see him.'

'Yes, I shall—whatever the changes.'

'I was sure you would.'

'I want to share Aunt Gwendoline's fortune with him. I am not sure how things stand now.'

'The marriage contract?' Vincent stared at her in mild astonishment. 'Did you not bother to read it before you signed it, Cassie?' She shook her head. 'I have, of course, made a settlement on you, which should cover your needs, and is I hope generous. But should you require anything more, you may have the bills sent to me. I am well able to provide for my wife, and wish to do so. Your inheritance remains your own. Once we are married, you can dispose of the capital as you please.'

'And you will not mind?'

'I shall not mind,' he assured her gravely. 'I am not marrying you for the sake of your fortune. Indeed, it would not matter to me if you had not a penny to your name.'

'This is the first time we have talked properly,' Cassie said, her eyes searching his face. It was not easy to read what was in his mind. 'Indeed, we have scarcely been alone like this before.'

'No, we have not,' Vincent said. 'Perhaps we ought to have taken more time for such walks, Cassie?'

'Yes,' she said, a shy but determined look in her eyes as she gazed up at him. 'I hope you will not think it impertinent in me if I ask you why you asked me to be your wife?' He was silent and she saw that she had shocked him. He had not expected her to ask such a question, but she needed to know the answer. 'I am not particularly attractive, and you do not need my fortune. People said it was a matter of honour, but…'

'In a way it was at the start,' Vincent said, knowing he must be honest with her. If he did not speak now, it might be too late. 'After the news of your father's death, Jack was greatly worried about what would happen to you…'

Cassie's face went white as she guessed what he was about to say. She took a step away from him, the pain of her disappointment sweeping over her so fiercely that she hardly knew what she said as she cried out, 'No! Do not say it, I beg you. Jack made you promise to ask me, didn't he? I know it, so do not try to deny it.'

'I cannot deny it,' Vincent said. 'He had asked me before and I would not, but that night…'

'You promised to ease his mind, didn't you?' Her face had drained of colour. 'And then when he died…'

'Cassie, it was just at the beginning…'

'No! Do not come near me.'

Cassie gave a little cry of despair as he held out his hand to her in silent appeal, then she turned and ran from him. At first she ran in blind panic, not caring where she went or what she did, wanting only to get away from this pain inside her.

She had to get away from him. She could not bear to hear his excuses. La Valentina had been right, he wanted her only as a means of securing his heir.

She gathered speed, her heart pounding as the tears streamed down her cheeks. Oh, it hurt so much—so much that she felt she would like to die. Nothing penetrated her misery, though she knew Vincent had begun to follow. Not at once but for some seconds now. He must surely catch up with her soon.

She redoubled her efforts. Then, after she had been running for a moment or two, she heard a scream. It was the cry of a wounded animal, a terrified scream that made her turn cold inside, and instinctively she turned towards it, her own hurt pushed aside as she followed the sounds of terror and pain.

'Cassie! Wait! You must wait for me…'

Vincent's cry only served to spur her on. Her instincts told her she must hurry or it would be too late. She knew Vincent was following her but she did not want him to catch her. Nor could she bear that some woodland creature should be in such agony. Its pitiful cries were tearing her apart.

Suddenly, she stopped dead as she saw the poacher bending over his cruel trap. He had caught a young deer by the leg and was about to beat its head in with a thick cudgel.

'Stop! Stop that at once!' she cried.

She ran straight at the poacher, throwing herself on him so that he was knocked off balance. He was taken by surprise and hit out with his stick, striking her a glancing blow on the head. It felled her instantly. She lost consciousness at once and was not privy to the violent scene that took place as she lay senseless on the ground.

'My God! You've killed her. You will hang for this.'

The poacher dropped his stick as he saw Vincent, recognising authority and fearing it. 'No, sir. It were an accident. Honest. I never meant—'

'Be quiet, sirrah! You are a murderer and a poacher,' Vincent said, his face white with anguish. 'I promise you this, if the hangman doesn't get you, I shall.'

With one furious blow, Vincent knocked him to the ground, where he lay whimpering, dazed and writhing in pain from a dislocated jaw. He did not attempt to move. To run would be useless. He was doomed. He knew it as Vincent took a tiny pistol from his coat pocket and shot the deer through the head, to put it out of its pain from the leg which had been nearly torn through and could never heal. The next shot would surely be for him if he dared to so much as flick a finger. But it did not come. He might

not have existed for all the notice the aristocrat took of
him.

Kneeling down by Cassie's side, his pistol back in his
pocket, Vincent touched her face, which was still warm.
She whimpered slightly and his heart stopped. She lived!
God be praised, she lived. He spoke to her softly, willing
her to open her eyes and know him, but she did not move
even as he lifted her very gently in his arms.

Then he turned on the rogue who had struck her. The
man was standing now, fear stamped all over his cowardly
face. Vincent would have liked to kill him there and then,
but he knew he must take care of Cassie. Revenge could
be sought later, for now her well-being was his only concern.

'Run for your life, coward,' he muttered, eyes blazing.
'For if I find you in this life I shall kill you. You would
sooner love the hangman's touch than mine if she dies.'

And with that he strode away, Cassie lying limp and still
within his arms.

Chapter Ten

Cassie was just beginning to stir as Vincent carried her into the hall. He had been seen coming towards the house, and besides a worried-looking footman who was foolish enough to offer to take her from him, thereby getting his head snapped off, he was greeted by a small reception committee.

'What *have* you done to her?' cried Lady Longbourne, giving him an angry stare. It was obvious that she blamed him. 'Oh, my poor, dear Cassie!'

'Knew you were a pugilist,' Septimus said with a beetle glare that hid his concern. 'Didn't think you practised on ladies, Carlton. What happened?'

'Out of my way,' came the curt reply. Vincent glared at no one in particular, his face as black as thunder. 'If any of you has the least semblance of sense in your heads, someone see that her bed is ready. And send for Janet!'

Cassie moaned, her long, dark lashes fluttering against her unnaturally pale cheeks. 'My head…it hurts. Please do not let him…do not let him…'

'You are quite safe now, my love. Your poor head will be better very soon,' promised Lady Longbourne as Vincent carried her past and on up the stairs. She followed him but at a discreet distance, looking distressed. The anger and despair in her son's eyes had shocked her. What could be the matter with him? She had never, never known Vincent to be so abrupt—or to look so out of control.

Janet was waiting with the bedcovers drawn back when Vincent swept into the room a fluttering maid had hurriedly indicated as Cassie's. He laid his precious burden down very carefully, frowning as she uttered a little cry of pain.

'What happened, sir?' asked Janet, shaking her head over her mistress.

'There was a trapped fawn and a poacher in the woods.' Janet nodded and clicked her tongue in dismay, understanding perfectly. She had no need to be told whose fault it was. 'I called to her to stop, but she would not listen. She just ran straight at him, unheeding of her own safety. He was taken by surprise and hit her. There was absolutely nothing I could do...'

'No, sir, of course not. If that isn't Miss Cassie all over. She is always so impulsive. Especially where animals in pain are concerned. It has always been the same.'

A cry of anguish issued from Cassie's lips. Her eyes opened, reflecting her pain as she looked directly at Vincent. 'The fawn...what happened?'

'I was forced to shoot it. It was too badly injured, Cassie. There was nothing else to be done but put it out of its misery.'

'No! Oh, no...' Tears welled up in her eyes. 'Too cruel... too cruel.'

'You were more important,' Vincent said, his face set in an unreadable mask, which she took for anger—or indifference. 'I did not know how badly you were hurt. I had to get you home.'

Cassie made a murmur of denial. She turned her head so that it was away from him, tears running down her cheeks.

'It was hurt, you should have helped it...'

The words were little more than a whisper, but they struck Vincent to the core, because they held so much meaning for him. If she cared so much about an injured animal, what must she feel if she knew he had been the cause of Jack's being injured and brought near to death? If she knew that he had been forced to leave her brother wounded on the ground and ride on? She would surely hate him!

'Cassie, I am sorry…please forgive me.'

She kept her face averted, a little sob escaping her.

'Perhaps it would be best if you left her to me, sir?' Janet suggested. 'I know how to look after her. She'll be better in a while.'

Vincent stared down at Cassie, his eyes dark with anguish. Her words and the way she held herself were rejecting him. He sensed that just at this moment she could not bear to have him near her, and it cut him to the heart.

'I shall fetch the doctor to her,' he said to Janet, then turned and walked from the room, his face so stern that Lady Longbourne felt a little faint. Her heart was racing quite madly, and she was sure she was on the verge of swooning.

However, this was not the time to give way to her own sad health, so instead she went into Cassie's room and sat down on the edge of the bed, holding the girl's hand in her own and kissing it.

'There, there, my dearest one,' she soothed, taking the cold cloth Janet had finished soaking in water and laying it on Cassie's forehead. 'I dare say you will have a nasty bruise, and I am sure your poor head hurts, but we must hope no more harm will come from this.'

Cassie smothered a sob, turning her head to look at her. 'It does hurt,' she said, 'but not so very much. What makes me cry is the thought of that poor creature…it was in such pain. I wanted to help it, but Vincent shot it. That was so unkind of him—he should have done something to help it.'

Lady Longbourne replaced the cloth with another supplied by the anxious Janet. 'You know I do not always agree with Vincent,' she said. 'But on this occasion I believe he acted for the best, my love. It must have been quite difficult for him, you know. A wounded creature in a trap, a dangerous poacher—and you unconscious. I imagine he did what he felt right in the circumstances.'

'His duty, you mean?' Cassie sounded almost bitter. 'Yes, I dare say he did the right thing—but not the kindest.'

Lady Longbourne saw the tears well up in Cassie's eyes once more. 'I think you are wrong, dearest. In this case it was kinder to act quickly. He could not help the fawn and you—and you were naturally more important.'

Seeing that Cassie was in great distress, Janet touched her ladyship's arm. 'Forgive me, ma'am, but I think it would be best if you leave her to me now. She's fretting and she needs to have a good cry, get it out of her system. I've seen her like this before, ma'am, and I know what to do.'

Lady Longbourne bowed to the experience of the woman who had nursed Cassie through many a crisis. 'Yes, perhaps I should leave her to rest.' She bent to kiss Cassie's cheek. 'Try to sleep, dearest. I shall visit you again after the doctor has been.'

Janet closed the door after her. Cassie had pushed herself up into a sitting position against a pile of pillows. Her face was pale and stubborn, her eyes dark with hurt.

'Why don't you just lie still and rest, child?'

'I hate lying in bed,' Cassie said. 'I think I shall get up.' She swung her feet over the side of the bed, then moaned as her head spun giddily. 'Oh, I feel dizzy.'

'What would you expect after a bang on the head?' Janet glared at her. 'Lie back at once, you foolish girl! I've warned you what would happen time and time again. If this isn't the outside of enough. Causing all this fuss—and with the wedding only three days away! What did you think you were doing? Poor Lady Longbourne must have had a dreadful fright. To say nothing of his lordship. You were very unfair to him, Miss Cassie, and so I must tell you. You did not thank him once for helping you. And that was very rude. I am surprised at you, and I do not mind telling you so.'

'Please do not scold me, Janet.' Cassie lay back against the pillows. Her maid's sensible tone had calmed her more than all the fussing and sympathy ever could. 'I know it was very foolish of me to do what I did—but that awful man was going to hit the fawn and I couldn't bear that. So I rushed at him and…I do not recall what happened then.'

'He hit you instead of the deer.' Janet's expression was grim. 'If you ask me, it was a blessing his lordship was there with you. Had you been alone, goodness knows what might have happened…' She shook her head over the thought, her tongue clicking in distress. 'You might have been killed—or worse.'

'That would have been very shocking, wouldn't it?'

'It would have caused a lot of people a lot of grief,' Janet said severely, secretly pleased that her scolding was working. Miss Cassie was coming out of the mopes. 'There are several of us who would have found that very difficult to bear, I might add. If you do not care for yourself, you should care for others.'

Cassie saw that her maid was battling with tears and was touched. She made an effort to stop feeling sorry for herself and smiled, holding out her hand.

'Yes, I know. I do not know why you should love me, when I have been so very much trouble to you, Janet—but I know you do. I am very grateful for it.'

Janet sniffed hard. 'Well, as to that—I am not the only

one. There's Miss Sarah, Lady Longbourne—and his lordship, naturally. And I dare say a few others.'

Cassie closed her eyes for a moment. She knew Vincent did not love her. Oh, he liked her well enough. They often shared the same jokes and they were comfortable together. He was concerned for her welfare, as he would be for any lady of his family—but he did not love her. Not as she wanted to be loved.

She opened her eyes and looked at Janet. 'Jack loves me,' she said. 'At least I have him.'

'Now, Miss Cassie.' Janet seemed alarmed, as if fearing that the bang to her head set Cassie's wits a-wandering. 'You know poor Master Jack was killed in France.'

'No, he wasn't,' Cassie said, and now she was smiling, her own hurts temporarily banished. 'He *was* terribly wounded, Janet. Everyone thought he must have died of his injuries, but he wasn't killed. I do not yet quite understand what happened, how it came about that he was reported killed, but I shall soon. He is coming here to see me tonight. I am to meet him in the library, so that we can be private together.'

Janet stared at her. She laid her hand on the girl's brow, but it was cool. She didn't think Miss Cassie was feverish, but it sounded too good to be true. 'How do you know all this?'

'Lord Carlton told me just before…' Cassie paused, swallowing hard. 'I had seen Jack once or twice in London, but he is so changed I did not know him. Do not look so disbelieving, Janet. I have not gone mad. I promise you, it is true. Jack is alive and coming here tonight.'

'God be praised!' Janet sat down on the edge of the bed with a little bump. Her legs had turned to jelly and she was all of a quiver. 'Oh, my goodness me. I'm all upside down. Master Jack not dead. It's a miracle, Miss Cassie.' She crossed herself. 'A miracle... I do not know how to take it in, and that's a fact.'

'Yes, I know. It is so wonderful. I can hardly believe it myself—but it is true.'

'And he's coming here tonight?'

'Yes. I shall meet him after everyone else has gone to bed—because he feels a little awkward about the way he looks, you see. He has a scar at his temple, I think—and his hair may be grey, though I believe he was wearing a wig when I saw him. He followed me in London, waiting to get his chance to speak to me, but in disguise. He did not want me to know him until he was ready, you see. I think he was afraid that I might reject him. But he has since revealed himself to Lord Carlton—and now he is coming to see me.'

'Mercy on us!' Janet cried. 'Well, if that's the case, miss, you lay your head down now. If you want to be up to seeing Master Jack later, you had best get some sleep now.'

'Must I?' Cassie pulled a wry face. 'Oh, I suppose you are right—and I do have a bit of a headache.'

Cassie did her best to sleep that afternoon. The doctor had visited, pronounced her lucky to have got off so lightly, and left her something to help her sleep if her head hurt too much. She thanked him politely, but the medicine remained untouched. Her head did indeed feel rather sore, and very tender where the bruise was coming through, but that was not the reason for her restlessness.

She could not forget what Vincent had told her just before she ran away from him. He had asked her to marry him because of a promise he had made to her brother! Jack had been worried because their father had brought the estate almost to ruin, then shot himself, leaving her to manage alone.

It was so typical of Jack to seek to protect her, but he

should not have done it. She did not want to be married
for such a reason! It was humiliating—to think that Vincent
had pitied her! And he must have done or he would not
have made such a foolish vow.

Oh, how could he do that? How could he allow her to
believe he truly cared for her when all the time it was a
sham?

Cassie tossed restlessly from side to side. She would
never, never have consented to be his wife had she known.
Oh, it was all too hurtful and too confusing. She did not
know what to do about the situation: it was such a tangle!

She could withdraw, of course. That would be so very
shocking. The wedding was only a few days away, the
guests invited, presents received. What a scandal it would
make if she cancelled everything now. She shuddered to
think of all the upset it would cause—but it would give
great offence to Lady Longbourne and it would also hurt
her deeply. No, it was not to be thought of!

Cassie smothered a sob. She felt wretched and very
weepy. She was truly fond of her kind hostess, who had
done so much for her. After the tiring visit to town Lady
Longbourne had undertaken for her benefit, her advice and
genuine concern! It would distress her terribly if Cassie
withdrew now.

Oh, what a mess it all was! Cassie's mood gradually
changed to anger as she lay staring at the ceiling. It was
all Carlton's fault. He had deceived her, allowing her to
believe he truly cared for her. His proposal had misled her.
Why had he been so emotional that day? Oh, he was so
very tiresome! She was extremely cross with him.

And yet she liked him so well, had missed him when he
went away for a few days.

Who was she fooling? Cassie forced herself to face the
truth. She was head over heels, helplessly in love with Vincent. It would break her foolish heart if she were never to

see him again. Yet how could she marry him, knowing what she did?

It was an impossible situation, and kept her tossing from side to side as she sought a way out and could not find one. No matter what she did now, she was destined to be miserable.

Cassie must have slept for a while. She woke feeling tired and listless, lying in the darkness for a moment or two, then suddenly remembered why she had not wanted to fall asleep. She jumped out of bed, in a frenzy of nerves mixed with excitement. As she stood, she was relieved to find that she no longer felt dizzy. A quick wash in cold water from a jug on her washstand left her refreshed and wide awake.

The house seemed very quiet. There was no sound from downstairs. She thought it must be very late. Perhaps Jack was already here, waiting for her.

She tidied her hair, wincing a little at the soreness of her temple, then pulled on a fresh gown Janet had left ready. It was an old one, which fastened at the front and was easy to manage. Taking a last glance at her reflection, she went out into the hall and hesitated, listening.

There were still candles burning, so perhaps not everyone had yet retired. Cassie moved softly along the carpeted landing and down the stairs, not wanting anyone to hear her and come out to ask what she was doing at this hour. She knew that all her friends would urge her to return to bed, and she was determined to see Jack. Nothing must stop her! She prayed that he had not been and gone already.

A clock striking midnight somewhere in the house made her jump and look guiltily over her shoulder. Reaching the hall, she fled through it to the green salon. It was empty as she had hoped, and led directly into the library. The connecting door was opened slightly, and she could see light coming from inside. Jack must be here!

Her heart began to race, and she went swiftly towards the open door, her mouth dry with a mixture of excitement and fear. She wanted to see Jack so desperately, and yet she was afraid of the changes she might find—not in his looks, which did not matter, but in the essential core of him.

As she paused outside the library door to gather her nerves, she heard their voices: Jack's and Vincent's. They appeared to be arguing—and about her! She knew she ought to go in at once, but somehow she lingered.

'How could you let it happen?' Jack demanded in outrage. 'Damn you, Vinnie! What were you about to let that ruffian hurt her? It was your duty to protect her. You should have done something. Stopped her! Good grief, Vinnie, you must have known she was in danger. She could have been killed!'

'She was too far ahead of me,' Vincent protested, sounding guilty. 'I called her to stop, to wait for me, but she carried on unheeding. I was not close enough to prevent what happened. She simply would not listen to me.'

'I should just imagine she would not listen after what you'd said to her. Why on earth did you tell her about that stupid promise? You must have known how she would react? Why blurt it out like an empty-headed fool?'

'I felt I owed her the truth,' Vincent said. 'Naturally, I said nothing about the others—or that we drew straws to see who went first. And I would be grateful if you kept that to yourself. Goodness knows what she would think then. Your sister is a very independent woman, Jack. And headstrong. I tried to explain, but she would not give me a chance. When she ran away from me in the woods I hesitated, and then I could not catch up with her. Now she is angry with me for shooting that wretched creature—but what else could I do? I had to get her home, and deal with the rogue who felled her.'

'Well, at least he got his just deserts.'

'I've not finished with him yet, believe me.'

'Let it go,' Jack advised. 'Revenge is empty. Besides, you'll have your hands full with Cassie.'

'I dare say you are right. She does seem to have a mind of her own.' A husky laugh escaped him. 'As I am beginning to learn to my cost, Jack.'

'You don't know the half of it,' Jack said. 'She has the devil of the temper, though you might not think it to look at her.' He sighed. 'Oh, well, I suppose it cannot be helped.'

'I shall apologise, of course, and hope she will forgive me.'

'And you think she is too unwell to see me?' Jack said. 'I had best go and—'

Cassie pushed the door wide. Both men swung round, their faces white with shock and guilt.

'My God!' Vincent looked horrified. 'How long have you been standing there?'

'Long enough.' Cassie was furious. With both of them. She took a few steps into the room, her whole body bristling with temper. 'How dare you! How dare you make plots behind my back? I am not a piece of baggage to be disposed of over a casual chat by the fire.' Her gaze fell on Jack. ' How dare you beg your friends to marry me, Jack? How dare you tell my brother to go away because I am too ill to see him, Lord Carlton?' She gave him a freezing look. 'Who gave either of you permission to dictate my life?'

Neither of them uttered a word. Caught in the act like two schoolboys with their hands in the toffee jar, they simply stared at her. She was too angry for them to try and soothe her ruffled feelings. It was clear that she had heard every word of their discussion and was outraged, as well she might be. Cassie had every right to feel aggrieved after the way they had been discussing her.

For several seconds there was complete silence, broken only by the monotonous ticking of the mantle clock. Outside, a branch rattled against the window as the wind rose. Vincent found his tongue first.

'Forgive me. I was told you were sleeping and must on no account be disturbed.'

'You were misinformed, sir. As you see I am awake, and perfectly recovered from what was merely a slight bump on the head. I really do not know what all the fuss has been about.'

'It was a little more than a slight bump, I think.'

He received a scorching look and retired from the field gracefully.

'Sorry, Cassie.' Jack ventured a sortie next. 'It was my fault and mine alone. I just couldn't bear to think of you all alone in the house if anything happened to me—and at the mercy of that bore Kendal. I meant it for the best, but I realise now that I was mistaken.'

'I was at no one's mercy,' she replied, her face beginning to soften as she looked at her beloved brother and saw the scars. Her poor, dear Jack! How he must have suffered. And she was not there to help or comfort him. 'You could not know, of course, but Aunt Gwendoline died and left me her fortune. I am of age, and financially independent. So I may do as I please.'

'Did she have a fortune?' Jack looked startled. 'I swear I never knew of it. I don't think I ever met her. Besides, I wasn't myself out there, Cassie. Everything seemed upside down. I had a terrible feeling that I was going to die. Forgive me, please? After all this…I came to see that I had made a wretched tangle of things…' He touched his temple. 'I am a bit of a mess myself, I'm afraid.'

'Oh, Jack…' Cassie's outrage faded as she saw the uncertainty in his eyes and realised how vulnerable he was. He really had thought she might reject him. 'Oh, my dearest darling…what a fool I am for pinching at you for such nonsense. It is wicked of me. Of course I forgive you. Nothing matters except you. I am so very glad to see you, Jack. So very, very glad you were not killed after all.'

She rushed towards him and was caught up in a bear hug. Tears began to run down her cheeks as she took his face between her two hands and kissed him, over and over again on his cheeks, his lips, his temple, until he began to protest.

'Hey, come on, Cas!'

'I love you, I love you, I love you. And don't you dare to doubt it ever again!'

'No, no, Cassie, don't eat me. You are as bad as that spaniel we once had! Do you remember Roxy?'

'Yes, yes, of course I do,' she cried and slipped her arm through his, glowing up at him as the memories came flooding back. 'She was forever licking one's face. You once said it wasn't worth washing after Roxy had finished licking you because there couldn't possibly be any dirt left—and Nanny Robinson dragged you off to the bath and scrubbed you. You are unkind to liken me to Roxy, Jack.' She gurgled with laughter. 'I should be cross with you, but I am so very, very glad to see you.'

'I am glad to see you,' Jack said. 'Vinnie had to dragoon me into coming, fool that I am. I thought you might disown me.' He glanced over his shoulder. 'Where is he?'

'He must have slipped out,' Cassie said, looking towards the door and frowning. 'How odd—I did not hear him go.'

'Well, if that isn't just like him. Wouldn't you know it!'

Cassie frowned. 'I suppose he thought we would prefer to be on our own for a while. And he was right. I want to hear everything, Jack—and don't leave anything out. I shall know if you do.'

'Yes, you would,' he said, looking rueful. 'It doesn't make very pretty hearing, Cassie.'

'As if I should care for that! I want to know how it happened—and why everyone thought you were dead.'

Jack pulled a wry face. 'Vinnie reported me dead. He saw me fall and thought the shot must be fatal, as it should have been, of course.' He grinned and touched the indentation at his temple. 'Louise says my skull must be made of iron. That ball should have entered my brain, but it merely splintered the bone. I can only think that the shot did not have a full charge of powder. Had it penetrated a fraction further, I would certainly have died.'

'You always were a bonehead,' his sister said, teasing him in her old way. 'So who is Louise—and how was it that Vincent thought you were dead? Did he not stop to make certain?'

'He could not,' Jack said, frowning. 'We were on a mission for Wellington and he carried vital papers that he dared not let fall into enemy hands.' He flushed as he recalled the way Vinnie had found him cowering in the baggage tent. Had his friend not dragged him with him on that mission, he would have been drummed out of the army for cowardice—and perhaps shot as a deserter. There would have been no Louise to save his life then. 'I—I should have been on the field of battle that day, but Vinnie had chosen me to ride as his escort. It was my job to draw enemy fire if we were attacked, while he went on. We rode into an ambush, and I was shot, but he escaped somehow.'

'And he left you to die? How could he?' She frowned and seemed about to condemn Vincent once more.

'No, no, it wasn't like that. Please listen before you jump to conclusions, Cassie. Vinnie did the right thing. Had I been carrying those papers, I must have made the same choice. It wasn't easy for him, but that's the way it is in war. Vinnie had to ride on, he could not do anything else.'

'Yes, I suppose so,' she admitted, slightly reluctant. 'But surely…afterwards?'

'I wondered after I recovered my memory,' Jack said. 'But in my heart I knew Vinnie would not have simply forgotten me. He did go back to where I was shot, Cassie. He searched for me everywhere, but Louise had already found me. She took me to her home, an old château hidden away in a hollow, which is not easy to find unless you know of it. Vinnie told me there were a lot of fresh graves in the woods near where I was shot. The French peasants had been out burying any bodies they found, their own countrymen or English. Vinnie thought I must have been found and buried by someone who did not know who I was. Indeed, had it not been for Louise, I dare say that would have been the case.'

'Yes.' Cassie reached up to stroke his face, as she began to see how it must have been out there in the aftermath of a bloody war. 'I do sort of understand, Jack. I suppose he could not have done anything other than what he did. It seems very hard to me, but in war these things must happen.'

'Be thankful that you did not have to make such choices. Louise faced them more than once.' Jack's expression was grim. 'I believe it cost Vinnie some grief,' he said. 'He blamed himself for taking me with him on that mission, but it was not his fault. He did the right thing at the time. Promise me you will not hold it against him?'

'No, I shall not blame him for something he could not help,' Cassie said, an odd look in her eyes. She knew in her heart he had done the only thing he could when he shot the wounded deer, though it had hurt her deeply. 'But now you must tell me everything else, Jack. Who is Louise— and what is she to you?' A smile touched her lips. 'I think she must be rather special.'

'Yes, she is. Very special,' he replied, the look in his

eyes giving him away. 'I owe my life to her, Cassie—and my sanity. If it were not for her, I should have been buried alive. She saw my finger twitch and made her people carry me home. She nursed me when everyone else said it was hopeless and I should, for pity's sake, be allowed to die.'

'And is she pretty?' Cassie asked, her feelings mixed. Jack had never loved anyone else as much as her, but he did now.

'She has hair like dark honey and greenish eyes,' Jack replied. 'But she isn't pretty like Sarah Walker—I think she's beautiful, but that isn't it either. She has...soul.' He blushed and looked embarrassed, as if ashamed of having spoken so openly of his innermost thoughts.

'Then I am glad you have her,' Cassie said, her feelings of slight jealousy banished by her love for him. If Louise had touched him so deeply, she could only be pleased for his sake. 'Now, tell me the whole of it, dearest.'

Jack's story was long in the telling, for he left no detail out, and Cassie's throat was tight with emotion as she lived through her brother's terrible ordeal. By the time he had finished she knew that she owed a debt of gratitude to the French girl that she would never be able to begin to repay, and she had already begun to love her for her true kindness and generosity of soul.

'So you love her,' Cassie said, smiling as she reached for his hand. 'And she loves you?'

'I cannot see for the life of me why,' Jack said with a self-conscious laugh. 'But it seems she does.' He smiled at his sister. 'Do you know, you and she are very alike. I think I would have loved her had I known her, even if she had not saved my life.'

'I am so glad, my dearest.'

'You will love her, Cassie.'

'I already do, for what she has done.' She looked into his eyes. 'You will be married?' He nodded. 'And you will live in France, of course. Louise could not leave her family or her home. And you will be happier in a new life, more comfortable amongst strangers who accept you as you are and do not pity you.'

'How well you know me,' Jack said and bent to kiss her cheek. 'I shall miss you, of course.'

'As I shall you,' she replied. 'But your life will be with Louise now. You must think of her first. That is only natural.'

'But you will visit us,' Jack said. 'Vinnie will bring you. I am going to sell the family house. With the money from the sale, I can at least make the château comfortable for us all.'

'You will share Aunt Gwendoline's fortune,' Cassie said. 'I want you to have half of it, Jack.'

'Not half,' he said. 'You were always too generous, Cassie. A thousand or two to set me up, if you like—but not half.'

'Half,' she replied, a glint of determination in her eyes. 'Do not argue, Jack. I have already discussed it with Carlton, and besides, I have made up my mind.' She gave him such a glare that he burst into laughter. 'It is not a laughing matter!'

'Miss Stubbornhooves!' Jack cried, grinning at her. 'That donkey was nothing to you, Cassie.'

'Well, yes, in this instance I am prepared to be stubborn,' Cassie replied and laughed. 'Major Saunders told me you used to recount those stories about me round the camp-fire. That was too bad of you, you know.' She reached out to touch his face lovingly. 'You really shouldn't have asked your friends to make that promise. It wasn't fair—to them, or me.'

'I know. I am sorry. Honestly.' He arched his brows at her. 'Forgive me?'

'Perhaps…oh, of course!'

'Well, it turned out for the best, did it not? I always thought you and Vinnie would suit.'

Cassie dropped her gaze. 'I am not sure, Jack. I am not certain I wish to marry Carlton after all…'

Outside the library, Vincent froze with his hand on the door handle. He had been about to enter, having left them together for nearly an hour, and had imagined they would have had time enough to say all they needed to one another. It seemed he had returned too soon—or perhaps too late.

'Not marry him?' Jack cried in astonishment. 'What on earth are you talking about, Cassie? Have you lost your senses? Your wedding is only three days away. You cannot change your mind now. It is impossible. Only think of all the fuss and turmoil it would cause! The gossips would have a field day…'

Vincent walked in before Cassie could answer. She glanced at his face, her heart pounding wildly as she saw the expression on his face. He was so angry! She has never seen him look that way before, his eyes bleak and cold…so cold! But surely it was more than anger…something else she did not understand. Was it pain she saw reflected there? Guilt? Or regret? She could not be certain, but she knew it had struck an answering chord in her.

'The scandal does not matter,' Vincent said quietly. He was looking at her and it was concern for her she saw in his face now. It smote her like a blade in her heart. 'I will not have Cassie forced into something she does not want for the sake of people's tongues. Let them do their worst. I shall naturally accept the blame—'

'Damn you, Vinnie!' Jack jumped to his feet, bewildered and angry himself at this sudden and disturbing turn of events. 'Are you saying you don't want to marry my sister? By God! If you dare to jilt her, I'll give you a bloody nose.'

'You could try, of course,' Vincent replied, a smile on

his mouth. 'I very much doubt you could do it—unless you have been taking lessons, of course.'

'I damned well will!' Jack put his fists up. 'Come on, you scoundrel. I'll give you a run for your money, if no more.'

'Stop this!' Cassie stepped between them, her eyes blazing with temper. 'Stop acting like a pair of fools. You will not fight, either of you. I never heard of such nonsense. I refuse to allow it. If you are not careful you will rouse the house—and I dare say neither of you would care for that.' She saw by their faces that she had struck home. 'You may settle this amicably if you please.'

'If he jilts you, I'll kill him,' Jack muttered. 'I don't know what he has done to make you unhappy, Cassie, but I won't have him disgrace you like this.'

'He has done nothing wrong,' Cassie said. 'Oh, stop looking at Vincent like that, Jack! He is your best friend. Besides, he isn't jilting me. I am just not perfectly certain I want to get married after all. I think I might like to wait a while and think things over.'

'You don't want to do that,' Jack muttered, still glowering at his lifelong friend. 'Get left on the shelf if people think you're contrary. Men don't like that sort of thing.'

'Being a wife is not necessarily the only way for a woman to live.'

'Getting cold feet, Cassie?' Vincent's eyes glittered as he looked at her flushed face. 'Want to cry off, make me look a fool? That would give me my own again, wouldn't it?' He smiled oddly as she hesitated, her expression revealing her uncertainty. 'The only thing is—it makes you look bad. You might find some of your friends would not want to know you when you next go up to town, unless you were thinking of retiring to the country.'

'Oh, you impossible man!' Cassie cried, catching the note of mockery in his voice. 'Can you never be serious?

Pray what is all the fuss about? I merely said I was not
sure I wanted to marry you—and then you offered to jilt
me. I must suppose that I have given you the excuse to cry
off.'

'I've changed my mind,' Vincent countered promptly,
his eyes challenging her. 'You shall be the one to decide,
Cassie. I'll give you until the evening of the dance to make
up your mind, whether you wish to be my wife or not.'

'That's not fair,' she said, flushing angrily as he turned
to leave. 'Where do you think you are going, sir? You just
cannot walk out. We have too much to discuss.'

'I shall be at Carlton House,' Vincent replied. 'You can
send word if you want me to return.'

'You cannot do that!' Cassie cried, distressed and confused by her own emotions. 'Vincent! You surely cannot
mean it?'

'Give me one good reason why I may not?' His brows
rose, his eyes daring her to answer him.

'Because…because I refuse to jilt you,' Cassie said, her
face pale. 'I cannot be the cause of so much pain to Lady
Longbourne. It is not fair of you to make me do it, Vinnie.
You must see that it would be quite impossible.'

'Why?'

Cassie shook her head, face flushed as she wrestled with
pride and common sense. 'You are putting me in an awkward position. I must appear foolish or contrary. What will
everyone think of me?'

'That you are very wise to have cried off before it was
too late?' He looked at her hard.

'No, of course they will not. Why should they? Anyone
who knows you would think I had gone mad.' Cassie said,
turning to her brother for assistance. 'Tell him, Jack!'

'You have to marry her, or jilt her. Vinnie, you know
you must do one or the other. You cannot possibly make
Cassie jilt you. No, no, you must see it!'

'I do not see why,' replied Vinnie, a flicker of amusement in his eyes. 'Cassie is the one who changed her mind. I am still perfectly willing to go ahead with the wedding. Indeed, I consider myself the injured party. If I were a vengeful man, which I am not, of course, I should go to court and sue for breach of promise.' He turned his intent, wicked gaze on her. 'So—what is it to be, Cassie? Will you marry me or not?'

'Oh, you…you awful man!' she cried, her eyes sparkling with suppressed fury. 'I dislike you very much. I should be out of my mind to marry you, but I cannot see what else to do as you are so very disobliging. Very well! You win, though by methods I cannot think anything but disreputable. I shall marry you, sir—but only because it would cause so much fuss if I didn't. Besides giving grief to Lady Longbourne, of whom I *am* fond.'

'That's told me, hasn't it, Cassie?' Vincent was unrepentant. 'A matter of honour, then?' His mouth quivered at the corners, and it was obvious that he was enjoying himself. 'I would have this quite clear if you please, my love. You are consenting to be my wife, because you do not want to let everyone down?'

'No—yes!' Cassie glared at him. 'If it were not for the harm it would cause to people I care for, I would jilt you this instant. You are an impossible man and—and I do not like you. At this particular moment, I detest you!'

'But you will marry me?'

'Yes, I shall marry you,' Cassie said, giving him a look that would have felled any other man. 'If only to make your life utterly unbearable. And do not think I cannot do it, because I assure you I can—and will!'

With that, she gave a choking cry of despair and ran from the room, leaving her brother and Vincent to stare after her.

Jack was silent for a moment, then he looked at Vinnie.

'What do you make of that? Damned if I've ever known her to be quite so contrary. Not sure why…'

'I seem to remember telling you earlier that your sister was both headstrong and stubborn.' Vincent's eyes gleamed. 'Perhaps you had forgotten?'

'Yes, I remember,' Jack said mournfully. 'Dash it, I know it all too well! You wouldn't think she had such a temper, would you—not in the general way. She is usually the sweetest creature, but if she gets a bee in her bonnet it is best to steer clear for a while. Regroup and come about another day, that's my best advice. You would do well to heed it.'

'Do you think so?' Vincent smiled to himself. 'I find it all rather interesting.'

'That's because you do not know how far she can go to get her own way. You'll come off worst, old friend. I'm warning you—Cassie will get her way in the end.'

'No, do you say so?'

'Women always do,' Jack said ruefully. 'You should have heard the language Louise used to get me off my back and stop me feeling so damned sorry for myself—and *she* is a milk-and-water miss compared to my sister. You have no idea what you are taking on, Vinnie.'

'Oh, I think perhaps I do. Cassie is capable of many things,' replied Vincent a hint of satisfaction in his eyes. 'I have always believed temper and passion go together.'

Jack's gaze narrowed. 'Damn it, Vinnie! You had no intention of jilting her—or of letting her jilt you, had you?'

'No, of course not.' Vincent chuckled. 'I merely gave her her head, to see what came off it.'

A long, low whistle escaped Jack. 'Well, blow me down! You *are* in love with her, aren't you?'

'Desperately,' Vincent admitted. 'Until a few minutes ago, I believed the passion was all on one side, that she wished only for a comfortable marriage. But do you know,

Jack, I think…I really think that she might just care for me a little.'

'She is in love with you, of course!' Jack said. 'That's why she was so cross.'

'Yes…' Vincent nodded, a smile in his eyes. 'But do you think she is prepared to admit it?'

Chapter Eleven

Alone in her bedchamber, Cassie threw a few cushions around before tearing off her clothes and depositing them on the floor. She then pulled back the covers, fell into bed and burst into a flood of frustrated tears, ending at last with her face buried in the pillows. Her heart was aching and she felt both exhausted and miserable.

What was she to do? Carlton had turned the tables on her and she was caught in a trap largely of her own making.

Oh, that wretched, wretched man to make her so un-happy! She disliked him very much. Indeed, she wished she had never set eyes on him. It would be the greatest pleasure to her to tear him limb from limb. She pounded at the pillow, which had become unaccountably wet and lumpy, then turned onto her back. For some minutes, she lay staring at the ceiling.

'Oh, bother,' she said and sighed. 'Why should I care? He is a complete shamster, a liar and a cheat and I shall make him pay for this. Oh, he will be sorry! To deceive me so—and then refuse to do the decent thing and jilt me!'

If there was a tiny bud of satisfaction deep within her that he had refused to jilt her, Cassie was not yet ready to allow it room to grow. Her feelings had been badly bruised by what she had heard as she eavesdropped outside the library door—which only went to show that Janet was right when she said listeners never heard good of themselves! And it just served her right for not going into the library at once.

Cassie reached for her kerchief and blew her nose. She was not exactly sure of how she felt about anything at this precise moment. She had been very close to telling Carlton she would not marry him, but at the last moment something had stopped her. And in her heart, she knew it was because she loved him.

'You are a complete idiot,' she scolded herself severely. 'If you love him and he does not love you, you will be miserable. You had much better run away now, tonight!' But she did not want to, of course.

She knew that she would not be able to bear it if, after she had conceived the child she knew would be expected of her, her husband left her to return to his mistress.

But she would be desperately unhappy without him.

Cassie realised she was caught in a trap. Whichever way she turned, she could not escape the feelings inside her. Besides, she had for the second time that evening promised to marry Carlton.

Why had he been so ungallant as to insist she must jilt him? Cassie could not be sure. If he had wanted to change his mind about marrying her, it would have been easy for him to insist that he did the honourable thing and stood aside. But like the wretch he was, he had turned it all back on her—even saying that he might sue for breach of promise!

And now she had a throbbing headache.

'Bother, bother, bother!' Cassie said, and put her head under the bedclothes. 'I am sure I do not care what you do, my Lord Carlton. You are quite odious, and I want nothing to do with you!'

*   *   *

Despite her fears that she would not sleep a wink, Cassie was awakened from her uneasy dreams by a young maid pulling the curtains back. She sat up, yawned and blinked in the bright sunlight pouring in at the window.

'What time is it?'

'Past eleven, Miss Thornton. We were given orders that you were to be allowed to sleep in a little this morning.'

'Oh…thank you. I was tired.' Cassie wondered who had given the order, but did not ask. 'Where is Janet?'

'She was feeling a bit under the weather, miss, so she stayed in her room this morning. She thinks she may have taken a summer cold, and was afraid of passing it on to you. What with the wedding so soon and all. It would be shocking if you were to take it, miss.'

'Janet ill?' Cassie was suddenly wide awake. 'I must go to her as soon as I am dressed. She is rarely ill. She must feel dreadful if she has kept to her bed.'

'It's just a cold, miss. Best you stay away from her for a day or so. You do not want to catch a cold before the wedding.'

'Nonsense! I shall visit her as soon as I am dressed. I would not dream of doing otherwise.'

Nothing would do for Cassie but that she must make sure Janet was not in danger of neglect. However, she soon discovered that it was only a chill. Her maid had stayed away from her for safety's sake, and was sitting up in a chair nursing a hot drink.

Cassie kissed her, despite Janet begging her not to, and promised that she would make sure she was supplied with lemons, brandy, hot water and sugar until she was feeling better.

'For I know that is what you would prescribe for me, dearest—and you must take care of yourself. I could not go away without you to look after me, so you must be better in time for my wedding.'

'Now don't you go troubling your head over me,' Janet scolded. 'You will have lots to do, and I can manage very well.' She sneezed into her handkerchief. 'There, you would not be told! Now you will catch it and the wedding will have to be postponed.'

'I never catch colds,' replied Cassie blithely. 'If you are sure you have everything you want, I shall go downstairs now. I really must walk down to the vicarage and see about those vases.'

'You should sit quietly with a book,' Janet advised, frowning at her. 'But I suppose you will not be told. So if you must go to the village, take Lady Longbourne's carriage. If there are poachers about, you should not walk in the woods.'

A flicker of pain showed in Cassie's eyes as she recalled the incident of the previous day. She could not bear that a creature should be hurt in that way, though she knew deer must be culled sometimes, but poaching was barbaric.

'Yes, perhaps I shall take the carriage,' she said. 'Do not worry about me, Janet. I shall be quite safe. That particular poacher will not dare to return.'

She was thoughtful as she walked down the stairs. She had been too upset after the incident to really think about what must have happened after she was knocked unconscious. Vincent had shot the fawn—had he shot the poacher, too? Oh, dear! She did hope not, though she also hoped he had been punished for his crime. She rather wondered from something Jack had mentioned the previous evening whether Vincent might have knocked him down, since it would appear that he was quite handy with his fists.

She was thoughtful as she reached the bottom of the stairs. hearing voices in the front parlour, she was about to turn away when Lady Longbourne came out to her.

'Ah, Cassie, my love, how are you this morning?'

'I am much better,' Cassie replied. 'Quite well—except for this horrid bruise, which looks so unsightly.'

'Well, I dare say we shall manage to cover it for the wedding—if we pull a little of your hair lower.' Lady Longbourne looked at her, seeming oddly uneasy. 'Now, my dear, there is someone waiting to see you. I believe you were expecting Major Saunders to call? Some idea of his giving you away, I think?'

'Oh, yes, I was,' said Cassie, remembering that he had been kind enough to offer his services. 'Yes, I must certainly speak with him.'

She went straight into the parlour. Major Saunders had been perched uncomfortably on the edge of his chair, but he sprang to his feet as she entered, coming at once to greet her.

'Miss Thornton,' he said, obviously very concerned. 'Lady Longbourne has been telling me that you met with an accident yesterday. Are you well enough to come down? I wondered if you might decide to postpone the wedding?' He could not quite conceal his eagerness. 'Just for a while, you know…'

'No, I shall not need to do that,' Cassie said, her cheeks slightly flushed. His admiration for her was quite obvious and she wondered if she had been wise to accept his offer to stand up with her. 'How very shocking that would be of me, to upset all dear Lady Longbourne's arrangements for the sake of a little bump on the head.'

'Far more than that from what I have been told,' he said, looking at her with undisguised approval. 'You were quite a heroine, it seems—though perhaps impetuous.'

'To no avail, I fear,' Cassie said on a sigh. 'Carlton was forced to put the creature out of his misery. All I did was cause a lot of fuss and distress for everyone.'

'You are too hard on yourself.'

'No, I do not think so,' Cassie replied seriously. 'It is

time I ceased to rush in without thinking. I am no longer a child to be playing foolish tricks. I should have waited for Carlton to act.'

'I think you were brave,' said Major Saunders. 'I like you very well as you are, Miss Thornton. You were not in any way at fault in my estimation.'

She felt that he was implying some criticism of Lord Carlton, but could not imagine what. 'Thank you, sir.' She blushed. 'You are too generous.'

'I only wish I might always be of service—there to champion your cause with my support.'

She wished he would not look at her quite so intently. He was a companionable man and she liked him well enough, but there could never be more than friendship between them. Surely he must know that? He could not think that she had a preference for him?

'It was good of you to call,' Cassie said, getting up and walking over to the window to cover her blushes. 'I was so very grateful for your offer to give me away, but I regret I must now refuse. You see…I shall ask Jack to do so. He will naturally expect it—'

'Jack?' Major Saunders rose and came over to the window to stand beside her. She glanced at him and saw he looked thunderstruck. 'What are you saying? Jack alive? Impossible! Carlton told me himself. He was certain he was dead.'

'It seems I made a mistake,' Vincent's voice drawled from the doorway, causing both Cassie and Major to swing round sharply. Vincent smiled his lazy smile. 'Good to see you, Saunders. I'm glad you could come down for the wedding.'

He crossed the floor to shake hands with the visitor. Cassie moved away and sat down on the sofa.

'Carlton…' Major Saunders shook hands, but was still shocked, still frowning over the startling news. 'Asked for you earlier, of course, but they said you were out. I had hoped to give Miss Thornton away, but…' He shook his head. 'This is wonderful news, of course. Hard to credit— but wonderful.'

'Yes, it is.' Cassie smiled, her happiness shining out of her. 'I could hardly believe it at first, but we have talked. Where is Jack at the moment, Vincent?'

'We rode over to see Kendal together,' he replied. 'I am afraid it was quite a shock for Mr Thornton. He was embarrassed and wanted to move out at once, but Jack wouldn't hear of it, of course. He has arranged to stay there until the wedding, and I think they may come to some arrangement between them as to the purchase of the property. However, both Mr Thornton and Jack will be dining with us this evening.' He raised his brows as he looked at the Major. 'I know you were invited to the dance, but perhaps you would care to dine beforehand?'

'What? Oh, yes, delighted. Thank you.' He looked at Cassie, still seeming stunned by the news. 'Well, I am disappointed you will not be needing my services, Miss Thornton, but very pleased for you, of course. It is excellent news, excellent.'

'Yes, I think so.'

'Well, I shall not keep you. I am sure you have a great deal to do.'

'Yes, I am afraid we do,' Cassie agreed. 'I have to see Mrs Walker about some vases…'

After the Major had taken his departure there was silence for a moment, then, as she turned to leave, Vincent laid a hand on her arm, his eyes seeking hers.

'You will take the carriage, Cassie? Please, as a favour to me. I do not believe there is any danger now—but just to be certain?'

Cassie bit her lip, then lifted her head to meet his dark gaze. She flushed, still feeling bruised from the previous night. 'Yes, I shall take the carriage, thank you—but only because Janet had already made me promise her I would.'

Vincent nodded, his face grave. He knew at once that she was still angry with him and felt it best not to push it further at that moment. Cassie was both stubborn and proud, and if they were to come to an understanding, he would need to be patient.

Cassie blinked hard as she went out, finding that she did not like to be at odds with him and missing their old, comfortable companionship. How very foolish she was!

She knew she had been unnecessarily rude and wished her retort unmade. Yet she was irritated by the restrictions laid on her. She had always enjoyed the freedom to walk alone. But of course she had never expected to come across a poacher in broad daylight!

Had she known it, poor Harry had already been taken to task over the incident by an angry Lord Carlton.

'If your gamekeeper had been doing his job properly, it could not have happened!'

'I never dreamed…' Harry was seriously disturbed. 'I hadn't bothered to employ a keeper, because I was not in residence, but now I see I must do so in the future. It could have been…' He hesitated and coloured. 'I mean, it might have been worse if you had not been there.'

'No, be honest, Harry! You meant it might have been Miss Walker, did you not?' Vincent raised his brows as his brother flushed guiltily. 'I do not imagine that she would have reacted to a poacher in quite the same way as Cassie. But if you want your woods to be safe for your future wife and family, you must take the proper steps to safeguard them. It is the price you have to pay for the privilege of your position.'

'Yes, I take your point.' Harry frowned. 'Vinnie, do you think Mama…I mean, would you have a word? About Sarah? See how she feels about the idea?'

'You should properly speak to Mama yourself,' Vincent replied. 'But I shall of course back you up if she cuts up rough over it. Miss Walker seems a very pleasant girl to me—and she is Cassie's best friend, which makes things comfortable for the family. I see no reason why you should not marry her if it is your wish. I'll settle a few thousand on her so you need not fear the expense of a wife.'

Harry's ears went purple. 'Good of you, Vinnie. I didn't expect it—or want it, come to that. But it might help persuade Mama that I do not need to look for an heiress.'

'Consider it done.'

Cassie was not there to hear their discussion, of course. She was not aware of many things going on behind the scenes, and so her doubts continued to plague her as she was driven to the village in Lady Longbourne's comfortable carriage.

On her return home, Cassie went straight up to her room. She discovered a small package on her dressing table and opened the attached card.

'To my future wife. Love, Vinnie.'

Cassie opened the box and discovered a tiny silver statue of a deer and its fawn lying together. She gasped with pleasure as she picked it up and saw how beautifully it was fashioned and marked.

In the bottom of the box was another card, its message brief.

'Forgive me. You were and are more precious.'

Cassie's eyes stung with tears. How thoughtful Carlton was to give her this. She would treasure it more than all the Carlton jewels—just as she did the ring and pendant she was sure had been made specially for her.

Jack must have told him she liked daises, of course. He must have commissioned them long before he had asked her to marry him. She wondered why he had waited so long if it were merely a matter of honouring his promise to her brother.

Lady Longbourne was secretly shocked by Sir Jack Thornton's appearance, but she was of course too polite to let anyone see her feelings. She presided over the dinner table that evening, her curious eyes noting certain changes in the people gathered there.

Vincent seemed in a better humour than of late. He and Jack had slipped into their old, comfortable companionship and spent most of the evening insulting one another. It was very odd, but she had frequently noticed that gentlemen who were the best of friends saw this sort of behaviour as the greatest fun.

She could not herself see what was so amusing about calling one's friend a great oaf or a mad-hammer, out and outer over the fences. But it caused a great deal of hilarity from the two friends, and Cassie seemed to approve of their banter.

There was something different about Cassie that evening. Lady Longbourne could not quite put her finger on it, but the girl seemed quieter somehow. She laughed, but her eyes were thoughtful and her manner oddly shy when she looked at her fiancé.

Perhaps that was not so very surprising, thought Lady Longbourne, wondering if she ought perhaps to have a quiet word with Cassie about the intimate side of marriage. She did after all stand in place of a mother to her, and although she was certain Carlton would be gentle with his wife on their wedding night, it was always best to be prepared. If Cassie were nervous, it might help her to set her mind at rest.

Her thoughtful gaze travelled down the table to Major Saunders, and then she frowned. If ever she had seen a man in love struggling against his feelings, it was him. He did try, but somehow could not keep his gaze from straying to Cassie again and again, and his eyes betrayed him.

He looked extremely agitated, as though he found the situation intolerable, as of course he must in the circumstances. She did hope he was not going to do anything foolish!

Lady Longbourne was well aware that Cassie had found the Major attractive when they first met, and she could not help the prickle of alarm that started at the nape of her neck and trickled down her spine. She would not be surprised if some trouble came of this before the night was out. Lady Longbourne was quite aware that her elder son was possessed of a violent temper when roused, though he had never treated her to a display of it—at least, not since he was a small boy and had defied his father over some trivial matter. For which he had been soundly thrashed, despite all her pleas in private to her husband.

She dreaded to imagine what Carlton would do if Major Saunders attempted to seduce Cassie, and by the growing desperation in his eyes she knew it was a definite possibility.

She would have to keep a very strict eye on things that evening! If at all possible, she would make sure that the Major never had a chance to be alone with the object of his infatuation!

Cassie met Lady Longbourne's eyes down the table and smiled. She was too caught up in her own private thoughts to have noticed the burning glances directed her way by the love-sick Major Saunders. Her wedding day was approaching very fast, and she had begun to think more and more of the moment when Vincent would come to her as a husband.

She was, despite Lady Longbourne's fears, perfectly aware of the things every young girl should know at such a moment, and her nervousness was not because of what would happen. The kiss Vincent had given her before they left London had made Cassie realise how much pleasure she could know in his arms, and she was torn between her longing and her pride.

It was too bad of Carlton to have made a promise to her brother—and then to have drawn straws! What would he have done if he had lost? Or perhaps he had! Wasn't it usual for the loser to draw the short straw? Oh, it was too bad of him! What was she? A wooden spoon or a consolation prize?

A sudden thought occurred to Cassie. Had Major Saunders been one of the officers who had drawn these infamous straws? She glanced down the table and smiled at him, making up her mind to ask him if she got the chance to speak to him alone that evening.

It could not make any difference, of course. The wedding must go ahead, but at least she would know what had happened.

After dinner was over, the guests drifted into the long gallery. The room had been cleared of furniture, the carpets rolled back for dancing. A group of musicians was already beginning to play rather romantic background music.

Some twelve persons had sat down for dinner, and another twenty had been invited for the dancing and supper. It was more than the gallery could comfortably hold. But card tables had been set up in a salon adjoining the temporary ballroom and no doubt some of the older guests would find their way there before too long.

'I shall join Felicity at the tables for a rubber or two,' Sir Septimus informed Cassie. 'But you will save at least one dance for me, I hope, m'dear?'

'Yes, of course, sir,' Cassie said and handed him her card.

It was Cassie's special night. She looked radiant in a

gown of pale green, the hem embroidered heavily with silver daisies, and she was wearing the daisy pendant and of course her engagement ring, having spurned the more expensive diamonds which were a part of the Carlton heritage. Her simple gown, together with her natural air of modesty, was much remarked upon, and more than one gentleman congratulated Carlton on his choice of a bride that evening.

She and Vincent opened the dancing together. They were alone on the floor for a minute or two, their guests clapping their approval before joining in.

'Thank you for your gift,' Cassie said, gazing shyly up at him. 'It is beautiful, and I shall always treasure it.'

'You are beautiful,' he replied, bringing a flush to her cheeks. 'I am very proud of you this evening, Cassie—but will you forgive me?'

'For acting as you did over the injured fawn?' Cassie nodded, not daring to look up at him. 'I believe you had no choice. The poor little thing was in pain. It would have been cruel to let it suffer, I see that now. Had I not been so foolish as to rush in the way I did, you might have driven off the poacher and had the leisure to see what could be done. I am as much at fault in this as you—perhaps more so.'

'Thank you. You are generous.' Vincent frowned. 'I can promise you that you will never be at risk of such an occurrence in my woods. I have keepers whose main function is to make sure they are safe.'

'Then you will not mind if I walk there alone sometimes?' Cassie felt relieved. 'You will not expect me to stay always within the formal gardens?'

'That is your choice, though I hope you will allow me to accompany you on your walks sometimes?'

'Yes, of course.' Cassie blushed and dropped her gaze.

'Have you forgiven me for other things?' Vincent asked. 'Or is what I did unforgivable?'

She raised her head to look at him with wide, serious eyes. 'I am not sure. I am hopeful that I may find understanding when I have thought more on your reasons. When we have the leisure, perhaps we could discuss them?'

'You are very right, Cassie. This is not the moment for what I must say to you.' He smiled down at her as the music ended. 'Let us agree simply to be friends for the moment—if you can bear that?'

'Yes, of course,' she replied, giving him a look that was more powerful than she could ever have guessed. 'I think we have always been that, at least. Even when I made you climb the tree twice to rescue me.'

Vincent chuckled, his laughter warm and husky. He led her back to the side of the floor where Jack was waiting to claim her for his dance. He himself was engaged to dance with Sarah, and after that his aunt Felicity and his mama. There were also Sarah's sisters and her mother. Sighing inwardly, he prepared to do his duty as the host.

Cassie was enjoying herself very much. She had danced several times with Jack, twice with Harry, twice with Sir Septimus, who had surprised her by his agility, once with Major Saunders and a second time with Vincent. It was now almost time for her to dance with the Major again, but before that she wanted to go upstairs and freshen herself.

She took a few minutes to tidy her hair and gown, and was about to leave when Sarah came into the bedroom. Her face was alive with excitement, her eyes glowing. Cassie guessed her news before she began to speak.

'Harry has proposed!'

'A few minutes ago,' said Sarah, twirling round in a surge of happiness. 'He is speaking to Papa now, but I am sure—I know he will agree!'

'I am so happy for you, dearest,' Cassie said as the two girls embraced. 'Has Lady Longbourne been told?'

'Harry says Lord Carlton prepared her and she was not surprised. It seems she would prefer him to be happy than to marry simply for money.'

'Then everything will be comfortable for you,' Cassie said and embraced her again. 'We shall be sisters, and you must persuade Harry to bring you to visit us often. I am not sure, but I think we may ask Lady Longbourne to make her home with us, but of course she will divide her time between us. I do not think she should be allowed to live by herself again—do you?'

'Oh, no,' Sarah agreed. 'There is no need for it. She is so good at arranging things and telling one who one ought to invite and what one ought to wear. I do not know how I should manage to entertain all Harry's friends and relatives without her.'

Cassie nodded her approval. She had not yet spoken to Vincent about her plans for his mother to have her own rooms permanently in all of their homes, but she would find the right moment—after they were married—and hoped to persuade him of its convenience.

She left Sarah to refresh herself, knowing that the next dance must have already started. Major Saunders would be thinking that she had abandoned him!

However, when she reached the hallway leading to the ballroom, it was to find Major Saunders sitting on a hard-seated chair. He sprang to his feet at once and came towards her, his manner so urgent that Cassie was startled.

'I am sorry to keep you waiting, sir,' she apologised. 'I meant to be only a minute or two, but was delayed.'

'The dance is not important,' he replied, his face flushed with colour. 'Please, Miss Thornton, may I beg your indulgence? Just a few moments of your time to speak privately with you?'

Cassie hesitated, some instinct warning her against this private tête-à-tête. 'What can you have to say that needs to be said in private, sir? I do not think that—'

'Something of great importance,' he replied. 'Please, I beg you, give me a hearing. Will you not step across the hall into the green parlour? I give you my word as a gentleman that you will be quite safe.'

He seemed so very agitated. Cassie allowed herself to be persuaded against her better judgement. She nodded and turned towards the parlour, feeling slightly apprehensive.

'Well,' she said, turning to face him after he had followed her inside. 'What can be so important, Major Saunders?'

'I could not allow you to marry Lord Carlton without being sure you understood the situation…'

'I beg your pardon?' Cassie stared at him in surprise. 'You could not allow… Forgive me, but I fail to see of what concern my actions are to you, sir?'

'Forgive me! I was too abrupt.' His agitation grew visibly and he took a hesitant step towards her, his face going from red to white and back again as if he were suffering some extreme emotion. 'You think me impertinent, as perhaps I am, but I shall risk your displeasure for the sake of your future happiness. No, no, do not look at me so! I beg you to listen for your own sake.'

'Very well, sir. Since you think it is so important, you may speak.' Cassie's heart was pounding frantically. What on earth had he to say to her?

'I must tell you first that I am devoted to your service, Miss Thornton. If you wished to—to leave this house, I would escort you safely wherever you wished to go. And to guard your honour with my life.'

His dramatic statement made her frown. 'I am indebted to you, sir, but why should I wish to leave? I am about to be married—'

'To a man who does not love you,' said Major Saunders. 'He asked you to marry him only because of a promise to Jack. There were five of us that night around the fire. Jack made us all promise. Carlton drew the short straw...' He looked at her as if this news must make her turn pale or faint. 'I am sorry to tell you this...but I felt you should know before it is too late.'

Cassie stared at him, her expression giving nothing away. 'Why are you telling me this, sir? If you also drew a straw...you were equally at fault. And it was ridiculous, of course. Five grown men drawing straws to determine who had the dubious honour of asking a woman none of them really knew to marry him. I must tell you, I can think of nothing more foolish.'

'No, no, you much mistake the matter,' Major Saunders cried, his eyes flashing fire. 'For me it would have been a prize beyond anything. I was even then halfway in love with you. And when we met, I knew what I had lost...what Carlton had cheated me of!'

'Cheated you?' She was bewildered. 'What can you mean, sir? I do not know how you could have been cheated.'

'Carlton presented the straws, but they were all of the same length. I saw him break his own behind his back, so that he made sure of winning. He was determined to be the one to ask you first.'

'I see...' Her face gave nothing away of the turmoil inside her. 'Thank you for telling me this, Major Saunders. I am much indebted to you for your concern. However, it changes nothing. You see, I already knew about the straws, and that foolish promise.'

His face registered shock and disappointment. 'You already knew? Did someone tell you?'

'I heard the story from Carlton's own lips,' Cassie said. She lifted her head, looking at him proudly. 'Both he and

Jack have confessed their parts in this foolishness, and we have laughed over it together. It was all nonsense, of course. And completely unnecessary. Carlton and I have had a private understanding for years. I thought everyone knew that. It was mere liking and friendship when we were children, of course. But it has blossomed into—'

She was allowed to go no further. Major Saunders gave a cry of despair, then grabbed at her in what was clearly a frenzy of disappointment and blighted love.

'No! No, do not say it,' he cried desperately. 'I cannot bear to see you so deceived. He has a mistress still. I dare say you do not know her, but everyone thought he would marry her. Do not waste yourself on this loveless match. Please listen to me, Miss Thornton. Come away with me now. I beg you…'

Cassie averted her face, giving a cry of distress as he tried to kiss her. She pushed against his shoulders with both hands in an effort to hold him off.

'Please, sir,' she cried. 'I must ask you not to do this. Let me go this instant!'

'Take your hands off her, Saunders, or by heaven I'll kill you!'

Vincent was suddenly there in the room with them, but this was not the polite, smiling gentleman Cassie had come to know and love. He was so angry, so violent! Old Carter, one-time landlord of the Hare and Hounds, might have recognised this grim-faced avenger, as might a certain poacher who had not yet stopped running for his life—but Cassie did not know him. As Major Saunders hastily let her go, she gasped and stepped back, watching with wide, scared eyes.

'You damned scoundrel!' Vincent yelled and hit out furiously.

One punch was enough to send his victim to the floor, but not in this case enough to knock him senseless. He lay on the floor, shaking his head and staring up at Vincent with every appearance of being every bit as angry himself.

'You will meet me for this, Carlton!'

'With pleasure,' Vincent replied. 'Name your seconds, sir.'

'No!' Cassie cried, her heart leaping with fright. They must not fight! Something might happen to Carlton, and she really could not bear that. 'Please do not fight over this. It does not matter. I am not hurt. Major Saunders merely forgot his manners for a moment.'

'Be quiet, Cassie,' Vincent said in a harsh voice she had never heard before. 'This is a matter of honour. It will be settled between gentlemen in the proper manner.'

'I say, what's going on?' Jack asked, coming into the room. He watched as Major Saunders rose somewhat unsteadily to his feet and rubbed his chin. 'Vinnie? Did you knock George down? What for?' His eyes narrowed suspiciously as he saw Cassie's flushed face and sensed her distress. 'Did he offer you some insult, Cassie?' Her uncomfortable silence was enough to answer him. He fired up at once. 'By God, sir! You will answer to me for this, Saunders. Name your weapons—pistols or swords.'

'Hold your heels!' Vincent growled. 'I am before you here. Cassie is engaged to me. I shall teach this bounder a lesson.'

'She's my sister, damn it!' Jack muttered angrily. 'You aren't married to her yet. You can take your place in line. I want first go at him.'

'She is my fiancée. And my wife the day after tomorrow.' Vincent glared at him. 'If I do not manage to kill him—if he should kill me—you can finish it for me.'

'Why do you not draw straws for the privilege?'

Cassie's sarcastic tones stopped them mid-argument. They both turned to look at her in surprise.

'You may as well. Why not, you have done it before, I

dare say?' she said, her eyes flashing with temper. 'It is all of a piece, I am sure. I have never heard such nonsense. You will neither of you fight a duel over something which is nothing but foolishness. I will not have either of you risking death or injury before my wedding.'

Or there might not be a wedding!

'Cassie...' Jack said warily, seeing the jut of her chin. 'You don't understand. A challenge has been issued. It has to be answered for the sake of honour.'

'I do not see why. You can all apologise to each other, shake hands and forget it,' Cassie said. Oh, how foolish they all were! Could Carlton not see that she was terrified of something happening to him? 'Major Saunders can apologise to me, and then he can take himself off and put an end to this. He has been very foolish, but I am prepared to forget the incident. And I might forgive both of you—if you are sensible.'

Jack looked at his best friend's face. Cassie had thrown down the gauntlet in no uncertain manner, but it was not wise to challenge Carlton in such a public way.

'Cassie, I think you ought to be a little careful—' he began but got no further.

'I shall not be dictated to in this manner,' Vincent said coldly, his face stiff with pride. 'You are my fiancée and—'

'I shall not forgive you if you do this,' Cassie cried, her face pale but determined. 'If you persist in this foolishness, Carlton, I shall never, never be your true wife!'

She would threaten anything to stop this happening. It must not happen, because she could not bear the thought of losing him. Until this moment, she had not really understood the depth of her feeling for him—the agony she would feel if she lost him.

Cassie had never believed anyone could mean as much to her as her brother, but Vincent did. Without her truly realising it, he had become a part of her, so much so that she could not bear the thought of life without him. And she would do anything, even run the risk of losing his affection, rather than see him badly wounded or dead.

'Cassie, my love! Not be Carlton's wife?' cried Lady Longbourne, stumbling in mid-scene and misunderstanding what was going on. 'You mean to call the wedding off? Oh, no, my love, do not say so!' For a moment she looked bewildered, then her accusing eyes turned vengefully on Major Saunders. 'This is all your fault, sir. Oh, you wicked creature! How dare you try to seduce Cassie away from us? Viper! I know your motives. I know you covet her fortune, besides being head over heels in love with her, I dare say.' Her eyes filled with tears. 'Oh, Cassie, you cannot leave us. I do not know how I should go on without you. Please, Cassie, if you love me, you must not run away with this awful man.'

'I am not going anywhere with anyone,' Cassie said. 'Indeed, I think I would be far better off staying here with you, Mama. I doubt it is ever worth a woman marrying anyone.'

'But, Cassie dearest, you must marry Carlton. Everyone will be so shocked if you do not.'

'Really, Mama,' Vincent said looking exasperated. 'I think Cassie and I can sort this out between us—'

'But she said she would not marry you…she will never forgive you for…well, I am not perfectly sure why, but you must have done something to upset her if she will not marry you.'

'I did not say I would not marry him,' Cassie said. 'Just that I shall never forgive him if he kills Major Saunders all over a silly misunderstanding.'

'Kill…!' Lady Longbourne gave a shriek of despair. 'You *are* in love with that viper!'

'No, of course I am not. I have never thought of the Major as anything but an amusing friend of Jack's,' replied

Cassie. 'But I will not stand by and let Carlton murder him. I am, of course, perfectly prepared to marry Vincent—but if he persists in this wretched duel—'

'*A duel?*' Lady Longbourne gave a yelp and clutched at her son's arm. 'Carlton, I feel most unwell. Forgive me, I am afraid I am going to faint…'

'Mama?' Vincent looked at her frowningly. 'Do not be foolish. This is not the time, Mama…Mama? Mama!' He was shocked into action as she began to crumple before his eyes. 'Mama dearest. Forgive me. Please do not faint!'

Lady Longbourne was not a sylph. It took both Vincent and Jack to carry her to the sofa, where she lay limply until Cassie waved her vinaigrette under her nose. She moaned a little, opened her eyes and promptly burst into noisy tears.

'Do not leave me, Cassie,' she wept. 'I cannot bear it. You have become more dear to me than my own. If you go away, I shall simply have nothing left to live for…'

It was barefaced blackmail and they all knew it, but how could Cassie resist such an appeal? She bent over her soon-to-be mother-in-law, patting her hand comfortably.

'Do not upset yourself, dearest. This is all Carlton's fault. I am sure he will on reflection see the error of his ways, and this can all be brought to a satisfactory conclusion.'

Lady Longbourne's eyes flicked on her son, giving him a warning he would be wise to heed. 'Go away, Carlton. If you care for me at all, you will do the right thing.'

Vincent knew when he was being offered a way of escape and silently blessed his rather clever mother. 'As you wish, Mama.' He glanced at the other gentlemen. 'Perhaps we should retire to the library and discuss the matter further?'

Lady Longbourne clung relentlessly to Cassie's hand as she made a movement to go after them. 'No, no, you must stay with me. They will resolve their differences, my dear, as gentlemen do, in their own rather peculiar way.'

Cassie's eyes sought and held Vincent's. 'I meant what I said. I shall not easily forgive you if you fight a stupid duel over this.' Surely he must know what she was really saying to him, with her heart?

Do not risk your life...I cannot bear it.

Vincent inclined his head, but said nothing as he went out. But she noticed an ominous glitter in his eyes as he glanced in her direction once more before closing the door behind them.

'Have they gone?' Lady Longbourne asked faintly, holding her lavender-scented kerchief to her lips.

'Yes.' Cassie looked at her in concern. 'Do you feel very ill? Shall I send for the doctor?'

'Fiddlesticks to the doctor!' said Lady Longbourne, sitting up with a sudden display of energy. 'I never felt better in my life. But you know, my love, you should not have issued an ultimatum to Carlton like that, not in front of the other gentlemen. It is always a mistake. He could not back down, his pride would not allow it. They would have thought he was petticoat-led!'

'But I do not want either Carlton or Jack to fight. Nor do I particularly wish Major Saunders to be killed. He did startle me with his declaration, but only for a moment. If he had not come in, I could have settled it myself. I was never in the least danger. I am very cross with Vincent for making all this fuss.'

'But you do wish to marry Carlton, don't you?' Lady Longbourne looked at her in bewilderment. Cassie nodded, her cheeks flushing. 'Then I am not sure what can be done. They will fight, you know. There is no possibility of Carlton backing down from a challenge.'

'Oh, no! I must stop them...' Cassie looked anxiously over her shoulders towards the door, the fear catching at her once more. 'Why must men be so foolish?'

'There is not the least need to worry,' said Lady Longbourne, a little smile on her lips. 'They will probably choose pistols and fire in the air. I dare say they are all feeling a bit silly by now, but for the sake of their honour, they will go through the motions.'

Cassie looked at her in surprise. 'Do you think so? That is rather foolish, is it not? How can you be sure they will not try to kill each other? Vincent was very angry. He knocked Major Saunders down—and he looked fit to murder.'

'The same thing happened once to me. Vincent's father was very angry, as I recall,' said Lady Longbourne reminiscently. 'He caught me kissing Sir Bertram, you know. We were in love for years, long before we were free to marry, but did not…well, I was not Bertie's lover. It was just a silly kiss under the mistletoe. But Carlton—my husband then, of course—insisted on fighting him. Bertie told me years later that they both fired into the air, then went off and got drunk together. They were friends, you see, and in the end they saw how foolish it was to fall out over a kiss.'

'No? Really?' Cassie looked at her, then began to laugh as she saw the ridiculousness of it all. 'Do you think Carlton…? Oh, no! It is too bad of him. Of them all…to make such a scene when they know it is no more than a storm in a teacup.'

'You will marry him, won't you, Cassie?'

'I think—'

She was interrupted as the door opened and Sir Septimus came in. He glared at Lady Longbourne as he saw she was sitting on the sofa.

'I might have known I should find this. What are you sitting there for, Emmeline? Everyone is waiting to go into supper.'

'Oh, dear,' said Lady Longbourne and stood up at once. 'That is too bad of me. Do forgive me, Septimus. I only came for a moment…my poor head, you know. But then, I am such a silly goose. I wonder you can put up with me at all.' She tucked her arm through his, then turned back to wink very naughtily at Cassie. 'Come along dearest. It was good of you to rescue me, but we really must not keep our guests waiting for their supper.'

Chapter Twelve

It was some considerable time later. Jack and Vincent were sitting together in the library, sharing a bottle of Sir Harry's very tolerable brandy. Sir Harry had been with them for a while at his half-brother's request, but had now returned to the dance, having played his part as Vincent's second.

'This is an awkward situation,' said Vincent as he poured brandy into two glasses. 'What do you think she means to do, Jack? Will she marry me and then keep me at a distance—or will she throw me to the wolves?'

'I did warn you,' Jack pointed out as he took the glass Vincent had refilled for him. 'There's no denying Cassie is a little contrary at times. She can fly off the handle for nothing...well, very nearly nothing. She does have a mind of her own.'

'Yes, I recall you saying so before.' A faint smile curved Vincent's mouth as he sat down in a rather worn leather armchair and stretched his long legs out in front of him. The window was open, silk curtains moving gently to and fro in the light breeze. 'She was rather magnificent, wasn't she—and completely in the right of it. I should not have lost my temper in front of her. I ought properly to have taken Saunders outside and thrashed him in private.'

Jack nodded wisely. 'Much the better course. What the fair ones don't know, don't hurt them. Of course, you couldn't back down in front of the ladies,' he said, waving his hand expressively as he took a sip of his brandy. 'Good stuff, this! Louise has a few bottles of excellent cognac in her cellars. You must sample it one day, Vinnie.

'As I was saying, a challenge issued has to be met. One couldn't look oneself in the mirror otherwise, naturally—and for two pins, I should have shot Saunders between the eyes. Still, he's not such a bad fellow. I suppose he couldn't help falling for her—and he did the honourable thing. Firing into the air when you had held your own fire and might have shot him had you liked. You could do no less, of course—bad form to shoot a man down after that.'

'Oh, very…' Vincent chuckled, his good humour long restored. 'It would have ended after I'd knocked him down if he hadn't been such a fool and challenged me in front of Cassie. Once I'd thought about it, I had no desire to kill him. To be honest with you, Jack, I've seen enough bloodshed to last me a lifetime.'

'Lord, yes!' Jack looked at him thoughtfully. 'Do you suppose she means what she said? She can be too stubborn for her own good—doesn't like to back down. Makes her pinchy.'

'Yes, so I have observed,' Vincent replied, recalling a young girl stuck in a tree, who would not let him take her down until he had first taken her kitten to safety. He had been obliged to give in to her on that occasion, and to retire with some loss of dignity after discovering his breeches were torn in a very revealing place. 'So what do I do now? I called my trump card the other evening. I cannot use it again.'

Jack thought for a moment. 'Cassie might respond to persuasion,' he suggested. 'If you can make her see the amusing side of all this, she would probably come down off her high horse. Especially when she knows neither of us is actually harmed. It was her anxiety for us that made her explode like that, you know.'

'Yes, I do know.' Vincent's eyes smouldered. He was finding this situation rather amusing and not a little intriguing, and was using Jack as a sounding board for his thoughts rather than seeking advice. 'I am not sure whether I should seek to persuade or use a more masterful approach, Jack. Show her who is in charge?'

'Doomed to failure!' Jack looked alarmed. 'She will simply stick her hooves down and refuse to budge.'

'Like that damned donkey she stole, I suppose?'

'Very much, only worse,' Jack said gloomily. 'You don't know Cassie if you think you can push her. Much better use the velvet glove, Vinnie.'

'You might be right,' Vincent said, a glint in his eyes. 'But for some unaccountable reason, I am reluctant.' He took a thoughtful sip of his brandy. 'Do you know, I think it might be far more amusing to see just how far Cassie will go to defy me?'

'Brave man,' Jack said and finished his brandy. 'Rather you than me, that's all I can say.'

The next morning, Cassie rose, feeling heavy-eyed after a night spent tossing restlessly from side to side. She had regretted her impulsive words to Vincent almost as soon as she had uttered them; if Lady Longbourne was right, her stance against the duel had been quite unnecessary. Indeed, she had begun to feel a little foolish and apprehensive. What if Vincent had taken her at her word? Supposing he decided he did not wish to marry such a temperamental woman? It would just serve her right if he did call off the wedding.

She wanted to apologise to him and yet how could she climb down from her principles? He was very much at fault, but she wished she had not made such a thing of it all.

'Bother!' she muttered as she got up and went over to the window. She was just in time to see Vincent mount his horse and ride off. Now where was he going? They were due to be married the following day and nothing was resolved between them. They had so much to say to one another. 'Oh, you wretched man! How dare you just go out riding as if nothing had happened?'

Cassie's mood swung back to indignation. It was not for her to be sorry! Vincent must apologise for his bad behaviour the previous evening. If he did so, she might forgive him. Yes, certainly she would do so, for it would make everything so uncomfortable if she did not... Bother! Bother! Bother!

Her indignation kept her going until she was met by a rather anxious Lady Longbourne downstairs in the parlour.

'Oh, there you are, Cassie,' she said, fluttering about like a distracted moth. 'I spoke to Carlton not half an hour ago. Oh, my dear! If ever there was such a contrary man! He is in a fit of the blues and says the quarrel between you is all his fault and he perfectly understands why you do not wish to marry him. He has taken himself off to Carlton House and says he shall stay there unless you send for him. He says he would not for the world force you into a marriage you could not like—and that the blame is all his. If you will not have him, he will own to having jilted you by reason of fighting the duel you forbade.'

'Oh, the provoking man!' cried Cassie, irritated beyond bearing by such a message. How could he be such a wet goose as to send his mother to tell her such a sorry tale? It was ridiculous, and most unlike him. 'How could he do this to me? And to ride off like that! He might at least have waited to talk to me.'

'I do not think he could bear to face you,' said Lady

Longbourne, dabbing her eyes with her kerchief. She gave
a little sob, hoping she was not doing it too brown. 'I have
never seen him in such a way. It seems to me he cares for
you very much, my dear—and I dare say he will do something quite dreadful if you do not tell him he may come
back and marry you.'

Cassie gave her a darkling glance. 'If he gave you that
impression, ma'am, you may depend upon it that he was
bamming you. I do not believe that anything I said to him
last night would cause Vincent to contemplate suicide. No,
no, he has sent you as his ambassador in the hoping of
forcing me to relent, but I am up to his tricks, and I shall
not yield.'

'Oh, Cassie,' her ladyship said, looking disappointed.
'Do you not think you might? Perhaps he is not so very
low as I led you to believe, but I am certain he cares for
you deeply. Besides, ladies are supposed to be yielding.
Men expect it, and one can always find some method of
getting one's own back later, you know.'

Cassie giggled as she saw the mischief in her friend's
eyes. 'You are a very wicked woman, Mama.'

'I know…but I prefer a comfortable life to confrontation,' said Lady Longbourne with a sigh. 'Do you not think
you might forgive him, my love?'

'He should have waited to speak to me. Had he done so,
I might very well have forgiven him, this time.' Cassie
tossed her head, her eyes sparkling.

'Shall I send someone to fetch him back—so that you
can discuss the situation?' Lady Longbourne looked hopeful. 'Just to talk, Cassie. You need not give in just at once.'

'No, indeed, you shall not,' Cassie said. 'He may come
if he wishes or not. I have an appointment with Mrs Walker
to arrange the flowers in the church.'

'But why arrange flowers if there is to be no wedding?'
asked a bewildered Lady Longbourne.

'Because I enjoy it,' countered Cassie blithely, then
kissed her. 'Do not worry, dearest. I am sure Carlton will
return as soon as he has thought things over.'

Lady Longbourne watched as she walked away, seemingly unconcerned. Then she went inside the house and
penned a rather incoherent note to Cassie's brother, begging
him to use his powers of persuasion on either his sister or
her son.

> For if they cannot be brought to see sense, they will
> throw away something precious—and beside, what am
> I to do with all the wedding food?

Vincent was lounging on an old-fashioned wooden settle
in Jack's parlour when the note was sent over to Thornton's
House. Jack passed it over to him, frowning as it was read
and returned without comment.

'You've really put the fox amongst the hens now,' he
said. 'Cassie will never ask you to return. She is too proud
to beg. Besides, why should she? You should have spoken
to her yourself this morning, Vinnie.'

'I had a fancy to have her send for me.' Vincent's expression was unreadable, but there was a glint in his eyes.

'Well, she won't. I know Cassie. You can whistle until
the cows come home, but she won't send.'

'Why do you not try to persuade her for me?' Vincent
fixed him with a winsome smile. 'Ride down to the church,
Jack. Tell her you think she ought to marry me even if she
does not want to—then come back and tell me what she
says.'

'Are you mad?' Jack stared at him suspiciously. Vinnie
was a great one for pulling the wool over one's eyes and
he had a nasty feeling he was doing it now. 'If I did any
such thing she would very likely box my ears. And, besides,

it would not serve. She won't change her mind—unless you ask her, of course.'

'Beg her?' Vincent's eyes flashed with fire. 'Would you have me go down on my knees?'

'Well, perhaps you need not go as far as that…' Jack stared at him in exasperation. 'Damn it, man! The wedding is tomorrow, you cannot risk it.'

'There is plenty of time…'

'You always had a steady nerve,' Jack said, admiring him. 'Well, I wish you luck.'

'And you will truly not try to persuade her for me?'

'No, damn it, Vinnie. This is something you must do for yourself.'

'Yes, I dare say you are right.' He glanced at his watch, which was a very fine gold one and engraved on the back. He listened to it chime the quarter hour, then replaced it in his waistcoat pocket. 'I should imagine Cassie has left the church by now, and since she is walking, I shall catch up with her on her way home if I leave at once.'

Jack stared at him, eyes narrowed in suspicion. 'You intended that all the time, didn't you?'

'Of course.' Vincent smiled his lazy smile. 'I believe Cassie may have had time to think things over and will very likely have cooled down by now…'

Cassie took a last look round the church before leaving. She was pleased with her work. It truly looked quite beautiful and the lilies she had arranged everywhere had a pervading scent which seemed to waft pleasantly round the ancient building. The sun was pouring in through a stained-glass window high above her, shedding a rainbow of colours on the worn flagstones. It was such a peaceful place to be and she was sure that just being here for a while had helped her to sort out her confused feelings.

At least, there was no doubt in her mind now. She knew exactly where she was going in her life and why.

Tomorrow she would take her vows here as Vincent's wife. She was smiling as she left the church. For a while she *had* been ruffled by Vincent's message but, thinking it over, she had come to the conclusion that it had been meant to say something far different than it would at first appear. Vincent might well have decided not to marry her, but had he done so, he would not have sent his mother with such a message.

No, he was testing her, teasing her, attempting to make her give way. She supposed she might have to in the end, because she did want to marry him, even if he was the most trying wretch! Not because it would cause too much trouble to cancel the wedding at the last moment, but because she loved him. She loved him so much she could not imagine her life without him.

The sun was warm on her head as she walked. She looked about her, remembering all the times when, as a child, she had played in these fields and ridden the bridle paths on her pony. Soon her family home would be sold, Jack would go back to France—and if she came here again it would be to visit Harry and Sarah. There was a tinge of sadness in the realisation, but the world moved on and she must move with it.

Entering the woods near Longbourne, Cassie knew a moment of disquiet, but refused to let herself be afraid. If she once gave way to fear, she would never be able to walk alone again. Besides, the poacher she had disturbed would not dare to come here again. She felt a brief moment of pity for him. He must be in terror of his life. If Vincent had threatened to kill Major Saunders just for trying to kiss her, she did not dare begin to imagine what he might have done to the poacher who had knocked her senseless!

She smiled to herself as she recalled the incident with

Major Saunders the previous evening. When one stood back and looked at it from a distance, it was so ridiculous!

After she had been walking for some minutes, she heard a cracking sound just ahead of her, as though someone had trodden on a stick. She took a deep breath, but would not let herself call out to ask who it was. Instead, she bent and picked up a fallen branch herself, preparing to defend herself if necessary. Then, as she came into a clearing, she saw Vincent sitting on the trunk of a felled tree and knew that he was waiting for her. She dropped the branch and went forward, her heart beginning to leap like giddy lambs in spring. He looked up and smiled as she approached.

'Hello, Cassie. Have you a few moments to spare?'

'Yes, of course,' she said. 'So you did not go to Carlton House after all?'

'Did you really think I had?'

'Only for a few seconds.' She shook her head at him. 'Really, Vinnie! Your poor mama seemed to imagine you were about to throw yourself in the river or sink into a decline.'

'But you did not believe her?' Vincent laughed as he saw the expression in her eyes. 'No, I thought not. Serves me right for sending you such a ridiculous message, does it not?'

'It was very foolish of you,' Cassie said in a scolding tone. She held her smile inside her. He must not be forgiven all at once. It would not be good for him to imagine he could always have his own way. 'Did you think I would not know it for a Banbury tale?'

'If I did, I should have known better, but I must confess it was done in a puckish mood.' He made room for her to sit on the log beside him, his eyes quizzing her as she sat down. 'I fear I do have a rather odd sense of humour, my love. In fact, we have both been a pair of fools, wouldn't you say?'

'I think we might have been more open with each other,' she said, fixing him with a look that made him wince. 'Why did you not tell me about the promise you made to Jack? It would have cleared the air and I would have understood, had you explained. And why did you break your own straw?'

'Did Saunders tell you that last night?' She nodded and he sighed. 'I thought at the time he had seen me, but he said nothing then. I did not tell you what had taken place, because I knew you would be angry. You were so very annoyed with poor Kendal, who was only doing what he considered the decent thing. He may be a pompous bore, my love, but he means well. He had no idea you had been left a fortune by your mother's aunt.'

'Yes, I know,' she said on a sigh. 'I have realised I misjudged him, and I have apologised.'

Vincent nodded, his eyes warm with approval. 'I was sure you would when you were ready. Imagine the quandary I found myself in, Cassie. You had opened your heart to me over this matter, and I could not but take notice. You would have been furious had you discovered that stupid promise.'

'Yes, I suppose so—but you have not told me why you broke your straw.'

'I wanted to make sure I was the one to ask, because I felt I owed it to Jack. He was in a terrible state that night, and would never have spoken the way he did had he been able to think clearly.'

'But why did you feel you owed him something? He had no right to ask such a thing of you—of anyone.'

'I owed it to him because I felt responsible for his death. I forced him to come with me that day, Cassie. We rode into an ambush and when he fell I believed he could not have survived. I rode on and left him lying there. For months after that I was torn by guilt and indecision. I felt it was my duty to ask you to be my wife, but I was sure you would hate me for being the cause of your brother's death. And if I did not tell you the truth, it would always be between us…it was my fault, Cassie. All he has suffered was because of me.'

'No, no, that is not true. Jack explained it all to me. He told me that you had no choice, that in your place he must have done the same and ridden on.'

Vincent looked grave. 'It haunted me. I blamed myself a thousand times for taking him with me on that mission.'

'So you waited for months to come to me, because your conscience was troubled…' Cassie turned her clear gaze on him. 'What made you decide to ask me at last?'

'My life was empty,' Vincent said. 'I missed Jack terribly. I was haunted by guilt—and Mama told me I ought to marry. It was in my mind that I might as well make a marriage of convenience.'

'Yes, I do see. I imagined it must have been something of the sort. You needed a wife and you could honour your promise at the same time. It must have seemed a good compromise. You thought I would be grateful for the offer. After all, I am not pretty and you believed me to be penniless.'

Her face was pale, her gaze averted. When he took her hand in his it trembled and when she turned to look at him, her eyes had the look of a wounded doe.

'Do not look like that, my darling,' he said softly. 'Please, I beg you. You know that is not how I feel now, do you not? Surely you must know, Cassie!'

Her cheeks washed with deep rose as she saw the intent look he gave her, a look so terrifying, so full of promise, that her heart almost stopped beating. 'I…I was not sure. It has sometimes seemed to me that you felt more than mere liking, but then—'

'A great deal more,' Vincent replied, his voice husky

with passion. 'Indeed, I have been at pains to disguise my feelings for you for fear of scaring you off, my love. You told me you wanted only a comfortable arrangement. You did not wish for love…' There was a sparkle of wickedness in his eyes now. 'I remember perfectly that you made your conditions for marriage very plain to me.'

'Yes, I know I did.' Cassie hung her head. 'Was that not very foolish of me? Jack and I had been so very close, you see. We shared our thoughts and our jokes, sometimes without even a word being spoken. I believed I could never be as close again to anyone else. Indeed, I may have been a little afraid to love, lest I somehow lost that person and was hurt again. All I wanted was a complaisant husband and a position in society. Some people were very odious after my father shot himself, you know.'

Vincent caught her hand, holding it tightly in his own. 'Well, you have your place in society for what it is worth, my dearest.' He smiled at her, a twinkle in his eyes. 'But I believe you discovered last evening that I have a very serious fault. I cannot contemplate another man making advances to my wife with any degree of complacency. I think I might well have shot to injure or kill had Mama's timely intervention not given me time for reflection.'

'I must say, I thought she acted her part very well and deserves some credit,' Cassie murmured, a gurgle of laughter escaping her. 'She must have learned how to faint at will long ago.'

'You mean she is a shameless blackmailer who will use all her feminine arts to get her own way?' Vincent smiled ruefully. 'Of course I have always known it. Mama does not like scenes or loud voices. She uses her vulnerability to get her own way. She is not brave enough to stand and fight as you do, my love.'

'But her way has its uses,' Cassie said, 'if it enabled you to go off and settle your own affairs in your own time?'

'Saunders fired in the air, as I did.' Vincent looked at her. 'I could not back down, Cassie. I had to go through the motions for the sake of honour.'

'Yes. Lady Longbourne said it would be that way.' Cassie gave him a wicked look. 'She told me that your father and Sir Bertram once fought a duel over her—and that it ended with them going off to get drunk together.'

'No? Did it?' Vincent laughed. 'I had no idea—though I knew she was in love with Bertie even before my father died. He was riding home after an evening spent in gaming and hard drinking, you know—and fell from his horse. He died almost instantly. Mama waited the full six months before marrying again, and I do not believe they became lovers until after the wedding. Which showed quite remarkable restraint on his part, don't you think?'

'I think it must have been one of those very special relationships,' Cassie said, gazing up at him thoughtfully. 'That is why she will not marry again. You must not hope for it, Vinnie.'

'I shall not again,' he replied. 'It was only because she seemed to have no purpose in life. I hated to see her so unhappy—but she is so much better now. She has become so fond of you.'

'As she will be of Sarah,' Cassie said. 'And her grandchildren, Vinnie. I am sure she will be devoted to them, and of course we must all see that she is not on her own for long.'

'Her grandchildren?' Vincent's brows rose quizzically. 'Am I to take it that you will marry me?'

'I might,' said Cassie, her eyes bright with challenge. 'If you can convince me that it would be in my interests to do so.'

Vincent was amused at the mischief he sensed going on in her head. 'And how am I to do that, Cassie?'

'Well…' she replied, appearing to consider. 'You might

start by kissing me the way you did in your study. And you might continue by telling me why you want to marry me.'

'As if you did not know the answer,' Vincent said, reaching out for her. 'For once in his life, Septimus was perfectly right—you are a wicked jade!'

'You still have not told me,' Cassie cried, jumping to her feet as he tried to put his arms about her. 'Time is running out, Vinnie. You must soon make up your mind.'

She threw a teasing look at him and started running. Vincent did not hesitate this time, but pounded after her, catching her before she had gone more than a few yards. He grabbed hold of her, swinging her round to face him, then he bent his head to kiss her lips.

It was such a long, tender, passionate kiss that it had her near swooning in his arms. She swayed and sighed when he released her at last, then smiled up at him confidently before nestling her head against his shoulder.

Vincent kissed the top of her head. 'You smell of flowers,' he murmured huskily. 'Do you know you have bewitched me, Cassie? I have been able to think of nothing but you for weeks.'

She looked up, pulling a face at him. 'And I have been breaking my heart for you.'

'No? Have you?' He touched her cheek, running one finger down it and over her chin, to the little hollow at the base of her throat. His face held a kind of wonder that made her want to hold him close for evermore. 'You gave no sign of it, Cassie. I was not sure you cared particularly for me at all. Did you have no idea that I adored you?'

'There was one moment when I thought you must love me,' she said frowning. 'Why were you in such torment when you proposed to me, Vinnie?'

'It was my idiot half-brother.' He explained what had happened and how he had felt about the resulting gossip.

'I was torn in two, Cassie. I thought you might hate me for ruining your chances of being a success if I let you make your début with such rumours flying around. For had you not been wearing my ring, they would have thought there was something smoky. I cursed Harry a thousand times, let me tell you. I wanted to be open with you, and yet I was afraid to tell you the truth.'

'Which was?' Her eyes gazed into his.

'That I was falling desperately in love with you, of course. But I would have preferred to wait, to give you a chance to know me. I did not know how to be with you, Cassie. I had never felt so—so lost and vulnerable. And I was terrified of losing you if you heard the story of the straws from one of Jack's friends.'

'You need not have been afraid of losing me.' She reached up to touch her lips to his. 'And as for that nonsense last night—you must have known why I wanted to stop you fighting?'

'Because you thought one of us might be killed?'

'It was mostly you, Vinnie. I knew Jack was in no danger. You would never have given way to him. I knew you would fight the duel yourself. And I did not want you to die.' She lifted her head, eyes flashing. 'I dare say you had not thought—but it would have quite ruined our wedding, you know.'

'Oh, Cassie! You little witch!' Her future husband was entranced. 'Shall I ever have best of you? Shall I ever teach you to show your husband the proper respect?'

'You may try,' she replied, demure now. 'But I am not perfectly certain you will succeed.'

'Nor am I,' said Vincent, a rueful look in his eyes. 'But if we can meet halfway, as we have today, I confess that would please me best of all.'

'Oh, yes,' Cassie agreed. 'I believe there may be hope for that, my dearest Vinnie.'

He held his hand out to her. 'Should we go home now? I fear Mama may have the hysterics if we do not reassure her that she need not throw away all the wedding food.'

'Oh, I do not imagine she doubted it for a moment,' Cassie murmured. 'She is much wiser than you may imagine...'

Chapter Thirteen

'You look so beautiful, my dear.' Lady Longbourne dabbed at her eyes with her lace kerchief, and for once the tears were quite real. 'I do not recall who once said to me that you were a plain gel, but whoever it was, they were very wrong.'

Cassie smiled and shook her head. 'It is the dress, Mama, and the diamonds Vincent sent me. I am still plain little Cassandra Thornton, who used to live down the road.'

'Well, you were a little plain as a girl,' her ladyship admitted judiciously. 'But you certainly aren't now. There's a glow about you. I am sure Carlton may think himself fortunate to have such a lovely bride.'

'Perhaps he does,' Cassie countered. 'But there is no accounting for the thoughts of gentlemen who are in love with one. I dare say he will recover soon enough.'

'Bertie never did,' said her ladyship with a sigh. 'He kissed my hand and told me I had given him perfect happiness only a few moments before he slipped away from me. Do not believe those who would tell you romance does not last, my dear. It is very much up to you as a woman to keep it alive.'

'You are very wise,' said Cassie and kissed her cheek.

'I shall think myself very fortunate if I inspire such devotion in my husband as you did in yours.'

Lady Longbourne patted her hand. 'I believe you already do,' she said in a choking voice.

Cassie glanced at herself in the mirror. She *was* looking quite handsome in her splendid gown of cream satin and lace, and the pretty headdress of silk flowers into which she had woven one of the Carlton heirlooms. She hoped Vinnie would approve of the use she had made of his grandmother's diamonds, but she wanted to wear the simple necklet he had given her on the day they became engaged.

She was still unable to imagine why Vinnie loved her, but she could not doubt that he did. The kisses he had given her in the woods, before they had walked hand in hand back to the house, had left her in no doubt of his feelings.

'If I were not a gentleman,' he had whispered hoarsely against her ear, 'I should make love to you now. I do want you so desperately, Cassie, and I am not as patient as Sir Bertram.'

'Are you not, my dearest?' She had smiled up at him and touched his face, a hint of mischief in her own. 'This honour thing can be rather a nuisance at times, don't you think? Tell me, Vinnie, why do gentlemen set such store by it?'

'Careful, minx! You are pushing me to the limits.'

'Perhaps that is what I wish to do—you see, I am not a gentleman.'

Cassie sighed as she recalled his very satisfactory response to her teasing. She turned as Lady Longbourne fussed over the last details of her dress, and then she sneezed three times in a row.

'Cassie!' Lady Longbourne looked at her in dismay. 'I hope you are not about to go down with a cold, my dear?'

'No, of course not,' Cassie said, sounding a bit nasal.

'Poor Janet warned me I would catch hers, but I never take chills. I have not had a cold in years.'

'Do not tempt fate, dearest,' Lady Longbourne begged her, looking faintly anxious as Cassie sneezed again. 'You do look a little flushed, now I come to think of it. I thought it was merely excitement, but after this I wonder.'

'You must not worry.' Cassie studied herself in the mirror. She *did* indeed have a high colour and she *was* feeling a little warm. 'No, no, I am sure it is just excitement. I shall be fine…'

The church was overflowing with friends of the bride and groom. Cassie walked to take her place beside Vincent, supported by her brother's arm. Jack's appearance caused some comment, as was to be expected, but most people had by now heard the news and thought his gaunt looks explained the reason for his having been reported dead. He had clearly suffered, and they were all genuinely glad to see him home.

Everyone thought Cassie looked very well, especially for a girl who had always been thought a little plain. One or two did remark on her high colour, which was really not like her at all.

Cassie smiled as Vincent turned to look at her, a smile of welcome in his eyes. She managed an answering smile for him but was beginning to feel really rather odd: a little light-headed and not quite well. Lady Longbourne had insisted on giving her a little brandy with sugar and hot water before they left the house. She wondered if perhaps the unaccustomed glass of strong spirits might have gone to her head, and hoped she would not say anything foolish when it came time for her to make her vows.

She did manage to say the right words, however, and to walk proudly from the church as Vincent's wife. Her hand trembled on his arm as they were showered with rose petals, but she only smiled when he looked at her inquiringly. It would have been so missish of her to let anyone guess that she had started to feel quite ill. But she did wish the bells were not quite so loud. Her head was aching terribly and she felt shivery.

Cassie was made of sterner stuff than to give in to a mere chill. As soon as they were back at Longbourne, she slipped upstairs to tidy herself, patting her face with cool water because it felt so hot. She asked Janet, who was now on her feet again, to make her a glass of brandy and sugar water.

'You've caught my cold,' Janet said, looking at her in dismay. 'I knew you would. I was afraid of it from the start. And it has come out on your wedding day!'

'Well, it cannot be helped,' Cassie said with a little shrug. 'At least it's only the fever so far. I have not got a red nose, so I must be grateful for that.'

Janet was helpless to prevent her going down to join her guests at the reception. It would have ruined everything had she retired to bed, but it was obvious that she was far from well.

The brandy helped, though it had the effect of making Cassie feel even more light-headed than before. However, she managed to keep smiling as she stood with Vincent to receive the congratulations of her friends.

'You look a bit flushed,' Jack remarked to her later as he kissed her cheek. 'You feel hot. What's wrong, Cassie? Are you ill?'

'It is just a bit of a cold,' she said in a low whisper. 'I shall be perfectly all right when we are all sitting down.'

She did indeed feel better when she was seated, though she could not bear to eat anything. The toasts and speeches seemed to go on and on for ever, and she began to wonder if it would ever be over. From time to time she sipped her wine, which seemed to help. Everything was muted, somehow distant, as if everything was far away. Her head ached, her throat was sore, but it did not feel as if it was happening to her. She was floating away towards the ceiling.

'What's wrong, Cassie?' Vincent asked, looking at her in concern. 'Are you ill? You look very flushed.'

'No, no,' she assured him. 'I am perfectly well.'

She smiled at him reassuringly. She even managed to cut the cake, her hand trembling beneath his on the knife handle, but it was when the music struck up and everyone called for the bride and groom to dance that she finally came unstuck.

She rose to her feet willingly enough, but when she tried to move she felt her legs had turned to jelly and she stumbled against Vincent. He held her, steadying her, a look of suspicion in his eyes as he caught a faint whiff of brandy.

'Have you been drinking spirits, Cassie?'

'Janet made a toddy for me…only a little brandy with hot water and sugar.' She gazed up at him a little unsteadily. 'Are we going to dance?'

'If you are sure you can manage it?'

'Of course I can.' She gave him an indignant look. 'Do you think I am insh…inshtoxicated?'

'Not at all, my love,' lied Vincent valiantly. 'I am merely intrigued to know why…'

At that moment Cassie sneezed violently and then sat down on her chair with a bump. 'Do you know, I think I shall not dance,' she said, giving him a rather owlish stare. 'My legs feel all at sea.'

'To say nothing of a slight dizziness, I suppose?'

Cassie was now looking decidedly feverish. 'My head aches,' she said. 'I am very sorry, Vincent, but I think, I really think that…' She gave a little sigh and would have fallen from her chair had he not been there to support her.

Lady Longbourne came hurrying up to them at that moment. 'Oh dear, I was afraid of this,' she said, looking rueful. 'She has a nasty cold. It started this morning and I gave her a glass of brandy. Quite a strong one.'

'And Janet gave her another,' Vincent said, a wry smile on his lips. 'She has eaten nothing, but she did drink some wine.'

'Oh, how unfortunate,' said Lady Longbourne. 'It seems the fever has quite overcome her, poor love. I suggest you carry her upstairs, Carlton. I believe it may be best if you delay your journey until tomorrow or even the day after. You must see that Cassie really is not fit to go anywhere but her bed?'

Cassie opened her eyes as Vincent bent to lift her in his arms. She smiled up at him enchantingly. 'Take me to bed, Vinnie,' she said. 'I am so very tired.'

'You are ill, my love,' he said as his arms went beneath her knees, and he caught her up. 'You foolish girl. Why did you not tell me how you felt before this?'

'Wanshted to marry you.' She gave him a dreamy look as her arms curled about his neck. 'Didshn't want to postpone the wedding for a silly cold.'

Vincent hid his amusement as he glanced at his mother. 'You will make our apologies, Mama. Please ask everyone to dance and amuse themselves. I shall of course return after I have seen Cassie settled, to thank them for coming.'

'Of course. Poor Cassie…'

Vincent strode from the dining room, carrying his bride and bravely ignoring the startled looks from his guests. He knew he could trust his mother to explain away Cassie's rather curious behaviour. For himself he cared little what others might think, but he suspected that his young wife might feel very embarrassed when she remembered her wedding reception.

She was half asleep when he laid her very gently on her bed. Janet was waiting to attend her, and looked apologetically at Vincent as she realised what was wrong with her young mistress.

'I think this is partly my fault, sir. I made her a hot toddy.'

'Yes, she did mention it.'

'She asked me to make it strong so that she could get through the reception without feeling the effects of the cold, sir. I think I must have given her too much brandy.'

'Mama also gave her a strong brandy before she left for church—and though she ate nothing downstairs, I know she drank at least a glass of wine.'

'Oh, dear, how unfortunate.' Janet smiled as she saw that his lordship had a wry amusement in his eyes. 'Miss Cassie—or her ladyship, as I should say!—has hardly ever been ill, sir. I warned her not to come near me when I first took the cold, but she would—and now look what's happened.'

'We must hope it is not the influenza.'

'Oh, no, sir, I do not think it. I was over my cold in three days. I dare say her ladyship will be the same.'

Cassie gave a little moan and opened her eyes. She smiled up at Vincent invitingly.

'Are you going to kiss me?'

Vincent chuckled and sat down on the edge of the bed. He bent over her, kissing her very gently on the mouth.

'I dare say you are hoping to give me your cold, you little wretch, but I shall brave it.' He stroked her forehead, which was very hot. 'You must rest now, my dearest love. Janet is going to give you a nice hot drink of lemon barley, and then you must sleep for a while.'

She caught his hand. 'Do not leave me, Vinnie. I want you to stay here and cuddle me. I like being kissed. It is excessively nice.'

'Yes, so I believe.' He kissed her again, very softly on the mouth. 'I should like nothing more than to stay with you, my love, but I think you should go to sleep now. And I must not neglect our guests.'

Cassie murmured something and closed her eyes. Her head ached, but it was so comfortable in her bed and she seemed to be drifting away on a fluffy white cloud.

'You leave her to me, sir,' Janet said. 'She will sleep it off now, I think—and knowing her, she'll be right as rain in the morning.'

'Well, we must hope she is better.'

Vincent walked to the door, then glanced back at his bride who was snuggling down like a sleepy kitten in the covers. He smiled ruefully to himself as he left her there. It was not going to be quite the wedding night he had anticipated, but Cassie's rather delightful behaviour had encouraged him to think that she was well worth the delay.

Cassie awoke the next morning feeling wretched. Every bone in her body ached and she had a dreadful suspicion that everything was not as it ought to have been. She sat up, moaning as the room seemed to spin around her and she realised she was in the bedroom she had been using this past week or so at Longbourne.

Why was she still here? What had happened? Oh, no! She rather thought she must have fainted at the wedding reception. How very lowering!

She saw a jug of barley water on the table beside her bed, reached for it, poured a little into a glass and took a swallow. Her throat felt better. So why did her head still feel as if it had a hundred and one drums banging inside it?

She was just thinking about getting up, when the door opened and Janet came in, carrying a tray.

'I thought you would be awake, your ladyship,' Janet said, giving her an intent look. 'I have brought you a little thin gruel and something to ease your head.'

'Gruel?' Cassie pulled a face at her. 'Must I, Janet? Could I not have rolls and honey?'

'Do you feel up to them?' Janet stared at her uncertainly. 'I thought you might still have a sore throat?'

'It feels much better,' Cassie said. 'But I do ache all over. I suppose it must have been the fever. I felt so strange yesterday. As if nothing was quite real.'

'Yes, I expect you did,' Janet said, not quite meeting her eyes. 'I dare say it was the fever—though the brandy and wine may have played its part.'

'Oh, dear,' said Cassie, looking conscious. 'Do you suppose I was a little intoxicated, Janet?'

Mindful of his lordship's instructions when he had looked at his bride earlier that morning, Janet hesitated.

'No, of course you were not intoxicated,' Lady Longbourne said as she breezed in, wearing a very fetching pale-apricot dressing robe and a lace cap. 'You had a nasty fever, and you may be sure I told everyone how brave you were to go through with the wedding at all.'

'I did feel quite ill,' Cassie replied, a faint blush in her cheeks as she began to remember certain things. 'But—but it did not seem to be happening to me at all. I do hope I did not do anything foolish during the reception?'

'Certainly not. I am always the same when I have a cold,' Lady Longbourne assured her. 'Drink the tisane Janet brought for you, my love. I believe you may find it will make you feel much better.'

'Thank you.' Cassie picked up the glass and took a tentative sip. It tasted unspeakably awful, but she swallowed it down without a word of complaint. 'Perhaps if I feel better, I shall get up later.'

'I should stay in bed today, if I were you,' her ladyship advised. 'People have been asking about you already. There are several bunches of flowers for you and concerned messages. I shall send them all up to you directly.'

'You are so kind. Everyone is.'

Lady Longbourne smiled and went away.

Cassie tasted the gruel and pulled a face. 'Please take it away, Janet. I would much prefer a pot of hot chocolate and some rolls.'

'As you wish, your ladyship.'

'Please,' Cassie begged, horrified. 'Do you think you could call me Miss Cassie as you always did—at least in private?'

'Yes, miss.' Janet smiled at her in approval. 'I should think I could...in private, mind. You must remember your dignity in front of the other maids. And there must certainly be no more escapades! His lordship will expect you to behave like a lady now that you are his wife.'

'Yes, Janet. I know I have to behave properly in future. Please do not scold me...' Cassie closed her eyes as the hammers began again. 'Forget about breakfast, if you please, I think perhaps I shall just have a little sleep...'

When she opened her eyes again, it was to find Jack standing at the foot of her bed. He was holding a wicker basket, which he placed into her hands as she yawned and sat up, smiling at him sleepily.

'Lady Longbourne thought I ought not to come up to your bedroom, but Vinnie said it was all right, so here I am. I leave for France later today, Cassie, and I wanted to make sure you were all right before I go.' He looked at her anxiously. 'You are, aren't you?'

'Yes, of course. I am glad you came, Jack. I should have hated it if you hadn't. What have you brought me?' A mewing sound came from inside and she opened the top to see a little ball of white fluff. 'Oh, a kitten! How lovely. You spoil me, Jack. That beautiful silver necklace you gave me as a wedding present, which I know belonged to Grandmother and is something I have always loved—and now this.'

'You deserve far more,' Jack said, bending to kiss her cheek. 'I am so fond of you, dear Cassie. It was a rotten shame your being ill for the wedding. I cannot say I blame you for getting a little squiffy. I would have done the same in your shoes.'

'Oh, no, was I?' Cassie stared in dismay. 'What must people have thought?'

'No need to worry. Lady Longbourne convinced everyone you had a virulent fever which had laid you low, but Vinnie told me you had been knocking back the brandy. I believe he secretly found it all rather amusing.'

'Did he, indeed?' Cassie scowled. 'Well, you may both think it funny, but I was feeling very ill.'

'Of course you were, and it is not a bit funny,' her brother said, but could not prevent a chuckle escaping. 'No, no, I am sorry, love. I know you were feeling under the hammer. Do not poker up. It may be ages before I see you again, and I do not want to quarrel with you.'

'It will not be so very long,' Cassie said, her outrage fading as swiftly as it had flared. 'Because I mean to ask Vincent to bring me to visit you and Louise when we are on our honeymoon.'

'That *is* good news.' Jack looked pleased as he bent to kiss her cheek. 'I hope you will love Louise as much as I do—and now I ought to be off.'

She caught his hand. 'Take care, Jack—and whatever happens in the future, always remember that I love you.'

'I love you, too, Cassie.' He smiled, let go her hand and went out of the door.

Left to herself once more, Cassie decided that she really was feeling much better. Her headache had gone, and her throat was not at all sore, though she did still have the sniffles and was obliged to blow her nose once or twice.

However, that was nothing to make a fuss about, and certainly would not oblige her to stay in bed.

She decided to get up, dressing herself in a plain gown that she had owned for some time which was easy to fasten by herself. On no account was she going to send for Janet, who would be sure to scold her and try to make her stay in bed.

She brushed her long, glossy hair, leaving it hanging loose on her shoulders, because she could not be bothered with putting it up in its usual style. A glance in her mirror told her that she did not look exactly elegant. Indeed, some of her London friends would think her positively dowdy, but she wanted to escape before anyone could tell her she ought to go back to bed.

Almost everyone had been in to visit her except Vincent. Cassie was frowning as she went downstairs, clutching the kitten her brother had given her. Why hadn't her husband visited her? She knew he had been in earlier, when she was asleep, but not since she had first woken. Was he cross with her for embarrassing him at the reception?

Cassie could not perfectly remember what had happened, but she seemed to recall Vincent carrying her upstairs. Had she really clung to him and asked him to kiss her? Oh, how shameless of her! What must he have thought?

She slipped out of a side entrance, hoping to avoid being seen, and made her way slowly to a small, walled garden she knew was hardly ever used. It was warm and sheltered, and on that summer afternoon, very peaceful. Just the place to be alone with her thoughts.

Cassie found a dry patch of grass beneath the apple tree, spread her shawl on the ground and sat down. She stroked the kitten on her lap, talking to it as she tried to think of a name for her new pet.

'Shall I call you Fluffs or Snowy?' she asked, holding the kitten and kissing it on top of its head. 'Or are they both too ordinary? I really ought to think of something better...' She yawned. 'Pray forgive me, Fluffs, I do not know what has happened to my manners.'

Setting the kitten down on the grass beside her, Cassie started to pick daisies and make them into chains. She hung them round her neck, then, beginning to feel sleepy, lay back on the grass and closed her eyes. It was so warm and tranquil here in this garden... When she opened her eyes again some twenty minutes or so later, it was to find Vincent sitting opposite her.

He smiled as she yawned, stretched and sat up. 'You looked so peaceful. I was reluctant to wake you—and the ground is very dry so I did not think you would take harm.'

'Have you been there long?' Cassie glanced at him a little shyly. He looked so handsome, dressed casually in just a pair of pale cream breeches, top boots and a white shirt. She hoped he could not read her mind, or he would know how very much she wanted to put her arms around him.

'A few minutes. Janet told me you had gone out, so I came in search of you. I did not think you would have gone far, and a gardener happened to see you come here.' His eyes went over her, bringing a flush to her cheeks. 'Is your cold better today?'

'Yes, much better,' she replied. 'It was so foolish of me to collapse like that yesterday. I never take colds as a rule.'

'Are you sure you should be sitting out here? Would you not have done better to stay in bed for another day?'

'I hate lying in bed for no good reason. Besides, it is so warm I am sure I shall not make my cold worse. I was playing with Fluffs...' She looked about her, frowning. 'Oh, no! She has gone. I should have watched her. She does not know her home yet. I am afraid she will be lost.'

'Fluffs?' Vincent raised his brows.

'A kitten. Jack gave her to me. She is an adorable ball

of white fluff so—' She stopped speaking as they both heard the pitiful mewing. Cassie looked up at the branches of the apple tree and gasped. 'Oh, no! You foolish kitty. How did you get up there?'

She jumped to her feet as if about to climb after the kitten, but Vincent caught her arm, firmly restraining her. 'No, Cassie. You must wait here. Leave this to me. I do not want to have to rescue you and that ridiculous animal.'

'There is no need to be cross, Vinnie. I wasn't going to climb the tree. I am not a child anymore. Besides, Janet has already told me I have to learn to behave as a lady. There are to be no more escapades, no more scrapes.'

His brows rose in disbelief. 'I shall believe that when I see it!'

She laughed as he began to look for a foothold, his expression somewhere between resignation and doom.

'Do be careful, Vinnie,' she urged. 'Some of those branches might not bear your weight. Perhaps we should send for one of the gardeners to bring a ladder?'

'I am not yet too old to climb a tree!'

Oh, dear! thought Cassie. He was cross! She refrained from answering, watching anxiously as he began to climb very slowly and carefully. Several small twigs and leaves came fluttering down to shower over her. The apple tree was old and in desperate need of pruning. She held her breath as Vincent inched his way towards the kitten, who was crouching in a fork between two branches and watching his advance nervously.

'Here, kitty,' Vincent said, making a coaxing noise that caused Cassie to smile to herself. 'Kitty…kitty…' He was just below the kitten and reached out to try and grab it. The startled creature lashed out with its claws and scratched his hand, making Vincent swear and almost lose his balance. 'Wretched creature!'

The kitten arched its back, hissing angrily. Vincent made

another grab, but it leapt at him, landing on his head so that he swore again and jerked involuntarily. The kitten then made a death-defying leap onto Cassie's chest as she stood beneath the tree looking up. Its claws went through the thin material of her gown and she gave a little shriek. The kitten sprang to the ground and ran off into the bushes. Vincent glanced down at her, lost his balance and caught at a branch which was not strong enough to hold his weight. There was an ominous cracking sound, a rather rude oath from Vincent, and then he came sliding and slithering down the tree to land on the ground with a bump. He lay on his back, eyes closed and very still.

'Vinnie!' Cassie cried. 'Oh, Vinnie, my dearest love!' She rushed to his side, kneeling down and bending over him in acute distress. 'Vinnie, speak to me! Are you hurt, my love? Oh, please do not be hurt. I cannot bear it if you die. Please do not leave me.'

She was running her hands over his face, her own pale with fright, when he suddenly reached out and pulled her down on top of him. In another moment he had rolled her over so that she was beneath him on the ground. She stared up at him, her fear draining away as she saw the wicked intent in his eyes.

'Oh, you wretch,' she whispered, suddenly breathless. 'You scared me. I thought you badly hurt.'

'I shall no doubt have bruises all over,' Vincent retorted drily. 'I shall look to you to tend them for me, my sweet.'

'Would you like me to rub liniment in for you?'

Cassie's tone was deceptively earnest and earned her a scowl from her husband. 'I know I am ten years older than you—but do you think me so decrepit?'

Her suppressed giggles made his eyes smoulder. 'You are a minx and a jade, Lady Carlton. You need to learn respect for your husband. I believe I shall have to discipline you.'

His mouth gently took possession of hers, but the kiss quickly deepened, their bodies straining against each other's with such urgency that both were shaken. Vincent released her ruefully, touching her face with the tips of his fingers.

'I do not believe this is quite the place or the time, my love. I was sent to find you because nuncheon is served.'

'We must not delay, then,' Cassie said, eyes bright with mischief. 'How very shocking it would be if I were to miss nuncheon. I do not know how I should ever face anyone again.'

'We could always sneak up to your room and pretend I could not find you.'

'Yes.' Cassie gurgled with laughter. 'I suppose we could.'

They walked hand in hand towards the house. But as they approached the door, Sir Septimus came out, carrying his wife's dog, which he dropped none too gently on the lawn.

'Wretched animal,' he said on seeing them. 'All such creatures ought to be drowned at birth, if you ask me.'

'Uncle, I have never agreed with you more in my life,' Vincent said. 'Especially kittens. Fluffy white ones.'

'Oh, Vinnie!' Cassie cried. 'We forgot Fluffs.'

'We shall send a footman to look for her, Cassie. And if one is not sufficient, we shall send more.'

'Yes, Vincent. Just as you say.'

'And how are you this morning, Lady Carlton?' asked Septimus. 'I must tell you, you had us all worried yesterday—but you seem to have made a remarkable recovery.'

'Oh, I am much better now,' said Cassie and promptly sneezed. 'Colds usually do not affect me at all. I cannot think what made me so unwell yesterday.'

'Nor can I,' murmured Vincent and gave her such a look that she blushed. 'It was quite unaccountable.'

Septimus looked at him, eyes narrowed as he caught their bantering mood. 'Humph!' he said. 'Carlton, I must tell you that you have torn your breeches. What on earth have you been doing?'

'Climbing trees,' replied Vincent. 'Excuse me, Uncle. I believe we must go and change before we join you all for nuncheon.'

His hand closed over Cassie's arm, and he propelled her into the house and towards the stairs. As they reached the top of them, however, they were met by Harry.

'Glad to see you up and about, Lady Carlton,' he said. 'Vinnie, may I please have a word?'

'Later, Harry. I must change my clothes.'

'Oh…sorry.' Harry frowned. 'You've torn your breeches, Vinnie, did you know?'

'Climbing trees,' Cassie murmured, eyes brimming with laughter. 'It is a sad fault in a man of his advanced years—but I hope to cure him of it in time.'

'Jade!' Vincent's grip tightened on her arm. 'Excuse us, Harry.'

He steered Cassie past his astonished brother and into her bedroom, kicking the door shut behind them. Then he reached out for her, pulling her fiercely into his arms.

'Do you know how very much I—?'

The door opened again. 'Cassie…' began Lady Longbourne, then stopped, a faint colour in her cheeks. 'Do forgive me, Carlton. I did not realise you were here. I came to see if Cassie had returned and would be coming down for nuncheon.'

'I am here because I wish to be with my wife, Mama, and because I need to change my breeches—and, before you tell me, I *know* they are torn.'

'Really, Vincent! What have you been doing?'

'I am tempted to tell you,' Vincent replied, his patience quite at an end. 'Except I have not been doing anything, because there are too many interested persons in this house. In answer to your question, no, Cassie will not be coming down to eat. As soon as we have both changed, we shall leave for Carlton House. A picnic basket may be prepared for us, and if we feel hungry we shall eat when and as we choose—but alone. Certainly alone.'

'Well, there is not the least need to lose your temper, Carlton,' his offended mama said and frowned at him.

'I am not losing my temper,' said he, but was. 'I merely wish to be alone with my *wife* for a few minutes. I do not think that too much to ask, do you?'

'Dearest Vinnie.' Cassie touched his hand, making him look at her. 'I think you are a little cross, my love, and you know there is no reason for you to be. We have the rest of our lives together. And as it happens, I am very hungry.'

'Are you, my darling?' Vinnie looked down at her, his impatience melting away as he realised she was right. She was his now and he did not have to grab at his happiness. 'Very well. We shall be down in ten minutes, Mama.' He smiled at her sweetly. 'And please shut the door behind you as you leave…'

Chapter Fourteen

Changed into the breeches he had worn for his wedding, Vincent did full justice to the cold meats, bread and raised pies set out for their meal. He noticed that Cassie ate only sparingly of some bread and butter and a little chicken. Indeed, she did not seem particularly hungry at all. His eyes gleamed. Later, when they were alone, he would challenge her on this point.

However, nuncheon over, the new Lady Carlton seemed very willing to set out on the journey to her future home. She kissed all her friends, and went out into the courtyard where the carriages were drawn up ready, horses champing at the bit, grooms, and footmen everywhere.

Lady Longbourne was tearful. She clung to Cassie affectionately for some seconds.

'Enjoy yourself, my love. I would not for the world have you come home before you are ready—but I shall look forward to a long visit when you are settled.'

'Do not forget you have Harry's wedding to plan, Mama,' said Cassie, kissing her. 'Besides, I shall write and tell you of all the places we visit—and I shall collect lots of interesting things to show you on my return. And you must come to us whenever you wish, of course.'

'You are such a sweet, generous gel. Carlton is fortunate to have found you, my dear.' Lady Longbourne let her go at last and blew her nose.

'Goodbye, Lady Carlton,' Sir Septimus said when it was his turn to take his leave of her. He kissed her hand. 'I dare say you know how to keep this young cockerel you've married in hand. But if he gives you any trouble, send for me. I shall engage to set him right.'

'I shall most certainly,' said Cassie, and impulsively kissed his cheek. 'And of course you and your family will naturally always be welcome to visit.'

Sir Septimus glowed and insisted on handing her into the waiting carriage himself. Vincent watched with amused indulgence, then climbed in after her and signalled to a groom, who closed the door.

'Are you not riding today?' she asked, deceptively innocent.

'No, I am not,' replied her husband. 'At least I shall have you to myself all the way to Hamilton.'

'Hamilton? Your estate in Surrey? I thought we were to go to Carlton House?'

'That was Mama's plan,' said Vincent, a little smile about his mouth. 'But I have decided that Carlton is too close to Longbourne. It would not surprise me if my dear mother does not decide to pay a visit there within a few days...'

'Vincent!' Cassie cried, quite shocked. 'How can you think she would do such a thing?'

'I know my family,' he replied wryly. 'And now that you have assured Septimus he will be welcome at any time, I dare say we shall never be rid of him.'

She looked at him doubtfully. 'Do you not like to see your family, dearest?'

'Naturally. But not all the time—and not while we are

on our honeymoon. It is the strangest thing, I dare say, but I have a fancy to spend a little time alone with you, Cassie.'

She laughed as he gave her a smouldering glance. 'Well, at least we are alone now. And I can get rid of this…' She began to undo the ribbons of a very pretty straw bonnet. She took it off and laid it on the seat opposite then sighed. 'There…that is very much better. Do you not think so, Vinnie?'

His eyebrows rose. 'I thought it suited you well, my love—did you not care for it?'

'It looked well enough—indeed, it is one of my favourites,' she replied a sparkle in her wicked eyes. 'But now you will be able to kiss me so much more easily—will you not?'

'Ah, yes, I perceive now that it is a very good idea,' he murmured with satisfaction. 'I had not thought of that, but it was a good notion of yours, my love.'

And with that, he took her in his arms and began to kiss her in a way that was most agreeable to them both.

Hamilton Manor was indeed much larger than Carlton House, as Vincent had once told her. It was considerably older, of course, and built of mellowed red bricks with three wings at the back, which made it look rather like a capital E, a style much favoured at the time it was built in the age of the great Elizabeth. However, despite its age, it had been kept up and inside many modern improvements had been made to make it more comfortable.

'Oh, how lovely,' Cassie murmured her appreciation when she was helped out of the carriage late that evening. Although it was too dark to get more than an impression of the outside of the house, the courtyard gardens were filled with the perfume of roses and honeysuckle. 'It smells so gorgeous. I think this garden must be absolutely lovely when one can see it properly.'

'I am sorry to arrive so late at night,' Vincent apologised, for it was close to the witching hour. 'But I thought you would rather sleep in your own home than an inn tonight.'

'Yes, oh, yes, I should,' Cassie agreed and valiantly tried to smother her yawns. 'I am excessively glad to be here, Vinnie. And I shall see the gardens in the morning.'

She was escorted into the house, where a few of the servants who had been ordered to wait on their master's arrival had hastily gathered in the large entrance hall.

'Forgive me for giving you so little notice,' Vincent said to his butler. 'It was a last-minute change of plans. I trust our rooms are ready, Morton?'

'Oh, yes, sir,' the butler replied. 'Your instructions were that we might expect you at any time. We have been in readiness since yesterday, my lord. A cold supper is laid in the morning room, should you wish for it.'

'Thank you. I knew I might rely on you. If Mrs Morton would show her ladyship upstairs, please? My wife is a little tired from the journey. You may send a tray up to her rooms in ten minutes. Only the porter need remain on duty after that. Her ladyship's maid will unpack the small trunk. Everything else can wait until the morning.'

'Yes, sir. Thank you, sir.'

Cassie had been briefly introduced to the more important members of her household. She was too tired to remember their names, but Janet would remind her in the morning. She followed Mrs Morton up the main staircase and along the landing to a suite of rooms in the west wing. As she was shown into the first rather pleasant sitting room, which was furnished in shades of blue and cream, she was relieved to see her faithful Janet was already in her bedchamber, waiting for her, her night things unpacked and ready.

As she walked into the bedroom itself, Cassie looked about her with a feeling of pleasure. The walls were covered with a green silk paper which had a repeat pattern of self-coloured daisies running through. The bed hangings, covers and upholstery were all of a lighter shade of green with borders of exquisite embroidery which was made to look like looped daisy chains.

'It is just like a summer meadow,' she said. 'Even on wet days when I cannot go out, I shall feel as if I am outside.'

Mrs Morton nodded, smiled and went away, leaving her new mistress to the ministrations of the faithful Janet.

Standing still as Janet helped her out of her travelling gown, she sighed with relief. Warm water had been carried up and Cassie went behind a magnificent painted screen to wash and pull on the soft, filmy nightgown Janet had spread ready for her. She was then helped into a very elegant satin dressing gown.

She sat down on the stool in front of her dressing table, glancing at the pretty silver-gilt brushes and trinkets set out there.

'I have not seen these before—oh, they have my initials on them. Carlton must have had them engraved for me.'

'You will find a rather special desk in your private sitting room,' Janet told her, looking rather like the cat who has just found the cream. As Lady Carlton's personal maid, her own position had suddenly shot up several notches, and she was feeling very pleased with what she had found here: it seemed she, too, was to have her own sitting room! 'All the trays and pens have your initials, Miss Cassie. His lordship has been to a great deal of trouble to make things nice for you.'

'Yes, he has, hasn't he?' Cassie smiled at her maid in the mirror. 'I believe we shall be very happy here, Janet.'

'Yes, Miss Cassie. I am sure we shall.' Janet finished brushing her hair and laid the brush down with a smirk of satisfaction. 'Is there anything else I can do for you, miss?'

'No, thank you, Janet.' Cassie stood up and kissed her

cheek. 'You may go to bed now. I shall not need you again tonight, and I am very sure you must be quite exhausted.'

'Goodnight then, milady. I hope you will be very happy.'

Cassie smiled but made no reply as Janet left through the sitting room. She heard her pause to direct the butler where to set the tray he had just brought up for his master and mistress's supper, then the door closed behind them both and all was quiet.

Cassie removed the silver top from a pretty blue glass perfume flask and tested a little of the scent on her fingertip. It smelled nice so she applied some behind her ears and to her wrists. Then she heard the door of the dressing room open and Vincent walked in. He had changed into a long, dark blue dressing robe, and she noticed his feet were bare, which made her very aware of the change in her situation.

He smiled at her as she stood up, sending delightful little shivers down her spine. 'I love your hair like that, Cassie, loose on your shoulders. You look lovely.'

She blushed, her gaze dropping as she saw the flame of desire in his eyes. 'Oh, Vinnie. I am not pretty. You know I'm not.'

'Pretty?' His eyebrows rose as he moved towards her. 'No, you are not pretty, Cassie—you are beautiful.'

She gazed up at him, eyes wide, mouth soft and inviting. 'I think you must be seeing through the eyes of love, Vinnie.'

He took her by the hand and led her to a long mirror set in the corner of the room, then turned her to face it. His arms went round her from behind, his lips against the softness of her hair.

'To me you are the most beautiful woman in the world,' he murmured huskily, and she felt a tremor run through him. 'Look into your eyes as I do, Cassie. You have a beautiful soul. Your beauty is not just skin deep, it comes from within—it is the kind of beauty that the years cannot take from you.'

At that particular moment Cassie's eyes were dark and glowing with the love she felt for him. And, knowing herself truly loved, she *was* beautiful.

'It is the candlelight playing tricks,' she said, laughing and turning within the circle of his arms to slide her own arms up about his neck. Her perfume and the softness of her flesh had an intoxicating effect on him, and Vincent moaned with longing deep in his throat. 'Kiss me, Vinnie,' she whispered huskily. 'Make me yours, my darling. I do so very much want to be all yours.'

'You are not too tired?'

'No,' she said, and in that moment the tiredness fled, leaving her eager and willing as he caught her up and carried her to the bed. 'No, I am not tired at all.'

Vincent's loving was beyond all that she had imagined or ever hoped for. His kisses roused her to a quivering ecstasy so that when his mouth moved ever lower, seeking out the secret, tender places of her body, she melted with pleasure.

'Oh, Vinnie…I do love you so.'

'And I adore you, my lovely wife.'

Now she was ready for him, moist and trembling with the passion his tender caresses had aroused in her, and though his entry caused her some initial pain, she was soon swept away on a rising tide of desire and sweet pleasure that lifted them both to joy such as neither had ever known. For only when passion is mixed liberally with love can the meeting of flesh with flesh be so complete, so right, so true, so all consuming that two people become one indivisible being.

Later, when they lay still and content, wrapped together in the warmth of perfect understanding and love, Vincent began to talk…to tell her of the things which had for so long lain hidden in his heart.

'Somehow I never forgot the girl who made me climb a tree twice for her,' he whispered softly against Cassie's ear. 'When I went to London, I was young and, like many men, sure of my own pride and manhood. There were women…' His arms tightened about her as he felt her stiffen. 'But the pleasure I found in their arms was fleeting. And I soon tired of them. I had friends. Jack was my closest, always. He invited me to stay at his home many times, but I was always too busy to come, or so I told myself. Then the war came. We both joined up as officers on Wellington's staff—and one night, Jack asked me if I would marry you should he die.'

Vincent kissed the nape of Cassie's neck. She snuggled back into the curve of his body, the warmth of him making her feel safe and content.

'I refused. I did not believe I could make you happy by offering such a marriage, and I was so restless within myself that I hardly knew what I wanted. My friends thought I was very brave because I risked death without a thought, but I had no fear of dying.'

'But if you refused Jack…' Cassie turned her head to look at him. 'I don't understand?'

'I refused the first time when he asked only me, but then, after your father died, he asked five of us at the same time. I had no choice but to promise when the others agreed. So I made sure I drew the short straw. If anyone was going to offer you a marriage of convenience, it was going to be me.'

'Why?'

'Because I had never forgotten your spirit. I still thought of you as a child who refused to give in. I believed some of the others who had given their promise to Jack might attempt to crush that spirit—and I was not prepared to risk that.'

'And yet you did not come?'

'I had everything prepared,' Vincent said. 'Yet still held back. I think perhaps I was afraid. Some years had passed since we had met. I thought you might have grown up into a very proper young lady, and I did not want you to have changed. I wanted you still to be the girl who had made me take her kitten first.'

Cassie turned on her side so that she could look at him. 'But I was such a plain, naughty child, Vinnie. I was so stubborn—and you ripped your breeches coming back for me. When you went off at once, I thought you must be cross.'

'Embarrassed,' he confessed with a laugh. 'I rather think there was more of me on view than was decent.'

'Yes, there was,' she said, and laughed. 'But you forget. Jack often swam naked in the river when we were children. I was quite used to a gentleman's anatomy.'

'Wicked jade! If it didn't spare your feelings, it did mine.'

'Oh, Vinnie! You were my white knight, but instead of carrying me away on your charger you went off as if the devil himself were after you.'

Vinnie kissed her at the base of her throat, just at the pulse spot. 'No wonder I adore you,' he murmured huskily. 'I have never met anyone like you. Something about you touched me even then.' He ran his fingers down the ridges of her spine, making her gasp as desire shot through her like hot threads and she arched against him. 'I cannot say that I loved you that day. It was not love then—just a fleeting thought that we might be kindred spirits.'

'You mean because I was always getting into scrapes—as you did when you hung a pair of corsets on the church spire at Carlton?'

'Who told you that?' Vincent stared at her in surprise. 'Was it Harry?'

'No. Miss Simpson. She told me a lot of interesting stories that night, Vinnie—and many of them were about you.'

Vincent chuckled, much amused. 'I see I must pay more attention to that lady in future. I have underestimated her.'

'You went to hide yourself in your billiard room, I expect?' She touched his cheek. 'At first I wished I might come with you, but afterwards I was quite glad I stayed.'

'What else did you learn from her?'

Cassie nestled closer, pressing her lips against his naked shoulder. 'Reading between the lines of what I heard and what I had myself observed, I came to think that perhaps you might sometimes have been lonely.'

Vincent smiled and cupped his hands over her buttocks, pressing her closer to him so that she could feel the pulsing heat of his manhood and know that he wanted her again.

'How strange that you should see it. I do not blame Mama for preferring Harry to me. He is always so easygoing, as you know—and she loved his father very much. I fear there were times when she came close to hating mine. And perhaps he deserved it. He was a violent man, and not kind to his family.'

'Vinnie, dearest…'

'She loved me as much as she could,' he went on, 'but I reminded her of things that hurt her. There was always an emptiness inside me, but I do not believe it was Mama's fault. I think I should still have had it had I been her favourite son. I have always known that I was searching for something—someone.' His arms tightened about her, his mouth against her hair. 'And now I have found my special person. The one woman who can make me whole.'

'Oh, Vinnie…' Cassie began to weep, her tears making his shoulder damp. 'Do not set me on a pedestal, my love.

I am not sure I can measure up to the image you have of me.'

She got no further. His mouth was on hers, tongue teasing, probing as it sought entry. And then he rolled her on to her back, taking her with such a hungry yearning that Cassie moaned with pleasure as everything else was swept from her mind, and she knew that she was indeed a part of him. She would never need to feel jealous of La Valentina again, for she knew Vincent was hers and hers alone.

And she knew that she too had found a safe haven for all the love and sweet passion she had held inside her for so long.

Cassie woke to find the bed empty. It felt cold and for a moment she wondered where Vincent had gone. To his own room perhaps? She got out of bed, pulled on her wrap and went through the connecting door to investigate. His bed had not been touched, the covers still turned down as they had been the previous night, and his room was empty. However, she saw his dressing robe thrown carelessly over a chair and guessed that he had dressed and gone out. Perhaps for an early morning ride.

She wished that he had waited so that she might have gone with him. She would ask him to do so another day.

Returning to her own bedchamber, Cassie wandered over to the window and gazed out. It was so beautiful! She had not dreamed of such a lovely view.

The park led to a lake, which glistened in the morning sun, and beyond that were gentle hills that seemed to stretch away into the distance and out of sight. Then something caught her eye and she drew a sharp breath of delight, for there, wandering at will—and only a short distance from the house—was a herd of deer presided over by a magnificent stag. There were at least fifteen and she saw two fawns keeping close to their mothers. They seemed to be grazing on food which had been specially put out for them, and were obviously quite tame.

Hearing a slight noise behind her, Cassie turned and saw her husband had entered the room. He was dressed for riding and had obviously been out, for his face had the glow of exercise and fresh air about it.

'Do come and look,' she said, holding out her hand to him. 'The deer are almost up to the house.'

'It was Grandmother Hamilton who started to feed them near the house,' he said, smiling at her pleasure. 'Grandfather grumbled when they sometimes broke into the kitchen gardens and trampled on the vegetables, but she loved to see them so he kept up the feeding even after she died—in her memory. I went out this morning early to make sure the food was there. I wanted you to see them when you woke up.'

'Oh, Vinnie, how thoughtful you are,' she said, gazing up mistily at him. 'You knew how much that would please me. It is a wonderful surprise.'

'I always want to please you,' he said, kissing her hand. 'Now, hurry and get dressed, my love. It is a little cooler than of late, but a lovely morning. And I want to show you my best surprise.'

'Now what have you been up to?' she asked, eyes sparkling.

'You will find out when you come down.'

He went away again. Cassie rang for Janet, and it was not quite five-and-twenty minutes later when she went down to find her husband impatiently pacing the hall and waiting for her. He looked up, a look of such delight coming into his eyes as he saw her that her heart filled with love for him. He held out his hand, and she ran gladly down the last few steps to meet him.

He was so impatient!

'What is it, Vinnie?'

'Come outside and I shall show you.'

She let him lead her outside, and then she gave a cry of pleasure as she saw the light curricle and a pair of beautifully matched grey horses standing in the courtyard, their manes and tails shining like pure silk in the sunlight.

'Are they for me, Vinnie?' She looked at him in dawning wonder. 'Oh, you knew it was what I wanted—something I could drive myself. And the horses! They are such thoroughbreds!'

'Nothing but the best for you, my love,' Vincent said, a glint of satisfaction in his eyes as she went over to pat and fondle the horses. 'It took me quite a time to find the right pair. And I had the curricle made specially light so that it will be easy for you to handle. Once I have taught you how to drive it, you will become known for your style.'

'I shall be like Letty Lade!' Cassie cried, laughing. 'Or perhaps not quite…'

'You will be known as the dashing Lady Carlton,' Vincent told her, a wicked gleam in his eyes. 'But I warn you, I shall be a hard taskmaster, Cassie. You will not be allowed to drive in town until I am satisfied you can do it with style and safety.'

'No, of course not,' she said. 'When can I have my first lesson, Vinnie? Can we go now? Oh, please, do say yes. I cannot wait to try my skill.'

'I do not see why not,' he said and smiled. Then he gave her his hand and helped her up on to the box. It was as he was showing her how to hold the reins lightly in one hand that they saw a horseman ride into the courtyard. Vincent frowned. 'Good grief! I think that is Harry…what in the name of blazes is he doing here?'

Harry came riding up to them. 'Thank goodness I caught you,' he said. 'I came on ahead to warn you, Vinnie. Mama had a terrible quarrel with Septimus yesterday, just after you left. She set out not two hours later for Hamilton. I persuaded her to stay at an inn last night, and came to warn you—she will be here within the hour.'

'Of all the…' Vincent swore furiously. 'Could you not find some way to prevent her, Harry?'

'She would not have it that you were here,' Harry said, looking apologetic. 'I told her I thought you had changed your plans, but she knew best. She was certain you were at Carlton, and said she would not dream of intruding on you there, and that she was certain you would not mind her coming here, because she refused to stay another moment in Septimus's company. And he would not budge, you know how thick-skinned he is, Vinnie.'

'Well, you can just ride back and tell Mama that we *are* here, and she can turn round and—'

Cassie laid a gentle hand on his arm. 'Do not be so unkind, Vinnie darling,' she said. 'Your mother is very welcome to stay for a few days if she wishes—besides, we shall be going to France very soon, to visit Louise and Jack.'

'Are we never to be alone together?' Vincent glowered down at her. 'Damn it, I want you to myself, Cassie.'

Cassie leaned towards him and whispered in his ear. Harry could not hear what was said, but whatever it was, a change came over Vincent's face and he was smiling again.

'No, you are very right,' he said and laughed huskily. 'She cannot follow us there, can she?'

Cassie blushed as she looked at Harry. 'Would you go on up to the house and let Mrs Morton know Lady Longbourne is expected, please, Harry? And pray tell Mama that we are very sorry but we shall not be able to welcome her personally as we are going for a drive—a rather long drive, as it happens, that may keep us away most of the day. However, she is to make herself quite at home, and we shall all dine together this evening.'

She turned to smile up into the frustrated eyes of her husband.

'And now, Vinnie—perhaps you would like to drive for a while? Just to show me how it is done?'

'Make a quick getaway, you mean?'

'Exactly so, my dearest.'

Vincent laughed and whipped up his horses, leaving a cloud of dust behind as he drove them out of the courtyard, through the park and away over the gentle hills.

Harry stood watching for a moment, then smiled to himself as he turned his horse. There was no doubt that Cassie was up to every trick in the book, and he rather thought he might need a few of them himself in the future…

* * * * *

The Chivalrous Rake
by
Elizabeth Rolls

Award-winning author **Elizabeth Rolls** lives in the Adelaide Hills of South Australia in an old stone farmhouse surrounded by apple, pear and cherry orchards, with her husband, two smallish sons, three dogs and two cats. She also has four alpacas and three incredibly fat sheep, all gainfully employed as environmentally sustainable lawn-mowers. The kids are convinced that writing is a perfectly normal profession and she's working on her husband. Elizabeth has what most people would consider far too many books, and her tea and coffee habit is legendary. She enjoys reading, walking, cooking, and her husband's gardening.

Elizabeth loves to hear from readers and you can contact her at books@elizabethrolls.com or via her website at www.elizabethrolls.com

Chapter One

Jack Hamilton glared across his bedchamber at the retreating back of his doctor. He'd always considered shooting the messenger to be an irrational and sadly ill-bred response to unwelcome news. Right now he could definitely see the attraction it held for some.

A month! A whole damn month! By that time the hunting season would be nearly over. And what was he supposed to do with himself in the meantime? Play shove ha'penny? When he was situated within easy distance of the Quorn, the Belvoir *and* the Pytchely?

He caught the commiserating look on his valet Fincham's face and uttered a malevolent curse under his breath, directed at his own unforgivable cow-handedness in letting Firebird come down in the first place. Marc would roast him finely when he heard. For a moment he considered not informing Marc of his accident, only to dismiss the idea. The last thing the Earl of Rutherford would want to do would be to come all the way to Leicestershire in the depths of winter to discover that his host couldn't go hunting.

Jack comforted himself with the thought that if he wrote, Marc's ribbing would, perforce, be on paper. He didn't have to read it if he didn't want to.

He reached for his brandy glass without thinking and swore loudly. Wrong arm.

'Er, Mr Hamilton…'

Jack looked up.

The doctor stood by the open door, a rueful smile upon his face. 'It might be an idea to wear a sling until that collarbone knits…'

'A *sling*?' Jack could scarcely believe his ears. 'What the hell do you mean, a sling?'

Wilberforce answered readily, 'Piece of cloth to support your arm—it goes around your neck and ties—'

'I know what a sling is, damn it!' growled Jack. 'What the deuce do you think I need with one? I'm not a child!'

'No, sir. Of course not.'

The doctor's placatory tone failed to convince Jack and he resolutely ignored Fincham's snort of laughter. At least he had the decency to pretend to be coughing.

''Tis just that I have observed that gentlemen such as yourself—er, *active* gentlemen, that is—have a tendency to forget their injury and use the arm. A sling would serve to remind you to rest the arm.'

Jack snorted. 'I'll be reminded of that every time I see my hunters eating their heads off, thanks very much!'

'Very well, sir.' A faint grin crossed the doctor's face. 'Sorry to have been of service, sir.'

'*Sorry to have*…oh!' An unwilling chuckle broke from Jack. 'I take you. Sorry, Wilberforce. It's my own stupid fault. Thank you, and pray give my regards to your wife. I understand you're expecting a happy event.'

The recently married doctor grinned. 'That's right, sir. I'd best be getting back. Alice said she'd wait supper. I wish to God she wouldn't—no saying when I'll get home some nights, but she likes to do it! Good night. And cheer up—at least it wasn't your neck!'

The expression of disbelief on Mr Hamilton's face and

the disgusted snort that accompanied it suggested that, in his opinion, he might as well have broken his neck.

With a friendly wave, and thoroughly unsympathetic smile, the doctor departed.

Jack reached for the brandy, carefully this time, and took a sip. It might serve to sweeten his temper.

It didn't.

His head ached. His shoulder ached and he felt thoroughly dissatisfied with life. With a disgusted mutter at his melancholy mood he got to his feet, cursing as his broken collarbone, and recently relocated shoulder, protested the unwary movement.

'Will you be going to bed now, Mr Jack?' asked Fincham, gathering up Jack's riding coat and discarded shirt.

Jack stared at him. '*Bed?* At this hour? Didn't you hear the doctor? I broke my collarbone, not my blasted neck, Fincham!' He picked up the coat Fincham had laid out for him.

This time Fincham grinned openly. 'No, sir. Be putting you to bed with a shovel if you'd done that. Here, I'll help you with that!' He came over and, ignoring Jack's protest, assisted him into the coat.

It was a good thing, thought Jack, that he disliked tight coats and preferred to be able to shrug himself in without assistance. As it was, he suppressed a curse at the jolt of pain.

'Thanks,' said Jack. 'I'll get out of your way and go down to the library.'

He'd better write that letter to Marc. No doubt he and Meg would be just as happy to remain at Alston Court and dote on their two-month-old son. Probably they'd just accepted his invitation at the christening because they felt sorry for him.

Gathering up his brandy, he left the room. His mood did not improve on the way to the library. *Poor old Jack. All alone up there in Leicestershire.* That sort of thing.

Oh, for God's sake! What the devil was the matter with him? He must have taken more of a bump on the head than he'd realised. Of course Marc and Meg weren't visiting out of pity. They'd accepted because they were friends. He had no closer friend than Marcus Langley, Earl of Rutherford. Not even Marc's marriage had interfered with their friendship.

He sat down at his very untidy desk and reached awkwardly for a pen and paper. He muttered a few imprecations as he realised the quill needed trimming and reached for the pen cutter.

Dear Marc, No doubt you will find this highly amusing but I feel I ought to warn you...

He finished the letter and folded it. Lucky Marc. A wife like Meg and now a son. He couldn't imagine how life could possibly hold more for a man—except, of course, for all the other sons and daughters the pair of them were looking forward to.

He shivered slightly and glanced frowning at the fire. For some peculiar reason his library, which he had always found a companionable sort of room, seemed cold and empty.

He'd noticed that ever since he returned from the christening of Marc's heir—his godson. He'd been conscious of the quiet. Even after the other visitors had left Alston Court, Marc's principal residence, he'd been aware of a sense of life, a hum of purpose, about the place. The way it had been when he'd stayed there as a boy.

It was as though Marc's marriage and the birth of his first child had brought the place back to full life.

Not even a broken collarbone and dislocated shoulder during the hunting season would bother Marc now. Jack grinned. He could only think of one aspect of a broken collarbone that would seriously discompose Marc. And he was fairly sure the inventive Earl of Rutherford would come up with a solution to that as well.

Disgustedly Jack faced the true cause of his recent irritability—he needed a wife. Which was all very well—he had known that for some years. Increasingly his various affairs had left him dissatisfied and restless. He wanted more than a discreet liaison with someone else's neglected and bored wife or a fashionable demi-rep. He wanted someone who was his, and his only. But finding the right female was far easier said than done.

For the last four Seasons he'd been actively, if surreptitiously, looking. He could do without every ambitious mama in Town thrusting darling little nitwits into his arms. He could certainly do without Sally Jersey introducing him to every heiress in sight.

He wanted a love match, not a marriage of convenience for an heir on his side and social advancement on hers. So he'd looked very carefully. So damn carefully that not even the girls he'd considered, nor their mamas for that matter, had realised his interest. And on each occasion the girl in question accepted some other fellow before he'd even got as far as becoming particular in his attentions. Which didn't really worry him—except for the inconvenience of having to select a new target.

All of which suggested that he hadn't cared in the least about any of them, which surprised him. They had, all of them, been nice, quiet, gentle, scholarly girls—bluestockings, even, who wouldn't have bothered him in the least. So why hadn't he felt the least flicker of interest in any of them?

Logically, all of those young ladies should have been perfect. Except for the unavoidable fact that he had thought them all a trifle dull, boring even. And he couldn't, not with the most vigorous stretch of his very fertile imagination, picture himself in bed with any of them.

He sipped at his brandy thoughtfully. Of course, desire and passion were not necessarily the best guides when choosing a bride. They had a tendency to ambush a man at his weakest point, sapping his self-control, rendering common-sense useless. There were safer ways to choose a wife.

It didn't really make sense. None of those girls should have been dull. They were all attractive, charming young ladies. They had all been interested in the same sorts of things he enjoyed. And they had generally agreed with him…

It would be nice to have a wife to come home to. Someone to talk to in the evenings instead of turning to his books. Someone to warm his bed—and his heart. A nice, sweet, companionable girl who would soothe his irritable temper when he broke his collarbone. Someone who wouldn't turn his ordered life upside down. Someone like Meg.

He grimaced. What the devil was he doing, languishing over his best friend's wife? But he had to admit, if Meg had not been well and truly married to Marc before he laid eyes on her, he probably would have courted her. She was just what he liked in a woman. Gentle, charming, unswervingly loyal. Easy to get on with. Elegant loveliness and dignity personified. She was tall, too. Smaller women always seemed to be daunted by his height. Meg didn't always agree with him, of course…in fact, she had even been known to disagree with Marc. Strongly.

He dismissed the thought. Marc *could* be a trifle unreasonable at times. Especially where Meg's safety or health was concerned. He grinned. Marc had been taken thoroughly by surprise in his marriage. *He* was far more rational in his approach to love. You worked out in advance what you liked in a woman and then looked for her. In a rational, logical way.

It hasn't worked yet, has it?

He frowned. The last thing you did was to permit the responses of your body to serve as a guide. Passion and lust were all very well, but he wanted a woman to respect and care for, not just take to bed. Passion and lust could lead a man badly astray in fixing his affections. Capricious guides at best, they were damned deceiving at worst.

He snorted as he picked up a book. He'd learnt that lesson early. Only a fool repeated his own mistakes. Besides, he was older now, more experienced and he was in full control of his responses and desires, as a man should be. So. There it was. He needed a young lady like Meg. Easy. Except the only girl like Meg *was* Meg and she was not only married to, but shatteringly in love with, his best friend.

The right girl must be out there *somewhere*, and this year, when he went to London for the Season, he was going to make an all-out effort to find her. Because it was in the highest degree unlikely that she would come seeking him out up here in the wilds of Leicestershire.

Two mornings later Jack stalked through the wintry wilderness of his garden on his way back from a walk in the woods behind the house. The stark lines of the bare trees, dusted with a light fall of snow, failed to please him. They looked contorted, dead. The whole world appeared unspeakably bleak and dreary.

Even the rambling seventeenth-century house looked uninviting. It even managed to look empty. Which was completely and utterly ridiculous. It had a full complement of staff, all of them hell-bent on cosseting him to death.

He'd had a shocking night, and getting out of bed had been worse. Never before had he realised just how inconvenient a broken collarbone could be, not to mention the residual ache from the dislocated shoulder. Every muscle in his upper body appeared to be connected to his shoulder, reminding him with every step that his hunters were enjoying an unforeseen holiday.

At least he'd managed to escape from the servants, along with their everlasting hot possets, cushions and commiserating looks, to get a breath of air. He hadn't counted on this blasted north wind, which sent spasms of pain through his shoulder and neck every few minutes. He'd have to try and sneak into the library without anyone catching him.

And he was definitely sick of all the callers. His neighbours had developed an appalling lack of tact. He really didn't need to hear all about the capital run the local pack had enjoyed two days ago. And he definitely didn't need to have his incapacitated shoulder treated as a sort of matrimonial godsend. He ground his teeth. If just so much as one more simpering chit was inspired to present him with her own... *special salve for injuries just such as yours, Mr Hamilton*! Well, he wouldn't be responsible for the consequences, that was all.

At least he'd told Evans to deny him to any further callers for a few days. It would be very hard to explain precisely why he'd stuffed a pot of salve down a young lady's bodice. With this in mind, he swung around a garden wall and crashed into the person coming the other way.

A thoroughly blasphemous and graphic exclamation escaped his lips even as his reeling body automatically registered the undoubted femininity of his assailant.

'Blast it, girl!' he went on, toning his language down slightly. 'Don't you ever look where you're going?' He probed cautiously at his shoulder. It *felt* as though everything was still there. Unfortunately. It certainly all ached in the right places. And, as he got a good look at his blushing assailant, a few of the *wrong* places made their presence felt, too. Good Lord! He was an experienced man of six and thirty—not a green youth of twenty to rise to the bait like a trout!

'Just as much as you do through a brick wall, I dare say!'

He blinked and looked down at the girl. He'd never seen

her before as far as he could remember, but something within screamed recognition.

Affronted mint-green eyes glared back as he took in her outmoded and very damp scarlet cloak, muddy boots and untidy hair. Straight and wet, it hung down her back and over her shoulders in dark mahogany strands. He thought it would be auburn when it dried. Dark brows lifted expectantly and he stared back.

What was the world coming to when young ladies assaulted him in his own garden? Who the devil was she anyway? And why did he feel such an overwhelming urge to lift her chin up and wipe the smudge off her tip-tilted, freckled nose? Or kiss it off?

Whoever she was, she had no right to be traipsing about his garden! Even if she did make him feel like a green youth of twenty—*especially* if she made him feel like a green youth of twenty! She had no right to do anything of the sort when his shoulder ached far too much for him to take any pleasure in it.

'Are all the men in Leicestershire as rude as you?' she enquired, pleasantly.

Jack felt his temper straining at its leash. What the devil did she have to be affronted about? He was the one who'd been practically assaulted in his own garden!

She told him, 'Your initial choice of epithet I might forgive, under the circumstances. But you could at least apologise now for using such disgraceful language to a lady!'

Jack glared back. Little vixen! Stung to fury, he allowed his eyes to rove over her, assessing her shapeless, dowdy clothes and general air of untidiness.

'Naturally I would apologise to a lady,' he drawled. 'You must forgive me if I fail to recognise the species when it invades my garden without invitation. I gave quite clear instructions to my servants that I was not at home.

Might I suggest that you return to your carriage? No doubt, if you are a lady, we shall meet at some party or other.'

His gaze lingered on the flare of temper in her eyes, the flush on her cheeks. And he had the distinct impression that her figure, under that appalling excuse for a cloak, would be altogether delightful. There was something about the way she held herself... In fact, she was altogether an attractive little package...and she was shivering in the bitter wind. What on earth were her parents about to be letting her risk her health and reputation in this manner?

He added impersonally, 'I can assure you that the warmth of your carriage will banish your chill far more effectively than my poor self.' Thoughtfully, he continued, 'Damp muslin may have been all the crack twenty years ago, but I can assure you, damp kerseymere doesn't wear well in Leicestershire in the middle of winter!'

The flush flamed to out and out scarlet and the mint-green eyes narrowed. 'Are you Mr Jonathan Hamilton?'

He bowed. 'I have that honour.' Lord! She looked like an angry elf.

She snorted. 'Then Papa must be all about in his head!' With which baffling statement she swung on her heel and headed back towards the house.

Jack followed more slowly, taking time to appreciate the swing of her stride, the lithe grace of her every movement until she disappeared towards the carriage drive. Thoughtfully he headed for a side door. With a bit of luck he could get to the library without any of the staff ever knowing he had escaped. He could make discreet enquiries about his caller later.

Suddenly the winter's day looked brighter. Branches wove an austere tracery against the scudding clouds. It would probably snow again later. He always liked watching it drift down against the windows, liked the blustery howl of the wind...invigorating...got the blood moving. And the house had suddenly sprung to life again, golden stone glowing a mellow welcome. He quickened his stride, no longer noticing the pain of his shoulder.

An apologetic cough caught his attention.

Jack looked up from his book with an irritated frown for his butler. With a bit of luck Evans would think he'd been here in the library all morning. 'I'm not at home, Evans. To anyone. I thought I made that clear.'

'Yes, sir. Quite plain. Indeed, I have denied you, but now that you have returned from your walk—'

'No buts, Evans. I'm not at home…walk? How did…I mean, what walk?' He returned his gaze, if not his attention, to his book. He might have known his escape would not go unnoticed. Perhaps if he ignored Evans, he might go away.

Unfortunately Evans had a tenacity to rival his damned collarbone.

'The walk you took in the woods, sir. If you could just tell me which rooms Mrs Roberts should have made up…'

Jack stared. 'Rooms? What rooms?'

'That's what Mrs Roberts wants to know,' pointed out Evans, with all the confidence of having been butler of Wyckeham Manor before the present master was breeched.

The stare became a glare. 'What guests, Evans? I'm not expecting anyone. Er, am I?'

'Dr Bramley, sir. And—'

'*Bramley?* The Reverend Dr Edward Bramley? My father's cousin?' Relief, it couldn't be disappointment, swept through him. Dr Bramley could have nothing to do with the little hornet in the gardens. Must be coincidence. Putting his book on the wine table, Jack asked, 'What the devil is he doing here? Has he come to stay?'

'Er, yes. The young lady seemed to think—'

'Young *lady*? Evans, in case it has escaped your notice, the Reverend Dr Bramley was, *is*, a gentleman somewhat older than my father would be if he were alive. Unless, of course, the laws of nature have changed...' His voice died away as cold horror washed over him. Perhaps Dr Bramley *could* have something to do with the little hornet in the gardens.

'No, sir,' said Evans in soothing tones. 'The laws of nature are much as they were. Miss Bramley is his daughter.'

Given that piece of information, Jack wondered if the laws of nature had, after all, been suspended. His memories of Dr Bramley, while admittedly sketchy, were of a vague, impractical, unmarried, and certainly celibate, scholar, who had trouble telling a bull from a cow. The only women he'd ever shown the least interest in were firmly ensconced between the pages of Greek tragedy. He couldn't for the life of him imagine Dr Bramley siring anyone, let alone that outspoken little hornet!

'Good God! And they have come to stay?' Mentally he began to rehearse his apology.

'Yes, sir. Shall I show Dr Bramley in, sir?'

'Well, of course you should show him in!' said Jack.

Evans departed swiftly, but not quite swiftly enough to hide the broad grin on his face. Refusing to ponder just what his butler found so amusing about the unexpected visit of an elderly cleric, Jack levered himself out of his chair very carefully.

A few moments later the door opened.

'Dr Bramley,' announced Evans.

Jack's first thought was that his elderly cousin had changed very little. Still the same short, spare frame, his face smiling vaguely. A few more wrinkles and much less hair, but he would have known him anywhere.

'Dr Bramley!' said Jack, coming forward. 'How pleasant to see you, sir. It must be twenty-five years since last you were here.'

The old man stared at him. 'Good gracious! You must

be right. It is Jack, isn't it? You look exactly like your dear father!'

Jack grinned. 'I'm glad to hear it. What brings you here, sir? I thought you were settled in Cornwall. Come and sit by the fire. You must be frozen.'

The old man nodded. 'Yes, I must say that gig was a little cold. Stagecoach wasn't much better, but at least we had our luggage. Ah, that's better!' He held out his hands to the blaze.

'Gig? Stagecoach? What in Hades were you doing in such conveyances? And what's this about your luggage?' If they'd come on the London stage then they must have fetched up at the Bell in Leicester after one in the morning!

Dr Bramley looked up absentmindedly. 'Hmm?' He rubbed his hands. 'Oh, this is nice! Stagecoach? Well, I don't really know, dear boy. Cressida took care of all that. Even managed to persuade the landlady to give me a bed in the smoking room. As for the luggage, she insisted it all had to be left at the inn.'

'Cressida?' was all he said aloud. *A bed in the smoking room? Of the Bell alehouse? Good God!*

'Haven't you met Cressida?' Dr Bramley frowned. 'Hmm…let me see… Twenty-five years, you say…I suppose not, then. She's only about nineteen, or is it twenty? Doesn't matter, she's not twenty-five yet, I'm sure.'

'And she is your daughter?' *Where the devil did she spend the night?*

Dr Bramley blinked. 'Well, yes…I have every reason to believe she's my daughter.'

'You believe…' Even allowing for the old boy's vagueness, it still rocked Jack to his foundations. 'How in heaven's name did that come about?'

Dr Bramley took that quite literally. 'Er…ah…in the usual way, you know.' He gave Jack a surprisingly penetrating look. 'At least, you look as if you'd know.'

Jack felt heat steal along his cheekbones. Lack of sleep

and his aching shoulder had obviously addled his few remaining wits—of all the atrocious questions to ask a clergyman!

His guest went on. 'Yes. Bit of a miscalculation on my part. I can't say I expected…not so quickly…and…er…easily…'

It might have been the heat of the fire turning Dr Bramley's bald head crimson, but somehow Jack doubted it. He changed the subject slightly. 'I didn't realise that you'd married, sir.'

The old man nodded. 'No, I didn't intend to. But Amabel was in such trouble, losing her post so unfairly as she did…just because that young scoundrel made up to her and got her dismissed… Anyway, I needed a housekeeper…so marriage seemed the best course all round.'

All Jack could glean from this was that his cousin had married as an act of charity.

'Who was Amabel?'

'Who was she?' Dr Bramley stared. 'I thought I explained. She was my wife. Dead now, poor soul.' He shook his head. 'Cressida's mother,' he added, plainly anxious that there should be no further confusion on the issue of his daughter's parentage.

Jack decided to leave it. 'And where is she now?'

Dr Bramley looked quite startled. 'Ah…in her grave, dear boy. Yes, definitely in her grave. I read the service, you know. Cressida dealt with that.'

Dr Bramley, Jack realised, had not changed one jot in twenty-five years. 'Er…I meant, where is Cressida?' He corrected himself. 'Miss Bramley, I should say.'

'Oh.' The old man's relief was palpable. 'Thought you had a touch of the sun for a moment. She's vanished. I dozed off, you know, in the parlour. The fire was so warm. When your man came back for me, she'd taken her cloak back and disappeared.'

'Taken her cloak *back*?' Jack seized on the bit that

didn't make sense. He knew where Cressida—Miss Bramley—had been.

'Yes. She lent it to me in the gig. Practically tied it on me. Makes a man of the cloth look a dashed fool wearing a bright red cape. At my age, too!'

Jack hid his smile. Lord, he'd give a monkey to have seen it. At least the wretched chit had had enough sense to try and keep her poor old father warm. A pity she hadn't had enough *nous* to hire something more suitable than a gig. And as for bringing the poor old boy all the way from Cornwall on the common stage in the dead of winter and leaving their luggage behind—he'd have a bit to say to her on that head! Which reminded him...

'Why on earth didn't you write, sir?' he asked. 'I would have been happy to send a chaise. Even to Cornwall!'

Dr Bramley looked puzzled. Pathetically so. 'But I did write. I remember *that*. Hmm. Maybe it went astray. You'd need to ask Cressida, my boy. She deals with all those sort of things.'

Miss Cressida Bramley crouched by the fire in the parlour into which the terrifyingly austere butler had ushered them and wished she had never thought of leaving it. In fact, she wished that she had never left Cornwall. Why was it that men took one look at her and decided that it was quite unnecessary to treat her with respect? Was it the freckles, the nose, or could it be her red hair?

And why, oh, why, had she been foolish enough to lash back at the tall, dark-haired gentleman in the garden? Who else could he possibly have been except their unsuspecting and now, probably, unwilling host? Obviously he had returned to the house and summoned her father. She could only hope that the Reverend Dr Bramley would make a better impression than his daughter.

Still, he didn't have to be *that* rude. Even if she had startled him, she hadn't bumped him nearly hard enough to have hurt him. Actually she found it hard to imagine anyone would be big enough to harm him. Not even Andrew with his tall elegance of figure had that breadth of shoulder.

Bitterly she jerked her mind away from the memory of Andrew. There was no point remembering…except as an object lesson in how gentlemen viewed girls of her background and circumstances, how little their avowed affection could be trusted. She'd remember that and forget the rest. For now she had better concentrate on her new surroundings.

She looked around the parlour curiously. From all Papa had said, his cousin, Mr Jonathan Hamilton, was shockingly wealthy. Rich enough to buy an abbey. He certainly wasn't spending his money on keeping his home furnished in the latest style of elegance. Even to her inexperienced eye, most of the furnishings and décor were at least seventy to eighty years old. Exactly what the Dowager Lady Fairbridge had stigmatised as '…so dreadfully dowdy…' and encouraged her son to replace the moment their period of mourning had expired.

Yet there was no suggestion of faded fortunes about this room. It might be old-fashioned, but all the furniture was of the finest quality, waxed and polished lovingly, and she could see that the chairs had been reupholstered quite recently. That was why she had crouched near the fire. Sitting on those expensively plump and comfortable chairs in her present damp state was out of the question.

She rather liked this room. It had an air of comfort, as though someone really lived it here and didn't just use the room to impress visitors with how important and wealthy he was. The austerity of the furnishings appealed to her. She had felt terribly uncomfortable in the newly refurbished drawing room at Fairbridge Hall, as though she hardly dared breathe for fear she would sully something.

Perhaps Mr Hamilton was one of those bluff country

squires who couldn't stand change and new-fangled ways. Perhaps he lived here all year round in rural obscurity and wouldn't mind being saddled with a vague, scholarly cleric and his daughter. Certainly the rambling house, nestled against the darkness of the woods, felt welcoming, home-like.

A vision of Mr Hamilton as he had appeared to her in the garden did not lend much credence to this bit of wishful thinking. Granted his heavy cloak had hidden the rest of his attire, but even so she had received the impression of great elegance.

She shivered. If only she hadn't had to leave all their luggage behind at the inn in order to persuade the landlord to loan them that wretched gig! She could have got out of these damp clothes at once.

At least her cloak had kept Papa dry in the gig—if she'd been looking after him properly, he wouldn't have had a chance to give his cloak to that rascally beggar in the first place. So it was all her own fault that she was damp and cold. And going out in the garden in damp clothes, even with the cloak, had been absolutely henwitted.

And now she would have to conciliate a host she felt more like slapping and trust that he possessed enough family feeling to let them stay until she thought of what they were to do next.

'Borrow a dress from the housekeeper, I think,' she said to the dancing flames.

'An excellent idea, Miss Bramley,' came a familiar drawl. Cressida spun around, lost her balance and sat down on the floor with a thump. She stared up at her host, furiously aware of her undignified appearance.

Judging by his expression, Mr Hamilton was equally aware of it. He went on, 'Bringing luggage would have been even better, but I have no doubt that Mrs Roberts will be happy to lend you something.'

He stepped forward and Cressida swallowed. She hadn't

realised that anyone could be so tall. He must be well over six foot, and something about the way he moved suggested leashed power, a very masculine power that his style of dressing did nothing to disguise.

His buckskin breeches—situated on the floor she couldn't help but notice—were moulded to very long, muscular legs. His top boots might be splashed with mud, but she could see that they were beautifully made and well cared for. Dazedly she raised her eyes further. This gentleman did not bother with a skintight coat that nipped him in at the waist, but nevertheless his coat had been made by a master and it fitted comfortably over broad shoulders.

Nervously she lifted her gaze to his face and encountered a slightly amused, and more than slightly cynical, smile. His dark grey eyes set under black brows seemed to take in every detail of her forlorn and damp condition.

Suddenly realising that she was crouching by the fire for all the world like a bedraggled puppy, she began to scramble up and discovered a strong hand under her elbow, lifting her. A knife-thrust of shock went through her at the sensation of his long fingers closing around her arm.

'I can manage...'

His sharply indrawn breath sliced through her protest. Abruptly the hand withdrew. Off balance, she sat down again with an audible and painful thump.

'Bloody hell!' The words were jerked out of her forcibly. She blushed. That was not at all the sort of expression a clergyman's daughter, or any other young lady, ought to use at all, let alone in front of a gentleman. Especially when she had recently raked him down for using similar language.

'Quite, Miss Bramley.' The bland tone made her itch to slap him. Condescending beast!

The other hand was extended to her. Such a strong, capable hand. So safe...comforting.

What happened to condescending beast? How could a

hand look safe? Especially when its partner had just dropped her on the hearth stone on her derrière and made her look an utter fool.

She looked up, ready to tell him exactly what she thought of him. The lines of pain on his whitened face shocked her.

'Sir? Are...are you all right?'

His mouth tightened. 'Perfectly, Miss Bramley. Merely a trifling injury to my shoulder.'

Guilt consumed her. Had she cannoned into him that hard? And if she had, how on earth had she damaged his shoulder? She'd be surprised to learn that her head even reached it. Perhaps he wasn't as strong as he looked.

'Master Jack!' The wail of distress startled Cressida and she blinked as the butler bobbed into view behind his tall master. She hadn't noticed him. Somehow Mr Hamilton had filled, indeed overflowed, her vision.

'Why won't you do as Dr Wilberforce said, and wear a sling? You'll never remember not to use the arm!'

Cressida relaxed slightly. Obviously the injury had preceded their first meeting.

'Oh, shut up, Evans. Go and find Mrs Roberts. Tell her to hunt out one of her dresses for Miss Bramley.'

'I beg your pardon, sir?'

'You heard me... Oh, I see what you mean.' His hand still outstretched, he looked at Cressida assessingly. Up and down and back again.

As if I were a...a filly!

Still, she must have jarred him horribly. Rude as he was, she did not like to think that she had given pain to any fellow creature. Ignoring the outstretched hand, she got up and straightened her skirts.

She opened her mouth to apologise, but her host spoke first.

'Hmm. Yes. Definitely one of Mrs Roberts's smaller

dresses, Evans. And you might find some rope to hold it on.'

'Very good, sir.'

Cressida eyed the butler's retreating back narrowly. She could have sworn he was amused. Whether at her or his master, she couldn't hazard a guess. Drawing a deep breath, she turned back to her host.

He returned her gaze with a faint smile. She fidgeted with the ties of her cloak, and shifted slightly in her damp shoes. Abruptly she became aware of how cold and tired she was. Of how little claim she and her father had on this man. Especially if she could not even do him the courtesy of telling him the truth, not against her father's expressed wishes… And even if she did…would he understand? Or would he turn them out, too? She couldn't risk it. Papa had travelled far enough. Perhaps later she could explain to Mr Hamilton exactly what had happened; that it was her fault Papa had lost his living. Then she could leave once she had found a position. Surely Leicestershire was far enough from Cornwall that rumours would not dog her?

'Miss Bramley?'

'Sir?' She could have sworn he flushed slightly.

'Perhaps you might be able to explain to what I owe the honour of this, er, visit.'

Cressida met his eyes. Dark ice, their expression shuttered—she could read nothing beyond indifference. But his slight hesitation over the word *visit* suggested that he already suspected that it might be a rather long visit.

Duty. Papa is family. She flushed. So was she if it came to that. But she had never felt like family. Had always been conscious that, despite his absent-minded affection, she was an encumbrance her father could well have done without. No doubt Mr Jonathan Hamilton, even if he were prepared to help her father, would feel the same. Without the mitigating affection.

'Circumstances dictated that my father resign his living

in Cornwall.' At least it had the dubious merit of being the truth and nothing but the truth. The less said about the whole truth, the better. 'He…he could think of nowhere else to go.'

'I see.'

He did?

'Naturally I have no objection to your visit,' he drawled. 'It will enliven my dull existence considerably. But I would have appreciated a letter informing me of your intentions. Your father was under the impression you had sent one. Had you done so, I could have arranged better accommodation for you last night and a chaise to meet you this morning.'

Cressida felt her jaw drop, even as her hackles rose at the insufferable edge of sarcasm in his voice.

'L…letter?'

'Yes. You know the sort of thing…*Dear Cousin Jack, we've never met but I would like to inform you that my father and I are arriving for an extended visit. Please expect us on such and such a date. Sincerely, Cousin… er…Cressida.*'

'I beg your pardon,' she said quietly. Obviously it hadn't been enough to stand over Papa while he wrote the letter. Why on earth hadn't she insisted on posting the wretched thing herself? She could have dealt with a bit of mud and a few stones. No doubt her cousin thought she had omitted to write so that he could have no opportunity to refuse them.

She could only describe his smile as sardonic. Her temper began to rise.

She was not, absolutely *not*, going to try and exonerate herself in his eyes by passing the blame straight back to her father. And she wasn't going to lose her temper with him. At least, not openly.

His expectantly raised brows suggested that he awaited some sort of explanation. All sorts of inappropriate responses jostled on the end of her tongue. Biting them back, she reminded herself firmly that the meek shall inherit the earth. *Possibly…when snow lay in hell. And he'd wait as long for an explanation from her!* She choked that back as well.

'And when do you think your luggage will arrive?'

'When it is sent for.' She didn't trust herself to say more.

'Oh?'

Some of her bubbling anger splashed over. 'Yes,' she snapped. 'I felt that it would be inappropriate of me to give orders to your grooms before we had seen you!'

Shutting her eyes briefly, she reached for control, mentally rehearsing the little prayer Papa had printed out for her use at times when her lamentable temper threatened to slip its leash. *Lord, make me an instrument…*

'Of course…' his tone became pensive '…some might have thought it advisable to hire a closed conveyance, one that could take your luggage. Some might even have chosen to travel post from Cornwall, rather than expose an old man to the rigours of the stage. Not to mention a bed in the smoking room at the Bell.'

Some people had more money than they knew what to do with and ought to mind their own arrogant, misbegotten business!

…of thy peace… 'I dare say.' Cressida felt a glow of pride at the sweetly demure tone she achieved despite the memory of the landlord's pithy dismissal of her insistence that Mr Hamilton was expecting them. *Mr Jack's a real gentleman, he is. His guests don't in general arrive on the stage…* It was only his wife's kindness that had secured the bed in the smoking room. Much to the landlord's disgust, she had allowed Cressida to sleep in the bed of a chambermaid who had gone to spend the night with her family. Nothing, however, could budge him from his refusal to loan the gig without the surety of their luggage.

'If you've quite finished, I should like very much to get out of these damp clothes.'

He inclined his head gravely. 'Of course, Miss Bramley. I am sure Mrs Roberts is waiting.'

He strolled to the door and opened it.

She stared. Then, shaking her wits into place, she hurried towards the door. Obviously he observed at least the outward customs of gentlemanly behaviour.

'Naturally you and your father are welcome to stay for as long as you like,' he said, very politely. 'But you may wish to consider that mine is a bachelor household. You have no chaperon here, which may prove a trifle awkward.'

She stiffened. 'How very kind of you, sir. I hope that it will not be necessary for us to impose upon you for long. I…I have every expectation that a position can be found that will value Papa's scholarship. And in any event, I have formed the intention of seeking a post as a governess, or possibly a companion. So you need not fear that I, at least, will trespass on your generosity for too long or cause you any undue embarrassment.'

His frown returned immediately. 'The devil you will! Neither you nor Dr Bramley have any need to go careering over the countryside looking for employment. You are both entirely welcome to remain here. I meant only—'

She interrupted at once. 'Coming here was a short-term arrangement only. Just until I could think of something else.' Short of the workhouse. She forced that nightmare into the back of her mind. 'At least for myself. Papa may be content to be your pensioner—I am not. Good day, sir.'

She swept out. At least she'd had the last word.

His amused voice followed her. 'Oh, I don't think I'll offer you a pension, Miss Bramley! I'm sure you have many years of active service left in you.'

Temper flared. Eyes narrowed, she turned. 'I dare say. Might I suggest, sir, that you take your butler's advice and

put your sling on? It will probably help me to remember
to treat your infirmity with consideration.'

Noting his dropped jaw, she knew that this time she'd
really had the last word and stalked from the room.

Chapter Two

Jack sat back in his chair by the library fire. He couldn't think of anything else he needed to do right now. The Bramleys' luggage had arrived. Both his guests were partaking of supper in their bedchambers. And he felt as though he'd been hit by a falling tree.

What was it about that chit that tipped him so totally off balance that he couldn't control his temper around her? Damn it all! He hadn't even realised that he had a temper, always excepting his irritation over his shoulder, but Miss Cressida Bramley had discovered it at once. Top-lofty little baggage!

He snorted. She plainly didn't think much of him, either. And he was saddled with her and her father indefinitely. What on earth could have happened to force Dr Bramley to resign his living? Granted he was the world's most absent-minded dreamer, and probably hadn't been a very good minister, but Jack had yet to learn that such drawbacks could deprive a cleric of his parish. Quite the opposite.

Jack hunted through his memories. He hadn't seen Dr Bramley in twenty-five years. All he remembered was a vague, if kindly, gentleman who'd spent most of his visits here in the library and had to be dragged out for meals.

Reclusive, scholarly, bookish—how the devil could a man like that cause a big enough scandal to lose his living?

And how on earth had any female dragged him away from his books for long enough to get through a courtship and marriage ceremony, let alone beget a child? At the very least, finding answers to all these questions would take his mind off his shoulder.

In the meantime, he would have to come up with some way of persuading Dr Bramley and his stiff-necked daughter to stay without trampling on the latter's pride.

In the middle of these cogitations there came a light tap at the door.

'Come in.'

A slightly built, elderly groom came in.

'Evening, Mr Jack.'

'Hello, Clinton.' Jack smiled at his head groom. 'You'd better come over here to the fire. Has the luggage been collected?'

'Aye, sir. Fetched it meself from the Bell and ast a few questions like you wanted.'

Jack nodded. Spying on his guests left a sour taste in his mouth, but he did not wish to upset Dr Bramley, and asking Cressida any more questions was plainly a waste of breath. Besides, the wretched chit unsettled him. The sarcastic edge in his voice when he'd spoken to her had shaken him. It left him feeling completely out of control. Of her. Of himself.

He refused to think about the uncomfortable stirrings of desire in his blood. If he ignored the urging of his baser self, it would doubtless go away like other inconvenient desires he had walked away from over the years.

He gestured to a chair.

'Sit down, man. What did you find out?'

Clinton flushed with pleasure as he lowered his slight frame into the chair and perched respectfully on the extreme edge. 'Thank 'ee, sir. Well, they came off the stage, like the young lady said,' he began. He grinned. 'Seems the driver took quite a fancy to her...'

Jack stiffened, icy fury surging through his veins.

'What!' If she had suffered any insult...any familiarity...

Catching at his self-control, he met Clinton's startled gaze and forced his jaw to relax.

The groom added soothingly, 'In a manner of speaking, as ye might say. One of the hostlers mentioned it. Seems when the road got real bad, they said all the gents had to walk. Well, Miss Cressida wouldn't have none of that. Got out herself, she did, so's her pa could stay inside. Driver's got a lass himself and he looked after her real proper. Wouldn't have none of it. An' he told Sam hostler to make sure she was treated right.'

Good God. Jack throttled his reaction and schooled his features back to an encouraging smile.

'Could you find out why they were on the stage at all?' Even the fact that Cressida had sacrificed her own comfort and safety for her father didn't excuse the initial idiocy of coming by stage. Even the mail would have been better.

'Seemin'ly they ain't got a feather to fly with,' said Clinton with a shrug. 'Sam reckons as how the old gent give his cloak to some rascally beggar and most of their money as well. Landlord was a bit pressed for time an' wouldn't even lend 'em the gig without they left all their luggage. He says to tell you he's real sorry an' there's no charge for the gig. Seems as how his missus felt sorry for Miss Cressida and let her sleep with the maids for the night, while her pa had a bed in the smoking room.' He shook his head in wonderment.

'I...see.' And this time he did. Only too clearly. He'd made a complete and utter fool of himself. Worse—he'd behaved like an arrogant, conceited coxcomb. All because Miss Cressida Bramley's bright eyes had turned him upside down and inside out.

Clinton nodded. 'That's about all, sir.' He hesitated.

Jack raised a brow. 'Just say it, Clinton. I'll guarantee not to sack you.'

'No, sir.' He grinned at his master and then sobered. 'Not wishin' to say nothin' against a kinsman of yours, Mr Jack, but it don't seem that the Reverend did much to help Miss Cressida. Very vague he was, Sam told me. Seems she had to order the whole journey and she was real upset when he give away the last of their money.'

Jack could just imagine. Yet she had silently endured his criticism of her management. He must have gone insane. A chit of that age should not have had to travel on the stage at all, let alone manage the journey and listen to his criticism afterwards.

Why had she let him get away with it?

Too meek? Hardly! The little virago who had raked him down for rudeness in the garden was not the woman to turn the other cheek with becoming meekness. No Patient Griselda there! Far more likely that she would slap back. He recalled her snapping green eyes and short answers. Those blasted freckles had practically quivered with outrage, yet she had held her tongue. Why?

He could think of plenty of women who would have had no hesitation in dumping the blame squarely on the nearest person available, fairly or not. Plainly Cressida was not of that ilk.

'Very well, Clinton.' He nodded dismissal. 'Thank you. I'll come down in the morning to see how Firebird goes on.' Reaching into his pocket, he held out half a crown. 'You'd better have this. That was a cold errand you had.'

Clinton flushed as he took the proffered coin unwillingly. 'Pshaw. That ain't necessary, Mr Jack. I don't mind havin' a jaw with Sam, thankin' you kindly, sir.' He left Jack to some thoroughly unwelcome reflections.

These were once again interrupted by a tap on the door. 'Come in.'

No doubt Clinton had forgotten something… 'Oh, good evening, Dr Bramley.'

The old man, restored to his luggage, looked a far tidier proposition than he had earlier. He advanced into the room, glancing around avidly.

'My, my, my!' His eyes practically glazed over with ecstasy at the sight of all the books. Jack bit back a smile at this evidence of Dr Bramley's abiding passion.

The old man blinked up at the gallery circling the library. 'Is that new?'

Jack nodded. 'Yes. My father had it built just before his death. He worried about Mama going up and down the ladders and she worried about him…and it gave some extra space for all the books he acquired at the Roxburghe sale in 1812.'

Dr Bramley tut-tutted. 'Very sad that His Grace sold the collection. I only heard about the sale later or I should have come up to London.'

Jack breathed a silent prayer of thanks to a merciful deity as he tried to imagine the old boy coming to London and indulging his passions at a book sale which had lasted forty-one days.

'Yes,' mourned Bramley. 'My wife mislaid the information about the sale. To think that *The Decameron* went under the hammer. To have had the chance to buy it!'

'Blandford bought it,' managed Jack, choking inwardly. For something over two thousand pounds. Cressida had more to be grateful for than she knew. *Lord! And people think excessive gambling pernicious!*

'Ah, you mentioned your wife?' He was proud of the subtle, questioning tone he managed to infuse into his voice.

'Amabel?' Dr Bramley sighed. 'She died some years ago. I think. Yes. At least four. It might be five. Cressida would know.'

Jack tried to imagine either of his parents being uncer-

tain of how much time had elapsed since the death of the
other. He failed completely.

'I never thought of you as a marrying man,' he observed.

'Hmm?' Dr Bramley examined a volume and replaced
it carefully. 'Marrying man, did you say? I wasn't. Never
intended to marry. But I can't stand injustice. And I can't
abide hypocrisy. What happened to Amabel was both. Her
father was a friend of mine and she became a governess
after he died. The son of the house where she was employed wouldn't leave her alone. Dare say you know how
these things go. Eventually she was turned off without a
character. She had nowhere to go, no one else to turn to.
So I took her in. Married her myself in the end. Seemed
the best thing at the time.' He thought about that. 'Still
does, actually. I'm not terribly practical, you know.'

'I had noticed,' said Jack gravely.

'Yes, I thought you would have.' Dr Bramley frowned
as he examined a shelf of books. He held up two volumes.
'What are *these* doing together?'

Jack bit back a laugh. At the very least you'd have
thought the old chap had caught the books doing something scandalous. 'My father died before he finished sorting and cataloguing...'

'Good gracious! Still not catalogued?' He made it sound
like a major sin of omission.

Jack shook his head ruefully. 'Not fully, sir. My father
made a start and I've continued, but it's a big job and I
have other demands on my time.'

Bramley looked blank, as if quite unable to comprehend
how a man could possibly rate anything above his library.
'Well, well. I shall potter in here while we are with you.
No doubt Cressida will assist me.'

'Ah, yes,' said Jack. 'What a pity she didn't write to let
me know you were coming.'

'She didn't? That's a good specimen.' The old man

frowned absently as he stroked a little jade horse with one thin finger. 'Went to China with your father, you know. Before your time. Oh, no, of course she didn't. I did. That's what brought me down. Here.' He reached into his pocket and brought out a sealed letter. He handed it to Jack with a touch of embarrassment. 'I do apologise. I can't *think* why Cressida would have given it back to me rather than posting it herself, most odd, inconsiderate even. But better late than never. T'ang?' This last was muttered to himself as he picked up the little horse and examined it.

Jack didn't bother to argue with his guest's reasoning. He had better things to do with his breath. 'Quite,' he said, taking the letter. Inwardly he added to the apology he already owed Cressida. At this rate he'd be begging her pardon until Easter. Especially when she found out that she had been volunteered to assist in the library.

He thought about the library after Dr Bramley had retired. Time and more that he did something about it. What he really needed was a librarian of course. Someone to catalogue and keep track of everything. He knew by now that he would never manage to do it all by himself.

A librarian. Where would one find such a man...?

'Catalogue Mr Hamilton's library?' Cressida did not even try to hide her disapproval. 'But, Papa, you said his library is enormous. We aren't going to be here for that long. Just until you can find a living or another suitable post. We don't want to impose on him.' She set down her teacup carefully and marshalled every possible argument. A daunting task over breakfast.

Her father smiled seraphically. 'But it's all different now. If I catalogue the library, I will be doing him a favour. After all, it is one of the finest private collections in the country. No, no. It would be very ill done of me to be

thinking of personal advancement when it is clearly my
duty to remain here.'

'Perhaps he doesn't want his library catalogued,' she
suggested.

'Not want it catalogued?' Dr Bramley appeared shocked
at such heresy.

'If he hasn't had it done already...' She pressed on,
aware she was speaking to a brick wall.

'Of course he wants it catalogued!' spluttered the old
man through a mouthful of ham. 'I should not dream of
leaving until it is done.'

'Very well, Papa. I dare say I can find some mending
to do for him to earn my board.' She could hardly complain if her father had managed to find an eligible situation
for himself without the least thought that it would be impossible for her to remain here for any length of time without giving rise to gossip. He might recognise impropriety
when it walked up and bit him, but only if it had very big,
sharp teeth.

She gazed with sudden distaste at the plate of ham and
eggs to which she had helped herself. The last thing she
wanted was to be the object of someone's charity. Especially a man's. Especially Mr Jonathan Hamilton's!

Her father sneezed. She looked up, concerned. 'Papa,
are you getting a cold?'

He nodded. 'It was rather chilly yesterday. But don't
worry, I'm sure it will prove trifling and I shall be as right
as a trivet in no time. The library will keep my mind off
it.'

'Very well, Papa. We'll stay until it's done.'

Surely the library couldn't be that large. Perhaps Papa
had exaggerated its size. Yes, that was it. They could get
it done in a few weeks and then find some sort of post for
her father. She brightened at the thought. If their host could
be persuaded to furnish Papa with a reference, it would be
even better.

* * *

Blinking up at the ranks of books lining the library walls half an hour later, Cressida rapidly revised her estimate. Weeks? Good lord! It would take years! And she knew who would be scrambling up and down all the ladders, sneezing, while her father drifted from pile to pile in a blissful, dusty daze. Still, she had discovered what Mr Jonathan Hamilton spent his money on. His library.

The books, anyway. While many of the volumes swelling the floor-to-ceiling shelves, and piled haphazardly on the gallery and mezzanine floor, were of obvious antiquity, she could see that many were of much more recent date. A large *bureau plat* piled with more books stood by the fireplace and a very battered and comfortable looking leather chair sat beside it.

It was a strangely old-fashioned room, very plain and austerely functional as though its owners had taken little notice of changing fashions and styles. Rather like the rest of the house that she had seen. Pulling out a book that caught her eye, Cressida wondered if Mr Hamilton were not as wealthy as her father had intimated. In her experience, people of wealth updated their principal residence and furnishings quite regularly.

She put the book back. No, that didn't make sense. There were plenty of servants and no evidence of neglect. The house was beautifully cared for. And their host had all the appearance of a man of wealth. Indeed, she understood that the estate was extensive, and that there were others.

There was one thing she was quite sure of— 'If he really does want this catalogued, we'll certainly earn our keep. We'll be here for years,' she muttered.

'Oh, I do want it catalogued, I assure you.'

She swung around sharply, caught her toe in the edge of the rug and slipped. She felt herself caught and held against a powerful chest with arms that resembled steel bars. At first the thrill of delight that shimmered from her breasts to her toes held her motionless. Her whole body softened against the much harder, masculine one which appeared to have surrounded her. Stunned, she looked up into stormy dark grey eyes. Fire blazed there. She dropped her gaze to his lips. She had the oddest sensation of melting, yielding. Then, shocked at the sensations winging through her, she wriggled furiously. His harshly drawn breath stopped her. The lines around his mouth locked.

She stood still, blinking. Was that pain? Abruptly she remembered his injury. His jaw was set, the lips hard and straight. Goodness, he looked as though he would gladly throttle her. His arms tightened, sending more shockwaves rippling through her and then he released her, setting her away from him with a gentleness at odds with the sudden chill in his face.

Stepping back a little further, she said crossly, 'You really are an idiot, sir! Why don't you put it in a sling?'

His jaw dropped. 'A…a sling, did you say?'

'Well, of course! How else are you to recover if you keep using it?'

She thought for a moment that he might choke. On what she couldn't hazard a guess.

'Oh,' he managed to mutter at last. 'My shoulder.'

It was Cressida's turn to be nonplussed. 'Obviously,' she said. 'Unless you've managed to dislocate anything else since I saw you yesterday.'

He turned purple. 'It is bandaged,' he pointed out in a very strained voice.

She sniffed. 'I dare say. But you need something to remind you not to use that arm.' Seeing his raised brows, she flushed. Drat the man. Why was she wasting her time in trying to make him see sense? No doubt he would only resent it. Especially since she had just called him an idiot.

'I beg your pardon,' she said stiffly. 'I did not mean to interfere in your affairs. I hope I did not jar your arm too badly.'

'Never mind my curst arm,' he snapped. 'That's the least of my problems now! I take it you object to the idea of remaining here.'

'Yes,' said Cressida. 'I do.'

He blinked. 'You're very direct, aren't you?'

She shrugged. 'It saves time. Do you truly want this library catalogued or don't you? I may as well inform you that Papa has decided that it is his duty as a scholar to do so. And I can tell you right now that it will take him years!'

She gestured wildly at the towering shelves. 'Was it your suggestion or his? And who did you think would assist him? He's far too old to be climbing the ladders, even with that gallery.'

'Well, of course, I would be—'

'With that shoulder?' She saw his flush with intense satisfaction. 'I understand it to have been dislocated as well as the broken collarbone, so—'

'For God's sake! Anyone would think that you and my staff expect me to be permanently disabled!' he growled.

She snorted. 'The way you keep using the wretched thing, you probably will be!' She tried to ignore the wry amusement that softened his rather harsh features, the twinkle lurking in his eye. Why did he have to be so attractive? Why couldn't he be old and fat and bald? Then he wouldn't make her feel like a cat having its fur stroked the wrong way.

'Anyway, I'm sure you aren't here all year. And I can tell you that to catalogue this is a massive job!'

Disgustedly, she surveyed the library again. 'If you wanted it done, why not employ a...a librarian?'

'That's exactly what I have done,' he said blandly. 'I'm so glad you approve.'

'Then what is Papa going to—?'

'I've employed your father,' he explained. 'I've pottered

at the library myself but, as you so rightly point out, I need a curator. Now I have one.'

'Now you...' Speech failed her completely. Her jaw dropped open. What did he mean?

'I just saw your father in the breakfast parlour. He has accepted the post of librarian here,' said her outrageous host. 'He was more than happy with the arrangement we came to.'

'Is it...a...a permanent position?' It would be just the thing for Papa, if only it didn't smack of charity. He would be safe.

He won't need you any more. Independence had never looked more depressing.

'I can assure you, Miss Bramley, that my library is not about to disappear,' he responded drily. 'I even add to it on a regular basis. I collect old books and manuscripts, as well as keeping up with whatever interests me in modern trends of literature. Your father will be invaluable.'

'Not with the modern poets, he won't!' said Cressida at once, ignoring the intangible feeling of being suddenly cut adrift.

'And just what does your father class as modern poetry?' he asked.

'Anything later than Spenser,' she answered promptly.

'I see.' He appeared to be trying not to smile. 'Very well, I shall put you in charge of ''modern'' poetry, and I dare say novels as well.'

She bit off the automatic refusal and nodded vaguely instead. There was no point in arguing with scholars. They rarely heard anything they didn't want to hear. Not that Jack...Mr Hamilton looked like any scholar she had ever met, but looks could be deceptive. Anyway, if Papa had found a position like this, then it was time and more that she got on with her own life. He probably wouldn't even notice that she had gone with all this to keep him busy.

The thought of not being needed, by anyone, swamped

her. She shivered slightly. And then saw Mr Hamilton watching her curiously.

'Is something wrong, Miss Bramley?'

Nothing was wrong. Nothing at all.

She changed the subject. 'I suppose if I don't climb up and down all those ladders, you will,' she said. 'Very well. I will act as my father's assistant for the time being.' In a very few weeks she'd be twenty-one and her own mistress.

'You'll do no such thing,' snapped her host. 'There's nothing the matter with my shoulder, if that's what you mean. And young ladies do not scramble up and down ladders!'

Cressida bristled. 'Certainly not. Young ladies ascend and descend ladders with a modicum of grace and dignity. And they do not put up with wholly unconnected gentlemen telling them what they may or may not do!'

Belatedly she realised that he had again prodded her into losing her temper with him. Just what was it about him that set her all on edge?

'I beg your pardon, Cousin Cressida.'

He spoke gently, humbly even, with not the least trace of sarcasm.

'You…you what?' She could not remember anyone ever, in her whole life, offering her an apology.

'Beg your pardon,' he repeated obligingly. 'That's what a gentleman is supposed to do when he offends a lady.'

He *was* mocking her after all! She turned on him fiercely.

'Let me tell you something, Mr Hamilton. I want nothing from you, nothing! Not even your spurious apologies! Do you hear me? And I would infinitely prefer that you did not call me Cousin. I have no claim on you. Our connection is of the remotest nature. Since I am to act as my father's assistant I am, in some regards, in your employ. I should vastly prefer that our relationship remain quite formal.'

He exploded with satisfying force. 'Let me tell you something, my girl; any employee who spoke to me as you do would be dismissed instantly!' Dark grey eyes blazed into hers. His lips were white with fury. 'I'll make one thing quite clear; yes, I do want my library catalogued and I will certainly pay Dr Bramley for his expertise, but at no time will I consider you and your father to be anything but my guests! And members of my family. And I'll call you what I damned well please, *Cousin Cressida*!'

Cressida knew when she'd lost a battle, but that didn't have to prevent her having the parting shot. 'Spoken like a true gentleman. Good morning, Mr Hamilton. I shall ask Papa when he wishes to make a start. In the meantime I shall offer to assist your housekeeper with the mending!'

Jack stared at the door, which had shut in his face with something perilously close to a bang. He couldn't remember the last time anyone had raked him down like that. Always excepting the trimming she'd given him yesterday. And he hadn't even managed to apologise for that. What the devil was it about her that put him all on end? Apart from that annoying talent of hers for getting the last word. That would drive a saint to blasphemy.

And he was definitely no saint. The nagging ache in his groin assured him of that. Not that he would have described the sensation as *dislocated*...

Obviously it didn't help that every time he saw her, he wanted to take her in his arms and kiss her senseless. Not to mention the other things he'd like to do with her. None of which were at all eligible for a young lady to all intents and purposes under his protection. Or in his employ, as the top-lofty little peagoose had put it. As though she were a chambermaid! He'd tripped over a chambermaid before, but the only reaction he'd had had been to pick up the linen she'd dropped and apologise.

With Cressida he'd ended up instantly and painfully aroused the moment he felt her breasts crushed against his chest. And that little wriggle—he'd felt her thighs shift against him. He groaned at the memory. God, she'd be sweet. When she'd looked up, her lips slightly parted, it had required all his self-control not to take her mouth. Her lips had looked so soft, so pink. All warm and moist, like raspberries. Thinking about it left his body aching with desire.

Only the realisation that she had not the least idea of the effect she had on him had stopped him. *Or did she? Was he about to repeat one of his own mistakes? With his eyes wide open?*

Grimly he remembered Selina. Lord, it must be fifteen or more years ago. Just after he came on the town. Selina Pilkington had tied him in knots. The number of times he had conveniently found her alone…the times she turned her ankle, lost a shoe, stumbled during a dance. She hadn't tried to get herself compromised, not really.

She had been far more subtle than that. All those times her breasts accidentally brushed his arm, the times she stumbled during a dance and he had found those same soft breasts crushed against his chest. Looking back on it, she hadn't been subtle at all, but subtlety would have been wasted on a cub of twenty…especially a chivalrous, young fool like Jack Hamilton.

By the end of that long-ago Season he had wanted her so badly he had been prepared to offer for her and to hell with his parents' unspoken misgivings. It had taken Marc, cynical, observant Marc, to make him think.

Going to offer for her, are you? Hmm. Prefer a filly that doesn't go lame all the time myself…

They had an invigorating bout of fisticuffs and afterwards, as they mopped up, Jack remembered to ask Marc precisely what he meant. Marc pointed out brutally that Miss Pilkington was perfectly surefooted, and never lost her slipper unless Jack was by.

She's leading you around like a puppy, old chap. Every-

*one else knows that Lady Pilkington has the chit ear-
marked for the highest bidder. You always seem to forget
that, for a mere commoner, you're quite a prize.*

So why the devil wasn't Lady Pilkington coursing the
even-more-eligible Viscount Brandon, heir to the Earl of
Rutherford?

Marc grinned. *What? After I greeted them in the park
while I had Harriette Wilson on my arm? Thanks. My
sense of self-preservation is a bit more highly developed
than yours!*

Jack laughed at the memory. He'd nearly called Marc
out over that incident. Greeting two delicately bred and
virtuous females while squiring the most notorious demi-
rep of the day had caused an uproar. Of course Marc apologised profusely—and claimed he hadn't remembered it
was Harriette with him…that he'd thought Lady Pilkington
had nodded to him…

In the end, that bout of fisticuffs with Marc saved him.
With a black eye and a swollen lip, he went into the country for a few days until he could present a more creditable
appearance. A few days became three weeks. Marc had
brought a couple of very lively little fillies along…and
Jack discovered that he was not really in love with Selina
Pilkington at all. He just had a surfeit of wild oats of which
to dispose.

By the time he got back to town, Miss Pilkington was
casting her lures to Viscount Ripley. The engagement was
announced a few weeks later. At which Jack breathed a
hearty sigh of relief.

Looking back on it, he couldn't really blame Selina for
her tactics. All was fair in love and war. Girls had to
marry. Society dictated that it should be so. And then proceeded heartily to condemn any enterprising female who
went beyond the very faintly drawn line in her matrimonial
campaign.

But he loathed a tease…and if Miss Cressida Bramley

thought she could bamboozle him with a few well-placed wriggles, then she could think again.

Oh, for heaven's sake! Of course she wasn't like Selina. She'd been reared in the depths of Cornwall by a vicar and a bluestocking mother... He frowned slightly, remembering Dr Bramley's explanation for his marriage. Had Cressida's mother simply overplayed her hand in the age-old game of hunt-the-husband? Had she played her trump card and lost it? And was Cressida going to try a similar ploy?

Good lord! What maggot had got into him to be feeling so suspicious and hunted? Cressida could know very little of the desires of men and the teasing games that marriage-minded, up-to-snuff young ladies could play. And as far as he could tell, she didn't like him above half.

Since when did a female intent on seducing a man into marriage abuse him like a Billingsgate fishwife, just because he had teased her a little?

Of course, it would help if she liked him before *he* seduced *her*...

Seduced her? Where in Hades had that come from? He had absolutely no intention of seducing any girl of good character, let alone his cousin! He'd end up having to marry her and he was damned if he'd marry any girl just because he couldn't keep his hands off her.

What he *was* going to do was put her over his knee and spank her if he caught her so much as touching a needle and thread in connection with mending! After all, he was a mature and responsible man of thirty-six, in full control of his actions and reactions.

Cressida didn't stop until she had reached her own room. Moodily she stared at the snow whirling down outside the window. She couldn't even go for a ramble to work off some of her fury. No, she was trapped. And she

was making the same mistake she had made before; allowing her attraction to a man to blind her judgement.

Jack Hamilton might behave like a gentleman at the
moment, but it would be rank insanity to depend on his
continued good behaviour if he thought she was attracted
to him. No doubt he felt that her position as his guest and
his cousin's daughter put her off limits. Until he knew the
truth about her.

Andrew certainly hadn't hesitated—why should Jack?
Granted, he didn't seem to be the sort to wrap it up in
pretty lies about love, but that wouldn't change the truth.
He'd offer her exactly what Andrew had. Apparently in a
gentleman's eyes that was all she was worth. And Andrew
had only offered that because nothing better was on offer.
He'd made it quite plain that she had little to recommend
her to a man of discrimination.

And surely her mother's warnings were sufficient to
keep her safe this time? That and her own experience.

The best thing she could do would be to stay out of
Jack's…*Mr Hamilton's*…way until she could leave and
find respectable employment of her own. Papa would be
safe here. There would be nothing to upset him. He would
be taken care of far better than she could ever do it. With
that library to catalogue and care for, he'd never notice
she was gone.

Shivering slightly, she went over to look out at the
snow. It was heavier now, hiding the woods and gardens.
Cold, so cold. She'd never realised the world was such a
chilly place. Perhaps she ought to be grateful to Andrew
for teaching her that.

Chapter Three

The following morning was Sunday. Jack stood up as Cressida entered the breakfast parlour. He saw at once that she had dressed for church. She carried her scarlet cloak over her arm and held a bible and prayerbook. All in all she was much tidier this morning, her hair tightly braided and coiled, not a stray wisp or tangle to be seen.

'Good morning, cousin.' She must have got over her annoyance by now. And he, of course, was fully in control. Of himself and everything else. Calm, reserved, the soul of dignity. He smiled determinedly. 'You won't mind if I go on with my breakfast?' He sat down again.

His smile bounced off a cool wall of propriety. 'Of course not. Good morning, sir. Is my father down yet? I assumed that he would wish to attend church this morning.'

Jack took a sip of coffee. 'Dr Bramley finds himself unwell this morning. He—'

'Is his cold worse?' The coolness had dropped from her voice and Jack glanced up. He could not doubt the concern in her voice, her eyes. The outspoken, impertinent chit obviously had a considerable affection for her father.

'It's nothing to worry yourself about,' he said soothingly. 'But he should not be going out until he feels better. I assured him that I would escort you to church myself.'

'Oh.'

Miss Cressida Bramley neither looked, nor sounded, as though this arrangement met with her approval.

'I…I'm not quite sure that I will be going to church this morning,' she said.

Jack's mask slipped a trifle and he glared at her. What the devil had he done now? And what had happened to his resolve?

'Really?' He managed to infuse his voice with boredom. 'Then why have you brought down your bible and prayer-book?'

She glared in her turn. 'I can read the service for myself, sir. There is no need—'

'In a cloak?' He let his amusement show. 'There are fires laid in most rooms, cousin. Obviously you intended to go to church. You will be perfectly safe with me. The village of Ratby is quite close. The closed carriage and a couple of hot bricks will keep you warm this time.'

Heightened colour washed over her cheeks. 'You needn't rub it in, sir. I am quite aware that I ought to have left Papa in the warmth at the inn with our luggage while I drove out here in the gig, but at the time—'

'You should have done *what*?' Jack nearly choked on a mouthful of beef.

'Left Papa at the inn.' She looked at him as though she thought him a bit simple. 'He wouldn't have caught this horrid cold if I'd—'

'Driven an open carriage with an unknown horse, by yourself, over unfamiliar roads, in the depths of winter!' he finished for her. 'For God's sake, sit down and have some breakfast before I spank you!'

Belatedly he realised that as invitations went, this had little to recommend it.

Plainly Cressida thought so, too. Green eyes narrowed

into chips of ice. 'Naturally I am all eagerness to avail myself of such a gracious offer!'

She stalked over to the table and sat down.

'Coffee?' asked Jack, feeling slightly dazed. Where had that surge of protective outrage come from? After all, she had managed the gig, found her way here, and, from all he knew of Dr Bramley, it was highly unlikely that he had been of the least help with either horse or route. If ever a female was capable of looking after herself, it was Cressida Bramley.

She was family, though, and as such he really ought to look after her. Delightful and erudite as Dr Bramley was, he obviously depended on Cressida rather than the other way round. For some reason that bothered him considerably. Almost as much as the knowledge that sitting in the intimacy of a closed carriage with Miss Cressida Bramley for any length of time would be pure torture. A handful of snow would be far more to the point than a hot brick.

'Is there any tea?'

He raised his brows. 'Of course.' Rising to his feet again, he made a fresh pot at the urn and brought it to her. The gentle summery scent of rosewater drifted from her braided hair. It wreathed and beckoned, entwining itself around his senses. Abruptly he put the pot down and moved away. So much for being in control of himself.

'Now, church—' he began, daring to breathe again.

She interrupted. 'There is not the least need for you to put yourself out, sir. I will remain here this morning in case Papa requires anything. And if I wished to attend church I am quite capable of walking there. I drove through Ratby on the way out here. As you say, it is not far.'

Jack took a grip on his temper. 'Cousin, I am not exactly a heathen. I have every intention of going to church myself. And since my head groom will probably refuse to let me use the curricle, we will take the closed carriage anyway.' He shut off every mental and physical reaction to the thought. 'And your father is probably asleep again. The staff will look after him.'

To his chagrin she frowned, nibbling at her lower lip as she mulled it over. He gritted his teeth. No doubt she was looking for a polite way of refusing.

'Oh. Well, in that case, I suppose it's all right.'

Obviously she hadn't found one.

Sitting next to his cousin in church, Jack reflected that he had never had such an unflattering response to an invitation in his life. Usually people liked him, didn't they? *You don't usually tell girls to sit down and eat their breakfast on pain of being spanked.*

That had been a whisker. He very much doubted that his shoulder would permit such a thing. And besides, he'd never raised a hand to a woman in his life. But the hollowness of the threat didn't excuse the impropriety of making it. He concentrated on the lessons, read in the Rector's quiet, assured voice. Something had to give his thoughts a more proper direction than imagining his hand on any of Cressida's curves, let alone her... A rustling of pages and the rumble of feet on wooden boards recalled him with a thump.

Belatedly he realised that the congregation had risen to its collective feet. Blast. It was time for the hymn and he didn't have his book ready.

He was still hunting for the right page when the hymn began and his fingers faltered helplessly in their task. He stood, caught in delight as the knowledge dawned on him that he'd brought a lark to church. Dazed, he listened as Cressida's achingly sweet voice soared effortlessly against the ragged singing of the congregation. It pierced him in its loveliness, haunting, alluring. And she stood, apparently quite unaware of the shock she had dealt him, simply singing, looking straight ahead, not bothering even to glance at her book.

Pulling himself together, he sought hurriedly in his own book for the right page. His suddenly nerveless fingers fumbled and he dropped the book with a thud.

Cressida's book suddenly appeared before him. Flushed with embarrassment at his clumsiness, he muttered a swift thanks and began to sing. He enjoyed the opera when he was in town, but he'd never understood why Ulysses had risked his life to hear the Sirens. Now he knew. Never before had he realised that a girl's voice could entwine itself in a man's senses like perfume.

An accomplishment. That's all it was. One of the skills a young lady ought to have. Nothing else. And he was not about to be snared by a young lady's *accomplishments*.

As they left the church at the conclusion of the service he said politely, 'I don't know when I've enjoyed the hymns quite so much, cousin. Thank you.'

Green eyes, wide with puzzlement, blinked up at him. 'They were lovely tunes, weren't they? But I don't know why you should thank me. I assume the Rector chose them.'

'I meant your voice, cousin. It's quite lovely.'

He snorted to himself. Typical of a female to angle for the more obvious compliment!

'My *voice*?' She looked up at him blankly. 'There's nothing special about it.'

It was Jack's turn to stare. She meant it. She really meant it. She truly didn't think that her voice was at all special.

Dazed, he pulled himself together in time to greet the Rector at the door and present Cressida. In doing so he became fully aware that practically the entire parish was either hovering around the porch or treading on his heels in an effort to discover who Cressida might be. He had absolutely no doubt at all that the Bramleys' arrival in the neighbourhood had been duly noted and commented upon.

'My cousin, Miss Bramley, Rector. She and her father are my guests. Dr Bramley finds himself unwell this morning. A most tiring journey from Cornwall.'

Cressida, he saw, blushed scarlet at his unthinking words. An absurd sense of guilt swamped him. Damn! He hadn't meant to imply that she hadn't looked after her father. Much against his will, he was forced to acknowledge that, given her youth and inexperience, she had done remarkably well. Especially when hampered with a travelling companion who could be counted upon to disburse every penny they possessed to the poor.

The local Squire and his lady came up with their daughter.

Jack groaned silently. Miss Stanhope was the front-running local candidate for the position of Mrs Jack Hamilton. It had all been decided by her very decisive mama. She was an heiress, well bred, well brought up. Her lands would round out his own estates very nicely and, since he had taken no other bride in the last few years, it could only be surmised that he was waiting for Miss Stanhope to grow up.

Jack was only too happy to wait. Until hell froze over. As far as he could see, Miss Stanhope had bearen hell to it by several lengths.

'Morning, Jack. How's that shoulder, m' boy? Glad to see you up and about,' boomed the Squire. 'And who's this? Cousin, did I hear you say?'

Jack felt his hackles rise at the expression of avid interest on Sir William Stanhope's rubicund face as he made the introductions. His wife was eyeing Cressida's worn cloak and morning gown in a way which suggested she already had the chit firmly labelled—*poor relation*—and no danger to her matrimonial plans for himself.

His teeth gritted, Jack presented Cressida.

'Miss Bramley.'

The faint tone of condescension and the way the Squire's lady held out two begrudging fingers sent a flare of anger through Jack. Lady Stanhope's habit of looking down her very long nose at those she considered her social inferiors would have sent most women cross-eyed.

He shot a sideways glance at Cressida, half-expecting her to give Lady Stanhope a set down.

'Lady Stanhope, I'm honoured to meet you.'

Jack blinked at the low, deferential voice. Was this the same little termagant who'd raked him down in the garden when they met, and practically every other time she'd seen him, including over the breakfast cups this morning? He thrust aside the acidic little voice that suggested his own behaviour over the last two days would not have given Cressida a favourable view of *his* manners.

Vaguely he realised that Sir William was repeating himself and responded. 'That's right, sir. No more hunting this season, and if my staff had their way I'd be laid up in bed with a hot brick!'

Sir William chuckled in very masculine way. 'Better ways to warm your bed than that, lad!' Then he cast a rather conscious glance at the ladies. 'Not with your cousin in the house of course, but you know what I mean!'

Smiling determinedly, Jack changed the subject at once by asking after Sir William's hunters. That should get the old boy safely off the dangerous subject of beds and how to warm them.

Nodding occasionally as Sir William thrashed out the benefits of applying fomentations to the leg of an injured horse, he kept track of Cressida's conversation with Lady Stanhope and her daughter.

'*Where* did you say you were from, Miss Bramley? Cornwall? Ah, near St Austell. I have a cousin there. She married *very* well, of course.'

To his absolute horror he heard the words '...position

as a governess, or companion' uttered in unnaturally polite accents.

Sharply he swung around in time to see Lady Stanhope's nose elevate itself by a few more degrees.

'Well, as to that, I should need to be quite assured of your credentials, Miss, er, Bramley.'

And even worse, Miss Stanhope's contribution: 'Oh, I don't think I know *anyone* who has to do that! How lowering it would be!'

His eyes narrowed. 'My cousin is funning you, Lady Stanhope,' he cut in smoothly. 'She has absolutely no need to seek employment. Dr Bramley will be remaining with me to assist with my library and Miss Bramley will naturally remain as well.'

Lady Stanhope appeared to have bitten into a lemon. 'Unchaperoned, Mr Hamilton? I venture to—'

Sir William interrupted. 'Pshaw! Fiddle faddle, my lady. Jack's a man of honour! No one in their right mind would think anything of it! Girl's got a father. Clergyman, ain't he? Used to visit years ago when Jack was a lad. Family! Nothing in it.'

Jack had the distinct impression that, had a table been handy, the Squire would have administered a substantial kick under it to his wife.

Lady Stanhope looked thoroughly unconvinced and said with grudging insincerity, 'Well, of course, one would not like to suggest anything in the least improper, but society does view these things...'

'I'm sure, Lady Stanhope, that your understanding would count for a great deal,' said Jack basely. The words nearly choked him, but he had the satisfaction of seeing Lady Stanhope rolled up. Any appeal to her social influence and standing was a certain winner. The part of his mind he reserved for cynical comment on social double standards and out-and-out hypocrisy suggested another, even more ignoble, reason.

He dealt the death blow without hesitation. 'I should be sorry to think that in having family members to stay, I would in any way be jeopardising either Miss Bramley's reputation or my own.' The effort involved in maintaining a straight face nearly killed him. Especially as he saw all the possible ramifications of the situation occur belatedly to Lady Stanhope.

Before anything else could be said, he made his farewells and hustled Cressida towards the carriage, bestowing polite, if hasty, greetings upon the rest of the congregation.

Cressida kept her mouth firmly shut until the carriage door closed behind them and the horses were set in motion. Then her much-tried control deserted her.

'Just what did you mean by telling Lady Stanhope that I don't need a job?' She had spent the entire walk to the carriage reminding herself not to curse at him and was justifiably pleased at her restraint. There! She could rein in her temper if she really tried. All it took was strength of mind.

'Exactly what I said,' he replied.

Her eyes narrowed at his cool, dismissive tones, but she began the usual litany, *Lord, make me an instrument of thy peace…*

'I consider you to be under my protection…'

'You *what*?'

The Lord's Instrument of Peace exploded in impious fury.

'Not like that!' he snapped. 'You are my cousin—'

'A distant connection!'

'Cousin!' he repeated. 'Your father intends to remain within my household. I can hardly permit his daughter to go out and make her way in the world! You have not the least idea of the dangers you would be exposed to, nor the least idea of how to protect yourself!'

'I'm perfectly capable of looking after myself!'

'Well, you shouldn't be,' he growled.

'And how do you propose to stop Lady Stanhope's gossip?' she asked.

His grin would have incited a saint to violence. Cressida had to lace her fingers together tightly within her battered old velvet muff.

'I already did.' He looked as smug as a fox in a henrun. 'Lady Stanhope is hardly likely to gossip when the end result would be that the neighbourhood's most eligible bachelor would find himself obliged to offer the protection of his name to a poor relation instead of offering for her daughter.'

Cressida took a very deep, careful breath. And another. Then she counted to ten. Satisfied that she had expurgated all the more unladylike elements from what she wished to say, she took another breath and began.

'Might I ask what gives you the idea I'd accept your *obliging* offer,' she asked. Her dulcet tones surprised even her.

'Oh, I've no doubt you'd refuse. At first.'

Her ladylike mask slipped a trifle and she glared. 'I'd refuse—utterly.'

His raised brows made her long to hit him.

'Really? Then it's just as well Lady Stanhope hasn't had time to realise that your intellect is disordered, or your reputation would have been in tatters before we reached the carriage.'

It had been shredded before she left Cornwall, but he didn't need to know that. Instead she managed to ask, with only a hint of sarcasm, 'And might one be informed why not wishing to marry you is evidence of a disordered intellect?'

He shrugged. 'Apparently I am considered to be an eligible match.'

'You're a conceited coxcomb!' The words burst from her. How dare he insinuate that she would leap at the first man to offer like a cock at a blackberry! She swept on in fury. 'Not every woman considers wealth as her primary motivation for marriage. Some consider being able to respect their husband to be more important than a respect for his purse!'

'Are you saying you don't respect me?'

She glared at him suspiciously. Was he daring to laugh at her?

'Let me put it this way,' she said dangerously. 'I always find it difficult to respect a man who offers me a spanking before breakfast! So I'll wish Miss Stanhope joy of you, sir. No doubt you will deal extremely together! Far be it from me to prevent a match so obviously made in heaven!'

This time there was absolutely no doubt. Jack Hamilton stared at her in apparent disbelief for a split second and then fell back against the squabs, laughing uproariously.

'Will that be all, sir?'

'Hmm? Oh, yes. Thank you, Fincham. I won't need you again tonight.'

'Goodnight then, sir.'

'Goodnight.'

The door clicked shut behind Fincham, and Jack eased himself into bed. Being helped out of his clothes was bad enough. Being assisted into bed was unthinkable.

He wriggled his shoulders carefully against the soft feathers in an unavailing attempt to find a comfortable position for his shoulder. And the hot brick wrapped in flannel at his feet was driving him demented. Sir William's words taunted him ceaselessly—*Better ways than that to warm your bed...*

As if he needed the reminder! His body was making no bones about suggesting all sorts of ineligible ways to warm his bed. And all of them were utterly impossible. Never before in his life had he found himself fantasising over the seduction of an innocent. That he could have been doing so in church actually shocked him. He couldn't remember when he'd last been shocked by his own desires. He was used to them by now. Come to think of it, he couldn't remember ever having wanted a woman so much in his entire life.

The whole thing was impossible. He could not, under any circumstances seduce a gently bred girl living in his house who was also his cousin. Not unless he was planning to marry her. And Miss Cressida Bramley was not at all the sort of girl he planned to marry.

She'd drive him mad. Pert, outspoken, far too independent and damnably hot at hand—she was the last woman on earth a man desiring a peaceful life of domestic harmony should marry. Even if he did want her like hell burning. He gritted his teeth. Burning passion was not, in his opinion, a valid reason for matrimony.

She did make him laugh, though. That crack of hers about finding it difficult to respect a man who offered to spank her before breakfast… He smiled at the memory. Most females would have had the vapours after what he'd implied. Not Cressida. She'd ripped back at him and given as good as she got. And then thrown it up at him when he'd had the hide to ask if she respected him.

Still, she wasn't the sort of girl he wanted to marry, so he'd better keep his thoughts safely occupied and his hands off her. He frowned into the darkness. He could keep his hands off her easily enough. Especially if he avoided speaking to her or looking at her. His thoughts were another matter entirely. In fact they were being thoroughly uncooperative—they kept on reminding him that he was lying in bed. Alone.

Over the next three days Cressida came to the conclusion that she'd been quite wrong about Mr Jack Hamilton. Far from showing the least inclination to flirt with her, let alone seduce her, he ignored her presence as much as he could. He greeted her politely at breakfast and thereafter barely spoke to her except in connection with the library, and even then he scarcely glanced at her.

Cressida relaxed. Men intent on seduction were all sweetness and light, flattering. They didn't ensconce themselves at one end of the library and grunt when one brought them a pile of musty old tomes. They didn't brusquely point out a smudge of dirt on one's face and then retire into one of the aforesaid musty old tomes. And they certainly didn't hand one to a seat at the dinner table and then remove their hand as though it had been stung. It mightn't be flattering that he disliked her, but at least it was safe.

She liked him, though. Too much for her own comfort. She liked the consideration with which he treated his staff. Even the lowliest maid would greet him with respectful pleasure. The upper servants were even more respectful—in front of their underlings. But Cressida shook with laughter as she remembered Evans catching his master sneaking back into the house after a walk. The scolding the master of the house had received for not wearing a muffler had been all the funnier for being couched in such polite terms.

And the memory of Jack's—Mr Hamilton's—face as he bore with it, and promised to remember next time, never failed to make her smile. He'd been as meek and mild as a lamb. Which puzzled Cressida. Because generally, she didn't think he was a very meek sort of man. He exploded like gunpowder every time *she* mentioned the word *sling*.

After three days Cressida came to the conclusion that Jack Hamilton considered her too far beneath his touch even to converse with. Yet she couldn't bring herself to dislike him. He treated her father with affection and respect. That was all that mattered. Her birthday was not far off. After that she'd have to leave. If she could find a position. First she had to find someone willing to give her a reference.

* * *

Jack drew a deep breath and opened the library door. It was doubtless the last breath he'd take free of dust until he came out again. And he'd need all his self-control not to watch surreptitiously as Cressida scrambled up and down the ladders. No matter how many times he told himself that he was concerned she'd slip, that he was ready to leap to the rescue, he knew it for a lie. He was completely and utterly fascinated by the tantalising glimpses of shapely ankles, not to mention slender, rounded calves.

He routinely thanked a merciful God for the presence of Dr Bramley at the other end of the library. Not that the old chap would notice anything less disturbing than the rape of all the Sabine women at once, but his presence did somehow help Jack keep a rein on his desires. That, and the rising suspicion that he'd met a female who left Selina and her parlour tricks for dead.

He stepped in and found a scene of charming domesticity, without the soothing presence of Dr Bramley.

Cressida sat in a chair by the fire, her legs curled up under her, not an ankle in sight, sewing. The warmth of the fire had brought a flush of colour to her normally pale cheeks and its flames were mirrored in the deep auburn of her hair. For once she did not have it scraped back into its braids or an equally unflattering bun. It hung loose over one shoulder, half-hiding her delicate profile.

So thick, so silky. A man could slide his hands into it and burn…

Memory froze him. All those times he had unexpectedly found Selina unchaperoned… Then he saw what Cressida was sewing. And forgot everything.

'Just what the bloody hell do you think you're doing?' he roared, slamming the door behind him.

Cressida gave a shriek of surprise, cursed vigorously and sucked her finger. The shirt she was mending fell to the floor, along with the work basket she had knocked off the wine table in her fright. Buttons, thread and pins tumbled everywhere.

Jack viewed the scene with satisfaction. Total confusion; just like himself.

He stalked over and bent to pick up the shirt. It was snatched from his grasp.

'How dare you!' blazed Cressida.

'This is my home,' he informed her, noting a smudge of dust on her nose. 'I'll dare anything I like. And I have maids to do my mending!'

Her eyes widened. 'How very nice for you, sir. I congratulate you.'

Jack throttled the urge to shake her. Or to kiss away the dust. 'The next time I find you doing my mending…' He left the sentence hanging and held out his hand for the shirt.

To his smug satisfaction, she gave it to him without further argument. Hah! Maybe she was learning that he was not to be baited like this. How dare she insinuate herself into his household in this way. Mending his shirts, indeed!

'Nothing to say, Cressida?' He couldn't resist teasing her a little.

'Have I your permission?' she asked sweetly.

'Don't be henwitted,' he growled. Perhaps he had been a little overbearing.

She smiled, and every nerve in his body sat up and screamed a warning. 'You might find it a little tight over the shoulders, but I dare say one of the maids could let it out for you. And lengthen the arms, of course. And I'm not quite sure that it will do up around your neck.'

Green ice glittered in her eyes as she warmed to her theme.

'Of course…' her voice dripped honey '…it's entirely possible that it won't even get over your thick head!'

A horrible suspicion formed itself in Jack's mind. Oh, hell and the devil! Surely not?

He shook out the shirt and bit off a curse. The damn thing was far too small for him. He seriously doubted that he would even get it over his shoulders.

'And perhaps you would be so good as to lend Papa one of your shirts while I make him another, since you have taken such an unaccountable liking to this one, sir.'

Heat washed over Jack's cheekbones in a crimson wave. He couldn't remember ever feeling so foolish in all his thirty-six years. And he certainly couldn't remember the last time he had blushed. If he ever had.

'I...I beg your pardon, Cressida.' The words came stiffly. 'It...it was just that I thought it was my shirt...that you were...' He hesitated.

'Going to ruin it?' she suggested. 'Rip it to pieces? Or sew up the sleeves, perhaps?'

He smiled wryly. His younger sister, Nan, had done just that on several occasions. Sneaked into his room and sewn up all his shirts when he had annoyed her. She had a quick tongue, too.

'Would you?' he asked.

She flushed in her turn. 'I'd be more likely to sew up your mouth,' she shot back at him. 'And you needn't bother apologising. You swear at me all the time and I've had quite enough insincerity to last me a lifetime! At least your language is preferable to that. Now, if you wouldn't mind giving Papa's shirt back to me, I can finish mending it!'

He handed the shirt to her and knelt down beside her chair. Damn it, she was right. He *did* swear at her. And he could hardly explain why.

I beg your pardon, cousin, but I keep swearing at you because I can't take you to bed. As an apology it lacked a certain something.

'What on earth are you doing?'

'Picking up your things.' He suppressed a curse as he pricked his finger on a pin. 'Good lord! How many of these damn—er, dashed pins do you have?' They were everywhere.

'Absolutely no idea,' returned Cressida. 'Why don't you count them while you're down there and tell me? They go in that box.' She indicated a little wooden box and reached down for it. Just as Jack did.

Their heads nearly collided. Their eyes did.

Jack found himself gazing into stormy green eyes, inches from his face. He froze. Such long lashes. She was staring back, her gaze startled. He was close enough to feel her sweet breath on his lips. Shaken, he made the mistake of looking down. Softly curved pink lips parted slightly…would they really taste of raspberries? He leaned closer and raised his hand to her jawline, feathering gentle fingertips over it. They strayed to her throat. Soft, silken. He hadn't known a woman's skin could be quite that delicate. The need to taste her lips throbbed in time to the rhythm of his blood, luring him on. He leaned forward. Just one taste, just one…

Her eyes widened in shock and he heard the sharp intake of breath as she jerked back out of reach and scrambled to her feet, bumping him as she did so.

Taken by surprise, Jack lost his balance and crashed to the floor.

White-hot talons of pain raked his shoulder.

'Bloody hell!' He shut his eyes and set his jaw against all the other curses that rose to his lips and breathed deeply until the nausea subsided. To be replaced by suspicion. *Damn. She hooked you again.*

'Sir?'

He opened his eyes unwillingly to find Cressida leaning over him, the shock in her eyes replaced by worry. Equally fraudulent, no doubt.

'Are you all right? Is your shoulder paining you?'

'Not at all,' he lied.

Her mouth flattened. 'Here, let me help you.'

Before he could protest she was kneeling beside him, her right arm under his left shoulder, trying to lift him to a sitting position. A different sort of pain shot through him as her soft breast brushed against his body. Heat flooded his loins as he sat up.

'What the devil did you do that for?' he asked savagely. Damn the chit and damn his response to her. She didn't even like him, yet she was baiting him just the way Selina had. And even knowing what she was up to didn't help. He rose to the bait every time. Literally.

Cressida felt the heat steal into her cheeks again. What on earth was wrong with her? He'd made a mistake and he'd been trying to atone for it. Of course he hadn't been going to kiss her. What would a man like Jack Hamilton want to kiss her for? He made it quite plain that he disliked her.

She must have imagined that softer glow in his eyes, the dawning smile that had turned her heart over. He was glaring at her now. As for his caress—perhaps she had a smudge of dirt on her face…or, or something. He looked like he'd rather strangle her.

'I…I didn't mean to knock you over,' she said. 'You…you startled me.'

He snorted.

'I'm terribly sorry,' she said. 'I…was mistaken.'

'Mistaken?' He looked puzzled. 'Mistaken about what?'

Too late Cressida realised the trap she had set for herself. She floundered.

'I…er…ah…nothing,' she said shortly.

'Nothing?' He appeared to have recovered all his usual self-command, even sitting on the hearthstone unconsciously rubbing his shoulder.

'Don't do that,' she said, reaching for his hand. 'You'll jar it again.'

She found that her hand was held in a gentle steel vice. A vice that made her hand tremble, sent tingling shocks right through her.

She tugged. 'Let me go!'

'When you tell me what you were mistaken about.'

The steel vice shifted slightly, a large thumb rubbing over the back of her hand.

Cressida trembled. If she tugged hard enough she could free herself. But she might tip him over again, hurt his shoulder.

'Will you promise to let me go and not to laugh if I tell you?' She felt like a complete idiot, and if she didn't end this scene quickly Papa would come back from his rest and find them on the floor together. She shuddered to think of his likely reaction.

'You have my word of honour as a gentleman,' said Jack.

She swallowed. She really hadn't needed the reminder that he was a gentleman.

'I...I...well...I thought you were...goingtokissme.' She finished the sentence at a flat gallop and charged on. 'I realise that it was silly of me and that you don't even like me, but I just thought you were and I didn't want you to, so...I really didn't mean to knock you over.'

'You thought I was about to kiss you?' His voice was even.

'Yes.'

'May I ask what gave you that impression?' Very even. Quite mild.

'I...I don't know...you just looked...as if...as if you were...' She trailed off, hot with shame and embarrassment. Of course he hadn't been.

'Going to kiss you,' he finished. 'And you think I don't like you and that I'll believe you didn't want me to kiss you.'

He levered himself off the ground carefully. Instinctively Cressida reached to help him.

'No!' he snapped. She ignored him and slipped his arm over her shoulder, supporting him as he rose.

He removed his arm and stepped away immediately.

'Do not do that again, Miss Bramley,' he said. 'I am fully awake on all suits. You will find me a difficult mark.'

What was he talking about? And *Miss Bramley*? He'd been calling her Cressida, much to her fury, for days. She was shocked to discover how much it hurt to become Miss Bramley again.

'Not...not help you? Why not? It was my fault you landed on the floor. You mustn't think I will hurt myself. I'm quite used to helping Papa when he has the gout.'

For a moment she thought he might explode. His face reddened and he seemed to swell with affront. Was it somehow dreadfully improper to help him up?

His eventual answer was not at all what she expected.

'Because you were perfectly right.'

Right? About what? Kissing me? Then she knew. He disliked her so much he couldn't bear to have her help him or touch him. *Stupid little fool that you are! Of course he didn't want to kiss you! Andrew wouldn't have either if anything better had offered. He told you so. Freckles, red hair and that nose...*

'I was going to kiss you.'

Shock froze all her wits.

'Why?' she asked blankly. And then cursed herself. Slapping him: yes. Telling him what a licentious beast he was: quite unexceptionable. But asking him why he'd wanted to kiss her? She ought to be in Bedlam.

His voice became colder. 'Gentlemen have these little lapses of taste from time to time. Might I suggest that it is not at all the thing for you to be alone in a bachelor household—'

Pain slashed through her.

'No, you may not!' she interrupted. 'Next time you have one of your *little lapses of taste*, I suggest you go out and bury yourself in a snowdrift for a few hours! In the meantime, I shall give thanks to God that I am not, in the general way, up to your exacting standards!'

Flaming with fury, she swept up the shirt and headed for the door.

'Cressida!'

She swung around.

'Go to the devil! And I much prefer *Miss Bramley*! Good afternoon, sir.'

Jack blinked at the slam of the door and then groaned. Someone ought to have smothered him in his cradle. And if his mother and sister ever discovered just what a nodcock he was making of himself they'd rectify the omission. How on earth was he to explain his confusion to Cressida when he didn't understand it himself?

And in the meantime, how was he to apologise since every time he got near her they had another fight? He swore. She might have a point in recommending a snowdrift. Something had to cool him down! Maybe he had imagined that she was teasing him on purpose. Oh, lord. No doubt she'd gone up to her room. It would be cold up there. Guilt lashed at him. She'd been sitting comfortably by the fire, mending her father's shirt...her *father's* shirt, he reminded himself mercilessly. And he had barged in and practically accused her of trying to trap him into marriage.

He found that he was pacing around the room, restless, unable to settle to the work he had intended to do.

He had a sneaking suspicion that she hadn't had the least idea what he was talking about. For which he ought to be devoutly grateful. Her freckles had been close to dancing in fury anyway.

Her room would be cold, though. The bedchamber fires would not be lit until closer to dinnertime. *Oh, for good-*

*ness sake! She can light the fire, can't she? She's not stu-
pid!*

His pacing took him past the window seat where Cressida often sat. Especially when he was in the library. He
winced. Well away from the fire. She either sat here or
was scrambling up and down ladders for her father.

A couple of books lay on the seat. He glanced at the
one on top. Hmm. Not his taste. Mrs Radcliffe and…he
picked it up to see the other… Good Lord! Southey's *Life
of Nelson*. Eclectic, if not downright catholic. A reluctant
grin tugged at his lips. Predictability was not one of Cressida's leading traits.

Why didn't she take the books up to her bedchamber to
read?

The answer came like a body blow. She felt unwelcome
in his home. He kept noticing little things that told him
how deeply she felt her poor-relation status. How determined she was not to be thought encroaching. Like these
books. She was obviously reading them. Yet they remained
there. She never took them up to her room. And she would
never ring and ask for the fire to be lit or light it herself.

If he wanted her to have a fire in her room, he would
have to light it himself. Or at least arrange for someone
else to light it. Cressida wasn't *that* unpredictable. If he
tried to walk into her room right now she'd throw something at him. He felt like throwing things at himself.

He crossed to the fireplace and tugged the bellpull. His
gaze drifted to the familiar items on the chimneypiece and
caught, puzzled. Something was missing. What was it?
Then he knew. Where the devil had that little T'ang horse
got to? It had been here last night in its place. Where could
it be now?

Chapter Four

Cressida stormed up to her room and slammed that door as well. Then she sat down on her bed and clenched her fists. She wasn't going to cry. She *wasn't*. She had nothing to cry about. Just that he thought wanting to kiss her was a lapse of taste.

Scowling ferociously, she went over to the dressing table and stared into the mirror. Her hair wasn't nearly as carrotish as it had once been. It was more auburn now. And since it was winter, the freckles on her nose were mere ghosts of their usual summer splendour. Hardly noticeable, really. But how she hated her nose! It turned up slightly, and there wasn't much she could do about that or her green eyes. She had filled out a bit, though. Actually, she'd filled out a bit too much in places. Her velvet evening gown had been made for a skinny sixteen-year-old. The more ample charms of twenty were nearly bursting out of it. Some lace, perhaps…

She glared at her reflection. There! See? She wasn't attractive at all. Maybe it was a lapse of taste. In which case she ought to be duly grateful.

She sat there for some time, trying to convince herself, only to be interrupted by a discreet tap on the door.

'Who...who is it?' If it was Jack... She looked around for a missile.

'It's Nell, miss. Come to light your fire.'

The door opened and a rosy-cheeked maid came in. She smiled at Cressida and said, 'Master thought as how you might be cold and asked me to light your fire, miss.'

Cressida felt her jaw drop.

The maid, taking silence for assent, dealt quickly with the fire and straightened up. 'There y'are, miss. Master said to ask you if you wanted tea on a tray.'

Tea. On a tray. She couldn't remember anyone, since her mother's death, making a fuss of her. Except Andrew. And that definitely didn't count. Did this?

'I...I don't think...'

The maid smiled. 'Why don't you have a nice rest, miss? I'll bring the tea up later. Just ring when you're ready.'

She bobbed a curtsy and left. Cressida stared at the door, trying to imagine the response of Andrew's mother, Lady Fairbridge, if a maidservant had addressed her with that degree of familiarity. It was even harder to imagine the maidservant addressing Lady Fairbridge with such open-hearted friendliness. Yet she kept on noticing the way Jack's staff looked after him. Fussed over him and his shoulder. Where had they learnt such things?

She could see it drove him to distraction at times, yet he never snapped at them. Just tried to dodge their ministrations without hurting any feelings. She had never seen servants behave like that before. Nor the affection Jack plainly felt for the senior members of his staff.

And now he had sent a maid to light her fire and offer her tea. Why?

To wheedle his way into your good graces, suggested a very nasty, suspicious little voice.

No, that's not like him. Especially if he doesn't like me. He wouldn't bother.

Kicking off her slippers, she curled up on the bed and drew the counterpane over herself. Still pondering the question, she fell asleep.

When she woke up, the deepening shadows told her that the afternoon light was nearly spent. Yawning, she sat up and looked around. Much to her surprise the fire still blazed brightly. How very odd. Surely it would have died down. She must have been asleep for a couple of hours. Had the maid come back? A warmth that had nothing to do with the fire stole through her at the thought that someone had cared enough to come and build up the fire while she slept. Even a maid.

Stretching deliciously, she swung her legs off the bed—and saw her workbasket sitting on a chair. She frowned. In the dim light it looked odd. What was that on top of it?

She went over and stared. Snowdrops, and the books she had been reading. A bunch of snowdrops tied with a silver ribbon lay on top of the books with a sealed piece of paper tucked under them.

With trembling fingers she reached for the note. Carefully she broke it and read.

My dear Cressida,
    You have every right to be angry with me. I behaved disgracefully. That was what I meant about a lapse of taste—that I was going to kiss you. Wanting to kiss you is not a lapse of taste.
    I hope I found all the pins, but I forgot to count them.
    Please accept my apologies.

                                                            Jack.

There was no mention of the snowdrops. It was unnecessary. She lifted them to her face and breathed their freshness. No one had ever given her flowers before... She caught herself up. Andrew had given her flowers. An expensive posy he had bought, probably on a whim, in Truro.

Jack, on the other hand, had gone out on a chilly winter's day with an aching shoulder and found what flowers he could. Simply because he knew he had hurt her feelings. And he had sent up the books, which she would never have dreamed of taking from the library. Was he trying to tell her she was welcome?

She had been right the first time. No one had ever given her flowers before—only a calculated lure.

How is it different? Except that the lure touches your heart this time and not merely your vanity. How can you tell? You were wrong last time and just look at the consequences. Will you risk your father losing this post?

She trembled. Surely this was different.

The differences screamed at her. Andrew's attempted seduction had been carried out in a situation of the utmost inconvenience, from his point of view, in front of an entire community. Jack, on the other hand, had the distinct advantage of having her in his own house. He had every opportunity to seduce her…

Oh, don't be such a confirmed ninnyhammer! Why on earth would he do such a thing? He doesn't even like you, let alone find you attractive. Just because he said he wanted to kiss you…men have these indiscriminate urges. Mama said so. He asked the maid to bring your things up because he felt guilty. Nothing more.

A light tap on the door distracted her.

'Come in.'

The maid put her head in. 'Oh, you're awake. I'll bring up the tea, shall I?'

'That would be lovely. And thank you for building up the fire again. Did you bring my sewing up?' She indicated the workbox.

'Me, miss? Oh, no. I've been in the stillroom helping Mrs Roberts. We all have.' She smiled and left.

He had been into her room. The impropriety of his behaviour crashed into her. He had actually entered her room.
While she was sleeping. And there was no one else on this
corridor. Her father's room was in the same corridor as
Jack's. Well out of earshot, even if he didn't take laudanum as a sleeping draught.

*And I couldn't scream for help anyway. Just look what
happened last time Papa decided to ask a man's intentions.*

She couldn't quite believe that she was thinking this
way about Jack Hamilton. Suspicious, hostile. Just because
a handsome man had admitted that he wanted to kiss her
and had given her a bunch of snowdrops to apologise for
his tactlessness. He was a gentleman to the tips of his
fingers. How could she possibly believe that he would behave so shabbily?

She *didn't* believe it. Just because he had entered her
room? It was his house after all and, even if entering a
woman's room while she slept was the height of impropriety, there was a big jump from impropriety to dishonour. She didn't believe it was a jump Jack Hamilton would
make.

But it would be much safer to behave as though she did.
At all costs she must keep her distance. And make sure he
kept his.

By a stroke of Providence, Papa had fallen feet first into
a post that would suit him perfectly. Especially since he
would no longer have any practical need for her own presence. He would be looked after far better than she could
ever manage.

She would take no more risks that might ruin her father's peace. And she would definitely ignore the little
voice that suggested she was even more worried about disturbing her own peace. Because she was as far beneath
Jack Hamilton's touch as a daisy to the sun that warms it.

Jack shifted uncomfortably in his seat and tried to concentrate on what Dr Bramley had to say on the subject of

mediaeval manuscripts. It completely failed to hold his attention. He ached too much.

His shoulder was fine. It hardly twinged at all now, except when he forgot not to use the arm. His problem sat at the opposite end of the table, picking at her dinner. He must have been out of his mind to leave those flowers. Just because the little baggage had somehow managed to convince him that, under her fury at being caught out, she was genuinely hurt.

Of course she hadn't been hurt. If she had, she wouldn't be sitting there in that green velvet gown she always wore to dinner. If ever a gown was built to make the most of a lady's assets, that one was. She was practically popping out of the damn…dashed…thing. She would be if it wasn't for that inadequate scrap of lace pinned in the neckline. All that did was veil her charms, while doing nothing to disguise them.

He couldn't even tell the maid who waited on her to lay out something else. Even *his* servants would gossip if he did that. He grimaced inwardly—dash it all, even he'd gossip!

He had to hand it to her. She was up to all the rigs.

She had scarcely glanced his way all evening since he had handed her to her chair. She had made it plain that she had read his note and accepted his apology. And then she had retreated behind a wall of silence, responding politely when he spoke to her, but offering nothing of her own.

Hah! Probably miffed because you bubbled her.

Her father didn't seem to notice the arctic atmosphere.

'You know, dear boy, that manuscript is far too ornate to be…'

With an effort Jack dragged his mind back to the subject at hand and listened attentively. Dr Bramley was probably right, but…

'What does Cressida think?' he asked. Now she'd have to respond with something more than a *yes* or *no*.

She glanced up from folding her napkin.

'What do I think?' She placed the napkin precisely by her plate. 'I think it is time I relieved you gentlemen of my company and left you to your port.'

Oh, curse it! He stood up, swearing silently.

She rose and went to her father. 'Goodnight, Papa.'

He looked up vaguely. 'Goodnight, my dear. Did you leave the laudanum by my bed?'

Jack caught the faint frown on her brow. Even if she did drive him to distraction, he couldn't deny her protective affection for her father. He had the oddest notion that there was very little she wouldn't do for the old man. It was part of her charm and Jack was very far from denying Cressida's charms. Merely his own reaction to them.

'I did, but, Papa, don't you think—?'

'Thank you, my dear. My stomach, you know.'

She bent to kiss him, providing Jack with a distracting insight into her charms. 'Well, don't take more than a few drops. Goodnight.'

Jack watched her leave the room, his gaze rivetted on the supple line of her back, the graceful, tempting curves of her waist and hips. He would have to do something about this. The more he thought about it, spending a few hours in a nice cold snowdrift had a great deal to recommend it and would be more to the point than a hot brick.

It might serve to remind him that passion could distract a man from all the other ingredients of a suitable marriage—such as interests in common and a comfortable friendship with each other. He shouldn't be thinking of how vulnerable she had looked, sleeping with her cheek cradled in her hand and the quilt slipping off her shoulders. And he shouldn't be thinking of the grateful little wriggle she had given when he tucked the quilt more securely around her.

Damn…*dash* it all, he shouldn't even have been there! He'd make quite sure he never did anything so corkbrained again.

'What the deuce have you got there?'

Jack's voice broke Cressida's concentration.

She looked up from the papers and frowned. How utterly typical of him to change his routine just as she was feeling comfortable with it. She had spent three days carefully avoiding the dratted man and she certainly hadn't expected to see him at this hour. He usually went for a walk after lunch.

No doubt he would think she was encroaching. Maybe she shouldn't have started rummaging through the box, but it was all so interesting, before she'd known it she'd been curled up in the window seat in the pale, wintry sun with dusty old papers strewn everywhere. Papa had slept badly the night before and was a trifle feverish, so she had persuaded him to remain in bed.

'You did say you wanted the library catalogued and everything sorted, didn't you?' she asked.

'Well, yes.' He looked amused. 'But that looks like my great-grandmother's box of papers. There won't be anything interesting in there.'

She snorted. How typical of a man. They always assumed that women had nothing interesting to say or pass on.

'Does it ever occur to you that, without women, you men would starve?' she asked. 'After all, I have noticed that you do like jam. There are several recipes for preserves in here. Plum jam, medlar jelly, even one for quince paste. Although I can't believe quinces would do very well here. Too cold. And you do like your furniture polished. Probably by this, judging by the scent of lavender in the house.' She waved a recipe for beeswax polish laced with lavender at him.

Jack stared at her.

She went on. 'Think about it. Her household-accounts books are here. You can read about all her expenses, how the house was run and who came to stay, even what she wore when they entertained the Duke of Rutland. It's fascinating. You…you know how they *lived*, what they enjoyed, what they had for breakfast. You can *see* it. That's just as interesting as Thucydides and his everlasting Peloponnesian War.'

His entire world tilted. And he found himself wondering what Thucydides had liked for breakfast. He could remember his great-grandmother living in the Dower House. She had died when he was about ten. She liked ham and eggs for breakfast without fail. One morning she asked her maid for a cup of tea instead and died five minutes later without any further warning.

He looked at the papers strewn around the window seat. Some were covered in his great-grandmother's spidery hand. Some looked even older. All her papers had been brought up to the house after her death and placed in this old deed box. Then it had been forgotten. He hadn't thought about the old lady in years. He did now.

He and Nan had liked nothing better than to run down to the Dower House and visit her. She'd always grumbled about how much they ate, even as she filled their plates with cake and biscuits. And they grinned and ignored everything except the twinkle in her eye. Lord, he could almost smell her special spice biscuits now, warm from the oven.

As a child he had wondered how she managed to know they were coming and order the biscuits so that they had just come out of the oven as they arrived. Years later he noticed that the side door he and Nan always used to sneak out of the house was visible from the Dower House drawing room half a mile away. He could just imagine the old lady bustling off to the kitchen and giving orders to the cook. And then going back to await her visitors and grumble that if their noses were any sharper, they'd cut themselves off their owners' faces.

Before he knew it he was picking up bits of paper and scanning them. He looked up to see Cressida watching him oddly.

'Are you looking for something in particular?'

He flushed, feeling remarkably foolish. 'She…she had a recipe for spice biscuits,' he began. And stopped. Impossible to put into words how the memory of those biscuits affected him. It wasn't merely that he wanted to taste them again; somehow they reminded him of his childhood, long days fishing with Nan, learning to ride and visiting the Dower House.

Cressida frowned and picked up a small pile, flipping through it. She set it down again. 'No, that's not it. I was sorting them into categories, you know, herbal remedies…' She looked up with a perfectly straight face. 'There's one here for comfrey salve. You could rub it on your shoulder. When you don't take your sling off.'

'My valet got some from Mrs Roberts,' admitted Jack with a smile. Somehow her teasing felt comfortable. 'He supervises me putting it on nightly!'

Cressida's returning smile warmed him. 'Oh, well,' she said, 'I shan't worry, then. Now, where was I…household cleaners and…ah! here we are…special spice biscuits. Hmm. Cinnamon, ginger, nutmeg.' She looked up with a faint twinkle. 'Does that sound about right?'

Jack's mouth started to water. 'Er…yes. Yes, it does.'

She cast him a mischievous glance. 'Just listen to this!' Her voice took on the reedy accents of old age: 'Tell Cook double batch. Jack and Nan impossibly greedy!'

Still giggling, she scrambled off the window seat and headed for the door.

Jack felt suddenly bereft. 'Where are you going?'

She turned back with a smile. 'To my room, of course.

Your great-grandmama's writing is a little hard to make out. I'll copy this out and give it to Cook. You can have your spice biscuits for afternoon tea.' The smile turned wistful. 'Things like that are important, you know. Every time I wear a piece of Mama's jewellery, I think of her. I dare say these biscuits are just the same. Maybe *your* great-grandchildren will remember them one day.'

With that she was gone, leaving Jack staring after her. How in Hades did she understand what he felt when he hadn't even been able to put it into words? And how the *devil* could she make a biscuit recipe seem as important a part of his family's traditions as the coat of arms over the fireplace? He shook his head and went back to the box of papers.

Then he paused. This was something Cressida was doing. She obviously found it interesting. Perhaps she wouldn't like it if he interfered. Reluctantly he put the papers down. He should let her get on with it in her own way.

But not in the blasted window seat. She needed a desk. Then she'd have space to sort the piles out and somewhere to write.

He looked around the library. His father's *bureau plat* that he used now stood near the fireplace, absolutely littered with books and papers. And there was another desk that he had cleared for Dr Bramley, similarly festooned with papers, manuscripts and books. Oddly enough, Dr Bramley's desk was somewhat more organised than his own. Probably because Cressida helped him.

There was nothing in here; but what about that writing table in his mother's private sitting room? Perfect. It had one drop side so it didn't take up much room when not actually in use. And if it were placed here, at right angles to the window, Cressida could use the desk when she needed it, or read on the window seat if she wished. He had a funny feeling that she liked the window seat. Perhaps because he had always liked it.

She had looked so comfortable, sitting there with the sun on her hair. In that light there had been just the suspicion of a scattering of freckles on her nose, oddly childish and endearing. And when she'd first glanced up at him, her eyes had that oddly focused, yet abstracted, look her father had when he was interrupted. As though she had been dragged back from another world. He liked seeing her there. She looked…right. Of course, when it was too cold over here, he could insist she came to the fire…

Something else occurred to him. She hadn't choked him off, found an irreproachable excuse to be elsewhere as she had without fail since he'd been addlebrained enough to enter her bedchamber. He hadn't realised quite how much he looked forward to seeing her. To having her tell him he ought to be wearing a sling.

Determinedly he got up and went to the bell pull. He'd have the table brought in before she got back. And he needed to make quite sure she knew it was for her own use. He began to consider exactly what she would require and a queer sense of satisfaction warmed him. Complete. That was it. He felt complete.

Cressida stared at the elegant mahogany writing table. It stood at right angles to the window seat and all her papers had been placed neatly upon it. Where on earth had it come from?

A discreet cough interrupted her wonderment.

'Is it in the right place, Miss Cressida?'

She turned and found Evans smiling at her in a most avuncular way.

'Oh, oh, yes! But…'

'The master assured us that was the right spot, but if you'd like it moved…'

How had Jack known how much she loved the light in

the window seat? This way she could read there and move to the desk when she needed to write…

'Oh, no, it's perfect,' she assured Evans. 'But who moved my papers?' Her fingers flickered over them. Yes, they were all in their piles, just as she had sorted them.

Evans chuckled. 'Mr Jack did that. Wouldn't let us touch them. He said as how you'd found old Lady Kate's biscuit recipe and were taking it to Cook.' His smile became reminiscent. 'I remember those biscuits. Cook wouldn't. She only came twenty years ago. Quite a newcomer, but I dare say she'll manage.'

A giggle escaped Cressida. Twenty years, and he could still describe the cook as a *newcomer*! Then she saw the twinkle.

'How long have you been here, Evans?'

The twinkle deepened. 'Me, Miss Cressida? I was born here. My old dad was butler to Mr Jack's granddad. When I was a lad Lady Kate was already down at the Dower House. She made those biscuits for his dad before Mr Jack and Miss Nan.' He blinked slightly. 'Now, if that table's right, I should be getting back to my pantry.'

Cressida sat down at the table and stared blindly at the neatly arranged papers. He'd done it himself. He'd made quite sure her papers weren't disturbed and he'd given her a space to work. With shaking fingers she reached out to touch the little brass standish. He had thought of everything. Sand in the pounce-box, ink, quills, everything. Even a steel pen-trimmer so the ink wouldn't sputter. A lamp.

Why? Why had he bothered?

Then she remembered the way he had sat with her on the window seat, his delight when she had found the recipe for him. She had always been aware of his attraction for her, but she had ignored it, telling herself he disliked her, that he was overbearing, bossy.

There was nothing overbearing about the man who had

sat there as excited as a little boy at the prospect of a treat, for all he'd tried to hide it. And the man who had found her a desk and then gone to the trouble of equipping it? She shuddered to think of what her foolish heart could do with that sort of encouragement.

He was just being kind.

She groaned. That sort of observation was useless. There was nothing wrong with him being kind. It was an endearing trait, especially when free of any hint of condescension. Except that to fall in love with Mr Jack Hamilton would be about the most henwitted thing she could possibly do.

Just the thought that he might be coming to like her a little warmed her. Literally. Even her feet felt warm. She frowned. How very odd. So far from the fireplace, this corner of the room was usually rather chilly, yet her feet did feel warm.

Puzzled, she bent down and looked under the desk and stared in disbelief at the brass box with its pierced sides and lid. An old-fashioned foot warmer. Her heart shook within her. He'd even filled it with embers.

She sat up slowly and stared unseeingly at the standish. She would have to be careful. It would be so easy to kick that box over and embers could very quickly become a dangerous all-consuming blaze.

Jack was heading back to the library when Evans caught him. He'd left Cressida to discover the desk for herself, but now he wanted to see her. See if she liked it. Had he remembered everything?

'Ah, Mr Jack. There you are.'

At the butler's triumphant tones, Jack turned warily.

'Yes, Evans? Is there something…?'

Then he groaned. Evans had his *visitors* face on. 'Not now, man! Who is it?' Evans could deny him, say he'd gone out for a walk. He would if that would make the old chap feel better. Then he saw the admonishing frown.

'The Stanhopes, sir.'

Blast! Evans only called him *sir* when he wished to remind him of his obligations.

'Oh, very well!' he grumbled. The Stanhopes! No doubt with Miss Stanhope's everlasting eyelashes raising a breeze calculated to send his shoulder into spasms.

'Where did you billet them?'

Evans's outraged expression put him right at once. 'The drawing room. Of course. Sorry, Evans. I'll go at once. Have some tea sent up.'

A thought struck him. 'Oh, Evans—you might mention to Miss Bramley that I have visitors. Tell her that tea will be served in the drawing room.'

A visit of ceremony from the Stanhopes would be far more entertaining if Cressida were there. Besides, it would serve to demonstrate to Lady Stanhope that he regarded Miss Bramley as family. *Not* a poor relation.

The first thing to go wrong was that her ladyship had decided to push the pace a little on his pursuit of Miss Stanhope.

'I understand it is *all the crack*, as you younger people say, for ladies to drive themselves. I thought perhaps we, Sir William and myself, might presume upon our long friendship and ask if you would mind very much showing dear Alison how to handle *the ribbons*.' She gave a tinkle of laughter. 'Dear me! The expressions one must use! I believe one must handle them *in form*.'

Jack thought his own expression must be quite something, but he choked back the instinctive response that, yes, he would mind very much. He'd seen dear Alison's hands on a horse's mouth when she rode and the thought of entrusting his horses' delicate mouths to her was enough to make him blench. The confounded wench didn't even *like* horses. He'd never seen her pet her mount at all, let alone speak to it, or encourage it. Miss Stanhope only communicated with a horse via her whip and spur.

He was in the middle of denying himself the honour of attending to Miss Stanhope's education when he discovered that Evans had sent in the spice biscuits, along with the usual sandwiches and scones. Sir William, he knew, adored biscuits. Dash it all, he'd once seen the man demolish a whole plate of shortbread! Where on earth was Cressida? If she didn't show her front soon, all the biscuits would be gone. Even as he watched, Sir William started on his third.

Still fending off disaster... 'Do but consider, Lady Stanhope, the dangers attending a young lady driving herself!' He racked his brains for some way of distracting Sir William from the biscuits.

'Have you tried the scones, Sir William? The blackberry jam was particularly good this year.' Good God! He sounded like his own mother.

Sir William waved his efforts at hospitality aside. 'Don't you fret yourself about me, m' boy. I'll do very nicely with these biscuits!'

Jack watched with barely concealed hostility as several more biscuits met their end. How many more could the man eat in the time remaining? A visit such as this should not last more than half an hour. Stealing a surreptitious look at the gilt clock on the chimneypiece, Jack calculated that there were at least fifteen minutes to go and that there wouldn't be a single biscuit left. No doubt Cressida had decided to abandon him to his fate and remain safely in the library.

On cue, Lady Stanhope asked, 'And where is your little cousin, Miss...Miss Brambly, is it not?'

'Miss *Bramley*,' said Jack, with icy emphasis, 'is in the library, I believe.'

Lucky wench! Except that she was missing out on the biscuits.

'Ah, I see,' said Lady Stanhope. 'Very wise. And I dare say she is more comfortable taking her tea there. I had a cousin who had to be *told* it would be more agreeable if she took her meals in the library. So unpleasant. She actually came to the drawing room! Such airs as she gave herself!'

The inference that Miss Bramley was being kept in her place nearly choked him.

Hanging on to the tenets of hospitality, he said politely, 'Naturally, since I usually take my tea in the library, it is very much more comfortable if my *guests* do so as well.'

Changing the subject, he asked when the Stanhopes were planning on removing to town for the Season.

'Oh, well, as to that. I am not quite decided when we shall go up,' confided Lady Stanhope. 'To be sure, it was most enjoyable last year, and dear Alison did very well, very well indeed—so kind of you to dance with her—but it was so tiring for her. We might go a little later this year.'

Jack's shoulder went into spasms at the mere thought of dancing with Miss Stanhope again. He made immediate plans to spend the Season buried in Leicestershire. The countryside was prettier than London in spring anyway.

'And you, sir? Will you be going up to town early?' Miss Stanhope cast a languishing glance at him, lashes aflutter.

Jack ruthlessly trampled his innate honesty. 'Oh, at the earliest opportunity, Miss Stanhope.' He could almost hear their plans undergoing rapid revision at this thoroughly misleading reply. Excellent. He'd make all the arrangements to go up, he'd even remove to his lodgings in town if necessary. Then, the moment the Stanhopes were safely ensconced in whatever house they had hired, he could come back. Now all he had to do was persuade Sir William to leave the biscuits alone.

He barely stifled a groan as Miss Stanhope reached for a biscuit. Lord! If she started in on them! Somehow he had to get rid of his unwanted guests.

Inspiration struck as her hand hovered greedily over the plate.

'Good God! There's that dashed mouse again! Cheeky little beggar.'

Feminine squawks of outrage rent the air and Jack, to whom such noises were usually anathema, viewed the success of his admittedly shabby stratagem with ill-concealed triumph. Jerking back in horror, Miss Stanhope had knocked the wine table. Even as he watched, it tottered and fell, scattering biscuits and Sir William's tea across the carpet.

The visit came to a swift end. Miss Stanhope and her mama evinced such an ardent desire to remove themselves from the vicinity of a mouse that Jack wondered about the advisability of actually importing a few rodents. There must be some in the stables, and if they actually saw one next time…

He saw them out with an apology whose graciousness was only rivalled by its insincerity.

Then he turned back to survey the casualties. The top of the wine table had hit the fender, adding a new dent to the piecrust edge. Nothing to worry about there. It was a shame about the broken tea bowl and saucer, but the plate hadn't broken and who cared about a few broken biscuits? They'd be better than no biscuits.

He piled the wounded on to the plate and headed for the library again, still weighing the advantages and disadvantages of mice.

Chapter Five

Cressida looked up from her desk as Jack entered the library. She stiffened, half-expecting to see the Stanhopes troop in behind him. Then she frowned, refocusing on Jack.

Why on earth was he carrying a plate of...he came closer...biscuits? Worse—why was he smiling in just that particular way that made her heart turn upside down? Despite the foot warmer, she felt a chill ripple through her.

She mustn't fall in love with him. She mustn't.

'Have...have your visitors left?' Curse her voice! Did it have to wobble like a jelly just because he had walked into the room? Apparently it did. And she was tolerably certain that had she been standing, her knees would have wobbled with it. Because he was still smiling at her as he lowered his big frame on to the window seat and had put the biscuits beside him with an inviting gesture.

'They have, thank God,' he said, stretching out his long legs. 'Coward! You might have come in. I barely saved the biscuits for you!'

For her? He'd saved them for her?

'I...thought I should get on with shelving the books Papa had finished.' It had the merit of being partly true. She had shelved them. It had taken, oh, all of ten minutes.

She hurried on. 'I must thank you for the desk, sir. I am very much obliged to you.'

'Are you?' His deep voice stroked her senses.

'Well, yes. Yes, of course I am,' she said, trying to ignore the shivers of pleasure in her heart. 'It…it was very kind of you. You thought of everything.'

He smiled and she nearly fled. It was worse than the last one. Warm and inviting. Tempting beyond all belief.

'Then come and sit beside me and have a biscuit.' The smile deepened, enough for a foolish girl to drown in. 'Tell me what else you found in Lady Kate's box.'

She swallowed hard. After all, he had sat with her on the window seat earlier and the ceiling had remained in place. It wasn't Jack that was dangerous, merely her own silly fancies. As long as she remembered that he was simply being kind, she would be safe.

'I found a recipe for apricot ratafia,' she offered.

'You surprise me,' he said drily. 'She loathed the stuff. Always drank her brandy unadulterated. Would you like a biscuit?'

'Yes, please.' She took one from the plate and the faint, but unmistakable, aroma of nutmeg teased her. 'Oh! Are these…?' She bit into it and smiled. Lady Kate's biscuits. No wonder Jack had remembered them all these years.

She finished the biscuit and turned to him unguardedly, smiling up at him. Then she saw his eyes. They were all she could see. Heated and intent. On her. She knew what he was about to do. Every nerve, every muscle sang with the knowledge. Her brain screamed a warning. *Run!* Her heart, useless organ, had melted and taken her body along with it. She stayed.

He leaned forward and took her lips in the gentlest, sweetest caress imaginable. She stilled in shock, her lips parting on a soft gasp of surprise. A large hand framed her jaw with exquisite care and she found her head tilted back even as an arm like steel encircled her and drew her closer.

Dazed wonder held her motionless. Not frozen—spreading heat surged in her blood. Her breath jerked in as his tongue traced the shape of her lips in a silky caress.

And then her body responded instinctively. She pressed closer yet and opened her mouth a little more, innocently pleading.

Her response was more than Jack's very rocky self-control could take. Lord, but she was sweet. And the sensation of that trembling mouth opening beneath his was a temptation to make strong men weak. Even her shock, and he could practically taste that, felt sweet. With a groan of pleasure he took what she offered, deepening the kiss and sliding his tongue over hers, gently plundering.

His mind reeled. She tasted of biscuit, of summer, of Cressida. And of desire.

Need ripped through him in a wave of heat that shocked him. He barely retained enough control to pull back before it swamped him, but he did it. He forced his arms back to his sides and dragged his mouth from the soft surrender of hers with every muscle screaming in protest. Hard as iron, his body rebelled savagely against the dictates of honour. Breathing hard, he stared down at her as her eyes slowly fluttered open.

What on earth was he to say? He hadn't meant to kiss her, but that smile…it was more than flesh and blood could resist. How could he apologise? He couldn't read the expression in her eyes. They were shuttered, but her mouth, soft and pink, quivered slightly.

'Excuse me, sir.'

Excuse me, sir?

He watched in stunned disbelief as Cressida stood up and walked from the library without another word.

Excuse me, sir? What the hell sort of a response was that?

* * *

In the quiet chill of her room Cressida made her decision.

She had to avoid him. Totally. She must never be alone with him again. Not because she feared him, but because she feared her own response. Wonderingly she touched her lips and felt an echo of pleasure. She had thought kisses to be something a man took and a woman endured. With Jack she had been invited to share.

Her fingers fiddled aimlessly with the fringe on her shawl. She had to face the truth: with Andrew, her danger had come from him, from the fact that he had attempted to force her acceptance of his demands. With Jack, the danger came from within, from her own desire to accept whatever he might be prepared to offer.

Worse, it was not just a physical desire she felt. She enjoyed being with him, teasing him, laughing with him and stopping him using his arm. In short, she cared about him. From caring it would be a very short step to love.

A step that would lead straight over a cliff. A small, frightened corner of her mind whispered that she was already poised to make that step, that her weight had already shifted. Somehow she had to pull herself back. It was one thing to be pushed to the brink of disaster, quite another to leap over oneself. Surely she wasn't that foolish. Was she?

Jack glared at the empty corner near the window seat. As far as he could tell Cressida had not used her desk at all. She no longer sat in the window seat. She no longer browsed on her own account, but came to the library only with her father and she confined herself strictly to helping him.

She had even taken to breakfasting in her room. On tea and toast he had ascertained. Dash it all, she'd starve to death! She was always hungry in the mornings, but now she never came down.

He knew why: Dr Bramley often came down late and Cressida had no intention of finding herself alone with her host.

Excuse me, sir.

He shouldn't have kissed her. She'd responded, though. Hadn't she? His body ached with longing as the memory of her softly surrendering lips coursed through his blood. And her shock.

Memory took him back further. To the day he'd found her mending her father's shirt and nearly kissed her. She hadn't wanted him to kiss her then. She'd said as much. Maybe she hadn't wanted him to kiss her at all. Maybe she was avoiding him to make quite sure it didn't happen again.

Didn't she know she only had to *tell* him?

An infuriated growl escaped him. Hell! *He* didn't know it. How should she? He ought to be grateful to her for removing temptation from his path, but damn it all—he missed her!

He missed her flitting up and down the ladders, missed her constant queries and arguments about the most logical places to shelve books. He missed her laughter and, above all, he missed *her*. The sheer fact of her being there.

It didn't help that he wanted to kiss her again. Resolutely he closed his mind to all the other things he wanted to do with her.

He couldn't understand it. The whole situation defied all logic. He had never been the sort of person to be ruled by his desires. If a desire was inconvenient, or its fulfilment would be dishonourable, one stepped away from it. Without hesitation. Certainly one did not wander about snapping at all and sundry as if one had a permanent headache. Which one did, of course, owing to unrelieved tension and a build up of sleepless nights.

Perhaps she'd told her father where she could be found?

Startled at the carefully phrased question, Dr Bramley gazed around the library.

'Dear me. Isn't she here? Hmm…no… Wait a moment, she did say something about going out…for a walk or some such nonsense. But she brought me enough books to keep me going for the time being. She can put them back on the shelves later, I dare say, so don't worry that we'll get behind, dear boy.'

Jack suppressed a curse. Cressida knew perfectly well that he spent a couple of hours on estate business in the mornings before coming to the library. So she came down early, did as much as she possibly could, left her father supplied with a mountain of books and fled. Before the owner of the books showed his front.

Tactically he had to applaud her. After he had wrung her neck. But to do that he'd have to find her. So far he had not had the least success in tracking her down. She had to be in the house somewhere. She couldn't possibly have been serious about going out. It was far too cold for her to be outside. She'd catch her death!

He frowned. Headstrong little peagoose! He'd better make sure. One of the servants would know if she had gone out…

Jack shook his head as he remembered this, striding towards the stables. Cressida ought not to be wandering about alone beyond the house and gardens. And God alone knew where she had gone to. Certainly neither her father nor the servants knew where she was. Jack took scant comfort from Evans's assurance that *Miss Cressida was well wrapped up, sir.*

He'd have to find her and see for himself, make quite sure she didn't do this again. It was his duty as her cousin, her host, the head of her family… Oh, devil take it! He just wanted to see her.

His mind froze, recalling another girl who had tantalised, held out glimmering lures and then retreated in maidenly coyness. Was Cressida playing that game after all? He couldn't quite believe it, yet all the outward signs were there. And, by God, it was working! Here he was, running after her like a puppy with a ball!

His steps slowed. Perhaps he should return to the house and ignore her ploy, if ploy it was. Then he shook his head. No. Even if she was a scheming little hussy, she was, in a manner of speaking, under his protection. She ought not to be out on such a cold day. And, no matter what Clinton had to say on the matter, he was going to have a horse saddled so that he could go after her.

He set his jaw. Cressida was avoiding him again. She had been for two days. Ever since he'd had the table brought in for her, she had adopted an air of cool propriety. She agreed politely with whatever he said, offered no opinion of her own and when he had accidentally knocked his shoulder in her presence, had not so much as muttered the word *sling*.

He shouldn't have kissed her, of course. That had only added to his confusion.

Jack swung into the stable yard, swearing under his breath.

He'd never known anything like that kiss. Lord, he'd always expected kissing an untutored innocent to be rather boring. The jolt of desire that shot through him at the sweet hesitation as she accepted his lips had shocked him witless. He'd thought he knew what it was to want a woman. He hadn't had the least idea. Never before had he wanted, damn it, *needed* a woman to the edge of insanity. His body hardened in a rush just thinking about it.

If he'd been thinking clearly, or rather, thinking at all, he'd never have kissed her. As it was, now she probably expected an offer from him! He muttered a few more curses. That would be insanity: allowing his unruly passions to choose his bride for him.

Where the devil was Clinton? Might as well get the

argument over and done with. It would serve to take his mind off the increasingly permanent pain in his breeches. Not to mention the cynical voice suggesting that young ladies in expectation of an honourable proposal from a wealthy man did not commonly avoid him as though he had sprouted horns and a tail. Unless, of course, she thought that by so doing she could fret him into offering faster... He ground his teeth and changed direction. He'd check on Firebird first, *then* yell for Clinton.

'Just keep his nose out of my book, Danny. I'm nearly done. Next time I'll leave the sugar outside!'

The unexpected voice coming from his injured hunter's stall stopped Jack dead in his tracks. What the devil was Cressida doing in there?

'Aye, Miss Cress'da. Got a long nose 'as Firebird.'

Good God! That was Daniel, Clinton's youngest boy. What were the pair of them up to?

A soft chuckle set his heart pounding. 'He certainly has! A long whiskery nose. I couldn't have done this without you. And I've got a surprise here for you as well.'

An embarrassed and wholly unintelligible mutter followed.

'I wouldn't dream of offering you money, Danny. Hold still...'

A long pause, followed by, 'There. All done.'

The sound of tearing paper.

'I did two. Do you think your parents would like this?'

There was a gasp. 'Cripes, Miss Cress'da! It looks jus' like me! I didn' know you was doing that! Thought you was jus' doin' old Firebird. You shoulda tol' me.'

Cressida's warm laugh greeted this. 'No. You'd have gone all stiff. Give it to your parents.'

'Aye, miss. Can I let Firebird go now?'

'Just let me put my book away safely...there. All right you big, slobbering idiot, here it is.'

Jack looked over the half-door to discover Danny Clinton, clutching a piece of paper, perched on the edge of the manger and Cressida seated on an upturned bucket as she fed sugar to his favourite hunter.

Something inside him turned over at the sight. The big chestnut towered over her, yet she sat with his long aristocratic nose in her lap, rubbing his ears with her free hand and crooning nonsense to him as he crunched up the sugar.

'Morning, Mister Jack,' piped Danny.

Something resembling a squeak escaped Cressida's lips and she jerked around. Firebird just crunched faster and shoved his face against her, imperiously demanding more sugar.

'Hullo, Danny,' said Jack, smiling as he entered the loose box.

He turned his attention to Cressida. 'There you are, my dear. Your father was wondering where you were.'

Her eyebrows nearly disappeared into her hairline as he uttered this lie.

'Really? Was that before or after you drew his attention to my absence?'

'Look at this, Mister Jack,' enthused Danny. 'Miss Cress'da did it for me mam and da'.' He held the sketch out proudly.

Biting down hard on all the things he would have liked to say to Cressida, Jack took the proffered sketch. And stared.

'Good God!'

Anyone who looked at this sketch and couldn't see that the lad was bubbling over with mischief would have to be blind. Anyone who had ever seen Danny would recognise him instantly from this. It was uncanny. Somehow, in a few strokes, Cressida had conveyed all the boy's energy and his love of horses. The grubby hand stroking a satin nose was somehow reverent. And the horse; Cressida had seen straight past the powerful, raking hunter to the gentle giant whiffling at an urchin's pockets.

He looked down at Cressida as he handed the drawing back to Danny, but she was busying herself putting all her sketching equipment away. From what he could see the back of her neck was absolutely scarlet. Unfortunately for his peace of mind she was bent over nearly double finding everything.

He swallowed hard. At least she was well wrapped up instead of wearing summer muslins. He hated to think of what the sight of that sweetly rounded bottom would do to him under those circumstances.

'Tell your mother I'll get that framed for her if she would like, Danny,' said Jack, sending a heartfelt prayer of thanks to God for the lad's restraining presence as well as Cressida's voluminous skirts.

Danny swelled. 'Coo. A picksher of me on the wall! Not but what it's really of Firebird. I was jus' holding him acos he wouldn't keep his nose out of Miss Cress'da's face. Bye, Mister Jack! Bye, miss. An' thank you!'

Jack forced himself to think about that as he watched Cressida pack up. Absently he scratched Firebird's ears. Some artists might have seen it like that. Many would probably not have bothered even to include the boy, let alone make him such an integral part of the sketch. They would have just concentrated their efforts on the magnificent hunter. Cressida had elected to show the affectionate bond between the two, the intangible link that was symbolised by a grubby hand on an aristocratic nose.

And she had sent the boy away with a sketch for his mother. Jack did not doubt for one moment that Bess Clinton would have the treasure framed to hang in pride of place in the parlour. Did Cressida have the least idea what a priceless gift she had bestowed?

He watched as Cressida straightened up and turned to face him. It didn't help much. She was slightly flushed from bending down. All he could think of was how much more flushed she'd be if he kissed her the way he wanted to. Gently at first, of course—but after she'd got over the surprise and responded to him... His whole body shook with longing. Madness. He'd be in over his head the moment his lips touched hers.

'Were you looking for me? Did Papa want some more books fetched?'

The quiet question dragged him back from his discreditable imaginings. He was damned if he'd admit to her that he had been looking for her. That he'd been worried.

'Your father has plenty of books,' said Jack. 'And although I did wonder where you were, I came to the stables to see Firebird, since it is my fault he has that bandage on his leg.' God in heaven keep him from saying, or worse, doing, the wrong thing. Stick to horses. They were always a safe subject. No one could get into trouble talking about horses.

The flush on Cressida's cheeks flared anew. How could she have possibly thought that he would look for her. No doubt he hadn't really wondered where she was. That was just a polite fiction.

'I'll get out of your way then.' She headed for the door, carefully giving Jack a wide berth.

Not wide enough. Shock tingled through her body as she felt her wrist caught in a gentle, inescapable grip. She stiffened, her immediate instinct to tug herself free. Then she realised; he had used his right hand. If she pulled hard enough to free herself, she would hurt him. Again.

She stood still. 'You are cheating, sir.' With a massive effort she kept her voice polite.

'Cheating, Cress? In what way?'

Ignoring the assault on her name as a red herring, she answered. 'You are holding me with your right hand. You must know perfectly well that if I try to free myself I'll hurt you.'

Damn his eyes! How dare he smile like that!

'I did, of course, but I can't say I was sure that you did.

Call it a gamble, my dear. Once in a while they pay off. Tell me—do you do much sketching.'

'Not enough,' she said shortly. 'I'm very out of practice.' Would he never release her wrist?

'My mother used to sketch a great deal,' said Jack. 'Come to think of it, she still does.'

The affection in his voice struck at Cressida. 'Your…your mother is still alive?' She had never thought of Jack as having a mother. She knew his father was dead.

He looked surprised. 'Oh, yes. She lives in London most of the year now.'

'Oh, not here?'

Jack shook his head and said with a grin, 'No. Mama says if I want a woman to manage the house I can marry one. But I keep the Dower House prepared for her. She was here for Christmas with my sister, Lady Barraclough, and her husband and all their family. They left just before I broke my collarbone, thank God.'

'Pardon?'

'They fuss,' explained Jack. 'Worse than you and the staff.'

'I don't fuss.' This came out between gritted teeth.

'No? Then why haven't you thumped me on the shoulder and jerked your hand free? Or wouldn't that suit your plans?'

What plans?

Recovering quickly, she riposted, 'Good manners and common decency! Don't you recognise them?'

He grinned. '*Touché*. My mother and sister would be proud of you.'

She ignored that. The female relatives of eligible gentlemen were not wont to approve the daughters of impoverished clergymen.

'Was there something you needed to know, or would you be so kind as to release my wrist? Stop that, Firebird!'

The big chestnut, despairing of any more sugar, had started tugging at his bandage with his teeth.

Jack swore. Releasing Cressida, he stepped forward, caught the horse's halter and brought his head up.

'Idiot horse. You have to leave that on a bit longer, old son. It's there to help you!'

She should have bolted, but temptation shimmered.

'My, my,' said Cressida. 'Just like a certain gentleman who won't wear a sling, perhaps?'

Jack glared at her as he petted Firebird.

'Not at all. I fail to see any resemblance.'

'Really,' asked Cressida. 'I can see several. Stubborn, quite incapable of taking advice. Nosy, of course. Shall I go on?'

Jack shook his head. A dangerous light glinted in his eye. 'Before you do, I ought to point out one salient difference.'

'Oh? Intelligence?' asked Cressida in dulcet tones, ignoring the warning in his voice. If she was impertinent enough she'd put him off her completely. Gentlemen, she had noted, hated backchat.

'Apart from that, of course,' said Jack with a slow smile. 'Firebird is a gelding.'

Cressida felt her cheeks burn as she took in his meaning and saw the devilish glint in his eye.

'Oh…ah…is…does that make a big difference?' Somehow she'd managed to blush even more deeply.

Jack appeared to be choking, but he straightened his features almost at once. 'Quite a big difference,' he said gravely.

She hardly knew where to look. On consideration, his face seemed the safest option, but the bland expression, so wickedly at odds with the twinkle in his eyes, was hardly reassuring. Apparently she had said something monumentally stupid.

'Quite a number of Mama's sketches are still here,' he

added conversationally. 'Indeed, she did quite a few of my father's favourite hunters. Perhaps you might like to see them?'

Shock and then anger flared. Her own mother's well-loved voice echoed from the vaults of memory,

Above all, my love, be very suspicious of any gentleman offering to show you his…etchings, indeed any artworks, or his family jewels for that matter…

Mama had never explained precisely what these terms alluded to, but she had made quite sure Cressida knew how a virtuous young lady should respond.

She spoke as coldly as she possibly could.

'How very kind of you, but if that is tantamount to offering to show me your…*etchings*, then I must beg to be excused. I fear that I do not deserve such an honour.'

His dropped jaw afforded her considerable satisfaction. No doubt he had not expected her to understand. Well, now he would know that she did, that she was no ignorant miss for his plucking, but knew precisely what she was about. Even if she didn't know why etchings and family jewels were so dangerous.

He took one swift step towards her and stopped, hard control in every line of his powerful frame. Her breath came in on a gasp as she registered the clenched fists, his eyes like shards of steel. She *wouldn't* step back. How dare he intimidate her like this?

'If you weren't your father's daughter and my guest…' He paused for breath. And then continued, each word clipped and furious. 'I'd put you over my knee and spank you for that piece of vulgarity!'

'Why, you—'

He cut her off ruthlessly. 'And if you were a man I'd call you out. Instead—' Abruptly his hands gripped her shoulders and he jerked her forward, bringing his mouth down on hers in a hard, brief kiss. As suddenly as he released her and stepped back. 'And that was definitely a lapse of judgement, not taste!' his voice grated. With that he turned on his heel and strode out, slamming the stable door behind him.

Cressida leaned against the side of the stall and wondered if her insides would ever stop shaking.

Jack stalked out of the stable yard, barely acknowledging Clinton's startled greeting beyond a grunt. Plainly, horses were not a safe subject after all. And if he didn't get himself under control soon, he was going to murder someone—probably Cressida. If he didn't seduce her first, that was.

Good grief! There he was, thinking about seduction again. When had he last seduced a gently born damsel of good, if decided, character and virtue?

Never.

Good character? A damned tease, more like.

Here he was, worrying that she intended to tease him into marriage and she had the gall, the unmitigated *gall*, to imply that he'd offer her a slip on the shoulder! That he'd actually seduce her. What the devil had he done to warrant that piece of missishness?

Naturally, having opened the floodgates on that line of thought, answers came in a veritable deluge.

You threatened to spank her. You told her you wanted to kiss her. You went into her room, while she was asleep, no less! To leave snowdrops. Then you did kiss her. Twice. And threatened to spank her again.

Put like that, he could see that Cressida had every excuse for a bout of missishness.

Even the desk, he realised with a stab of hurt, could be construed as buttering her up. And as for his efforts just now…he groaned. Why had he ever thought horses a safe topic of conversation?

He picked up the pace as he headed back to the house along a path edged with lavender. Usually, he walked through here slowly, enjoying the fragrant fronds brushing against him. Not today. The soothing scent of lavender always hung round Cressida's clothes. Now it infuriated him.

He'd never seduced a virgin in his life and he'd certainly never tampered with the affections of gently born girls who might reasonably expect an offer of marriage. Not even the girls he'd thought of offering for. He hadn't got that far. Certainly he'd never got as far as making dubious comparisons between stallions and geldings!

And what in Hades had he been about to kiss her again? Let alone like that. As though he meant it as an insult. When in truth he had been longing to reassure himself that her lips really were as sensuously yielding as he remembered. Never had he known a kiss to be so sweet with innocence and the promise of pleasure.

Most of his carnal dealings had been restricted to the Fashionable Impure, the demi-reps—women who made their living as courtesans. He'd also had a few discreet affairs with women of his own class; widows and married ladies blessed, or cursed depending on one's point of view, with husbands who couldn't care less, as long as the paternity of their heirs wasn't called into question. Nothing that could have prepared him for Cressida. Certainly the couple of kisses he'd stolen from Selina hadn't done so.

It wasn't that he objected to causing scandal—a nice juicy scandal kept society's wheels turning—it was just that he had always considered that the purpose of an affair ought to be mutual pleasure. Leaving a woman facing an enraged spouse did not fit into his definition of mutual pleasure.

He swung around a corner, which brought the main drive into view, and came to a dead halt. Damn. There was a chaise approaching the house. Well, with a bit of luck the occupants hadn't seen him. Evans could deny him in good faith if he stayed out of sight.

He stood partially behind a rose arbour and watched the chaise. Funny. Neighbours wouldn't use a post chaise just to pay him a visit. They must have the wrong place. But those bays—a bang-up set-out of blood and bone—looked rather familiar. Part of his mind toyed with that while he went back to the more pressing problem.

What on earth was wrong with him that he was thinking of seducing Cressida? He had nothing but loathing for hardened rakes who seduced, or worse, forced innocent girls and left them to their ruin. Even if the girl was a tease, a gentleman should have enough control for both of them. So if he intended to seduce Cressida...that meant he had suddenly become the greatest scoundrel unhung...or that he was intending to marry her.

Marry her? Marry that hot-tempered, outrageous little baggage, who twisted him in knots and had him saying things he'd never said to a gently bred female in his life? Not to mention the things he wanted to do.

Those bays really did look very familiar...

Marry her? He'd be lucky to finish proposing before she tore strips off him! Besides, he was damned if he'd let the little minx tease him into it. Marriage to Cressida Bramley was the last thing he wanted. She'd turn his ordered life upside down. So he couldn't possibly *intend* to seduce Cressida Bramley. He just wanted to. There was a difference, he hoped. Her ability to tip him off balance shortened the odds considerably. But, since she was nothing in the least like the sort of female he planned to fall in love with and marry, he'd better start working on his self-control.

Oh, hell and the devil. No use thinking about it. Concentrate on those Welsh bays! They were just as good as Marc's team... He looked again. God in heaven! They *were* Marc's bays!

Dazed, he watched as one of his footmen rushed out to let down the steps of the chaise. He couldn't quite believe

it until he saw the tall, athletic form of the Earl of Rutherford leap down and hold out his arms to someone in the
chaise. A tiny shawl-wrapped bundle was handed down to
him. Jack watched with suddenly envious eyes as his
friend cradled the precious burden in one arm and held the
other hand up to his wife. They had both come. With little
Jon, Jack's godson.

'Marc! Meg!' He strode towards them. 'What the devil
are you doing here?'

Marc swung around and grinned. 'Visiting. Aren't we
welcome?'

'I can probably find a garret for you,' Jack assured him.
'Hello, Meg, sweetheart.' He enveloped the Countess in
an overwhelming hug, lifting her quite off her feet.

'Jack! Put me down, you great bear! You'll hurt your
shoulder.'

Jack groaned. 'Heaven help me. Another female fussing
about my blasted shoulder.'

He set her down anyway and cast a wicked grin at Marc.
'Nothing to say about my manhandling your wife, old
chap?'

Marc shook his head. 'Not yet. We all know Meg has
ways of dealing with idiots! If you're lucky she'll just
thump you in the shoulder.'

'Oh, never mind that,' said Meg. 'Jack, what did you
mean by sending Marc that idiotish letter telling us not to
come, because you couldn't hunt? Of all the stupid notions! How you could possibly think we wouldn't come is
beyond me!'

'Come in out of the cold,' urged Jack. 'My godson
won't like it at all. How is he?'

'Asleep,' Marc informed him. 'And long may he remain
that way. He becomes very grumpy when he doesn't have
enough sleep.'

'Like his papa?' suggested Jack.

Marc grinned wickedly. 'I've discovered certain compensations for losing sleep. However, let's get him inside and see what sort of nursery your housekeeper has arranged. We'd have been here days ago, but we travelled in short stages to make sure he didn't get too tired or cold.'

Jack smiled. 'I'll ring for her at once…' Then the oddness of Marc's comment hit him. 'Hold hard there. Did you say *has* arranged? Are you expected?'

'Of course we are,' smiled Meg. 'I wrote to Mrs Roberts telling her to expect us by today!'

'My God!' said Jack deeply. 'They never said a word! Piracy! Piracy and mutiny—one of these days I'll turn the lot of 'em off without a character between them!'

'Well, when you do,' said Meg cheerfully, 'just let me know. We'll have them all happily!'

Chapter Six

Cressida stared at the door of her bedchamber, devoutly wishing that she didn't have to go beyond it. An Earl and a Countess. Jack's intimate friends. Here. She flushed at the memory of the last time she had come under the eye of a Viscountess. No doubt a Countess would be even more dismissive. Especially if she had heard anything about the scheming Miss Bramley.

Perhaps she should send a message down that she had the headache. If she sat here fretting for very much longer it would be the literal truth. How on earth she was going to face Jack at dinner, after that conversation in the stable, with a Countess at the end of the table, defeated her.

And that was another thing—how ever was Jack going to arrange the seating? They had been dining at a circular table in a small parlour. With such exalted guests, would Jack use the main dining room?

She sighed. Cowering up here was out of the question. If the maid who waited on her was to be believed, Lord Rutherford's estates were nowhere near Cornwall. They couldn't possibly have heard what amounted to village tattle—she was being ridiculous, oversensitive.

She stood up swiftly and smoothed down her gown. It might be old fashioned, and have been remodelled from a cloak of her mother's, but it was the only one she had and at least it was velvet. The soft, rich green still glowed in the firelight and the ivory lace she had pinned into the rather low neckline gave it a more modish air.

No doubt the Countess would be festooned with diamonds, like Andrew's mother, Lady Fairbridge. Well, she had nothing, save her mama's cut-steel necklace of flowers. She lifted it out of its box and smiled sadly. No matter that she wouldn't exchange it for a thousand diamond necklaces, she did just wish that the rest of the world didn't judge so much on what one could afford.

Love didn't seem to work that way.

Cressida slipped into the drawing room, wishing that there were more people, furious with herself for being nervous.

What do an Earl and Countess matter to you? Why should you care?

She couldn't see the Countess at first. Jack's large body hid her as he laughed at something she had said.

Cressida stiffened. No doubt he found her far more entertaining than his gauche, not to mention rude, little cousin. He hadn't even noticed her come in.

Oh, for goodness sake! How could he? He has his back to you.

It was the Earl, tall, tawny haired, with eyes of a much lighter grey than Jack's, who came forward.

'Good evening. You, I take it, must be Miss Bramley. Jack is far too busy flirting with my wife to introduce us, so I'll presume on your relationship with him and save him the trouble. How do you do, Miss Bramley? I'm Rutherford.'

He held out his hand with a friendly smile.

Cressida swallowed. What on earth was she meant to do when a whole, live Earl held out his hand and appeared to invite her to address him simply as *Rutherford*? Remember her place, that's what.

'G…good evening, my lord.'

She placed her hand in his and wondered what he would do with it. And why, although he was quite as handsome as Jack, she didn't suffer a single palpitation as he bowed over her hand.

A faint smile as he straightened drew a hesitant answering smile from her. Then, 'I don't bite, you know.'

'D…don't you?' *Oh, help! Can't you do better than that?*

But his shoulders were shaking and his rather cool grey eyes had warmed with laughter.

'No, Miss Bramley. Whatever whiskers Jack has told you about me, I don't bite!'

She felt heat stealing into her cheeks. And felt it drain away as she realised Jack's eyes were upon her. Cold, aloof. Oh, bother him! Why did she always have to feel as though the world tilted every time they were in the same room? And why didn't she feel absolutely disgusted and outraged at his behaviour this afternoon? Surely any self-respecting clergyman's daughter would have been shocked!

Then, as Jack moved, she saw the Countess of Rutherford, standing with an expectant smile on her face, eagerness in her smoky blue eyes.

Why, she looks as though she wants to meet me! And, *Good heavens! She's no older than I am.*

Jack was bringing the lady forward.

'Meg, may I present my second cousin, Miss Cressida Bramley? Miss Bramley, this is Lady Rutherford.'

Lady Rutherford stared at him, opened her mouth and shut it again.

'How do you do, Miss Bramley,' she said, and held out her hand.

Cressida took it shyly. Lady Fairbridge had never offered more than two languid fingers to anyone she considered her social inferior. Did Lady Rutherford imagine that her relationship to Jack somehow elevated her?

The Earl turned back to Cressida. 'You know, I thought I was acquainted with all Jack's relations, including your father, I might add. I'm on Christian name terms with all those of my generation. There's no reason to make you an exception.'

Cressida could think of one perfectly valid reason. And the reason's dark grey eyes were boring into her all of a sudden. She couldn't—wouldn't—call him *Jack*. After this afternoon she doubted that he even wanted her to. Indeed, his manner of presenting her to Lady Rutherford suggested it.

His very next words confirmed it. 'How very kind of you, Marc. But I'm afraid Miss Bramley prefers to observe all the niceties governing social conduct. She frowns upon any hint of familiarity.'

The chill in his voice cut at her. Desperately seeking to change the subject, she looked about. 'Is my father not down yet? Perhaps I should go and find him.' And send a message back down that she had developed a sudden headache and retired for the night. If she cried enough, it would be true.

'Dr Bramley has retired for the night,' Jack informed her. 'He is feeling unwell. His stomach, I believe.'

'Oh, then pray excuse me...I should go up to—'

Jack cut her off ruthlessly. 'He has everything he needs. I saw to it myself. He has no need of you, Miss Bramley.'

Shocked, Cressida stared up at him. No, her father had very little need of her in this house. At least in Cornwall she had been useful to him, running the house and helping with his parishioners. Here everything was done by one of the staff.

'One of the maids has instructions to go to him should he ring for anything.'

'Thank you,' she said bleakly. 'But if Papa is not down, there is no need for me to—'

'Nonsense,' said Lady Rutherford. 'Jack's shoulder must be aching for him to be such a curmudgeon. You can't possibly leave me with only these two for company. Come, Miss Bramley...Jack's a grouchy old bear this evening and he and Marc will talk forever about some horrid mill or Jack's last curricle race!'

Her lovely smile beckoned, easing Cressida's hurt. *Has no need of you...has no need...no need...* The words echoed mercilessly. She would have to leave, find a position. But how was she to do that without a reference?

Two hours later Cressida followed Lady Rutherford from the dining room in a daze. This was not the sort of aristocrat she was used to. Why on earth would a Countess make the least effort to include Miss Cressida Bramley in the conversation, let alone rake her host down for being *a grouchy old bear*?

And why would such an exalted being as an Earl chat to her at all? Let alone about parish duties and the way they fitted in with the duties of a landlord! If she didn't know better, she'd think they actually liked her. *Maybe they do.*

She shied away from the thought as if it had stung her. *They wouldn't like you if they knew the truth. Lady Rutherford would be shocked and Lord Rutherford would refuse to have you anywhere near his wife.*

Out in the hall Lady Rutherford turned to her and said with a smile, 'Will you excuse me, Miss Bramley? I must go upstairs.'

There. Why would she wish to spend her evening with a dowdy nobody? But perhaps she might be prepared to write you that reference... 'Of course, my lady. I quite understand,' said Cressida very politely. She found to her discomfort that Lady Rutherford's smoky blue eyes were looking at her with disconcerting penetration.

'I don't think you do,' said her ladyship. 'I need to go upstairs to give Jon his feed. He's not weaned yet, you see.'

Cressida blinked. 'You feed him yourself?' Lady Fairbridge had expressed very strong views on how disgusting such a procedure was and that no female of consideration would so demean herself. Then she flushed. Who was she to question a Countess?

Lady Rutherford only smiled. 'Of course. I know it's not fashionable, but it's so lovely. At home I have him brought down to the library after dinner and Marc sits with me, but I suspect poor Jack would find that a little hard to cope with!' Her giggle was infectious. 'Just imagine his face!'

'You're very fond of Ja— Mr Hamilton, aren't you?' asked Cressida, shivering at an unbidden vision of herself nursing Jack's child while he sat by.

Lady Rutherford nodded. 'After Marc, there is no one dearer. He is such a kind, *chivalrous* soul. Now, I must be off. I shall see you in the morning. Perhaps your papa may be better. Goodnight, Miss Bramley. I dare say I shan't come down again. Feeding Jon always makes me so terribly sleepy!'

'Goodnight,' responded Cressida.

She walked slowly towards the library. What would it be like to feed a baby? She had never understood why Lady Fairbridge had found the whole idea so disgusting. Cuddling a baby was wonderful, and just think how content Rosie the house cow had been when she had a calf. Surely it wasn't all that different for a woman? Why else would God have given women breasts?

A fire was lit in the library and the curtains were all drawn. She looked longingly at her desk, but knew she mustn't stay. With Lady Rutherford upstairs, it would be most improper.

No, she would take a book and go to bed after checking on Papa. She yawned. Was the sky still clear? She might go for a walk tomorrow if the weather held.

She went over to the long window and tweaked the curtain back to peer out. A full moon was rising over the woods and she sighed with pleasure. Unhesitatingly she slipped behind the curtain and sat down on the window seat, drawing the curtain closed to banish the light of the room.

Silver light glimmered over the woods and snowy gardens. Trees stood frosted with silver against a sky that pulsed with stars. She smiled up at them, recognising Orion and his dogs, the Big Dipper and other friends her mother had shown her. As a child she had been convinced that the stars were windows in heaven that God and the angels could peep through.

Gazing up as she leant against the window, she wondered if her mother could peep through. What would she think of her foolish daughter? Would she be disappointed if she could see what a muddle Cressida had made of everything?

Look after Papa, darling. He's very kind, but so vague. And he was so good to me that I have always tried to repay that.

She hadn't looked after Papa properly. Instead she had put him in the position where he had tried to protect her with disastrous results. She had cost him his living. But at least he could be happy and safe here. Mr Hamilton…Jack…would look after him. Cressida smiled to herself sleepily. Even if he was a grouchy old bear, he liked Papa. It would be nice if he liked her, too… But she would have to warn him, explain what sometimes happened if Papa was upset. Surely if she warned him about this little idiosyncrasy before she left, he would understand... After all, Papa meant no harm.

The stars blazed down and the moon gleamed through the window as she dozed.

She awakened, cold and shivering, to hear voices.

'Thought you'd be upstairs with Jon, but Lucy said he went straight off to sleep and you'd come down for a book.'

She stretched sleepily. Good heavens, that sounded like Lord Rutherford.

'Yes. I thought you'd be talking to Jack for a while. Where is he?'

That was Lady Rutherford.

'Gone up. Come here, sweetheart.'

Cressida blinked at the husky growl. The Earl had spoken affectionately enough to his Countess at dinner—but this! Perhaps she ought to let them know she was there... She hesitated for a moment, embarrassed to be caught hiding in the curtains like a child. Silence ensued. Had they gone?

A sob mingled with a deep groan. 'Meg...God, I want you. Kiss me again...'

Stunned, Cressida peeped out between the curtains and nearly sprained her jaw.

Lord Rutherford sat in one of the chairs by the fire with his Countess in his lap...what on earth was he doing, kissing her like that? It looked as though he was biting her lower lip, devouring her. Was she enjoying it?

Logic and memory told Cressida that no woman could possibly enjoy being mauled by a man. Observation told her that the Countess was not being mauled and that she was enjoying it very much. She was pressing herself against the Earl, threading her hands through his hair to draw him even closer. And surely those were whimpers of pleasure... Good lord, his hand was on her breast! A shaft of pure fire shot through her own breasts, merely watching the Earl's fingers shift and tease…and release his wife's breast from her bodice…heat, yearning, a melting ache…just like she had felt when Jack kissed her. It hadn't been at all like that with Andrew. He had grabbed and demanded, terrifying her…intent on nothing but his own pleasure. *Just as well. If you hadn't fought him in the end, you'd be in a worse mess now…Papa would have been too late.*

Eyes wide, she watched as the Earl traced kisses down his wife's throat…and lower. *What would that feel like with Jack?* Now the little sobs she had heard, became intelligible.

'Marc?'

He lifted his mouth from her breast. 'More?'

'Yes…oh, yes.'

'Little wanton.'

He teased affectionately before returning to her breast while his hand caressed its way over her waist to her hip and lower until it slipped under the heavy velvet skirts…the aching heat in Cressida's breasts rippled lower. It was obvious from the way the velvet bunched over his elbow just where the Earl's hand was… Her breath jerked inwards at the thought of Jack touching her so intimately.

Shocked, she felt her own thighs melt in longing as the Countess shifted slightly in her husband's arms…allowing him greater access. Cressida heard his murmur.

'So soft…Meg, dearest Meg…'

Shaken, Cressida drew back silently into the silver-lit window embrasure. She should not be here. No wonder girls were told little or nothing of the marriage bed. Her body ached and burned just watching. And listening. Desperately she pressed her hands over her ears to shut out the sweet sounds and stared out into the silver night…so lovely…so peaceful… Would they stay there for very long? It was bitterly cold behind the curtain, cut off from the warmth and light of the room.

Blushing, she took her hands away from her ears. Just for a moment, just to find out if they were still there…

'…should go up, dearest. If we stay any longer…'

Cressida's cheeks scorched to flame and her knees wobbled as Lord Rutherford seduced his wife with hot, loving words, describing exactly what he wanted. Words that spoke of her pleasure as much as his…

She sank on to the window seat, trembling. If they ever found out she had overheard this… Could she open the window and slip out? Would they hear? She might freeze to death, but at least she would no longer be intruding on their privacy…their intimacy… Ashamed of her accidental intrusion, she looked closely at the latch. It would open easily enough, but would the window creak? Would the draught catch the curtains and alert them to her presence? Perhaps if she only opened it a crack, enough to slip out. Her hand went to the latch. Cold moonlight mocked her, the snowy garden no longer looked inviting.

'Marc?'

She barely recognised the Countess's voice. So husky, so…aching. She should go at once.

'We must go up. This isn't *our* library… What if Jack walked in?'

A masculine chuckle Cressida could only describe as wicked answered this, even as she stilled her hand on the latch.

'Almost, my love, you tempt me. But poor old Evans would have a seizure. Come along, little tease. Time for bed.'

Somehow Cressida doubted that the Earl intended sleep in the near future. She breathed a silent sigh of relief as she heard them getting up.

'Here. Let me settle your skirts. No need to shock Evans too much.'

'What about your cravat?'

'Have you ruined my cravat *again*, woman?'

'While you were strewing my hairpins around the floor.'

'Baggage. Find them in the morning. It'll give Jack something to occupy his mind if he spots them.'

'Speaking of Jack…'

'Yes, sweetheart…is that your earring?'

'Oh, yes. Whatever do you think is bothering Jack?'

'Nettle rash.'

'Pardon?'

'Nettle rash. In his breeches. Now, stop worrying about Jack's problems and come to bed and worry about mine.'

Nettle rash? Startled, Cressida peeped out through the gap again. What on earth did Rutherford mean?

'Oh?' The Countess reached up and twined her arms around his neck. 'I wasn't aware you had any problems in bed.' Her voice was outrageously provocative as she shifted her hips sinuously against her husband.

'I don't,' growled the Earl, lowering his mouth to hers briefly. 'I have you instead.'

He led her from the room, shutting the door firmly behind them.

After waiting a few minutes to make sure they had really gone, Cressida emerged. The chair they had occupied looked no different. She had sat in it herself earlier in the day. Much sat in, saggy. It was wickedly comfortable, but required a massive effort to pull oneself out. Jack always gravitated to it when he didn't want to use his desk. And winced every time he dragged himself out of it.

Firebird is a gelding…

Colour scorched into Cressida's cheeks as she recalled her longing to feel those long fingers on her throat and jaw again. Had *he* ever sat there with a woman in his lap, seducing her? Loving her? Cressida shook her head. Such a thing had never occurred to her. Certainly not between the married couples she had known. Between her parents there had been gentle affection and, on her mother's part, gratitude. Lady Fairbridge and her late spouse? She nearly giggled at the thought of that august lady being seduced by anyone, let alone the gross and frequently inebriated peer.

Andrew? The fourth Viscount Fairbridge. A shudder tore through her. He had terrified her. The more since she had trusted him, had thought he loved her. Even afterwards she had blamed herself. Until she found out what he really wanted of her. Love had nothing to do with what Andrew had wanted from her.

What did Jack want from her? His kisses had been so different from Andrew's demands. Were his feelings different, too? Had he just been teasing her when he made that outrageous remark? He had certainly been furious at the interpretation she had put on his words. Insulted.

And why did she keep looking at that wretched chair and imagining Jack in it instead of the Earl of Rutherford? Of course, Jack sat in that chair all the time. It was his. But did she have to imagine what it would be like to be nestled in his lap?

Abruptly she turned to the ladder. She'd shelve all those books Papa had put on the finished pile and then choose something to read in bed. Tucking a pile of books under her arm, she scrambled up the ladder. She trod on the skirt almost immediately and cursed as she grabbed frantically for the ladder. Books cascaded merrily to the floor.

'Drat!' She picked up her skirts and got down carefully. This skirt was quite a bit longer than her morning gowns. It nearly touched the ground. Cressida looked around guiltily, half-expecting the books to indict her on grounds of impropriety as she tucked her skirts up into the sash at her waist.

No one would come in at this hour.

She picked up the books again and re-ascended the ladder. Happily she glanced at the books as she began to shelve them. Latin poetry…hmm…she'd read most of these…Virgil, Horace, Catullus, she shelved them without

a second glance. Ovid? She knew her father had copies of
Ovid, but he had never permitted her to read any. Why
not? All she really knew about him was that he had offended the Emperor and got himself banished.

Curiously, she opened one of them…what was it called?
Ars Amatoria… Mentally she translated…*The Art of Love*?
Good heavens! She hesitated…perhaps she ought not to
read it. Papa always said many of the classics were quite
unsuitable for a female. He'd only taught her Latin and
Greek because he loved to share his knowledge and there
was no one else to teach.

Oh, bother it. It was only a book, after all. What harm
could a book do? She thrust away the knowledge that
many would consider it quite improper for a female to read
anything more inflammatory than a sermon to improve her
mind, an etiquette manual, or a household list, that some
considered even the mildest novel to be corrupting. Anything called *The Art of Love* would certainly not qualify
as *improving*.

Defiantly, she opened the volume and began to flick
through the pages. Very quickly she could see why her
father had put Ovid on the proscribed list. Scandalous…no
wonder that moralist Augustus had exiled the poet to the
Black Sea…she read on, entranced at the outrageous advice the long-dead poet offered to men intent on the pursuit
and seduction of women… Goodness! it was a sort of etiquette manual for lovers and a great deal more to the point
than the one she had telling young ladies how to go on.
She noted with interest that the poet agreed with Lord
Rutherford and felt women should enjoy the procedure as
much as men, although the phrases he used didn't make
much sense… And then she found the poet's advice to
women intent on being seduced.

Her eyes widened as she scanned the dancing couplets.
A couple of choked giggles escaped as she read the advice
for accomplishments and bodily care to attract a lover. Not

so unlike her own etiquette manual after all...until she came to some extremely graphic and explicit advice near the end.

Her cheeks flamed. She had lived in the country all her life and had seen enough horses, cattle, dogs and sheep to have grasped the mechanics of the act of procreation. But, goodness gracious! She had certainly never realised just how much *variation* was possible. *The Mirror of Graces* didn't mention anything like this!

'What in Hades do you think you're doing up there at this hour?'

The furious voice came from just beneath her. Forgetting her precarious perch on the ladder, she spun around and slipped.

Swearing, Jack leapt forward. She landed heavily in his arms in a tumble of green velvet.

'Oof!' he grunted as he staggered under the impact.

Having temporarily given up on sleep, Jack had come down for a book. Something dull and turgid preferably. The last thing he had expected, or wanted, to find was the object of his fantasies perched above eye level with her skirts hiked above her knees. It didn't help when he'd been fantasising about her legs, to discover that the limbs in question were every bit as graceful and silken as his heated imagination had surmised.

That was bad enough. Realising that she was shelving his books, at midnight for God's sake, put the finishing touches of guilt to his response. But he hadn't meant to startle her into falling off the ladder. He ought to put her down immediately. Anything to halt the inevitable effect her soft, feminine weight had on his very shaky self-control. Anything to get those startled, indignant eyes further away from him. Before he added to their surprise by covering her soft pink lips with his mouth and kissing her, and himself, senseless.

Any man of resolution, not to mention honour, would

have set her on her feet by now. Plainly he possessed neither honour, nor resolution, because she still lay in his arms, staring worriedly into his eyes as though she thought he might bite her.

He wouldn't have cared to bet any sum that he wasn't about to do just that. Her pulse, beating wildly in her throat, cried out for his lips...

'J...Jack? Do you think you should put me down now? Your...your shoulder...'

Shock rippled through him. She had called him Jack, at last. And she lay so sweetly, so trustingly in his arms.

You blithering ass! She's worried about hurting your shoulder. And then, insidiously: *Or did she wait for you? Did she intend something like this?*

Abruptly, he set her down, but found he could not release her. He shifted his grip to her shoulders, his hands sliding sensuously over the old, worn velvet. Only the fine trembling of her body told him of her tension. Her eyes met his steadily, wide, puzzled. *Does she understand? Is this a clever trick?*

Then the tip of her tongue slipped out to sheen the soft invitation of her lips. He fought a brief, hard battle for his self-control and lost. The longing to kiss her throbbed in his blood, surged to a blazing need to feel her mouth helpless under his. Maybe that would answer his questions. Common sense suggested he retreat immediately. He ignored it. *How far would she go?*

'I shouldn't do this,' he whispered hoarsely.

Cressida trembled at the heat in his eyes. 'Do what?'

'This.' Slowly, hungrily, he lowered his mouth to hers.

She had plenty of warning. She knew what he intended, and had every chance to escape. She chose to stay.

At first his kisses were gentle, teasing, a feathering of firm, warm lips over hers. One large hand cupped her chin, tilting her face up. The other arm cradled her against his body, pressed her against the hard wall of his chest along with that wretched copy of Ovid.

He kissed her as he had kissed her in here once before. Tender and ravishing all at once, shot through with fierce restraint. A gasp shuddered through her as she felt his teeth close lightly on her lower lip, felt his tongue stroke the captive flesh in a hot, silky caress. The book fell unheeded, all theory forgotten as her hands slid instinctively to his shoulders, clinging for support as her knees shook.

Heat poured from him, into her. Inviting, imploring her response. Not forcing her abject surrender. Willingly, she parted her lips for him and sighed her pleasure as his tongue found and laved the sweet inner surfaces. Never had she known that a man's arms could be so gently inescapable. That long fingers could brush over suddenly sensitised skin with the delicacy of a butterfly, leaving tingling fire in their wake. Her last vestige of fainting reason noted that Jack, if not familiar with the letter of the text she had just been reading, was thoroughly versed in its spirit.

One hand curved over her nape, caressed the soft skin there. Instinctively she tilted her head back further to increase the sensuous pressure of his teasing fingers. His fingers speared into her hair, loosening the pins which pattered to the hearth as her hair cascaded around her shoulders. And she felt his lips trail fire down her exposed neck, felt the hot probing of his tongue in the hollow at the base of her throat.

His other hand curved around the softness of her waist and hip, holding her against him. Never had she been so conscious of a man's power as she was now; when it was held in check. She knew, none better, that if he wanted to, he could overpower her in a trice. That knowledge should have terrified her. It didn't. Instead she pressed herself closer to his heat and hardness, sliding her hands over his shoulders and shivering as his hand flexed on her hip.

Slowly, tenderly that hand shifted over the curve of her waist, burned over her ribs until it rested just below one soft breast. A languorous, seductive thumb brushed her nipple which flamed to aching life. Her cry of shock was muffled by his mouth, which came back to hers in swift need, taking all he had previously claimed and asking for more. His tongue traced her lower lip, probed gently. With a sob, she obeyed the unspoken command and opened her mouth.

His groan shuddered through her as slowly, inexorably he stroked his tongue into her mouth, taking it in a surge of silken penetration. Heat took her body in slow pulsing rhythms that throbbed with fiery pleasure. His hand at her breast stroked and caressed through the heavy velvet, dragging the material across the burning peak. She heard a tearing sound, felt the fragile, old lace give where she had pinned it to her bodice…a warning bell rang. Then his loins shifted against her in the same compelling rhythm as his tongue, deep in her mouth. Need melted her, her thighs trembled with want… This was so different…surely it was different…

How can it be different, you little fool? Because he uses tenderness rather than force? Seduces rather than attempts to force you? The end result is still the same. She should stop him. Should have already stopped him. She should not even have let him kiss her again.

She didn't want to stop him. Then: *What if he doesn't want to stop? What if you can't stop him?* And hard on its heels: fear. Streaking through her, freezing her blood, just as one long finger slipped beneath the torn lace to trace the swell of her breasts above the bodice, gently stroking silken skin. Desperately she tore her mouth free and gasped, 'No! Please, let me go!' She pushed at his chest and realised just how helpless she was against his strength.

Jack felt the frantic change, the desperate attempt to escape. The temptation to hold her a little longer, take her a little further along the path that beckoned in shimmering delight, tugged at him. He mustn't. Didn't dare. He couldn't trust himself to pull back if this went any further. At some point his intention to teach her a lesson in the dangers of teasing had burned to ashes in the consuming need to teach her the delights of passion. He had his answer. She would go far enough to drive him insane. He released her, stepping back, dragging air into his lungs.

Forcing his voice to glacial boredom, he began, 'Perhaps that may show you…' Then he saw her face. 'Cressida?'

She didn't reply. Simply stared at him, through him, her face accusingly white and strained, as though she looked on a nightmare. For a moment he wondered if she would faint. Unconsciously his hand reached out to her. Her gaze snapped into focus and she jerked back out of reach.

'No!' The harsh fear in her voice stabbed into him. Then she whirled and fled.

Shame, mingled with frustration, lashed him. Even if she had teased, he should have had more self-control than to terrify her. He was supposed to be a gentleman, supposed to have enough control and discretion for both of them.

But did she tease on purpose? Experience hooted derisively that he could even question it. Lord! She could give Selina Pilkington tips. She was bolder, too. Selina had never permitted more that one or two chaste kisses.

Bolder? Or more innocent? Did she really know what she was doing? Some deeper instinct told him that she'd had no idea. And even if she had, he should not have behaved as he had. There were other ways to explain to a girl that her ploys were unacceptable. Far less risky ways. He'd deal with it in the morning. For now he'd go up to bed. With a book.

Savagely he thrust away the knowledge that he'd rather go to bed with Cressida. If only this were London. At least he could have gone out and found a woman to ease his frustration. On the heels of the thought came a shattering realisation; it wouldn't work. He didn't want some anonymous woman for a quick tumble in a strange bed. He wanted to make love. To Cressida. In *his* bed. He had never wanted that before. A man's bed should be reserved for his…wife. Wildly his mind sheered away from the implications of *that* thought.

A book. He needed a book.

His gaze lit on the one she had dropped. She'd been perched on the top of the ladder reading. A reluctant grin curved his lips. He did the same thing himself. That was partially why the library was taking so long. Neither he, nor his father, had ever been able to resist the temptation to browse.

The book looked familiar… He frowned. No, it couldn't be. Surely not. The book lay there, silently assuring him that it could be. Dumbfounded, he picked it up and read the title. It was. He thrust it into a space as though it had burned his hand. Not quite what he'd had in mind for bedtime reading. He couldn't see that it would advance the cause of peaceful sleep one iota.

As he turned to leave his foot scrunched on something. Glancing down, he saw the scatter of hairpins his unrestrained embrace had shaken from Cressida's auburn tresses. They had wound about his hand, a burning silken snare. The memory tore at him.

Grimly he set his jaw against it and bent down to pick up the pins. He would return them in the morning. If Cressida had started taking tips from Ovid, the sooner he made his opinions known, the better. Ovid's ideas could be unsettling enough in writing; he shuddered to think what their effect might be made flesh, so to speak.

And there was something else. *He* would not take advantage of Cressida's ploys and use them to his own ends. He hoped. But another, less scrupulous, fellow might. Had she fully realised the danger she courted? Had her sudden panic just now been genuine, or was it all part of the tease?

His eyes narrowed as another plan wreathed in his brain. With a bit of luck he'd teach Miss Cressida Bramley a lesson she wouldn't forget in a hurry. And he'd make damned sure that *he* was well and truly chaperoned this time.

Chapter Seven

'I beg your pardon, Papa?'

Cressida pushed a lock of hair out of her face and turned to look at her father. He was frowning up at her from his desk.

'I said that volume should not go there. It was on the other pile, my dear. It should go over *there*.' He pointed to a section of shelves further along.

She sighed and rubbed her eyes again. They felt unpleasantly scratchy from lack of sleep. And her hair kept collapsing into her face since she had not enough hairpins to keep it up this morning. Normally such a thing would not have bothered her one whit. This morning she felt thoroughly annoyed about it since, in addition to tickling her face, it reminded her of how disgracefully she had behaved the previous night.

'Sorry, Papa,' she said aloud, even as she cursed silently and twisted her hair up into yet another inadequate knot. She had come down early to find her hairpins but they were nowhere to be seen. Which puzzled her exceedingly. If a maid had found *her* pins, then why were Lady Rutherford's pins still scattered around the hearth where they had fallen? And why was she so irritable this morning?

Could it be the lack of sleep? Or could she be sickening for something? Certainly she ached in some odd places...

Dispiritedly she returned to her shelving, placing the books automatically, not even remotely interested in browsing. A glance down at her father found him doing just that. His faint frown and pursed lips spoke of total absorption. A reluctant smile curved her lips. An earthquake might shift him, but not much less.

What on earth should she say to Jack this morning? She bit her lip. She had behaved like the veriest wanton last night. If Jack were not a man of honour... She trembled at what would have happened. She had thought about it all night.

He would have forced you... He wouldn't have needed to use force. If he hadn't released you, you would have surrendered.

The thought sent more tremors feathering down her spine. Especially since those odd aches intensified. Fear. It had to be fear. Anything else was impossible. She dared not contemplate anything else as she had in the chilly darkness. It would be madness to believe...to hope again.

But why had he kissed her so? No one but a fool would doubt Jack Hamilton's sense of honour. And no honourable man kissed a girl as he had without... No. Impossible. She had to stop this stupid dreaming. Now. Before she gave herself away. Besides, she could not accept an offer without telling him why they had left Cornwall. And even if he gallantly renewed his offer afterwards she would not accept. She could not offer Jack a tarnished name as a marriage portion.

She stared unseeingly out at the gloomy day. The sparkling magic of the previous night had been replaced by grimly lowering clouds. More snow. She shivered despite the heat of the fire, wishing she had a warmer gown.

Or that she could become colder. Once you were cold enough you no longer noticed it, she had heard tell. You drifted off into a false sense of warmth and security. Once you were colder than the snow…

The sound of a throat being loudly cleared dragged her back.

'Hmm?' She looked around vaguely. And grabbed for the ladder. Blast it all! Why did he keep sneaking up on her?

'Perhaps I might have a moment of your time, cousin?'

It sounded as if he had asked several times from the note of languid boredom in his voice.

'My…my time?' Cressida could not control the wobble in her own voice.

'Yes,' he said. 'Privately.'

Privately?

'No,' she said baldly. And added belatedly, 'Thank you.' Somehow it sounded thoroughly inappropriate. Hurriedly she went on. 'I do not think it…it would be at all saf—a good idea,' she amended, 'for us to be alone, after…after…' Her voice failed. *After you kissed me? After we kissed each other? After you nearly seduced me? After I nearly ruined myself?* Nothing seemed quite right. Prudently she remained at the top of the ladder and left the sentence to finish itself in Jack's mind.

'My dear cousin, while I laud your prudence, the other end of the library will suffice. Your father's presence is surety enough while I return your property.'

He held up a single hairpin, no more.

One was quite enough. Cressida could feel the blush extend much lower than her cheeks and throat. That only increased the heat of the blush. Surely it was only embarrassment at the memory and not the memory itself. Numbly she came down from the ladder, praying that he wouldn't try to assist her.

'Cressida?' Her father's voice brought them both up short.

'Y…yes, Papa?'

'Jack taking you for a walk, m'dear?' He smiled fondly. 'Better fetch your cloak, then. It looks cold out.'

'I...er...I don't think...'

'Just to the end of the library, sir,' answered Jack. 'With your permission.'

She noted the change in his tone at once. To her father, he spoke...kindly...with not a hint of the cold hauteur he had used with her.

Coolly he possessed himself of her hand and placed it on his arm to conduct her to the far end of the library. Fury seethed in her breast. She had no choice. If she objected and Papa heard, then he would take her part instantly. She knew that now.

The sun had broken through briefly and light poured through the north windows, gilding the worn Persian rugs with frosty brilliance. So cold, so bright. Her hand on his arm felt cold, too. As though it had frozen there. Yet she could feel the heat pouring out of him. Why couldn't it warm her hand?

He halted her right by the windows near her desk, in full light, although, as she looked up at him in unspoken question, the sun cravenly retreated behind the overriding gloom of the day. She did not have that option and would not take it anyway.

He dropped the formality at once, holding her hand between his and rubbing his thumb over her palm in a way that sent tremors of pleasure through her. Shocked she tried to jerk her hand away. How could such a simple caress send heat flooding through her?

His fingers tightened slightly. 'Cressida, you were perfectly right to call a halt to last night's...er...proceedings,' he began.

Proceedings?

'It was most inopportune of me to leap so far ahead without discussing the situation with you.'

What situation?

'Yes, indeed. I should have spoken earlier, but my passions ran away with me.'

Oh, dear God. Surely he doesn't mean to make an offer…? If he thinks that he compromised me…

'It was most inconsiderate of me to push matters so far. Naturally you will wish to know my terms and assess the matter in a rational light. Your father, of course, may disapprove…'

'Why would Papa disapprove?' She heard herself ask the question as if from a great distance.

He smiled. 'My dear Cressida! Most clergyman would disapprove of their daughters taking such a step. Indeed, most men. I should not be making such an offer had you not clearly signalled that it would be welcome.' His smile flayed her. 'I quite understand that I am probably your first. If that is indeed the case, of course I will be only too happy to compensate accordingly.'

'What…what exactly are you suggesting, sir?' Her lips felt stiff, chilled. The answer already battered at her mercilessly, but her heart refused to accept the appalling blow that loomed.

'That you should be my mistress, of course,' he said calmly. 'I'm only human, my dear. After the lures you cast out, I should have to be dead not to notice your charms…'

'Cressida?' Dr Bramley's puzzled voice broke in on them.

'Y…yes, Papa?'

'There was a copy of Ovid here yesterday. Do you know where it is?' Suspiciously, 'I do hope you haven't been reading it.'

'I…er…ah…' She floundered. 'It must be…'

'Oh, yes. I see it now. However did it get *there*? Thank you.'

Scarlet, she turned back to Jack.

'I'm sure you found it instructive,' he said pensively.

'And, of course, putting theories into practice is even more instructive.'

'You…you think I wish to be your…your mistress?'

The world had shattered around her into shards of ice, shining, deadly. Andrew had shamed her, dented her pride. The knowledge that Jack thought of her in such terms left her chilled to the bone. Knowing deep in her soul that if not for the bitter ice, she would feel her heart tearing apart.

He shrugged. 'But of course. In a girl better connected, or less intelligent, I would have assumed she wanted to tease me into marriage…but in your circumstances…'

She knew the litany by heart. *No connections, your mother's reputation dubious, no dowry, not even beauty to tempt a man… This is what comes of allowing your heart to override your judgement. Another man who thinks you will become his mistress.*

Something must have shown on her face.

'Cressida?' Faintly surprised. 'Is that it? You thought I might offer marriage?' He laughed gently. 'No, no, my dear. That is impossible. I do sympathise with your circumstances, indeed, I am very sorry for you, but marriage! You will do very nicely as my mistress…'

He went on, outlining exactly what she could expect of him. What he would expect of her. Every word sliced into her as he reduced her to a filly at auction. And he had offered pity.

'No.' Her shaken voice cut across his summary of the financial agreement.

'Not enough? There is, of course, room for negotiation.'

He didn't sound even remotely concerned as he raised his offer. The indifference in his voice shook her wits back into order. Later there would be time to weep with disillusionment. She realised that, despite her caution, her mistrust, some deep unacknowledged corner of her heart had hoped, had believed, he loved her. Now, if it killed her, she would give the arrogant beast a setdown he would never forget. Pride, after all, had its uses.

''Tis not that, sir.' She forced herself to sound as uninterested as he, not to betray by so much as a tremor the pain that ripped her apart. 'I gave the matter considerable thought last night, and have come to the conclusion that I was vastly mistaken in thinking I should like to become your mistress. On reflection, I believe that it will not amuse me at all. I am sure your offer is more than generous, but I believe it will suit me better after all to look elsewhere.'

Her voice she could control. Just. She could do nothing about the fiery blush that scorched her cheeks and throat. To disguise it, she bent to fiddle with her slipper. To her horror, she could feel the heat behind her eyes become blinding. In a moment it would spill over. Retreat. She had to escape.

Abruptly she stood up. 'Perhaps, sir, you would be so good as to give me my hairpins? I should like to put my hair up properly.' She risked a glance at him. Only to regret it instantly.

Steely grey eyes bored into her. 'Miss Bramley, if I find you casting lures at my good friend, Lord Rutherford, you may rest assured that you will be ejected from this house by the following morning.'

Cressida lost her temper. Completely. How dare he suggest that she would do such a vile thing! Well, if that was what he thought of her, then she was only too happy to assist him.

'Oh?' she said sweetly. 'Do you think he might be interested? I had the impression that Lord Rutherford was so enamoured of his Countess that he would scarce notice another female, but if you think—'

'Good morning, Jack. Good morning, Miss Bramley.'

As one they turned and Cressida felt all the blood drain from her face. Indeed, from her body. Nausea swept her as she faced the Countess of Rutherford, who hadn't even bothered to attempt putting her hair up; it hung nearly to her waist.

'Just looking for my hairpins,' she said. And flushed delicately pink.

Cressida began to breathe again. *She couldn't have heard.*

Then, coming closer, 'Oh.' The Countess went even pinker. 'You've found them, Jack.'

Jack's face had gone brick red. 'They're not...I mean...they belong...'

'They're mine,' said Cressida. She reached out to take them from his hand and dropped the lot as her fingers touched him.

For his part, Jack felt as though her soft touch had scorched him. He wanted more than anything in the world to drag her into his arms and kiss her until she knew she belonged to him.

She had thought of becoming his mistress. His offer hadn't shocked her in the least. Somewhere, deep down, that hurt. And she had changed her mind. That hurt even more. She had said she didn't want him. Rage consumed him, fraying the edges of his self-control.

'Here, let me help you.' Meg had bent down to pick up the scattered pins with Cressida. 'Miss Bramley? Are you all right?'

Meg's concerned tones sliced at Jack. Lord! If she only knew what the little hussy had said.

'It's...it's nothing. Some dust in my eye. Thank you. I...I think your pins are still by the fireplace. I mean... there are some there.'

She had risen to her feet, and was hurrying from the room, but not quickly enough. Something glinted on the ends of her lashes and slid down her cheek. Guilt and shame lashed at Jack. Along with the horrible suspicion that he had just made a dreadful mistake.

'Cress!' He started after her instinctively, but a small hand caught his wrist.

'You've probably said quite enough for one morning.'

Turning, he found Meg's normally gentle eyes had hardened to blue steel.

'Miss Bramley can put her hair *up* without your assistance, Jack,' she pointed out. 'And, since you were obviously in the middle of a fight when I walked in, she would probably prefer to cry without your further assistance.'

'Damn it, Meg! You don't know what—'

'No,' she said. 'And I don't want to.' She paused. 'Yet. Right now I need to find my hairpins.'

'Cressida, my dear…'

Jack turned towards Dr Bramley, who was peering at them in obvious puzzlement.

'Oh. That's not Cressida.' Dr Bramley made this pronouncement with an air of discovery, as Meg turned. 'Has she left the room?'

Speech failed Jack. He nodded feebly.

'I thought she might know where that little jade horse and the ivory Buddha have disappeared to,' explained Dr Bramley.

Jack frowned and looked to the place where the Buddha had always sat. It was gone. Anger shot through him. If one of the servants… No. Impossible. They had all been here for years. Yet the T'ang horse was missing and now the Buddha… Could they have been broken accidentally and a maid was too scared to confess?

Meg had found her pins and was engaged in putting her hair up in front of a mirror.

'Is it the T'ang horse, Jack?' she enquired through a mouthful of pins.

'Yes,' he said shortly. His father had given it to him for his twenty-first birthday. An accidental breakage was one thing, but if someone had stolen it… He set his jaw. Whoever it was would find themselves the recipient of a dubious honour—namely, being the first servant he had ever dismissed without a character.

And he still had to decide what to do about Cressida. More and more the memory of those tears convinced him that he had made a complete and utter codshead of himself. Had he really asked a gently bred, virtuous girl to be his mistress? Chills of horror slithered up and down his spine. *What the hell would you have done if she'd accepted?*

Cressida stared at the very solid drawing room door and gathered up all of her courage. It was only a door after all. And the woman on the other side of it was just that—a woman. Even a Countess could only say no and after Jack's offer this morning, she would have to take the risk. She had no choice now.

Taking a deep breath, Cressida opened the door and went in. 'Lady Rutherford?'

At first Lady Rutherford did not respond. Then her head came up from her book with a jerk. Cressida noted that her rich brown curls were very elegantly braided and anchored with what was no doubt an army of hairpins.

'Oh, heavens! I'm so sorry, Miss Bramley. Half the time when people address me by my title I don't realise who they mean.'

Cressida blinked. How could a Countess possibly forget her rank and title?

'Is there something I can do for you, Miss Bramley? Do sit down.'

Nervously, Cressida approached. She hardly ever came in here. Jack only used it for receiving visitors, but Lady Rutherford had said that if she were to use the library, Dr Bramley would be driven demented by little Jonathan. So she had taken over the drawing room. A large wicker basket sat by her chair, containing, Cressida surmised, Viscount Brandon, heir to the earldom of Rutherford.

Cressida perched on the edge of a chair near the fire and

twisted her fingers together. She had rehearsed her speech for an hour. It ought not to be so difficult. If only she didn't keep on thinking about hairpins.

Dragging in a deep breath, she plunged in, reminding herself to whisper. 'Lady Rutherford, could you write me a reference as a governess? If I were to speak to you in French and Italian, demonstrate to you my proficiency in sketching and music—and I can use the globes, of course, and all the other things that a governess is supposed to be able to do—could you please write me a reference?'

Lady Rutherford's lovely smile dawned. 'If you were to speak to me in rapid and fluent French or Italian, I should probably have to apply to my husband for a translation!' she said in a normal tone of voice. 'And as for music and sketching! I've not the least doubt that your skill far out-shines mine. Oh, and don't worry too much about Jon,' she added. 'He's nearly due to wake up anyway and nothing less than a musket blast would wake him.'

'But…but surely…a…a Countess?' Cressida could not keep the note of amazement out of her voice. 'I thought…that all…'

'That all elegant young ladies of birth and fortune were educated?' Lady Rutherford's voice held amusement and a faint hint of embarrassment. 'You see, I wasn't reared like most future countesses. I was taught none of the things you take for granted. After I married I spent quite a lot of my allowance paying for tutors and the like. Until Marc found out and told all of my teachers to submit their bills to him!'

She grinned. 'So while I'll write you that reference gladly, you should consider the fact that some people might consider my opinion a trifle suspect! Shall I ring for tea?'

'P…pardon?' She was going to write the reference. And despite Lady Rutherford's disclaimer, Cressida knew that most people would take a Countess's word on anything. Absolutely anything.

'Tea. Or should I say, *thé*?' Lady Rutherford laughed. 'I've been sharing the governess my sister-in-law's daughters have. For French and Italian conversation. If you and I speak French to one another, then my reference will be even better!' She rang the bell.

'Just French conversation, or would you like Italian as well, Lady Rutherford?' Cressida found herself asking.

Lady Rutherford swung around. '*Would* you?' A faint frown creased her brow. 'I'll write that reference anyway, if you really want me to. I didn't mean to *blackmail* you. And I do mean to pay you, after all…'

'No!' gasped Cressida. 'I can't possibly take money from *you*, Lady Rutherford.'

'Do you think you could just call me Meg?' asked Lady Rutherford plaintively. 'It seems so silly when you are Jack's cousin and he and Marc and I are all on Christian name terms. I've never known Jack to be so idiotish before.'

'I…I don't think Mr Hamilton wishes to be on such terms with me,' said Cressida. And at once realised that she had uttered the biggest whisker of her life. Having offered her a *carte blanche*, Jack was no doubt prepared to be on far more informal, not to say intimate, terms with her.

'That,' said Lady Rutherford, viewing her flaming cheeks with evident interest, 'is very definitely his problem, not ours. If you call me Lady Rutherford again I won't write my best reference.'

An indignant squall from the basket interrupted them.

Cressida watched entranced as Lady Rutherford knelt down and picked up her son, crooning to him softly. Longing flooded her. This could never be hers. Never. You could miss what you'd never had. Seeing another woman nurse a baby in her arms as she unbuttoned her bodice with deft fingers, seeing the baby settle contentedly to his feed, brought an almost physical pang of need.

'Do you really want to be a governess?' asked Lady Rutherford.

'Not much,' admitted Cressida, shutting her heart to what she really wanted. 'But now Papa is safely settled here, there isn't much choice. I...I couldn't possibly stay here permanently.'

'Hmm. I suppose not. People can have such dreadfully commonplace minds about that sort of thing.' Lady Rutherford wriggled her shoulders a little.

'Do you need a cushion?' asked Cressida.

'Oh, yes, please.'

Careful not to disturb the baby, Cressida slipped a cushion behind Lady Rutherford. 'Is that all right, Lady—'

Blue steel flashed up at her. *'Meg.'* She really meant it. She wanted to be friends.

'M...Meg.'

'Lovely. That's much more comfortable,' said Meg happily. 'When Jon's finished, why don't we give him to my maid to look after and go for a walk before it snows again? It's a little cold to take him out.' She smiled. 'You can tell me exactly what to put in this reference. In French, of course!'

'Or Italian,' suggested Cressida, with a perfectly straight face.

Meg grinned. 'Indeed. Now, if you wouldn't mind tying that ribbon to the door knob in the hall, Jack and the male servants will know not to come in just now.'

Jack looked at the list in his hand and swore again. While helping Dr Bramley, he had surreptitiously checked the entire library and discovered a number of other small, but very valuable, items missing. He didn't care so much about the monetary value, but some of them were of great sentimental value, heirlooms, gifts, things which spoke to him of his father and grandfather. And even that paled into insignificance beside the hurt he felt at the betrayal of trust implicit in these thefts.

Someone he trusted, someone he knew, had sneaked in here and stolen these things. Under ordinary circumstances he would have expected the maid who dusted in here to notice, but with the library in such a muddle, she might well have thought they had been put away.

Unless she took them, thinking they wouldn't be noticed.

He ground his teeth. Loathsome to be so suspicious, but someone had taken them. He'd better make enquiries. Perhaps Evans or Mrs Roberts had put them away for safe-keeping.

Without telling you? And why not move all the jades and ivories?

'Something wrong, old chap?'

He turned. So preoccupied had he been, that Marc had come right up to him.

'Hello, back from your ride?' said Jack. 'Where's Meg?'

Marc grinned. 'Met her in the gardens.' He dropped into a chair and stretched out his long legs, crossing one muddy, booted ankle over the other. 'Walking with your cousin. Chatting in French, actually. She's very fluent, I must say.'

Jack nodded. 'Yes, she said that she was making progress.'

Marc flicked him an amused glance. 'Miss Bramley, I meant. Not Meg.'

Dr Bramley looked up from his desk. 'Fluent? Cressida? I should think so. My wife, poor Amabel, was most particular about her French. And Italian. She sings very nicely, too. Having been a governess herself, Amabel was very well qualified to educate her.'

'Did she also teach her Latin?' asked Jack feelingly.

'Er, no.' Dr Bramley looked rather conscious. 'I'm afraid I did that. And Greek. I do like teaching, you know.

She has such a quick mind. And I must say, her way of looking at things often gives my own thinking a jolt. Salutary, most salutary. But I did warn her that people would think it most improper if they found out. And I never let her read the more *explicit* texts, of course.'

'Of course not,' said Jack in a slightly strangled voice. Since when did a chit like Cressida wait for permission? She had certainly given his own thinking a jolt. And not just his thinking.

Dr Bramley returned to his catalogue and drifted back into the past.

'I believe,' said Marc, with a provocative grin, 'that Meg and Miss Bramley intend to concentrate on French in the afternoons and Italian in the evenings while we linger over our port. I wonder when they mean to fit in Latin?'

Jack snorted. 'You'd better hope they don't,' he muttered. 'Or you'll find Meg up a ladder reading Ovid!'

'Really?' purred Marc in a soft voice that reached only Jack. 'Is that how Miss Bramley lost her hairpins? How simply fascinating. Yes, I dare say Ovid would come under the heading of *more explicit*.'

Jack controlled himself with a violent effort, reminding himself that not only was his shoulder not up to planting Marc a facer, but that it would not be at all consistent with the role of host. And the last thing he wanted was for Dr Bramley to know anything about those confounded hairpins.

'Have I moved any of the ivories or jade, Mr Hamilton, sir?'

Betsy's eyes widened in shock and Jack could see the sudden tension stiffening the maid's body as she realised that she had been caught in a servant's worst nightmare.

'Oh, no, sir. I thought you must of moved them. Being as how all them books is being shifted and sorted. Or I'd of said something to you as w…well as Mrs Roberts.' Her voice shook. 'P…please, sir, I…I wouldn't never…'

'You mentioned something to Mrs Roberts?' asked Jack intently. Thank God! That practically cleared her. Betsy was hardly the sort to try a bluff like that!

Mrs Roberts spoke up. 'Betsy did mention the little horse, Mr Jack. Several days back. She said as how you must have put it away. I didn't think anything of it. She's a good lass, sir.'

'Indeed she is, Mr Jack,' said Evans firmly.

Jack smiled reassuringly. 'I can see that. Very well. Thank you, Robby. Evans. And you, Betsy. Can you by any chance recall how often you noticed things missing?'

'Oh, yessir!' she said eagerly, the tension ebbing from her visibly. 'Most every morning. I noticed cos I'm allus so careful to dust them gentle like. Like friends they are. Makes you think. Someone all those years ago carvin' them. Like they're still alive an' talkin' to you.' She flushed. 'Bit silly, I suppose.'

Jack shook his head. 'Not at all, Betsy. That's one of the reasons I like them. Off you go. And don't worry. You're not suspected and none of the other servants are going to know that we asked you anything. So don't mention this to anyone.'

'No, sir. Thank you, sir,' she gasped and removed herself.

Jack looked at his housekeeper and butler. 'It's not her. Can't be. But if she thinks things are missing most mornings, then all I have to do is slip down to the library one evening after you snuff the lights, Evans.'

Evans nodded slowly. 'Aye, Mr Jack.' He sighed. 'I just can't think who'd be daft enough to do such a thing. Even if one of the servants was in trouble of some sort, I'd have thought they'd come to me. Or Mary, here.' He indicated Mrs Roberts. 'And asked us to approach you.' He shook his head. 'But night after night... It has to be someone inside the house.'

Mrs Roberts bristled. 'And when I find out who it is, I'll give 'em what for. The very idea! Stealing! In *this* house!'

Chapter Eight

Jack glared at the drawing-room door. Never had he felt so unwelcome in his own house. Yet he hesitated to open that door. And open it he must. An apology spoken through two inches of solid oak was no apology at all. He knew she was in there. For the last two days Cressida had eschewed the library entirely, leaving it to himself and Marc to assist her father.

He saw her at meals, or with Meg, who had become the most over-conscientious chaperon he'd ever been cursed with. No doubt Meg would be in there now. He double-checked the door handle. No ribbon this time. Never before had he realised just how much nursing a baby could do.

He walked in to find Cressida with his godson asleep in her arms. Meg was curled up on the sofa, stitching industriously at what appeared to be a dress.

'Oh, hello, Jack. I found this in the attic,' she said cheerfully, indicating the brown velvet in her arms. 'Yards of it, in an old gown. No wonder our grandmothers never had more than two or three. This must have cost a fortune! You don't mind, do you?' She looked back to her task.

He shook his head, dazed. Of all wives, Meg was the last to need to make her own gowns out of someone else's cast offs. He looked closely at the velvet.

'Is that shade of brown going to suit you, Meg?'

The flashing needle stilled, but she didn't glance up. 'For goodness' sake, Jack! It's amber and it will look ravishing on *Cressida*. That green gown is all very well in colour, but a girl changes between sixteen and twenty, in case you hadn't noticed. More than can be accommodated by letting out seams. It's time she had a new one and this is my *thank you* for all the French and Italian conversation, since Cressida won't let me pay her.'

Understanding flayed him. He'd thought that Cressida wore a skin-tight gown to display her charms. It had never occurred to him that she might not have another. And she had refused Meg's money. What a damned fool he had made of himself.

Reluctantly he turned to his quarry. His heart lurched. Cressida had his godson nestled in her arms. Her head was bent over him, and Jack could see her lips moving as she whispered tenderly to the child.

He didn't fully understand the body blow of savage longing that pierced him like a two-edged sword, but it left him breathless and shaken. He wanted that little scrap of humanity to be *his*. *His* baby, *his* son and heir snuggled in Cressida's arms. His and Cressida's. Clutching at logic, he reminded himself of all the reasons that Cressida would not make him a suitable wife. Outspoken, outrageous, hot-tempered…

He still had an apology to make. 'Er, Cress…' She looked up. Slowly. He blinked. Lord. If looks could kill, he'd be lying dead on the carpet. Hastily he corrected himself. 'Ah, Miss Bramley, would you care to come for a walk?'

He received the distinct impression that she would have liked to tell him to go to hell, but she smiled sweetly and said, 'No, thank you. Sir.'

He gritted his teeth and tried to ignore Meg's amused gaze. Cressida had been like this for days. So polite he couldn't fault her. A shining example of feminine virtue and propriety. He could have cheerfully throttled her. How the hell was he meant to apologise for his insulting offer if he could never get her alone?

'There is something I wish to speak to you about privately,' he said. Perhaps Meg would take the hint and remove herself.

She certainly heard the hint. 'Oh, don't mind me, Jack.' She had bent virtuously over her sewing.

He couldn't throttle Meg. Marc would object. And he was rather fond of her himself. Most of the time.

'Miss Bramley,' he tried once more.

She looked up from the baby again and this time Jack found himself gazing into shuttered green. Not even anger showed. Her voice was very quiet. 'My opinion has not altered. You can have nothing to say to me, sir, that cannot be said in front of Lady Rutherford.' She lowered her gaze back to the baby.

His jaw dropped. And then he pulled himself together. If the little devil thought that he would offer her a grovelling apology publicly, then she could... *She isn't expecting an apology. She probably thinks you mean to press your offer.*

He hesitated. Long fingers clenched into fists as he looked down at her shining auburn hair, neatly confined in a chignon. The urge to stroke the gleaming fire burnt into him. Damn it all, she wouldn't even look at him.

Why should she? You made her a shameful offer with her father at the far end of the room. And you cavil at making an apology with someone else present?

He'd have to do it. 'Miss Bramley...Cressida...' he began. What the devil had happened to his neckcloth to make it so tight? He tugged at it irritably. 'I...I made a complete fool of myself the other morning. What I said...suggested...was shameful. My...my assumptions, all of them, were insulting and I apologise unreservedly.'

He dared say no more. He very much doubted, since Meg was still speaking to him, that Cressida had told her the full story. Shifting nervously, he waited.

She looked up. His head lurched and he had to harden every muscle in his body against the urge to bend down and take her in his arms to kiss away the sadness in her eyes.

'Another lapse of judgement, sir?'

He nodded.

Her lips tightened. 'Very well. I dare say it was not altogether your fault. I…I am well aware that my own judgement is sadly lacking in…in such matters. If my—'

Suddenly he realised want she was about to do. Namely apologise because *he* had asked *her* to be his mistress.

'*No!*' Furiously he glared at her. And spoke very softly. 'Cressida, you will not attempt to shoulder any of the blame for my behaviour. I won't have it. Do you understand me?'

Speechless for once, she nodded, but Jack took little satisfaction in having reduced her to silence.

Quickly he turned on his heel and stalked out. If anything, his apology seemed to have caused her more hurt. Before, when she had looked at him, he had seen only cool indifference. Now he had seen the hurt he had caused her, quivering like a wounded creature hiding in the green depths of her eyes. A wary, suspicious creature, expecting nothing but pain.

The little clock on the chimneypiece reminded her sweetly that it was five o'clock in the morning. The sort of time on a winter's morning that any sane young lady should be tucked up in bed. Not sitting in a draughty library before the fire had even been laid. On her birthday.

Cressida shifted the lamp closer, edged her feet nearer the footwarmer and wrapped her shawl tightly about her shoulders against the chill of the room. She read the advertisement again. If she got the position it would be the closest thing to a birthday present she could expect.

A thorough knowledge of French, Italian, music and watercolour sketching. She should have a mind improved by proper reading...impeccable references...

She'd just ignore that bit about proper reading. After all, she had at least *read* the requisite sermons and moral treatises considered necessary to improve the frippery female mind. If hers wasn't improved by the experience, that was her business, not her employer's. In every other particular, she was qualified for the job. She certainly had impeccable references. Meg's glowing testimonial to her capabilities sat on the desk before her. And Lord Rutherford would frank it for her. Meg had said so.

Yawning, she pulled a sheet of paper towards her and began to draft a reply. Her eyes felt unpleasantly scratchy. Perhaps she should go up to bed again. She might be able to sleep now. No, she might as well reply to this and get it off today... She had been unable to sleep all night, surely she could stay awake long enough to finish this... Resolutely she dipped her pen in the standish...

'Lawkes!'

The startled shriek jolted her awake. Dazedly she shook her head. Where was she?

'Oh, it's you, miss! Lor', I thought as how you was the thief for a minute there!'

She turned around to find a housemaid, fully armed with dusters, bucket and brushes standing just inside the door. 'Thief? What on earth are you talking about? Betsy, isn't it?'

Betsy nodded delightedly. 'That's right, miss. I do feel a silly. But I didn't see 'twas you just at first, hunched over like you was. An' with all Mr Jack's things missin'...well, I was about to run out into the corridor an' yell!'

'Oh,' said Cressida, cold dread flooding her. She felt her way carefully. 'Nothing has turned up yet, I take it.'

'Nothin', miss.' Betsy shook her head. 'All them nice little bits of jade an' ivory. Real pretty they was. Mr Jack's real upset, I reckon. Mrs Roberts reckons as how the little horse was given him by his pa, for his birthday…'

She prattled on, but Cressida took very little in. She remembered the jade horse. T'ang, Papa had said, pointing it out to her. Jack had said nothing about any thefts. Why not?

'…think at first that Mr Jack might of thought I'd taken stuff, but Mr Evans and Mrs Roberts spoke up for me. Mr Jack's a real gentleman, he is, and he took their word…'

A real gentleman… Yes, he was. And thank God for it. Many another so-called gentleman would have accused the nearest servant and had her charged. Even if not proved guilty, that would be enough to condemn her to either the workhouse or prostitution.

Nausea swept her and left her shaking. Dear God, what should she do now? She could not stand by and take the risk that some innocent servant might be blamed. Even gossip could destroy a character overnight. She would not wish that fate on another soul.

Betsy looked around indulgently at the piles of books and folios. 'Reckon I'll just be clearing out the fireplace, miss. Shall I light it for you when I'm done?'

'Hmm?' Cressida blinked. 'Light the fire? Oh…n…no, thank you, Betsy. I…I won't be here much longer.'

Please God, she would be away from here entirely in a matter of weeks. Then—could she leave? And she had still to decide what to do about the missing items.

Betsy finished her work and left, and Cressida sat on, her letter forgotten in front of her. Vaguely she knew that she must finish it, send it off, but suddenly it had lost its importance. She turned around to stare blindly across the room at the fireplace, as if hoping to find answers in the dancing firelight.

Firelight? Her mind focused abruptly. The fire had been lit. Betsy had ignored her instructions and lit the fire anyway. They were all so kind. That no longer surprised her. Lady Fairbridge had always maintained that servants took their tone from their mistress. Or, in this case, from their master.

Bitterly she faced the truth. She had fallen in love with Jack Hamilton. A man who, even if he had cared for her enough, ought not to marry her. She knew, none better, that, at his level of society, love was not enough to justify a union. A bride must bring a dowry, increase a family's wealth and power. She had nothing and no one, except her father. Above all, a bride must bring an untarnished name. As far as the world was concerned, she was ruined. Damaged goods.

He might not know that her reputation had been ruined, but he knew well enough that he could not possibly marry her. So he had offered her what he could. What he thought she expected. Then, somehow, he had realised his mistake. He had apologised.

And he had spent the last two days trying to make amends for his error. At least, she assumed that was the reasoning behind all the odd little attentions he had been paying her. He had been trying to assure her of his regard. His respect. He couldn't possibly know that the mere touch of his hand, tucking hers into the crook of his arm sent heat waves pouring through her. That every time he spoke to her gently her heart leapt and danced. That his eyes on her as she sang to her own accompaniment after dinner in the evenings felt like the sweetest caress...a featherlight brush of tenderness possible only in dreams...

'Good God! What the devil are you about now?'

Jack's stunned accents tore into her dream. She must have dozed off again. Blinking her eyes to clear her head, she found Jack standing at her elbow with the reference in his hand, staring at it as though he had been personally insulted.

'What in Hades is *this* for?' he growled, flinging her precious reference down in front of her.

She snatched it up and glared back, but spoke in tones of sweet reason, guaranteed to annoy him. 'It's a reference. *Most* employers require one. For respectable positions, anyway.'

'For *respect*—' He appeared to be choking. 'You don't need a position as a governess!'

'Yes, I do,' she contradicted him flatly. Much easier on her heart if they had a good fight. As long as she didn't permit herself to dwell on how handsome he looked with his storm-dark eyes.

'What do you want to be a governess for anyway?' he snarled.

She didn't, not particularly, but she met his fulminating eye squarely. 'Because, apart from your own generous offer of employment, of course, it is the only occupation for which I have any qualification. And while it may not be as well paid as the position you offered, it is infinitely more to my liking.'

For a moment she thought he might strangle her. 'I apologised for that,' he growled at last. 'You can forget this tomfoolery. I forbid it!'

There was no pleasing some people. He didn't really like her, for all his kindness. Made it quite plain that she could not remain in his home unchaperoned, and then, when she made plans to leave, he complained about it.

'And just how do you propose to stop me?'

His eyes glittered with triumph. 'By having your father stop you, that's how. You have to obey him. By law.'

Anger shot through her. 'Not since midnight, I don't,' she flashed at him. 'I might *choose* to follow his advice out of respect and affection, but I certainly don't have to obey *your* vicarious orders!'

Oh, damn! She bit her lip. The last thing she had meant to do was draw attention to her birthday. Perhaps he hadn't noticed.

'What do you mean, *since midnight*?'

Of course he had noticed. The wretched man noticed everything.

'That is none of your business!' she snapped.

She could practically see his mind working, adding it together. And getting four.

Abruptly the anger drained from his face. 'It's your birthday,' he said, in tones that wrenched at her heart. 'Your twenty-first birthday. And instead of waking up excited, wondering what presents you will receive, you're down here, writing bloody job applications, knowing full well that your father probably won't even remember to wish you a happy birthday.'

Words struggled in her throat. 'It's…it's not that,' she managed. 'I…I don't m…mind…' Her voice wobbled helplessly as she fought back tears. His anger she could deflect. Tenderness slipped past her guard.

Dragging in a deep breath, she set her jaw and forced her voice to a semblance of normality. 'I came down early to write this letter privately. I had no intention of disturbing you. Indeed, I had no idea that you ever came down this early.'

His jaw looked as though it had turned to solid, chilly granite. But she knew it wasn't. That it was quite warm and deliciously scratchy…

'I came down to check something,' he said quietly. 'Cressida, you cannot become a governess. You must realise that.'

He had come down to check something… What? To see if anything else had disappeared? Oh, God. What was she to do?

'Cressida?' She flinched back as he moved towards her.
If he touched her again… He stopped instantly. 'I'm sorry.
I didn't mean to startle you.'

She shuddered at the note of concern.

'Are you all right?'

'Yes,' she lied. 'I had better go.'

He looked as if she had struck him. 'Damn it, Cress!
You must know by now you've nothing to fear from me!'

Tears pricked hotly. 'I don't fear you.' Her voice
sounded queer, unfocused. 'I…I know that you will force
nothing on me.' Gathering up her unfinished letter and the
reference, she left the library.

Jack stared at the shut door. *I know that you will force
nothing on me.* Her words could have but one meaning.
She thought that he might still seduce her, so she was
intending to remove herself from his home, his life, as fast
as she possibly could.

A governess! God in heaven! He could just imagine
what the outcome of that would be. Most ladies were reluctant to employ young and attractive governesses. There
was always the danger that older sons, or husbands, could
become entangled. Most of them worried more about the
sons—who could find themselves obliged to marry the girl
they had ruined. Always assuming she had connections
with enough power to force the issue. And so many governesses were used as drudges by the mistress of the house.

He shuddered to think of what could happen to Cressida.
I know that you will force nothing on me. There were
plenty of men who would be only too happy to force whatever they liked on her. Good God! Hadn't her mother's
experience taught her that?

He stalked over to his desk, swearing in frustration.
What the devil had Meg been about to write her that
blasted reference? Cressida didn't need a job—she needed
someone to look after her. A pleasant, kindly…husband.
That was it. He firmly ignored the outraged response from

his baser self at the thought of another man possessing Cressida. Curse it all! He couldn't offer for her himself. She wasn't at all the sort of girl he'd imagined as his wife. He just had a bad case of lust. So logically he ought not to mind her marrying someone else. Someone who could make her happy. He wanted that above all things.

A…a curate or some such thing. Someone meek and mild, who wouldn't mind that she was a bit of a bluestocking. The only problem was that she had no dowry. Very few curates could afford to marry a girl who could bring nothing to her marriage.

He frowned as he sat down. There was a very simple answer, of course. He could provide her with a dowry. If she'd accept it, which he took leave to doubt. Cressida, among all her other faults, had the devil's own pride. His fingers drummed on the desk as he thought it through. Somehow there had to be a way of furnishing Cressida with a dowry without wounding her pride.

In the meantime, it was her birthday. Since Dr Bramley had said nothing he probably wasn't aware of the date. Blast it all, he wasn't even sure of her age! With a violent effort of imagination, Jack tried to envision what it would be like to wake up on your birthday and know that not a single present, nor birthday greeting, would come your way. That no one would make a fuss, or care in the least.

Well, he cared. And she'd have at least one present. Now, what the devil could he give her? He was her cousin, after all. A small token would be quite unexceptionable. He frowned, thinking. What would she like? Most women liked jewellery, of course. And the only jewellery he had ever seen her wearing was that cut-steel necklace of flowers.

Of course, a gentleman ought only to give a girl the most trifling of gifts and *never* jewellery, but he was her cousin… What about those carved ivory beads he had picked up on his travels years ago? The ones he had intended for Nan, but she had been married to Barraclough by the time he returned and had more jewels than she knew what to do with.

They'd be in his bedchamber somewhere. Just as well— if they had been down here, the thief might have taken them.

'Ah hah! Here she is at last!'

Cressida stopped dead just inside the drawing room as the Earl of Rutherford announced her entrance. She wasn't late, was she? She had taken rather longer dressing than usual. Her new gown looked so nice, she had experimented for quite a while with her hair, trying to achieve a new style.

His lordship came forward and offered her his arm. 'Happy birthday, my dear. And congratulations. Jack tells me you attained your majority today.'

She felt her jaw drop and her eyes flew to Jack's face. No one had said anything all day. She had assumed he had not said anything.

He was watching her with an odd smile as Rutherford led her into the room.

Meg came forward and tilted her head as she examined the gown. 'Hmm. Just right for you. And this will add the finishing touch. Stand still.' She slipped a lace fichu around Cressida's shoulders and twitched it into place. 'There. Perfect. Happy birthday, Cressida.'

She ought to say something. Something gracious, like *thank you*, but the words stuck in her throat, lost in the choking lump there. She saw Meg's smile through a haze of tears.

Her father came to her with a self-deprecating smile. 'I'm sorry, my love, I forgot the date until Jack reminded me. But I do have a present for you. I always meant you to have it on this day. Happy birthday.'

He put his hand into his pocket and drew out a small, oval-shaped object.

Recognition robbed her of speech even before he kissed her and handed her his present. Her fingers trembling, she took the miniature of her mother and gazed at it. Tiny, on ivory, it showed her mother as a young girl, smiling gently out at the world she had left.

'And Jack has something for you,' went on the old man. 'He asked my permission to give it to you, so you need feel no impropriety in accepting it, my dear.'

Jack had something for her? Biting her lip, she turned to him.

He approached her hesitantly. 'It's nothing much,' he muttered. 'Mere trumpery. But I thought they'd look pretty with that gown...' Flushing deeply, he handed her a small wooden box.

Carefully she put the precious miniature down on a side table and opened the little box. A necklace of carved ivory roses met her gaze in accusing innocence. Ivory. And Jack had given it to her.

Horror struck, she stared at it. She mustn't accept it, she couldn't. Papa didn't understand...and she could never tell him.

Even as she fought for the words to decline the gift, she became aware of Jack gently taking the box from her numb fingers.

'Here. Let me.' His deep voice caressed her senses even as deft fingers unclipped her mother's necklace and laid it down carefully. Then the ivory necklace was placed around her neck. She trembled uncontrollably as she felt his fingertips brush her sensitive nape as he did up the clasp.

'There. All done.' His voice was suddenly harsh, tight. Wildly at odds with the gentle, lingering touch on her throat. Then it was removed abruptly as he stepped back.

'Jack...I can't accept...'

He interrupted. 'Yes, you can. Your father and I discussed it. There is no impropriety attached.'

The sudden intensity in his voice told her he had misunderstood. That he still felt guilty over his disgraceful offer and thought her reluctance stemmed from that. She fell silent. She would have to explain, but not here, not now.

Rutherford came forward and said, 'Not being your cousin, there would be every impropriety attached to me offering you a gift. London is full of people, Meg among them, who will tell you that my reputation is disgraceful, but I would like to extend an invitation: Meg and I would consider ourselves honoured if you would come to London and visit us for the Season.'

Six months ago such an invitation would have sent her into the boughs with delight. Now all she could do was try not to cry as she mumbled something non-committal. She would have to explain herself to Jack in the morning. After she had put things right.

Jack shifted restlessly in his chair, stifling a yawn. After three and he still couldn't get to sleep. This chair had always seemed extremely comfortable, but that was before he tried to sleep in it. Under those circumstances a man discovered every single lump and sag a chair had to offer.

He knew perfectly well that his inability to sleep could not be blamed entirely on the chair. He doubted that he'd sleep properly in his own very large and comfortable bed after finding Cressida writing a job application on her birthday. His eyes felt as scratchy as his temper, but every time he closed his eyes visions of Cressida arose to haunt him. Cressida making her way in the world as a governess, ordered about by an unfeeling mistress, her quick wits and sharp tongue curbed by polite necessity. Her green eyes lowered and shadowed. Her birthday forever forgotten.

They were the more cheerful efforts of his imagination.

The ones that really bothered him involved men. Those ones had him pacing back and forth in a fury of frustration as he plotted ways and means to stop Cressida's insane scheme. In his more rational moments he knew there was little he could do to prevent her doing precisely what she wished.

He ran his hands through his already untidy hair and frowned. Riding roughshod over Cressida just didn't work. She didn't appreciate it any more than he would. Guile? He rejected it out of hand. He'd tried it once and she had called his bluff. He still shuddered to think what would have happened if she had taken him up on his offer. Lord, he'd have had to offer for her.

Would that be such a bad thing?

What!

You do like her, you know. And you'd never be dull with her around.

He'd never have any peace either. She had turned his peaceful existence inside out. But the disquieting thought persisted. Maybe he didn't want that old, peace any more. Maybe he wanted a new sort of peace.

He wriggled his shoulders again. Maybe he should just take himself up to bed and forget about the thief for to-night. If he could think of a way to persuade Cressida to accept a dowry…or him. The idea was shattering. That irritating voice had understated things a trifle. He didn't merely *like* Cressida. Whatever he felt, liking was too pale a word for it. He shied away from the idea. Bed. Much the best place. As long as he didn't dream—

The click of a latch effectively banished all thoughts of retiring to his warm, comfortable bed and its distracting dreams.

A light glimmered as the door opened and a small, slender figure came in. He knew instantly who it was, despite the dark. Something about the walk as she crossed to her desk. And…roses…he could smell roses.

What on earth did she want at this hour? Surely not another job application! He couldn't quite see what she was doing…the candle flickered so much… Why didn't she light a branch, or the lamp on the desk?

He shifted slightly in preparation to stand up and let her know that he was there… And saw it. An ivory in her hands, a pale glimmer in the candlelight.

Shock held him and then vanished in a surge of blinding rage. Bloody hell. Here he'd been sitting worrying about her, trying to think of a way to furnish her with a dowry so that she might make a creditable marriage and all the time the little baggage had been providing herself with one. His mind lurched away from the thought that he'd been within a whisker of admitting something to himself. Something he hadn't quite believed…

Thank heavens he hadn't. She'd been robbing him blind. But he had her now and, by God, he'd make her pay for betraying his trust.

He spoke as he stood up. 'You'll find it easier to see what you're doing if you light the lamp, my dear.'

Chapter Nine

She nearly dropped the satchel as the icy voice came out of the darkness. Fright choked her, only to ebb as she realised who stood near the fireplace. And flared again as she remembered just what she was doing.

'J...Jack?' She cursed the shake in her voice and fumbled with the satchel, trying to slip the tiger back in. She hadn't wanted him to know...not like this.

'The same.' His tall figure coalesced out of the shadows into the uncertain light. 'Allow me to help you.'

'N...no. That's quite all right,' she stammered. To her horror she realised that he held a branch of unlit candles. Fear froze the blood in her veins as he took one and reached out, lighting it from her single taper.

The flickering light as he lit his branch threw queer shadows on his face. Surely it was a trick of the light that made his mouth look so hard, so flat, and gave that savage blaze to his eyes. Surely he didn't—*couldn't*—believe that she would...

He spoke again as he set the branch down on her desk. 'Much better. Now we can see what we're doing.' He reached out for the satchel and removed it from her nerveless fingers. He did believe it. She could see his eyes properly now. Hard as tempered steel, they narrowed as he delved into the bag and drew out the ivory tiger.

'How very odd.' His sarcasm sliced at her. 'It was a necklace earlier this evening.'

'I…I can explain…' she began. Explain what? He'd never believe her…

'Of course you can,' he agreed coldly. 'It remains to be seen though, to whom you make your explanation. To me. Or to a magistrate.'

A magistrate!

'No!' The cry wrenched itself from her without warning and frantically she forced back the ones which would have followed. Dear God, no! Anything but that! It would mean hanging, transportation at the very least. Bile rose in her throat at the thought, a strangling terror.

'Jack, please, no! You must list—' She caught back the cry. The truth was impossible. His fury scorched her. She didn't dare tell him the truth. Not while he was still so angry. Perhaps when he calmed down… Shaking, she faced his coruscating rage.

His words bit into her. 'Listen? To you? After you have insinuated yourself into my household and then robbed me? A pity you outfoxed yourself. You might else have snared a richer prize.'

Dazed, she could only wonder vaguely what he meant. 'Prize?'

His lip curled. 'Oh, yes. All your teasing. Followed by that sudden and uncharacteristic bout of modesty. For Lady Rutherford's benefit, no doubt. It might have worked. I might have been prepared to offer more than a *carte blanche* and a trumpery necklace.'

She stared and swallowed as he held her wide gaze trapped. Deliberately he placed the satchel on the table and came swiftly towards her. She retreated sharply, flinging up a hand to ward him off. Too late. He caught her wrist in a crushing grip and brought her up close.

His face set in hard planes as he said coldly, 'As it is, you have attempted to rob me. What can you give me in return to settle the debt and convince me not to call a magistrate?'

She could tell him the truth... Terror shot through her at the thought of his likely reaction. She bit her lip. That would be worse than useless. It might ensure her own safety, but at what cost? If she paid his price, it would give her a breathing space, time to find a way out... Nausea rose. That he could believe her capable of such a betrayal...it stabbed to the depths of her soul.

What else can he believe?

Shuddering, she met his eyes and forced the words from her throat. 'There is only one thing I possess that you could have the slightest use for.'

A sardonic smile played about his lips. 'Assuming, of course, that you haven't already traded it to buy off an earlier outraged victim.' His gaze narrowed. 'Is that it? Is that why your father had to resign his living?'

The accusation took her by surprise. Rage flared. 'You bastard!' Her free hand swung up and caught him across the cheek with a ringing crack.

With a startled curse he caught that hand and imprisoned it as well. 'A little late for outraged virtue, Cressida,' he noted. 'You've offered yourself to me in exchange for my forbearance. After all, the stakes are high. Transportation or the gallows. Or...'

He left the sentence hanging and she shuddered as the room blurred around her, blackness swirling in. Frantically she shook her head to clear it...she couldn't afford to faint. No matter what he said to her. Or did.

Abruptly that cruel grip on her wrists disappeared. Bereft of its support, she staggered, clutching at the desk to steady herself. But her limbs felt stiff, leaden and an icy void had opened inside her, cold leaching out of its black depths, numbing her from within, sealing off pain and fear.

His voice ripped at her again. 'Are you refusing me? Are you daring to risk your life against your...*honour*?'

She shut her eyes against the roiling nausea, against the scorn in his voice that made the word *honour* an insult.

'Did it ever occur to you, I wonder, what might happen if some other poor soul, one of the servants perhaps, was accused of your crimes? Or what your father's shame and despair might be if you were found out?'

Tears scorched behind her eyelids, threatening to spill over. She could not bear any more. 'Please...stop. I am not...refusing you...' She clenched her fists so hard the nails bit into her palms. 'If you want your...your recompense...' She shut her eyes, attempting to hold back the flood. Anything would be better than hearing him flay her character any further and imagining what his reaction might be if he knew the truth. No doubt he would kick them out. He would never know the truth...

'Just let me go—I will find a job, somewhere for my father... The...the truth would kill him. Let us settle this now.' She shut her eyes, fully expecting to feel his hands drag her back against him.

Silence. A fraught, seething silence which lengthened until her nerves screamed for something, anything to relieve the tension.

'Get out.'

Her eyes opened to meet steely, grey daggers.

'I'll take no woman under any sort of coercion. Get out,' he repeated, 'before I change my mind. But rid yourself of the notion that your father should suffer for your sins, or that you will be leaving. Now that I know what you are, you will behave here. But I won't send you out with Meg's reference, knowing the truth. If you attempt it, I'll make sure your employer is apprised of the truth.' His lip curled. 'If you wish for *employment*, I'm sure I can find an occupation for you, complete with a discreet cottage on my land.'

'No,' she whispered, but even as she spoke, feeling began to return, and with it, terror. If they didn't leave...

'Out,' he said, very softly. 'Before my anger at what a damned fool I am gets the better of my judgement.'

She whirled and fled, the door banging behind her.

Jack sank into a chair with a harsh groan and dropped his head on his hands. He felt as though he had been ripped apart. She was a liar, a thief, a conniving little tease. And she was also the finest actress he had ever met. All he wanted was to go after her and comfort the pain and despair he had seen in her face.

Yet he knew what she had said about sparing her father was just to save herself. She knew him well enough to know that he would not willingly destroy her father. Just as she must have known that he would never coerce any woman into submission, no matter what she had done. In short, his sweet little cousin had played him for a fool. And he had had his eyes wide open while she did it.

He swore. There was nothing more to be done now. He had caught his thief. He might as well go up to bed and get what sleep he could. Later this morning he would have to make a decision about Cressida. If he allowed her to leave and take up a position elsewhere, it could only be a matter of time before someone else caught her. Someone who would have no hesitation in hauling her before a magistrate... He shuddered. Better for her to face the gallows than transportation.

Or be forced to become your mistress?

She's a thief, for God's sake! Damn it to hell, most men would have just dragged her to the nearest magistrate.

She's your cousin. And destitute. Saddled with a father who gives his last penny to a beggar, along with his cloak. Can you blame her?

So why the devil didn't she come to me for assistance, advice?

He'd never sleep. Not now. Not with this churning in-

side him. It was going to take him quite a while for his
emotions to catch up with his intellect and realise that he
couldn't possibly be in love with a thieving little jade…

He might as well put back her evening's haul. Obviously
she had been to a few other rooms before coming in here.
Sadly he picked up the tiger he had taken out of the bag
and looked at it. And frowned.

He must be imagining things…no, he wasn't. That
damned tiger had been here in the library after dinner. On
Dr Bramley's desk. He remembered seeing it when he
came in, wondering how the thief decided what to take.
The tiger had been up on a high shelf…until Marc had
brought it down that morning.

Cressida hadn't come to the library after dinner.

Doubt seeped through him in icy waves of merciless
horror. If it had been here in the library earlier, how the
hell could it have found its way into Cressida's bag?

With shaking fingers he opened the bag and looked in.
Bundles. Little packages, carefully wrapped in handker-
chiefs and scraps of amber velvet and tied with string.

He opened one at random and stared, dumbfounded as
the T'ang horse fell glimmering into his hands. What on
earth? Why would a thief bring all the spoils of previous
raids along with her? It didn't make sense. Unless she got
cold feet. Unless she was putting them back.

He swore softly. Had she realised the danger? His gaze
fell on the tiger again. How had that got into the bag? *Had*
it been on Dr Bramley's desk?

They had all come in here after dinner. Except for Cressida. She had gone straight up to bed. Meg had been alone
with little Jonathan when the gentlemen came in. She had
said Cressida had a headache. That she had gone straight
from the dining room… He knew the headache was a lie.
She had been upset about something. And the tiger had
been here. He was sure of it. So how…?

All at once the scene rose before him… Marc, standing

where he was now, glancing down at Meg, laughing at something she had said...and Dr Bramley, seated at his desk, fidgeting aimlessly with his papers...he'd seemed even more absent-minded than ever... The tiger had been there. He distinctly recalled the old man knocking it over and picking it up again; he'd gone up to bed shortly afterwards...

Cressida couldn't possibly have taken it. His whole body sagged with relief. Thank God, thank God... Thank God for what? That he had accused her of being a thief? That he had threatened to...to force her to become his mistress? Honesty compelled him to abandon that euphemism. Savagely he confronted what he had done—he had, in effect, threatened to rape her.

He shuddered, sickened at his own lack of control, his brutality... *She must have known you wouldn't do such a thing, that it was an empty threat...that you would never force yourself on a woman...*

He shut his eyes in pain, remembering the fear and despair in her face. She hadn't known. Why should she? And he had finished up by telling her that he would take her as his mistress.

She couldn't possibly have taken that tiger. Only one person could have done that. Which meant Cressida had been trying to right the wrong. She had been putting the things back. And she hadn't trusted him enough to tell him the truth. Instead she'd risked her life and honour to keep the truth from him.

Slowly, with shaking fingers, he unwrapped each of the small bundles and placed them one by one on the desk. Scraps of amber velvet fluttered to the floor. Material left over from the gown Meg had made for Cressida.

He groaned. He knew now why Cressida had gone straight upstairs after dinner. Why she had been so upset when he gave her the necklace. She had painstakingly wrapped every single one of his treasures to protect them.

After which she had waited until the dead of night to put them back where they belonged.

Leaving the jades and ivories on the desk, he went slowly upstairs. He'd never felt so exhausted in his life. He had to pass Cressida's door on the way to his room. Unconsciously his stride slowed until he found himself standing outside her bedchamber in the dark corridor.

Should he knock? Tell her he knew she hadn't stolen anything and apologise now. His hand lifted, hesitated. And then he heard it—a queer, muffled sound, the sound of a girl weeping. As though her face was buried in a pillow. As though her heart would break, knowing that there was no one to trust, no one to confide in.

Silence. He waited, hardly breathing. Another sob came. Barely audible, it felt like a shell exploding in his stomach. His hand went to the latch, and stilled.

He dropped his hand and leaned against the panelled wall. His shoulders sagged. What would she think if he walked in, after what he'd said to her in the library? His stomach clenched. She'd probably think he'd changed his mind about not settling the 'debt' here and now. Even if he knocked…she'd be terrified…as she had been in the library.

Only until you explain… Explain what? You don't understand yet yourself.

Grimly he faced the real reason why he should not open that door. He didn't trust his own reactions. He wanted to hold her, comfort her, yes. But beneath his horror at what he'd done, and said, desire lay in wait. He'd never been in control of himself where Cressida was concerned. And tonight, when he'd accused her of theft, and told her she could become his mistress or face a magistrate… despairingly he acknowledged that he'd be the last person she would want anywhere near her now.

Let us settle this now…

Her broken words tore at him as another muffled sob

came from behind the door. He shut his eyes, trying to banish the image of Cressida weeping, her face buried in the pillow, choking back tears.

Bitterly he remembered his thoughts before she came into the library. The realisation that he cared for her. That turning his life upside down might not be such a bad thing. Oh, hell! He might as well admit it: he loved her. At last he understood Cressida's ability to drive him demented. Why he always felt so totally out of control with her. Why everything always felt so out of place with her.

His body had worked it out before his brain had even woken up to what his heart was saying. This was the girl. The one above all others that he wanted to cherish, protect and possess. At last. The knowledge stunned him. It didn't feel in the least as he'd expected—a sort of polite, gentle affection. The sort of affection a logical, sensible man ought to feel. This was a wild burning in his soul, an urgent need to possess and protect. And all the other feelings were there as well: tenderness, friendship.

Love. People said it all the time until the meaning faded. The word had seemed so bland, so colourless to him. Yet what he felt was like a rainbow burning, shot with life and passion. He couldn't begin to imagine a word that would come close to expressing it. He'd have to make do with *love*.

And in the space of half an hour he had given her cause never to want to see, let alone speak to, him again. Somehow he thought that Cressida might find a declaration of love a trifle hard to accept after what had passed between them. He shuddered. There was always the chance that she might find it utterly repugnant.

Dr Bramley looked up at Jack, plainly dazed and with the beginnings of horror in his lined, old face.

'You…you say *Cressida* had all these? That you caught

her with them? But…she wouldn't… Jack, I do assure you—'

Jack interrupted gently. 'I think she was putting them back, sir. And I know she couldn't possibly have taken that tiger. It was on your desk last night. Do you recall?'

The old man shook his head, whether in denial or confusion, Jack couldn't tell. 'Then, are you saying…?'

'I'm asking,' said Jack softly. 'Can you think of any reason for Cressida to have had them and to put them back without telling me she had found them?'

'Yes,' said Dr Bramley. 'I suppose I must have taken them.'

For all he'd realised the truth, this mode of confession still floored Jack. 'You…you suppose?'

Dr Bramley seemed to have aged ten years. His face looked grey and pinched. 'It's the confounded laudanum. I take it for the stomach cramps. To help the pain and it lets me sleep at nights.' He groaned.

Jack blinked. He'd known the old man took laudanum, but plenty of people took laudanum without ill effects…although, come to think of it, he knew his mother refused to take it. She had always said it gave her nightmares and affected her memory…

'I'm sorry, my boy, but you know, I do tend to forget things anyway. The laudanum makes that even worse and when I stop taking it after a bout of stomach cramps, it's worse still. And that confounded habit of mine of picking things up and fiddling, I just slip things in my pockets without noticing.'

'But wouldn't you notice them after a while, sir?'

Miserably the old man shook his head. 'Probably not. My wife used to find all manner of missing household items in my bedchamber. Usually put in my valise, for some reason. It never seemed to matter very much…at home, you know. I…I never thought it could happen somewhere else.'

His scared old eyes met Jack's. 'It's been much worse since Amabel died. She looked after me, you know. As Cressida does. But it's not quite the same. I...I became very fond of her, you know. Despite the circumstances of our marriage. And one day Cressida will have to leave. She will have to find a position of some sort... I...I have nothing to leave her, you know, and there is no one else to look after her.'

So the old man had lashed himself into a frenzy of worry, which probably made the stomach cramps worse—and he took laudanum for the pain. Jack swore mentally as he untangled the whole sorry mess. What to do now? First he had to deal with the frightened old man before him.

'Stop worrying, sir,' he said gently. 'As you said yourself, these things don't matter much at home, and this is your home now. I will explain it to the staff and tell them that it is just a case of absent-mindedness. And if anything else goes missing, we know who to ask.'

He took a close look at the shaken old man and strode across to a side table. 'Here.' He poured a generous measure of brandy. 'Drink this.' Placing it in Dr Bramley's hand, he forced a smile. 'There's nothing to worry about.'

After taking a careful sip, Dr Bramley asked the question Jack had been dreading. 'What did you say to Cressida?'

'I...I thought at first that she...that she had...' He gritted his teeth. 'I threatened to haul her before a magistrate.' *Or into my bed.*

Bramley nodded, wincing. 'And then I suppose she told you the truth.'

All the breath left Jack's lungs in a rush as though he had been dealt a body blow. Did the man know so little of his daughter?

'No,' he said quietly. 'Dr Bramley, I think you have not understood how furious I was. I will not distress you with the things that I said to your daughter, but rather than expose you to my anger, she told me nothing. She allowed me to think that she was the thief, despite my…threats.' He could not bring himself to tell the old man the whole. Not yet.

'She…she did that?' Dr Bramley dropped his face into his hands and shuddered. 'Dear God…' his voice came muffled '…what have I done? What have I done?'

'Sir—' Jack felt desperate '—it wasn't your fault…'

'There is something else you need to know, Jack,' said Dr Bramley. 'The reason I had to resign my living and leave Cornwall. You…you see, this is not the first time I have accidentally appropriated things in this way…'

Jack emerged from the library, his face white, fury surging through every vein in scalding torrents. If he ever got his hands on that *bastard*, Andrew Fairbridge, he'd make the elegant Viscount rue the day he was born. He'd horsewhip him! And then he'd thrash him to within an inch of his life!

What sort of a man made up to a gently bred girl, leading her to expect an honourable offer, and then tried to give her a slip on the shoulder? What sort of man waited until he knew the girl to be alone on a wintry evening with her father out administering the last rites to a dying parishioner and then came around to offer her a *carte blanche*?

His fists clenched. Andrew Fairbridge was damned lucky that several hundred miles of bad roads lay between Cornwall and Leicestershire, because otherwise he'd be dead in short order.

He strode through the front hall, seeing it through a red mist of rage, scarcely hearing Evans speak to him, and mounted the stairs. Nightmare visions of what Dr Bramley had found when he arrived home made his stomach clench.

Thank God that his parishioner had not spent the whole night dying. That Bramley had got home in time.

Jack swore savagely as he thought of Cressida, struggling with Fairbridge, despairing. His booted feet hit the floor with unwonted fury as he imagined Fairbridge's insolent disavowal of any honourable intent towards Cressida.

He could well imagine Lady Fairbridge's fury at her son's indiscretion. Especially when the Rector of the parish arrived on the doorstep, hot on the Viscount's heels, to demand he do the honourable thing and marry Cressida. Marriage to a dowerless girl without connections would not have been part of Lady Fairbridge's plans for her son.

Bramley's voice echoed in his head...*I only wanted to protect her. She begged me not to go. Said she would rather die than marry any man under such circumstances, but I ignored her. And then it snowed and I had to spend the night up at the Hall...and the butler found the snuff box in my pocket the next morning. He'd seen me pick it up...* Jack felt sick as he remembered the old man's tears. *They told me if I tried to force Fairbridge to marry Cressida, that they would have me taken up for theft...*

And then they'd taken away his living and made quite sure that Cressida's name was ruined anyway, put it about that she was loose, available to the highest bidder, just in case anyone questioned Fairbridge's conduct.

His jaw hardened. Someone was going to question Fairbridge's conduct all right. He was going to call the villain out over this. With swords, so that he could carve Fairbridge's apology out of his sorry hide, one slice at a time.

He pulled up short. Damn. If he challenged Fairbridge, then the cur would have his choice of weapons. And Fairbridge preferred pistols, as did most gentlemen these days. Not that Jack had the least objection to pistols, but he wanted to kill Fairbridge slowly. Very slowly.

He strode around a corner and cannoned into someone.

A soft, female someone who bounced off his body with a very unladylike exclamation.

'Damn it…I mean, dash it, Jack!' said Meg. 'What are you doing, charging around like a mad bull?' She eyed him thoughtfully. 'Are you feeling quite the thing? You look terrible. And have you seen Cressida? Evans says she went out ages ago.'

Jack felt all the blood drain from his face. She had gone out? That must be what Evans had been saying to him. Where? And why? Surely she hadn't left?

'Was she…carrying anything?'

Meg stared. 'For a walk? I shouldn't think so. Evans didn't say. He just thought she ought to be back by now.'

Of course she wouldn't have left. Jack lashed himself for even thinking it. She'd never leave her father. Not now. Not when she believed he had to be protected from… He shuddered.

'Jack?' Meg's puzzled voice dragged him back. 'Are you sure that you're all right? Is your shoulder hurting?'

His shoulder was fine. But his self-respect and heart had taken just about as much battery as they could deal with. He'd just been raging at Fairbridge's treatment of Cressida and her father. What he had done last night was just as bad, if not worse.

He met Meg's eyes reluctantly. 'I'll go and find her, Meg. Don't worry. It's my fault. We…we had a disagreement.'

Her nod lacerated him. She didn't seem surprised at all. 'I see. That explains why Evans thought she was upset.'

Jack headed towards the stables. Clinton might break a blood vessel, but it couldn't be helped. He'd have to ride. Wilberforce had only told him not to hunt. He hadn't actually said not to ride and Clinton could do as he was damn well told for a change.

'Ride? Damn it all, Mr Jack, sir. Doctor said as how you weren't to ride this month!'

Jack glared. 'He only told me not to hunt, man! Just saddle Pericles and be done with it.'

His headgroom glared right back and snorted. 'Told me not to saddle a horse for ye this side of Lent is what he said! Hunting, my—' his eye fell on his youngest son, listening avidly to this sterling example of how to conduct yourself with your betters '—foot,' he concluded lamely.

'You take yourself off, young Danny.' He turned from the boy and rounded on Jack. 'Now, see here, Mr Jack, you shouldn't be riding until—'

Jack swore. 'Damn it, Clinton! Miss Bramley went out some hours ago. I need to ride after her. She should be back by now—God only knows which way she went!' He cast a worried glance at the sky. The clouds were getting heavier by the minute. If it snowed, or rained... He had to find her.

Clinton wavered visibly. 'Miss Cressida? Well now, ye should have said. I'll saddle up and go after her, and you—'

'No.' Somehow Jack managed to speak quietly, but Clinton paused and took a very careful look at his master.

'Pericles, you said.' He sighed. 'Yessir. But I'd take it kindly if'n ye make quite sure the Doctor knows this was your idea!'

'Mr Jack, sir...'

'Yes, Danny?' Jack tried not to sound too quelling, but, judging by the look on Danny's face, he'd failed conspicuously.

Danny gulped. 'Ah...um...Miss Cress'da...she went up through the woods.'

Jack blinked. 'She did?' That was something. At least she'd be sheltered from the worst of any weather.

Danny nodded vigorously. 'Yessir. Saw her when I was

walkin' Firebird out a couple of hours back. You know that clearing where all the snowdrops is? She was there.'

Relief poured through him. At least he had the general direction now. And it had rained last night. He should be able to follow her easily enough.

Riding out five minutes later on the big grey, Pericles, he acknowledged to himself that finding Cressida was one thing. Persuading her to remain within his household in any capacity would be quite another. Especially the capacity he had in mind for her.

Chapter Ten

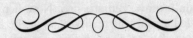

Cressida set her shoulders against the bitter north wind and trudged on a little faster. Her heavy list boots squelched depressingly through the mud of last night's rain. She shouldn't have come so far, but she needed to think without having to worry about interruption. The only problem was that she felt so horribly tired. And her brain had frozen along with her heart, and her body wasn't far behind. She should have turned for home an hour earlier than she had.

She couldn't get past the knowledge that Jack had thought she was a tease and out to snare him... A tear slid down her cheek at the thought. If only he knew, she'd never accept an offer from someone like him, let alone someone she cared for that much. She had nothing to offer but a ruined name...

You won't have to refuse him! He thinks you are a thief, remember? He'd rather take you as his mistress!

She stepped over a fallen branch. She couldn't blame Jack for jumping to conclusions. After all, he had caught her with all the jades and ivories. What else was he to think?

That you found them? That you were putting them back? In the middle of the night? Without bothering to light a

*lamp or a few more candles? You couldn't have looked
more guilty if you'd tried!*

But he'd sounded as though he hated her. As though he
had always despised her. Grimly she ploughed on. It would
be easier if she could dislike him, or at the very least feel
indifferent. But she couldn't. She cared for him as she had
never cared for Andrew. How she could ever have confused a schoolgirl's admiration for a handsome face for
love she didn't know. But she had. Now her childish infatuation paled against the reality of what she felt for Jack.

*He threatened to take you before a magistrate... What
will happen if Papa keeps on getting muddled and moving
things? What if Jack finds out?*

Now she was trapped. She couldn't leave alone. And
she couldn't persuade her father to leave. Not without telling him what had happened. And she couldn't do that. The
chill bit into her and she shivered, walking a little faster.

She would have to tell Jack the truth. She would have
to trust him. There was no other choice and she had meant
to tell him this morning anyway. All last night had done
was make it more difficult. It did not absolve her of the
obligation. She picked up the pace a little more. Better to
get it over with sooner rather than later.

Another fallen branch loomed. Hurrying, she stepped
over it, catching the hem of her cloak on it. The jerk as
the snag brought her up short threw her off balance and
her foot slipped in the treacherous mud. With a startled
shriek Cressida flailed wildly, trying to save herself. The
muddy ground and branch leaped up to meet her and she
felt a shock of pain shoot through her ankle as she fell.

Jack looked up at the lowering sky. Damn those clouds!
And damn that leaden smell of snow threatening on the
wind. It probably wouldn't be too serious this late in the
season, but he couldn't bear the thought of Cressida out
in it, perhaps lost, cold and abandoned.

She isn't abandoned, you idiot! She went for a walk and you're looking for her.

But Cressida didn't know he was looking for her. She didn't even know that he had found out the truth. Desperately, he pushed Pericles into a hard canter, ignoring the jabbing pains in his shoulder. The big grey gelding's hooves thudded on the muddy path, flinging up gouts of mud. He was already mired to the belly and Jack wasn't much better. His heavy frieze cloak kept out the cold and damp but it was liberally spattered with mud.

He rode with fierce concentration. The slipperiness of the path demanded his attention, but he searched the way ahead constantly for a glimpse of Cressida through the trees. He could see her tracks, clear in the path. At least he hoped they were hers. He'd left the snowdrops a mile back, following the bootprints on. Surely she wouldn't have gone much further, not with that sky.

Something cold and soft landed on his face. Several more fluttered past his face and drifted to rest in Pericles's mane.

'*Hell!*' The exclamation burst from him and the horse's ears flickered back curiously even as he snorted his disapproval of the snow landing on his nose.

'Sorry, old man,' said Jack. 'You'll have to pick up the pace a bit more.' He sent Pericles into a gallop, praying that he wouldn't bring the horse down and setting his jaw against the pain pounding in his shoulder to the beat of flying hooves.

And then he saw it—the flash of scarlet through the grey tree trunks. Was it? His heart stood still as he reined Pericles in hard, peering ahead—it was! His heart leapt and the breath he'd been unconsciously holding rushed out of him. She was safe—in a manner of speaking.

There was something odd about the way she moved, something jerky, quite unlike her usual light step. Pericles shifted restlessly under him in the cold wind and Jack gave him the office to move.

What had Cressida done to herself? He cursed as he saw the stick she was leaning on, saw that she was limping. Oh, God! Well, at least if she was walking on it, she hadn't broken her ankle, but still…if he hadn't savaged her last night, she wouldn't be out here. Guilt flayed him and he nudged Pericles into a trot.

Her glance flashed up and he saw the exact moment she realised who was riding towards her, the moment she froze in her tracks and stumbled as she dropped the stick, falling headlong on the muddy path.

'Cress!' Flinging himself off Pericles, he was beside her in a moment, reaching for her. Her tired, numb voice checked him.

'There was no need to worry yourself, sir. I wasn't running away from…our…agreement.' She struggled to a sitting position and he saw her face. Set, and pinched blue with cold and pain.

Sick horror churned as he realised what she meant. Why she thought he had come after her.

Shaking, he lifted his hand to her cheek and froze as she flinched away, refusing to look at him.

'Cress, for God's sake! I didn't come out because I thought you had run away from me. You *can't* think I came out to drag you back to…' His voice cracked. What else was she to think after the things he had said to her? 'I came out because I was worried about you, because I had to find you…and tell you…I saw your father this morning. He told me what happened in Cornwall, why he lost his living, how Fairbridge duped you.'

'He…he told you?' She couldn't hold her voice steady. Just the cold, she told herself.

'Everything,' he assured her. 'Except that you hadn't stolen anything. I mean, he did tell me, but I already knew that.'

How? She couldn't think clearly. Her ankle throbbed and she was so horridly cold. All she wanted was to curl up and go to sleep. In her dreams Jack would miraculously know all the things she had omitted to tell him. He would have forgiven her and he would ask to marry her...

The sensation of strong hands lifting her heavy, muddy skirts and rolling her stocking down jerked her back to grim reality. Frantically she grabbed at her skirts and pushed them back down, shoving his hands away.

'Cress, I'm trying to see how badly your ankle is hurt. That's all.'

Meeting his gaze, she was slightly reassured. 'That's all?'

'That's all.' He flipped her skirts out of the way again and unlaced her boot. 'It's a little cold for tumbling maidens in the woods.'

She jerked her foot away and stifled a cry of pain.

'Did I hurt you?' He caught her ankle in long, gentle fingers and probed carefully around the swelling.

Biting down hard on her lower lip, she eventually managed to lie without her voice shaking. 'My ankle is perfectly stout, thank you.'

'Um-hmm.' He sounded as though he'd barely registered her words and kept turning the joint this way and that.

Cressida went back to biting her lip.

'Perfectly stout, is it?' He slipped her boot back on. 'Well, that explains why you were using the stick, of course. And limping. But even if you weren't lying through your teeth, we need to get home a trifle faster than you can go on foot.' He laced her boot lightly. 'I'll tie that up for you at home. Your father will be having a fit if he realises that you are out.'

She cried out in shock as he gathered her into his arms and lifted her. 'Come along. We need to get home, before this blasted snow gets heavier.' Flakes swirled around them in a drifting dance.

'You…you aren't angry with Papa?' Relief breathed through her. He had always been kind to her father. And now that he knew the truth, her father would be safe. She could count on Jack to protect him.

'No. I'm not angry with him.'

She fought the urge to rest her head on his broad shoulder. Forever.

'Only with you.' His voice sounded clipped as he swung her up onto his horse and settled her safely in the saddle before vaulting up behind her. She shuddered uncontrollably as his arms came around her to take up the reins.

'Sir, I…I can walk.' She couldn't sit, *lie* there, cradled safely against his large body, knowing that he disliked her, that he was angry with her. Especially not when her entire body wanted to sing aloud with joy.

'The devil you can.' His terse response sounded as though it had been bitten off. 'I'd rather get home before dark, thank you.'

She held herself stiffly, trying not to watch as he transferred the reins to one big, capable hand. Then she realised that he had unbuttoned his cloak, was putting it around her and easing her against his chest.

'What are you doing?' She gasped as she felt one arm settle around her waist, anchoring her to him.

'Making sure you don't fall off and keeping both of us warm.' He buttoned the heavy cloak up around the pair of them. 'Cress, why the devil didn't you tell me the truth last night?' The arm tightened.

'Why do you think?' she whispered.

'Because you thought I'd drag your father off to the nearest magistrate! Is that it?' Every word came clipped and savage. 'Damn it, Cressida! The risk you took!'

Anger flared. 'I risked what was mine to risk!' A horrible thought speared her. 'You....you did not tell Papa what you...suggested, did you?'

'No, I did not!' A savage pause. 'And the word is *threatened*. My confession stopped short of admitting to your father that I'd threatened to take you as my mistress. Willing or otherwise.'

Relief rushed through Cressida. If Papa didn't know, then he wouldn't try to force Jack to marry her.

'That's all right, then,' she said, wishing that his arms weren't cradling her so tenderly and that her wretched heart would calm down. *He wants to get home quickly. If it wasn't snowing, you'd be perched up here alone while he led the horse.*

'No, it's not all right. Cressida, I have to know—did you care very much for Fairbridge?'

A knife turned in her heart. She shut her eyes and repressed a shudder. 'At the time...I...thought I did.' She couldn't go on, couldn't explain how youthful admiration for the dashing Viscount had bubbled over into infatuation when he finally noticed her. Andrew was charming, he was wealthy. And he had noticed her.

'And you believed that he intended marriage?'

'Yes.' *Wretched little fool that I was, I believed his lies.*

'It was never very likely, my dear.' His voice was very gentle.

'You don't have to rub it in,' she replied savagely. 'Do you think I believed it easily? That a girl with no beauty...' she felt him tense, '...no connections and less dowry could possibly have caught a man of wealth and position? At first I ignored his attentions, but eventually he told me that he loved me, that he wished to court me...'

'He told you *that*? He used those words?'

'Yes,' she whispered. 'He told me that his mother would not approve, but that he wanted me anyway. That his mother would come around to the match in the end...'

'Did he actually ask you to marry him?'

She nodded against his chest. It felt so powerful beneath her cheek. So very reassuring. She ought not to be telling him all this, he would think her a wanton and a fool, but she had to tell someone. It had all been bottled up for so long.

'Then what?'

'He…he said that since we were betrothed, we should meet more often. Privately. I…I was coming to the house daily to tutor his younger sisters in French conversation, so it wasn't hard. He would meet me afterwards and escort me home…' She trembled.

'Cress, did he…?'

'He kissed me.' She shuddered, remembering. 'I didn't like it very much. He said that I was a little prude, that he would school me better after we were married… That was when I began to wonder if I really wanted to be married. I began to avoid him. I thought he would forget about me soon enough.'

'He referred to marriage between you, actually used the word?'

'Yes.'

'And the night he came to the Rectory?'

She tried to ignore the churning nausea. Chills that had nothing to do with the drifting snow coursed through her. 'He said that his mother had refused to countenance the match. That she would need some extra persuading to give her consent. That he wanted me, and if I was carrying a potential heir, his mother would come around—'

'What?' The explosion rocked her. Arms which had cradled turned to steel.

'I was furious. I realised then how he'd duped me and I refused, so he…he…' Shaking, she fell silent, unable to go on.

'He tried to force you?'

She couldn't tell from the icy softness of his voice what he felt, only that he felt it intensely. Anger? Scorn? Disgust? Desperately she fought the tears which threatened to spill over her cold cheeks. 'He didn't believe that I meant it when I refused him.'

The choked whisper froze Jack's blood. Hearing what Dr Bramley knew of the story had enraged him. But this! Andrew Fairbridge was a dead man. The effort of reining in his fury kept him silent for a moment. He breathed deeply, trying to ignore the heady scent of rosewater that hung about her hair. Light and teasing, it stroked his senses, urging him to rest his cheek on the snow-starred silk of her hair. He dropped a featherlight kiss on the top of her head and heard the suppressed sob.

She had cared for that bastard, had trusted him. And he had taken her trust and dreams and trampled on them with about as much thought as he would have given to robbing her of her virtue. Less, in fact. He'd wanted her virtue.

She was speaking again. 'After Papa realised that, and that…Lord Fairbridge had mentioned marriage to me, he went straight up to the hall to demand that Lord Fairbridge marry me—' She broke off. The tremors that coursed through her shook Jack to his soul. 'I begged him not to go. By then…I…I didn't want to marry…anyone… I felt sickened…by what had happened…by what he wanted of me, but Papa wasn't listening. He…he has a…a tendency to be chivalrous and—'

'I know the rest,' said Jack, desperate to spare her part of this painful recital. 'He was taking laudanum for his stomach cramps and what with that and his upset over what had happened, he pocketed Fairbridge's snuffbox and the butler saw him do it.' He ground his teeth in rage. 'So Lady Fairbridge offered him the choice between prosecution and dropping his threat of a suit for breach of promise.'

Silence, cold and muffled by the falling snow.

'Yes,' said Cressida eventually.

He realised at once. There was more, something her fa-

ther had no inkling of, something Cressida would prefer
not to say.

'What else?'

'N…nothing.'

He pulled Pericles up and transferred the reins to one
hand. With his free one he caught her chin. Gently he
forced it up, willing his long fingers to remain still on the
silken skin, ruthlessly suppressing the urge to cover the
trembling lips with his own and kiss her until the whole
world whirled into oblivion.

'What else? Tell me, sweetheart.' He could not help the
endearment, it slipped from him before he knew it was
there.

And she shuddered. 'Andrew never really wanted me,'
she said quietly. 'All he wanted was to ruin me so that he
could force Papa to resign the living.'

'*What?*'

She nodded wearily. 'He…he came to see me again.
Two days later on the Sunday afternoon. By then everyone
in the village knew what had happened. I…I couldn't even
leave the house without being insulted, let alone go to
church. That…that was why the letter Papa wrote to you
never got posted. I couldn't go and he must have forgotten.' She drew a deep breath. 'Papa was resting when Fairbridge arrived…'

Sheer terror at what might have happened held Jack in
an icy grip.

'Yes?' He scarcely recognised his own voice.

'He told me to tell Papa that it would be necessary to
leave the living…that my behaviour…and his act of
theft—' She broke off on a sob. 'That was when I realised.
His younger brother had just taken orders. They wanted
the living for him. I had played right into his hands.'

Every drop of blood congealed to solid ice in his veins
as he understood her determination to protect her father
this time and heard the self-loathing in her voice.

Shivering, she went on. 'He told me that I could still be his mistress. I...I was so angry I picked up the poker and...'

'Clubbed him with it,' suggested Jack, when she paused. It was the least of what he'd do to Fairbridge when he caught up with him.

'N...not exactly,' said Cressida. 'I did swing at him, but he grabbed it. Only it was still hot from me stirring up the fire a moment before. So he screamed and left me alone.'

Despite his mingled fury and horror over what had happened to her, Jack choked slightly. 'I can just imagine,' he said unsteadily. There was, after all, a certain rough justice in Cressida having fought the brute off with a red-hot poker. A certain irony that he doubted Cressida appreciated.

But if she had flatly refused to consider becoming Fairbridge's mistress, then why...? 'Last night,' he said, very carefully, 'When I...asked...demanded...that you... Damn it all, Cressida! You didn't refuse! You let me think that you were a thief and that you were prepared to...to...' He couldn't even say it. The very thought shamed him.

'It was Papa's life this time...you were so angry... and...'

He couldn't let her go on. 'Don't, Cressida,' he said harshly. 'Don't remind me. I behaved as badly as Fairbridge, but I swear to you, I would never have acted on any of those threats. It was just that—'

He broke off. This was neither the time nor the place for this particular conversation. She needed warmth, food and sleep. He needed time to sort out his tangled thoughts. One thing seared itself into him with blinding clarity: he was going to protect Cressida one way or another, whether she liked it or not.

'Never mind,' he said quietly. 'All that matters is that you're safe. We'll sort it out tomorrow. For now we'll get home, bind up your ankle and you can have a sleep.'

She didn't answer beyond nodding her head, the movement caressing his chest.

Silence enveloped them apart from the squelch of Pericles's hooves and an occasional disgusted snort as snowflakes settled on his nose. Jack tightened his hold as Cressida relaxed, grew heavier until he knew she was asleep. Warm and trusting, she slept in his arms.

The wood, which he had scarcely noticed on the way out, suddenly leapt into life despite the gently falling snow. In sheltered places violets glowed purple and the elm blossom defied the cold, its tender green veil banishing winter. Spring was here and Cressida was exactly where she belonged. And the first thing he was going to do when he got home was burn that curst reference Meg had written for her. The future Mrs Jonathan Hamilton had absolutely no need to hire out as a governess.

Chapter Eleven

'N<small>O</small>.'

'Damn it, Cressida! I want you to marry me, not be my mistress!' Her unhesitating, not to say uncompromising, response flayed his conscience raw.

She faced him unflinchingly, her chin set at a stubborn angle, her mouth a flat line.

'No. I won't marry you.'

Jack cursed inwardly. Not even he could misconstrue that refusal. She wouldn't accept his proposal. He bit his lip. How the devil was he meant to protect her and see that she was kept safe and happy if she wouldn't marry him? Now that he knew the whole story, governessing was doubly impossible. Fairbridge had ruined her reputation beyond all repair save by a creditable marriage. The savage hypocrisy of society ensured that, even though she had saved herself, she was considered fallen. Soiled. If she married him, then she was safe beyond the tongues of all save the most hidebound. And even they would not dare cut her. They might murmur, but, by God, they had better do it damn quietly!

Frustrated, he frowned at the girl facing him quietly over his desk. She still looked as though she hadn't slept enough, but at least that haunted look had gone from her eyes. Small comfort when the tension in her frame was almost palpable.

He ran his hand through his hair. 'Cress, it's the only way to protect you from this mess. Don't you see…?'

'Why do you wish to protect me?'

'Why do I… *Why?*' Sheer disbelief robbed him of coherent speech for a moment. Then he said, carefully, 'I should have thought that was obvious.' He got the impression that she was choosing her words.

'I'm afraid not, sir.'

He clenched his fists. *Sir.* She held him at a distance with that cool formality.

'You see,' she continued, 'I have no idea why you think I need protecting, or why you should be the one to do it.'

One thing at a time. Jack took a very deep breath. 'Sweetheart, Fairbridge may not have ruined *you*, but he has certainly ruined your reputation. For most people that is enough. And Fairbridge made quite sure your credit was destroyed from what you said. He is not the only member of society with estates in Cornwall. Others who move in society will have heard the tale by now. If you try to find employment as a governess, it will only be a matter of time before word gets back to your employer.'

He watched contritely as she whitened. No need to add the obvious. She'd be turned off at once without a character, if she were lucky and it was her mistress who found out. The master of the household might well decide to hold his knowledge over her head and sample the wares before hurling her to the wolves.

'I see.' The tight control of her voice told Jack that she did, indeed, see. 'And why do you think that you ought to protect me?'

This was the tricky one.

'My behaviour towards you has been appalling. I've insulted you, asked you on two separate occasions to be my mistress…' He gritted his teeth. Now was not the moment to try and explain his earlier confusion, his overwhelming desire for her. He could well understand that she might be more than a little suspicious of male passion. As for his love…he didn't even know how to say it convincingly, but he'd have to try.

'Cressida, you are a member of my family. Our fathers were the closest of friends. And you were staying in my house where you ought to have been safe from insult. My own honour demands that I offer for you. And you must know that I…that I care for you. We…we would get on well together.' There! He'd said it!

Sort of.

A racking shudder nearly tore her apart. Despair and acceptance combined. His honour. No more. And certainly no less. Honour, chivalry, kindness. Everything any sane woman could desire in her husband. He was even a little fond of her. But they wouldn't make him return her love. And without that… She had no choice. Loving him as she did, she could not permit him to make such a sacrifice.

Swallowing tears, she answered. 'Very well, sir. You have satisfied the demands of your honour. And I must satisfy mine, which demands that I refuse you. Since my reputation was in tatters before we met and the circumstances had nothing to do with you, then—'

The expletive Jack uttered was no less shocking for being so softly uttered.

She felt her eyes widen in disbelief.

He flushed. 'I beg your pardon, Cress. But that is the most complete and utter—' He caught himself. 'It's arrant nonsense.'

'No, it's not.'

'Sweetheart…'

'No! I won't! I…I can't!'

I mustn't.

Frantically she fought for control, her fists clenching so hard the nails dug into her palms. She could resist anything but his tenderness. She loved him for his kindness and his chivalry, but she could withstand them. Against his tenderness she had no defence. It would shred her resolve in minutes and she'd be sobbing in his arms, confessing that she loved him. He'd never let her go then. He'd feel doubly responsible. She couldn't, simply couldn't, trap him like that in a web of his own decency.

'Please, don't ask me again, Jack. I can't bear it.'

'Damn!' Something inside Jack ripped apart at the broken whisper, and he strode around the desk and lifted her to her feet. He wanted to kiss her like he wanted to keep breathing. He shut his eyes and fought the urge. She needed comfort. So instead he enfolded her in his arms and held her gently, his cheek resting on her hair, one large hand caressing it, long fingers tugging it free of the ribbon.

He realised what he had done as he felt the cool, silken tresses spill over his hand, slide between his fingers as they wove their own soft spell of enchantment. He should release her, step away. Before he ruined everything again.

He could feel her resistance, then it was gone and she yielded, softening against him with a shuddering sob. He would let her go in a minute. As soon as he could. When he stopped breathing. She felt so utterly right in his arms. Sweet and relaxed. Warm soft breasts were pressed against him as she wound her arms about his waist, leaning against him trustingly. This time he would get it right. He had to take this slowly. Give her time to realise that he wasn't going to ravish her. At least not before he had managed to ask her father's permission to marry her. Hopefully not before her father had actually tied the knot. Tightly. He wasn't going to make any promises he couldn't keep, but he certainly wasn't going to kiss her now. He had to give her time to come to know him.

Her cheek shifted against his chest. Through his riding coat, waistcoat and a linen shirt, Jack felt the unintentional caress scorch into him. Every muscle in his body hardened as his hand came up helplessly to trace the line of her exposed cheek. So soft, so delicate. His blood took flight as the image came to him of that soft skin rubbing over his bare chest. His fingers shook as he stroked, found the corner of her mouth. Dear God. Nothing had ever been softer. Nothing had ever yielded quite so sweetly.

What was a man to do against that sort of temptation? His hand had found its way beneath her chin, urging it up gently. Need shuddered through him as he realised that a single teasing finger was all the encouragement she required. That she was responding—to his need and her own. That all she had ever done had been to respond honestly.

Shame lanced through Cressida.

'No.' She turned her head away from him. 'No. Please let me go.' This time she did not struggle. She knew he would release her. Even if he truly wanted her, his sense of honour would not permit him to force anything from her.

His arms dropped from her.

'Cressida…'

She had turned away from him.

He watched her go, his heart aching as he saw her straighten her shoulders and lift her head. The quiet thud of the door closing echoed in his soul.

She was going to leave. Nothing he could say would have the least effect on her decision.

How the devil was he supposed to go back to life without her?

The question stopped him cold. *Life without Cressida?*

He couldn't imagine it. He didn't even want to imagine it. *Without Cressida.* It sounded unspeakably dreary and empty. Chilly, too. Like his bed. And his heart wouldn't be any better.

He had to stop her leaving. He groaned. Why shouldn't she leave? He'd done everything to convince her that he held her in the lowest possible regard and, to crown his follies, he'd just proposed a marriage of convenience dictated by his conscience. His declaration of love had been tacked on the end like an afterthought. She had every reason to dislike him.

He couldn't force her into marriage. But only in marriage would she be safe. His own and the Rutherfords' sponsorship would go a fair way, but she needed a husband. The violent surge of irrational rage caught him by surprise. The thought of Cressida married to any but himself had him pacing back and forth. *It's unthinkable.*

Well, it has to be thought of. If she won't have me…

He came to a halt by the window out onto the terrace and stared out into the bleak, bare garden. He found it hard to believe that it would ever bloom again. How could he possibly have been so stupid, so caught up in his theorising about the ideal wife, not to see the truth when it had literally hurled itself into his arms?

His fist clenched unconsciously. He'd been a blind fool, but Lord! He'd never expected love to be such a damnably confusing complaint. Never in all his life had he been knocked endways by a woman. He hadn't expected to feel so…so bewildered by the whole thing. He'd always thought that love, when it finally came, would be a gentle, warm sort of thing. Naturally he had expected to feel desire for his wife, but not this fierce urge to possess at all costs.

No. Not at all costs. Not at the cost of Cressida's peace and happiness. That seemed to be the other queer thing about love. Her needs, her desires, ranked far above his in the order of things. He would give his right hand to spare her any further pain. Or even his life. And that was exactly what it felt like. His life. It wouldn't be worth living without Cressida.

If she couldn't bear the thought of marriage to him, then he would have to let her go. Protecting her was more important than possessing her. Or at least it damned well ought to be. His entire being howled in protest at the idea of her belonging to another man.

Savagely he forced himself to consider practicalities in a detached, rational manner. If Cressida were to marry— he ground his teeth—she needed to meet eligible men. Unfortunately, except for himself, eligible men were not exactly thick on the ground up here in Leicestershire. At least they were of course, but they were hunting foxes, not brides. And the end of the foxhunting season was nearly upon them anyway.

London. They'd have to take her to London. Introduce her into society. As his cousin and the friend of Lady Rutherford, she would be accepted. No doubt the Fairbridges would be in town. His mouth set in a hard line. Fairbridge would keep his mouth shut if he knew what was good for him. Reluctantly he abandoned any idea of calling the bastard to account for what he had done. It would cause gossip that might damage Cressida's chances.

Then he faced the biggest hurdle. Money. They would need money to buy her a suitable wardrobe to figure in fashionable society. And, above all, she needed a dowry. Very few eligible men were prepared to offer for a girl who was literally penniless. Not even those with more money than was good for them. A girl needed a dowry.

So he'd have to furnish her with one. A respectable amount. Enough to make her an eligible match, but not enough to interest the fortune hunters. It wouldn't make more than a small dent in his yearly income. He sighed as he faced the real problem. He'd thought before about a dowry for Cressida. God knew he had more money than he knew what to do with, but she'd never accept it. Not from him. Probably not from anyone but her father. He'd have to hoax her...

A calm, sympathetic voice broke in on his thoughts. 'I take it your proposal didn't go too well.'

Reluctantly, he turned to face Marc. 'You could put it like that. How the devil did you know?'

'What? That you were going to offer for Cressida? Or that she refused you?'

'Both,' responded Jack. He might have known that Marc would know what was afoot. After all, he'd told him the whole sorry story last night over a bottle of brandy.

Marc shrugged. 'Anyone who knows you could have worked out that you would feel obliged to offer for her under these circumstances. What remained to be seen was if she would accept you.' He strolled over to a side table and poured two glasses of brandy.

'Bit early for that, isn't it?' asked Jack irritably, perfectly aware that he was behaving badly.

With a faint smile, Marc shook his head. 'Not in the circumstances. Actually, in my humble opinion, you should have had one before you proposed.' He came over and shoved a cut glass tumbler into Jack's hand.

'I did,' growled Jack, with a brief nod of thanks. 'How did you know she refused me?'

Marc hesitated for a moment and then said unemotionally, 'Just that girls don't usually cry their eyes out after accepting an offer of marriage from one of the wealthiest men in the country. Even if he is a mere Mister. I knew you'd asked to see her this morning, so the rest was easy.'

Pain stabbed Jack. 'She was crying?' His voice came out hoarsely. Oh, hell! Could he do nothing but hurt her?

Marc nodded. 'Anything I can do, old chap?' He sipped his brandy.

Jack took a mouthful of brandy. It burned its way down, warming him very slightly. Almost as much as Marc's quiet presence.

'I'll need help getting her married off.'

Marc choked and spluttered over his drink. Obligingly Jack thumped him on the back.

'I…I beg your pardon?'

'You heard me.' Jack didn't feel up to actually repeating what he'd said. Just the thought of it was enough to rip him apart. Saying it made it seem real, as though it had already happened.

'Mmm. I *heard* you,' agreed Marc. 'But I'm damned if I understood you.'

Goaded to the end of his patience, Jack snapped, 'I should have thought the reasons were absolutely bloody obvious!' Then he groaned. 'Oh, lord. I'm sorry, Marc. Just ignore me. It's all such a confounded mess!'

'Love is a bit like that,' commented Marc. 'But I can guarantee one thing: watching her marry someone else won't help matters in the least!'

Silently Jack agreed. But that didn't alter the facts. Cressida had refused even to consider marriage to him. He couldn't force her to marry him. She had said she couldn't bear it. So he would have to bear it instead. If he couldn't possess her and protect her himself, then he would have to see that someone else did it. And pretend that he didn't care.

In the meantime Cressida needed a dowry.

It was only after he and Marc had thrashed out all the details, and Marc had gone to find Meg, that Jack recalled his words. *Love is a bit like that.* No surprise, nothing. Just a calm acceptance of the fact. Now he thought about it, he had never actually told Marc that he had fallen in love with Cressida.

But Marc had seen it all along. Probably before he had seen it for himself. No doubt Marc's perspicacity sprang from personal experience and long friendship. He bethought himself of Marc's final suggestion.

You know, old chap, there's no need to be quite so self-sacrificing. Once you've given her the opportunity to meet other eligible fellows, you can always court her yourself. If she can see that you are courting her because you want her, that there is no obligation on your part…take my word for it, no woman appreciates knowing that a man has offered for her from the promptings of honour.

Hope gleamed dully.

'Good heavens!' The uncharacteristic exclamation from her father broke through Cressida's fog of tiredness. She really hadn't slept well in the last two weeks. Not even knowing that her father was safe, that Jack understood his odd lapses and was perfectly happy to ask him to check his chamber from time to time if things went missing, had the power to raise her depressed spirits.

'How can this be?' Dr Bramley had a letter in his hand, an odd circumstance in itself.

'Who is it from, Papa?' asked Cressida, helping herself to a scone. They had so few acquaintances apart from those in Cornwall. She could think of no one who knew they were here.

'A firm of solicitors, Chadwick and Simms.' He looked up at Jack. 'Mr Simms describes himself as your man of business.'

It seemed to Cressida that Jack looked up from his breakfast with a complete lack of interest.

'That's correct, sir. He is. I mentioned your residence here in a letter a couple of weeks ago.'

'Well, that explains how he knew where to find me. But good heavens! What an amazing thing.'

'What is, Papa?' Cressida asked patiently.

'This letter, of course. I didn't even know he had died! Sad. All getting old now. But Morwell!'

'Papa! Who was Morwell?'

'If you mean Thurston Morwell, he was a distant family connection,' interjected Jack. 'He died last year.' He turned to Dr Bramley. 'My father often spoke of the tour the three of you made on the continent.'

Dr Bramley nodded. 'Very close we all were, but I

didn't expect this! Goodness me! Why, I shan't know what to do with such a sum of money!'

Cressida nearly dropped her scone. 'Money?'

Dr Bramley waved the letter at her. 'Apparently he left me ten thousand pounds! Dear me, just think what I can do with that. There must be so many poor, deserving souls I can help now!'

She bit back a groan of despair. Would Papa never, just for one moment, give some thought to his own security and well-being? Perhaps at the very least she could persuade him to invest the money safely in the Funds and subscribe to charity out of the income.

'Papa, do you think—?'

'Yes, indeed, I shall have to talk to the Vicar about how best to lay out this little windfall,' continued Dr Bramley enthusiastically.

'Papa—'

'With respect, sir, I have a suggestion for you.'

Jack's deep voice cut across Cressida effortlessly. 'You might find a worthy cause somewhat closer to home, if you think about it.'

'I might?'

The scone slipped from Cressida's suddenly nerveless fingers, landing on the floor at the Earl of Rutherford's feet. Just what the devil did Jack mean by that? He *knew* how little money they had. Where was Papa to go if the wretch's next accident out hunting resulted in a broken neck rather than a broken collarbone?

Jack's next words crashed into her just as Lord Rutherford handed her another scone.

'Settle the money on Cressida, if you feel that you have no need for it. She wouldn't need to become a governess, then. And the Rutherfords and I can take her up to London and introduce her to society. She would marry well with a respectable dowry.'

The floor tilted in a most disconcerting way as her

breath slammed out of her and the scone disintegrated in her suddenly trembling fingers. Had he taken leave of his senses? London society? If the Fairbridges once got wind of her in London, they'd destroy her. And Papa needed the money!

Dr Bramley, however, had welcomed the idea with enthusiasm. 'Of course! I never thought of that. It *would* provide a dowry for her. What an excellent idea! Well, that's settled then.' He smiled happily at Cressida. 'I'm sure you will be very happy, m'dear.' He turned to Jack. 'I dare say you could give instructions to Simms, could you? You'll know how these things are done.'

Lord Rutherford handed her yet another scone.

Breathing deeply, Cressida reached for self-control. Just to be on the safe side, she took a large bite of the scone. If she had a mouthful, she couldn't say all the blistering things that she wanted to say to the pair of them. Saying them to Papa would be a waste of breath. And saying them to Jack would have to wait until she caught him alone.

She cornered Jack in the estate office. He'd been there all morning with his agent. Now he was finally alone.

'Come in.'

His deep voice answering her firm tap sent shivers up and down her spine. Stiffening her spine and quelling the shivers, she went in. All she had to do was say exactly what she had spent the last three hours thinking about. All he had to do was listen. It ought to be simple.

He looked up and smiled as he saw her. Simple suddenly developed problems. How on earth was she supposed to concentrate when he looked at her like that? Determinedly she started.

'Papa needs the money, I don't.' Oh, bother. That was several sentences into her prepared speech. And those dark grey eyes had crinkled up at the corners distracting her even further.

'You're always direct, Cressida,' he observed.

She flushed to the roots of her hair. 'What I meant to say was—'

He interrupted smoothly. 'That you are concerned about your father's well-being if he gives away all his legacy. That you don't want a dowry because you have no intention of marrying and that you don't want to go to London because you will doubtless meet Fairbridge and his mother there. Does that about sum it up?'

Now his smile brought tears pricking hotly behind her eyelids. Unable to speak, she nodded. That covered nearly all her objections. The only one missing was the one about needing to escape before she succumbed to the temptation of telling him that she regretted refusing his offer. Or rather that she regretted having to refuse it. *He doesn't love you. His offer sprang from motives of chivalry and family loyalty.*

'There are answers to all those concerns, my dear,' he said gently. 'Your father is perfectly safe here. He has enough money for his needs and, even if I were to die, I have altered the terms of my will slightly to ensure that he is secure. He will receive a pension in the event of my death and the use of a house on the estate.'

'You had already done that?' she whispered.

He nodded. 'That was how Simms knew where to find him. I sent my instructions to him. The necessary documents came in the same post. It's all done and on the way back to London.'

'I see.' He had made quite sure of her father's security. Her heart ached. Kind, loyal, he was everything a woman could want in a husband.

'I still can't go to London. I…I don't want to marry.' She would never be able to bring herself to marry anyone else, even if anyone offered, which was doubtful.

He disabused her of that misapprehension at once. 'With ten thousand pounds, even with a slight misunderstanding in your past, you are perfectly eligible. Not a prize for the fortune hunters, but dowered well enough to gain a respectable offer.'

She shuddered at the thought. Marriage was unthinkable now. She could not give herself to another, loving him as she did.

He went on in a low voice. 'Even if you feel repugnance towards marriage after…after what has happened, the money will serve to make you independent. As a governess, you would always be at risk.'

She snatched at the chance. 'Very well, then. I don't need to go to London. You haven't thought, my reputation—'

His voice turned molten. 'Believe me, Cressida, if Fairbridge dares to open his mouth about what he did, I'll shut it for him. Permanently.'

Horror washed through her in an icy black flood. He meant to challenge Fairbridge. And Fairbridge was a crack shot…

'Jack, no…you mustn't…' Fear choked her, images of Jack wounded, dying, dead. Dazedly she clutched the edge of the desk for support and met his implacable gaze.

'Don't waste too much sympathy on him, Cress,' he advised. 'He certainly wasted none on you or your father.'

He thought she was worried about *Fairbridge*?

'Please, Jack, I don't want you to call him out…' Her voice broke in anguish that he could think she was frightened for Fairbridge. Yet if she told him the truth…she could find herself sobbing out her love for him. There would be no escape then.

'I won't be able to if you come to London,' he said quietly. 'The last thing I want to do is stir up talk. Calling that…' he paused, took a deep breath '…calling Fairbridge out would be a last resort, if he talks. But he won't. He won't dare. I'll make quite sure he knows what he's risking if he does.'

'But—'

His voice cut across her harshly. 'You can't stay here, Cressida. It's impossible.'

Icy pain stabbed through her as his words went home. Knowing she had to leave, and knowing he wanted nothing more devoutly, were two entirely different sorts of hurt. 'I see.' She forced her voice to quiet indifference. 'Very well, then. When do you wish me to leave?' The words rang between them with merciless clarity.

Equally cold, he replied, 'Marc and Meg intend going home in a few days. They have suggested that you go with them and that they will take you up to town at the start of the Season in a couple of weeks, as Marc suggested on your birthday.'

As soon as possible.

A shiver knifed through her. He must really want to get rid of her quickly if he wouldn't even let her stay for another two weeks.

Unconsciously she clutched the edge of the desk, staring blindly at the bookshelves beyond him with their ranks of old estate books. The fire crackled mockingly, offering a warmth she could not feel. The cold striking through her came from deep within. She shivered again as the chill tightened its grip. Soon she would not feel the cold or the pain. She would be frozen.

'Go up to your chamber, Cressida.' Jack's harsh voice drew her momentarily from the ice of the abyss. 'I'll have a tray sent up to you there.'

'Thank you,' she said tonelessly. She wouldn't cry. She wouldn't. Tears were warm. And they hurt too much. They would thaw out the ice, leaving her exposed to hope. And more hurt.

Jack watched her leave, battling the urge to leap to his feet, grab her and kiss her into submission. Hell, she needed warming! She looked so cold and tired. As though all the life had been drained out of her. *Better a fire and dinner on a tray than you pressing an unwanted suit on her.*

Thank God she had agreed to go to London! Lord, he hadn't even been able to sit in the same room with her for five minutes without wanting to make love to her! Just as well he'd been seated at the desk the whole time. Otherwise she'd have known exactly what was on his mind.

He had spent the last two weeks trying to show her that he cared about her. She had spent the last two weeks trying to avoid him. Every time he entered a room she froze. If she could, she made a quiet excuse to remove herself. And if he touched her in any way, he could feel the tension coiling within her.

There was no point remembering the sweetness of her mouth under his, the feel of her curves fitting so perfectly against his body. If she had ever felt anything for him, if there had ever been the potential for her to care for him as he now cared for her, then he had destroyed it the night he accused her of being a thief and offered to take her as his mistress.

Morosely, he returned to his estate tallies. Usually it was a job he enjoyed, but now all he could think of was how much he would have liked to show Cressida how it was done. How much he would have enjoyed seeing the quick comprehension flood her vivid face. How much he would have enjoyed her laughter and questions as they shared the task. As they shared their lives. He'd thought he wanted a wife who would leave his life much as it had been. A smiling, undemanding presence on the edges of his world that could care for. Fate had ignored him and sent him exactly what he needed. And he, damned fool that he was, had handed it straight back without even realising it.

Cressida wandered out into the garden and looked up at the house. Mellow golden stone smiled back at her. She blinked back tears. This might have been her home. It still could be if she went to Jack and accepted his offer. But he wanted her to go. He had offered when she had nothing to recommend her to anyone else. When his honour demanded it. Now she had a dowry, connections. She had suddenly become eligible. And Jack had arranged for her to leave.

She would be going to London for the Season and she might as well enjoy it as best she could. Never mind that she had no intention of accepting any offer of marriage. After the Season was over, she would find herself a small cottage in the country where Papa could visit her occasionally. She had ample money to live simply. And if she found somewhere near Lord Rutherford's principal seat, then she would have a friend close by.

She was a great deal better off than she had been when they left Cornwall. Papa had a safe and respected position, she had an independence and at least one dear friend. So why on earth were the budding flower borders disappearing in a haze of tears? She dragged a handkerchief out of her sleeve and blew her nose violently. Surely in time her pain would fade? Wouldn't it? She drew a deep breath. Whether it faded or not was immaterial. What she had to do now was behave as though it had done so already.

Chapter Twelve

'Are you quite sure about this neckline, Meg?' Cressida looked at the silk-clad vision in the modiste's mirror and blinked. Surely that could not possibly be her? Why, she actually looked elegant, pretty even. The shimmering blue-green silk did odd things to her eyes as well. But the un-accustomed exposure of her cleavage... 'It looks very low.'

Meg's sister-in-law, Lady Diana Carlton, chuckled.

Meg glared. 'Tell me, as an academic question—if you saw it on another woman, me for instance, would you think it scandalous?'

Caught by surprise, Cressida considered the matter dis-passionately. Meg had worn a gown cut low across the breasts just the previous night. It had looked lovely. And there was no mistaking Lord Rutherford's opinion. His of-ten rather cold grey eyes had flared as they rested on his wife gowned for a ball.

'Well?'

A reluctant smile tugged at her lips. 'No. I wouldn't. But you are a Countess...'

'Granted,' said Meg, 'that gown would not do for a girl of seventeen in her first Season, but you are one and twenty, possessed of a respectable fortune and Jack Hamilton's cousin to boot. Di agrees with me.' She turned to Lady Diana. 'Don't you, Di?'

Lady Diana nodded. 'Perfectly unexceptionable. Indeed, I can think of only one person who will be at all shocked by that neckline.'

The modiste added her mite. '*Ravissement, mademoiselle! Les gentilhommes* will be, 'ow do you put it? *Bouleversé?*'

'Bowled over?' suggested Meg.

'*Exactement!*' enthused the modiste. 'An' *moi*, I tell ze truth. It does my business no good if you wear the wrong dress! Now, consider if you please, ze pelisse...'

Cressida gave up. If Meg, Lady Diana Carlton and a fashionable modiste all thought the gown appropriate, who was she to argue? If they all said no one would be offended, then no one would be offended. Except, of course, for that mysterious someone alluded to by Lady Diana. Oh, well. One person couldn't matter all that much, surely.

Jack glared at the swirl of dancers in puritanical disapprobation. Why had he never before realised just how disgracefully low women's necklines had become. Brazen hussies! Lord, he wondered that they didn't all contract an inflammation of the lungs. While he, on the other hand, felt far too hot. Just thinking of that gown Cressida was almost wearing, as she pranced about Almack's Assembly Rooms with every gazetted rake in London, was more than enough to heat his blood. His cravat felt as if it would choke him! As did his satin kneebreeches, which, in deference to the immutable laws of Almack's almighty patronesses, he had donned with much cursing and reluctance.

Just what the hell had Meg been thinking of when they ordered that gown anyway? Chaperons were supposed to bait the trap and display the goods, so to speak. But damn it all! The bodice practically grazed Cressida's nipples! Which was precisely what he wanted to do. With his teeth.

He clenched one fist and glared a bit harder. Thank God no one had yet given Cressida permission to waltz here. The sight of her whirling in the embrace of one of his lecherous friends would probably consign him to Bedlam, worrying if she were about to fall out of her gown.

The music drew to a close and he watched possessively as Cressida came off the dance floor with Lord Parbury. He'd always considered Parbury a friend, but what the devil did the fellow think he was up to, flirting like that with the chit? There! She was laughing again. Practically giggling. Dash it all, he'd never found anything Parbury uttered worth laughing over.

But at least she was happy again. Somewhere, between Leicestershire and London, Meg had managed to dispose of the sad, dispirited girl who had left Wyckeham Manor. In her place was the outspoken, impertinent elf of old. Flirting with all the *ton*'s most eligible bachelors, with the notable exception of Mr Jack Hamilton.

To his utter horror he saw Lady Stanhope, with dear Alison in her wake, sailing in his direction. Good God! He could end up dancing with the wench! Panicked, he reacted instinctively and found to his immense surprise and annoyance, that he had automatically moved to intercept Cressida and Lord Parbury as they headed back towards Lady Rutherford.

'I'll escort Miss Bramley, Parbury. No doubt you have other fish to fry this evening.' He really couldn't help the growl in his voice. It just happened. Something about his stiff jaw, no doubt.

Parbury's answering grin didn't help in the least. 'But none so charming as your little cousin, Jack, old fellow. Permit me to congratulate you on acquiring such a lovely ward.'

'She's *not* my ward!'

'I'm *not* his ward!'

The hasty denials tumbled over each other in their vehemence.

Lord Parbury choked, an endeavour in which Jack felt seriously tempted to assist. In the nick of time he recalled the impropriety attached to strangling a peer of the realm within the sacred portals of the Marriage Mart.

'Of course not, old chap,' Parbury said soothingly. 'But you do such a sterling imitation! Have you been taking lessons from Rutherford? I note he's got the jealous-husband routine down to a fine art. Miss Bramley, if you will excuse me, I'll leave you to your cousin. I'm sure he will return you safely to Lady Rutherford. Perhaps you might care to drive with me one day in the Park?'

Cressida replied with what Jack considered to be quite unnecessary enthusiasm. 'I should like that very much, my lord.'

'I shall call, then,' he assured her as he bowed gracefully over her hand. 'Your servant, ma'am. Evening, Jack.' He strolled off and Jack's hackles subsided somewhat.

Only to rise again as Cressida asked resignedly, 'Very well, Mr Hamilton—what's wrong with him?'

'Damned rake and libertine!' growled Jack as he started walking. If they stayed still, Lady Stanhope would have every opportunity for a broadside.

'What? Another one? But Meg assured me he was a friend of yours!' She looked up at him challengingly. 'Don't you have *any* respectable friends?'

Jack wondered which he wanted to do more—throttle her or run his finger along beneath the edge of her bodice.

Dragging in a deep breath, he forced himself to accept that neither alternative would meet with society's approval. Then he found a use for the breath he had taken—enumerating to Cressida exactly which of society's single men he considered suitable dance partners for her. A detached and irritatingly astute part of his brain suggested that there could only be one motive for leaving out every unmarried man between the ages of twenty and sixty.

He only realised the danger his preoccupation had invited when it was breathing down his neck.

'At last! My dear Mr Hamilton, I vow it has been impossible to come at you. But I knew you would like to see dear Alison, so I have persevered!'

Lady Stanhope came up with the quarry in full cry, Alison close on her heels.

'Ah, Miss Bramley. How very singular. Do you know, I have just had the most interesting chat with my cousin.' Lady Stanhope paused and bestowed upon Cressida the full benefit of her long-nosed stare. 'My cousin who lives in Cornwall, I mean. The Dowager Lady Fairbridge. I understand you to be quite well, ah, known to her.' Her eyes glittered with malice.

Every nerve in Jack's body flared to full battle alert. The presumptuous *cow*! 'Yes, indeed, Lady Stanhope. Miss Bramley's father did mention the connection. Perhaps you might be good enough to convey to his lordship's mother my desire to further explore the issue with her son.'

Lady Stanhope discovered herself to be dangerously exposed to superior firepower and beat a hasty retreat.

'Jack! Please…' He felt Cressida's hand tighten convulsively on his sleeve. 'Can't I go home? She knows! They must have talked. I *knew* this would happen! Please, let me go.'

He looked down into her stricken face. 'Tell me, Cress. If it were not for the Fairbridges and Lady Stanhope, would you enjoy London?'

She stared as if she thought he had gone mad. Stupid question. What female would not enjoy the social whirl, the shops, the opera, the gossip? 'Well, of course I would. Only…only not all year.' Her eyes grew distant. 'Not even every year. Just imagine; never seeing the spring flowers, never seeing the woods go mad with bluebells and the trees bud. I suppose coming up to town for a week or so would be nice, but...isn't being at home better?'

His heart lurched violently, but his response died in his throat as another voice chipped in.

'Hello, hello! Jack, old man! Is this your little cousin? I heard she was charmin'. Quite charmin'. Lord Danville, Miss Bramley. Perhaps you might have a dance free for me?'

Meg, having watched Jack chase off Lord Parbury, with mingled amusement and consternation, turned to Lady Jersey in exasperation. 'What is wrong with him!'

The Countess of Jersey didn't reply for a moment, being fully occupied with Lady Stanhope's forlorn hope. Then she shrugged. 'Who knows? He's a man, my dear. Could it be that? Mind you, my love, he did see off Lady Stanhope in fine style. Much must be forgiven him for that effort. Such a tedious creature!'

Despite her annoyance, Meg laughed and then frowned as she watched Jack don full battle dress for the inoffensive Lord Danville.

'Goodness me,' breathed Lady Jersey as Jack saw off Lord Danville. 'I always thought Jack's eyes were grey! A delightfully stormy grey for the right woman, no doubt, but I do believe I detect the merest hint of green this evening! How splendid! And such utterly splendid sport to see dear Jack engaged on two fronts.'

Meg laughed again behind her elegant chickenskin fan and darted a glance sparkling with challenge at her friend. 'Sally, are you feeling suitably meddlesome this evening?'

The Queen of the *ton*, and its most inveterate gossip, didn't bat so much as an eyelash. 'But of course, my dear. Did you have something particular in mind, or just general nosiness?'

Meg smiled seraphically. 'Wouldn't you say that my protégée's behaviour is unexceptionable, Lady Jersey?

And you are a Patroness, after all. What use is power if one doesn't wield it?' She gazed pointedly at Jack. 'Isn't the next dance a waltz?'

Lady Jersey smothered a grin and said unsteadily, 'I believe so, Lady Rutherford. How deliciously convenient. After all, only a madman fights on three fronts at once.'

Their eyes met and saw that they were in agreement just as a deep voice behind them said, 'My dance, I believe, my lady. Hello, Sally.'

Meg swung around, struggling to quell her laughter and aware from the palpable suspicion on Marc's face that she had not succeeded in the least. His glance flickered from one laughing countess to the other.

'Hmm. Should I ask, or would ignorance be safer?' He possessed himself of Meg's hand and kissed it.

'Much safer, my lord,' she said, smiling at him. 'But if you watch Sally…'

His gaze followed Lady Jersey as she stalked her quarry through the crowd… 'Good God! She's not? Is she?'

'Dear Jack,' purred Lady Jersey, 'how splendid, simply splendid, to see you here! And Miss Bramley! I do hope you are enjoying yourself, my dear. You seem to have danced every single dance this evening. Lady Rutherford and all your well-wishers must be delighted at your success.'

Cressida blushed and stammered a disjointed response as Jack eyed the peeress warily. There was no escape. What the devil was Sally about now?

He found out.

'Miss Bramley, it would be such a pity to break your run, so to speak, but the next dance is a waltz, of course. So I just popped over to say how much pleasure it would give all of us to see you take part.' She smiled with what Jack considered to be wholly malicious intent as the orchestra struck up. 'Goodness me, how vexatious. There is no time to find you an eligible young man. But perhaps Mr Hamilton might care to oblige? Just this once, of course! When it is perceived that you have our approval, you will be swarmed under with eager gentlemen.'

She sailed off with a final wave, having completely out-flanked her opponent.

Even as he realised that he had won several battles, only to lose the war, Jack wondered which would be the greater trial—watching Cressida take the floor in a waltz with any other man in London, or dancing with her himself. Grimly he looked down at Cressida and discovered her biting her lip.

'There is absolutely no need for you to put yourself out, sir. I quite understand that you do not wish to dance with me. Perhaps you might escort me to Lady Rutherford.'

His heart clenched at the carefully indifferent tone. He'd hurt her. Again. Understandably, she saw only that he didn't wish to dance with her. And drew the obvious conclusion.

'It will be my great pleasure to escort you to Lady Rutherford,' he said huskily, and drew her into the dance.

Shocked green eyes flashed to his face. 'Jack? I mean—'

'Jack,' he said firmly. God, but she felt sweet in his arms, just as he remembered, so warm and silken, her waist so deliciously supple under his hand... He smiled down at her, consigning all his misgivings to hell. As he whirled by, he bestowed upon Lady Stanhope and dear Alison the most radiant of smiles and then returned his adoring gaze to Cressida. They could report *that* to the Fairbridges.

'But...but you said you would escort me to Meg,' she protested, her own gaze fully focused on the top button of his waistcoat.

The curve of his lips deepened as he answered. 'Meg, if you will but look about you...' he swung her around expertly '...is dancing with Marc. But don't imitate them,' he warned, observing that the Earl of Rutherford had, as usual, drawn his Countess scandalously close and was doubtless whispering sweet nothings in her ear, very much as he wished to do to Cressida. His whole body tingled at the thought of drawing her closer, feeling her thighs, not just the silken skirts, slide past his.

His arms tightened instinctively before he could check himself. To his utter horror he realised that he had encouraged her to do exactly what he had just warned her against. That his unthinking, possessive action had brought her dangerously close, that the dreamy, summery scent of rosewater was wreathing its enchantment, seducing his senses.

He stifled a groan and concentrated on dancing, trying to ignore the pounding of his blood. She looked so lovely this evening. The blue green silk Meg had helped her choose did something to her eyes. Or was that just his heart? And her hair looked so silky, so soft, he ached to stroke it, to feel the sensuous slide of it through his fingers.

Desperately he fought the urge to tighten his hand on her back, to bring her closer still. Music swirled around them, the rhythm sweeping them along. She felt like thistledown in his arms, moving with him so lightly and easily.

How could dancing with Jack be so totally different from practising with her dancing master? Or the Earl of Rutherford? Cressida pondered this dizzily as Jack whirled her around the room. After the initial shock of dancing in a man's arms, she had found dancing with Signor Ridolpho and Marc quite easy. Indeed, the Earl had been only too happy to help her practise the steps when he found her practising with Meg in the drawing room at Rutherford House.

Dancing with Jack was another matter entirely. Not a single shiver had feathered up and down her spine dancing with Signor Ridolpho. Not even the devastatingly handsome Earl of Rutherford had made her feel flustered. He'd teased and instructed her in the steps and her heart had remained unmoved in its place. Now it pounded so hard, she could not think rationally about Lady Stanhope's half-voiced threat.

Dimly she knew that between them Lady Stanhope and Lady Fairbridge could destroy her, but Jack's arms encircled her like steel and she felt safe. His body radiated heat and power and her wretched heart had bolted like a runaway horse. Her whole body tingled at the nearness of his. Her breasts felt most peculiar, flushed and aching, so that she longed to press against him to ease their torment. Or to increase it. And she felt safe. She had never been in more danger.

The room had become insufferably hot. She'd expected to freeze in this light gown with its scandalous neckline, despite Meg's insistence that she'd be quite warm enough. Meg had been right. Blushing like this would warm a marble statue. And the look on Jack's face didn't help in the least. Set in stone, his expression suggested that he had slammed the lid on something unwanted.

'Is something bothering you?'

Her question obviously caught him off guard. He tried to dissemble. 'How did you...? No! Why?' The flush of colour on his cheekbones, as well as the near slip, betrayed him.

Aware that he had slipped, Jack tried to relax slightly, to smile at her. But the hard tension sang in his body, pounded in his veins.

'Because you look as though you are in pain,' she said as he whirled her around. 'I thought perhaps your shoulder...'

As he shook his head, he caught Marc's amused, and not unsympathetic, glance. The Earl of Rutherford would have a very fair idea just which portion of Jack's anatomy was in most discomfort. And it certainly wasn't his shoulder.

'My shoulder is quite all right,' he said tightly. The rest of him might have tied itself in knots, but his shoulder had recovered nicely.

The end of the dance came eventually, leaving Jack uncertain as to whether it had been joy or torture. To his absolute horror he could see any number of eligible gentlemen with their eyes firmly on Cressida. Sally Jersey had given the chit permission to waltz. As far as the men were concerned, that was enough. Open season.

Seeing that he was about to be besieged by half the men in London, he turned Cressida towards the refreshment tables. 'A glass of lemonade, Cress.' He was tempted to down one himself if it had enough ice in it. Something had to cool him down. A languid voice stopped him in his tracks and made every muscle in his body leap to full battle alert.

'Miss Bramley, how charming to meet you here. Do you know, I couldn't quite believe it when my mama informed me that you had come up to town.'

Jack felt Cressida's hand freeze on his arm. He looked down sharply as she turned. Her face was quite composed, her voice utterly calm.

'Good evening, Lord Fairbridge.'

Somehow Jack contained his simmering rage as he looked the Viscount up and down. A mill at Almack's was out of the question, yet he could not control the instinctive clenching of his fists, or the note of contempt that crept into his voice.

'My cousin has mentioned her *acquaintance* with you, Fairbridge. You might wish to consider the fact that she is under *my* protection now. I do hope Lady Stanhope conveyed my message to you.'

The barely leashed menace in his voice brought Cressida's head around with a jerk. Never, even when he had been angriest with her, had she heard that particular note. And his eyes—they had gone hard, like stone, flint. Cold and dangerous. She had always thought of him as civilised, quiet, scholarly. A thorough-going gentleman. Evidently she had missed something.

So, apparently, had Lord Fairbridge. 'Your cousin, is she, Hamilton?' The Viscount did not seem to have noticed Jack's narrowed eyes and clenched fists. He was busily engaged in removing a speck of dust from his coat sleeve. 'Miss Bramley never mentioned that.' He favoured Cressida with his most charming smile. 'And how does your father go on, Miss Bramley? I trust he has recovered from his indisposition.'

She could barely bring herself to answer civilly. This was the man who had plotted to deprive her father of his living and then threatened to have him transported.

He could still do it if you offend him. Fear shivered through her. Jack and the Rutherfords might be able to salvage her reputation if Andrew gossiped, but if once he went to Bow Street, nothing would save her father. So she forced a smile to her lips and spoke lightly. 'My father is very well, my lord. I shall tell him you asked when next I write to him.' The lie nearly choked her.

'You're looking as fine as fivepence, Miss Bramley.' His eyes wandered and Cressida wished, not for the first time, that she had resisted Meg's ideas on necklines far more strenuously. His gaze seemed to creep over her with an almost tangible slither.

Never before had she been so conscious of the unyielding strength of Jack's arm as she was now, when her gloved hand lay on his sleeve. To the world it must look as though she had two eligible bachelors dangling on her string. She felt more like a lamb hiding behind a very large sheepdog to escape the jaws of a wolf.

'Miss Bramley, might I escort you to my mother?' suggested Lord Fairbridge. 'Mama said she would look forward to renewing the acquaintance.'

Dizzily, Cressida attempted to reconcile this assertion

with the matron who had stigmatised her as a scheming little slut at their last meeting. Perhaps she wanted to re-state her case.

'Then you might do me the honour of dancing with me,' he went on, his tone suggesting that he was the one be-stowing the honour.

Before she could even draw breath to respond, Jack saved her the trouble. 'Another time, Fairbridge,' said Jack. 'I have promised to return my cousin safely to her chaperon. And I believe Miss Bramley's card to be full this evening. No doubt Lady Rutherford will be happy to receive Lady Fairbridge should she wish to call in Gros-venor Square.'

Fairbridge looked startled. 'The Countess of Ruther-ford?'

For a moment Cressida thought the sheepdog had turned into a wolf. Only a fool would have thought Jack's smile friendly.

'Quite so, Fairbridge. I hope that clarifies the situation for you and Lady Fairbridge.'

She found that she was being led away inexorably. Re-lief sang through her. Perhaps seeing him would become easier as she gained confidence, but somehow she doubted it. Why ever had he come up to her? Did he intend to renew his *offer*? That didn't sound quite right, but she couldn't think what else to call it. Proposition? Proposal? No matter. The important thing now was to convince Jack that Fairbridge's presence didn't bother her in the least.

She could feel the anger surging out of him. His arm, under her white gloved hand, had turned to steel, and, when she glanced up, his jaw looked as though it had petrified. The fear that he might use the slimmest of pre-texts to challenge Fairbridge slammed back into her. Vi-sions of Jack, dead or maimed on her behalf, choked her. Forcing a deep breath into her lungs and offering up a mental apology for the lie she was about to utter, Cressida said, 'It's so nice to see a familiar face after so many strangers. How kind of him to speak to me. I wonder if Lady Fairbridge will call?'

How Jack managed to return a civil reply was more than he could understand. But he did. Wondering just how he could have been so stupid as to send Cressida up to London with a respectable dowry.

Much to Cressida's horror Lady Fairbridge did call. The very next day.

She had caught only fleeting glimpses of the Viscountess through the crowd at Almack's. The only dances she had free had been the waltzes and they were soon snapped up by eager gentlemen. But she had been conscious very often of a cold, considering gaze upon her.

She was sitting in the drawing room of Rutherford House alone, when the butler came to inform her that Lady Fairbridge had called.

He smiled kindly. 'Naturally I told her that her ladyship was not at home, but she said she would be happy to see you. I said that I would ask if you were at home.'

Cressida took a deep breath. Meg was upstairs, nursing Jon. What should she do? She could ask Delafield to deny her. The last thing she wanted was to confront Lady Fairbridge alone. On the other hand, it might be best to see her alone. No doubt she had observed her son last night and wished to make her opposition to any connection quite plain. A shiver took her. It would be better to see Lady Fairbridge alone. Then she could assure her that she had no interest in Lord Fairbridge. That she would prefer never to see him again.

There was no point in hiding.

'Please inform Lady Fairbridge that I am at home,' she said at last.

She did not have long to wait.

'Lady Fairbridge.' Delafield closed the door behind the dragon and Cressida rose to her feet, coming forward.

'How do you do, ma'am?' She might as well be polite. 'Will you not be seated?'

She was enveloped in a heavy cloud of ambergris and purple satin. 'My dear Miss Bramley! I am in tolerable health. So surprised we were to hear of your presence in town! How naughty of you not to write and let me know! But it's always so nice when old friends appear unexpectedly! And how is your dear papa? Recovered from his malady, I trust?'

Disbelief robbed Cressida of rational thought, let alone speech, as she emerged gasping.

'I...er...he's very well. I didn't think...that is...you were not...'

Her ladyship sailed on. 'Of course, Fairbridge was delighted to see you last night. I had no idea that Mr Hamilton was a connection. And how is his dear mama, Lady Anna? Such a charming creature, don't you think? Is she not in London?'

Lady Fairbridge disposed her amply cushioned behind on the sofa and patted the place beside it invitingly.

Cressida pretended not to see and moved to the bellpull. Stumbling over the words, she explained that Lady Anna Hamilton was staying with her daughter in Yorkshire, that she had never met either lady and would Lady Fairbridge care for some refreshment?

Lady Fairbridge indicated the place beside her again. Gingerly Cressida seated herself at the extreme end of the sofa. What had Jack done? He had assured her that Fairbridge would not dare to cause trouble. Could he possibly have issued enough threats to cause this *volte face*? Had he, in fact, informed Fairbridge that he owed Miss Cressida Bramley marriage?

Clinging to the conventions governing polite conversation, Cressida smiled and responded to her guest, searching for a clue that might explain the mystery. It came as she poured a cup of tea. 'Sugar, ma'am?' She held the tongs poised.

'Oh, just a teeny lump, my dear. Thank you.' Lady Fairbridge accepted the cup. 'What a happy circumstance for you, that little legacy! I heard all about it, you know. So handy for a girl!'

How had she heard? They had said nothing to anyone.

Lady Fairbridge gave a tinkling laugh. 'Now, my dear! You must not look so surprised. These things get about in the country. My cousin, Lady Stanhope, knew all about it!'

She rattled on, enumerating all the advantages of a girl with a respectable dowry. Shaking inwardly, Cressida saw the true significance of her dowry. It could turn the Vicar's daughter from a useful tool, no better than she should be, into an eligible débutante, courted by eligible bachelors and their mamas.

The delicate basaltware teacup she held rattled on its saucer. She took a deep breath to steady herself. Perhaps Lady Fairbridge had been misinformed. Could ten thousand pounds really be sufficient bait for a Vicar's scheming daughter to hook a whole, live Viscount? Or had rumour exaggerated her circumstances?

'Of course, it wasn't a terribly big legacy,' she said confidingly. 'Only ten thousand pounds, you know.'

Lady Fairbridge didn't bat so much as an eyelash. 'Of course not, my dear. But it still helps. Of course, I have a girl in my eye for Andrew.' She smiled conspiratorially. 'So important that he should settle down and secure the succession, you understand. A marriage of the right sort is so important.'

Listening to the clues dropped by Lady Fairbridge, Cressida came to the conclusion that the Dowager had an absolute paragon in mind for Andrew. Lady Fairbridge was understandably coy about stating exactly what she meant by a *respectable dowry*, but no doubt the girl had a dowry of land and enough liquid assets to make her own fortune seem paltry. She wished them joy of each other.

The advent of Lady Rutherford took the conversation into other channels. Meg apologised charmingly for not being present to greet her guest and said with a smile, 'But Miss Bramley is quite invaluable to me.'

Cressida continued to be amazed at this side of Meg—the glittering society hostess. Charming, delightful, but with a reserve that kept Lady Fairbridge at a distance. Skilfully she deflected all of Lady Fairbridge's questions and made it obvious at every turn that Cressida was a close friend.

Eventually Lady Fairbridge rose to take her leave.

Lady Rutherford rang the bell. 'Goodbye, ma'am. Shall we see you at Lady Verner's soirée this evening?'

Lady Fairbridge preened slightly. 'Oh, yes. Aurelia is always very select about whom she invites to her soirée. I have prevailed upon Fairbridge to escort me.' She cast an indulgent glance at Cressida. 'I dare say you and he will have a great deal to say to one another. I know he thought escorting his mama would be a dead bore. We shall look out for you.'

'How lovely. We shall look forward to it.' Meg's practised charm covered Cressida's very undignified gasp. Good God! Surely she didn't think…? *She* couldn't be Lady Fairbridge's well-dowered paragon…could she? With an Amazonian effort, Cressida managed to pull herself together to bid Lady Fairbridge farewell.

'So delightful to see you, dear Cressida. Perhaps you might escort me to my carriage? We shall not trouble Lady Rutherford to ring for her butler that way.'

Far too shocked to come up with a good excuse, Cressida acquiesced. Lady Fairbridge continued to expatiate on the elegance of Rutherford House until they reached the front door.

Then, 'Dear Cressida, I do hope you will feel inclined to pass over our little misunderstanding last winter. Dear Andrew…' she gave vent to a tinkling laugh '…I had no idea he was so constant! But he is of the same mind as ever, so I must withdraw my opposition and hope you will forgive him and…and…well, *you* know!'

Bile rose in Cressida's throat. Cold denials jostled on her lips, until she noticed the stolid-faced footman holding the front door open. If any hint of this got back to Jack, if he thought her unwilling to be pursued by Fairbridge… She shuddered. She would have to come up with some other way of putting Andrew off.

She summoned a smile and a few non-committal words and took herself back to the drawing room after seeing Lady Fairbridge into her landau.

Meg was on the sofa, fanning herself with the *Morning Post*. 'Phew! I do wish she'd wear less scent! Well, there you are. At least one mama with a hopeful son is courting you! What a pity it had to be her.'

'Do they really do that?' Despite her horror at the thought of being in Lady Fairbridge's matrimonial sights, Cressida found the idea intriguing. Besides, she wanted to head Meg away from the idea of Lady Fairbridge pursuing her.

Meg chuckled. 'Those with younger sons to dispose of do. They don't usually have to bother about the eldest sons. They might need a little prodding to get them out of the clubs and into the Marriage Mart, but their expectations will do the rest of the job for them. The younger sons, however, generally need to marry money. Or so Diana tells me.' She frowned. 'You can hint him away easily enough, I dare say. Or I can have Marc do so. Better not to ask Jack. His temper seems a little touchy at the moment.'

Cressida hesitated and then said, 'Meg, I think at the moment it might be best not to hint Lord Fairbridge away.' She wouldn't wager a groat on the likelihood of Marc not telling Jack and Jack wouldn't wait to be asked. He'd go and do his own hinting.

'Are you sure?' Meg sounded worried.

Cressida plastered a determined smile on her face. 'Oh, yes. There is no point in offending Lady Fairbridge. And I dare say that now I have a dowry, Andrew will look on me with greater respect. There cannot be anything to worry about!'

Just over a month later Jack sat in the reading room of Brook's, inwardly fuming. He would have liked to fume outwardly but Marc had not yet arrived to keep their appointment. He glared at the newspaper. Mindless drivel, all of it. He folded it and set it down with a snap.

What the devil was keeping…ah, there he was. No doubt he'd been tying his cravat for two hours.

'You took your time,' he growled.

'The gossip's getting worse, old man.' Marc ignored the snarl in Jack's voice as he sank into a chair. 'Apparently one or two hostesses have asked just how long Meg will be "obliged" to chaperon Miss Bramley.'

He leaned forward and poured himself a brandy while his best friend cursed fluently and at length, ending with, 'I swear I'll kill him!'

'Sssssshhhhhhhh!'

The indignant protest came from the opposite corner where a group of the commons were attempting to have a serious political discussion over a friendly game of hazard.

'You're interrupting play, old chap,' observed Marc laconically. 'Or the governance of the nation. But I dare say the former is of more consequence!'

Despite his rage, Jack laughed at this cynicism as he glanced at the group in the corner. 'Oh, they're all right. They just need something to keep their minds occupied while they talk politics.' Then he frowned. 'You're trying to head me off,' he accused.

'Mmm. I thought I'd succeeded,' answered Marc. 'If you must have it, while calling Fairbridge out might afford you satisfaction, it will not help Cressida in the least. You know how these affairs go: the moment someone reacts with a challenge, the rumour is confirmed. Besides, there's nothing to suggest that the talk started with him *per se*. Let's face it, little though you, or even I, might like it, to all appearances he's courting the girl.'

Frustration howled, but Jack forced himself to nod his head curtly. 'Very well. I'll have to think up some other pretext to put a ball into him. Any ideas?'

Marc spluttered over his brandy. 'Ah, not just off hand.'

'Damn it, Marc!' said Jack in savage undertones. 'You nearly took a horsewhip to Winterbourne in front of Sally Jersey when he tried to abduct Meg! Are you seriously telling me that I have to sit back and let that bastard Fairbridge ruin Cressida?'

Marc was silent for a moment. Then, very quietly, he said, 'Jack, it's quite possible that he really does mean marriage this time. The circumstances have changed. Cressida is no longer unprotected. Don't you think it's possible that Cressida's dowry was a big enough bait to land him?'

Jack felt sick. It had never occurred to him that Fairbridge would have the hide to renew his pursuit of Cressida. And while she didn't encourage him, neither had she discouraged him. She smiled at him, danced with him and strolled in the park as she did with a dozen others. But whereas the others paid attention to other young ladies, Fairbridge had singled out Miss Bramley exclusively.

Then the rumours had started. Nothing much. Just a suggestion that Miss Bramley was not quite up to the rig. That *poor Jack Hamilton and the Rutherfords have been sadly taken in*…nothing a man could get his hands on and choke to death.

The idea of any man possessing Cressida appalled him. The idea of Fairbridge possessing her sickened him. His whole being revolted at the thought. Parbury would be bad enough… He snorted inwardly at this idiocy. Parbury was a rattling good fellow. His objection to Parbury was plain jealousy. His reaction to Fairbridge was revulsion. Revulsion at the thought of a man who had offered a gently bred girl a slip on the shoulder and then offered marriage when she acquired a dowry.

He'd always loathed the *ton*'s prevailing attitude towards marriage, but this took hypocrisy to hitherto unplumbed depths.

He took an irreverent gulp of brandy and relaxed slightly as it burnt its way down. Fury at his helplessness ate at him. If only she'd married him! They'd be at home in Leicestershire right now, probably having a cosy evening in the library. Although he somehow doubted they'd be cataloguing many books. A practical study of Ovid would be far more to the point.

Then he groaned. What would be the point of marrying her if the stubborn, loyal little idiot was secretly eating her heart out for a blasted fortune hunter? His body might burn with desire every time he set eyes on her, or thought about her, but he wanted more than that. He wanted all of her. Body, mind, soul and heart. He wanted her love.

Marc signalled for a waiter. 'Another bottle of brandy, if you please. And an extra glass.'

'Thanks,' said Jack morosely. 'After all, if I can't do something, I may as well end up in my cups.'

Marc grinned. 'On a third of a bottle of brandy? I somehow doubt it.'

Jack stared at him. 'A third? What are you…? Oh, hello, Toby.' He forced a smile for the benefit of Marc's brother-in-law. 'I didn't realise you were in town.'

Sir Toby Carlton disposed himself in a chair with languid grace and sent a shuddering look at the far corner. 'Dear God. Aren't they a trifle over-enthusiastic? Gambling *and* politics.' He shook his head and then responded to Jack's remark. 'Came up this morning.'

Despite his gloom, Jack smiled. 'You found the energy to come to Brook's so soon, and you complain about others being overly lively? This is unheard of for you, Toby.'

Sir Toby looked pained and gestured at Marc. 'Blame him. He sent me a letter saying I had to come up immediately, and if I didn't, he'd fetch me himself. I came. And what does he do? Descends upon me the moment I arrive with instructions to go around to Boodle's and memorise the contents of the betting book for the last month!'

Jack blinked. '*Boodle*'s betting book?' He'd known Marc to do some odd things during the course of their friendship, but this had him fairly gapped. 'Why did you want Toby to look in Boodle's betting book?'

'Because he's a member and you and I aren't,' explained Marc. 'Wake up, Jack. I wanted to see if there was anything in the betting books that might refer to Cressida. There's nothing here, which was to be expected. No one would be corkbrained enough to put a bet like that in the book here, where you might see it. But there's nothing at White's either.'

'I'm a member there as well,' Jack pointed out.

'True,' said Marc, 'but you hardly ever go there, except with a friend for dinner. The likelihood of your poking your nose into the betting book there is remote.'

Jack nodded. It was true enough. He'd always preferred the slightly less aristocratic atmosphere of Brook's. 'But, why...' He broke off as his brain swung into action. 'Hold hard there...if there was gossip about Cressida, you think it would show in one of the betting books.'

Marc shrugged. 'You'd think so, but unless Toby found something...' He directed a querying gaze to his brother-in-law.

Toby shook his head. 'Not a thing.' He paused. 'Unless

you count a bet as to whether a certain Mr J. H. will take a bride with the initials C. B. this year.'

Jack's explosive *'WHAT?'* nearly drowned Marc's crack of laughter.

'Sssssshhhh!'

'Bloody impertinence!' growled Jack. For goodness' sake! In Boodle's of all places!

'Harmless, really,' said Toby, helping himself to brandy. 'No nasty innuendoes—ah, that's better—just the suggestion that the gentleman might take a bride, with those initials.'

Jack subsided. He frowned and racked his brains. 'Then, if the clubs and men aren't talking yet, it's unlikely that Fairbridge started the rumours, so who—?' Understanding crashed upon him with brutal force. 'Oh, my God! Lady Fairbridge!'

He groaned. This was worse. Much worse. While gossip in the clubs might be damaging to a woman's reputation, it could be killed. A few well-chosen threats in the right quarters would have dealt with it. If the society hostesses turned on Cressida, then she was ruined. No one would receive her. Doors would close in her face and her chances of marriage would be slim. And there was not a damned thing he could do to prevent it. He couldn't call Lady Fairbridge out... Or could he?

He might not be able to challenge her as he would a man, but he could certainly make things difficult for her socially. Especially since she had a daughter to establish. He clenched his fists. Damn the woman! Couldn't she see that Cress had no interest in Fairbridge? That she avoided him when possible and never granted him a waltz?

Lady Fairbridge had called on Cressida...been all sweetness and light according to Meg.

His brain tripped over that. Why would Lady Fairbridge call on Cressida if she disapproved of the connection and meant to ruin the chit?

'But…' He looked up from his brandy and found both his friends watching him.

'Can you make anything of it?' asked Marc. 'It has me foxed. Why would Lady Fairbridge gossip maliciously if she's still calling in Grosvenor Square behaving as though Cressida were an intimate friend of the family?'

Jack stiffened. Put like that… 'For a man who's puzzled, you certainly know how to sum up a situation,' he said. 'Conniving bitch! It's obvious, isn't it? Cressida Bramley, daughter of impoverished Vicar—totally unacceptable as a daughter-in-law. But Cressida Bramley, heiress to ten thousand pounds—there you have a potential bride for your son.'

Fury at the barefaced hypocrisy of Lady Fairbridge seared him. And the perfidy of Lord Fairbridge. He'd known that Cressida cared for him, trusted him. And he had used her mercilessly to ruin her father. Now, no doubt, he intended to stand back while his mother blackmailed the girl into marriage with him.

'There's something else you might consider, too, Jack,' said Marc.

Jack looked his question.

'Lady Stanhope is a cousin of Lady Fairbridge, remember. The pair of them are quite close.'

Jack swore as all the ramifications of that occurred to him.

'Stanhope?' Toby frowned. 'That neighbour of Jack's with the daughter? Interesting.'

Interesting didn't begin to describe Jack's opinion. Lady Stanhope would be only too happy to wreck Cressida's chances. Especially if she thought those chances involved Jack Hamilton.

'One-horse race,' said Toby, summing it up succinctly. 'If they blacken Miss Bramley's name enough, then the girl has no choice but to marry the only man to offer. Leaving Jack free for the Stanhope chit.'

Marc shook his head. 'It won't work. To my certain knowledge, Miss Bramley has already refused one more-than-eligible offer. At the time she might well have thought it was the only offer she'd ever receive and she didn't have a penny to her name. And unlike most girls her fortune is settled on her absolutely. She doesn't have to marry.'

Jack met his eyes reluctantly.

'Ah,' said Toby. 'But is Lady Fairbridge aware of this eccentricity on the part of Jack's ward?'

'She is *not* my ward,' snarled Jack rather more loudly than he intended.

'Sssssshhhhh!' The commons turned as one and glared.

Toby raised his brows. 'Oh? Dare say it's just as well. Always looks a bit off when a man marries his own ward. Anyway, we'd better go, or that lot over there will be issuing challenges. Besides, shouldn't be bandying a lady's name around in here. Come on, Jack.' His glance took in Jack's immaculate evening dress. 'Di told me to meet her at Lady Wragby's ball. And I understand Meg will be there with Miss Bramley.'

With a growl that both Marc and Toby took to be assent, Jack heaved himself out of his chair and stalked out.

'Di didn't exaggerate, did she?' murmured Sir Toby as he rose.

'About what,' asked Marc.

'About the peculiar effect love has had on our hitherto unflappable friend.'

Marc grinned as the door banged behind Jack to the indignation of everyone else in the room. 'Hmm. Just as well I didn't mention the bet in the book here on his likely marriage this year.'

Toby looked interested. 'Oh? Who placed that bet?'

'I did,' said Marc. 'Couldn't get a taker against, but Parbury was happy to wager a monkey against it happening within the next month!'

Chapter Thirteen

Not all the brilliance of Lady Wragby's ball, nor her ladyship's kindly greeting could make Cressida think the evening anything but a penance when she realised that Lord Fairbridge was in attendance. On her.

She managed to avoid waltzing with him, by dint of telling an outright lie, but was obliged to partner him for two country dances. After the second dance he commented on her heightened colour.

'I'll take you on to the terrace,' he said. 'No need to disturb Lady Rutherford. It's this way.'

Cressida baulked. 'Thank you, my lord, but I feel perfectly well and have absolutely no need of fresh air.'

Did he think she was all about in her head? Or that Meg and Di would not have warned her about going aside with any man on to the terrace? Not that she needed to be warned about Fairbridge.

She tried to pull her hand from Lord Fairbridge's arm, but he had his other hand clamped hard across hers.

The time had definitely come to hint Lord Fairbridge away, but he appeared to be impervious to hints. Grimly, Cressida considered more direct methods, only to dismiss them. Delivering a solid punch to Lord Fairbridge's nose would not only be impolitic in the middle of Lady

Wragby's ballroom, but also, for one of her height, down-right impossible. She might, just might, manage to hit his chin. If she kept on reminding herself of all this, it was even odds that her free hand would stay safely by her side.

If only he would take the hint and stop pestering her, then maybe the rumours would stop. They must be ema-nating from Lady Fairbridge. Didn't the horrid woman un-derstand that she would as soon sign a marriage contract with the devil himself as with her ladyship's precious son! All that conciliating air of hers must have meant that she was still terrified that an action for breach of promise would be brought against Andrew.

She flicked a glance at her companion, furiously aware that people had noted them together and Andrew's pro-prietary hand over hers.

'My lord, have you considered the distress your pursuit of me must be causing Lady Fairbridge? She has made it quite plain that she disapproves of me. And I have no desire to distress her.'

'Mama?' Fairbridge's tone bordered on patronising. 'I fear it is you who misunderstands, my dear Cressida.'

His dear Cressida nearly tied her fingers in knots in the folds of her apple-green silk evening gown.

'Mama has absolutely no objection to my pursuit of you—in fact, it has her blessing.'

It did? Then why…could it, after all, be someone else who had started the whisper that Miss Bramley was not quite the thing? But who?

She knew Jack had heard something. He was going about with the blackest, most excoriating frown on his brow. And it was usually directed at her. Especially when he had arrived this evening with Marc and Sir Toby. She thrust the thought back where it belonged—in a dark cor-ner of her mind. Thinking of Jack's anger and disappoint-ment hurt too much. No doubt he had counted on being able to get her off his hands easily.

Unfortunately most of the gentleman who danced with her didn't seem to be interested in marriage, Not with her anyway. They liked her apparently. They sent her posies, bouquets and strolled with her in the park. They flirted outrageously, but none of them ever gave the least impression of wishing to make her an offer. Which didn't really matter because she didn't wish to marry. Not them, anyway.

Even if she had felt inclined to accept an offer, the only gentleman seriously pursuing her was Lord Fairbridge, and she had no hesitation in dismissing him as a contemptible maw worm. She had to get rid of him.

She turned her scornful gaze upon him and he said, 'After all, you have to marry someone. And no one else is coming up to scratch, are they?'

Under cover of his hand, Cressida administered a savage pinch to his arm. And smiled beatifically as he jerked his arm away, swearing.

With another beaming smile, she responded, 'I fear you are mistaken, sir. I have no need to marry.' She clasped her hands before her in an attitude of maidenly decorum.

He smiled unpleasantly. 'Are you so sure you have no need to marry, my dear? After all, you seem to enjoy London society. It would be such a shame if London decided once and for all that it didn't like you.'

Somehow Cressida's fingers got themselves untangled and turned into fists, clenched in fury.

'So when would you like to be married?' he asked.

Heaven preserve her from domineering males who took everything for granted. But at least he'd asked her something!

'Never,' she answered with a wholly false smile. 'I have given the whole business much thought and feel that while such dreadful rumours persist, I cannot, in all honour, accept an offer from any gentleman.' She might as well get what use she could out of the situation.

'What!' His lordship's eyes bulged and his jaw hung slack. 'But you can't…I mean…no one will think anything of it once you're married to me.'

She sighed mournfully.

He glared at her, suspicion flaring in his face. 'This is all a hum. You have no other choice, my dear.'

'Blessed singleness is still a choice,' she shot at him.

'Not for a woman who wishes to ensure her father's safety, it isn't.'

The silken indifference of his voice shivered through Cressida. *No, not that. They couldn't!*

Trying to quell the inward shaking, she said, 'My cousin…'

'Will have little influence at Bow Street. Think on it, Miss Bramley. Think on it.'

Utterly dazed, sick and shaking, Cressida didn't even realise that she was standing beside the glass doors opening on to the terrace until Fairbridge shouldered her through them.

Jack moved steadily through the crowded rooms, searching for Cressida. He hadn't seen her for at least ten minutes and it bothered him. He smiled and nodded automatically at Lady Jersey, who had waved to him from a chaise longue. *Silence* holding court, he thought. No doubt gossiping over the peculiar and entertaining behaviour of Mr Jack Hamilton. And his *ward*'s matrimonial chances.

He simply couldn't understand it. Night after night he watched Cressida cut a swathe through the ballrooms of the *ton*. Her dance card was always full. Charming and eligible gentlemen flocked to her side—well, Meg and Di described them as eligible and charming. *He* thought they were a pack of rakes and libertines—but apparently none of them had made any serious overtures. Of any sort.

He nodded and smiled at Lady Gwydyr. Not automatically. He always had to remind himself to greet that haughty dame.

Some of the ladies were a little stiff with Cressida, but the support of Lady Rutherford, Lady Jersey and Lady Diana Carlton had kept the damage to a minimum. The gentlemen had ignored the rumours completely. So why hadn't he or Marc been besieged with offers for Cressida's hand? As far as he could see, the only man seriously pursuing her was Fairbridge.

The idea of that was enough to turn his stomach. What was wrong with all the others? Were they blind? Or merely mad? Even Parbury—the damned rake!—would be a better choice than Fairbridge.

A jovial gentleman nearly emptied a glass of champagne over him and he dodged, waving away the fulsome apologies proffered. It all served to remind him just how much he disliked this sort of thing anyway. What the devil was he doing at a squeeze like this? It was so crowded you could barely breathe. The answer presented itself to him with irritating ease—he was trying to find Cressida so that he could see if she had a dance free for him.

He snorted. No doubt Parbury had snabbled the supper dance. His eyes narrowed. There was Parbury now, chatting with Petersham. Comparing snuff boxes, no doubt. Fribbles! Oh, hell and the devil! Petersham had seen him. He couldn't cut them. After Marc, Parbury was one of his closest friends. And Petersham was always entertaining with his everlasting tea and snuff. Besides, they might have seen Cressida. Setting his shoulders, he forged a path through to them.

'Hullo, Jack,' said Viscount Parbury. 'I saw your… er…ward a few minutes ago. Danced with her, actually. You're a lucky dog! Isn't he, Petersham?'

Lord Petersham nodded. 'Charming girl, quite charming.'

'She's not my ward!' growled Jack.

'No, no. Of course not!' soothed Parbury. 'Didn't mean to imply that things aren't just as they ought to be. Everyone knows you wouldn't take advantage of the chit's situation. Just drop a hint in your ear though, old chap. While most of us are pleased to see you happy and willing to deny ourselves the pleasure of stealing the filly from under your nose, young Fairbridge ain't so particular. Came up to walk with her, you know. Not much I could do about it, beyond scribbling your name against the only dance she had left, but he's not at all the thing, that lad. You might want to hurry up the official announcement, y'know. Not the sort of feller to take a hint, and lord knows I've given him a few.'

'Which official announcement would that be, Parbury?' Jack kept his voice very casual. Parbury couldn't, simply couldn't, mean what he *thought* he meant.

'Your betrothal, of course,' said Parbury. He frowned slightly. 'You really ought to hurry it up. Settle these damned rumours. Tell you something else, too. Young Fairbridge appears to be in a spot of bother. Got in over his head in a card game a few weeks ago, my brother tells me. Apparently his trustees are cutting up stiff about settling more gambling debts. And they've been paying off his brother's debts. Not but what I understand they've managed to settle some family living on him now.'

Jack swallowed a few choice expletives.

'Exactly,' said Parbury, just as if he'd spoken. 'Ten to one Lady Fairbridge would rather someone else paid his debts this time, and there ain't no denyin' it; ten thousand is a tidy little fortune. Especially when it's wrapped up in a cosy little package like Miss Cressida.'

Jack managed to respond to that. It wasn't intelligible— fortunately—but it was a response.

Petersham, delicately raising a pinch of snuff to one nostril, added his mite. 'Shouldn't let Fairbridge…' he inhaled the snuff and smiled beatifically '…steal a march on you with Miss Bramley. Sheer waste. Like offering you snuff.' He put his snuff box back in his pocket.

'Did you say that my cousin is strolling with Fairbridge?' asked Jack. Much better to ignore the rest and just concentrate on the bits he could deal with.

Parbury nodded. 'Sorry, old chap, but short of telling him to…well, you know, in front of a lady and all that. And she didn't give me any hint that she *wanted* me to tell him to—' He broke off and bowed to Lady Sefton.

Part of Jack's brain registered Maria Sefton. Just enough to realise that he'd given her the cut direct. He kept going, trusting to Parbury and Petersham to make his excuses.

Upon occasion Jack found his height a nuisance. It was practically impossible to hide in a ballroom. Any horse under seventeen hands was utterly useless to him and most females seemed to have utterly fascinating conversations with his chin, or worse, the top button of his waistcoat. Usually he cursed his height.

Right now he gave sincere and heartfelt thanks for it, especially when he spotted Fairbridge edging Cressida out on to the terrace.

She knew perfectly well that she was in trouble. No properly brought up young lady went out alone on to the terrace with a gentleman. Quite apart from that, she had no desire to be anywhere alone with Lord Fairbridge. The gentle silver glow of moonlight mocked her.

'I am *not* going to marry you, my lord.'

Cressida didn't wait for Lord Fairbridge to open negotiations, but stated her position as clearly as she knew how. She couldn't, she wouldn't believe that even Andrew could be base enough to actually threaten her father to force her consent. She wasn't sure just how much more forcefully she could refuse an offer, but judging by what she could see of Lord Fairbridge's face in the light streaming from the ballroom, she would have to think of something.

He shrugged.

'You will, my dear. You have no choice. Either you marry me or your precious father will face a magistrate and see the inside of Newgate. Besides, if I keep you out here for long enough, someone is bound to catch us. Then you won't have any choice at all. You were happy enough to think I wanted to marry you down in Cornwall. Nothing has changed after all.'

She thought she might actually be sick. The marble flags of the terrace heaved under her feet and the buzz of chatter interspersed with the violins suddenly came from a vast distance as the night swirled around her.

Hard fingers clasped her arm, dragging her further away from the light and chatter of the ballroom towards the steps leading down into the garden.

Understanding came to her. If he could compromise her…it would not make the least difference to her reply, but the disgrace would hurt Meg. She baulked, trying to wrench herself free, but he grabbed her wrists in one powerful hand and bore them down easily.

'Stop! I told you—'

Her protest was smothered as he trapped her against the balustrade and forced his mouth on hers. His free hand thrust into her coiffure, seizing a handful of hair and holding her helpless.

Before she could do anything a savage voice ripped through the night. 'What the devil do you think you're about, Fairbridge?'

Jack's furious voice brought Fairbridge's head up sharply and Cressida pulled herself away from him, shaking. Nausea shuddered through her and she breathed deeply, trying to steady herself. A few hairpins pattered to the flags.

Jack. With Meg and Lord Rutherford on his heels. And Lady Jersey.

'Sealing my betrothal, Hamilton.' All the air left her

body as though at a blow. 'Your, ah, ward has just accepted my hand in marriage. Perhaps you and your companions might like to be the first to congratulate me.' A few more avid faces peered around the doors on to the terrace. From the dropped jaws it was evident that they had heard this announcement, had taken in her dishevelled appearance.

Horrified, Cressida fought for the breath to deny the claim, only to hear Jack's cold voice seal the trap.

'I see. My congratulations, on your good fortune, my lord. I shall wish you happy of it.' He turned on his heel and strode back into the ballroom, the growing crowd parting before him, only to swirl back, staring and whispering.

Only the balustrade against her back held Cressida upright as she watched him walk away from her, saw him disappear into the crowd.

Meg hurried forward, forcing Fairbridge to step away from Cressida. 'How very interesting to be sure, Lord Fairbridge. No doubt you will call upon my lord or Mr Hamilton in the near future to discuss the matter in a *proper* setting.'

'Indeed, Fairbridge.' Lord Rutherford stepped forward in his Countess's wake. 'Hamilton and I will look forward to it.'

Between them they escorted Cressida back into the ballroom. Desperately she searched the eddying crowd, but the press of silk and superfine defeated her. He had gone, but she could tell which direction he had gone in.

Half the crowd was staring at her, eyebrows raised. Fairly licking their lips in speculation. The other half was staring towards the main entrance. Even as she watched a tall, immaculately clad figure ascended the stairs and left the ballroom. Something about the purpose in his stride and the set of the broad shoulders told Cressida that his exit was permanent.

'You can't leave.' Rutherford's low voice held both apology and understanding.

Her stomach flipped over. Stay? With every eye on her for the rest of the night? She couldn't! Shaking, she looked up at Marc, ready to contradict him flatly.

His eyes held a challenge. 'One melodramatic exit is quite enough titillation for them for one evening. Any more and they'll expect it every night. Put your chin up and smile. Think of what you are going to do to Jack next time you see him.'

Her spine stiffened at the thought. Without thinking, she said, 'He's too tall!'

Marc choked. 'Then, my dear, I suggest you stand on a chair.'

From her other side, Meg muttered, 'I'd suggest you hit him with the chair and be done with it!'

Marc raised an eyebrow in mute query as Meg joined him in his bedchamber.

'And how do we handle tonight's little disaster?'

'Murder Jack.'

Her tones startled Marc considerably. She sounded as though she'd like to skin Jack. Inch by inch. And then use his hide as a hearthrug.

He went to her and drew her into his arms. 'Sweetheart, that's not going to help if Fairbridge has offered for Cressida and she accepts him. And right now that's exactly what everyone is expecting.'

He pressed a gentle kiss on her hair as she nestled against him.

'I know,' she admitted. 'But there was something odd about that announcement of his. Cressida looked absolutely stunned. I thought for a second she was about to deny it, and then Jack opened his big mouth. Now she's clammed up and won't talk about what really happened.'

Marc felt the tension in her and began rubbing her shoulders.

'Idiot,' she muttered.

'Who? Me?'

She chuckled. 'Not this time. Jack. Everyone thinks of him as in charge of Cressida. By reacting like that, he's made it much harder for her to reject Fairbridge's offer without looking like a jilt.'

'Mmm.' Marc rubbed a bit harder. 'You don't seriously think that would stop her, do you?'

'What the devil's wrong with him?' she burst out. 'Can't he see how unhappy she is? She loves him, for goodness' sake, and he's making her miserable!'

'He did offer for her,' Marc pointed out, duty bound.

Meg snorted. 'She told me. Because he felt obliged to.'

Marc smiled. 'Amazing, the stupid things a man will say when he's confused. And love is very confusing at first.'

Meg's eyes widened. 'Are you saying Jack knows he's in love?'

Marc laughed deeply. 'Oh, yes. He's got that far at least. Now, forget Jack and his problems for the time being. It's after three and there isn't a single thing you can do about any of it. Come to bed instead.'

Cressida sat curled up in the window seat and listened to rain spatter against the glass as she stared unseeingly into the night. Lamplight gleamed back from the rain-washed cobbles, dancing and flickering wetly. Light blazed from many of the houses and the clop of hooves drifted up to her as people began returning to their houses after the evening's entertainment.

She shivered. Anyone who had attended Lady Wragby's ball would be agog, waiting for the newspapers over the next couple of days. Enough people had heard Andrew's announcement and Jack's cold congratulations for the news to be at every breakfast table by tomorrow. The clock on the chimneypiece chimed and Cressida winced. By later this morning.

Her brain felt leaden, but unless she thought of something fast she was going to find herself betrothed to Andrew Fairbridge. Her stomach clenched and she began to shake uncontrollably. She couldn't do it. She couldn't!

She might have to. Breathing deeply, she fought down her panic and forced her mind to work. The most important consideration was Papa. He had to be protected. But she baulked at the idea of turning Papa's money over to Fairbridge to squander on gaming and…and…debauchery. She'd heard enough of the Viscount's reputation since coming up to town to have not the least doubt that his notion of marital fidelity would have nothing to do with his own behaviour and everything to do with hers. Not that she cared much about that. She wanted as little to do with him as possible. She simply hated the thought of giving her father's legacy to a family who would destroy him without a moment's hesitation… How tightly was the money tied up? How tightly could it be tied up?

She caught herself up with a violent shudder. What was she thinking? Was she seriously considering marriage to Andrew? She could taste bile in her mouth as nausea flooded her. What choice did she have? If a report was made to Bow Street, nothing could save her father.

How tightly was the money tied up? Marc had explained it all to her, but apart from the fact that she couldn't touch the capital and would have an allowance paid to her quarterly until her marriage, she hadn't taken much in. At that point she hadn't intended to marry.

She frowned. Women had very few rights. Anything she owned at the time of her marriage or inherited later would become her husband's property. Unless it was tied up in a trust. Could she have it tied up in a trust? So that they had the income but not the capital? Or would she need her husband's consent? She passed a hand over her aching brow. Her eyes were sore, too, from crying. She had heard that sometimes money was tied up very tightly with the capital settled on the next generation.

The first thing was to find out what could be done. She would send a message to Messrs Chadwick and Simms tomorrow.

'Now, is all that quite clear, Miss Bramley?'

She nodded at the little man. 'I think so, Mr Simms. Let me see if I have understood. The capital is not available to me, or, if I marry, to my husband. Instead it is settled on my children, to become theirs after my death...' She frowned. 'But what if I don't marry, or, even if I do, don't have children?' Would Fairbridge inherit the money under those circumstances?

Mr Simms smiled. 'I don't think we need worry about you not marrying, my dear. But in any case, if you die without children, then your husband would have no further claim on it. The capital would revert to Mr Hamilton, of course. Or to his heirs.'

It would? She stared at him blankly. 'I beg your pardon? Why would it do that?'

Mr Simms looked puzzled. 'Well, it seemed the logical solution when I drew up the deed of transfer for Mr Hamilton. He was quite adamant that your husband should not have any interest in the money. He was most concerned that you might become a target for a fortune hunter.'

A shiver took her. That was exactly what had happened. But why would Jack have directed that Papa's money go to himself? And *how* could he have arranged it? Surely no reputable lawyer would have...surely the money should go back to Papa's heirs, his old college, or school... Maybe Papa had designated Jack his heir...that would explain it, but something still didn't quite fit.

She knotted her brow, trying to think. The lawyer's

words came back to her—*when I drew up the deed of transfer for Mr Hamilton*... The truth crashed over her with all the force of a physical blow. There was only one possible explanation.

'Sir, under whose instructions did you settle this money upon me? My father's or Mr Hamilton's?'

If Mr Simms had looked puzzled before, he now looked totally bewildered.

'Why, Mr Jack's, of course. He has sole control of his fortune.'

She was never quite sure how she got herself out of the lawyer's chambers and back into the waiting carriage with her maid. All the way back from Lincoln's Inn the knowledge pounded into her with the rattle of wheels and hooves over the cobbles.

Jack's money. Jack had provided her with a dowry out of his own fortune. Slow tears rolled down her cheeks. Why had he done such a thing? Her brain just wouldn't work. Every time she tried to think, Jack's image got in the way. Every argument they had ever had echoed through her. And the kisses.

The memory of his mouth and hands possessing her sent fire coursing down every vein to pool, hot and mysterious, between her thighs. Nothing made sense. He desired her, yes. She didn't doubt that any more than she could deny her own desire. But what else did he feel for her? Why would a man settle a dowry of ten thousand pounds on a woman he disliked for whom he had no responsibility? That went far beyond family duty.

He felt enough for you to offer marriage. No. That was honour. He said as much.

More tears trickled down her cheeks. Just because she had fallen in love and hidden it, was no reason to suppose that Jack had fallen in love. After all, there was nothing particularly lovable about her. He, on the other hand, was eminently lovable, the big, chivalrous idiot that he was!

Grimly she faced something else. She could not marry. Least of all Fairbridge. Even if he could never touch the principle, she could not stomach the thought of Jack's money, Jack's decency, benefiting a man of that ilk in any way whatsoever.

The carriage had halted. She sat there dazed, lost in despair. How could she protect her father if she had to refuse Fairbridge? If only she could get rid of the money, Fairbridge would cease to want her! But there was nothing she could do to return the money to Jack. What Mr Bell had said about the terms governing trusts had made that abundantly clear. She had no power to touch that money or bestow it on anyone, not even St Peter himself.

'Miss? Miss? Are you all right?'

The concerned voice penetrated the fog of misery. Vaguely she looked up and recognised one of the Rutherford footmen holding the carriage door open for her. By the look on his face, he had been doing so for some considerable time.

With a confused apology she got down. Only one thing mattered. She had to make sure Papa was safe. As far as she could see there was only one way to do it. She would have to send for Jack.

He came straight after breakfast the following morning.

Delafield announced him in tones positively stiff with disapproval. 'Mr Hamilton to see you, Miss Cressida.' He shut the door of the breakfast parlour behind the disgracefully early caller with what could only be described as a near bang.

Cressida set down her coffee cup carefully and faced her visitor. She might have summoned him, but she really hadn't expected to see him before afternoon. After all, very few young ladies were out of bed at this hour of the morning. Most would not arise until noon or so after attending a ball, so what the devil did he think he was doing here this early? For most social aspirants, nine o'clock in the morning ranked as the middle of the night. Indeed, she felt as though it was the middle of the night, but her internal clock just couldn't get used to sleeping late.

'You wished to see me, Miss Bramley.'

She shivered slightly. A Gunter's ice would be a tropical delight after his gelid tones.

'Y…yes, yes, I did.' Furiously, she bit the inside of her cheek. Where had that despicable wobble come from? And why did he have to look so disgustingly attractive, even if his jaw did look as though it might break if he smiled? And if there wasn't a law against gentlemen with legs like that appearing in buckskin breeches before innocent maidens when they'd scarcely swallowed their breakfasts, then there ought to be. Along with a law about the maximum breadth of shoulder a gentleman was permitted to sport.

He strolled over to the chair opposite hers and raised his brows in mute query.

Fiery heat scorched her cheeks. 'Please, will you sit down, Mr Hamilton? Would you care for coffee?' She thought he frowned. No doubt, since he was in breeches, he had been riding and didn't wish to keep his horse standing.

He sank into the chair with his customary grace and stretched the long legs out comfortably. 'Thank you. Coffee sounds excellent. Black.'

She knew that. She knew all his odd little habits. Black coffee. The tiniest splash of milk in his tea. And he hated sugar. Except in spice biscuits, of course. She reached for the coffee pot, realising as she did so that she really ought to have rehearsed what she was going to say. At the very least she ought to have worked out if she was going to ask him about the money or just tell him straight out that she knew. Then, of course, she had the problem of explaining why she wanted him to take it back. And she must not, under any circumstances, let him realise the pressure Fairbridge had brought to bear on her...

'I did not see you at Almack's last night.' His voice sounded utterly indifferent.

'I wasn't there.' She concentrated hard on pouring the coffee. If he could state the obvious, then so could she. There was no need to tell him that she had spent the evening with a blinding headache—a very natural consequence after spending the afternoon crying her eyes out. 'I can't accept your money,' she blurted out. The coffee cup rattled in its saucer as she handed it to him.

It didn't seem possible that his jaw could harden even more, but somehow it gave that impression. His whole body seemed to stiffen. 'I beg your pardon?'

Oh, lord. If she had this wrong, then she would look the most complete henwit. 'That supposed legacy,' she said. 'It's all a hum. There was no money—'

'There most certainly is!' he snapped. 'What do you mean, no—'

'I mean there was no legacy,' she interrupted, blinking to force back the tears pricking at her eyelids. 'There is money, yes. But no legacy. You invented that, didn't you? And then persuaded Papa to settle the money on me, when all the time it was your money. You knew I would never accept a dowry from you, so you tricked me!'

His first sip of coffee scalded even as her words burnt into him. How the hell had she found out? The question screamed in his brain. He closed his eyes in pain. The money had served its purpose. Caught her a husband. Bile rose in his throat at the thought of the sort of pond scum ten thousand pounds could lure to the surface.

He forced his voice to normal. 'Cress, how did you know about the money?'

She told him in a voice that ached with tiredness, finally saying, 'When I found out the money came from you, I realised that I couldn't marry him, no matter what happened. You'll have to take the money back.'

He didn't quite follow that. 'Cress, the money is yours. Signed over. Even you can't give that money to anyone except in marriage. No matter how much I dislike your choice, I have no power to take the money back, or…or stop your marriage.' Except, of course, by standing up in the middle of the marriage ceremony and claiming her as his. Or, preferably, strangling Fairbridge.

She shook her head. 'No, Jack. Even tied up as it is, I can't marry Andrew and let him benefit from your kindness. I won't do it. I…I can't marry anyone. Least of all him. Not after he threatened—'

It seemed to Jack that she caught herself up with a gasp. Something was not quite right here, but he couldn't put his finger on it. And he didn't dare believe what his senses were screaming at him—that she didn't want to marry Fairbridge. He had to be wrong. She would have said something the other night. Wouldn't she? 'Cressida…if you want to marry Fairbridge…'

'*I don't!*'

He could only stare, his jaw dropped. 'You don't? Then why the hell didn't you tell him so the other night?' Anger surged through him. 'Good God, what a muddle! He called on me yesterday, trying to get my consent to a notice in the papers!'

'I did tell him.' The quiet despair in her voice stopped him dead.

'You refused him? Then why…?'

A shiver went through her and he watched in horror as she rubbed at her arms, hugging herself as if to keep warm or to protect herself.

My job, he thought savagely. *Both of them.*

'Andrew isn't used to taking no for an answer,' she said wearily. 'I said *no* and he grabbed me. You and the others came out on to the terrace and he announced our betrothal. You know the rest.'

'But you didn't say anything!'

'Haven't you ever found yourself in the situation where you are so stunned at what is going on that you can't say anything?' she asked angrily. 'And even if you could, you don't know what to say?' Her control broke. 'I had just refused him. Point blank. The last thing I expected was that he would announce our betrothal!' A tear spilt over and she dashed it away with a shaking hand. 'Or that you would congratulate him! What could I say after that? I was too busy trying not to be sick!'

A tangle of emotions battered at his self-control. Horror flooded him at the realisation that in his hurt fury he'd helped Fairbridge tighten the noose around her neck. And then he'd walked out on her. Because he hadn't trusted himself not to tear Fairbridge's throat out and then toss her over his shoulder in front of everyone.

He knew, because Marc and Parbury had told him, that she had got through the rest of the evening with her chin up and her smile gay. When no doubt all she longed for was a quiet corner in which to hide. And weep.

The need to take her in his arms and comfort her nearly overwhelmed him. He mustn't. He didn't dare. Not with the need to take her and show her incontrovertibly that she was his, and his alone, still pounding in his blood. She didn't want to marry Fairbridge. She had meant to refuse him. Even before she found out the truth about her dowry. That didn't mean she wanted to marry *him*. Did it?

'Will I be ruined when I don't accept him?'

That jerked him back to reality. 'No,' he grated.

Her next question rocked him. 'What if he…he may be very angry. Could he do anything to Papa? If he talked…'

'You and your father are perfectly safe.' He tried to control his fury, but his eyes narrowed. 'Fairbridge, however, isn't.' Scurvy bastard! If he tried to have a charge brought against Dr Bramley!

'Jack, please don't call him out. Please…'

She was on her feet, her eyes dilated with fear. His jaw tightened at the terror in her voice. Loyal, stubborn little idiot! Even after all this she could still care enough for the brute to worry about him…

'Jack!' His heart clenched as she came to him in a tumble of muslin skirts and gripped his arm. 'You must promise me! I couldn't bear it if you were hurt…please! You mustn't!'

She was worried about him? Slowly he covered her small hand with his large one. Did she care just a little bit? Could that little bit of caring be fanned to a blaze to match the need consuming him? He lifted her hand from his arm and raised it to his lips. So soft. Her hand trembled as his lips brushed over her fingers. Oh, hell. He'd have to try again. Surely he could convince her that he loved her. Couldn't he? After all, the rest of London had had no trouble in coming to that conclusion. Why couldn't the one person who mattered see it?

Drawing a deep breath, he plunged in. 'Cressida, do you remember that I once asked you to marry me?'

Chapter Fourteen

Pain lanced through her as she turned away, tugging her hand free of his. Remember? The memory quivered in her heart every time she thought of him. Unable to force a response past the choking lump in her throat, she nodded.

'Would you reconsider your answer and marry me?'

She shut her eyes against the pain of having to refuse him. But the constrained note in his voice pierced her. And he'd stiffened up again, as he always did when he touched her or danced with her. As though he could not bear to be near her, let alone touch her. Perhaps even his desire for her had died, leaving him with only guilt.

And now she felt guilty. He had cared enough to try to protect her, even to the extent of providing her with a dowry. She would give it back if she could, but she couldn't. There was absolutely no way she could hand that money over to anyone. Except by marriage, and that was out of the… Her churning thoughts faltered, tripping over the bitter logic of the trap fate had set for her.

Marriage wasn't out of the question. It was the only way in which she could repay him. She could marry Jack and repay her dowry that way. And it might even be the best way to ensure her father's safety. No. She shouldn't do it. He didn't love her.

A wave of cold chills washed through her. Why couldn't she do it? As far as the men of his world were concerned, marriages were generally made for very logical reasons—money, power, status, and an heir. If one was lucky, affection might develop.

But she wanted love. From him, anyway. She didn't deceive herself. If she had never met Jack, she might well have been content to settle for logic and affection. But she had met him and she could give him nothing except a tarnished name. And his own money. No doubt he didn't want love. Did it really matter if she did? She would not be lying when she took her vows. Merely terrified of betraying herself when she consummated them.

'I have nothing that you want, Jack,' she said painfully. 'No money, no connections. Only a dubious reputation and my...' Her fingers twisted together as she choked back the word *love*.

'You do have money, Cressida,' he pointed out. 'Not that it's an—'

She drew a breath so ragged it tore at her soul. 'Yes,' she said carefully. 'Your money. So, on that basis, I have no choice but to accept your offer.' She kept her eyes on the carpet, determined he should not see the tears burning her eyelids, threatening to become a flood of despairing grief.

Jack felt as though he had taken a full body blow from Gentleman Jackson himself. His plan to protect Cressida had backfired. Instead he had trapped her. She wouldn't even look at him. What he could see of her face was wreathed in shadows.

Fighting to keep his voice steady, he asked, 'Is honour the only reason for our marriage, Cressida?'

He thought she shuddered.

'What else could there be?' The bleakness in her voice struck through him.

Her next words shamed him.

'You desired me. That's all. You said yourself that was not enough for marriage. You even suggested that I should be your mistress—'

'That was because I thought you were teasing me on purpose and I was trying to teach you a lesson about the dangers of flirting!' he growled.

'Then you offered for me because you felt you had to,' she went on as if she hadn't heard him.

'I offered because I wanted to protect you!' he snapped, 'and because—'

She interrupted. 'I…I know you feel responsible—'

'Responsible be damned!' His voice was tight as he reached for her. 'What I felt was desire and—'

'No!' She panicked, jerking back from him. If he touched her now she'd betray herself. Her treacherous heart and body ached with the longing to yield to him. If he touched her, she'd break. Breathing hard, she fought for control. 'Andrew desired me. It wasn't enough. It wasn't enough for you either. Money made the difference for him. Honour has made the difference for you. And for me. I have no choice.'

He stopped dead and she watched him through a bright blur. His hand was still stretched out to her.

'My dear, you're wrong, I do care for you…very much. I…I love you, Cressida.' His careful, restrained tone of voice sent splinters of pain bursting through her. It was as if he had to force himself to say it. Maybe he even had to exert will power to keep his hand held out. If only he would let it drop, before the temptation to place hers in it and leave it there forever overwhelmed her resolve.

'You told me you wanted to marry me because your honour demanded it,' she reminded him. 'I can't think of any particular reason why you should love me, and you've never given me the least reason to believe that you do. But my honour demands that I accept your offer. It is the only way I can return your money.' The splinters lodged a little deeper as his mouth tightened and his hand sank back to his side. She should be glad he was no longer reaching for her.

Her eyes burning with tears, she stood up and said, 'Perhaps you will excuse me, Jack. I must write an answer to Lord Fairbridge.'

'You refused him, didn't you?'

She shivered at the hard note in his voice. 'Y…yes.'

'Then there is no need for either of us to give him any further response. The announcement of our betrothal will be response enough.'

A nod. That was all she could manage. Her throat ached with unshed tears. She had to reach the door somehow, before any of them fell. And then her room. Which meant she had to get past Jack, standing like a mountain before her, his eyes like gunmetal, hard and blank. His entire body looked as though it had turned to stone.

One step. She could take one step. She took it. Then another. One step at a time, because she dared think no further than the next step, Cressida walked past Jack. Slowly. The bright Persian rug on the floor swirled in misty reds and blues. He might reach out to stop her, sweep her into his arms and tell her what a little fool she was, that he really did love her, that their marriage would be based on love… If only he would kiss her, love her…

One step at a time she made her way to the door. He was there before her. Her heart shuddered to a stop, hope blazing up, unbidden, unwanted.

He opened the door for her.

One more step and she was through. The hallway was cold after the warmth of the breakfast parlour. She clenched her teeth against a sob of pain at knowing she'd been right. He was letting her go.

'I will arrange for the announcement in the papers the day after Meg's ball. We will make the announcement at supper.'

It was all he could say. His throat felt tight. His entire body screamed with the need to sweep her into his arms and kiss her. And then drag her back into the parlour, lock the door and show her how much he loved her. It wouldn't work. She'd think it was nothing more than lust. He would not lower himself to the level of Fairbridge by attempting to overcome her resistance by force.

Somehow he managed to shut the door on Cressida and on his own need. He stared blankly at the closed door and wondered just exactly where he'd gone wrong first. He'd misjudged her initially of course. He'd been quite pig-headed about that, as though he was determined to think the worst of her. Why? He wasn't usually that stupid, was he? His undeniable case of lust hadn't helped. He had to admit that. He'd scarcely been able to focus his mind enough to eat since he'd met her. But why hadn't he realised sooner that he loved her?

Because she's not the sort of girl you expected to love. With a dazed shake of his head, he thought about his imaginary, ideal bride. Quiet, gentle, submissive. Someone who wouldn't turn his world upside down. Lord, a marriage like that would have bored him to death.

A long scratch on one of the door panels caught his attention. What had caused that? And what was he doing, staring at the door? He really ought to go. Dear God. What was he to do now? He'd wanted her to accept his offer. Never had he imagined that she might accept it to return his money! He cursed fluently. As if he needed money! That was the final, cutting irony. That she should marry him to return a miserable ten thousand that he wouldn't have noticed missing anyway.

Disgustedly he wandered over to the breakfast table, sat down and sipped his now tepid coffee. At least they were betrothed. And if she had accepted on the promptings of honour, then she was unlikely to try and back out of it. It was grim comfort.

The door opened and he turned his head.

Meg gazed back and said blandly, 'Congratulations.'

He groaned. 'Don't, Meg. What the hell am I going to do? Did she tell you why she accepted?'

Taking the chair Cressida had vacated, Meg nodded.

'I never meant to trap her like that.' He felt sick at the thought. 'She doesn't love me.' Automatically he poured coffee for Meg and handed it to her.

She sipped and asked, 'Did she actually tell you, in as many words, that she doesn't love you?'

He ran his hands through his hair distractedly. 'She didn't have to! What the deuce am I supposed to think when the girl accepts me because she feels honour bound to return a paltry ten thousand pounds?'

Meg's coffee cup rattled in its saucer and a choke of laughter escaped her. 'Paltry? Ten thousand pounds, paltry?'

Jack had the grace to blush.

Sobering, Meg went on. 'Jack, all I could get out of Cressida was that you had renewed your offer and that she had accepted because of the money. Then she burst into tears. Apparently you told her that you love her and she doesn't believe you?'

The faintly questioning note got to him. 'Damn it, Meg! Of course I love her! The problem is her not lov—'

'Fudge!' said Meg roundly. 'Why would she be so upset about *you* not loving *her* unless *she* was head over ears in love with *you*?'

Jack left Rutherford House twenty minutes later with his wits in total disarray. She loved him? All he had to do was convince her that her love was returned?

Meg had been full of advice on how to achieve that end. Most of it was so obvious, that he blushed to think of it. Instead of growling at her all the time he could send her flowers, take her to Hatchard's and to Gunter's afterwards for an ice, drive her in the park, dance all the supper waltzes with her and utterly monopolise her company. In short, he could woo her properly and make a complete and utter spectacle of himself.

The prospect was enough to make him shudder. Sally Jersey would be in alt.

Gazing into the silken, glittering mob at Lady Harwood's ball that evening, Cressida wished with all her heart that it had not been necessary to attend, but Meg had explained how vital it was not to give the gossips the least idea that she was avoiding Andrew. Was he here already, or would he appear later? Would he approach her?

She had discussed with Meg exactly how she should handle him. They'd even practised it, with Meg borrowing one of Marc's coats and pretending to be Lord Fairbridge. The session had ended in laughter, which, oddly enough, had buoyed Cressida's confidence.

'Jack's in the far corner,' Meg told her. 'Talking to…good lord! That's Lady Anna! I had no idea she was in town.'

'Who is Lady Anna?'

'Who…oh, his mother, of course. Lady Anna Hamilton. Jack wrote to her. She's been staying in Yorkshire with Jack's sister, but—'

'*Jack*'s mother is here? *That* Lady Anna?' Jack had said nothing to her about writing to his mother. Had she come to town to rescue her son from his disastrous entanglement? She took a deep, if careful, breath. Despite Meg's assurances, she was never quite sure that something wouldn't fall out of her bodice one evening and this green silk gown made her very nervous.

'Yes, oh…he's seen us. They're coming over. Why don't we just wait here for them?'

An excellent idea, thought Cressida hollowly. Get it over and done with. No doubt Lady Anna would have any number of arguments that would persuade her son to withdraw his offer. Although she couldn't help hoping that the fashionable crowd would slow down Jack's progress towards them.

Lord Parbury came up. 'Evening, Lady Rutherford, Miss Bramley. Shocking squeeze, ain't it? Marc here this evening?' He chatted on and Cressida relaxed slightly, letting the conversation wash over her. No doubt Jack and his mama had been waylaid by other acquaintances. Lady Anna might have already convinced him of the foolishness of pursuing such an unequal match. Nothing had been made public. She could release him without anyone being the wiser. The thought did absolutely nothing to raise her spirits.

'Perhaps you might do me the honour of standing up for a dance, Miss Cressida?'

She forced herself to smile at Lord Parbury. 'Whichever you like, my lord.'

'Except the first waltz and the supper waltz,' came a deep voice. 'They're mine. Just bear that in mind, my lord.'

Outraged, Cressida turned to glare at Jack. And encountered a smile that would have melted a statue.

'*Yours?*' she challenged, despite the pounding of her heart and the breathless little voice that said he was welcome to the dances and anything else he liked to claim.

'Mine,' he affirmed with an absolutely wicked grin as he caught the dance card at her wrist. Her immediate reaction was to jerk it out of his hand, but the light caress of his fingers sent a wave of dizziness through her, even through her long kid gloves. She dragged in a deep breath as her heart raced and caught his mother's glance.

Familiar dark grey eyes twinkled at her out of a woman's face and an amused voice said, 'I apologise, my dear. I did my best, but as you've probably noticed, he's dreadfully stubborn.'

Cressida stared. Heavens! How alike they were! And realised that Jack had managed to write his name down on her dance card. Twice.

Lady Anna Hamilton continued. 'Since we have a little time before Jack claims you for the first waltz, perhaps you might like to walk with me a little. Your papa was used to visit a great deal years ago. We were sorry to lose contact with him after he moved to Cornwall. I'm so glad you came to Jack.'

She was?

By the time Jack claimed her for the first waltz her convictions had taken a severe battering. Lady Anna betrayed no sign that she disapproved of her future daughter-in-law. And it was obvious she knew. *You'll make Jack so happy. Thank you, my dear. He needed something to shake him up a bit.*

How could she possibly make Jack happy? And whatever did Lady Anna mean about shaking him up? She knew she drove him insane at times, but for the life of her, she couldn't see how that would make him happy.

She shivered as he swung her into the waltz. Judging by the impersonal way he was holding her, he probably didn't even desire her any more... *He doesn't love you. You know that. He's kind, chivalrous and protective, but he doesn't love you.*

She caught sight of Meg and Marcus in the whirling throng. They were dancing with eyes only for each other, close enough to have every tongue in the room wagging if they hadn't been married. She would love to dance like that with Jack, close enough to...

He whirled her through a turn and drew her closer to avoid another couple, close enough to feel the heat of his body, to smell the cologne he used and the faint, musky odour of himself beneath it. Close enough to feel his thighs brush against hers, melting every bone in her body. Close enough that he filled her entire vision as well as her heart.

'Jack…' Her voice came out as a sort of squeak. 'Do you think we're close enough?' Irony was not going to work with her voice wobbling everywhere. 'I mean, shouldn't you—?'

'Not nearly close enough,' he said softly. 'But I can't do anything about it now. If I kiss you, all hell will break loose.'

If he… 'What did you just say?'

There was no sort-of-squeak about her voice this time. It was unquestionable squeak.

'I can't kiss you here,' he said obligingly. 'You'll have to wait until later.'

Her mind whirled even faster than the violins. 'I…I don't want you to kiss me,' she lied.

He grinned. 'Do you know what a terrible liar you are?'

There was no answer to that.

Lord Parbury claimed her for the next dance. He confused her even more.

'About time,' he said without preamble. 'Lord, if I ever knew Jack to be such a slowtop! I'm sure you'll be very happy, m'dear. Lady Anna looks to be in alt, too.'

But…

None of it made sense. She found that Jack was constantly at her side between dances, but he no longer growled at her admirers, rather he chatted easily with men who were obviously his friends. And kept her hand anchored safely on his arm the entire time until he had to relinquish it for her to dance with someone.

Eventually, when he swept her on to the floor for the supper waltz, she asked, 'Why are you doing this?'

This time he didn't bother to wait for the excuse of a near collision to draw her closer. He simply did it and smiled that heartshaking smile. 'I'm showing you,' he said.

'Showing me?'

'You didn't believe me yesterday, so I'm showing you.'

His hand at her waist drifted scandalously low, sending

waves of heat through her. What hadn't she believed yesterday? Her brain had melted along with the rest of her. No wonder Meg always looked and sounded distracted after she'd danced with Marc.

What hadn't she believed yesterday? *That he loves you.* But... She stared up at him and found another smile on his face, even more heartstopping than the other one. Her jaw dropped.

'That's right, sweetheart.' He swung her around effortlessly and said, 'From now on the first waltz and the supper waltz are mine. Even if I'm not there to claim them at the start of the evening.'

A quiver of delight ran through her. That was the exact arrangement Marc had with Meg. No one ever solicited Lady Rutherford for either of those two dances.

'But—'

'No buts,' he growled softly. 'They're mine.' The possessive tone in his voice suggested that he'd like to claim a few other things as his while he was at it.

Marc and Meg joined them at the end of the dance and they made up a party for supper, gathering Parbury, Petersham and Lady Anna.

Cressida watched, entranced, as Jack attended to his mother, making sure she had everything she required. He did it all without seeming to realise, as though caring for his mother was second nature to him, something that was so deeply engrained it was a part of him. She thought back to all the times he had grabbed for her, despite his injured shoulder. And the writing table. Helping people was normal for Jack. Caring for people was normal. He did it without thinking.

And she could no longer doubt that he cared for her in much the same way. Her heart ached with unspoken love, even as she wondered if he would ever care just that little bit more. That little bit that included so much more than the promptings of honour and chivalry.

* * *

Over the next week Cressida's certainty about Jack's chivalrous intent wavered. He said not one word of love, but if she'd had a pocket, he would have been living in it.

As it was he made do with attending her everywhere, monopolising her company, taking her to Hatchard's book-shop—and Gunter's afterwards. He made good his threat to dance every supper waltz with her and no longer both-ered to wait for an excuse to drag her scandalously close. He just did it. Right at the start of the dance.

And he seemed happy to be with her. Content. Proud. He teased her, laughed at her, told her scandalous stories about all society's most starched-up pillars. He strolled with her in the park every day at the fashionable hour. In short, he made a complete and utter spectacle of himself in front of all society.

By the end of the week Cressida suspected that the raised eyebrows of London's gossipmongers were going to result in some permanent wrinkles. Yet apparently not a word was said in disparagement. Even the other gossip died away.

Meg remarked on that. 'They wouldn't dare, of course.'

Cressida blinked. 'They wouldn't? Why not?'

It was Meg's turn to blink. 'With Jack involved? He's made his intentions quite plain. No one would dare cross him!'

Cressida tried in vain to reconcile a Jack that no one would dare cross with the big, chivalrous mere Mister she was betrothed to.

'But he's not titled, or in Parliament...or...or anything like that,' she said. 'I mean, I know the family's very old and he's wonderful and kind, but...' Words failed her.

Meg grinned. 'And so disgustingly wealthy that he re-ferred to your wretched dowry as a *paltry ten thousand*. Quite apart from which, everybody likes him, from the patronesses of Almack's down. So with Sally Jersey and all the others beaming upon the whole situation, no one else will say a word.'

Cressida shook her head at the unfathomable ways of society. Apparently a mere Mister could wield a great deal of subtle power. Oddly enough, although she had seen Andrew and his mama on several occasions, neither had made the least push to approach her. And that worried her. Somehow she could not quite credit that the Fairbridge arrogance would be deterred by anything less than a public announcement of her betrothal.

She banished the thought. After all, she had never been happier. Only one thing niggled at the edges of her dream: Jack never kissed her, never touched her in any way that could be construed as lover-like. Unless you counted the way he waltzed with her. And even that had her puzzled. He seemed to be a mass of tension during and immediately after those dances.

Did he really want her? Or was it all a façade?

'Meg, I'm really not convinced about that…um, that nightgown. It's rather…well, you know!' Apart from anything else, she'd freeze in it!

Cressida was still fighting a valiant rearguard action as she followed Meg over the threshold of Rutherford House after a morning's shopping. The ball was the next day and Meg had commandeered her from Jack, announcing that there were several important items to be purchased for her protégée. Cressida had a sinking feeling that the contested nightgown had been the focal point of the expedition and that she had been cozened by an expert.

The Countess of Rutherford very properly ignored her protégée's craven attitude, as indeed she had done all the way from Regent Street, and smiled cheerfully at the footman holding the door for them.

'Good morning, Thomas. There are a few parcels in the

carriage. Could you please carry them up to Miss Cressida's chamber?'

Miss Cressida could only blink at this staggering understatement. The shopping spree Meg had dragged her on when she came up to London had left her breathless. This one beggared the imagination, leaving very little room in the carriage for passengers.

'Meg!' cried Cressida. 'That nightgown…'

Meg turned with an absolutely wicked grin on her face. 'Will be simply perfect.'

For what? wondered Cressida. Her appearance in a seraglio?

Meg answered the unspoken question. 'For your wedding night.' With a smile she called out to the footman, staggering up the steps under a pile of dress boxes. 'Thomas…is his lordship home?'

Thomas peered around the teetering pile. 'Yes, m'lady. His lordship is in the ballroom, fencing with Mr Hamilton.'

'Fencing!' Cressida forgot all about Meg's perfidious behaviour. 'In the ballroom?' It seemed an incongruous setting to say the least.

'Better than the library,' commented Meg. 'That's where they used to practise because Marc keeps the foils and *épées* in the cupboards under the bookcases.'

'Oh,' said Cressida weakly. Jack and Marc?

'Come and watch, if you like,' said Meg cheerfully. 'We can stand at the top of the steps just inside the doorway. They won't mind as long as we don't make any noise. Although I dare say they're only using foils with the buttons on. Quite harmless.'

Bemused, Cressida followed her to the ballroom. The doors stood slightly open and as they approached Cressida could hear the swift hiss and clash of steel, the thud of feet.

Meg frowned slightly. 'Funny. They usually talk while they practise.' She led the way into the ballroom and stopped short. Cressida peered around her shoulder and stifled a gasp.

She had never seen any swordplay before, but her heart nearly stopped at the fire and pace of the match. And the blades looked far heavier than she had imagined. More deadly. Swallowing hard, she clenched her fists. Dear God, if she didn't know that the two men below were the best of friends, she'd swear they were intending to kill each other.

She had experienced Jack's strength before, but never had she been confronted with his sheer athleticism. She had never realised that for all his height and powerful physique, he could still move with the speed and grace of a striking cat.

Plainly they had been at it for some time. Jack's shirt was soaked with sweat and clung to his body as he fought. Cressida's mouth went dry as she watched.

It seemed to her that he was attacking the whole time, constantly thrusting, only to be met with a parry each time and forced back by Marc's blade. The blades hissed and sang, clashing again and again until at last she felt Meg's hand on her wrist.

Reluctantly she turned her head and saw Meg gesture towards the door.

Once outside she gave voice to her question. 'Meg, were those foils? They look much heavier than I'd thought. And I couldn't see any buttons.'

The Countess of Rutherford shook her head. 'There weren't any buttons,' she said, sounding rather preoccupied. 'And those weren't foils. They were using Marc's *épées*.'

Épées? Duelling swords? Every drop of blood thickened in fear.

'Meg…' she began.

'Cressida, they fence all the time!' Meg assured her. 'I dare say they just got the *épées* out for a change of weight, or pace…or…or something.' She slipped her arm around Cressida's shoulders. 'No one duels with swords anymore. They all use pistols. If Jack were planning to challenge Fairbridge, he and Marc would be down at Manton's, culping wafers.' She grinned. 'At least I hope so. I'd have a bit to say if he practised for a pistol duel in our ballroom!'

Cressida refused to be diverted. 'But, Meg! What if he does challenge Fairbridge?'

Frowning, Meg said, 'He wouldn't be so idiotish.' But she didn't sound at all convinced. Then she brightened. 'Besides, if he did, it would be Fairbridge's choice of weapons, you know. And he'd choose pistols. So stop worrying. Jack and Marc like fencing because it's good exercise.'

Jack lowered his blade.

'Enough?' asked Marc calmly. He sounded very slightly winded.

Jack nodded. 'For now. We might have another session tomorrow.' He dragged a handkerchief out of his pocket and mopped his face. His shoulder ached liked the very devil, but a few more bouts with a fencer of Marc's calibre would take care of that.

'How does your shoulder feel?' asked Marc, glancing at him shrewdly.

Jack rolled it around and shrugged. 'Tired, but I don't think it slowed me too badly.'

His lordship snorted. 'Hardly! And there I was, counting on it to give me an advantage.'

'Did you need one?' Jack pulled on his boots. 'Did you notice Cressida and Meg? They came in part way through and left again.'

'Mmm. I saw them.' He picked up his coat from the balustrade. 'You'd better come upstairs and borrow a clean shirt,' he continued. 'You can't put your coat on over that one. Go on up and ring for my man. I'll put the blades away.'

'Do you think Cressida noticed we were using the *épées*?' asked Jack.

'I've no idea,' returned Marc. 'Any more than I've the least notion why you want to practise your swordsmanship. I feel it encumbent upon me, as your likely second at the impending bloodbath, to point out that in the face of a challenge from you, Fairbridge will opt for pistols. And so would I,' he added feelingly, shaking out his sword arm. 'No one in their right mind would accept a challenge from you in your current mood and then plump for swords!'

'It won't be my challenge,' said Jack quietly.

Marc stared. 'It won't?' His eyes narrowed as he thought about it. 'No,' he said slowly. 'Of course it won't. Hmm. I dare say it's better this way. Too easy to kill with pistols, and if you kill the bastard there'll be the devil of a kick-up. You'd be spending a very protracted honeymoon abroad.'

Jack smiled very slowly. 'That's not the point at all, Marc.'

Marc swore. 'Curse it, Jack! You're meant to be the level-headed one! Mr Jack Never-Seen-Him-Ruffled Hamilton. You can't be meaning to kill Fairbridge! You'd have to leave the country!'

Seeing Marc's genuine concern beneath his expostulations, Jack relented. 'I've no intention of killing him. But I've every intention of carving a few strips out of his hide. Slowly.'

He grinned at Marc's disbelieving stare.

The Earl looked at him narrowly. 'Let me be quite sure I understand what I'm getting myself into: you intend to provoke Fairbridge into challenging you, so that you can choose weapons, time and place. Would you mind very much letting me know the time and place so that I can make a note of it in my diary?'

Jack straightened up from pulling on his boots. He met Marc's eyes and stated, 'The next time he attempts to force Cressida to accept his suit. Then and there.'

'Any use my pointing out that one of the first duties of a second is to attempt a reconciliation?' asked Marc drily.

'You probably have more useful things to do with your breath. I certainly won't be wasting mine on apologies.'

'Hmm.' Marc appeared to consider this. He shrugged. 'Ah, well. At least I am spared the indignity of thinking up a convincing lie to explain to Meg just why I'm leaving our bed so early. Dawn appointments are always so inconvenient.' He appeared to consider something further. 'Er, Jack, have you entertained the possibility of Fairbridge trying to force Cressida's hand at our ball?'

Only a fool would have described Jack Hamilton's smile as pleasant. 'I'm counting on it.'

The Earl of Rutherford groaned. He didn't need second sight to foresee that the Countess of Rutherford's first ball was fated to go down in history as one of the Season's most talked-about entertainments. He could only hope that Jack Hamilton's legendary self-control would be sufficient to prevent him from actually killing Lord Fairbridge. Right now, Jack's assurances to the contrary would not have inspired him to wager any considerable sum on the chance.

Chapter Fifteen

Her hand anchored firmly on Jack's arm, Cressida came off the dance floor with him after the first waltz of the Rutherford House ball. Perhaps if she stood still for a moment her head might stop revolving. She refused to believe that her heart would ever stop spinning.

'The notice will be in the papers tomorrow.'

Her heart did more than spin. Then his voice registered. He sounded odd. Grim almost. Her heart plummeted.

She met his eyes. 'Jack…' She couldn't go on. Why did he look so strained? What was bothering him? He'd seemed happy enough at the start of the dance. But, as always, by the end of the dance he'd turned into a statue. Heavens, he looked as if a smile would break his jaw.

He smiled down at her. She'd never realised that it was possible to smile with a locked jaw, but he did it. What had she done wrong? Or was it just that he couldn't keep up the façade any longer?

Lord Petersham came up to claim her for the next dance and Jack watched her go, practically breathing a sigh of relief. Surely if he couldn't see her, or feel her, he would be able to control his urge to bundle her out of the ball-room and into a quiet unused parlour where he could give rein to the urgent need building inside him.

The past week had been hell. His control was in tatters, smoking around the edges. He hadn't dared to touch her in any way beyond keeping her hand on his arm except during their waltzes. And the temptation to kiss her senseless in the Rutherfords' carriage after an evening party had been appalling. He'd resisted, knowing exactly where that would have ended. And she deserved better than a carriage seat for her first experience of lovemaking. She deserved a bed and a wedding ring.

He drew a tentative breath. Oh, God. The light scent of rosewater hung about his clothes, clinging, seducing. And her face, turned up to his, worried and uncertain, haunted him. Something was bothering her. Had she realised just how much he desired her? Did that frighten her? He wouldn't blame her if it did. It frightened the hell out of him. One thing was certain. Their betrothal was going to be one of the shortest on record.

'Miss Bramley, my dear! How delightfully you look this evening! Have you seen Andrew yet? I believe him to be looking for you everywhere!'

Cressida stiffened as Lady Fairbridge enveloped her in a waft of scent. She drew breath to respond, but found herself sneezing instead.

Lady Fairbridge sailed on regardless. 'Good evening, Petersham. Perhaps you might leave me to speak privately with Miss Bramley.'

Thinking fast, Cressida smiled up at Lord Petersham. 'Thank you so much for a lovely dance, my lord. I shall look forward to our next.'

'So shall I, my dear,' he assured her, bowing deeply over her hand. 'Servant, Lady Fairbridge.' He favoured Cressida with a friendly smile and Lady Fairbridge with a brief nod and strolled off.

Reminding herself to breathe deeply and keep a tight

rein on her temper, Cressida manufactured a polite smile for Lady Fairbridge.

The Dowager's opening remarks nearly wiped it off her face. 'I saw you dancing with Mr Hamilton, my dear. Petersham is harmless enough, but you would do well to be a little careful with Mr Hamilton. I have noted that he always engages you for the first waltz and the supper waltz. A little too particular, my love, if you don't mind my saying so. Of course, I do understand that he is your cousin, but—'

'As a matter of fact, I do mind. Very much.' Cressida spoke as quietly as she could, but anger bubbled over. Firmly, she pinned the smile back in place.

Lady Fairbridge favoured her with an indulgent smile. 'Now, now, my dear! I quite understand that you and Andrew have had a little difference of opinion, but you must not tease him by encouraging the attentions of other men! That would be sadly unkind in you!' She lowered her voice to a conspiratorial whisper. 'He tells me that he has renewed his offer and I wish you to know the match now has my full support. You need feel no scruples in—'

'Refusing his suit,' finished Cressida. She hung on to her temper desperately. Words blazed on the tip of her tongue, but she quenched her rage and forced them back. She utterly refused to tell Lady Fairbridge that she and Jack were betrothed. The announcement would be made at supper. Then she would know. And Andrew would have to give up his pursuit of her.

Her eyes bulging, Lady Fairbridge stammered, 'You c…can't be serious! Refuse *Fairbridge*?' Her voice rose a couple of octaves, carrying even over the roar of conversation, so that several people turned in eager curiosity.

Cressida flinched. Good Lord! Did people have nothing better to do with their lives that they needs must take such a suffocating interest in one's personal affairs? Plainly she had made a serious mistake. This was not the right venue for this particular discussion.

Lady Fairbridge voiced exactly what she was thinking. 'My dear Miss Bramley, perhaps you would do me the favour of withdrawing to somewhere a little more private where you may explain yourself.'

Reflecting that it would all be much simpler if either Lord Fairbridge or his mother had ever learned to take *no* for an answer, Cressida agreed.

'Certainly, Lady Fairbridge, I will be only too happy to explain my decision to you.'

'Excellent,' purred Lady Fairbridge. 'I'm sure I can give your thoughts a happier direction. The library perhaps?'

Cressida hesitated. Meg had not intended the library to be used this evening. On the other hand, it would probably be empty and, since she had every intention of telling Lady Fairbridge very plainly exactly what she thought of Andrew's offer, that would be a distinct advantage.

'The library,' she agreed.

Jack saw her go and breathed a sigh of relief. Far better if she told Lady Fairbridge that she had refused the Viscount's offer. He couldn't bear to think of her so much as being in the same room as Fairbridge, let alone speaking to him. Her ladyship could convey the fell tidings to her precious son. While it would have afforded him immense satisfaction to carve a few chunks out of Fairbridge, the course of wisdom was to avoid scandal, not cause it.

Gloomily he turned and snaffled a glass of champagne from a passing footman. He'd never realised how boring wisdom could be.

Someone had lit the fire in the library and left one small lamp burning. Despite her simmering anger, Cressida had to suppress a smile as she saw Marc's *épées* lying on a console table. Jack had come around for some more fencing in the morning and Delafield had chased his noble master out of the ballroom when the housemaids and footmen complained. Obviously they had forgotten to put the blades away.

Turning to face Lady Fairbridge, Cressida stated baldly, 'I have refused Lord Fairbridge's offer. You cannot possibly believe that, after what has passed between us, his offer would be acceptable to either myself or my father?'

Her ladyship swelled with indignation. 'Your *father*? Do you tell me that he has the temerity to forbid the match? When *I* approve it? Do you imagine that you can attract a better offer? Think carefully, girl. I can ruin you!'

'You've already tried, haven't you?' flared Cressida. 'All those whispers! The suggestions that I was fast! They came from you!' It all made sense now. To someone like Lady Fairbridge, any husband would be better than none. So she had tried to make sure her son was the only one to offer.

Lady Fairbridge snorted. 'D'you think I'm stupid, girl? My cousin, Kate Stanhope, did all the talking! Lord! The ninnyhammer was convinced Hamilton was about to offer for you instead of Alison.' She laughed scornfully. 'The idea! Jack Hamilton to offer marriage to a little provincial nobody with a soiled reputation! He don't need to marry money! Unfortunately, not everyone can afford to be so choosy.'

Nausea left Cressida cold and shaking.

Lady Fairbridge was still talking. 'So you'll marry Andrew, my girl, or I'll ruin you. And your father will end up where he belongs. Hamilton can't call me out, and no one will support him if he calls my son out to account for my actions!'

Rage lashed Cressida, burning away the fear and nausea. 'Lady Fairbridge, you and your precious son may go to the devil!' she blazed.

The door opened and she spun around.

'Ah, Mama. I did tell you she was stubborn, didn't I?'

Lord Fairbridge sauntered into the room. 'I'll deal with it now, ma'am.' He bowed to his mother. 'Thank you for getting her here.'

Lady Fairbridge headed for the door, saying, 'You've got about ten minutes, Andrew.' She stalked out and shut the door firmly behind her.

Ten minutes? What in God's name did she mean by that? The question hammered in Cressida's brain along with the realisation that she had been trapped. Her every nerve focused on Andrew as he started towards her. Instinctively she backed up, circling until she had the sofa between them. It stood directly opposite the fire and she allowed herself a swift, desperate glance at the hearth. The fire irons were missing. She dragged in a deep breath. Only one thing would recall Fairbridge to his senses—she would have to tell him she was betrothed to Jack.

Lord Fairbridge laughed softly. 'I'm not a fool, my dear. I moved them earlier. Give up now. They will find us soon and you will have no choice but to accept my offer.'

Fury swept her, banishing all rational thought. 'When snow lies in hell!' she spat. 'You must be mad! What do you think my cousin will say to this?'

He shrugged. 'Why should I care? If he is fool enough to issue a challenge, I am a good enough shot to account for him. Anyway, why should he bother? I'm offering marriage. It's the best offer you'll get once my mother opens her budget.'

He smirked. 'And believe me, she can do so very convincingly. Bemoaning my *infatuation*, that your dowry was the final straw. She's a very fine actress. At this moment she is busily fainting in the ballroom and wondering feebly where I might be. And my cousin, Alison Stanhope, will conveniently remember that she saw me go in this direction. Any moment now, someone, probably several someones, will come in and find us.'

'Not much of a discovery,' she mocked. 'You on one side of the sofa and me on the other.'

His smile sent chills down her spine. 'If necessary, they will find you with your skirts around your waist and me on top of you.'

She jerked backwards, her knees shaking. He was much taller than she was. If he caught her... She shuddered, remembering his strength. All her senses at the stretch, she waited as he began to circle the sofa slowly. She edged away. If she could get to the other side, she would have a clear run to the door...

He vaulted over in an effortless move.

She had a split second's warning to whirl and run, but, hampered by her skirts, she had scarcely taken three strides before he was on her, spinning her against him and clamping a hand over her mouth. Struggling wildly, she was borne back towards the sofa.

'For God's sake, you little spitfire!' he hissed viciously as she kicked him on the knee. He forced her on. She fought the more furiously. If once he got her to the sofa...his very weight would subdue her.

She heard a tearing sound as her bodice ripped in the struggle and bit down savagely on his hand. Swearing, he loosened his grip and she managed to turn towards him, getting in one blow to his nose and spitting in his face.

She was free and leapt back.

He still stood between her and the door. The slow smile as he wiped his face said that he knew it.

Cressida fought to steady her breathing. Fear lashed her. She must not get caught in a compromising position. She couldn't bear for Jack to marry her under those circumstances. Somehow she had to stay out of Fairbridge's hands. Literally. If only she could get to the door, she knew the house and would be able to escape.

She couldn't get past him. If once she made a break for the door, he would be on her.

'That torn bodice will pretty well do the job for me when they find us,' said Fairbridge.

Cressida resisted the temptation to shrug. 'I'll tell the truth, that you—'

He interrupted. 'Became carried away by passion when I begged you to marry me.'

She smiled. 'And were so dreadfully disappointed when I told you I had accepted my cousin's offer instead.'

He froze. Then, 'You're lying. What would Hamilton want with a soiled little dove? *He* doesn't need your dowry.'

He came towards her, steadily, inexorably, but Cressida had seen what she needed. There would be only one chance. Abandoning caution, she darted for the door and, as Fairbridge charged after her, swung around, rushing at him.

He checked, startled. And swore as Cressida flung herself down in his path and rolled under his feet bringing him down heavily. Gasping for the breath he had kicked out of her, she surged to her feet in a flurry of silken skirts, coming up against the console table with a crash that nearly shook it loose from the wall.

Grabbing an *épée*, she whirled around to face him.

Every rib felt battered, but she said coolly, 'Checkmate, my lord.'

He came to his feet slowly and his eyes narrowed. 'If you say so, my dear.'

'I do,' she said. 'You are running out of time, my lord. If anyone comes in now… How many men, making an *honourable* offer to a woman, are held off with a sword?' She fought down the knowledge that being caught like this would spell ruin as surely as if Fairbridge had succeeded.

He did not answer, but waited. And waited.

The minutes stretched out until Cressida's arm began to ache with the strain of holding the sword up. At first it had felt light enough, but holding it up, and keeping it steady…

She could feel the fine trembling in her arm. She did not dare set her other hand to it. It would be too awkward. And too revealing. If Fairbridge did not already know that the sword was too heavy for her, Cressida had no intention of telling him.

All her nerves alight, she considered her situation. It was not really checkmate. He could still move freely. More like check. He could not approach her, but if she tried to move for the door, he would be able to take the second sword and disarm her. She could see the clock on the chimney-piece out of the corner of her eye and shivered. She had defeated Fairbridge and time would defeat her. Could she take both swords? Impossible. One sword was heavy and unwieldy enough.

As she watched him, he took off his coat. He was going to try and catch the blade through it.

Then she heard it. A hubbub of conversation from the hall. Numbness gripped her. This, then, was the end of her brief dream of happiness. Not even to return the dowry could she marry Jack in the aftermath of a scandal like this.

The door opened. 'Maybe he's in here…this is the libr— Oh! I say! Er…sorry to interrupt and all that, but, ah, Lady Fairbridge has…' Young Mr Guilfoyle's voice trailed off as his startled gaze landed on Cressida.

'Conveniently fainted in the ballroom,' suggested Cressida, hitching up her torn bodice.

'Oh…well, um…yes,' he said, eyes goggling. He seemed to recollect himself. 'Well, it wasn't convenient exactly, but…'

'I'll come at once,' said Fairbridge smoothly. 'My betrothed will excuse me if I don't give her any more fencing tips tonight.'

She would have consigned him to hell, along with all the people crowding avidly in the doorway, but she never got the chance.

'*Your* betrothed, did I hear you say, Fairbridge?' came a deep voice, pouring cold water on the excited simmer of incipient scandal. '*Your* betrothed?' Jack forced his way through the door with little or no regard for those in his way.

Cressida's heart lurched. She was vaguely aware that Marc stalked close behind him, but her eyes fixed on his face. Terror rushed through her. His face was locked in lines of savage fury. He was going to call Fairbridge out.

Only iron control kept Jack from launching himself at the Viscount's throat as he came through the door. There must be no misunderstanding about the situation. He had to make quite sure everyone understood what they had interrupted.

Swiftly he searched for Cressida. And felt his jaw nearly dislocate itself as he saw her, gripping one of the *épées*. By God, she had held the bastard off. With a sword. His little Cressida. Gallant to the last.

Marc's urbane voice came from just behind him. 'Hmm. What a redoubtable girl. And you're going to marry her. Good luck.'

Jack ignored that. 'I can think of three reasons why it is impossible for you to be betrothed to Miss Bramley,' he informed Lord Fairbridge. 'She has accepted *my* offer of marriage and the announcement of our betrothal will appear in the papers tomorrow. With her consent.'

A shocked hush fell over the curious crowd seeping into the library.

Jack stood and waited, cold patience holding him in check.

'Er, that's only two reasons at most, Jack, old fellow,' pointed out Lord Parbury, politely edging his way past Mr Guilfoyle. 'What's the third?'

'The third?' asked Jack, trying not to sing with triumph. 'The third is that Fairbridge has shown himself to be such a contemptible cur, that no woman of even moderate breeding and intelligence would choose to sully herself by such an alliance.'

This time the hush was deathly, but Jack didn't have long to wait.

'Why, you arrogant bastard! You'll answer for that! Name your seconds!'

Jack saw the choking fury in Fairbridge's face with savage satisfaction. 'Certainly, my lord,' he said promptly. 'Rutherford and Sir Toby Carlton will act for me. Choose yours quickly, Fairbridge. I have no intention of missing supper over this affair.'

'What the hell do you mean?' snarled Fairbridge. 'My seconds will call on yours! Or aren't you familiar with the rules governing an affair of honour?'

Jack permitted his lips to curve in satisfaction. 'Oh, I'm perfectly familiar with them, my lord. You, on the other hand, seem to be a little out of touch with the niceties of honourable conduct. Your challenge, Fairbridge. My choice of time and place.' He paused. 'And weapons, of course.' His glance roved around the library. 'Right here, right now. And no doubt Rutherford will be happy to lend us his swords. I repeat: name your seconds, coward!'

'Oh, I say, Hamilton! That's coming it a trifle strong!' protested Mr Guilfoyle.

'Is it, Mr Guilfoyle?' asked Jack. 'Let me ask you: what name would you give a man who courted a gently reared girl with promises of marriage and then told her his mother would never countenance the match and asked her to be his mistress instead? What name would you give him when, in the face of her refusal, he attempted to force himself on her? What name would you give him when it transpired that his whole intent was to ruin the girl and thus force her father out of his living? What name would you give him when he ensured the girl's name and reputation were destroyed?'

Mr Guilfoyle blanched.

Jack paused and turned slowly to Fairbridge. 'There are several names for the man who did all that and then attempted to force the girl into marriage when she acquired a generous dowry that would cover his gaming debts. Since there are ladies present I shall have to content myself with calling him: coward.'

'By God, I'll teach you a lesson, Hamilton!' exploded Fairbridge. 'Would you question the word of a gentleman over this little trollop?'

Jack shook off Marc's restraining hand. 'Yes,' he grated. 'I would. But the question doesn't arise, since you fail to qualify as a gentleman. But that will not deter me from teaching you a lesson for insulting Miss Bramley. Your seconds! Quickly. Or have you thought the better of your challenge? I'm sure we would all understand if that were the case.'

For a moment it seemed all too possible that Fairbridge would deprive Jack of satisfaction by dying of apoplexy. He turned purple and literally shook with rage. He looked around wildly. No one stepped forward.

'I'll act for myself!' he snarled. 'If I might examine the blades?'

'I'll act for Fairbridge,' said Mr Guilfoyle suddenly. 'Awkward affair. Rutherford's a second in his own house. His blades, too. Dashed irregular anyway. Not that I'm implying anything dishonourable, my lord,' he added hastily as Rutherford raised his eyebrows. 'But it's best to have everything all snug.'

'Oh, very well,' sighed Lord Petersham, edging past Lady Jersey. 'Excuse me, Sally. I must say this goes against the grain, but Guilfoyle has the right of it. I'll act with him. Just to oblige you, Jack!'

'My thanks, gentlemen,' Fairbridge sneered. 'How very gallant of you! Rutherford, Carlton! You may deal with Mr Guilfoyle and Lord Petersham.'

Marc nodded and went to Cressida.

She looked at him, dazed. When had her elegant, easy-going host been replaced with this cold, grim aristocrat? He met her glance and the chilly eyes softened slightly.

His quiet words reached only her. 'Don't worry, Cressida. Nothing will happen to him.' Then, a little louder, 'I do apologise that you were subjected to such unpleasantness under my roof, Miss Bramley. If I might have both swords, please?'

Automatically she moved so that he could reach the sword on the console table. She flinched slightly as his fingers touched hers. Puzzled, she looked down and discovered that she still held her sword, clenched tightly.

Jack was going to fight a duel. He had insulted Fairbridge publicly, openly questioning his honour. Fairbridge would be ready to kill. It was all her stupid fault. And even if Jack won…what if he killed Fairbridge? He'd have to flee the country, ruin his life just because she had made an unholy mess of everything. Shivering she looked at Jack. The expression on his face said very clearly that no arguments would alter his decision.

'Cressida, let go. You are safe now. Come, you must give me the sword.'

Again she looked down and discovered that Marc was uncurling her fingers from the hilt, one by one. She jerked back from him, still gripping the sword. Her voice came out queerly detached. 'I'll give it to him.'

Keeping the blade lowered, she walked steadily towards Jack. Fairbridge stood in her way, his blue eyes scornful. Coldness spread and firmed inside her, sheathing her resolve in bitter ice. Reaching Fairbridge, she stopped.

'You'll never live the gossip down,' he mocked. 'You know that, don't you?'

She nodded. 'I might have been naïve, my lord, but I'm not stupid.' She smiled at him gently. 'Of course, in that situation I have nothing to lose. They might as well have

something worth gossiping over.' So saying, she lifted the
sword in one swift motion and lunged.

Jack's roar of protest nearly drowned out the Viscount's
scream of shocked pain as he staggered back, clutching his
right arm just above the elbow. His forearm hung useless
and a slow trickle of blood squeezed from between his
fingers.

'*Bloody hell!*'

Rutherford strode past her, his dropped jaw radiating
disbelief. Lord Petersham, Sir Toby and Mr Guilfoyle all
converged on the disabled duellist.

Still dumbfounded, Rutherford turned back to Cressida.
Then the corner of his mouth twitched. 'I thought you
meant to give the damn thing to Jack.'

The guilty flush burnt her cheeks. 'I...I know you did.
I'm awfully sorry, my lord. I thought if you knew what I
intended...you'd stop me.'

The twitch became an outright grin. 'Don't waste your
apologies on me, my dear. Unless I'm much mistaken,
Jack is about to peel one out of your hide, since you've
saved Fairbridge from him.' He looked at her with an ap-
proving smile and added very softly, 'And a damn good
thing, too. Well done. I'm sure you'll both be happier in
Leicestershire than on the continent.'

Jack's voice sliced through the confused babble at the
door. 'Perhaps if everyone would like to remove themselves,' he said, 'I might be permitted to discuss the situation with *my* betrothed.'

They were alone and Cressida finally faced Jack's blistering anger.

'What the devil did you do that for?' he demanded.

Whatever had surged through her blood, giving her the
strength to face down Fairbridge and defy him, whatever
had kept her chin up while the others remained in the

room, Cressida had no idea. All she knew was that it had deserted her, leaving her drained and exhausted.

'I...I...' Cold, she was so cold. And she couldn't stop shaking. Shudders racked her until she could barely stand. She rubbed clumsily at her arms, but her hands felt cold, clammy. The room swung about her in sickening swoops.

If I don't sit down... She took a step and staggered as a wave of blackness hit her. Somehow she had made it to the sofa and he was there, enfolding her in his arms, pressing her head to lie against his shoulder.

'Sshh. You're safe now,' he murmured. 'Take a deep breath, relax. He won't touch you again.' His heat poured through her, but she continued to shake, wondering if she were about to laugh or cry. Nothing made sense. She was safe. Jack was safe.

And she had to release him from their betrothal. 'I...I'm releasing you...' she whispered. She felt every muscle surrounding her tense and his hand stilled on her hair. The breath he took shivered through her.

'Sweetheart, in case you hadn't noticed, *I'm* holding *you*. And I have no intention of releasing you. Ever. Under any circumstances.'

Oh, God. He's being chivalrous again! And after I made him look a complete fool in front of the entire ton*!* She struggled to free herself and sit up. 'But you must! It's quite all right, Jack. I know that I can't marry you after tonight. We...we don't need to say anything. Even if the notice is in the papers tomorrow...'

'It will be,' he interpolated.

She hurried on. 'No one will say anything. At the end of the Season I can go away and...and everything will be just as it was. People will forget and...and...' She would spend the rest of her life crying herself to sleep.

'That's your idea of *all right*, is it?' Jack asked in a very neutral voice.

Shakily she nodded.

'Well, it's not mine,' he said bluntly. 'You're forgetting something,' he went on. 'You've still got something of mine.'

Wildly she tried to imagine what. She had nothing of his, except…

'You want the necklace back.' Try as she might, she could not disguise the wobble in her voice. It might have little value, but to her it was all the riches of the Orient.

'I don't want anything back,' he said quietly. 'Not even my heart. I'll settle for yours instead.' He gave Cressida no further warning of his intentions. He moved with all the speed of a striking cat, and had her locked in his arms. Anything she might have said was lost as his mouth came down on hers in fierce possession.

His control fractured as she gave herself completely into his embrace. There was nothing gentle about his kiss, or about the arms that locked around her. Nothing gentle and everything possessive. Nothing mattered except convincing her once and for all of his love. He could feel sobs racking her and released her mouth to whisper kisses over her brow and cheeks.

'I thought he might kill you,' she whispered. 'If you had died…' Her fingers shook as she stroked his cheek, drew his mouth back to hers again.

He kissed her gently, his mouth drifting over hers as he murmured soothingly. Sobs still shuddered through her and he tasted tears on her lips, her cheeks. With clumsy, shaking hands he framed her face and wiped the tears away with his thumbs.

'Oh, Cress, you little idiot. If you think I'll let you go now…' His arms tightened around her and he sought her mouth again. She gave it unhesitatingly with a sweet generosity that seared him, her lips parting in wordless invitation. He took instant advantage, plundering the vulnerable softness in fierce possession. His hands roved, claiming every feminine curve until his control threatened to break completely.

'You have to marry me, sweetheart.' He felt her stiffen and he held her closer. 'I know. You thought I offered for you because I think you need protecting. It's partially true, because I can't help myself. Damn it, Cressida, I've been in love with you for weeks.' He corrected himself. 'No. I think I've been in love with you from the moment we met, but I was too curst stubborn to see it.'

'You love me? Really love me?' The aching hope in her voice turned like a knife in his soul. 'You don't just feel obliged to protect me?'

He shook his head against her hair, a soft auburn cloud, teasing his senses. 'No. I need to protect you. And I need you. Like I need to breathe.' He floundered, lost for words to tell her how he felt. 'I can't help it, Cress. Any more than you could help trying to protect your father, or worrying about me challenging Fairbridge.' His jaw clenched. 'You're mine. And I'm not going to let you wriggle out of our betrothal.' He waited, conscious that he hadn't said it all. That he didn't know how. All he felt for her seemed to have frozen his wits and tongue.

The quiet stretched between them as Cressida stared at him, trying to see his face in the fire lit shadows. She couldn't think, her heart still raced, her blood still burned in the aftermath of his kisses. He had said he loved her. He had said he needed her. That she was his. She couldn't doubt him. Only one emotion could possibly blaze with that sort of protectiveness and possessiveness. Her heart sang with the sincerity of his declaration, but still she hesitated. Was she doing the right thing in accepting him? Would he come to regret it one day? What would his mother and sister think of such a connection?

Before she could speak again, he slipped a hand into his coat pocket and brought out something that glittered, and flashed fire in the flickering light. Reaching for her left hand, he slipped the delicate marquise ring on to her third finger.

'It belonged to my great-grandmother.' Cressida could hear the smile in his voice and her fingers trembled in his gentle hold. 'She of the spice biscuits. My great-grandfather gave it to her on their fiftieth wedding anniversary.' He cleared his throat. 'I never saw her without it. She left a note saying I was to have it when Mama was ready to give it to me. I never understood why until she gave it to me tonight.'

He lifted her hand to his lips and kissed it. 'I'm yours, Cress. Will you be mine?'

She couldn't speak. The words, whatever they were, had stuck somewhere in her throat, clogged with tears of joy. But she did manage to nod and stroke his jaw with shaking fingers before he drew her back into his arms and kissed the tears away. His lips feathered over her eyes and cheeks, burning in their tenderness. 'Mine.' It was a low, possessive growl.

Her response breathed from her very soul. 'Always.'

Their kiss left him shaking with urgency. Desire hammered in his blood as he locked every muscle against the need to sweep her up into his arms and carry her to the sofa. Dazed, he reached for the easy self-control he had used with every other woman he had ever had. It wasn't there.

Even as he grappled with the knowledge and strove for something, anything to rein himself in, a small hand reached up and stroked his cheek. A butterfly's caress over his jaw, gentle and yearning. That did it. Scooping her up into his arms, he stood up and headed for the door.

'Jack? Why are we in my bedchamber?'

He drew a deep breath. 'Because I'm making love to you and the library is a trifle public.' Even as he spoke,

his hands skimmed over her waist, tracing the sweet curve
down and over her hip to flex gently.

'M...making love to me? Why?'

'Because I want you.' He kissed her gently on the lips.
'Because I can't help myself.' This time he traced her lips
with his tongue, tasting and biting until she opened her
mouth for him. Groaning, he took what she offered, sliding
his tongue deeply and rhythmically into the honeyed
warmth. He shuddered in delight as he felt her answer, felt
her body melt against his.

With an effort he drew back and said raggedly, 'Because
I love you, Cressida. You're mine. Do you understand?'

All the breath left Cressida's body as the reality of his
words finally hit her and the truth of what he had said
blazed in his eyes. Storm-dark grey, they held nothing as
soft as pity or chivalry. Only a hard-edged need, which
should have terrified her in its intensity.

'You...you want me that much?' she stammered. 'You
can't.'

'Oh, yes, I can,' he whispered against her mouth. 'And
I'm about to demonstrate.'

She gasped and shuddered as she felt him draw her
lower lip into his mouth and bite down gently. Heat
streamed through her, welling up endlessly as his mouth
plundered hers, tenderly, mercilessly. Eagerly she kissed
him back, sliding her own tongue against his, pressing herself closer and closer to his shockingly hard, hot body. Her
fingers sank into the surging muscles of his shoulders under the fine linen of his shirt. Heat poured out in waves,
melting, intoxicating.

When he finally broke the kiss she whimpered in protest,
wildly aware that her lips were swollen and tingling from
the pressure of his mouth.

'Cress.'

She could scarcely recognise his voice. It sounded
hoarse and strained.

'I'm telling you now; I need you to be mine. In bed.' He dragged in a deep breath. 'If you want me to wait until our wedding night, you'll have to kick me out and lock the door. Not very chivalrous of me, but it's the best I can do.'

She looked up in disbelief. 'You want me so much that you'd...you'd...take me n...now.'

He nodded, a rueful smile on his face. 'Right now,' he affirmed softly. 'As long as you swear you'll make an honest man of me as soon as we can get back to Leicestershire for your father to marry us.'

She trembled as she felt his powerful hands flex on her hips. Fire shot through her until she could scarcely think. His eyes, stormy with desire, didn't help her confusion in the least. Jack Hamilton, renowned for his chivalry, kindness and honourable behaviour under all circumstances, had actually begged her to go to bed with him before they were married. And the closest he could get to chivalrous behaviour was warning her to kick him out if she didn't want him to take her. He plainly had no intention of kicking himself out. She could see the tension in his body, the locking of every muscle. Except those hands, which didn't seem able to help themselves.

Why? What had driven him to this state?

He answered her unspoken question. 'Sweetheart, I can't explain. I don't understand it myself. I've never been like this with a woman. Unable to control myself. I thought I'd go mad when I realised what was happening...' He shuddered. 'And I thought I'd kill Fairbridge when I found you.' His jaw clenched.

'You'd have been angry no matter who the woman was, though,' she pointed out quietly.

He nodded. 'Yes. Angry, disgusted. And you're quite right. I would have helped any woman in trouble.' Shaking, he pulled her against his body again. 'But I wouldn't be in her bedchamber now trying to seduce her.' He kissed her gently. 'Chivalry didn't have very much to do with it, Cressida. Possessiveness, protectiveness; they were driving me. If you're expecting chivalry, we have a problem. I've none where you're concerned. Only love.'

Her mouth went dry and she had to force words past the tears clogging her throat. 'That…that will do to be going on with. Are you going to take me to bed now?'

His voice shook with raw need. 'Are you sure, Cress?' Even as he spoke his mouth sought hers.

'Yes,' she whispered against his seeking lips. 'I don't want chivalry. Only you. Now.'

His mouth answered her, taking hers in a kiss that both possessed and cherished. Without breaking the kiss, he lifted her into his arms effortlessly. Swirling streamers of heat writhed through her, coiling tighter and tighter as she again realised his power; and his passion, hovering on the brink of frenzy. She twined her arms about his neck, straining to get closer as he carried her to the bed and lowered her to it. Then nervousness assailed her.

Swallowing hard, she watched as he removed his shoes and stockings. Shyly she reached out and traced the shifting muscles in his shoulder, felt them flicker in response. Then he turned to her and took her hands, placed them at the top button of his shirt. Her eyes widened as shock lanced through her at the realisation that he wanted her to undress him.

Jack watched enthralled as understanding dawned in her eyes. He reined in the urge to tumble her back on the pillows and ravish her, as trembling, uncertain fingers fumbled with the buttons of his shirt. He set his jaw and endured, as light accidental caresses scorched his burning skin.

He had to touch her or die. Slowly he reached for the laces of her torn gown and felt her fingers still on the last button. Huge, questioning pools of green stared at him. One by one he loosened the laces. He shifted his hands to her shoulders and pushed it down to her waist. His blood thundered as he saw the chemise it had concealed. God alone knew what Meg had been thinking of when she recommended that little wisp of silken temptation. Sheer ivory silk, he doubted that it was warming Cressida, but it was certainly causing his already heated blood to boil over. Taut pink buds thrust pleadingly against the diaphanous material.

With a groan he tore his shirt off over his head and pulled Cressida back where she belonged, into his arms. Heat burned through him as his hands shifted over her, shaping and learning every delicate curve under the silk. Her mouth under his, yielding and passionate as he possessed it deeply, rhythmically. Small hands on his shoulders, stroking, exploring, a sweet fire on his body.

Cressida was far beyond thought. A sob of delight escaped her lips as he pressed her back into the pillows and followed her down. A strong hand beneath her hips lifted her slightly and swept the ruined gown away leaving her in just the chemise and a petticoat. Then the petticoat and chemise were gone and his hands roamed unhindered on her burning flesh.

Large, strong hands that wielded a tender power over her senses, beguiling, adoring. Instinctively she responded in the same way, stroking and exploring the curved muscles of his shoulders, his broad back. His groans and the shudders that racked him had heat pooling in her belly and lower. Never had she imagined that desire was like this, a burning, shimmering fire in her soul.

She cried out as she felt his teasing fingers slide lower, into her soft curls, pressing intimately into the melting heat between her thighs. Shivers coursed through her as she felt his hand stroke her inner thigh, lightly, possessively. His mouth came to hers again, licking and biting tenderly at her lips. 'Open for me, little one.' The velvet-dark voice caressed her heart as surely and intimately as his hands and mouth caressed her body.

Frantic with need, she opened her mouth, wanting to feel him inside her, filling her mouth, ravishing her with his kiss. He continued to tantalise with light, teasing caresses. She had to have more. Her entire body sang with longing. Distantly she could hear someone sobbing, begging, 'Please…oh, please…'

Her own voice, torn from her throat. Her body, arching against his in sensuous pleading as her thighs parted in surrender.

He gave her more. His fingers teased with such shattering intimacy that she cried out, scarcely able to comprehend what he was doing. Heat coiled in her. She arched again and felt his other arm slip beneath her, holding her as his mouth blazed fire over her throat to one breast.

He thought he might die. He'd never known anything like this in his life. Not this hot, sweet wanting that burned in his blood and soul. Never had he needed to take a woman like this. Never before had he known, to the depths of his soul, that he couldn't stop, short of death. That he needed her like he needed breath.

He needed to feel her all around him, all that soft, wet heat holding him safely. Now. He groaned. Not yet. He circled her swollen breast hotly, lifting her into the savage heat of his mouth, drawing the sweet flesh deep, moulding the taut peak with his tongue, scoring with his teeth in fierce restraint. He felt her body's response as urgent heat welled up between her thighs, spilling helplessly over his fingers. Burning in passion's grip, he pressed gently at her entrance with one finger, felt her still in sensual shock.

Words were beyond him, but he had to make sure she understood. Releasing her breast he took her mouth again, deeply, intimately, his tongue penetrating and retreating in rhythmic surges. And felt her response, felt her kiss him back, draw him deeper. Locking every muscle in his body against the savage need to open his breeches and sink himself to the hilt in her sweetness, he continued to play, sought out the secrets between her thighs even as he plundered her mouth and drank her cries of pleasure.

She couldn't think, only feel as he taught her the secrets of her own body. And want. She wanted him inside her. Now. Empty, aching, she wanted to feel him deep within. Desperately she lifted against him, fire raging through every vein as she fought to get closer. Through his breeches she could feel the hard male flesh riding against her hip as he lay half over her. Instinctively she reached for it, sliding her hand over the front of his breeches, between their bodies. His whole body jerked, tightened and she felt one probing, wicked finger slide within as his thumb found a place that laced her body with jagged lightning.

Shock held her motionless, her hand still on the throbbing front of his breeches, dazed at the intimacy of his touch, at the pleasure rippling out from her very centre. He stroked gently, deeply and she felt his flesh stir under her hand.

'Am I hurting you?' The words were harsh, ragged, spoken against her mouth. As if he could barely force them out. She couldn't even answer. She could only cling tightly and move against him as her response pulsed hotly between them.

He needed no further answer. Jack clenched his jaw, his entire body, against the need to take her. Now. At once. Five minutes ago. She felt so soft and hot, her body tightening sweetly around him. He ravished her mouth instead as talons of desire raked him mercilessly.

Trembling fingers continued to stroke over the front of his breeches. He shuddered at the pleasure and tried not to think about how it would feel without a layer of satin muting her curiosity. Releasing her mouth, he rested his brow on hers and whispered, 'Are you trying to kill me?'

At once she stopped and took her hand away. 'Jack? Am I hurting you?'

'No,' he groaned. 'You're killing me. There's a difference.'

Her innocence burnt at his control. It was time. Gently he withdrew his hand from the lush sweetness between her thighs, savouring her sob of protest. He kissed it tenderly from her lips and sat up.

Her eyes were dazed, so dilated that all he could see of the green was a smouldering rim around the black. Cat's eyes, burning in the night, and like a cat she arched her body towards him in need.

Slowly his fingers went to the front of his breeches, where he held her suddenly focused gaze as he unbuttoned them. Her breath caught somewhere in her throat as she watched the breeches slide off, revealing the tip of that arrow of black hair, which pointed to…

He reached for her.

'Jack…' It had never occurred to her that her lack of height and small frame would be such a problem, but as she gazed, stunned, at his body, she realised that it was. Heat pulsed between her thighs as she remembered his finger teasing and probing, sliding deep…her entire body quivered in sensual need…but it had to be impossible.

His hands slid over her shoulders, drawing her up against him. He knelt in front of her and pulled her into his arms, his lips feathering over her face, gentle hands roving over heated skin so that fire flickered and spread, melting through her veins. His mouth settled ravenously over hers, devouring, seducing. The hot penetration of his tongue brought her pressing urgently against him, feeling the rasp of his hair roughened chest on her swollen, aching nipples.

She felt the buried groan, deep inside him as he shifted against her sensuously. A gasp escaped her as his hands stroked and cupped her bottom, and brought her gently

against his loins. And he rocked. Back and forth, his hard
length pressing into her soft belly. She clung to him, stroking his shoulders, his back, feeling the taut muscles flicker
and tighten under her hands.

'Touch me.' The husky whisper seared through her.

Her hands stilled. 'There?' Heat flooded her at the
thought of touching him so intimately.

'Yes. There.' He caught her hand and brought it between
their bodies, curving her fingers around him. So hot, so
silky smooth. And hard. The heat at her core redoubled in
a melting surge.

Then his hand slid away, between her trembling thighs,
searching and finding. A sob of anticipation escaped her,
but his fingers, traced, circled, teased. No more. And she
needed him. Needed to feel him inside her. Urgently she
shifted, trying to move his fingers to the right spot.

'Are you still scared?'

Had she been scared? She looked up into the burning
grey eyes and whispered, 'No.'

He took her mouth and brought her to him, pulling her
across his thighs so that she straddled him, his hands resting possessively on her hips.

'Jack?'

'It's all right,' he murmured, taking tiny biting kisses
on her lips, as one hand slid between her thighs. 'Like
this.' And he pressed her down, opening her hot, swollen
flesh with gentle fingers as he did so. Her eyes flew open
as she felt him, hard and blunt at her entrance, pushing
inside.

She tensed in shock and felt his body turn to iron as he
stopped. His mouth drifted down her throat, licking, suck-
ing at the wildly beating pulse. His hand between her
thighs moved and a lightning bolt struck through her as he
pressed knowingly. And his mouth found her breast, drew
the burning peak deep into the heat of his mouth. Every
nerve in her body exploded with a fiery need.

Jack felt the change at once. Every muscle locked against the urge to thrust deep into the melting heat that spilled over him, he rocked her body against his. Teasing her, torturing himself. And felt her press down further, enveloping more of him in silken heat. Tight, so tight. He shuddered and took her mouth fiercely, needing to be inside her, caressing her mouth with the intimate penetration of his tongue.

He drank the little cries of pleasure from her lips and rocked gently, encouragingly, his hand on the sleek curve of her hip urging her lower. All at once he felt it, a constriction, barring him from her most intimate depths.

He could barely breathe as he gripped her hips and lifted her. Carefully, with exquisite slowness, he lowered her again, his gaze on her face. This time she felt it, too. He could see it in the ripple of awareness as her eyes opened, hear it in the sharp intake of breath, felt it in her fingers digging into his shoulders.

Cressida had gone beyond frantic. Nothing existed beyond his hands burning on her body and his hard male flesh stretching, tantalising her. She wanted more, much more, but he had stopped, was holding rigidly still, his face harsh with restraint. And it felt as though he could come no further.

'Jack...' Her voice broke on a gasp as he shifted inside her, increasing the pressure.

'Stay still,' he ground out. 'It's all right. Just...stay... still.'

He moved again and fire splintered deeply, melting beneath her heated skin.

'Please...oh...please.' She clung to him, her hands sliding over his shoulders, her mouth capturing his in desperate entreaty, shredding at his control. She felt his grip on her hips flex, then harden as he lifted her. A broken cry of pleasure rippled from her and she tightened instinctively around him.

Fiery need scorched through the simmering remnants of Jack's control. With a groan of ecstasy he caught her lips and plundered as he brought her body down to meet his thrust. His mouth took her shocked cry as she shuddered against him. He set his jaw, fought the urge to tip her back on the pillows and ravish her. Every muscle and nerve turned to steel as he cradled her protectively and soothed her with kisses and tender murmurs, waiting for her body to ease in acceptance.

He slipped his hand between them to fondle her breast. Felt her pleasure—hot, liquid silk spilling between them. She shifted slightly and he felt it again, searing his shuddering flesh. He brushed his mouth over hers and closed his eyes on a groan as her whole body softened against him, around him.

He heard his name, whispered against his mouth on a sob of pleasure and held her tightly to him as he withdrew a short way and pressed in again slowly, finding only hot, yielding sweetness that held him in loving intimacy.

'Mine,' he whispered. 'Every hot, soft inch of you. Always. I'll never let you go.' Supporting her every inch of the way, he tipped her back into the pillows and came down over her, bracing himself on his elbows, still fully sheathed within her. She lay beneath him, eyes dilated with passion, her soft lips swollen and quivering. One small hand came up and traced his cheek, his jaw and the corner of his mouth.

The butterfly caress drew an aching groan from deep within him. He turned his head slightly to capture her finger with his lips and draw it into his mouth. Gently he bit down and groaned again as he felt the shudder of her response ripple through her.

Cressida cried out wildly as he moved deeply within her body in the oldest dance of all. Instinctively she caught the rhythm and matched it, lifting to meet his thrusts, knowing that she was both possessor and possessed. Lover and beloved.

The knowledge bloomed within her, even as her body flamed to incandescence beneath him, the tension coiling and spiralling, tighter and higher with every thrust and with the fierce mating of their mouths.

The tension wound tighter in the sweetest anguish, threatening, promising to break, to tear her apart. So close. She sobbed in her need and felt his hand slip under her hips, long fingers caressing and squeezing. Then his hand flexed, tilting her into his thrusts, holding her there helpless in the storm of his possession.

She broke, fire exploding through her with a shuddering cry that he stole from her lips even as he had taken her body and soul. Ecstasy held her stretched on the quivering rack of fire, burning her to her soul.

The shuddering pulses of her release stripped the last of Jack's control. White hot with raw, aching need, he took her again and again, in thrall to her passion, his own consummation breaking over him in an endless wave.

Stunned, he collapsed on top of her, every muscle relaxed and heavy. Joy sang through every vein. His. All his. Every soft, sweet, stubborn inch of her. Forever.

Jack lay steeped in contentment, as dawn stole into the bedchamber. He ought to leave, before one of the maids came in, but he couldn't. Cressida lay, a warm, trusting weight, in his arms. Her cheek rested on his shoulder, one rounded arm reached across his chest and a silken thigh lay trapped between his. If he left he'd disturb her. And she hadn't had a great deal of sleep.

Chivalry, it appeared, was dead. Only need and passion remained. No chivalrous man behaved as he had done, sneaking into his betrothed's bedchamber and then preempting the wedding night. Several times. He certainly didn't lie there in the pearly light of dawn pretending the only reason he hadn't left was fear of waking her. Not when he was, in fact, waiting for her to waken of her own accord so that he could have her again. And make quite sure she was convinced that he loved her, of course.

She stirred against him with a sleepy, questioning murmur that heated his blood even further. He rolled and settled her beneath him, taking her mouth even as her eyes fluttered open.

When he finally broke the kiss she smiled up at him and wriggled helpfully.

'Did I tell you I love you?' he whispered, brushing his mouth over hers again.

'Yes.' She twined her arms around his neck and drew him down to her.

He held back, resisting her sweet temptations. 'Did I convince you?' His loins shifted against her.

'Oh, *yes*.' She arched under him.

He lowered his mouth to hers. 'Good. Because I'm going to convince you again.'

Ten days later Cressida stood beside Jack facing her father before the altar. The bright crisp morning was dimmed to a gentle glow in the old church at Ratby. Very few people had been asked to come from town, but, none the less, the pews were full enough for Cressida. All the people she cared for were there. And the one she cared for most stood right beside her.

The words of the marriage service flowed over and through them in loving benediction. The only difficulty about the swiftness of the wedding had been Dr Bramley's uncertainty as to whether he should perform the ceremony or give his daughter away.

'Who giveth this woman to be married to this man?'

'I do.' The Earl of Rutherford's deep voice was a blessing in itself.

Her eyes full of tears, Cressida smiled up at Jack, as

Marcus placed her hand in his. Jack had solved even this problem. He had told her father that since his home would hence forth be the dower house at Wyckeham, he was not really giving his daughter away. And that there was no one he'd liefer be married by.

He smiled back at her as he repeated his vows steadily. The formal measured words only confirmed what his eyes told her. *Mine. Always.*

* * * * *

The Regency

LORDS & LADIES
COLLECTION

More Glittering Regency Love Affairs

VOLUME NINETEEN

Tavern Wench by Anne Ashley

Alone in the world and too proud for charity, vicar's daughter
Emma Lynn earns her money by cooking – in a tavern! But
her independence has a heavy price – a tavern wench isn't fit
to mix with the gentry and Emma has had to turn her back
on the Polite World. But Mr Benedict Grantley, baronet's
heir, isn't going to let Emma's principles stand in his way.

The Incomparable Countess by Mary Nichols

For one long, hot summer Frances and Marcus had meant
everything to each other. And then he had betrayed her
by marrying someone else. Having learnt to suppress her
youthful desires, Frances, Countess of Corringham can't deny
she's pained to hear that Marcus, Duke of Lascoe is looking
for a new wife to care for his motherless child…

On sale 7th March 2008

www.millsandboon.co.uk

If you've missed any of the volumes in the
Regency Lords & Ladies Collection, you can
have them delivered straight to your door

Please add 99p postage & packing
per book

DELIVERY TO UK ONLY

Post to: End Page Offer,
PO Box 1780,
Croydon, CR9 3UH

E-mail: customer.relations@hmb.co.uk

Just fill in the attached form and ensure that you
include full postal address details.
Please pay by cheque or postal order
(payable to 'Reader Service'). Prices and
availability subject to change without notice.

Order online at: www.millsandboon.co.uk

Allow 28 days for delivery

Volume	Authors	ISBN & Price	Quantity
1	Nicola Cornick & Anne Ashley	978 0263 84570 9 £5.99	
2	Ann Elizabeth Cree & Anne Ashley	978 0263 84571 6 £5.99	
3	Paula Marshall & Meg Alexander	978 0263 84572 3 £5.99	
4	Francesca Shaw & Meg Alexander	978 0263 84573 0 £5.99	
5	Joanna Maitland & Mary Brendan	978 0263 84574 7 £5.99	
6	Elizabeth Rolls & Mary Brendan	978 0263 84575 4 £5.99	
7	Anne Herries & Anne Ashley	978 0263 84423 8 £5.99	
8	Elizabeth Bailey & Anne Ashley	978 0263 84424 5 £5.99	
9	Sylvia Andrew & Claire Thornton	978 0263 84425 2 £5.99	
10	Meg Alexander & Claire Thornton	978 0263 84426 9 £5.99	
11	Mary Nichols & Paula Marshall	978 0263 84427 6 £5.99	
12	Anne Gracie & Paula Marshall	978 0263 84428 3 £5.99	
13	Helen Dickson & Joanna Maitland	978 0263 85105 2 £5.99	
14	Julia Justiss & Joanna Maitland	978 0263 85106 9 £5.99	
15	Claire Thornton & Georgina Devon	978 0263 85107 6 £5.99	
16	Gayle Wilson & Georgina Devon	978 0263 85108 3 £5.99	

The Regency
LORDS & LADIES
COLLECTION

*Two glittering Regency
love affairs in every book*

MILLS & BOON®

www.millsandboon.co.uk

The *Regency*

LORDS & LADIES
COLLECTION

*Two glittering Regency
love affairs in every book*

MILLS & BOON®

www.millsandboon.co.uk

The Regency
LORDS & LADIES
COLLECTION

More Glittering Regency Love Affairs

Volume 17 – 4th January 2008
One Night with a Rake by Louise Allen
The Dutiful Rake by Elizabeth Rolls

Volume 18 – 1st February 2008
A Matter of Honour by Anne Herries
The Chivalrous Rake by Elizabeth Rolls

Volume 19 – 7th March 2008
Tavern Wench by Anne Ashley
The Incomparable Countess by Mary Nichols

Volume 20 – 4th April 2008
Prudence by Elizabeth Bailey
Lady Lavinia's Match by Mary Nichols

Volume 21 – 2nd May 2008
The Rebellious Bride by Francesca Shaw
The Duke's Mistress by Ann Elizabeth Cree

Volume 22 – 6th June 2008
Carnival of Love by Helen Dickson
The Viscount's Bride by Ann Elizabeth Cree

M&B

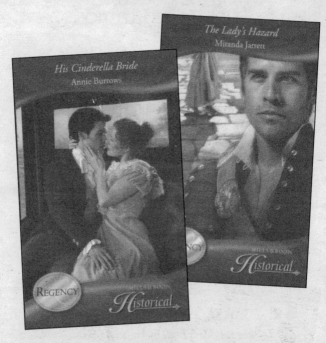

100 Reasons to Celebrate

2008 is a very special year as we celebrate Mills and Boon's Centenary.

Each month throughout the year there will be something new and exciting to mark the centenary, so watch for your favourite authors, captivating new stories, special limited edition collections…and more!

Celebrate 100 years of pure reading pleasure with Mills & Boon®

To mark our centenary, each month we're publishing a special 100th Birthday Edition. These celebratory editions are packed with extra features and include a FREE bonus story.

Now that's worth celebrating!

4th January 2008

The Vanishing Viscountess by Diane Gaston
With FREE story The Mysterious Miss M
This award-winning tale of the Regency Underworld launched Diane Gaston's writing career.

1st February 2008

Cattle Rancher, Secret Son by Margaret Way
With FREE story His Heiress Wife
Margaret Way excels at rugged Outback heroes…

15th February 2008

Raintree: Inferno by Linda Howard
With FREE story Loving Evangeline
A double dose of Linda Howard's heady mix of passion and adventure.

Don't miss out! From February you'll have the chance to enter our fabulous monthly prize draw. See special 100th Birthday Editions for details.

www.millsandboon.co.uk